石
水

Lindsey,

Thank You for
Your music, Some
of it helped with the
writing of this novel.

May Luck Bless You.

5/24/16

Stones and Water

By

Phillip Michael Gomez

This is a work of fiction. Names, characters, places, and incidents either are the product of the author's imagination or are used fictitiously. Any resemblance to actual persons, living or dead, business establishments, events, or locales is entirely coincidental.

STONES AND WATER

ISBN-13: 978-0692500460 (Phillip M Gomez)
ISBN-10: 0692500464

Dedication

For my Mom and Dad, Maida and Chris Gomez, who encouraged me to choose the hard path to success where the rewards are more rewarding.

For Shari Lynne Gomez, my best Friend and Wife who has been there to bring me back to the present from the past, and also for her fellow Teachers who have one of the toughest jobs of educating our youth.

For those in Uniform who have walked in the Valley and seen more than they wished to.

Table of Contents

Acknowledgements

What started out as a recommended method of therapy when I was diagnosed with combat related post-traumatic stress disorder (CRPTSD) has finally evolved into a fictional historical novel. Merging my two passions of history and Aikido into this story of love, war, and devotion has been my way of combatting my memories of the past. It provided the means to balance myself on the fence that separates peaceful tranquility, many of us take for granted, and the realistic horrors on the other side many of us on the peaceful side wish to deny exists.

I have so many to thank for the words written in this book that have provided insight into the characters of the story. I start off by giving thanks to my wife, Shari Lynne Gomez. At a time when I needed someone the most, she was there when I was asleep and awake. No matter how difficult of a time I was having, Shari was there to provide the unconditional love and devotion I needed when my world was not making any sense. Shari, being a public school teacher, inspired the occupation of the character, Reuben. Although I have dedicated this book to my mother and father, I also wish to dedicate this book to her and those in the teaching profession.

I have my sister, Pattie Stark, to thank for being the first person to read the first draft of this book and the initial editor. Although editing is not her profession, she provided much insight to the story and its content. We may not have been close as brother and sister, but I always knew she would be there if I needed encouragement, just as I would be there for her. This story has brought us closer and for that, I dedicate the chapter, "Wha'cha Doing" in honor of our family and the many road trips we spent together in the back seat of our parent's cars, from the Chrysler to the VW Bug.

I first met Tony Zusman back in 1997 when I returned from Adak, Alaska. Tony was one of two people who introduced me to the hobby of living history reenacting. Being that we both came from the Southwest, we hit it off as friends right away. Of all of my friends, Tony was the most open-minded and unbiased person I have ever known. He had his own beliefs, but was always open for new ideas and thoughts. He was very understanding when I was diagnosed with CRPTSD and supported me in my most trying times. Tony was a very good friend and even took the time to visit my parents while he was on vacation in the Southwest region. Unfortunately, Tony passed away long before his time. Because of the loss of my friend, the hobby of reenacting has never been the same, giving me no desire to participate knowing he will not be in the camp. Tony's outgoing personality, wit, and his deep sense of caring inspired one of the most caring characters in this story, Doctor Lawrence Chelmsford. For Tony Zusman, I dedicate the chapter "Don't Cry For Me Renee" in memory of Tony's friendship and loyalty.

Mike Baldwin and I became friends because of our fondness of history. As the years went by, our friendship developed into one of trust and reliability. Like that exercise where two people sit on the ground, back-to-back, and use each other as support to stand on their feet, that is how our friendship grew. In his time of need, I was there for him to lean on, and in my time of need, Mike was there for me, even when he was deployed. Together we kept each other on our feet. When Mike advanced to chief, he was concerned our friendship would suffer since he knew of my distrust of chief petty officers. I put his thoughts to ease when I told him I was his friend long before he was promoted and I viewed him as a friend, not a chief. When he was promoted to Ensign, of all his acquaintances in his chief's mess, he asked me to be the one to render his first salute at his pinning ceremony, and I was honored to do so. The Navy has separated us, but Mike Baldwin will always be a dear friend no matter where he is. Mike's brotherly friendship inspired the two characters, Max Warren and Todd Stevens. For Mike Baldwin, I dedicate the chapter "Remember the Ribbon" for a friendship that has no bonds between officer, chief, and enlisted.

I met the Kusner family during my active years of living history reenacting and found them to be the most loving, dedicated, and devoted family I have ever met. George, Sherry, Samantha Kusner, Ashley, Dylan, and Derek Beerbroer seemed like the ideal family. There are not many families like them anymore these days. They did everything together, from school activities to household maintenance. They also brought that love and devotion into their friendship with me. I could always count on the Kusner family if I needed anything, especially a laugh like the time we were on our way to a living history event. We met at my house to caravan together and unknowingly, both Sherry and I had worn our black Punisher t-shirts. George's only comment was, "Is there anything about you two I should know about?" George and Sherry's family provided me with the inspiration of the love and devotion for the Duran family in this book. For George, Sherry, Ashley, Dylan, Derek, and Samantha, I dedicate the chapter "Is That Fresh Baked Bread I Smell" for a strong friendship that even distance cannot sever.

Kamala Grogan Rheaume and I used to visit in the passageway near the water scuttle to discuss our individual personal issues at our last duty station before we both left the Navy. Because of our similar backgrounds, we seemed to be the only ones in the command we could relate with. I always liked Kamala's last name and it was that name that inspired the name for the character, Renee. For Kamala Grogan Rheaume, I dedicate the chapter "Can We Call Him Riley" in memory of her German Shepard, Riley.

When Ashley Frantz and I first met, she thought I was going to be a serious piece of work, to put it mildly. She was a beginning Fifth Kyu Aikidoka, and I was a ShoDan, First Degree Black Belt, with no school to claim. After our first training session, she told me how lucky she was when I found my way onto the mats of Mid-Atlantic Aikido in Virginia Beach. Although our sensei was responsible in her achievements in the Art, I felt I played a huge contributing part in her training and was honored when she asked me to be her primary uke when she tested for ShoDan. I have Ashley to thank for many of the techniques described in the story. There were many times, sometimes unknowingly, she provided me the movements of techniques both Reuben and Renee used. For Ashley "Kiai Kitty" Frantz, I dedicate the chapter "Please, Let Me Take Reuben His Kutto" in honor of her input to this story and her dedication to the art of Aikido.

I was in search of a new school and about to give up to take up training on my own when I got a phone call from Bruce Williams, who asked me to assist his class for a demonstration.

Because of an act of fate all due to irony, it was on the mats of the newly formed Mid-Atlantic Aikido in Virginia Beach where I found my new school. We were only three students at first, but the training environment was just what I was looking for. Sensei Bruce was instrumental in helping me achieve the rank of NiDan, Second Degree Black Belt, and Fukushidoin, certified assistant instructor. Sensei Bruce's open-mindedness, skill, and wit inspired one of the most beloved characters of this story, Akagi Genda-San. For Sensei Bruce Williams, I dedicate the chapter "Bushido" in honor of his friendship and Mid-Atlantic Aikido.

Cady Moore-Callahan and I met in the gym where I work and hit it off as friends right away. Her bubbly, bright attitude could cheer up the grumpiest of individuals. It's that bubbly, bright attitude that inspired the character, Aarleen. Cady's cheerful attitude was more than just the inspiration for Aarleen's character. If you knew how physically active Cady is with marathons, triathlons, surfing, motorcycling, and almost anything that causes one to break out in a sweat, you would get exhausted just watching her do time on an elliptical machine. She kept up that physical activity while she continued her studies of becoming a physician. When I found myself not wanting to write, even dreading it, it was her on going persistence that kept my fingers clicking away on the keyboard because I knew no matter how tired she was, she would keep going. For Cady "Wildkat" Moore-Callahan, I dedicate the chapter "My First Entry" in honor of her support and cheerfulness.

I met Waverly Byth Adcock (author of *Cradled in the Blue Ridge)*, Carl Brandt, and Bruce Houle during my early active years of living history reenacting. Our two groups merged many times at events and shared a common flaw of living history reenacting, going off script, especially during tactical scenarios. We often found ourselves in heated water from the staff of the Corps due to our shenanigans on the field and in the camps. However, when it came down to the Corps needing a tactical edge, because of our antics to go off script, we were often asked to provide diversions during many tactical scenarios such as the trench around Fort Branch. Whether it was deploying to the left instead of the right during tactical scenarios or going off to create our own tactical during the spectator events, one thing was certain, we had a good laugh around the campfire in the evening and recreating the events during the School of the Cup. For being a fun influence in my life, I have dedicated to Carl, Waverly, and Bruce the chapter, "Aishite'ru yo, My Precious Wickham Girl."

Growing up, I always had a form of social anxiety. After Desert Storm, it had gotten worse. I was in both individual and group therapy for a few months before I transferred from Rhode Island to Guam where there was no follow up treatment. For eight years, I had no outlet or anyone I could associate with having the same experiences I had. It was in 2000 when I was finally diagnosed with CRPTSD, and began formal treatment. It was still hard for me to associate with others and I had difficulties discussing my time in the military. That was until I got my motorcycle. I was riding my bike behind a truck with a logo of a gold and red skull with a black spade on a black background, and around the logo read, "Combat Veterans Motorcycle Association." I googled the association and found the National website of the CVMA and submitted an application. It was approved and I found a group of vets I could associate with.

Although I still tend to be quiet, unsociable, and introverted amongst these brothers and sisters who have also walked in the valley, I am still very grateful for their company. They make me feel I am not alone. I know if I ever need a lifting spirit, all I have to do is reach out to the group and know I will have brothers and sisters at my side. For my brothers and sisters of the Combat Veterans Motorcycle Association, Virginia Chapter 27-1, I dedicate the chapter, "Remember Me As Your Friend, Not A Soldier." It was after I joined the Virginia chapter when I found out the truck I was riding behind belonged to Edward "Amerbadas" Lonecke who has become a good friend and brother.

When my story was finished, I was curious if it was good enough to publish. I asked my wife if she knew anyone who would be interested in reading the entire story and provide input. She recommended her friend Barbara, and her husband Don, Speight. I dedicate the chapter "She's My Girl" for Barbara and Don's positive feedback and their willingness to be my experimental readers.

I am also grateful to Erica Wright and Amanda Conley-Powers. For Erica, who proofed some of my earlier work and provided me with informative publishing and copyright information, I dedicate the chapter, "Stones and Water". For Amanda, I dedicate the chapter "RENEE!!! Get Out Here! I'm Not Ready For This!" for reminding me I had unfinished business, and for the anecdote of her daughter reflected in the chapter. As both being caring, devoted mothers, I want to thank Erica and Amanda for their very informative insights of motherhood which was very helpful and needed for this story.

Thank you, Sara Davis, for keeping the 6th Virginia Inf'y, Company C "The Woodis Riflemen" alive. Tony would be very proud. For that, I dedicate the chapter "Gift of Tranquility".

Forward

This is a fictional story set in a historical time period. The story is not intended to focus on any historical facts and is not meant to be used for any type of research. This story is for entertainment reading only. Many of the names, places, situations, and locations have been made up. An armchair historian may arrive to a certain part of history in the story and think, this never happened, and they would be correct. There are several factual historical events referred to in the story to aid the reader of the time that portion of the story is taking place. Several places referred to in chapter four, for example, *"Don't Cry for me Renee,"* did not exist in Mexico during that time period. My hometown of Santa Rosa, New Mexico, which is mentioned in chapter four was founded in 1865 by Don Celso Baca. At that time, the settlement was called, Agua Negra Chiquita (Little Black Water). It wasn't until 1890 the name was changed to Santa Rosa, being named after the chapel Don Celso Baca built in honor of his mother. I also mentioned the village of Puerto De Luna, located ten miles Southeast of Santa Rosa. Puerto De Luna, or PDL as it is commonly called, was established in 1863, and was the county seat of Guadalupe County until 1891 when Santa Rosa took over that distinction. I mention these two locations and other surrounding villages such as Anton Chico, Colonias, and Villanueva to pay tribute to my family and friends who live in these communities and may have ancestors who originally settled them. Appreciation goes to Yolanda Sena for her input of my hometown area history.

This story revolves around how I overcame the use of anti-depressants for CRPTSD that was making my life much worse by numbing my emotions and memories, rather than learning from and dealing with them. There are many ways to deal with PTSD, and the most common is with anti-depressant drugs. Those who suffer from PTSD that chose not to use anti-depressants, use other means of positive outlets to deal with their condition such as art, music, and in my case, the Martial Art of Aikido and writing. I am in no way saying I am an expert regarding PTSD and don't advocate the non-use of anti-depressants. If they work for an individual, than by all means do what it takes to keep you getting out of bed in the morning and keep living. In my case, after four years on the anti-depressants, I found myself signing up for an Aikido class when I retired from the Navy. I did what any novice Martial Artist would do and buy several "how to" books on Aikido. I initially bought three, all recommended by the Sensei of the school. I also bought a small pocket sized book for two dollars, but I put that one aside. And so I read the "how to" books and went to class. At that time, my only goal was to make it to class on time. Then one day when I believed I had enough of life and wanted to go to sleep forever, I had my enlightenment. I had a plan and the means, but something inside kept urging me to attend class before I did anything drastic. I gave into that urge and found myself bowing in for class and partnered up for the first exercise called tae no henko. My partner was a huge Second Kyu with an ego to match. He whipped me around like a rag doll and when it was my turn, I could not budge him and grew more frustrated with life. That was until I caught a glimpse of O'Sensei Morihei Ueshiba's picture on the wall. His eyes in the picture calmed me and made me think of all the darkness in my life and how it could be put to good use. I closed my eyes, breathed, and then I did something I had not done in a long time, smile. That evening, I did the best tae no henko I have ever done in my life, taking the balance of that egotistical Second Kyu, and learning that in Aikido, there is no revenge... but there is *My Turn*. After class, I went back home and pushed aside the "how to" books and grabbed the small pocket sized book I bought for two dollars called *"The Art of Peace"* and opened it to page 86. The passage on that page caused me to realize what was missing in my life, balance.

"Be grateful even for hardships, setbacks, and bad people. Dealing with such obstacles is an essential part of training in the Art of Peace." ~ O'Sensei Morihei Ueshiba

The story itself is of love and devotion shared between two individuals who endured so much to be together. It is a story of family, friendship, separation, and overall self-victory in the most stressful of times. It is a story that will take the reader away to a more simple time, a time where nothing mattered except family and friends. It is a story of adventure and self-victory almost anyone can relate to. As you read this story, do not dispute the historical facts within the pages because there are none. As the author, I wrote this story with the most common question almost all history enthusiasts have, "what if?"

Part One

Fate is an Awesome Power

Filled with Irony…

STONES AND WATER

APRIL 6, 1865

Sailor's Creek, Virginia

The American Civil War has waged on for four years.
General Robert E. Lee's Confederate Army of Northern Virginia finds itself battling for existence. Depleted of supplies and ammunition, the Confederate troops are still determined to fight their way through to Lynchburg to establish a new supply source, and join up forces with General Joseph E. Johnston's army in the West.

It is a pivotal time in American history, not because of the battle to be fought this day, but because it will mark the beginning of the end of a long bloody struggle that has separated many families.

One such family's linage continues through traditions not learned in America, but in a land where the sun rises, and richly disciplined teachings saved one man from his own demise to become a protector, not only for his family, but for those he led.

Prologue

Try as hard as he could, Colonel Margin could not block against the major's second thrust. The major's blade found its target though the colonel's heart. The major pulled his blade free, smiled, and nodded approvingly with his victory as he wiped his blade free of blood on the colonel's shoulder, a crude and disrespectful act. The colonel looked blankly at the wound, and back to the major for a moment, fell to his knees, and forward to the ground, his eyes still open as he died.

"HAZZA!!! That's one less rebel we have to parole!" shouted a loud-mouthed sergeant raising the major's arm in a victory salute. The other soldiers in blue likewise cheered their superior's win with pride.

The major's talent with a sword had been legendary in the ranks of the Union Army. He was fencing champion during his full tenure at West Point, and was permitted to teach the art to the lower classmen. He never tired of exhibiting his skills, and when the opportunity to use captured Confederate officers as "practice" arose, many soldiers cheered when his blade hit its mark, and took down his victims in cold blooded murder.

Union soldiers patted the major on his back congratulating him on his victory, while the Confederate captive officers looked on with fear, with the exception of one. Reuben Duran, like the others, was sitting on the ground being guarded at musket and bayonet point. As his fellow Confederates sat trembling, Reuben remained calm, his eyes closed, and meditated on wonderful thoughts of his childhood special friend who he never stopped loving, even after she had been arranged to be married to another by her father. He meditated about her long, dark, brown hair and how it would wave in the breeze, and her large, beautiful, brown eyes that would sparkle with joy.

"Reuben, how in the world can you be so calm when we are about to die most heinously?" whispered a fellow Confederate officer.

Reuben didn't respond. His thoughts were of more pleasant times such as being on the farm his father inherited, the games he played with his older brother and younger sister, and the walks home from school with his special friend.

"Time for the next victim, I mean partner!" shouted out the loud-mouthed sergeant. The other Union soldiers laughed.

"The Major has already won seven victories, perhaps he needs to rest," responded another soldier.

"Nonsense," said the major. "Sergeant, pick the next sword!"

"With pleasure, sir!" replied the sergeant.

"Wait!" called out a lieutenant. "Major, you need to look at this sword. I believe you will find it quite familiar."

"Bring it to me," said the major.

The lieutenant presented the sword to the major. Immediately the major's eyes opened wide as he took hold of the sword.

"I know this sword!" proclaimed the major. "This is the sword that got me reprimanded and relieved of my position in Norfolk! DURAN!!! We meet at last! Show yourself!"

Opening his eyes at the sound of his name, Reuben calmly stood and stepped forward to the major. He walked up to the major dangerously close causing the sergeant to raise his rifle, aiming it to his head. "That's close enough, Johnny. If that's your sword, take it and let the game begin," he said, in a very mocking manner cautiously eyeing Reuben through the sights of his rifle.

The major smirked at Reuben and said, "I hoped I would come across you, and here you are."

Reuben let out a low grunted laugh and had a mischievous look on his face, a look his special friend from his youth found so adorable.

The major's face turned red with fury as Reuben remained calm. The exact reaction Reuben wanted.

Furious, the major threw Reuben's sword at him. Reuben caught it calmly. "You're not going to last long with that sword. It's going to be a pleasure claiming that sword as a prize, and melting it down to a worthless lump of ore!" said the major showing an overconfident cocky smile.

Reuben raised his sword and stepped back a few paces. He held out the sheathed sword in both hands, the hilt pointing to the left, and in a sign of respect, bowed forward to the major, never taking his eyes off of him. The major's cocky smile faded at the odd gesture from Reuben.

The major took his ready stance with his sword drawn and said, "Before we begin, I must ask from what alma mater you hail? I already know it is the Virginia Military Institute, but for me to claim victory over your school, you must proclaim it yourself."

Reuben stood before the major, tucking the sheathed sword beneath his belt. He took the ready stance with his right arm relaxed at his side, hand open, and fingers extended outward, energy flowing from his fingertips. His left thumb gently pushed the guard free from the sheath.

"Can't you hear, Johnny? The major asked you what school you attended!" shouted the sergeant. He began to laugh loudly.

Reuben maintained his posture with his eyes fixed on the major's center.

"Now, now, Sergeant, that will do," responded the major with the cocky expression returning to his face. "By the looks of these rebel officers, the Confederate army is promoting anyone these days, school or no school. But I do know you hail from VMI, Captain, so just claim your school."

Reuben kept his focus on the major's center and waited for his first move.

The major, in a more serious manner, asked Reuben again, "From what school do you hail, Reuben Duran? What school do I have the honor of discrediting this afternoon?"

The loud-mouthed sergeant took on the seriousness of the major's question and stepped closer to Reuben. "You heard the major! Answer him, damn it, where did you go to school?!"

石
水

In the year of our Lord, 1837, a destiny begins of a romantic tale.
Adolescent awkwardness, and confusing feelings...

Wha'cha Doing?

It was in the spring of 1837 when Aaron's father died leaving him the farm, where he was raised, located on the banks of Tamden's Creek in Norfolk County, Virginia. Although Aaron didn't follow in the footsteps of his father, he did appreciate the gift of the farm where he spent many happy years with his mother and father growing up. It was in very prime condition and well kept. His father employed several slaves belonging to James Wilcox to help with the running and upkeep of the farm. Aaron not only received the farm from his father's will, but also a great sum of funds to keep these individuals employed for many years.

Miles McDurand escaped noble persecution at a time when common citizens of Scotland were bearing down on rich landowners. Although Miles McDurand was viewed as a fair and just man, his social position made him a target. Fearing for his wife and son, he packed as much wealth as he could, a very sizable amount, and escaped to America, Norfolk, Virginia to be exact. Upon arrival, he changed the family name to Duran, bought a small farm in the country, and began to live a simple anonymous life with a secret financial security.

Aaron was especially happy to receive the farm. He enjoyed that simple life as a child yet, his father encouraged him to be more, especially in this land of opportunity, an opportunity that would lead to law school and becoming the predominate attorney in the city of Norfolk.

There were so many wonderful memories on that farm, memories to which he wanted to introduce his children, Monroe, Reuben, and Lucy. His hopes were his children would be able to appreciate life both as farmers, and well educated citizens of this country.

After school was let out that spring, Aaron moved the family to the farm for their first experience of working the land. They had visited the farm time-to-time from their home in the city, but never spent a considerable amount of time there. Monroe, wanting to become a lawyer like his father, didn't quite take to the farm. He spent most of his time inside reading and studying. Lucy enjoyed living on the farm, and learned a lot from a Negro woman named May, one of the servants of James Wilcox, which Aaron's father had hired to help with upkeep of the house. But it was Reuben who took to the entire life of the farm, the animals, field work, and daily chores. Reuben was overwhelmed with questions for his father and hired help regarding the working of the farm, and when it was time to move back into the city, he hated to leave. But he found comfort the following spring he would return.

Reuben started his seventh year of schooling, very eager once again under the tutelage of his mother, Coleen, one of the best educators in the city school. He always liked learning and reading was his favorite topic. He read almost everything he got his hands on, but he was becoming more interested in farming topics because of the summer he spent on the farm. Reuben was anxious to try some of the ideas he had read about, and discussed them with his father. Although his father was happy his son took to the farm, he constantly reminded Reuben there was more to life than being a farmer.

However, this did not stop Reuben from accompanying his father on occasion to check on the farm and to pay James Wilcox for the use of the workers. Although they lived in a state with the institution of slavery, Aaron could never bring himself to refer to the hired workers as slaves, which in legal terms, that's what they were.

It was on one of these trips when Reuben met Noah, one of the slave children belonging to James Wilcox. James Wilcox owned a large plantation about two miles further up Tamden's Creek. He owned many servants and field hands, several he hired out to Aaron to do some fieldwork on his farm. There were the two sisters, May and June, who worked in the house. Of the two, May was older. Jasper, who took June to be his wife, had four children: Able, Kay, Noah and Alice. Alice worked in the house, but spent most of her time caring for the animals. Able, Kay, and Noah worked as field hands along with their father. Henry was an uncle to May and June, and an older servant who did almost everything from helping in the kitchen to gathering up the crops, and was for all intents and purposes, lent to Aaron at a reduced cost because of lameness.

As by the law, the money Aaron paid the workers went to their master, James Wilcox. James Wilcox, as agreed, was to use the money to pay for clothing and extra food for the hired slave workers. However, Aaron secretly compensated the workers with produce from the farm, an act that earned the respect and admiration of the workers.

Reuben never interacted with Negroes before, except for asking questions about farming, until he met Noah. Noah was about the same age as Reuben. They became good friends and spent lots of time together, as it would allow. Aaron would make special trips to the Wilcox's for Reuben to say hello to Noah and his family.

It was difficult at this early age for Reuben to understand the concept of slavery, but accepted it as a way of life in the country he was raised in. He felt, like his parents, the owning of others was not right. However, since his family did not own anyone, the topic didn't seem to matter.

Once again, spring came and it was time to make that "summer vacation," as Reuben called it, to the farm. Monroe and Lucy, although they enjoyed the farm, didn't seem to enjoy it as much as Reuben. However, their brother had a way about him that would cause them to enjoy the spring and summer months, especially for Reuben's very creative, younger sister Lucy, who adored Reuben very much.

Reuben once again took to the farm even more so this year because of the research he had done and because of his friend, Noah. But it wasn't always work that had to be done on the farm. There were games to be played, fish to be caught, playful mischief and shenanigans to be masterminded by the three siblings and Noah, and a new friend to be made.

Franklin Wallace and his wife, Margret, were visiting with the Wilcoxs, along with their nine year old daughter Renee, this one particular summer. James' wife, Monique, was Margret's sister, so the Wallaces made frequent visits and stays at the Wilcox plantation. Franklin Wallace enjoyed the relaxing life away from the city and his wharves, while Margret enjoyed spending time with her sister being that they were close.

Renee attended the same school as Reuben and his siblings, but it wasn't until this summer when Renee and Reuben took notice of one another.

In the beginning of Renee and Reuben's friendship, Franklin Wallace didn't mind it too much. James Wilcox introduced Aaron to Franklin Wallace and praised him as one of the best attorneys in the state, and how he had used his services more than once with great results. In time, Franklin Wallace would also use Aaron's law talents in drafting contracts for his export and import shipping business which would make him the most successful shipping agent in the region.

At first it was adolescence awkwardness between Renee and Reuben, but soon, they were to become best friends. Although Renee was being raised as a "proper daughter and lady of the South," away from her parents, her true nature as a child at heart was unleashed. Reuben provided her with some of his clothes so she wouldn't ruin her expensive dresses she was only allowed to wear.

Aaron and Coleen could not help but feel sorry for how Renee's parents strictly raised her. They did as much as they could to make her feel like a part of the Duran family when she visited. Aaron, often accompanied with Coleen, would ride to the Wilcox plantation to pick up Renee to bring to the farm and visit with their children. They assured Franklin and Margret Wallace, Renee was well cared for in all proper Southern aristocratic manners, just as their children were. However, once they were well on their way and the carriage was out of sight, Renee became free to the ways of true childhood, and once on the Duran farm and clothes changed, she and Reuben were off to do chores and play.

If her parents, especially her father, found out about her playful side, they would have never allowed Renee to visit the Duran farm, which she adored and visited frequently. As far as Franklin and Margret Wallace were concerned, because Aaron was a successful man and his wife, a highly praised educator, they were people from which their daughter could benefit. With the Wilcoxs not having any children, it was also logical for Renee to have friends her own age to help keep her occupied while Franklin Wallace and his wife visited the Wilcox plantation.

Renee and Reuben first met one warm summer day under the oak tree by the creek when James Wilcox brought Franklin Wallace over to introduce him to Aaron. Franklin Wallace had been having contract disputes with other shipping companies and James Wilcox felt Aaron would be a great help to Franklin Wallace's problem. James Wilcox had mentioned how Aaron found legal loopholes in many of his grain and crop contracts he had signed making them void causing him to double his earnings in less than a year.

As James Wilcox and Franklin Wallace were about to depart to the Duran farm, Renee begged to come along, especially when she heard the Durans had children. Although strict with the ways of raising their daughter, Franklin Wallace still, at that time, had fatherly instincts so he allowed her to come along to meet the Duran children.

Franklin Wallace found Aaron Duran to be a genius at contract interpretation. This one visit alone saved Franklin Wallace thousands of dollars in gold and silver, to which he was entirely grateful.

"You see, Mr. Wallace, the contract states specifically. The vessel *must* dock at your Norfolk wharves to unload its cargo. However as you mentioned, it docked in Portsmouth and unloaded its cargo at your one wharf there, thus causing a breach in contract. It's a minor technicality, but still a breach, nonetheless."

"What does that mean, exactly?"

"It means, you do not owe them any payment, and the shipment still belongs to you. In fact, this company owes you two hundred and fifty dollars. You see, it states here, *'If delivery of cargo is postponed by* any *means, the shipper will pay a fifty dollar a day late fee to guarantee continued business.'* Hmm, I sure wouldn't want to be that ship's captain when he returns back to England. That's if he ever does."

"How is it they owe me two hundred and fifty dollars?"

"You said it took them five days to move from your one wharf in Portsmouth, to your wharves in Norfolk because of other ships docked outboard from the delivery ship, and could not move. There's your five day delay in delivery, if you take this agreement literally, which is the purpose of a contract, to avoid misunderstandings."

"Aaron Duran, you are a genius! Anything my man, name it, I owe you nicely."

"Well, if you can, lead me in a direction of purchasing a piano for my daughter Lucy?"

"Done," Franklin Wallace said, gratefully.

Franklin Wallace was so grateful of Aaron's legal knowledge, he forgot all about Renee when he and James Wilcox were leaving. Franklin Wallace remembered when Coleen asked if Renee could stay for dinner, since their daughter Lucy was having a good time with her visit. For Lucy to have another girl to visit with, instead of her brothers, would be a good change for her. Coleen assured they would bring Renee back to the Wilcox plantation afterwards.

"Why not... let the children visit," said Franklin Wallace, feeling thousands of dollars richer.

As the adults were discussing legal matters in the dining room, Lucy sat across from Renee in the parlor. Although Lucy was a couple of years younger than Renee, she was grateful to be with another child close to her age, even though she wasn't saying much at first.

"Why are you dressed like that? Are you going to a party? Can I come?" asked Lucy.

Looking embarrassed, Renee answered, "No, my parents always make me dress like this. You want to know a secret?"

Lucy smiled and moved over next to Renee. "Yes please, I won't tell, I promise," she answered.

"I don't like dressing like this. It's uncomfortable."

"I bet. You want to come up to my room? I have a few games we can play. Some of them, I made up."

Not exactly what Renee had in mind, but it was better than sitting on the porch doing nothing at the Wilcox plantation, so she agreed.

Lucy and Renee spent close to an hour in Lucy's room playing checkers. Renee found Lucy very creative. She would make up interesting rules, making an otherwise dull game of checkers incredibly adventurous and fun. What really impressed Renee were Lucy's musical abilities when she played a small tin whistle for her.

"My GrandDa came from Scotland and he said this was a popular instrument with children there. He taught me a few songs. I made up some of my own. Here, listen."

Lucy played a few songs Renee recognized immediately, and some songs Lucy made up that sounded very pleasing.

"You're very good, Lucy."

"Thank you, I love music. Da is going to get me a piano sometime so I can play all day."

Renee took a shine to Lucy and began to wonder what her brothers were like. She was about to find out when Coleen lightly knocked on the open door to tell Renee her father left her to stay for dinner, to which Renee was elated.

"Lucy, where are your brothers? Perhaps you should introduce Renee to them."

"I would, Mama, but Monroe is reading, as usual, and Reuben is outside with Noah by the creek. I can't take Renee out there or her pretty dress might get dirty."

"Hmm, I see what you mean. I'm sorry, Renee, but once Monroe gets into his books... he is lost forever. He wants to be a lawyer like his father," said Coleen walking to Lucy's closet.

"Yeah, he's kind of stuffy."

"Lucy, don't talk about Monroe like that."

"Sorry Mama. What are you doing?" asked Lucy.

Coleen pulled out one of Lucy's dresses, too large for her, and put it up against Renee's front and nodded.

"Well, even though Monroe is too busy to be pried away, Lucy can introduce you to Reuben. He's closer to your age anyhow. You don't mind changing into one of Lucy's dresses so yours won't get ruined do..."

Renee began undressing before Coleen could finish her thought.

Once Renee was dressed in Lucy's dress, an older pair of her shoes, and her hair unpinned, Lucy lead Renee by the hand out of her room. As they were about to go downstairs, Monroe emerged from his and Reuben's room. He was rather tall, slim, and nicely dressed. His brown hair was groomed nicely and looked as if he spent most of his time indoors.

"Mama, where's Da? I need to borrow one of his law books!"

"Quiet down, Monroe. We have company," said Lucy. "Here, this is Renee. She's visiting from the Wilcox plantation up the road."

Renee was about to offer her hand in greeting, except Monroe ignored it and said, "Yeah, yeah, nice to meet you. Mama!" he yelled as he went down the stairs.

Lucy shrugged her shoulders and said, "Well, that's my oldest brother, what do you think?"

"Hmm, kind of stuffy," said Renee with a chuckle.

"See, I told you. You'll like Reuben. Can I tell you a secret, Renee?"

"Sure, I told you one of mine, so it's only fair."

"I'm not supposed to pick, but Reuben is my favorite brother. Monroe is great, but I guess since he's the oldest, he's more like a grown up. Reuben is fun and he plays with me all the time. We sometimes play jokes on Monroe. Yep, I love both my brothers very much, but I like Reuben the best. You won't tell anyone will you? Like I said, I'm not supposed to pick."

"I promise, Lucy."

Lucy was about to continue down the stairs until she turned to Renee with a thoughtful look on her face and asked her, "Do you think liking someone is more important than loving them? I mean I love Monroe, but I don't really like him, if that makes any sense. But Reuben, I both like and love him."

Renee, although very young herself, found Lucy's question very perplexing, especially coming from a girl a couple of years younger. "Gee, I don't know, Lucy. I suppose you really can't truly love someone unless you like them first," she said.

"Hmm, fair enough," said Lucy and continued to lead Renee down the stairs.

As they made their way to where Reuben and Noah were, Lucy pointed out various areas of the farm. She told Renee about her grandfather and how he came to America. Although she didn't understand the details of why he left Scotland, she did make it clear he picked this one place because it seemed hidden from the main road.

"I don't know why he left Scotland, but something tells me, he did *not* want to be found," Lucy explained.

They were walking the path between the main planting field and barn as Renee marveled at the beauty of the Duran farm. It was far smaller than the Wilcox plantation, but it had a beauty all of its own. By viewing the enclosed landscape with trees that lined each side of the farm, she began to understand Lucy's grandfather's reasoning for the solitude the land had to offer. This is the perfect place to grow up, she thought.

When they reached the end of the field, the land sloped downward. Renee was awed at the beautiful scenery of the creek winding its way to a bend of grassy land covered by a huge oak tree. It was the most perfect tree she had ever seen. The trunk was wide and limbs covered with leaves which gave off the impression of a huge green mushroom.

As they neared the oak tree, Renee saw two boys sitting near the water, both wearing shoddy clothes, obviously dirty from work and play. They were sitting on the grass with a pail between them and each had a fishing pole. Renee began to smile. She had never been fishing and was thinking this was going to be a wonderful experience until the two girls neared the tree and Renee began to hesitate.

"Oh dear," said Renee, concerned.

"What's wrong?" asked Lucy.

"One of those boys is a Negro. I'm not allowed to talk to Negros."

"Why not?" asked Lucy. "They're people too. Come on! That's Noah, and the other one is my brother, Reuben," said Lucy, pointing at the two boys.

Renee stopped altogether and Lucy asked, "Is everything okay, Renee?"

"Lucy... does your father own any servants or slaves?" asked Renee rather awkwardly.

"Nope," answered Lucy, in a matter-of-fact type of manner. "Noah and his family belong to Mr. Wilcox. My Da hires them to work on the farm. My parents don't like the thought of people owning other people."

"Really, my father owns several servants for our house. I feel it's wrong too, but I'm only a child so what can I do about it?" replied Renee.

Lucy answered with bright childhood innocence, "Well, you can come and meet Noah and talk to him and not tell your parents. You'll find he's just like any other boy... icky."

Why not indeed, thought Renee. If the Duran children could talk with them, then why not me too? I just won't tell my parents like Lucy said.

"Hey Reuben, hey Noah, I brought a new friend to meet you! Her name is Renee."

"Quiet, Lucy. You're going to scare the fish away," said Noah.

Lucy pointed to Noah. "That's Noah, he's always telling me to be quiet."

Renee walked up to Noah. She was excited to meet a Negro child her age. At this young age, it was difficult for Renee, as it was for Lucy and Reuben, to understand the relations between coloreds and whites.

"Hi, Noah, it's nice to meet you."

"Nice to meet you too, now be quiet."

Just like any other boy... rude, thought Renee.

Renee turned her attention to Lucy's brother Reuben and immediately understood what Lucy meant about liking and loving someone at the same time. Although he was busy tending to his fishing line, she could see why Lucy picked him as her favorite brother. He was nowhere near anything like Lucy's other brother. Reuben was all boy, from his unkempt brown hair on the top of his head to his toes wiggling in the grass. But it was his eyes that caught her attention most of all. Even as he was in deep concentration attaching a hook to the line, his brown eyes gave off a spark of sincerity with just a hint of mischievousness.

Renee walked over to Reuben and asked, "Wha'cha doing?"

"I'm getting ready to fish, what's it look like, silly?" said Reuben with a smirk on his face that Renee thought was cute, even at her young age.

Although his response was playfully sarcastic, she still found him interesting. Thinking what Lucy said about Reuben being fun and her favorite, she thought it might be fun to tease him a little and try to get him to notice her.

"You're doing it wrong," she said not really knowing what he was doing.

"What are you talking about? You don't know how to fish," he replied as he looked at her with a perturbed look, but faded quickly as he got his first real glimpse of Renee with her bright, brown eyes, adorable smile, and long, dark, brown hair cascading over her shoulders.

"Bet I can catch a fish before you do," said Renee.

Reuben looked at Noah. Noah snickered saying, "goofy girl."

"Go on, Noah, give her your fishing pole and let's see how good she is," said Reuben.

Noah handed Renee his fishing pole and took a seat next to Reuben.

"Well, what are you waiting for? Get to fishing," Reuben said with more playful sarcasm.

Renee looked to Lucy who was motioning her on. She went to the water's edge and put the line in the water.

Reuben and Noah started laughing hard.

"What's so funny?" asked Renee.

"You didn't bait your hook!" exclaimed Reuben, rolling in the grass laughing.

"Okay, okay. I forgot! Will you bait it for me, please?" asked Renee, feeling like a fool. Geez oh geez oh geez he's going to think I'm just another stupid girl, she thought.

Reuben and Noah stopped laughing and sat up.

"You've got to be kidding?" said Noah.

Renee looked to Lucy who had her little hands in fists silently cheering her on.

Renee stomped her foot and thought to herself, I need to do something to really get Reuben's attention, or he's going to think I'm just another prissy girl.

"Okay, I'll show you," she said as she knelt down, reached into the pail, and pulled out a good sized worm. She rolled it around with her fingers and stuck it onto the hook. She was about to put the line in the water until she took the worm off the hook and looked at it.

Both Reuben and Noah looked at each other questionably, and then looked back at Renee.

"This worm is too long," she said. She put it in her mouth, bit it in half, spit one half in the pail, and put the other half on the hook.

"WHOA! That's nasty!" yelled Noah.

Lucy cried out, "EWWW! YUCK!"

Reuben stood up, looked at Renee with admiration and said, "THAT WAS GREAT!!! What did you say your name was again? I'm Reuben."

At that very moment, Renee and Reuben fell in *"like"* with each other, even when Renee threw up shortly after with Reuben right next to her supporting her head as she heaved.

14

And so it went on for the next several years, moving back to the city for the fall and winter months where Renee and Reuben went to school together, and back to the farm in the spring and summer. With the Wallace and Wilcox close family relationship, Renee spent many days at the Wilcox's plantation and many overnight sleep overs with Lucy at the Duran farm so Renee and Reuben seemed to be together all year round.

Franklin Wallace did more than deliver on his gratitude for Aaron's legal assistance. Not only did he locate a piano for Lucy, and at a decent cost, he gave it to the Duran family as a gift. Aaron and Franklin Wallace's relationship thrived for a few years until the friendship of his daughter and Aaron's son seemed to be developing into a relationship, a relationship that would cause concern for Franklin and Margret Wallace.

It was about his fourth year on the farm when Reuben began to get an interest in teaching. He had always respected his mother's teaching abilities and enjoyed teaching the hired help on the farm of all the latest farming concepts he read over the school year. He even secretly taught Noah the basics of reading and writing, which of course, was illegal for persons of color. He began to entertain the idea of becoming a teacher like his mother, or even a college professor, both professions being agreeable to his parents. Renee also felt Reuben would make a good teacher and encouraged him.

Renee and Reuben began to get much closer. A friendship Renee's father didn't appreciate. He was also becoming very concerned with the time she was spending with the Duran family. She was always invited to participate in their family outings and holidays. Franklin Wallace was concerned Renee and Reuben would take their friendship to a different level. Although Aaron had a very respectable career as a lawyer and was considered a prestigious citizen of Norfolk, Franklin Wallace could not take a chance of his family name being stained by a family whose son was inviting thoughts of becoming an educator, a respectful occupation, but not a high paying one. Therefore, on Renee's thirteenth birthday, he put all concerns to rest when he made an arrangement with a shipping colleague from Charleston, South Carolina, for Renee to marry his son once she turned eighteen. This put an end to any notion of Renee and Reuben becoming romantically involved and also, such a merger of both shipping companies would be extremely profitable for Franklin Wallace.

The day when Renee heard about the arranged marriage, she became horribly upset and went to visit with Reuben. Reuben didn't know how to handle the news. For all Reuben knew, they were childhood friends who could, and have, shared good times together. However, this issue had them both confused about their feelings toward each other. Reuben gave her a hug like always, but this time, the embrace had a deeper meaning and neither one of them wanted to let go. They remained good friends, but knew nothing more could become of their friendship because of the arrangement Renee's father had made.

That same year, Reuben turned 16. Monroe was starting his first year of college at William and Mary in Williamsburg, Aaron's alma mater. He had aspirations to study law like their father. This gave Aaron the opportunity to introduce Reuben to higher education and took him to visit Monroe at the college for a few days. On their journey, Aaron paused in the trip, and stopped at Fort Monroe to visit a legal colleague with whom he had attended law school, Major Steven Tombs. In making this visit, Aaron inadvertently introduced Reuben to Military life. The moment Reuben passed over the moat and into the fort, he was in severe fascination. He had endless questions for Major Tombs, making it difficult for Aaron to visit his friend. Major Tombs acquired the service of a corporal to give Reuben a tour of the fort. Reuben stopped at almost every point of interest. He was mesmerized at watching soldiers doing every day drills and had the opportunity to shoot an army musket at the target range. The sergeant of the range was impressed with Reuben's loading and shooting ability.

At the end of the day, it was too late for Aaron and Reuben to continue on to Williamsburg so Major Tombs set them up with quarters for the night, a postponement Reuben did not find disappointing. He experienced eating dinner in the mess hall with the other soldiers, listened to the endless tales, and found the sounds of the bugler playing evening retreat soothing when he turned in for the night.

He was awakened early by the sounds of reveille and eagerly cleaned up and dressed to see the morning's evolutions of the fort. Again he had breakfast in the mess hall with his father and Major Tombs. Although he didn't want to leave, he also wanted to see Monroe and visit his new world to see if it was as fascinating as the fort. If so, he would have a very hard decision to make.

They arrived at William and Mary in midafternoon and met up with Monroe at his dormitory. It was much less active than the fort and Reuben found it extremely dull. Most of the time was spent visiting Monroe, which Reuben enjoyed, but kept bringing up the visit at the fort. As Aaron and Reuben traveled back to Norfolk and nearing Fort Monroe, Reuben stretched every which way to get another look at the fort as they passed. There was no doubt in Aaron's mind Reuben would pursue the career of a soldier, much to his dissatisfaction.

As much as Aaron desperately encouraged Reuben to attend William and Mary like his brother, Reuben was too mind strong and began to change his reading habits from farm almanacs for research and literature for educational knowledge, to books of military instruction and history. He began to cherish the heroics of the Generals of the Revolutionary War of Independence and the Second War of Independence of 1812.

The year was 1842, Reuben was 16 years old, head of his school and was being considered by the administrators of William and Mary for next year's session, but to his father's grief, Reuben still wanted to become a soldier. Even Renee and Noah tried to change his attitude because they felt Reuben would make an excellent educator. Renee was especially not happy with Reuben wanting to become a soldier. He's too good natured and caring to carry a musket, she thought. But then, she thought it may also be for the best because he would leave, and the confusing feelings they have been sharing would go away.

At his wits end, Aaron called upon Major Tombs at Fort Monroe and asked what it would take for him to secure a seat at West Point. Aaron felt by attending a military academy, Reuben would still be furthering his education. Major Tombs, Aaron, and Reuben spent one evening discussing the matter, but being Reuben had never ventured out of the state of Virginia, he didn't welcome the notion of traveling up the Hudson into New York. Instead, he said he would have no ill feelings, and would even honor the notion of attending the Virginia Military Institute in Lexington. With the agreement settled and the assistance of Major Tombs, the following year, Reuben would begin his upper education as a cadet at VMI.

石
水

In the year of our Lord, 1843, a romantic tale continues.
First time away from home and deep hidden emotions…

She's My Girl

The days leading up to Reuben's departure for the Virginia Military Institute were both exciting and sorrowful for everyone in the Duran family, especially for Lucy. Although Monroe was the older brother, Reuben seemed to be the one always coming to her rescue, and Lucy loved Reuben for that. Monroe was more distant. He could not help but feel green with envy for the attention Reuben was receiving from their father who Monroe was trying to model his life after. He had a distain for Reuben choosing to attend the Virginia Military Institute, which he considered a lower educational venue than his alma mater of William and Mary.

One other person who found it very difficult with Reuben leaving home was Renee. Although she disagreed about Reuben taking up a military education, she admired him for the brave move to take up such a disciplined life. Reuben was her best friend, a relationship she would gladly keep instead of her arranged wedding to be held in the next few years. Sadly, she would cry herself to sleep thinking she didn't want to forget about Reuben, but it was best for her future. Hating herself for having such thoughts, Renee's hope was in time, with his absence, she would distance herself from Reuben, and eventually forget about him altogether. But even at a young age, Renee could not allow herself to think of forgetting the boy with whom she grew up and for whom she had affectionate feelings. Knowing it was a relationship that could never be, she began to put pen to paper and write her thoughts in the form of passages. It was this one passage she accidently gave to Reuben's mother as a homework assignment before her father pulled her out of the city public school where she and Reuben attended, and enrolled her into Norfolk's prestigious Wickham Finishing School for Girls to prepare her for the life of a Southern aristocratic wife.

I raise my walls around my heart
But your spell causes them to crumble
And my heart bleeds love into your hand
A hand I long for but cannot hold
I allow myself to be tortured
With painful dreams of happiness
Happiness longed for but unattainable
But nothing is unattainable so I am told

The passage Renee wrote moved Coleen to tears and amazed her how a girl of Renee's youth could have such emotion in her writing. She confronted Renee about the passage, a confrontation that led to much embarrassment for Renee, until Coleen assured her what she read will never be known, but needed to know one thing for certain.

"Renee, my darling, this passage is so passionately filled with so much emotion that I must ask you a serious question."

"What's that, Mrs. Duran?"

"These words, are they how you feel about my son?"

Renee looked at Coleen with her adorable, large, brown eyes, a hint of sorrow within, and without looking away, Renee said as her eyes began to water, "Yes, Mrs. Duran. Please don't be mad."

"Oh, sweetheart, I could never be mad at you, especially for being so truthful," said Coleen as she reached and took Renee into her arms. "But remember, my dear Renee, both you and Reuben are still very young. You both have your entire lives ahead of you. Do you understand?"

"I do, but that doesn't make it any easier," replied Renee as she affectionately rested her face on Coleen's shoulder, something she could never attempt with her own mother.

Coleen moved to cup Renee's face in her hands and gently spoke to her in a motherly way, "I know it's hard and you must believe me, although he doesn't show it, it's just as hard for my son. You must promise me two things."

"Yes, Mrs. Duran?"

"Whatever you do, first, never give up faith and love. Second, continue to write these marvelous passages. Your words are a true gift from God and they will leave your mark on this world."

Renee again embraced Coleen and held her tightly as she said, "I promise, to both."

As for Reuben, like his mother said to Renee, he held his emotions and affections for Renee deep within himself. In order to cope with the dilemma, his focus became to be more toward his future studies at the institute. Major Tombs was able to secure Reuben access to Fort Norfolk for some advance study and military drill, both of which he took to immediately and impressed many of the officers and non-commissioned officers of the fort. Most of his spare time was spent at the fort, and when Reuben wasn't at home when Renee came to visit, she could not help but feel she had lost her friend.

The times Renee and Reuben did get to spend with each other were often in the Duran home. With his access to Fort Norfolk, the Duran family didn't make it out to the farm as often as in previous years. Their visits were usually held in the parlor with the family or on the front doorsteps on their own. They both tried to avoid looking at each other directly when they visited and they no longer physically teased one another. Their discussions tended to be more mature in nature, such as her father's business on how her arranged marriage would make it more profitable. They also discussed his plans after VMI, if he were to make the army a career, or use what he learned to continue the avenue of education to become a teacher or university professor like he had discussed in the past.

狼

As quickly as the summer began, it was coming to an end, and time for Reuben to depart on his educational adventure that would lead him to Lexington, Virginia. Never having been on a train before, Reuben was excited. He was in a bitter-sweet time of his life, wanting to see what lay outside the Norfolk region, but not wanting to leave his family behind. Will I be so homesick, they will send me home in disgrace, is what he worried about the most. After all the troubles his father went through to secure a seat for Reuben, he didn't want to let Aaron down. He knew taking on a military education wasn't what his parent's wished for him, but they still admired his determination to seek out the unknown wonders away from where he lived all his life.

Monroe felt a combination of relief, and also disbelief. He was relieved Reuben was leaving and hoping their father would now share as much enthusiasm for Monroe's studies of becoming a lawyer much like Aaron, but also found it difficult to see his younger brother leave. Wishing he was as brave as Reuben, Monroe also felt discontent toward him and guilt for having such feelings. What has he ever done to me that I should dislike him, Monroe often thought, especially now. Reuben was always supportive toward his older brother, and like Lucy, he always stood by his brother's side, many times protecting him from bullies who tormented Monroe because of his studious nature. Reuben knew Monroe harbored such negative emotions, but never let them seem as if they bothered him. Perhaps that is what caused Monroe to continue his misgivings toward his younger sibling. But for now, he put all that aside as they neared the train depot.

"I don't think you packed enough, son. That bag seems awfully light," said Coleen with much concern.

"I have what Major Tombs said I would need the most, underwear and socks. Everything else will be supplied, so please don't worry, Mama," answered Reuben as reassuring as he could.

"Oh, I hate to see you leave without much nicer clothes and heavier coat. It gets much colder in the Valley than it does here, from what I understand."

"Now, dear," said Aaron as he placed his arm around his wife's shoulder. "Reuben will be issued a very heavy wool coat. Probably warm enough to make him sweat in the coldest of weather."

The Duran family made their way through the station and onto the platform. Lucy was clutching onto Reuben's bag as if her life depended on it. Looking at the clock on the wall, Reuben noticed he had 15 minutes left with his family. He took his mother's hands and told her, "Mama, I love you so dearly. I will make you very proud." He embraced her tightly.

"I love you, my dear son," she replied as she began to sob. Reuben held her tenderly and kissed her for reassurance.

He turned to Monroe. "Listen, brother, you may not understand, but I love you with all my being. It's you who has encouraged me to continue learning. It may not be in a prestigious university such as William and Mary, but it's still education, all thanks to you." He offered his hand and Monroe took it in both of his.

"Make me proud, little brother. Make me proud to tell my classmates I have a cadet as a brother," he answered as all of his angered emotions toward Reuben suddenly disappeared.

Reuben now turned to Lucy. She released his bag, letting it drop to the platform and leaped into his arms. She began sobbing into Reuben's shoulders and he held her close. He said softly into her right ear, "It's up to you, baby sister. It's up to you to keep this family strong, you hear me? At least until I return."

Lucy lifted her face to look at her brother, "I will. I promise."

Reuben now looked to his Father. As Aaron began to offer his hand, Reuben went to embrace him. No words were spoken, but the emotion between the two could be felt by all. Reuben released his hold as he stared into his father's eyes. Aaron cupped Reuben's face with his hands and kissed him on his forehead. "You will do wonders, boy. You will do wonders."

Aaron released his son and reached into his inside jacket pocket and retrieved a small black velvet bag. "Here, son, as with Monroe to help him get to classes on time, your mother and I got you this watch. No son of ours is going to be tardy to any of his classes."

Reuben took the watch from the bag and looked it over. It was marvelous. He embraced his parents in gratitude.

"Well, I hope it's my turn to say goodbye," said a soft voice behind Monroe and Lucy.

Everyone turned to see Renee looking as radiant as ever. Her long, dark, brown hair was flowing over her shoulders just as Reuben liked, as if she wore it that way just for him.

Aaron and Coleen released their embrace on Reuben and turned him to face Renee. The rest of the family cleared a path for Reuben to meet Renee. Expecting only a hand shake, Renee was taken by surprise when Reuben took her into his arms and tenderly hugged her. She raised her arms and wrapped them around Reuben and held him tightly. It was an embrace they had been longing to share, and no matter what the consequences, they were going to enjoy it.

The affection the two were sharing at this moment should have been awkward for everyone present, but it wasn't. It was welcomed and looked upon with sheer warmth and delight. As for Renee and Reuben, without speaking, neither of them wanted this moment to end.

A tear began to run down Renee's cheek. She so wanted to express her love for Reuben in words and a kiss. Instead, she placed her face on his shoulder.

"I can't believe you actually came to say farewell. I didn't think your father would let you come."

Renee lifted her head to look into Reuben's eyes. Her eyes were still glistening with fallen tears, yet she could still produce the bright smile that always brought joy to Reuben's heart. "He didn't," she replied. "I couldn't miss coming to say farewell with your family for the world, so I snuck away," she continued with a hint of a giggle.

Reuben chuckled in return saying, "I'm going to miss our adventures and shenanigans so very much," and pulled her back into his embrace.

22

"ALL ABOARD... ALL ABOARD! Engine 73 now boarding for Petersburg, Amelia Court House, Buckingham, and Lexington! ALL ABOARD!"

The call from the conductor felt like a spike being driven through Reuben's stomach, and caused both Renee and Reuben to hold each other tighter. He released his hold on Renee and took his bag from Lucy who began to sob uncontrollably. Coleen was about to console her, but Renee took Lucy into her arms with the warmth and love of an older sister.

Reuben entered the passenger car. Quickly he took a seat directly above his family and raised the window. He leaned outside raising his hand as the train began to lunge, creeping forward. As it began to gain momentum, Lucy couldn't contain herself any longer, broke free from Renee's hold, and began to chase after Reuben. Renee followed after her.

As she caught up to Reuben's window, Lucy reached and pulled the purple ribbon holding her hair. "Reuben, here, take my ribbon for luck!" she yelled.

He reached down and grasped her hand and let it slide away leaving the ribbon in his just as the car cleared the platform. Lucy came to a stop at the edge and waved as Reuben waved back.

Renee caught up to Lucy and took her into her arms again and they both watched as the train rolled away. A sudden fearsome chill ran through Renee as she felt a premonition. A premonition in the near and distant future, Reuben will fall victim to severe tribulations and she will need to be stronger than ever before, not only for her sake, but for his as well.

狼

Reuben roamed the corridor admiring the workmanship of the dormitory. The moment he arrived at the Institute, he was in so much wonder of all the surroundings. All his thoughts of homesickness had long vanished. He was now on his own and it was a magnificent feeling. He wondered if this is how Monroe felt when away in Williamsburg attending William and Mary.

Unlike other newly arriving cadets and classmates, Reuben adapted immediately to the direct orders of the senior cadets instructing them as they were being indoctrinated. All the days Reuben spent observing the soldiers and officers at Fort Norfolk was a great influence, and made a valuable impact. One of the instructors took notice of Reuben, strict and obedient, yet calm and reserved. The instructor nodded in approval. He noticed how, unlike the other new arrivals, Reuben remained quiet, but alert and very detailed. He followed directions quickly with no comment.

Once initial indoctrination was completed, the new arrivals were marched to their dormitory where they would be spending their next four years of study. As Reuben neared the door which would lead to the inside of his cell, he took in a big breath and said to himself, "So this is where your new life begins. Make it a good one."

Reuben opened the door and entered the room to find it was occupied by another new cadet sitting at one of the two small desks facing the large window. He was about Reuben's age, his height, but with blond hair and grayish eyes. He turned to see Reuben standing in the doorway, rose and stepped toward him.

"Greetings, my friend, Adam Stanns is my name. Welcome to dormitory C, room 2D," he said in a very pleasant manner as he presented his hand.

Reuben looked him over, stepped closer, accepted Adam's hand, and said, "Hello. My name is Reuben Duran. This is the room I have been assigned."

"Grand, grand," said Adam gleefully as he shook Reuben's hand feverishly. "I got here yesterday and it has been lonely. I'm finally glad I got a roommate. I'm from Culpepper. From where do you come, Reuben?"

Reuben enjoyed Adam's pleasant tone. Although they just met, Reuben felt as if he made a new friend, the first of his new life.

"I'm from Norfolk."

"Norfolk you say. I've been there. Got family there, I do. Maybe you know them, Jonathan and Ester Allister. They're family from my mother's side. Have you ever been to Culpepper? It's not as big as Norfolk, but much nicer, looks wise. No offense. I just prefer the country towns than the big cities. You don't say much, do you?"

Reuben chuckled, "You really haven't given me a chance."

Adam laughed at himself. "I guess you're right. As I said, I've been here by myself since yesterday. Here, let me help you get settled in. As you can see, I set myself up on this side of the room… first come first serve, you know."

Reuben found Adam's demeanor odd, but amusing. He was reminded of one thing his father had told him.

"Son, when you go away, you'll meet all kinds. Don't be afraid, but don't be complacent. Embrace, but be aware of new experiences and people you meet. It takes all kinds to make this world of ours go round."

For Reuben, Adam was a new kind of person. A kind of person he felt would make a good friend, and as soon as Adam was able to be quiet for a moment, Reuben began to tell him about his family and life story which Adam took much interest.

As Reuben was placing school items on his desk, he looked over and noticed an open image case sitting upon Adam's desk. The image was of a young girl wearing a formal gown standing with her gloved hands folded in front of her. Her hair was in fashion, pulled tight.

"Ah, I see you took notice of Mary Alice," said Adam as he walked over to his desk. He picked up the image and walked over to Reuben and presented it to him for a better view.

Reuben accepted it and carefully held it as he looked it over.

"Mary Alice Colbert is my girl back in Culpepper. She's the most beautiful girl in the world I tell you. She and I will be married after I graduate from VMI, and she will follow me to all my assignments. Her father owns one of the largest horse farms in Virginia. In fact, some of his horses are used right here at the Institute."

Reuben nodded approvingly and handed Adam back the image. "She's very pretty, Adam. You're a very lucky man." Reuben gave a quick thought to Renee. If only things would be different for them he thought, then maybe he could call Renee his girl. That quick thought caused Reuben to slump in sadness, and Adam noticed.

Adam placed his image of Mary Alice on his desk and turned his attention to Reuben. "How about you, Reuben, do you have a girl back in Norfolk?"

Looking outside the window toward the mountians, Reuben breathed out heavily, "No, not exactly."

"Not exactly, what does that mean?"

"I have a friend back home. She's my best friend, not exactly my girl, if you understand my meaning."

Adam felt as if he hit upon an open wound. Trying to defuse the awkwardness in the room, he cheerfully placed his arm around Reuben's shoulders. "Well, no matter, Reuben, my friend. Perhaps on one of our furloughs, you can come along with me to Culpepper so Mary Alice can introduce you to one her friends. Now mind you, her friends are pretty and all, but not as beautiful as my Mary."

Reuben nodded and said, "You know, Adam, it would be nice to meet new people. Maybe that's what I need. But for now, I think we better get ready for what this school has in store for us."

"Agreed Reuben, Agreed."

狼

Reuben was having the time of his life and adjusting very well to the surroundings of VMI. Unlike many of his fellow classmates, he adapted to the ridged discipline, rules, and regulations easily. He was prompt and diligent in all manner of his duties. He lived by the philosophy of the sergeant major that provided much of Reuben's instruction at Fort Norfolk.

"Mind your own business and keep your damn mouth shut. If you have a question, keep it to yourself, more than likely another will have the same question, so let him ask it. If no one asks the question you have, then it isn't important so forget about it. And never volunteer, it only gets you into the shit."

It was a philosophy that had been serving Reuben very well. Following it, he learned exactly what and when to ask without repercussions. Unfortunately, the one who always seemed to bear the brunt of many asked questions was Reuben's friend and roommate, Adam.

Adam was proving not only to be a good friend, but a great study asset as well. Reuben feared he would fail because of the one course of study he detested more than any other subject, mathematics. He discussed this fear with Adam and it was Adam who came up with the solution, Adam would tutor Reuben. Adam was a mathematical genius and was able to apply mathematics in everyday situations that Reuben could understand. In return, Reuben tutored Adam in his worst areas of study, English and military protocol and drill. With the help of the other, they both excelled in their respective weakest subjects of study.

The daily routine of school and duties fell into place for the two roommates. They became so in tune with the schedules, they could tell the time by not looking at a clock.

The one day all the cadets looked forward to was when mail arrived. Reuben received letters from his mother and father. They kept him informed of all the happenings of the city and the farm. Lucy would also send him letters on her own which surprised Reuben because he thought she was too young to use the post. One time she even included a letter from Noah. It was a short letter, but it made Reuben feel good Noah still remembered what he had taught him about reading and writing.

Lucy also mentioned she would visit Renee at her school. She wrote they had to visit in secret behind, what Lucy called, the old gloomy school Renee's father made her attend.

Lucy would mention in her letters that Renee always asked how Reuben was doing and for her to send him Renee's regards. Lucy explained in one of her letters Renee had tried to send him a letter herself, but Renee's father caught her, became furious, and tore up the letter. She wrote how sorry she felt for Renee because how strict her father had become. Lucy heard he was very angry with Renee when he found out she came to see Reuben off at the train station.

As cruel as it felt, Reuben tried not to think of Renee's situation. He felt she wouldn't want him to concern himself with her troubles, but for him to focus on his studies. It was hard for him not to think of her, especially when Adam would, once again, shout for joy when he received a letter from Mary Alice Colbert.

Adam received a letter from Mary Alice almost every mail day, and every time he received a letter from her, he felt it was his duty to read her words to everyone within earshot. With every letter he went on and on about how lucky he was to have the most beautiful girl in Culpepper waiting for him. Of course, Reuben had to bear Adam's good fortune twice, once in the courtyard, and again in their dormitory cell.

And so the days for the two cadets turned into weeks, and then months until the Christmas season was upon them, and that meant Christmas furlough.

狼

The great ballroom was trimmed beautifully for the festive occasion. There was no doubt Christmas was in full swing in the city of Norfolk, although one wouldn't know it amongst the attendees to this ball. The ballroom housed all of Norfolk's socially elite families and politicians. The orchestra played wonderful waltzes, but no one was paying attention. Functions like this in the beginning were more for the so called influential members of society to pay tributes to those who would provide support in one endeavor or other. It wasn't until much later when the occasion would begin to take on the appearance of a celebration. In the meantime, the group of beautifully dressed debutants from the Wickham Finishing School for Girls stood amongst themselves, making snide comments about other ladies' fashions, and obliged themselves discussing and conjuring up rumors of other debutants out of ear shot. That is, all but one debutant.

Renee, in a very pretty light green ball gown, was seated at a beautifully laid out table by herself. She was fondling a linen napkin with a fork as she was eyeing a black velvet bag that held an image case which was delivered to her moments before entering the hall. Renee's mood was gloomy as she wished she was anywhere else but in this ballroom. In her mind, she was dreading the upcoming trip to Charleston to spend the holiday with the Sinclair family at their invitation. In four years, she will be wed to young William Sinclair, her arranged fiancé.

She ignored the image case and began to fold the napkin into a tree, the way Lucy would when she set the Christmas table in the Duran household. When she finished, Renee placed the folded decoration directly in front of her and she looked upon it with delight. Memories of the times she spent with Reuben's family during the Christmas season were some of her favorite. She was always made welcome and felt as if she were a member of the Duran family.

How she wished Reuben would come home from VMI so she could visit with him before she was "dragged" to South Carolina. Renee had not spoken with him since the day he departed. She attempted to write Reuben a letter until her father caught her and he became furious.

"A true Southern lady does not write letters to other boys when she has a promised fiancé!" he yelled as he took the letter she had been working on and tore it into shreds.

Once her marriage arrangement was made, Franklin Wallace quickly pulled Renee out of the city public school where she and Reuben attended together. Franklin enrolled Renee in Norfolk's prestigious Wickham Finishing School for Girls to be prepared to become a proper lady of the South, and to learn the ways of social grace and culture to become a devoted Southern aristocratic wife, ideals Franklin Wallace strongly felt Renee lacked and would never learn while attending the regular public school.

Renee hated Wickham. The hooped skirts, gloved hands, curtseys, etiquette lessons, and boring, dull educational classes... she hated it all. The school's head mistress boasted the school teaches the girls to be proper, elegant, and non-judgmental, everything the over-privileged girls attending Wickham were not, although every student prided herself to be. It seemed Renee was the only girl who lived up to the head mistress' boasts, but her teachers and schoolmates were too upper crust and out of touch to notice. Renee constantly broke infractions because of her spirit to be free of social bonds. Had it not been for the groundskeeper, Martin Doogan, Renee would have gone insane.

Martin Doogan had been the groundskeeper for many years and saw a refreshing joy in Renee. Although he was superb at keeping the grounds of Wickham elaborate, to the faculty and students, he was only an attendant to serve the school, with the exception of Renee, who treated him as a respected elder, much the same way she treated Reuben's father. In return, Martin Doogan treated Renee as the only true lady of the school. He allowed her access to his workshop and sheds where she could pull the pins from her hair to let it cascade over her shoulders, just how Reuben liked it, and escape the tedious school routines.

Her thoughts of the Duran family's Christmas holidays were rudely interrupted when two of her finishing school classmates loudly seated themselves next to Renee. Elizabeth Rogers, a pretty brunette debutant dressed in a festive green dress, sat to Renee's right as Cynthia Garratt, with blonde hair and just as pretty wearing a soft colored lavender dress, seated herself to Renee's left. They were both giggling and fanning their faces as they were taught in school.

"My dear Renee, what are you doing here all by your lonesome? Did you not see that group of young men from Chandler Academy enter the room?" asked Cynthia in a cheerful manner. Chandler Academy was the equivalent boy's school to the finishing school Renee and the other girls at the ball attended. The boys that attended Chandler Academy were just as over-privileged as the girls of Wickham.

Cynthia Garrett had become Renee's nemesis at Wickham. She always pointed out Renee had a previous public education and wasn't good enough to attend Wickham. Cynthia led a group of girls who often harassed and tormented Renee. However, Renee was able to keep her nemesis in-check with the help of Martin Doogan, who knew scandalous secrets of the student's families. He also helped Renee by "suggesting" how to play pranks on Cynthia and her group, something she wished Reuben could be a part of.

"Oh, Cynthia, Renee cannot be bothered by those no-bodies from Chandler. She already has a handsome well to do man waiting for her," answered Elizabeth.

Renee rolled her eyes at the comment made by Elizabeth and went back to looking at the folded decoration.

"Yes, Renee, when do you and your parents depart to Charleston for your holiday visit with the Sinclair family? I do believe you will have a grand time," commented Cynthia. "I would sure love to see Charleston during this time of the year."

"We leave the day after tomorrow. We'll be away for a week," said Renee with no enthusiasm in her voice.

Elizabeth lightly clapped her hands and said, "How lucky you are to have your future secure with a handsome man who will play a part in his father's successful shipping business. I saw him when he came to pick you up from school a few weeks ago. He is one handsome boy."

"I agree," said Cynthia. "I saw him also, tall with light brown hair and blue eyes. Yes indeed, very handsome and much older than the boys from Chandler Academy. I understand he is attending University in South Carolina. Is that right, Renee?"

Not taking her eyes off the napkin, Renee answered, "Yes, the University of South Carolina in Columbia. He's studying law."

William Sinclair was close to Reuben's age. When Renee's father first boasted about William Sinclair to Renee of how intelligent and aristocratic he was, following in the footsteps of his father, Stephen Sinclair, the owner of Sinclair Southeastern Shipping, Renee thought, if William Sinclair is so great, then why does he need help securing a wife.

There was more to it than that Renee came to find out. Not only would her union to the Sinclair boy separate her from Reuben Duran, it would merge Franklin Wallace's shipping company with Stephen's, thus doubling his business and profits. As far as Franklin Wallace was concerned, the Durans were common, and a union with his daughter and their son would only damage his image.

The more she thought of her arranged marriage, the more she would fall deeper into depression. Cynthia and Elizabeth didn't make matters better by talking about how handsome and successful William Sinclair was, and how lucky Renee was whenever they would be with her. Renee knew they were doing so out of spite. She had overheard these two girls discuss with other, over-privileged girls, how ungrateful Renee was to be promised to a handsome young man with a great future ahead of him. They both knew about Renee's friendship with Reuben and at times, they would purposely provoke Renee to get her into trouble by teasing her about how Reuben and his family were not as privileged and socially acceptable as their fathers claimed the Durans to be. Such talk would cause Renee to break into a frenzy, and sometimes, physically attack Cynthia and other girls. These outbursts always got Renee in trouble with the school and of course, her father.

However, this evening, their conversation was sincere in nature, probably because of the holiday atmosphere in the ballroom. Cynthia's and Elizabeth's conversation about Renee's fiancé transitioned from William Sinclair's success, to being compared to the boys from Chandler Academy. Some of their comments caused Renee to smile and even laugh, not out of amusement of their discussion, but because she could not believe how so called "ladies of culture" could be so hypocritical. These moments of amusement were her silent way of criticizing these "ladies" without them being aware.

The conversation died down to topics of school lessons and the upcoming term after the holidays. Cynthia and Elizabeth discussed what they felt would be the most difficult subjects they were about to enter, and into the spring ball.

"Although the balls and dances are always with the boys from Chandler, I still look forward to them. When else will we get a chance to have a man other than our fathers dance with us?" commented Elizabeth.

"The boys from Chandler are not men, Elizabeth," replied Cynthia. "Unless you count the seniors of the school. Now those boys… or men, as I put it, are the ones I take my aim. They tend to take notice to girls our age, much like Renee's William. Men of older age tend to adore younger women, so if you can catch the eye of a Chandler senior, you may have a chance of a good future… Elizabeth, are you listening to me?"

Elizabeth's attention was focused on a very young girl entering the ballroom escorted by a boy in a cadet uniform. "Yes, Cynthia, I am listening, but I would rather have the eye of a man in a cadet uniform like that one escorting that girl into the hall."

"Oh yes, indeed," responded Cynthia. "Who is that I wonder?" she continued as both girls were straining for a better view of the couple entering the hall. Renee's attention was back on the folded napkin, placing sugar cubes at its foot giving the appearance of Christmas gifts under a tree.

"Heavens to be, it can't be," said Elizabeth in a surprised tone. "There is no possible way. Is that? Oh my goodness! It is! That's Lucy Duran and her brother Reuben!"

Renee's head shot up like a rocket. Quickly she looked toward the entrance of the ballroom but could not see them.

"Great sakes, you're right, Elizabeth, you're right. I did not know Reuben was a cadet. I wonder which school. Richmond? Certainly not the Virginia Military Institute," replied Cynthia.

Renee could not locate Lucy and Reuben and began to think the two girls were playing a cruel game with her, until she saw Reuben's parents and Monroe enter the ballroom. It was then when she rose, bumping the table causing some of the glasses to tumble over. Frantically she scanned over the crowd, which had grown, looking for Reuben when she caught the sight of a cadet uniform from the back. She gathered up the napkin she had folded, the image case, and headed off in that direction. She stopped suddenly, turned toward the two girls with their mouths gaping open. "Sorry, please excuse me. I have to wish Merry Christmas to my best friend, and yes, he is a Virginia Military Institute cadet!" she proudly exclaimed and was off.

狼

Lucy was all aglow looking radiant in a soft yellow gown with her hair tied up in a ribbon to match. She stood erect with pride walking next to her brother, arm-in-arm, in his VMI cadet uniform. She greeted everyone, introducing her brother who everyone knew, but indulged her, and also looked upon Reuben with pride as well. Not many boys from the region have the opportunity to attend VMI, so they also took it as a considerable achievement for the city of Norfolk to have Aaron's son represent the area.

They were making their way to the table the family usually occupies until Reuben slowed down his pace causing Lucy to follow. "Hold on, Lucy. I think we're way ahead of Mama, Da, and Monroe," said Reuben as he turned to locate them. As he did so, he turned into the most beautiful sight he had not seen in a long time.

"Renee! Is that you?!" he cheerfully exclaimed.

Without waiting for a reply, he wrapped his arms around Renee and lifted her off the floor in a warm embrace, which she returned.

"Of course it's me, you silly. Who else would take the time to come and wish you Merry Christmas?" she said just as cheerful, her eyes shining and a smile on her face. She actually felt a little ache in her cheeks for she hadn't smiled that big in a long time.

The moment they released each other, Renee went to embrace Lucy. "Merry Christmas, Lucy."

"You as well, Renee," replied Lucy, joyfully. "So what do you think of my handsome brother in his uniform? Does he not put the other boys to shame?" she said proudly taking his arm.

"That he does. Oh my, I do believe he's blushing," answered Renee with a gentle laugh.

Reuben did feel flushed and looked downward, until Renee, using her fingertips, lifted his chin saying as she looked strongly into his eyes, "So very handsome."

"Renee! Merry Christmas, my dear lass, Merry Christmas to you," said Aaron Duran as he, Coleen, and Monroe finally caught up to Reuben and Lucy.

Renee turned to face them and not only took Aaron's hand, but also hugged him, Coleen, and even Monroe in greeting.

"This is fantastic, do you have time to sit and visit with us, Renee?" asked Coleen.

Renee looked all around the room for her parents and didn't see a trace of them and happily replied, "Of course I do."

Lucy released Reuben's arm allowing Renee to take it, and took Monroe's arm. The three ladies were all escorted to their usual table and took seats.

They spent quite a while visiting at the table. The visit consisted of catching up on topics over the past fall months and memories of the Christmas seasons past. Renee showed Lucy the napkin she had folded earlier and soon they had all the napkins at their table folded into little trees.

The orchestra began to play a festive melody causing Monroe to stand, "Lucy, my dear sister… may I have this dance?"

"What a capital idea," said Aaron as he too took to his feet and offered his hand to Coleen. Coleen took his hand and they were off to the dance floor along with Monroe and Lucy.

"Well, Cadet Duran, are you going to ask me to dance?" asked Renee in a playful tone. She knew Reuben didn't care to dance and she continued to tease him about that.

"I would if I knew how to dance," he said. "But not to worry, they teach us how to dance next term between infantry and artillery drills so the next dance, I'll be ready."

They both laughed so hard, it caused others to notice, but they didn't care. They both were extremely excited to be together. They sat at a respectful distance, but could not take their eyes off of each other.

"So, how's school, Wickham girl?" asked Reuben in a teasing manner.

"Oh shut up, Reuben, that's not funny," she replied lightly slapping his shoulder.

"Yes it is."

Renee let out a little chuckle, "Okay, yeah, I'll give you that one."

"So what's it like, Wickham?" asked Reuben in a very serious and interested manner. "Is it as stuffy as we always joked about when we would walk by that school?"

Every day, after school, Reuben would walk Renee home and they would pass Wickham Finishing School for Girls, and thought of it as an institution that turned out the most snobbish girls in Norfolk. There were many times, Renee and Reuben, and sometimes Lucy, would sit across the street laughing and pointing out the most pompous Wickham girl of the day.

"Geez oh geez oh geez it's so stupid, Reuben, worse than we joked about because it's all true."

Reuben made a sour look and said, "Whoa, that bad, huh? Ha! I bet you're causing all sorts of agony for the other students and teachers though."

They both laughed. Renee told Reuben about Martin Doogan and if it wasn't for him, she would be living in an insane asylum. Reuben was happy she at least had one friend who could offer her some refuge. He was also happy to hear Lucy would secretly go and visit her.

Reuben noticed the black velvet bag Renee had resting near her since they had first seated themselves at the table. "What's that, if I may ask?" he asked, hesitantly.

Renee looked at the bag and reached to pick it up. She looked it over and said as she stared at it with no emotion in her gaze or tone, "It's my Christmas present for William Sinclair. It's a tintype image I had taken of me at Mr. Armon's studio the other day. He delivered it to me moments before I entered the hall." She wasn't enthusiastic in discussing the gift. "My father thought it would be a '*Wonderful*' gift for William Sinclair." She still couldn't bring herself to say William's name without including his surname.

Very timidly, Reuben asked if he could see it. Renee, still staring at the bag, took a tighter grip as if she was trying to crush it. She loosened her grasp as she felt Reuben's warm hands over hers. Her gaze shifted from the bag to his eyes. She felt a small amount of energy from his touch, and he had that childlike smile on his face she adored so much. Without saying anything, she loosened the draw string and handed it to Reuben. He gently took it. He looked it over and caressed the rose carved into the wood which Reuben found unusual because he knew Renee wasn't fond of roses. He turned it to the edge and carefully unhooked the clasp holding the halves together. Slowly opening the case like an antique book, he saw the inside was lined with black velvet.

The image itself was of Renee standing next to an empty chair, the chair representing the "throne" her future husband would be occupying. She was wearing a formal gown and her hair groomed tight against her scalp. Her eyes were emotionless looking off in a distance.

"Well, what do you think?" asked Renee.

Reuben could clearly see the pain in her emotionless eyes in the image, yet he couldn't stop looking at it. Without looking away, he said, "You're very pretty, Renee." He gently closed the case and hooked the clasp shut. He turned his attention back to Renee while placing the case on the table next to her and continued, "That picture does you no justice and doesn't capture the true heart and soul I've come to know and love."

Desperately wanting to embrace Reuben, she could only bring herself to smile brightly and her face was once again joyful. "Well, considering the circumstances for the image, I hope you can understand the way I look. Mr. Armon suggested the pose as '*the traditional devoted wife,* '" said Renee with a hint of sarcasm.

"Renee, you're anything but traditional," said Reuben in a mocking manner.

"Oh, you're so lucky we are in a formal setting or I'd be arm twisting you to the ground," replied Renee in a joking manner, then laughing after.

"So how are things with your father? Are you still giving him grief about living in Charleston?" asked Reuben.

Blowing air out of the side of her mouth, upward in frustration, Renee said, "You certainly know how to ruin a moment."

Suddenly feeling awkward, Reuben replied, "I'm sorry, Renee. I just wanted to know how you've been doing. If you'd rather not talk about…"

She cut him off, not allowing him to finish, "I want to hear all about your first term at VMI! Now that sounds exciting! Is the valley as beautiful as I've heard? All I've ever seen is harbors, rivers, and beaches, but never the hills and mountains in western Virginia."

"Oh, Renee, you'd love it. Especially with the changing of the color of the trees, it's a sight to see."

"Tell me about the campus of the Institute. How are your grades, Reuben? What type of classes are you studying?" asked Renee, excitedly.

"The campus is laid out nicely and with a wonderful view no matter where you are. My classes are very interesting. We study military doctrine and instruction, and of course, we have the usual history, sciences, English, and mathematics, and you will never guess what, my grades in mathematics are great. Imagine that!"

Looking very happily surprised, Renee replied "Great grades in mathematics? How could that be? Both your mother and I couldn't get you to understand mathematics at all."

"I have a roommate who is very smart in mathematics and shows me how they can be put to actual use. His name is Adam Stanns. He's from Culpepper. We have a mutual study agreement."

"Mutual study agreement?" asked Renee, truly interested.

"Yes, he isn't good in English and military drills, so I tutor him in both, and he tutors me in mathematics."

"He sounds like a good friend. How did you meet him?"

"I met him the first day I arrived. He had arrived the day before." Reuben chuckled under his breath.

Renee smiled, "What's so funny?"

"Adam is a good friend, but he does have one flaw. His girl, Mary Alice Colbert," said Reuben, smirking. "Don't get me wrong, she sounds like a wonderful girl, but that's all Adam talks about. He receives a letter from her almost once a week and he always reads them out loud to us over and over and over and over again. Since I'm his roommate, I get to hear them all over again later in the day." Reuben began to laugh at the thoughts of Adam bragging about "his girl". That was until he noticed Renee looking down and her smile fading away.

"What's wrong, Renee?"

Renee, looking up and with regret in her eyes, said, "Reuben, I'm very sorry I haven't sent you any letters. I did start writing you a letter, but my father caught me and he got very angry and tore it up."

"Please don't worry about that, Renee. I understand and I felt that's the reason why I've not received any mail from you. You are my best friend, Renee, and best friends always have a bond that is much stronger than mail," he said with a very reassuring smile.

Renee's smile returned, but still looked uneasy. Reuben was being as strong as he could. Deep inside, he longed to take Renee in his arms and hold her much more than one would hold a "best friend". He understood her dilemma of her arranged marriage and he hid his feelings well. Renee, on the other hand, knew Reuben was doing his best to hide his feelings toward her for her sake.

Quickly trying to ease the sudden awkward silence, Reuben said, "Mama tells me you've become quite a good poet. Is that true?"

Looking downward to hide her blushing cheeks, Renee let out a giggle. "I wouldn't say a good poet. I accidently gave your mother a passage I wrote before my father pulled me out of her class. I was so embarrassed, but she reassured me of my talent and thought it was full of emotion and told me I had a gift. She made me promise to keep writing."

"And are you? Still writing, that is? Will I get to read any of your work?"

Renee was suddenly at a loss of words. The thoughts in her written work, is a result of the pain she is going through with a love she cannot pursue. If he reads my work, he will know it's about him, she thought.

"I'm not sure, Reuben. They're kind of personal."

"Oh, I see," said Reuben rather disappointed.

Renee saw she hurt Reuben's feelings, but she couldn't bring herself to let Reuben have the opportunity to read her passages, or even recite them to him. It would make their dilemma that much more painful.

"I'm sorry, Reuben. Maybe when I think my work is good enough for you to read, I'll let you have a look at them," she said hoping that answer would ease the mild tension.

"I understand. You want to wait until you're a famous author, and then you'll make me pay to read your poems," said Reuben with a cheerful smile, which in turn caused Renee to again giggle.

Hoping to change the topic, Reuben quickly startled Renee by saying, "Hey, Renee, I have something for you. An early Christmas present, if you will."

Renee's face brightened up as Reuben turned his back toward her and he lowered his head. Reuben undid the bottom button from his tunic, grasped the button tightly, and tugged sharply. The button snapped off and Reuben turned back to face Renee.

"Hold out your hand."

Renee did so and Reuben placed a shiny VMI button in the palm of her hand. "It's not much, but it's all I have to give you."

Renee looked at the shiny button and suddenly clenched it in her hand and leaped forward and gave Reuben a very tight hug.

"Geez oh geez oh geez Reuben, this is the best gift I have ever received," she said holding back tears of joy. "Will you get in trouble for pulling a button off your uniform?"

"Don't worry, I can have it replaced. Besides, it's worth it because I know it will be in safe keeping."

"I will cherish it always," she commented more to herself as she cupped the button in both hands, looking upon it as if it were a lost treasure. It was a reaction which made Reuben feel warm inside causing him to feel relieved he could still bring happiness to his best friend.

Renee looked up and over Reuben's right shoulder. She saw her parents enter the ballroom and her smile faded. Reuben, seeing her expression change, slowly turned and looked into the direction Renee was focused on.

"I guess you have to leave now, huh?"

"Yes, I suppose. But I had such a wonderful time with you. The best I've had in a very long time," Renee said with a very charming smile and hint of affection in her eyes.

Franklin Wallace and his wife Margaret strolled quickly to the table once he noticed Renee sitting with Reuben. As they neared, Reuben smirked at Renee and said, "Watch this."

Reuben stood very erect and turned to Renee's parents. Standing at cadet attention, he held out his hand and in a very gallant charming voice he spoke. "Good evening Mr. and Mrs. Wallace. Permit me to wish upon you a most sincere holiday greetings from myself and the rest of my family. I do hope the upcoming year will prove most successful for you, your business, and your family."

Renee's father, completely dumbfounded, his stern expression of hidden anger turned to confusion. Renee's mother nudged him at his elbow causing him to startle. He took Reuben's offered hand and shook it in greeting.

"Ah... Happy Christmas to you as well, young Duran. My, my, you have really matured this past fall. The Institute has been very promising to you," said Franklin Wallace as he turned to his wife. "What do you think, Margaret, my dear?"

As he turned to his wife to make the comment, Reuben quickly looked toward Renee, winked his left eye at her, and turned back before Franklin Wallace returned his attention to Reuben. Renee found it difficult not to let out a laugh, lowered her head, and gently covered her mouth.

"Yes indeed and my, have you grown. That uniform suits you very well," replied Renee's mother, genuinely impressed.

Renee's mother was the foundation of a true Southern lady and wife of a powerful Southern businessman. She knew of Renee's unhappiness, but felt Franklin Wallace's word on the matter of Renee's life was law. Renee disliked and seldom spoke to her.

"Please pass on to your parents and family our greetings in kind, young Duran. Come Renee, we must leave. We have much to do before our journey to Charleston."

Renee, again gathered the folded napkin and velvet bag containing the image case, and stood with the assistance of Reuben's hand. "Yes, father. Goodbye, Reuben. Good wishes on your studies when you return to VMI."

"Have a safe trip," answered Reuben as he watched Renee's father shuffle her off toward the door of the ballroom. Just moments before they reached the door, Renee quickly turned to see Reuben watching her and she quickly gave him an affectionate smile and wave.

Once inside the carriage, sitting with her back toward her parents, Renee removed the shiny VMI button out of her little handbag. She grasped it tightly and held it to her heart, bowed her head down, and began praying for Reuben's safety and success.

狼

The days following Christmas furlough were once again filled with rigorous class work, military drills, and duties. Reuben and Adam spent almost every waking minute with their heads in books or on the parade ground. Adam made good on his promise to tutor Reuben in mathematics in their cell, and in return, Reuben made sure Adam was well versed in English subjects and military drill.

On the parade ground, Reuben was making very good impressions with the senior cadets as well as the faculty during military drills and parade. He excelled in military doctrine and protocols, and showed an uncanny ability to understand battlefield strategy. When looking at maps and charts of historical battles, he could see the flat graphs in three dimensions, and point out points of interest that even a most experienced army officer never saw.

As a student, Reuben maintained the philosophy of the sergeant major from Fort Norfolk to keep quiet and observe. It was a philosophy that kept Reuben from being disciplined, unlike Adam, who was given demerits, mostly for talking too much. The faculty viewed Reuben as quiet, modest, and reserved with a great attention span for details. Reuben never volunteered for any extra duties or activities, another piece of advice from the sergeant major. He was told by the sergeant major that extra duties and activities only attract unnecessary attention to yourself and distracts you from your purpose, education… or gets you killed.

And so the days turned into weeks. And the weeks turned into months. The routine of classes and duties became second nature and no longer was the lack of time complained about, it was accepted.

The only day set aside by all cadets, and even the faculty to take time for themselves is when the mail arrived. As for Reuben, mail day was met with not as much enthusiasm as the others. He did receive letters from his family and was much appreciative, but he always wished Renee's father would allow her to correspond with him. However, he understood and didn't want Renee to feel her father's wrath of trying to send him a letter.

For the class of '47, mail day was both a grand day, and also one to dread. Almost everyone received a letter, and the one who could always be counted on receiving a letter was Adam Stanns. He received at least one letter from Mary Alice Colbert on almost every mail day. There were a couple of times he didn't receive her weekly letter, and each time he moaned and sulked the entire day making everyone miserable. The cadets of the class of '47 didn't know what was worse, when Adam received a letter or didn't. When he received a letter he was obnoxious with his gloating, reading it out loud over and over, and praising how he was the luckiest man to have the most beautiful girl in the world waiting for him back in Culpepper.

Yes, it was another mail day, but this one would prove to be different. It will be different for Reuben because of what he will receive, and it will be different for Adam as well when he realizes Mary Alice Colbert is not the most beautiful girl in the world after all.

狼

This particular mail day, Reuben received a letter from his father. It was filled with the usual family news and greetings from May, Henry, and Noah and how well they are keeping the farm in order. He was about to start reading his mother's words until Adam hopped on the wall he was sitting upon and interrupted Reuben's mail time with his letter from his girl back in Culpepper.

"Hey, Reuben, did you hear my letter from Mary Alice? Here, take an ear to this." Adam cleared his throat and began to read a portion of his letter.

"My sisters continue to tell me how lucky I am to have such a handsome looking gentleman in uniform. My oldest sister, Clare, is at times so jealous she sometimes makes a spectacle of herself."

"Ha, what do you think of that, Reuben? Mary Alice's sister, Clare, is beautiful as well, but not as beautiful as my Mary. Hey, maybe you and Clare should meet." Adam continued.

"I am so proud of my Virginia Military Institute cadet. When you escorted me to the Christmas ball, I felt like a queen."

"There, Reuben, what do you think of that?!"

"Oh for crying out loud, Stanns, please don't tell me you're pestering poor ole Reuben with your letter from Mary Ellen? Can't you see he's trying to read his own mail?"

Carlton Edwards, a fellow cadet, strolled up the path to where they were sitting on the stone wall.

Reuben could not help but chuckle out loud at Carlton's comment.

"No, I'm not pestering Reuben! And her name is Mary Alice, not Mary Ellen, you jackass! Now what do you want? Don't you see Reuben wants to hear the rest of Mary Ellen's letter... I mean Mary Alice's letter!"

Both Reuben and Carlton could not help but laugh at Adam's outburst.

"Hey, calm down, lover boy, I'm just bringing Reuben another piece of mail that wasn't in the first batch," said Carlton as he walked past Adam and held out what looked to be a small package to Reuben.

"Thanks, Carlton," said Reuben as he took it with an inquisitive look on his face.

"A package, you've never received a package before. Who's it from?" asked Adam.

Reuben continued to look at it while turning it in all angles. He read who it was from.

"It's from my sister, Lucy. That's strange. She's too young to be sending any packages through the post," Reuben said.

He began to carefully open the package. Inside there was a folded letter and a hard object inside a green cotton bag with a drawstring. He unfolded the letter. Suddenly his eyes opened wide and his mouth gaped open.

"Well, what did your sister send you?" asked Carlton.

"It's not from my sister. It's from... Renee."

"Renee? Who's Renee?" asked Adam looking at Carlton.

Carlton shrugged his shoulders, shaking his head in wonder.

Ignoring his classmates, Reuben began to read Renee's letter to himself.

Dear Reuben,

For once I have taken pen to paper to do what I should have been doing since you first departed from Norfolk and write you a letter, and will continue to do so with Lucy's help being my mail carrier, even with my father's objections. As you had once told me, I am anything but traditional.

I don't have much time to write because I want to make sure your sister can get this package in the post for me before it departs for the day. We have secret visits quite often behind the back wall and elm trees at my school, and she's due for a visit today.

When I presented my gift to William Sinclair, I felt so terrible that I should have gotten you a gift especially after you gave me the button from your uniform which I carry with me always. Trust me, it's difficult to keep hidden, but I find it challenging to keep it with me without anyone finding it.

With that in mind, I paid a visit to Mr. Armon's studio shortly after we returned from Charleston to have another image of myself taken. Remembering what you said about me being anything but traditional, I convinced Mr. Armon to take this image of myself for you. I hope you will enjoy this one much more than the one I had made for William Sinclair, and I also hope it captured the true heart and soul you have come to know and love.

I also want to give you my sincere apologies for telling you I didn't want you to read any of my 'poems'. That was very selfish of me. With that being said, I wrote this for you to go with this gift.

I will miss the winter season
A season filled with a precious gift
We play an eternal game of hide and seek
My hiding place is before your eyes
Please come and find me
And replace my world with love
A world free of obligated lies

Your Friend Forever,
Renee

P.S. Now you will have something to read to your roommate, Adam, over and over and over again.

After reading the letter, Reuben smiled and chuckled at the postscript. He then folded it and carefully placed it in his tunic breast pocket. He brought his attention to the green bag which he knew to be an image case. He quickly took it up in his hands. He looked it over thinking the color of the bag was Renee's favorite.

"Well, are you going to keep us in suspense all day or are you going to open up that bag?" asked Adam quite excitedly.

"Yes, come on already, Duran, we all want to see what you got," said Carlton just as eager.

Reuben looked at both of them, nodded his head, and began to loosen the drawstring of the cotton bag. He gently removed the image case and looked at it admiring the carved butterfly in the wood. Quickly he remembered how Renee enjoyed chasing and catching butterflies and letting them go. Both Adam and Carlton began to inch closer for a better view of what was inside the case.

Finally, Reuben unhooked the clasp and opened the case. It was lined in velvet with Renee's favorite color of green. The image itself was so unlike the one she had made for William Sinclair. It was a close up image of Renee. She was wearing the same simple, sleeveless, common summer dress with a low neck line she kept at the Duran farm to change into during her visits. Reuben recognized the dress and had told her many times how pretty she looked in it, and it was his favorite dress of hers. Her long, dark, brown hair was unpinned and cascading over her shoulders, just the way Reuben liked it, but it was her face that caught Reuben's attention. Instead of an emotionless hundred acre stare in the distance like the one she had made for William Sinclair, Renee's eyes were fixed, as if looking into Reuben's eyes. They were wide and bright with happiness along with an open, very affectionate, adoring smile. Very unusual of other images Reuben had seen where the subjects stare off in a distance with no emotion. It was the most precious gift Renee could have ever given Reuben, and he couldn't take his eyes away from the image. And neither could Adam and Carlton.

"Oh great heavens, Reuben, she's beautiful. She's the most beautiful girl I have ever seen in my life," said Carlton.

"That she is, very, very beautiful," added Adam completely forgetting all about his "beautiful" Mary Alice, who he was praising as the most beautiful girl in the world moments before Carlton delivered Reuben his package.

Carlton placed his hand on Reuben's shoulder leaning in for a better view and asked with admiration in his voice, "Who is she?"

Without looking away from the image, Reuben said, "Her name is Renee." Knowing she was promised to another, Reuben added with pride, "She's my girl."

For the next three years as Reuben attended the Virginia Military Institute, Renee and Reuben continued to communicate through the mail, with Lucy acting as their mail carrier. They also continued their visits during Reuben's holiday furloughs and summer vacations always at the Duran home in secret from Renee's parents, and with the consent and collaboration of Reuben's family. Although Renee's father had already predetermined her future, Renee was determined never to split up her beloved friendship with Reuben. Reuben was also just as determined never to lose his best and special friend he deeply adored, and although she was spoken for by another, Reuben's love for Renee remained resolute. Without expressing it outwardly, they both knew that somehow, sometime, somewhere they would be together, as love intended.

石
永

In the year of our Lord, 1846, a romantic tale continues.
An adventure to say farewell, and the help of an old forgotten soldier…

<u>Remember Me as Your Friend, Not a Soldier</u>

Running as fast as her legs could carry her, Lucy made her way through city streets, alleys, and shortcuts she and Reuben learned while they lived in the city. She didn't stop to catch her breath because she knew her task was of the upmost of importance to her brother and she wasn't about to fail. She knew where her mission would take her and as Lucy ran, she prayed the one she was looking for was there.

Five minutes before she departed on her mission, Lucy was told by her brother, Reuben, "Please, Lucy, if you can, try to find Renee and ask her to come to the house after school to visit if possible. I only have one day to spend with you all, and then I have to board a ship that will take me to the war." Reuben knew his sister and Renee visited regularly. If anyone would know where to find her at any time of the day, Lucy would. He also told her, "If you can't find her within one hour, come back home so I won't miss out spending time with you."

"I'll find her before the hour is up," she assured him and was out the door without haste.

Only one day to spend with his family, and it wasn't a full day either. Being of "sound moral character," and selected for early commissioning, due to the newly declared war with Mexico as a second lieutenant in the United States Army, Reuben was granted a pass to visit with his family prior to reporting with his regiment for departure. To visit with his family was most precious, but if he could have just one moment to say farewell to Renee as well would be a heavenly gift. A gift Lucy wasn't about to fail him, so she ran to the one place she knew Renee would be, Wickham Finishing School for Girls.

狼

Lucy made it to the high, ivy covered walls of Wickham. There was a portion of the school located on a side road where the wall wasn't so high. It was near the rear side of the school, well hidden by large overgrown elm trees. It was the only place Lucy and Renee could visit without being noticed, and hopefully, Renee would be there. However, when Lucy arrived, Renee was nowhere to be seen.

That wasn't going to stop Lucy. She was going to find Renee even if she had to sneak into the school, and that's exactly what she began to do. She easily scaled the wall, and like a thief on the prowl for loot, she made her way across the school grounds and entered the building through what seemed to be a storage room. This was no longer a task, it was a quest.

41

As quiet as possible, she navigated through corridors, in and out of doors, and up and down stairs. Every room she passed, she would take a quick peek to see if she could find Renee. Almost every room was filled with girls listening to the teachers giving lessons. Not once did she think her quest was impossible.

She traversed one hall into another, stopping more than once to take a quick glance at the portraits on the wall, wrinkling her nose at their ludicrous poses. As she searched, she could not help but feel sorry for Renee having to be forced to attend such a *"stuck up stuffy school"* as Renee put it more than once.

Suddenly Lucy heard the echo of footsteps coming from around the corner. It sounded like several pair of shoes making the sounds. Lucy quickly glanced around for a place to hide. There was none, except to duck behind one of the large bookcase shelves that lined the walls. She quickly leaped to the dark side of the hall, and pressed her petite body against the wood of the shelf case and the corner of the wall. She covered her mouth to mask any sounds of breathing that might give her away.

The footsteps came closer and three girls about the same age as Renee passed Lucy, all chatting very quietly. There was another set of footsteps lagging behind the others and as the owner of the steps walked passed Lucy's hiding place, her eyes opened wide. It was Renee walking with her head down.

As silently as possible, Lucy began to follow Renee. Ahead, there was a turn in the hall and Lucy thought that would be her chance. When the three girls made the turn, Lucy acted quickly. She leaped up behind Renee, and with her hand, covered Renee's mouth from behind. Renee, very startled, began to struggle and squeal until she heard, "Shhh, it's me, Lucy."

Renee turned around with a look of dismay and fear. She said in a hushed angered voice, "Lucy, are you crazy? What are you doing here?"

Lucy glanced around checking if all was clear, grabbed Renee by the elbow, and pulled her away from the middle of the hall and stood against the wall. In a quiet voice, she said, "Reuben sent me. He's home for one day only and is hoping to see you before he's sent away. Can you come to the house after school?"

"Geez oh geez oh geez are you serious?!" she responded with excitement in her expression. "Let's go... now."

"Now? In the middle of school? You're the one who's crazy."

Renee straightened her posture, placed her fists on her hips and with a smirk on her face she said, "Come, Lucy, these are the kind of shenanigans you, me, Reuben, and even Noah, live for. Come on. Let's go."

With one quest achieved and another in the making, Lucy grabbed Renee's hand and led her the way she came. Renee made Lucy stop and motioned to their feet. Their footsteps were still a little too loud, so they both took off their shoes. Back through the same stairs and corridors Lucy previously ventured, the two made their escape. They were one room away from the storage room where Lucy entered the school. She opened the door and quickly ran over the threshold, only to run right smack into Martin Doogan, the school's groundskeeper.

狼

Martin Doogan, a tall, big, and strong man, had been the school's groundskeeper for many years. He kept the grounds in immaculate condition all year round. Although he was superb at his job, making Wickham a school for all the faculty and students to be proud of, because of his position, the faculty and students treated him as a second class citizen, with the exception of Renee Wallace. Renee treated Martin Doogan with dignity and the upmost respect. He reminded Renee a lot of Aaron Duran, very proud of his work and delightful to be around.

Renee felt he was a man with a troubled background, but she didn't pry. At times, she would come upon him and he would have a distant look of despair and anger at the same time. But when she would greet him, Renee's gentle voice always broke his inner spell, and he would be very grateful for her presence.

With Renee's open friendship to Martin Doogan, he in turn, also cared for her. He provided a haven in his sheds and workshop for her when she needed to escape the nonsense of this school, or when she just wanted to be alone with her thoughts. He knew of Renee's situations at home, for he was one of the few, other than the Duran family, who she confided about her difficult, confusing life. He knew about her arranged engagement to a boy she had no interest in, and the love for the one she so very much desired. Martin Doogan felt sincere pity for her. However, now he felt, and had the look of anger and disappointment.

"What's this game you're playing at, Miss Wallace, and who's this wee lass with ye? She isn't a student here," said Martin Doogan very sternly.

Wincing into her shoulders, Renee answered, "Ah, hello, Mr. Doogan. This is my friend Lucy. She's here to deliver a message to me."

Tears were forming in Lucy's eyes, her lower lip quivering, and she looked to Martin Doogan as if she was about to start wailing at any moment.

"Lucy, ye say," he said as he laid his eyes upon Lucy's gaze, begging for mercy. "Is this the very same Lucy who's the sister of the Reuben lad ye have told me about?"

"Yes, she is."

"Aye, and what's this message she came to deliver?"

"Her brother sent her to come and ask if I could come see him before he is sent away with the army to Mexico. Knowing he's going away for a long time, I just had to sneak away to go see him." Renee looked down, ashamed that the only friend she had in this school caught her breaking rules. He had caught Renee pulling pranks on some of the other over-privileged girls, and even provided materials and advice on how to make them work. But actually leaving school grounds during lessons, that was something else. She raised her head with a sad appealing look with hopes he would tell her to go back to whatever class she was supposed to be in, and he would quietly escort Lucy off the grounds to return home.

Looking up at Martin Doogan with her most appealing look, she quivered as she said, "Please, Mr. Doogan, don't be mad at me."

Martin Doogan just stood staring down at the two, sad, pitiful looking girls. "I'm not mad, Miss Renee, and will ye stop with that adorable, sad, doe-eyed, pathetic look of yours. It's not going to work on me."

"You're not mad? Then why do you look so angry?" asked Renee, her expression changing to a questionable glare.

"This isn't my angry look, this is my thinking look. I'm trying to figure out how to get ye two lasses off school grounds without anyone seeing ye. Ye can't go by way of the elms because Mrs. Fletcher has taken some students to the back gardens for reading."

Renee's face opened up with a huge smile as she wrapped her arms around the groundskeeper. "Thank you, Mr. Doogan, you're a saint."

Lucy stood dumbfounded and completely confused.

"Saint now, is that what ye say? I wouldn't go that far, lass. Now take little Lucy to the back dining room. I closed it off for cleaning. I have an idea so I'll meet ye there. Now hurry off, the both of ye."

Renee took Lucy by the hand and led her toward the closed off dining room as Martin Doogan quickly made his way to the linen closet.

狼

Renee led Lucy by the hand to the dining room as Martin Doogan instructed. He had closed off the dining room moments before his encounter with the two girls. He knew the two would be safe there from prying eyes, for the faculty forbade the students to go anywhere near when housekeeping was being done. Although they were safe, Renee and Lucy still hid underneath a covered table.

"When did Reuben come home, Lucy?" asked Renee in soft tones once she felt secure to talk.

"He arrived at Fort Monroe last week, but didn't get permission to visit until today," answered Lucy, also feeling much more secure and beginning to feel braver. She continued, "We tried to visit him at the fort the day before yesterday and got a chance to talk to him for a few minutes. He couldn't visit very long... army stuff, you know, whatever that is. He told us he might be able to get permission for a day visit before they are sent off, but didn't know when."

Renee began to nervously rub her hands together and look downward. She was so anxious for Martin Doogan to help them get out of the school so she could see her friend. She was so intent on seeing Reuben that she cared nothing of the repercussions of her leaving school during classes from the head mistress, or even her father.

"Oh, Renee, my brother looks so handsome in his uniform," said Lucy looking up with a proud smile on her face. With a very sorrowful look overcoming her face, Lucy looked at Renee and placed her hand on her shoulder. "I'm so very sorry things couldn't be different for you and my brother."

Renee looked off to the side of Lucy's stare, as if she was looking toward a very distant future. A slight smile came to her as she said, "We're both still very young. We still have lots of time for the unknown to happen."

She looked back to Lucy and they both smiled. Suddenly they were startled by the sounds of squeaking wheels of a large linen basket being rolled across the hard wood floor of the dining room. It came to a stop a couple of tables away. Renee put her finger to her lips indicating Lucy to be quiet.

"Miss Renee, where are ye and Miss Lucy?"

Relieved and delighted, Renee poked her head out from underneath the covered table they had taken refuge under and said, "We're here, Mr. Doogan, both of us."

"Come quickly ladies and hop in this here cart."

Renee helped Lucy out from under the table and they were both helped by Martin Doogan into the cart.

"Now sit back and don't make a sound. I'm going to cover ye with these tablecloths, push ye to the back gate where the deliveries are made, and there ye can make your *escape*."

Both the girls nodded in agreement and snuggled together as Martin Doogan carefully placed clean linens over them. He then placed a few dirty linens on the clean ones giving the impression of a basket cart full of dirty linens being taken out for cleaning.

Satisfied with the ruse of the cart, he said "Okay now, lasses, here we go. No noise now, ye hear?"

He rolled the cart out of the dining room, through the kitchen, and down the corridor connecting some classrooms to the main hall. Classes were in session and no one paid Martin Doogan any attention. Inside the cart, the two girls could not help but snicker at this adventure they were sharing. Renee felt a light kick on her rump and heard a "Shhh," from Martin Doogan for the two to keep quiet. They both covered their mouths.

A sudden bump was felt as the cart began to shake from the uneven ground, and birds could be heard. We must be outside, Renee thought. She began to hear girls reading out loud in the garden and estimated they were very close to the delivery gate.

They felt the cart come to a stop and heard heavy footsteps come from Martin Doogan walking around the cart. Then a sharp click and the creaking of the delivery gate swinging open was heard. More footsteps and the cart again was on the move. Now the sounds of the common street din were heard as the two felt them being pushed across the street. The common street sounds died down and then the cart stopped. They heard and felt the rustle of the linens as Martin Doogan removed the linens hiding the girls. Sunlight caused their eyes to momentarily close to adjust. They both opened their eyes to see Martin Doogan looking down with a happy grin on his face. He then helped them out of the cart.

Martin Doogan lifted Lucy out of the cart and set her down gently and turned to help Renee. As he lifted her out of the cart he said, "There ye go, Miss Renee, a successful escape."

As he set her down, she again wrapped her arms around the big groundskeeper. "Thank you again, Mr. Doogan, from the bottom of my heart."

"My pleasure, lass. Ye just give that lad of yours my sincere regards and tell him to keep his head down."

Renee looked at Martin Doogan questionably, "What does that mean?"

"He should know by now, that's if he values the veteran soldiers."

Renee suddenly realized why Martin Doogan had that distant despair and angry stare sometimes. She raised her hands to her mouth to hide a sudden gasp. Mr. Doogan was once a soldier himself and probably knows what Reuben is about to encounter, she thought to herself.

"What about your absence?" asked Lucy interrupting Martin Doogan and Renee's moment. "How are you going to explain where you've been for the rest of the day?" she asked quite worried.

"I seem to remember the head mistress assigning ye punishment for tripping Miss Garrett into the mud last week. I recall her saying you're to assist me in weeding the side garden sometime this week, a task that will take ye the rest of the day."

"But you did that weeding yesterday, Mr. Doogan," said Renee.

"Aye, ye know that, and I know that, but they don't. Now off, the both of ye. That lad doesn't have much time so ye need to make the best of it."

"Goodbye, Mr. Doogan," said Lucy as she grabbed hold of Renee's hand and took off running back home.

"Bye to ye, young Lucy, no more getting caught now, ye hear!" called out Martin Doogan as he waved them off.

狼

In the Duran home, Reuben was enjoying a nice, peaceful, relaxing visit with his parents and Monroe. Not soon after he sent Lucy on her task, Reuben went up to his room and changed out of his uniform, and into his comforting old clothes. For the time being, he wanted to forget he was Second Lieutenant Reuben Duran of the 9th U.S. Regular Infantry Regiment. He just wanted to be Reuben Duran for the day.

Every so often, Reuben would glance up at the clock on the wall. It had been almost 50 minutes since Lucy ran off to find Renee and deliver his message to her.

"So tell me, Reuben, of how many men are you in charge?" asked Monroe. "The whole regiment?"

"Oh, no. I only have a platoon of men, ten to be exact. But these men seem to be more in charge."

Puzzled, Monroe asked, "More in charge? Why's that? Are you an officer or not?"

"They are more in charge because they are more experienced, and if there's one thing I learned from the time I spent at Fort Norfolk before VMI, the non-commissioned officers, or NCOs, are the backbone of the army and a good leader takes their experience to heart."

"Are you a good leader?" asked Monroe in a mocking manner.

"My company commander granted me permission to come and visit with you, so yes, I'm a good leader."

Laughter roared out of Aaron at Reuben's response. "I see you have learned to be somewhat of a smart ass as well," he said as his laughter died down.

"Now that, I learned from you Da, the army just brought it out."

More laughter ensued from everyone in the room including Reuben's mother.

The laughter was interrupted by the sound of the door opening and Lucy running into the parlor. Prior to entering the house, Lucy told Renee that it would be a fun surprise for Reuben if she was to announce Renee since Reuben didn't expect for her to visit until after school, if she could come at all. Renee agreed as she pulled the pins out of her hair and letting it fall over her shoulders.

Lucy stood in front of the family panting from her running. Reuben stood to help her sit on the piano bench as Coleen poured her some lemonade.

"Did you find her, Lucy? Were you able to ask Renee if she could visit after school?" asked Reuben, excitedly.

"Not only did she succeed in finding and asking me, she brought me along," said Renee, unable to wait for Lucy to announce her presence.

Reuben rose and turned to face Renee entering the parlor, knocking Lucy off the bench.

"Hey you big brute!" shouted Lucy.

Reuben turned back to Lucy and knelt down to help her back onto the bench while everyone else began to laugh hysterically.

Aaron was the first one to stand and greet Renee still chuckling. "See, my girl, things are still crazy as ever in the Duran home," he said as he gave her a welcoming embrace.

"Hello, Renee," greeted Monroe. "It's been a while since you've visited."

"Hello, Monroe," she acknowledged and turned to Coleen who had a stern look on her face.

"Renee Wallace, what are you doing out of school?" asked Coleen and then turned to Lucy. "Lucy, was this your idea of getting Renee to ditch school? You know how I feel about students cutting classes and skipping school, including Wickham!"

Coleen, being a respected educator, always showed disappointment when students would skip school and her punishments were severe for students who were caught. Her looks of disappointment at the moment brought awkward silence to the parlor. That was until she replaced her angered look with a bright smile and opened her arms wide and said, "But for you to escape the walls of Wickham to come and visit my son, I'll forgive you, Renee!"

Renee quickly stepped into Coleen's arms and greeted her warmly.

Coleen released her embrace of Renee and gently turned her to face Reuben. Reuben stood next to Lucy, now sitting back on the bench. He was mesmerized by Renee's presence and stood with his mouth gapping open.

"You know, flies are going to enter your mouth if you don't shut it, brother," said Monroe as he stood to excuse himself from the parlor as more laughter followed.

"Hey, Reuben," said Lucy, disappointedly. "Why did you change out of your uniform? I wanted Renee to see how handsome you look in it."

"Not to worry, Lucy, he looks handsome in his old clothes also," said Renee. "And look, he still blushes."

There was no laugher spared at Reuben's expense and he could not help but laugh himself. Unable to wait any longer, Reuben stepped toward Renee as she did the same and they embraced in a long awaited hug.

Reuben offered Renee a place on the sofa and he sat next to her. A pleasant visit began and everyone was enjoying the conversations as if they were the old days, both in the Norfolk house and the farm.

After about half an hour of the visit, Lucy stood and reached across the piano and retrieved a frame and brought it to Renee.

"Here, take a look at this. Since Reuben isn't wearing his uniform, you can at least see what he looks like in this picture."

Renee took the offered picture frame and looked at it adoringly. She saw Reuben standing at attention with an American flag at his side. It was a very modest image, but Renee admired how brave and noble he looked in the picture. She felt pride Reuben was her special friend. Then she remembered what Martin Doogan asked her to say to Reuben for his sake, *"Tell him to keep his head down."*

Suddenly, as she looked upon the picture of a uniformed Reuben, her eyes began to water and a tear dropped landing on the glass covering the picture. She quickly jerked the frame away from under her face and with her sleeve, she wiped the tear off and handed the picture back to Lucy.

Coleen handed Renee a handkerchief as Lucy asked, "What's the matter, Renee?"

Renee wiped her eyes, smiled, and said, "Nothing, Lucy, I'm just happy you came to bring me to visit."

Coleen stood and said, "I believe it's time for us to let Renee and Reuben visit for a while alone. Come, let's prepare something to eat. We can't send Renee back home hungry considering she's supposed to be in school," Coleen continued as she winked toward Renee.

狼

"Are you all right?" asked Reuben once they were alone in the parlor.

"Yes, just a bit overcome. It has been an interesting morning, to say the least," Renee answered with a giggle. She began to tell of the adventure she and Lucy had in order for her to come and visit. She told Reuben about Martin Doogan's help. Reuben was glad she had someone she could talk and visit with knowing how upper crust with nothing in common her classmates were.

As she described the groundskeeper, she again felt despair and began to feel her eyes tear up again. Her thoughts of Martin Doogan knowing what Reuben will be facing weighed heavy on her. She wanted to tell, or warn, Reuben of what the groundskeeper knew, but thought now isn't the time. I should not cause him to worry about his own safety. That might frighten him, she thought.

She remembered seeing the old war widows from the Second War of Independence visit the resting places of their fallen husbands. There was a huge difference between the wives of those who survived and the wives of those who never returned or returned in a coffin. Is this the way that both types of wives felt before their loved ones left for war, Renee wondered as she looked up to Reuben. A tear fell from her left eye, and Reuben gently wiped it away with his fingertip.

Not knowing why Renee was on the verge of crying, he tried to cheer her up. "Hey, I have something for you," he said, delightfully. He stood and walked over to a military issued haversack, picked it up by its strap, and returned next to Renee.

As he sat, Renee wiped her eyes and watched closely as Reuben opened the haversack and retrieved the green pull string bag that held the image case Renee had sent Reuben after his first Christmas visit from VMI. Upon seeing the bag, she brought up her hands to hide her face and started to embarrassingly giggle.

"Oh geez, Reuben, don't tell me you carry that everywhere you go?"

"You bet I do. It's my favorite thing in the whole world," he said as he opened it and handed it to her.

She took it carefully and could not help but snicker at the image of her dressed and posed so unconventionally.

"You know, Mr. Armond almost didn't take that picture because he thought the way I was dressed and way I posed was, 'crude,'" she said looking upon the picture suddenly feeling special Reuben said it was his favorite thing in the whole world.

"So what made him finally take it?"

"I told him if he didn't, I would tell everyone he did take a 'crude' image of me and he kept it for his own personal enjoyment and that would cause him such scandal."

Looking at her in disbelief, Reuben shook his head and began to chuckle.

"This image isn't crude at all, Renee. Mama said it captures your true beauty as a caring person," said Reuben as he focused back onto the picture.

"Good lord, Reuben, you showed this to your mother?" she asked, shocked.

"Yes, but as I said, she loved it. Here, I'll call her over to tell you."

Just as he was about to call for his mother, Renee slapped her hand over his mouth and they both started laughing.

After their laughter died down, Renee said, "I do like that picture Lucy showed me."

Reuben smiled and again began to dig into his haversack. He pulled out a deep dark red pull string bag and handed it to Renee. She took it gently and looked it over.

"This is for you," said Reuben.

Renee's eyes opened wide and she quickly undid the string and took out an image case. It had a butterfly carved into the wood which made her smile. She undid the clasp and opened it. Inside she saw a picture of Reuben, not in his uniform, but in a similar type of image as the one Renee made for him. It was a close up image as well. He was wearing a common band collar button shirt in his usual fashion, the way he was wearing the one he had on now with a few buttons undone. His hair was roughly combed as if it were windblown, and like Renee's image, Reuben eyes had happiness in them and he had a wide smile. He looked very handsome and she couldn't take her eyes away from the image.

"It's beautiful," said Renee.

She asked as she was still looking at the picture, "Why didn't you have one done in your uniform for me?"

Reuben's smile faded and he rose and walked over to the piano where the picture of him in uniform rested. He picked it up and looked it over.

"After four of us were selected for early commissioning because of the war declaration, we went to get pictures made in our uniforms for our families and sweethearts. I thought of you. Not exactly my sweetheart, but my very special friend."

Renee stood up and walked over to Reuben. She placed her hands on his arm as he continued.

"I watched the others pose as heroes who have not done anything to be worthy of the term. I took this modest image for my family, but I couldn't bring myself to have one done in my uniform for you, Renee."

"How come?"

"I'm not naïve like my other classmates, Renee. I spent enough time with veteran solders at Fort Norfolk to know what it means to go to war. It means the possibility of not returning alive. Renee, the memories I have of you are fun, wonderful, and beautiful. I have used those memories to help me with the lives we have been dealt, and my separation from you. I'll continue to use those memories when I go away."

Reuben set the picture down and turned to face Renee. Now his eyes began to water. "Having an idea of what it means to go to war, I couldn't bring myself to give you a picture of me in uniform. You are my best and special friend, Renee. You always have been and you always will be. If something was to happen to me, and I don't come back alive, I want you to remember me as your friend, not a soldier."

Unable to contain herself, she wrapped her arms around Reuben and held him tightly. He held her also. She lifted her head and with her hands she cradled his face. "Don't talk like that. Do you hear me, Reuben Duran? You *will* come back. You *will!* Do you understand? I won't have it any other way. YOU JUST KEEP YOUR HEAD DOWN!" said Renee with severe emotion.

They both stood by the piano, arm-in-arm, holding back tears and trying to be brave for one another. Reuben, not being able to speak without it coming out as a sob, only nodded in agreement. Renee also nodded.

"Good, it's settled then. You better bring yourself back here alive, you shoddy farm boy."

Coleen and Lucy stood in the archway between the parlor and the hall. They accidently overheard their conversation. Holding back tears herself, Coleen cleared her throat and said,

"Hey you two, I have lunch set up. Let's have something to eat before Renee has to go home… after a hard day's afternoon of pulling weeds out of the school's garden."

"I told Mama that's what Mr. Doogan is having you do this afternoon to mask your absence from classes," said Lucy, wiping her eyes and causing everyone present to forget the last few moments and to remember this was to be a pleasant visit.

For the rest of the afternoon, it was just that, pleasant, very pleasant. Lunch was served and cleared away and there was enough time for Lucy to play a few songs on the piano Renee's father had given the Duran family several years back. Renee admired how wonderful Lucy's talent was and hoped one day Lucy could teach her to play almost as well.

It was near the time for Wickham to excuse classes for the day, so everyone walked Renee as close to home as possible, surrounding her so no one who could, would be able to recognize her. Aaron commented more than once about the irony of the situation to his wife helping a student skip school.

"Looks like you're going to have to look the other way if I ever decide to skip school, Mama," said Lucy.

Coleen looked sternly at Lucy. "Don't even think of it!"

"You all are crazy," said Renee, laughing.

They stopped one block away from Renee's house. They all said their goodbyes and gave Reuben some time to be alone with her for one last moment.

"Do you have your picture, Wickham girl?" Reuben asked, with the smirk Renee adored so much.

"Right here in my skirt pocket with the button you gave me, and don't call me Wickham girl, you shoddy farm boy," replied Renee as she playfully slapped his shoulder and giggled adoringly.

They embraced each other and before they let each other go, Reuben, lowered his face to kiss Renee on her cheek. She, however, turned her face just before his lips made contact and her lips met his.

"I'll be back, Renee, and I *will* keep my head down."

She smiled, turned, looked both ways, and began to run home. She got halfway up the block when she came to a stop and turned in time to see the Duran family turn the corner on their way home.

狼

The following day, Renee came to school concerned. Was Martin Doogan successful in his ruse of her accountability for yesterday afternoon? All her apprehensions were put to rest when she heard the whiny voice of Cynthia Garrett call out, "Hey look! It's the weed puller who is in love with a low class peasant she cannot have! What William Sinclair will ever see in you, I will never know!"

Laughter broke out from all the girls walking with Cynthia, but it died down once they heard Renee begin to laugh also. As she did, all she could think of was, if you only knew real love, Cynthia.

51

"Why are you laughing?!" called out Cynthia.

"If I have to explain it to you, then I suppose you're not as smart as you think you are," replied Renee with a mocking curtsey.

"See, what did I tell you all, crazy, absolutely crazy that girl is," said Cynthia and strutted off in a bad temper.

The first chance Renee got, she ran to Martin Doogan's workshop to tell him about her visit and to thank him again. As she neared the workshop, her pace slowed. The door was open and she peered through the doorway. Martin Doogan was sitting on a stool eating his lunch out of a basket. Renee knocked.

"Hello, Mr. Doogan, may I come in?"

"Always, Miss Renee, come and have a sandwich with me. My wife always packs extra."

Renee entered and sat on a shorter stool as she took the offered sandwich. She took a bite. "Mm, ham with butter. Perfect. Mr. Doogan, I'm really in your debt for yesterday."

"Have a good visit, did ye now?"

Renee rested her hands with the sandwich on her lap and dropped her shoulders and smiled. "It was the best. Here, look, he gave me a gift." She placed the sandwich carefully on the workbench and dug in her skirt pocket and pulled out the image case and handed it to Martin Doogan.

He also placed his sandwich on the bench, wiped his hands on his coveralls, and inspected them before he took the case. He gently took it in his hands, looked it over, undid the clasp, and opened it. Renee moved in closer to also look at the picture as she continued to nibble on her sandwich.

"Ah, is this your friend, Reuben, lass?" he asked very impressed.

"Yes, that's him," she said, adoringly.

"A fine looking lad." He slowly closed the case and handed it back to Renee. When she took hold of it, Martin Doogan, with his other hand, gently took hold of her hand.

Surprised, Renee said, "Is there something wrong, Mr. Doogan?"

"Miss Renee, ye have been a joy in my life here at this school. Ye have always had a way of making me smile when I'm haunted by the old days. I know what awaits Reuben when he gets to his destination, and what may become of him when he returns."

Renee showed concern. Why is he talking to me in this manner, she thought.

Martin Doogan became serious as he said, "What I'm about to tell ye will be difficult for ye to understand, but ye must prepare yourself. You're a strong young woman, stronger than all the other girls, and even the teachers in this here school. Stronger than ye, yourself, believe. But when Reuben returns, and from what ye have told me of him, he will survive and return, he won't be the same boy ye have known up until now. He will be different. He will no longer be a boy, but a man subjected to death. He will no longer have that spark in his eyes like in this picture. He will have the look I have when ye bring me back to the here and now. When he returns, he will need your friendship more than ever, even if he doesn't know it himself." He released her hand, and picked up his sandwich.

Renee sat, thinking of what Martin Doogan told her. "I think I understand, Mr. Doogan. There was a moment during our visit when he told me he knew what it meant to go to war, and it meant... he might not return," she said, hesitantly at the thought of him not returning.

Martin Doogan sat straight and snapped his fingers startling Renee. "There ye go, lass. He will be fine. If he understands he might not return, then he has accepted that fact, and that is the first step to any soldier's survival."

That eased the tension. Renee felt a little reassured and said, "He understands it'll be difficult, but he said he will use me to get him through, whatever that means."

Martin Doogan nodded his head and he placed his hand on Renee's shoulder. "That means, Miss Renee, he will use his memories of your friendship of the past to help keep him alive. And ye must do the same. Memories are a powerful tool. They bind friendships, or they can haunt ye like ghosts. But never lose faith and love in the memories of friendship. Now those are the memories that will keep ye near to him and him to ye."

A bell sounded for the start of afternoon lessons. Renee rose and wrapped her arms around Martin Doogan. "Thank you, Mr. Martin Doogan. You're a wonderful man," she said. She then made her way out of the workshop, glanced back, and gave Martin Doogan a warm smile.

Renee made her way to her next lesson, a poetry class she found boring and dull because the teacher, Mrs. Fletcher, only taught classical poetry. Every assignment was to write a synopsis on their meanings. Try as hard as she could, Renee was never allowed to turn in any of her original passages. Mrs. Fletcher would never take the time to look them over and every time Renee tried to turn in passages that came from her heart, it was never accepted as real poetry.

She began thinking of what Martin Doogan told her about memories. During this one class, as with many others, she spent most of the time drawing or doodling on the parchment rather than listening or writing about what Mrs. Fletcher was lecturing about. It always seemed she would write a barely passable assignment by the end of class and turn it in. Mrs. Fletcher would always shake her head and ask what nonsense Renee was about to turn in for the day.

However, as the end of this one lesson came and all the girls turned in their summaries for the day, Renee, the last one to turn hers in, handed her parchment to the teacher. Mrs. Fletcher snatched the page out of Renee's hand and glanced at the very short passage written on it.

"Wasted time, Renee Wallace, wasted time," said Mrs. Fletcher in a condescending tone.

Renee's only response was a smile. She snatched an apple from Mrs. Fletcher's desk Cynthia Garrett placed before class, took a bite, turned on her heels, and walked out of the classroom.

Mrs. Fletcher, appalled at Renee's behavior, took another look at Renee's assignment and noticed wet spots dotted the page, tears. She took a seat at her desk and began to read Renee's short passage. When she was done, her eyes watered up, and a tear rolled down her left cheek.

Please grasp my hand and take me with you
My purpose would be to keep you safe
Memories of our togetherness bond our closeness
But distance between us in my tears I do taste

Memories dearest fulfill my spirit
Treasured times and love we should share
Can you feel me in your heart
Run away we must to become one if we dare

I pray to almighty to keep you safe
To spare you of the danger of which war carries
And bring you home to my open heart
To live a life filled of sweet new memories

石
水
In the year of our Lord, 1847, a romantic tale continues.
Same sun, same moon, different places…

Don't Cry For Me, Renee

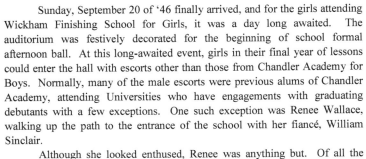

Sunday, September 20 of '46 finally arrived, and for the girls attending Wickham Finishing School for Girls, it was a day long awaited. The auditorium was festively decorated for the beginning of school formal afternoon ball. At this long-awaited event, girls in their final year of lessons could enter the hall with escorts other than those from Chandler Academy for Boys. Normally, many of the male escorts were previous alums of Chandler Academy, attending Universities who have engagements with graduating debutants with a few exceptions. One such exception was Renee Wallace, walking up the path to the entrance of the school with her fiancé, William Sinclair.

Although she looked enthused, Renee was anything but. Of all the girls in this graduating class, she had no desire to attend this ball or be escorted by her fiancé. She didn't participate in the decorating or promoting of the ball, activities so looked forward to by the girls entering their final year. Instead, her attention was on the events far south, events that seem difficult to hear about.

As often as she could, Renee would visit with Reuben's family to see if they received any information, but they were in the dark just as she was. She even asked her father at one time if he heard any news of the war in Mexico and his response to her was a resounding, "It is none of your business!"

She was a few steps away from entering the school's entrance as she looked up in the sky toward the sun and wondered if Reuben might be looking at the same sun this very moment.

"Come, my precious pet, you're lagging," said William Sinclair with a hint of cocky amusement and arrogance.

William Sinclair arrived the day before for this occasion. Starting his fourth year of studying law at the University of South Carolina, he strutted into the school as if knowing he had the prettiest girl at his side, and displayed her as if she were a trophy. Many girls from the ninth years to final years took to admiring him. Those who knew Renee best, such as Cynthia Garrett, felt he could do much better, like themselves for instance.

As they entered the auditorium, music from the orchestra was playing beautifully and several girls with their escorts were waltzing. Renee had her eyes on an empty table, but William Sinclair guided her to the dance floor and commenced to dance without asking Renee as she followed, forcing a smile.

I know he doesn't know how and doesn't care for dancing, but I wish it were Reuben holding me now, Renee was thinking behind her false smile. She looked around to the pairs of dancers thinking she didn't belong here.

The orchestra was about to start another waltz as William Sinclair began to bow for a fourth dance with Renee, when she held up her hand.

"I believe I have had enough for a now. How about we sit?" she asked.

William Sinclair nodded saying, "Perhaps you are right, my pet. Let me escort you to a seat, and I will get us some punch."

"That would be lovely," Renee replied. Oh geez, if I ever said that to Reuben, he'd never let me live that down, thought Renee with a silent chuckle.

After William Sinclair seated Renee, he excused himself and went to retrieve some punch. While he was away, she, uninterestedly, watched others dancing and having a good time. That was until she overheard a few boys sitting at the next table discussing the war in Mexico. She leaned back further into her chair and slightly turned her head to hear their conversation better.

"I'll tell you what, if I were down there, I would show them Mexicans how we fight up here in Virginia."

"I'm not even sure why we're there in the first place."

"Manifest Destiny, Thomas, Manifest Destiny. We have to show our strength. I'm with Clifford, if it wasn't for me starting my first year at university, I would be killing me some Mexicans."

"I hear there have been some pretty big battles already. Places called, Santa Rosa and Puerto De Luna, are a couple I heard about."

"Santa Rosa was in June, and Puerto De Luna was in July. We won at both, but I heard we lost over a hundred men combined from both battles."

Over a hundred men, geez oh geez oh geez, Reuben wasn't one of them. He didn't leave until June, and maybe he wasn't at Puerto De Luna, thought Renee with dire concern. She continued to listen.

"I'm still not sure. I think it's a wasted enterprise. After all, I got a look at some of those soldiers of ours, not the best we have to offer."

"Ha, I know what you mean. I heard some of the cadets from the Virginia Military Institute were made officers because of the lack of experienced officers."

"Bah, VMI cadets, what a waste. Do you know why those types attend a military academy? Because they're not smart enough to attend a real university like us," stated one of the boys, proudly.

Renee stood, turned to face the three, and slammed her white gloved fists on their table causing them to cower. "You three wouldn't be accepted to attend a military academy because you have no honor or discipline! At the first sight of blood, all of you would gag and run home to your mothers!"

William Sinclair cleared his throat causing Renee to straighten and turn to face him. "William, you're back. You know, I'm ready for another dance. Shall we?"

"Ah, sure. What about the punch?"

Renee took the glass cups from William Sinclair's hands, "There is plenty of time for that later. Come and lead the way," she said.

As William Sinclair turned to face the dance floor and offer his arm, Renee turned and placed the two cups on the boys' table, and pushed them over causing punch to splatter onto their jackets. She turned and took William Sinclair's offered arm and walked toward the dance floor.

As they were about to begin to dance, Renee caught a glimpse of Mrs. Fletcher and said, "Just a minute, William, I want to introduce you to one of my teachers." Her hope was Mrs. Fletcher would distract William Sinclair so she could be alone for a little while longer.

Looking very prideful, William Sinclair smoothed out his coat and tugged on his tie. "Certainly, that would be nice," he replied, quite smugly causing Renee to cringe in disgust.

"Excuse me, Mrs. Fletcher. I would like to introduce you to my fiancé, William Sinclair. William, this is Mrs. Fletcher."

Since the one class Mrs. Fletcher took the time to read the poem Renee wrote after her visit with Reuben before he left to Mexico, she began to take a serious interest in her work. Although the work Renee would turn in wasn't the given assignments, Mrs. Fletcher still accepted and graded them. After several moments talking with William Sinclair, Mrs. Fletcher assumed this was definitely *not* the man who the poems were about.

"Oh my, will you look at my glove, I got a punch stain on it," said Renee lying, hoping for an excuse to get some time alone. Mrs. Fletcher provided her with that much needed excuse.

"Dear me, you had better go dab some cold water on that before it comes permanent. Not to worry, I'll keep Mr. Sinclair occupied while you see to that."

"Thank you, Mrs. Fletcher. I'll be but a few moments," said Renee as she was making her way toward the back of the auditorium.

Once in the main corridor she ran up the staircase and sat in a plush leather bench next to a bookcase. Renee breathed in deeply a couple of times with her eyes shut. She opened her eyes, reached into her skirt pocket, pulled out Reuben's VMI button he gave her as a Christmas gift, and gazed at it.

"Ye never stop thinking about him, do ye lass?"

"Mr. Doogan, I didn't know you were here," said Renee, startled.

Martin Doogan had been leaning against the wall when he saw Renee sit down.

"Now why are ye not at your ball?"

"Come on, Mr. Doogan. You know I loathe those things. Oh damn, I can't believe I just said *loathe*. Do you have any idea how much Reuben would be laughing if he ever heard me talk like those girls down there?"

Martin Doogan chuckled. "As I said, ye never stop thinking of him."

"Every day, Mr. Doogan, every day, and the hard part is, I have no idea what's happening to him," she answered as her eyes began to fill with tears.

Martin Doogan took a seat next to Renee and consoled her by gently placing his arm around Renee's shoulders. She rested her head on his shoulder. With tears falling from her eyes, she said, "Oh, Mr. Doogan, I would give anything to know what's happening to him this very moment."

狼

"FUEGO!" BAM!
"FUEGO!" BAM!
"FUEGO!" BAM!
Second Lieutenant Reuben Duran, along with the rest of his platoon, laid low in a shallow arroyo bed, much like the creek bed behind his farm house, but with much less water. Mexican artillery six pound guns showered shots mere yards ahead of them on this 20th day of September.

"Jesus Christ, Lieutenant, that was close!" yelled Sergeant Sam Evers. "Just what the hell are we supposed to be doing here anyhow!"

Earlier in the day, prior to Renee entering the ball with William Sinclair, Reuben's platoon was placed on the far right side of the line to take up skirmish positions after the Mexican infantry fell back behind their artillery to regroup. Five platoons of Company B, 9th U.S. Infantry Regulars, were assigned to silence the enemy guns, a task Reuben thought was suicidal.

Muskets against cannons, what god damned idiot came up with that bright idea, thought Reuben as he peered over the edge of the arroyo bed. He saw the gunner of the cannon directly ahead of their position raise his arm to give the order to fire.

"FUEGO!" BAM!

Reuben ducked back down into the arroyo as did the rest of his platoon, however the shell didn't land anywhere near their position. Again, he peered over the edge watching as the gun crew reloaded their cannon.

"We're cannon fodder, Lieutenant! We got to do something and quick!" said Sergeant Evers as he was pushing the heads of the rest of the platoon lower into the sand.

Again, Reuben saw the gunner raise his arm, and drop it giving the order to fire, but this time Reuben didn't duck. He watched to see where the shell was aimed and saw it directly hit the first platoon.

"Holy shit, they got us marked in! We can't stay here, Lieutenant!"

"Mr. Evers, come here, quickly!" ordered Reuben.

Looking puzzled, the sergeant looked at the private next to him. The private shrugged his shoulders.

"Now, Sergeant!" ordered Reuben, more sternly.

Sergeant Evers crawled over the platoon to reach Reuben. "What is it, Lieutenant?"

"Look over the edge and tell me what you see."

Sergeant Evers did as he was told, took a quick peek, and dropped back. "All I see is a whole lot of chaos."

Frustrated, Reuben grabbed the sergeant's shoulder and raised him up as he also peered over the edge. "Again, tell me what you see."

As they were looking over the edge, the gunner lowered his arm giving the order to fire. Sergeant Evers was about to duck, but Reuben kept him above the edge.

"See that? Both those guns have changed the angle of their aim."

Reuben dropped back down in deep thought as Sergeant Evers continued to observe. After a few moments he dropped back as well.

Reuben looked at his sergeant directly into his eyes. "Are you thinking what I'm thinking?"

"That's crazy, Lieutenant."

"Crazy enough to work... take another look to the right, and tell me what else you see," said Reuben.

Sergeant Evers did as told and peered over the edge to the right and dropped back with an inquisitive look on his face. "I see nothing but brush, thicket, and the river's ridge. It just might be possible."

"Good, come with me," said Reuben as he started crawling toward the fourth platoon twenty yards away.

"Corporal, keep the boys low, we'll be right back!"

"What do you want us to do until you get back, Sergeant?" asked Corporal Rall.

"They think we're dead so play dead. This won't take us long."

Corporal Rall nodded as he watched the sergeant follow Reuben.

Reuben reached the sergeant of the fourth platoon moments before Sergeant Evers caught up. "Sergeant, where's Lieutenant Stanns?" he asked.

The Sergeant pointed further down the line as he kept his head low.

Reuben looked in the direction he pointed and called out, "Adam! Get your ass over here!"

"Jesus Christ, Reuben, what the hell are you doing here?!"

Bobbing his head in frustration, Reuben turned to Sergeant Evers, "Hold on, I'll be right back," he said as he began crawling over the fourth platoon to reach Adam.

"Adam, I have an idea to take out the two guns in front of us."

"That's idiotic, Reuben! We're all going to die here in this bloody ditch!"

"Oh, get a grip, Adam! What would your Mary think of you cowering like this! We have a chance to stop this nonsense, now what do you say?!"

"Do what you want, Reuben, I'm staying right here until it's over!"

Grabbing his tunic sleeve, Reuben pulled his VMI roommate closer to him, "Snap out of it, Adam!"

In return, Adam desperately started pushing Reuben away.

Reuben let go as he felt a tug at his own tunic. He looked back to see Sergeant Evers.

"Come on, Lieutenant, he's lost it!"

Reuben nodded, "Let's get back to the platoon, Mr. Evers!"

The two crawled back over the men of the fourth platoon. As Reuben made his way back to his platoon he grabbed a musket from one of the fourth platoon's men.

Sergeant Evers took hold of the fourth platoon's sergeant's collar and said, "Take charge of your platoon leader, Gilly, or he's going to get you all killed, damn it!"

When Sergeant Evers made it back to the platoon, Reuben was again peering over the edge of the arroyo.

"Any changes, Lieutenant?"

Reuben dropped back down and shook his head no.

"Shit, Mr. Evers, back in school, Adam was always leading us in drills and I didn't want to do any of the leading. What happened?" Reuben asked, not requiring an answer.

"Reality happened, sir, and you got a grip on that. He doesn't," he still answered as he sat next to Reuben.

Reuben looked at his platoon who had their eyes fixed on him. He heard another order from the Mexican gunner ordering his gun to fire. As it did, he didn't flinch as the others did.

"Sergeant, something needs to be done or many of us are going to get killed."

"Your idea, sir, I think we can pull it off ourselves."

Corporal Rall leaned up on his elbow and spoke, "Sir, if you have an idea, let's hear it. Anything is better than waiting here for a shell to land on us like the first platoon."

Reuben looked at Sergeant Evers who nodded in agreement.

Reuben motioned the men of the fifth platoon to gather. "Listen boys, I have an idea, but without your help, it won't be a plan. We've been together ever since we landed in this country, and so far it has been minor skirmishes until now. I've never volunteered us for any unnecessary details I didn't think it worth getting any of us hurt over. I would never put any of you in any danger I wouldn't go through myself. What I have in mind is dangerous and I'll lead the way, but I leave it to you. We were ordered to hold unless we find it probable to take those guns. Well, the gun in front of us, and the one next to it, are probable."

Several moments of silence passed when Private Jesseps said, "Well, I didn't come all this way to sit in a creek. What do you have in mind, sir?"

Reuben looked at each member of his platoon as they each nodded in reply.

"Looks like we have a plan, Lieutenant Duran, so let's hear it," said Sergeant Evers.

狼

Taking another quick look over the arroyo's edge, and estimating the distance they would have to trek to get to the first gun, then taking the ground into consideration, Reuben lowered back and nodded.

"Okay boys, strip off everything except cartridge and cap boxes. Load your muskets, but no caps, and remove your bayonets."

"Remove bayonets, sir?" asked Private Jesseps.

"That's right, Jesseps. They'll only slow you down, but you'll fix them just before we take that gun."

All the men of the platoon nodded including Sergeant Evers.

As Reuben was loading the musket he had taken, he caught a glimpse of his blue tunic. He raised his arm against the foliage on the arroyo's edge and shook his head.

"One more thing men. Strip off your tunics, put them to the side, roll in that patch of mud, and dirty up your shirts and trousers."

The men looked at him strangely as they saw him crawl and roll in the mud covering his shirt and trousers.

Sergeant Evers also had a questioning look until he looked at his tunic and the ground. He snapped his fingers and said, "Do as the lieutenant says, quickly boys."

After the men quickly rolled in the mud, the men of the fifth platoon looked as brown as the foliage around them. Reuben motioned the men to come closer as he was about to explain the plan.

"Okay, here's what I have in mind. Jesseps, you're with me. Osborne and Taylor, you're also with me, but staggered. The rest of you, skirmish pairs with Mr. Evans."

"We're going to skirmish across that field, sir?" asked Private Osborne, frightened.

"Yes, but we're going to crawl. No firing until I fire first. I'll take out the gunner. Osborne, you take out the number four man. Taylor, you're the best shot so you get the prize. You pop the number five man in the sack, and let's hope he has a shell in the bag."

"That's going to be messy, sir," said Taylor.

"Exactly. Once we open the wasps nest, Mr. Evers, come in quickly as support. I'll give the signal to fix bayonets and cap muskets just before."

"Lieutenant, all this is rather unconventional I would think. Isn't this more like what Indians would do?" asked Corporal Rall.

"That's right, Rall, and it works for them," answered Sergeant Evers.

Reuben nodded. "Okay boys, as low and quick as we can, let's cross that field and have some fun."

Not waiting for any replies, Reuben crawled up and over the arroyo's edge followed by Jesseps, Osborne, and Taylor. Sergeant Evers waited until they were five yards ahead before he began sending out the rest of the platoon in pairs, motioning them in the directions they should go. When the last two were over the edge, he followed.

With muskets loaded and slung across their backs, the men of the fifth platoon crawled their way undetected and were making progress. In less than five minutes, they made their way over forty yards, almost half the distance to the battery.

Sergeant Gillis took a look over the edge of the arroyo from his position and noticed movement in the brush heading toward the enemy battery. His mouth opened in amazement and quickly crawled over the men of the fourth platoon to reach Second Lieutenant Adam Stanns.

"Lieutenant, look to the right, sir. It's the fifth platoon. They're crawling to the enemy guns, look!"

Adam took a look. He couldn't believe what he saw. "Reuben, you crazy son of a bitch, what the hell are you doing?"

"Should we follow, sir?"

Adam slid back against the edge and shook his head no. "No, Sergeant, we'll only draw attention to them, but we need to do something," he said, thinking very hard.

If I were Reuben, what would he do, thought Adam as he looked down the arroyo toward the third platoon.

"I know. We need to keep the enemy's attention away from them. Send the men one at a time toward the third platoon and have them fire their guns once they get there. Yes, that should keep their eyes away from Reuben."

"Very good, sir, right away."

The fifth platoon covered another twenty yards as Reuben stopped. We've been too lucky so far, he thought. He looked down the skirmish line to see all his platoon was in position. Suddenly he heard musket fire coming from the arroyo. Annoyed, he looked back to see Adam's platoon taking pot shots in the air. He looked back toward the battery and saw their attention was focused on the musket fire.

"Good on you, Adam," Reuben said, and motioned his men to advance further.

They advanced another fifteen yards. Again he looked down the line of his platoon. Sergeant Evers waved his hand across his throat. Reuben nodded and gave the signal to cap their muskets and fix bayonets.

He breathed in several times and looked to Jesseps, Osborne, and Taylor. They nodded they were ready. Reuben winked, pulled back the hammer of his musket and waited until the number two gun crewman pulled out the rammer from the muzzle. Reuben rose to his knees, took aim at the gunner as he was about to raise his arm. Reuben squeezed his trigger and the ball hit the gunner square in the chest. He took off running toward the cannon with Jesseps following close behind.

Both Osborne and Taylor rose and aimed at their targets and fired. Osborne's target fell hard to the ground and Taylor's target exploded as his ball hit the shell case slung over his shoulder. Just as Reuben and Jesseps did, they also ran toward the cannon.

Sergeant Evers motioned to the rest of the men as he shouted, "Forward, men! Advance!"

Reuben made it to the cannon first as one of its crew drew a single shot pistol and took aim. Reuben flung his bayonetted musket like a spear catching the crew member in the neck. As he fell, so did his pistol. Reuben reached down and picked it up and pulled the trigger blasting another member of the crew in the face coming at him with a gun implement.

The rest of the fifth platoon arrived and began picking off anyone in a Mexican army uniform.

Sergeant Evers picked up the trail end of the cannon and shouted, "Turn the gun on the second position, boys, quickly!"

Privates Peters and Roberts took the wheels and guided the gun to where it pointed directly to the next cannon. With a few turns of the gun site, Sergeant Evers primed the cannon and looked at Reuben.

Reuben nodded and yelled, "Fire that piece of shit!"

Sergeant Evers lit the fuse.

The cannon fired and its load made direct contact with the next gun causing the limber also to explode. All the men of the fifth platoon were tossed to the ground by the huge explosion.

Sergeant Evers was the first to recover and as he stood, he saw Reuben laying face down. He looked like he was heaving and the sergeant ran to him. Grabbing him by the shoulders, he rolled Reuben over and to his amazement, Reuben was laughing.

Sergeant Evers brought his hand up to his forehead and knelt down next to Reuben. "For heaven's sake, Lieutenant, what's so damned funny?"

Reuben sat up taking in a breath as he said, "You should've seen your face when you lit that fuse. It looked like you crapped your pants."

"Lieutenant, look! The other gun crews are leaving their guns!" shouted Private Stewart.

Both Reuben and Sergeant Evers took a look and also saw the rest of the company advancing from the arroyo followed by the regiment.

"What do we do now, Lieutenant?" asked the sergeant as he helped Reuben to his feet.

He took a few steps to the end of the cannon and watched as the rest of their regiment gave chase to the retreating artillery batteries. He looked at the state of his uniform and shook his head.

"We've done enough, Mr. Evers. Let's go back and get our gear."

Sergeant Evers nodded, turned to the men and said, "You heard the man. Let's get to it."

Still holding the single shot pistol in his hand, Reuben looked to its owner. The bayonetted musket made a mess out of the man's neck and his head lay at a gruesome angle held together by a string of skin. Reuben knelt down and placed the pistol in the dead soldier's hand and laid it across his chest. He straightened out the victim's head and stood.

Sergeant Evers came and stood next to Reuben. "The boys are on their way back to retrieve the gear, sir," he said.

He looked down at the dead soldier and asked, "Are we going to take credit for this, Lieutenant?"

Reuben grunted and said as he motioned to the dead soldier, "Take credit for that?" he asked in a solemn tone.

He looked over the land and the carnage they caused. "Sergeant, I didn't do this for credit. I did this to survive. For your, the platoon's, and the company's survival. All I did was protect you and the others from dying. I'll never take credit for death, Sergeant."

Reuben patted Sergeant Evers on the shoulder and headed off in the direction of their original position.

Whatever doubts were left in Sergeant Evers' mind about Reuben disappeared on that ridge, and a new vision of him appeared in his mind, a vision that frightened him.

狼

When Reuben and Sergeant Evers caught up with the rest of the platoon, they were in the river washing the mud from their shirts. Reuben took the time to look at his uniform. He began to take his shirt off and wash it along with the rest of the men for which he was responsible.

"I'm sorry about your clothes," he said as he was wringing out water from his shirt. "I didn't think this part through. I'll see to it you all get some clean clothes somehow."

"Come on, Lieutenant, if it wasn't for this trick, we wouldn't have gotten that close and our chances wouldn't have been so good," responded Private Taylor as all the others nodded in agreement. "But if you do, make sure the shirt you get me is a little smaller than the one I have now."

Reuben chuckled along with the others.

Ever since Reuben was assigned as leader to the fifth platoon, Sergeant Evers had a strange feeling about him. The sergeant expected him to be like any other young junior officer, all out for glory and to make a name for themself, and their family. That began to change after he attended his first platoon officer's meeting. What was different about Reuben is when the call for only the platoon leaders to meet with the company commander, Reuben took the sergeant along, something every junior officer never did.

"Come along, Mr. Evers, I have a platoon leaders meeting."

"Sir?"

"Yes, come on."

"Begging your pardon, Lieutenant, the other platoon leaders never take their sergeants along to these meetings."

"I don't care about those other platoon leaders, I want you with me."

When the sergeant arrived at that first meeting, he was made unwelcome, but Reuben kept him by his side. At the end of the meeting, the sergeant questioned why Reuben wanted him there.

"Because I want you to know what I know, for the sake of the men," replied Reuben.

The next meeting, the company commander asked for three platoons to volunteer and enter an unknown village to hunt out enemy advance troops supposed to be garrisoned within the village. The sergeant hung his head low, shaking his head with his eyes closed. Reuben took note. When Sergeant Evers raised his head and opened his eyes, it was as he expected except for one thing. All the arms of the junior officers were raised to volunteer... except for his platoon leader who stood with his arms crossed.

The following day after the mission, the three platoons who were picked suffered many causalities. Sergeant Evers began to notice whenever volunteers were asked for, Reuben would look to him to see his expression. He's taking my experience in mind, thought the sergeant. He confronted Reuben about what he felt.

"Mr. Evers, I was not put in charge of this platoon to get them killed. It's my goal to see you all survive and if it takes my own life to make that happen, then so be it. One thing an old sergeant major once told me is, *'volunteering only gets you in the shit.'*"

From then on when Sergeant Evers nodded to volunteer, Reuben would raise his hand and was usually picked. These missions always saw some skirmishes, enough to keep the men sharp, but they seldom saw any serious action. However the fifth platoon always came back with foraged rations that were never issued. These foraged rations, such as eggs, sausage, and other food items were provided by friendly villagers.

Another side Sergeant Evers also revered about Reuben was his concern for the men. While other platoon leaders only saw to their men when needed, Reuben always made sure his men were never in need.

"I don't care what it takes, Mr. Evers, make sure the men have what they need before they need it."

"But sir, in order to do that, Corporal Rall and I may have to take, shall I say, certain liberties," hinted Sergeant Evers.

"I'll let you in on a little secret, Sergeant. Remember those socks I got for you and the men last week? I took those same certain liberties you're talking about with the fourth platoon."

"Lieutenant Stanns's platoon? I thought he was your friend."

"He is, a very good friend, but he isn't in charge of my men."

Today after the cannon incident, Sergeant Evers saw a different side of Reuben. A side that was very cunning, ingenious, and frightening. And so did another observer.

"Ah, Lieutenant, we have a visitor," pointed out Sergeant Evers.

Reuben rose from wringing out his shirt and looked to the river's edge where he saw a high ranking officer. Slipping on his shirt, he nodded to the sergeant and made his way to the officer.

"Forgive me for not saluting, Colonel, but as you can see, I'm not entirely in uniform."

"Come on, Reuben, I'm a doctor more than an officer, you know that."

Colonel Lawrence Chelmsford, a doctor in the army medical corps also had a unique feeling about Reuben when he first met him at Fort Monroe. Upon Colonel Chelmsford's routine examination of Reuben, he found him to be much more grounded than the other cadets who were accelerated into promotion because of the war. He noted Reuben seemed to have a pure grasp on reality the other cadets and some of the junior officers lacked.

As a personal project, Colonel Chelmsford began his own study on the effects of war on the individual psyche. The study became a personal topic of concern as he witnessed his father, a veteran of the second war of independence, who was still haunted by the memories he encountered during that conflict which ended thirty years ago. After lengthy informal discussions with Reuben, which included his family, how he was raised, and also his relationship with Renee, he took note Reuben may possibly be a candidate to study during this conflict.

"What brings you to this charming spot in the Mexican countryside, Doc?" asked Reuben rather informally.

"I should ask you. How come you're not with the rest of the regiment securing the heights after the enemy was chased off?"

Reuben looked toward the distant battery still engulfed in smoke from their attack. He turned to the colonel and with a look that reminded the colonel of his father, Reuben answered, "I believe my men have done more than enough for today."

Colonel Chelmsford nodded. "You know, Lieutenant, talk from the rear has it that the second cannon on the right exploded, possibly from an overheated cannon barrel or breach. Either way, the rear echelon is calling it a stroke of good luck."

"Whatever gets them through the day, Doc," said Reuben unemotionally as he looked up to the sun and momentarily wondered if Renee was looking at it as well this very moment.

Sighing loudly breaking Reuben's thought, Colonel Chelmsford said in a concerning manner, "Look, Reuben, I witnessed what you and your men did on the right with you leading the way up to that gun fully exposed. Don't forget, unlike other high ranking officers, being a doctor allows me to view the field from different positions. Of all the junior officers in this corps, you are the only one capable of concocting such a risky excursion, and make it work."

"So are you going to tell regiment it was my platoon that saved the day?" asked Reuben, sternly, "Because I don't need that type of attention."

"Well, how about your men?"

"Maybe so, but that sort of attention will only get them killed, and it's up to me to make sure they survive," Reuben answered as he watched the men splashing in the river. "Besides, they know what they did."

"Can I ask you a question, Reuben?" the colonel asked in a caring manner.

Reuben nodded.

Colonel Chelmsford took in a long breath and let it out, "Are you deliberately trying to get yourself killed, Reuben?"

Reuben turned his head from his men and shot a look of fury at the colonel. It slowly dissolved into a look of sorrow. "It would make life much easier for her if I were to die here," answered Reuben.

"A life she doesn't wish to have," added the colonel.

Looking back up to the sun, Reuben answered, "She doesn't have much of an option with regards to her life."

Reuben's logic and voice was reminding Colonel Chelmsford of his father the more he spoke. His father took on much responsibility during his war years and he suffered from it, up to the point when he took his own life with a single shot pistol pressed below his chin. He could see Reuben following in his father's footsteps, believing he had the responsibility for everyone who depended on, and also loved him.

Colonel Chelmsford placed his hand on Reuben's shoulder and told him, "Listen, Reuben, don't take on more responsibility than you can handle. If you do, you will travel a road where there's no turning back, and you will never be able to return to those who love you, and the one you love."

He removed his hand and began walking back toward the regimental encampment.

Reuben sincerely said, as he kept staring at the sun, "Thanks, Doc."

Colonel Chelmsford turned around. "If there's anything you need, Reuben," he said.

Reuben turned his attention to the colonel. "My men could use some clean uniforms. As you, *witnessed*, we had to improvise to do what we did."

The colonel smirked and replied, "I'll see what I can do, Lieutenant."

"Thank you, Colonel. And also, if possible, can you make sure one of those shirts is a size small?"

狼

It had been a very long day for Renee, beginning with church services with William Sinclair, the back to school formal ball with William Sinclair, family dinner with William Sinclair, and finally, an evening sitting on the terrace with William Sinclair. Renee began to believe this day would never end.

They sat on the terrace swing, Renee on one side and William Sinclair sitting on the other keeping with courting tradition. William Sinclair did most of the talking, mostly about himself and his achievements while Renee pretended to show interest in what he was discussing, of which she had no clue. Although she appeared to be listening, her thoughts were of how she and Reuben would spend their visits. At their unwedded age, those visits would be considered inappropriate by their gazing, touching, and holding. Instead of Reuben sitting on one side of this swing and me on the other, I would probably be sitting on his lap, she was thinking. Maybe him on mine, a thought that brought a smile to her face which she hid with the fan she was holding. At least those stupid fan etiquette lessons at Wickham are good for something, she thought.

"I said I must be taking my leave, Renee," said William Sinclair interrupting her thoughts.

"Oh, I'm terribly sorry, William. I had a momentary reflection of you and me walking into the ball this afternoon," she said. Yuck, she thought.

"That was fun. I did enjoy meeting Mrs. Fletcher. She says you have a wonderful talent with a pen. Perhaps one day you will honor me by reciting some of your work?"

"I believe once we are married, I will," she replied, thinking her passages about Reuben would be a smashing hit. "Come, I'll walk you to your coach as you say your farewells to my parents."

William Sinclair presented his arm and Renee placed her hand in the crook and they walked into the house to her father's den where Franklin Wallace and Margret were sitting.

William Sinclair thanked them for their hospitality and wished them good fortune. They too also walked William Sinclair to his coach to say their farewells.

Before he boarded, with his back to Renee's parents, he inappropriately leered at her, took her hand in his, and gently kissed her gloved knuckle. "Farewell, Miss Wallace, until our next visit."

Renee curtseyed as she shuddered in disgust at his leer, and quickly began to think of the day she ditched school to see Reuben one last time before he went away. How they stood in each other's arms by Lucy's piano with adoring looks for each other, a far cry from a gentle kiss on a gloved knuckle and an inappropriate, unwelcomed leer.

As the coach rode away, Renee and her parents walked back inside the house.

"Come, my daughter, tell us of your visit with young William," said Franklin Wallace cheerfully.

Being as enthusiastic as possible, Renee replied just as cheerfully, "Not now, father. I must go to my room and write down the day's events in my diary now that they are fresh in my head."

Renee's father laughed, "Well then, go and write. We can hear about it tomorrow."

"Thank you, father," she answered as she curtseyed to him and her mother before making her way up the stairs and into her room.

Once Franklin Wallace heard the door close, he said to Margret, "I do believe our daughter is finally taking a shine to William, and the prospect of becoming his wife."

"She is going to make a pretty bride," said Margret and walked toward the den.

Franklin Wallace stayed looking up toward the direction of Renee's room. "Thank God for that war in Mexico," he said silently to himself.

Renee entered her room, closed the door and leaned against it. "Geez oh geez oh geez I thought this day would never end. I can't believe how self-absorbed he is. Reuben has never been self-absorbed or vain like him."

She walked to her desk and reached behind to the secret compartment she rigged to hide her image case with Reuben's picture, and sat down. She yanked off her gloves and threw them to the floor and released her hair from the tight hair pins, shook it loose, and let out a long sigh of relief as it cascaded over her shoulders, just the way Reuben likes it.

Sitting in a relaxed position with her head back and eyes closed, images of Reuben came to her. She had seen paintings of tropical landscapes and wondered if they were anything like where he was. In her mind, she was comparing the oak tree on the Duran farm to the palm trees in the paintings.

"I would take the oak tree any day," she mumbled to herself.

Suddenly her eyes opened with thought. She sat up and retrieved her writing utensils and a page of parchment and began to write, not of her thoughts of this day, but of her thoughts of Reuben this very moment in the shape of an oak tree...

My dearest most secret love
Do you think of our tree wherever you are?
I think of it often during the day and especially at night
I clear my mind of memories of you so I can sleep
But I wake in the morning atop a wet pillow
I would give up all my worth to find you
So I can see you
To touch you
To hold you
So I can wake in the morning atop a dry pillow

Looking over her words, she nodded approvingly, extinguished the lamp, and placed the page amongst her other written passages in a small chest hidden high atop her closet shelf.

Walking to the center of the room, she unbuttoned her bodice and untied the hoop skirt's draw ribbon, and let her dress fall to the floor and dug out the VMI button from the dress skirt pocket.

Stepping over the dress, she retrieved the image case from the desk and hopped onto her bed. Placing the image case on her pillow, she untied her shoes, kicked them off, and pulled off her stockings. She sat on the edge of the bed and watched as she wiggled her toes. She was so exhausted from the pretending she did the entire day.

The only light in her room was of the moon shining through the window. She lay on her stomach, opened the image case, and placed the button on the velvet side. She gazed into Reuben's eyes in his picture.

She laid her head next to the image case and looked up toward the moon. "I hope you had a better day than I did," she said, softly.

狼

Reuben lay upon his bedroll looking up toward the moon holding the open image case with Renee's picture. He lowered his eyes to the picture. With his finger tip, he caressed the image of her face.

As he watched his finger trace Renee's face, he took notice of his hand and looked at his palm. It looked as if it were covered with blood. In a panic, he closed his eyes tight, shook his head, and opened his eyes to see his hand was clean.

He let out a sigh of relief and looked back up to the moon. "I hope you had a better day than I did," he said, softly.

狼

In the following days, the regiment was on the march making progress to the capital of Mexico. After a three day battle in which the fifth platoon took part with the house-to-house fighting within the village, they were supplied with new uniforms which included a small sized shirt, complements of Colonel Chelmsford.

The platoon was supposed to exchange their old uniforms for the new ones, but Reuben decided they were to keep the old uniforms with the eerie feeling they might need them again. So in turn, including Reuben, they carried the bundle of old clothes as they marched along.

It didn't take long for the truth to come out about what actually happened on September 20th regarding the enemy cannon incident. When the actual events were revealed, Reuben was called before a board of inquiry regarding his actions. He believed Colonel Chelmsford was responsible for reporting Reuben's platoon's involvement, but was angered to find it was his VMI roommate who reported the incident.

"Just who in the hell do you think you are telling regiment about our little stunt, Adam?"

"Reuben, I just believe credit should be given when credit is due. I didn't expect them to charge you with any infractions, believe me. You may have saved many lives and I believe that should be rewarded."

"I'm not mad or even concerned with the board. I can care shit about regiment. What I'm mad about is you betrayed your word to me you wouldn't say anything."

But with Reuben's nature, he got over his anger of Adam's naive good deed in a short time.

In a huge command wall tent, Reuben stood before the board of inquiry consisting of top regimental commanders. To the rear of the tent sat his company commander, Captain Waylon Masters and to Reuben's surprise, Colonel Lawrence Chelmsford.

Colonel Chelmsford had a difficult time being allowed to attend the proceedings, but because of his persistence and being a highly regarded physician, the regimental commander agreed to allow him to be present only as an observer.

Also standing in the rear of the tent was the regimental sergeant major.

Once proceeding protocols were made, the hearing began with the reading of Second Lieutenant Adam Stanns's report followed by the formal charges of disobeying lawful orders, conduct unbecoming of an officer by putting his men in undue risk, and failure to report said operations. Once the charges were read and discussed in turn, Colonel Norman Carrene asked Reuben how he pleaded.

With an emotionless expression, Reuben replied, "Guilty."

In sheer disbelief, all the officers, including the sergeant major, were stunned. They were expecting a long drawn out nervous justification of his actions, like any other junior officer would offer with hopes for clemency.

Colonel Chelmsford rather admired Reuben's arrogant attitude toward the whole affair. His attitude reminded the colonel of his father's attitude toward authority, brash and assertive.

After a long moment of awkward silence, the regimental commander had the sergeant major escort Reuben out of the tent while they deliberated over the charges and his plea.

Outside the tent, Reuben leaned against an army wagon with his arms crossed looking up toward the sun thinking of Renee. He began to have a sense he wasn't alone in his moment of solitude.

The sergeant major, an imposing individual, had an intense scowling glare toward Reuben. Reuben, feeling his personal thoughts were being rudely intruded upon, turned his head toward the sergeant major and made eye contact with his own intense glare, but his was one a hungry wolf would give before pouncing on its prey.

Feeling intimidation from a junior officer for the first time in his army career, the sergeant major's expression dissolved as he was forced to look away. Reuben returned to his thoughts of Renee.

After what the sergeant major thought was the shortest deliberation ever for a board of inquiry, he was asked to bring Reuben back in.

Reuben stood before the board as Colonel Carrene stated, "Second Lieutenant Reuben Duran, you have been found guilty on all charges. Therefore, you are sentenced to a... reprimand only. You are to return to your duties as platoon leader of the fifth platoon, Company B of this regiment."

He called an end to the proceedings and excused Reuben.

Just as Reuben was about to walk out of the tent, Colonel Carrene called out to him. "Officially, Lieutenant, what you did was inexcusable, unofficially... outstanding job, sir." The Colonel rose and saluted Reuben.

Not knowing the protocol of a senior officer's salute, he returned the salute and walked out of the tent without uttering a single word.

In the weeks to follow, the fifth platoon of Company B was assigned tasks similar to the one they performed at Anton Chico, unconventional. Regiment saw an interesting resource with Reuben's platoon, and wanted to make use of it, discreetly. What Reuben feared because of that one incident of survival was beginning to haunt him. No matter how hard he tried to get out of these assignments, he was overturned with no option but to perform the assigned tasks.

"Lieutenant, I have a job for your platoon. You recall the incident you were involved with at Anton Chico, do you not?" asked Captain Masters.

"Yes sir."

"Well, you and your men are to perform the same task on these gun emplacements on this ridge," instructed the company commander pointing to a map on his desk.

With a very puzzled look, Reuben replied, "Sir, may I remind you I was sent before a board of inquiry for that incident?"

Unmoved by Reuben's response, Captain Masters continued to look at the map and said, "This assignment isn't coming from me." The captain shifted his eyes from the map to Reuben. "It's coming from regiment. And that's between you and me, understand?"

Reuben would still share with his men where these assignments were coming from, and he also told Adam. Adam felt responsible for the position Reuben was in and did as much as he could to support his VMI roommate, even as far as suggesting rotating a few of his men into Reuben's platoon, but Reuben denied the idea.

"My men have already been exposed to this type of work. They know each other's capabilities and most importantly, know what to expect. Besides, the more individuals who know about these tasks, the more chances they will be exposed and I won't allow you to get in trouble or others to die. Do you understand, Adam?"

"I do, and you have my word, I mean it this time. But I will help you in any way I can."

Besides creeping up on cannons, other assignments included reconnaissance behind the enemy lines, the capture of prisoners to gain information, and neutralizing enemy outposts prior to regimental incursions. All of the activities of the fifth platoon went unreported as ordered by the company commander who got his orders from regiment. As far as the rest of Company B was concerned, fifth platoon was just another platoon assigned to the company. However, the men of Company B regarded them as anything but. Company B began to refer to them as the Lone Wolf Platoon, not because only they were given these dangerous assignments, but because of Reuben's menacing lifeless glare of his resembling a wolf on the prowl. A glare all of his men would eventually acquire from their activities.

After a few months of the fifth platoon's assigned activities, Colonel Chelmsford began to notice how Reuben and his men exhibited peculiar mannerisms quite different from the other men of Company B, or the regiment for that matter. Mannerisms of the men consisted of being more on the reserved side. They tended to keep amongst themselves, withdrawn from the others, and more alert.

The other platoons ridiculed them, thinking they believed themselves to be above the rest of the company because of the tasks they were assigned. But when Colonel Chelmsford would visit with Reuben and his men, he didn't get that impression at all. His diagnoses were on the bases the men of the fifth platoon found it difficult to associate with the other soldiers of Company B. He hypothesized the difference between how during battle, the company and regiment were at a distance not seeing the enemy close up, whereas Reuben and his men had an up close and personal view of the enemy soldiers they dealt with. That itself had a profound effect on the men of the fifth platoon.

It showed dramatically when soldiers of the regiment found themselves walking amongst the dead. They exhibited signs of tension, anxiety, and would avoid looking at the corpses as much as possible. However, the men of the fifth platoon would walk amongst the dead and step over them as if they were large stones or fallen tree limbs in their path, often taking useful items such as ammunition, food, and taking drinks out of the corpse's canteens. Their line of work seemed to turn them into emotionless individuals, void of any interest of others who lacked their experiences.

Colonel Chelmsford's notes on Reuben and his men were extensive and through his personal interest in the platoon, he began to have a better understanding of his father's difficulties after his wartime involvements. Serious concerns began to form in Colonel Chelmsford's mind for Reuben and his men and took them to regiment. Regiment's response was anything but concerning. As far as they were concerned, as long as the fifth platoon was providing positive results, they were a valuable asset not to be interfered with. However, they assured the colonel Reuben's platoon would be granted extra rations because of the work they performed, a remedy Colonel Chelmsford thought insulting to the fifth platoon. What these men need is to be rotated out of the field, or have them train other platoons on their tactics.

Colonel Chelmsford's answer and relief came in the form of the arrival of three fresh infantry regiments to replace and rotate two infantry regiments back to Fort Monroe. The colonel's and Reuben's regiment being one of the two.

狼

Reuben was sitting up against a tree with Renee's open picture case in his hand. He had a childlike smile and gleam in his eye as he gazed upon her image. He began to wonder what she could be doing this very moment as he looked toward the moon. His peaceful moment was interrupted when Sergeant Evers plopped down next to Reuben causing him to close the case.

"I'm sorry, Lieutenant, I'm not disturbing you, am I?"

"Well... no not really, what is it?"

"Oh, nothing, for a year now, I have seen you with that picture case and you have never offered a peek. Is it something special?"

Reuben smiled as he looked at the closed case. "You can say that, Mr. Evers."

"Tell you what, Reuben, here, look at this," said Sergeant Evers informally as he handed Reuben an image case of his own. After all they have been through, this moment was a sharing of friendship rather than a relationship between an enlisted man and his superior, brotherhood.

Reuben carefully took it and asked, "May I, Sam?"

"Of course."

Reuben opened the case to see a very pretty woman sitting on a plush chair with two small children, a boy, and girl, standing on each side of her. The image caused Reuben to smile and think of his mother and father.

"Is this your wife and children, Sam?"

Sam Evers nodded. "Her name is Cybil. The boy is Sam Jr., and the girl is Samantha. They are nearly adults now."

"You have a very handsome family, Sam. I feel honored you shared this with me."

"Will you return the honor, Reuben?" Sam Evers asked as he motioned to Reuben's image case.

Reuben smiled and nodded. He handed it over to the sergeant. The sergeant opened the case and when he saw the image of Renee, his jaw lowered.

"My goodness, is this your wife?" asked Sam Evers, not knowing exactly Reuben's relation to the girl in the picture since he never spoke of Renee.

"Not exactly," said Reuben in a neutral tone. He took in a deep breath, let it out, and began telling Sam the story about his relationship with Renee. When he was finished, Sergeant Evers closed the image case and handed it back to Reuben.

"That's a rough story, Reuben. If you don't mind me saying so, that story should be no reason why you should be taking so many risks. Even though she may be promised to another, it

73

sounds to me you are her true love and you dying would only devastate her, if I may be so bold to say," said Sam, hoping he didn't over speak his opinion.

Reuben opened the case and again gazed at her image. "Thank you, Sam. That's the most profound thing I have ever heard regarding our relationship. I never thought of it that way. Thanks."

"Either way, having a girl like Renee as a wife or a special friend would make any man forget the last twelve months of hell we have gone through," said Sam.

Their pleasant discussion was interrupted by cheers coming from the adjacent camp. Both Reuben and the sergeant looked to one another with questioning looks. They stood and walked to the rest of the platoon who were sitting around the fire pit. They were looking in the direction of the cheering.

Appearing out of nowhere, Adam tapped Reuben on the shoulder with a huge expression of happiness. "Have you heard, Reuben, we're being rotated back to Fort Monroe! We should be back sometime in August! I heard it myself from regiment."

Reuben and his men looked at Adam with expressionless faces.

"Oh, come on boys, we're going home!" said Adam, cheerfully.

Reuben placed his arm around Adam's shoulders and nodded. "That's good news, Adam, very good, right, boys?"

The men around the fire pit nodded silently looking at each other.

"What's with you boys? I bring you good news and you treat it like it's a job order."

"It is good news, Adam. It's just we have a big day tomorrow, you know, the gun batteries," said Reuben as he led Adam away from his men.

"I thought this would cheer them up, Reuben."

"It does. It does, Adam, and thank you. But remember, August is a whole month away. A lot can happen in a month, especially with the assignment the company has to do tomorrow."

Adam stared at Reuben in a peculiar manner as if he were trying to read a wall poster in a different language.

"What's the matter, Adam?" asked Reuben.

"How do you do it, Reuben? Time after time you do these assignments. I get scared at the sight of the enemy hundreds of yards, or even miles, away. But you, you deal with them face-to-face and hand-to-hand."

Reuben looked at his VMI roommate as he did when they first met back in Lexington, a soft innocent look which made Adam become his friend.

In a most sincere, honest manner, Reuben replied, "When I go into a fight, I believe, I'm already dead, therefore I have nothing to lose if I'm killed."

"But your family, Renee, don't you think of them?"

"No."

Looking horrified at Reuben's answer, Adam said, "That's inhuman, Reuben."

Reuben let out a small laugh.

"What do you find so amusing?" asked Adam, troubled.

Reflecting on what he told Adam about his feeling before going into a fight, Reuben replied, "I just had a deep sense of déjà vu. A sense that… a great man, perhaps a soldier… no, a warrior of the past may have made my words more elegant than what I said about believing to be dead before fighting."

狼

Nearly 8 o'clock in the morning, Sunday, July 4th, Renee was being escorted by William Sinclair, dressed in his Sunday best, along with both their parents from the coach to Saint Mary's for early morning services. Outside the church, Franklin Wallace proudly introduced the Sinclair family to business associates, elected officials, and acquaintances and boasted of how much the union of their son to his daughter will be prosperous for the city of Norfolk's shipping and trade industry.

Renee again pretended to be enthused, thinking this was going to be another long day of holiday events, and pretending she was having the time of her life. Dear Lord, I could really use something to pick up my spirits to get me through this day, she silently prayed.

She stood quietly with a fake smile on her face listening to all the high society drivel, and being introduced as the future Mrs. William Sinclair. Her jaws began to ache from holding a phony smile. Using her fan to cover her lower face, Renee would look away to drop and shift her lower jaw back and forth for relief. As she did so once again, she noticed a head pull back from peaking around a tree. She kept looking in that direction until the head peaked around again and motioned to Renee.

"Lucy!"

"Pardon me, my pet?" asked William Sinclair. "Did you say something?"

Clearing her throat, Renee said, "Nancy, an old classmate of mine. I just saw her. If you will excuse me, William, I need to discuss the prospects of her being a part of our wedding party." Oh geez, I can't believe I have to talk like this, and if Reuben ever heard you call me *pet*, he would beat you to a pulp, she thought and longed to hear Reuben call her Wickham Girl.

"Oh indeed, very well, but don't be too long. Services are about to begin shortly."

"I will be but a few moments," said Renee as she made her way to the tree.

Once she arrived at the tree and peered around it, Lucy was nowhere to be found. Was I seeing things, she wondered.

"Psst… over here behind the wall," said Lucy peering around the tall ivy-covered brick wall.

Quickly Renee made her way to the other side where she took Lucy in her arms elated to see her.

"Oh geez, Lucy, what a nice surprise to see you," said Renee thinking this is just the thing she was praying for earlier to lift her spirits.

"Not as nice as the surprise I have for you."

"What do you mean?"

"Here, listen to this," said Lucy as she unfolded a sheet of paper.

Dear Mr. and Mrs. Duran,

It is my pleasure to inform you that your son, Second Lieutenant Reuben Duran, is very well and will be returning with the rest of his regiment sometime within the month of August. I am pleased to say your son has served his country and flag with distinct honor in the highest regards.

> *Your Obedient Servant,*
> *Col. Norman Carrene*
> *9th U.S. Reg. Inf'y Regiment*

"Geez oh geez oh geez let me see that!" exclaimed Renee as she snatched the letter out of Lucy's hands.

She stood holding the letter in complete and utter disbelief.

Lucy could see Renee's lips move as she was silently reading the letter to herself. When Lucy saw Renee was finished, she asked, "Well, what do you think?"

Renee wrapped her arms around Lucy and they both began jumping up and down in sheer delight.

Renee released Lucy and again looked at the letter.

"Mama and Da sent me to tell you first thing this morning. The messenger delivered this message late last evening. We thought it was bad news, being it was late and all, but boy were we jumping around like crazy when Da finally read it. I knew you would be here. I hope that was okay?"

"Are you joking? I just finished praying for something to lift my spirits and you did it, Lucy. I wonder when in August? It doesn't say," said Renee still looking at the letter.

"Well, if I know my brother, he'll surprise us all the way he surprised us the day I helped you ditch school to see him before he left."

Renee leaned against the wall with a genuine smile on her face holding the letter to her chest. "Do you know what this means, Lucy?" she asked.

"What?" replied Lucy as she also leaned against the wall.

"This means I no longer will be crying myself to sleep every night wondering if Reuben is alive because he's coming home."

Lucy looked at Renee. "But you're crying now."

"I'm crying because I'm so happy, silly."

Renee looked up toward the sky and said, "Just think, Lucy, your brother could very well be looking up at the sun this very moment as we are."

狼

Lying on his side in his mud covered uniform, Reuben looked up to the sun and estimated what time it was. Again, on this Sunday, the 4th day of July, the men of the fifth platoon were assigned to use their unique talents, like they have done on more than one occasion to capture the cannon on the far left, and use it to blast the neighboring gun.

Slinging his musket across his back, he silently motioned to Sergeant Evers it was time to proceed. Nodding to Privates Jesseps, Osborne and Taylor, they crawled up and over the earthworks low to the ground. There was no need to look back to see if the others were off on their assignments for the men of the fifth platoon knew everyone's mannerisms all too well.

From his position, Adam kept a close watch on his friend. He had told Reuben if anything were to happen, his platoon would support Reuben's in any way for them to recover.

Taking the gun this time was much different because all the guns were silent. All the other times they crept up on cannon positions, the cannon crews were occupied with their tasks which made it easier for Reuben and his men to make their way across the open field undetected. This was the first time they attempted it with no commotion, and Reuben felt uneasy about the operation.

"If you want us to take that gun, let us begin our advance in the very early hours before daylight," he told regiment.

Their response was idiotic. "The general doesn't wish to be awakened too early to view the operation, so therefore you will begin your advance at 7 a.m."

Just as before, Reuben crawled, keeping his eyes on his target, the gun captain. Besides birds chirping, it was completely silent. This was a huge concern for Reuben, and unlike before, he would stop every five or six yards as the others followed his lead.

It had taken them three times longer to reach fifty yards. Every little movement Reuben saw from the battery, he would stop and evaluate.

He looked down the line to Sergeant Evers. The sergeant motioned to advance a little further. Reuben nodded in agreement. From this position, their success would be less likely.

狼

Back at the earthworks, all the platoon leaders of Company B had their eyes fixed on the fifth platoon's progress. They too thought it was idiotic for regiment waiting this late for Reuben to make his move. Although Reuben's platoon was regarded as a rogue platoon, the men of Company B also regarded them as very valuable.

All because of one incident for the sole purpose to survive, Reuben caused his men to be used for certain unique operations that required stealth, an assignment he tried desperately to get his platoon out of.

Moving down the earthworks at a crouch, the regimental messenger was making his way to Adam's platoon to deliver a message for his men to cross the field at an angle towards the far left to cover the flank once the operation is underway. The messenger got as far as the third platoon when he tripped, knocking over a loaded musket causing it to fire and hit a soldier in the groin who screamed out in agony.

Every man in Company B looked toward the musket shot in horror, and then back toward the enemy gun batteries.

"FUEGO!" BAM!

狼

The fifth platoon was about thirty five yards away from their target cannon, the distance they usually began their attack. Reuben started to evaluate if they should move ahead another five yards considering the unusual conditions. He looked to Sergeant Evers who waved his hand across his throat, the signal this is close enough. Reuben gave the signal to cap and fix bayonets and waited for all his men to give the signal they were ready.

Reuben pulled back the hammer on his musket, eyed his target, rose to his knee, and as he was about to pull the trigger, he heard gunfire and a scream come from their earthworks.

He looked back in fury as did the rest of his platoon. He was fully exposed and he heard the enemy give the order to open fire. Turning back his attention to their target cannon, he was knocked back. His shoulder felt as it were stung by a thousand wasps all at once. He looked to his shoulder and saw his mud colored shirt turning red.

He felt a tug on his arm and looked up to see Corporal Rall kneeling over him trying to lift him when a musket ball exited his chest followed by a spray of blood. Corporal Rall fell forward on top of Reuben.

Trapped under the dead weight of the corporal, Reuben struggled to roll out from underneath. He pushed himself up using his good arm and ordered his men to fall back.

Privates Jesseps and Peters began running at a low crouch toward the earthworks when they were shot down. Reuben yelled out in anger and looked at their target cannon.

The gun captain trained the gun directly at their position.

"FUEGO!" BAM!

The shell obliterated Privates Osborne, Taylor, Roberts, and Stewart. There was nothing left of them except a cloud of red and limbs falling to the ground.

Reuben crawled back and retrieved his musket. Using Corporal Rall's corpse as a shield, he leveled his musket, targeted the gun captain and pulled the trigger. He yelled out in agonizing pain as the musket butt recoiled against his wounded shoulder.

The gun captain fell dead on the spot. His death was answered by a hail of musket balls aimed in Reuben's direction. Reuben laid on his back reloading his musket as he felt musket balls hit the dead body of the corporal. He looked to his right and saw Private Allen's head explode from a musket ball making contact with his face.

Reuben capped his musket, rolled over, and took aim at another enemy soldier as another cannon blast blinded him with dirt and dust. His vision returned in time to see Sergeant Evers, who was carrying Private Matthews over his shoulder, blasted by canister fire from their target cannon.

In less than two minutes, with the exception of Second Lieutenant Reuben Duran, the fifth platoon of Company B of the 9th U.S. Regular Infantry Regiment ceased to exist.

From the earthworks, all the men of Company B watched helplessly as the fifth platoon were either dropping to the ground or exploding from cannon fire. From his position, Adam saw Reuben still fighting with a wounded shoulder. He looked down the line of his platoon. They also were witnessing the terrible drama being played out before their eyes. In a fit of rage, Adam, for the first time followed Reuben's demeanor and disobeyed the order to hold their fire as he gave the command, "PLATOON READY!"

On reflex, the men of the fourth platoon stood with their muskets at the ready.

"AIM!"

Simultaneously, their muskets leveled off aiming toward the enemy batteries.

"FIRE!"

All ten muskets went off at the same time.

The fifth platoon had always kept to themselves because the rest of Company B regarded their unconventional means of warfare tactless, but one thing was certain, they also knew the fifth platoon saved the lives of Company B on more than a few occasions. Now it was their turn to do what they could to save the fifth platoon. Following Adam's lead, the other platoon leaders of Company B began to give the order to open fire.

Adam gave the order to commence continuous fire to cover Reuben's retreat. He looked to see if anyone of the fifth platoon were nearing the earthworks when he saw Sergeant Evers, with Private Matthews over his shoulder, disappear in a blast of canister fire. With his jaw dropping, he glanced toward Reuben's position and saw him sitting on his knees looking toward the direction of the canister blast.

"GET DOWN, REUBEN, FOR GOD SAKES, GET DOWN!!!" roared Adam.

Reuben remained in his seated position exposed to enemy fire from muskets and cannons. Adam called out to his sergeant, "Sergeant Gillis, cover me!"

So unlike Adam of the past, he climbed out of the earthworks and sprinted toward his VMI roommate, and friend.

Reuben, sitting on his knees, helplessly witnessed the last two members of his platoon die before his eyes. He remained sitting, devoid of any feelings or emotions as enemy musket balls were hitting the ground all around him. From a distance he heard his name and looked to his left to see Adam running to him.

Wincing from his wounded shoulder, he shook his head thinking he was hallucinating. But again, he saw it was Adam waving his arm in a downward motion coming toward him.

A scowl came to his face and he began to rise, yelling for Adam to go back.

Adam made it to Reuben's side and he draped Reuben's good arm over his shoulder, "Come on, Reuben, I'll get you out of here!"

As Adam lifted Reuben to his feet, a musket ball entered Adam's chest and both men fell to the ground.

"ADAM, NO!!!"

Reuben covered the wound with his hand and put down pressure.

Adam looked up to his friend who had him cradled in one arm, while keeping pressure on the wound with the other.

"I don't want to be here anymore, Reuben. Please take me back to Culpepper."

"I'll have you there before you know it, Adam. Think of Mary, think of her hard."

"Mary Alice, my Mary. She's sweet, she's the best girl in the world."

"That she is, Adam. The best, the very best."

"I need her now. Momma, don't cry, it doesn't hurt too much."

Reuben began to tremble. Adam told him his mother passed on years before he entered VMI. After these long months of dread, Reuben lost all faith in a god that would let such chaos happen. He began to think of god as a sadist.

"Reuben? I can't see! Are you there?"

"Yes, Adam."

"You must leave me, Reuben. You must go back to your girl, Renee. I always thought she was so beautiful, more beautiful than my Mary. I'll protect you. You must go now and leave me." Adam coughed up blood and gasped a last breath of air and fell silent in Reuben's arms. Reuben closed Adam's eyes and cradled him.

Feeling light headed, Reuben fell to his back with Adam still in his arm. He began blacking out.

狼

"Quickly boys, quickly, get them out of here!"

Reuben was jarred awake by the rough handling of soldiers lifting him off the ground. He lifted his head to see about half a dozen soldiers of Adam's platoon surrounding him, half of them firing their weapons while the other half were carrying him and Adam back to the earthworks.

"Come now, let's go!"

Reuben looked to his left and to his surprise, he saw Colonel Chelmsford in his medical apron leading the solders back to the earthworks. Reuben's eyes closed tightly wincing from the painful handling as he was being passed to the soldiers in the trench.

"There you go boys, good job," said the colonel as he began attending to Reuben's shoulder.

Reuben pushed him away and rolled on to his stomach and began pulling himself toward his platoon's position in the works.

The colonel lifted and held him in his arms, but Reuben was still fighting to get free while pointing.

"What is it, Reuben? What do you want?"

"Haversack, picture…"

Colonel Chelmsford pointed to the nearest man, "You there, grab his haversack and bring it here, quick! Hold on, Reuben, hold on."

The private ordered to retrieve the haversack lifted one and looked to Reuben. He shook his head no and pointed. The soldier picked up another one and looked back and saw Reuben nodding his head yes and quickly ran back handing it to him.

Reuben was having difficulties opening the bag so Colonel Chelmsford took it from him, opened it, and began digging for what he knew Reuben wanted. He found the green drawstring bag and pulled it out of the haversack. Reuben immediately motioned to it with shaking hands.

The colonel was about to hand it to him, but stopped. He placed it in his apron pocket, pulled out a bandage and wiped Reuben's hands clean of blood. He retrieved the bag, opened it, pulled out the image case and handed it to Reuben.

Reuben took hold of the image case and rolled over onto his back and breathed a sigh of relief as if he'd been given a miracle remedy. He held it tight and close. As Colonel Chelmsford was seeing to Reuben's wounded shoulder, Reuben gazed up toward the sun and softly spoke, "Don't cry for me, Renee," before he passed out.

石
水
In the year of our Lord, 1847, a destiny continues of a romantic tale.
A long awaited homecoming, and a new friend from a faraway land…

<u>Bushido</u>

The sun was bright and the day cool and crisp with an easterly breeze flowing in from the bay. The window to the barracks officer's room was wide open allowing the fresh air inside. The bed was made regulation perfect, not because Reuben made it that way, but because he was not able to bring himself to lay on it. Instead he took to resting seated in the far corner of the room. His eyes were looking out to the bay, not in focus. They were the eyes not looking to the present. They looked to the horrors of the past, a past that has forever changed a young, happy, innocent boy into an unfeeling bitter man with no ambitions to continue. A man who would rather sit the rest of his life in a chair occupying a dark corner only to be forgotten.

He sat in his uniform pants and shirt with no shoes. He was to leave the fort today, however his trunk had not been packed, a chore he neglected to perform, like the previous days he was supposed to leave. A struggle had been ongoing within Reuben for the past several days to leave. His obligation to the army was over and he was glad of it, although, he did not want to leave the safety of the room. In many ways, Reuben wished for peace that can only be received by oblivion, lifelessness, and long-eternal sleep. If only the Mexicans were better shots and I were left for dead, he often thought to himself.

Reuben looked at the case with Renee's image wrapped in Lucy's purple ribbon. He had not seen her for over a year. The distance and news of the war must have made her think him wicked. The war in Mexico was evil. Invaders are what we were, Reuben thought to himself. What business did Virginia have in Mexico? Renee will never forgive me, especially after all the sins I have committed, Reuben thought. He could not understand why he had such deep thoughts and feelings for a girl who has been promised to another man. She would be better off with William Sinclair for he could offer her a safe and stable life, he thought as he wondered what possible use he could be to her.

狼

Today was the third time Aaron came to Fort Monroe to retrieve his son. The previous times, Reuben never left his quarters, not ready to face his family. Today will be different, Aaron hoped. Previously the entire family came and left without Reuben to accompany them home. Today it was only him and Renee.

When news of the 9th U.S. Regular Infantry Regiment was arriving at Fort Monroe on Tuesday, the 24th of August, the Duran family made the trip across the bay to welcome Reuben home. Renee desperately wanted to go, but her father didn't allow it, not when her marriage to William Sinclair was less than two months away.

That's all right, she thought. In the past, she always snuck out of her large house to visit the Duran home during Reuben's absence and she knew she would continue to do so, especially now that he's home, at least until she is forced to move to South Carolina with her newlywed husband. In the meantime, Lucy assured her she would give Reuben a hug for her until Renee could give him one herself.

The Duran family was excited until the last of the troops of the regiment disembarked the ships and Reuben was not amongst them. Deeply concerned, Aaron left Coleen and Lucy in Monroe's care so he could ascertain if Reuben did arrive on this day, or perhaps another ship had not arrived with more troops.

"What's his name, sir?" asked the regimental sergeant major.

"Reuben Duran, Second Lieutenant Reuben Duran. He's with Company B of this regiment."

When Aaron mentioned Reuben's name, the sergeant major went pale and looked as if he saw a ghost.

"Please follow me, sir," is all he could say, and led Aaron to what looked like a temporary hospital.

When they entered the huge tent, Aaron was sickened by the wounded soldiers lining the canvas walls. It was a sight Aaron never thought existed and it was horrifying. To the left were soldiers with missing limbs and to the right, men covered with so many bandages, one could not tell if they were human beings.

"Sergeant, where are you taking me and where is my son?" asked Aaron, frantically.

The sergeant major did not answer, but continued his walk through the ward until they emerged into a camp of wall tents with signs reading various clinics. They arrived in front of a tent with no sign and entered.

"What is it, Sergeant Major?" asked a captain.

"Where may I find Colonel Chelmsford, sir?"

"He's in the city at the hospital with a few patients, should be returning soon. Who is this gentleman?"

"Sir, this is Mr. Duran, Second Lieutenant Reuben Duran's father."

The captain had the same look on his face as the sergeant major had when he heard Reuben's name.

"What the hell is going on here?!" yelled Aaron in a rage. "Is my boy here or not? What have you done with him?!

"Please, sir, please... Lieutenant Duran is fine. He, in fact, is with Colonel Chelmsford and will return with him," said the captain as diplomatically as possible. He looked to the sergeant major and nodded for him to excuse himself.

The captain began to tell Aaron how Reuben was wounded before his regiment was rotated back to Virginia. He told how Reuben arrived three weeks earlier with the wounded and been here at the fort recuperating.

Extremely furious, Aaron, in an emotional outburst of rage demanded an explanation. "Am I to understand, my son, my boy, has been a row boat's ride away from his front doorstep for three weeks and no one took the time to notify us?! Now who in the hell has that authority and where is he?!"

"Please, Mr. Duran, if you will allow me. Your son is well. His wound is nearly healed."

"Then why in God's name was he not allowed to come home?!"

"He didn't want to, and he was the one who wished not to notify you, sir," said the captain with a remorseful expression.

With a look of disbelief, Aaron asked, "He didn't want to? Why?"

"I don't know, sir. You'll have to ask Colonel Chelmsford."

"And just who is this Colonel Chelmsford?"

"I am."

Aaron turned to see the colonel standing in the doorway of the tent. The colonel nodded to the captain to leave. When they were alone, Colonel Chelmsford introduced himself as Doctor Chelmsford. He went into detail of how he'd taken an interest in Reuben's health, both physical and mental. He discussed the activities Reuben's platoon was involved in and what type of effect they had on them.

Aaron stood with a terrified look. "My boy, what have you done to my boy?"

"Listen, Mr. Duran, Reuben *will* go home, but he's not ready yet. He has made progress and wants to go home, but is not willing. I intend to work with him some more to help him readapt."

"Readapt to what? What in Christ's name does he have to readapt to?"

"Mr. Duran, let me see if I can explain this in a manner you can understand. Reuben left here as a boy and spent a year having cannons aimed directly at him and those for whom he was responsible. He faced enemy soldiers and looked them in the eye as he had to... shall I say, liquidate them. The tasks his platoon were assigned are not common for every soldier in his company, or the entire regiment for that matter. For a year, Reuben faced guns, both cannons and muskets, blasting in his direction. Now those guns are silent. Mr. Duran, to go from one extreme like that to the next in a matter of days is traumatic to a boy who has now become a man in the harshest of ways."

Looking horror struck, Aaron lowered himself on a camp stool. Looking toward the ground he said sorrowfully, "What do I tell his family? What do I tell his friend Renee who is expecting him to be with us when we return home?"

"Tell them the truth. Reuben is going to need a lot of support and to do that you need to know what happened to him. As I said, I'll continue to work with him. Come back next week and we will see if his adjustment is better by then. As I mentioned, he does want to come home. He's afraid he may be a disappointment to you and his family."

"But we're proud of him, very much."

"I know, I know, but he must understand that himself."

After several more minutes of discussion, Aaron asked the doctor if he could at least see Reuben himself. Doctor Chelmsford nodded and took Aaron to Reuben's room in the medical officer's barracks.

Reuben acknowledged his father, but didn't speak. He didn't rise out of the chair he'd been sitting in when he would take refuge in this room.

Aaron spent close to an hour with Reuben while Doctor Chelmsford quietly stood on the far side of the room observing. Aaron spoke to Reuben about how happy and proud he was to have him home, and how much everyone missed him.

As he spoke, Aaron noticed Reuben had Renee's image case in his hand. It seemed to be the one thing that kept his interest.

"Listen, boy, we want you home very much, but we don't want to rush you. We'll come back next week and we'll take you back home then, okay?" asked Aaron.

Reuben's only response was a woeful nod yes.

Doctor Chelmsford escorted Aaron back to the family and he briefly told them what he had discussed with Aaron.

Lucy was distraught hearing Reuben didn't want to come home and ran toward the large parade ground where soldiers gathered for trips into Hampton and Chesapeake City to look for Reuben on her own. Aaron and Monroe ran after her. Monroe caught up to Lucy and struggled to bring her back as she was kicking and screaming.

"Reuben! Where are you? I want you home, Reuben! Renee wants you home! Put me down, put me down, I want my brother!" Lucy cried loudly as Coleen did what she could to console her, trying to be strong herself. All the while, Reuben watched from the window of his barracks room.

That evening, Renee arrived at the Duran home excited to see Reuben for the first time in over a year only to hear the depressing story of the day's events. She was devastated. That night she cried all night long, the first since the 4th of July when Lucy brought news Reuben was coming home.

The following week, the same drama unfolded when Reuben's family was told he still didn't want to come home. Again Lucy cried out Reuben's name, and tried to fight Monroe's and Aaron's hold on her as she screamed, "Come home, Reuben, we need you! Where's my brother? Damn it! Where is he?! Don't you love us anymore, Reuben? If you do, for Renee's sake, come home with us!"

The following morning after the second attempt, Renee lifted her head from a wet pillow.

The day before Aaron was to attempt to bring Reuben home for the third time, Coleen told Aaron she thought it would be best he go without the family.

"But he needs to know his family wants him home, and he won't know that unless we all go for him."

"I believe our son knows that. But he needs to know someone else wants him home. Aaron my love, it's time we go to you-know-who and beg for him to allow her to go with you tomorrow."

狼

"How is he today, Doctor? Will he come home with us?" asked Aaron, hopeful.

"I certainly hope so, Mr. Duran. He needs to get on with his own life and away from anything military. He wants to leave, but is frightened."

Colonel Lawrence Chelmsford returned from Mexico along with Reuben and many of the wounded shipped out prior to the entire regiment. As a physician, he provided medical care to the ship's wounded cargo and worked tirelessly, but his primary concern was Reuben and others like him. There were more such cases like Reuben he was unaware of because his attention was focused on the fifth platoon. It wasn't until the sorting of the wounded to be shipped home when he became aware of this phenomenon. Colonel Chelmsford couldn't coin a phrase to this condition except for, nostalgia. Through the study of Reuben and his men, he gained a better understanding of his own father. In the short amount of time under direct fire as he led Adam's platoon onto the field to bring Reuben and Adam back to their earthworks, Colonel Chelmsford had a mind opening look of the terrors Reuben, and others like him, live with day and night.

"Of what could he be frightened?" asked Aaron.

"Only he knows. Not being accepted perhaps. War does strange things to a man. It's not easy to explain. Lieutenant Duran, Reuben, is not the same man you knew before he went away. He's different now. In many ways, possibly for the better, for he has experienced a different world. A world of, if you will pardon me, death and suffering. A world sheltered from everyone else so he may be more grounded than an average man who never had such experiences, such as you, no offence intended."

"None taken, Doctor. However, there's more, correct?"

"Yes. Unfortunately he doesn't know how to cope with the experience thus causing an unequal conflict with the world he grew up in, and the world he has left. I spent the entire time in Mexico observing Reuben's platoon. As I earlier mentioned, because of one desperate act for survival, he and his platoon were used for unusual assignments involving uncommon tactics. These tactics caused Reuben and his men to literally see the enemy face-to-face in many situations. As time went by, I noticed the fifth platoon exhibit behaviors unlike the rest of the company who didn't take part in these types of tasks. Behaviors Reuben still has."

"What type of behaviors, Doctor?" asked Aaron.

Doctor Chelmsford opened a pad of notes. "I noticed irritability and outburst of anger, hyper-vigilance along with sleeping difficulties. Ah... reliving assignments he took part in, increased anxiety, especially in social situations. Feelings of detachment and withdrawal from others, which I found most interesting. You see, when I observed Reuben and his men with other company men, they couldn't associate with them. But when they were among themselves, they were at ease, even if there was no interaction. It was as if they had a silent understanding."

Aaron looked down to the floor. He thought of the times Reuben, along with Monroe and Lucy, had gotten sick in one form or another and Coleen cared for them making them well. How will she care for Reuben now? Reuben didn't even want to see anyone the last two times the family came to take him home.

Doctor Chelmsford went on to say, "It's a strange phenomenon. Many come back playing the part of the victorious hero, and then there are those like Reuben who feel remorse for what has happened. The ones that don't want to fight, but for some reason only known to them, are driven to fight, and in Reuben's case, to protect the men he was responsible for, and see to it they survived."

The doctor tapped his fingers on his notes. "Reuben's platoon's last engagement was a place called Villanueva. He was wounded there and he helplessly saw his entire platoon decimated mere yards away from him. And as his friend Adam tried to help him back to safety, he was shot and died in Reuben's arms."

Aaron looked up at the doctor. This was the first time Doctor Chelmsford spoke in detail of Reuben's last assignment.

My god, that poor boy, he thought to himself. He felt a gentle touch and looked at the small delicate hand resting on his forearm. Aaron took hold of the hand and looked to the bright, brown eyes of Renee sitting next to him.

After two unsuccessful visits to Fort Monroe, Coleen realized Renee was the key to bringing Reuben home. Aaron had mentioned to Coleen the last two attempts to bring him home, Reuben always had Renee's image in his hand. It took a careful amount of planning by Aaron and Coleen to get Renee's parents to allow her to help. As much as Renee wanted to accompany the family on the two previous trips, her father would not let her go. Aaron and Coleen nearly begged Franklin Wallace to allow Renee to travel to Fort Monroe with Aaron. Unfortunately Franklin Wallace remained stubborn. It wasn't until Coleen appealed to Renee's mother, with a hope she still possessed a mother's natural instinct for wanting the best for her daughter their persistence paid off. Margret Wallace was just as stubborn as her husband only because she was raised on the principles that the man's word is final. However, deep within her heart, she felt keeping Renee and Reuben apart was wrong. What would be Margret Wallace's only act of compassion toward her daughter's marriage arrangement, Renee's mother persuaded Franklin Wallace to approve Renee's visit.

When Doctor Chelmsford described Reuben's behaviors, Renee was reminded of what Martin Doogan once said to her...

"What I'm about to tell ye will be difficult for ye to understand, but ye must prepare yourself. You're a strong young woman, stronger than all the other girls, and even the teachers in this here school. Stronger than ye, yourself, believe. But when Reuben returns, and from what ye have told me of him, he will survive and return, he won't be the same boy ye have known

up until now. He will be different. He will no longer be a boy, but a man subjected to death. He will no longer have that spark in his eyes like in this picture. He will have the look I have when ye bring me back to the here and now. When he returns, he will need your friendship more than ever, even if he doesn't know it himself."

Although he could see the anguish in her face, Renee gave Reuben's father a hopeful smile everything will be all right.

"Well, are you ready to see Reuben?" asked Doctor Chelmsford.

"Yes," replied Renee, startling the doctor who expected Aaron to answer, "very much so, please."

With that said, all three stood and made their way to the officer's medical barracks. It was about a five minute walk, all in silence. Upon entering the barracks, Renee saw several men looking around aimlessly.

"These men are suffering the same affliction as Reuben in various forms," replied the doctor as he took notice of Renee taking an interest.

They climbed the stairs to the second floor where Reuben's room was located. They traversed the hall to room nine where a tag was pinned to the door reading LT. DURAN. Outside the door was a padded bench.

"Mr. Duran, I would like for you to go in first while Miss Wallace and myself wait for a while, give you a chance to lead up to Miss Wallace's presence," advised the doctor.

Aaron nodded and knocked on the door. He turned the door knob, opened the door, and went over the threshold. As he did so, Renee tried to gain a peek into the room. She saw it was dark, the only light coming from the window, but could not see Reuben.

She sat down on the bench staring at the door. On the other side was the boy she had not seen for over a year. The boy who has been her special friend since childhood. The boy she had confusing feelings for. The boy she wished could rescue her from her upcoming arranged wedding.

"May I ask you a question, Doctor?" asked Renee.

This was Doctor Chelmsford's first time meeting Renee, but from his visits with Reuben before, during, and after Mexico, and how Reuben described Renee, the doctor felt as if he already knew her.

"Of course, Miss Wallace, please."

Looking at the doctor, she asked, "I know you said there are others like Reuben you are concerned about, but why Reuben? Why are you so focused on him? Is there something about him that means something to you?"

Doctor Chelmsford's eyes widened and showed wonder in Renee's question. Beautiful, loving, charming, and very instinctive as well, he thought. No wonder Reuben loves this girl.

In a solemn manner Doctor Chelmsford answered, "He reminds me of my father. My father was in the second war of independence, and for the rest of his life he had difficulties because of it. The same difficulties I'm hoping Reuben will avoid."

"And did your father rid himself of those difficulties, Doctor?"

Doctor Chelmsford answered by slowly shaking his head no. Renee let out a little gasp while covering her mouth with her hands.

Seeing her concern, he shifted to face her more directly and took her hands in his and continued to say, "But my father didn't have any help or understanding and Reuben has, and I believe it has made a huge breakthrough in his recovery. A first step if you will. This is a form of illness never studied before because no one has recognized it ever existed, and those I have tried to convince say it still doesn't. I believe it does and I intend to see my theories through. Believe me, Miss Wallace, Reuben has had a head start, a head start my father never had and I'm sure he will be helped, if not by me, then by someone who will see Reuben for what he really is."

"What's that, Doctor?"

"A survivor, a protector and heaven knows we need as many of those as possible."

狼

"Son," said Aaron as he walked into the room closing the door behind him. "How are you, boy?" Boy, how absurd, Aaron thought. I'm not talking to a mere boy anymore. This is by far a man.

"I'm fine, Da," answered Reuben, not looking away from the window.

Aaron pulled up another chair and sat next to his son. He noticed Renee's image case in Reuben's hand and smiled. To him that was hope. "I've come to take you home, son."

Reuben glanced toward his father and tried to smile, but could only move the left corner of his mouth. He sighed, "Not today, Da."

Aaron's head sunk. Finally perturbed, Aaron grabbed hold of Reuben's arm causing Reuben to face his father with a look of a wounded, hungry wolf. A look Aaron had never seen in his son before, but he didn't back away.

"Damn it, boy, when? You can't stay here forever, you know. Sooner or later the army is going to kick you out and then where will you be? You have family and friends waiting to see you at home. Your home."

Aaron stood up and walked to the empty trunk and lifted the lid. "I don't know what happened to you, but it's never going to go away if all you're going to do is sit in that damned chair. How could you do this to your mother? How could you do this to Renee? She could really use your support right now."

Reuben stood up and walked across the floor holding the image case. He lifted it up, "I'd do her more harm if I came home. Damn it, Da! I have blood on my hands. No matter how hard I scrub, it doesn't come off, see," said Reuben, showing his palms to Aaron. There was nothing on his palms except for the image case in his right hand. "I can't get them clean. I just can't. How can I support Renee? She deserves someone with clean hands," he woefully said with tears falling from his eyes.

Aaron took his son's hands in his. Reuben tried to pull them away, but Aaron didn't let go. "Listen, son, I don't see any blood. I only see the hands of a man who wants to come home."

Reuben pulled his hands free and began to pace the floor looking down grasping the image case with both hands. "If I do go home, please don't make me wear that uniform."

Seeing a hint of hope, Aaron walked up to Reuben and grasped his shoulders. "Son, you can wear anything you want." He pulled him into his arms and embraced him tightly. Reuben didn't fight to break away. Instead he laid his head on Aaron's shoulder and began to sob quietly.

"I don't know, Da. I can't face Renee. I'm not the boy who was her best friend anymore. She may not even want to see me."

"You're right, son. You're not the same boy she knew before you left. You are now a man. A man she trusts and needs even more, but you're never going to realize that unless you leave this fort. You have learned a very hard lesson, Reuben, but now it's time to see if you have learned it well," said Aaron as he made his way to the door.

Sitting on the bench outside the room, Doctor Chelmsford and Renee saw the door open, and standing in the doorway was Aaron. Renee looked up and smiled with hope in her eyes. Aaron motioned for her to come in. She looked at Doctor Chelmsford, who rose and offered his hand to assist her. She took his hand, stood, and walked to the door. Doctor Chelmsford sat back down on the bench with a sigh of relief. He closed his eyes and began to pray for Reuben to accept Renee back into his troubled world.

Reuben watched Aaron open the door and make a motion for someone to enter the room. His feet became rooted to the floor when he saw Renee walk into the room and face him. She looked so beautiful, her face so soft and fresh. Her hair was loose, cascading over her shoulders, the way he liked it, and her eyes, Reuben never tired of looking into her eyes. But this time he was scared, ashamed, so he looked away.

Aaron placed his hand on her shoulder, "Go on, lass, to your friend." He exited the room and closed the door.

Renee walked toward Reuben, but he looked down and away from her.

"Hello, Reuben. I have missed you so."

She looked down at his trembling hands which were holding the image case. He stumbled back and she started to reach out to him. He raised his left hand to stop her from getting any closer and she stopped. Reuben looked around and found the chair and quickly sat, breathing hard. His hands were shaking. His head fell forward and hung there, eyes shut.

Renee stepped quietly toward Reuben and knelt down. She took his trembling hands in hers causing Reuben to look up and open his eyes. He didn't attempt to pull them away. Renee looked into his eyes. They were no longer the eyes of the young boy she used to play games of tag or go fishing with under the oak tree anymore. They were no longer the eyes of the boy who she held in her arms next to Lucy's piano when she came to see him before he left. His eyes were different now. They had more meaning, more understanding, and more pain. They were eyes her father never had, and definitely not the eyes her fiancé has. They were now the eyes of a man who saw more than his share of hell and caused her to see Reuben as a new love in her life. She felt proud of him. There had been several courting visits from her fiancé while Reuben was gone, but her thoughts were always of him and their friendship. The anguish and confusion she felt between her obligation and Reuben were very strong, but she knew Reuben needed her to be strong for him, just as Martin Doogan had told her.

Reuben looked at Renee as she stared into his eyes. All was silent, but he could hear his heart beat. It began to slow down quickly, something that hasn't happened after anxiety had taken hold of his body. In the past, it had taken Reuben a few hours to calm down, but now with Renee holding his hands, his shaking began to slow and his breathing returned to normal. He felt safe with her touch.

"I missed you so very much, Reuben, and I need for you to come home," said Renee as she caressed his face. "Please come home."

Reuben returned her caress using the back of his hand. Renee took his hand and turned it around having the palm of his hand touching her face. She leaned her head toward his hand, closed her eyes and smiled. Reuben scooted off the chair and joined her on the floor.

A tear started running down Reuben's face. The first tear Renee ever saw Reuben shed in an unhappy state that she could remember. She raised her hands to his face and leaned forward and kissed it away. They both rose helping each other while staring at one another. Reuben took Renee's face in his hands and leaned forward. His lips met hers. As they kissed, they hugged one another. When the kiss ended, they stood in the middle of the room holding each other with Renee momentarily resting her head on Reuben's shoulder. She lifted her head and they looked at one another, eye-to-eye. Suddenly Reuben's face had a hint of happiness in it. However, the thought of their separate futures still lingered in both their minds.

"I want to go home, Renee," said Reuben with a hint of highland Scot in his voice much like his father, which Renee never heard come from Reuben, and found it charming.

Renee's adorable smile came out and her eyes brightened up, the very look Reuben loved so much. "Well, I don't think you're going to get too far without any shoes on now, are you?"

"I suppose you're right," said Reuben looking down at his feet. "I need to pack."

"You're in luck soldier boy. I'm one of the best packers ever…" said Renee walking to the trunk and suddenly thought about what she said. "I'm sorry, Reuben. I didn't mean to call you that."

Reuben walked to Renee and again took her by the hand. "I will always be your friend, Renee, and as long as you don't call me soldier boy or lieutenant, I will never ask you to give me one of your Wickham school curtseys."

"Oh, Reuben Duran, if you ever do, I tell you, if you ever do, I swear, I'll kick you so hard in your giggleberrys, you'll be in a constant curtsey for the rest of your life, and that you can count on, you shoddy farm boy!"

"Wickham girl!"

"Don't call me that!" said Renee. She pulled her hand free and began to playfully slap his shoulder as he tried desperately to defend himself, both laughing as if they were children again.

From the hall, Aaron and Doctor Chelmsford heard the playful banter and laughter coming from the other side of the door. Tears came to Aaron's eyes as he said to Doctor Chelmsford, "Those two will never grow up, and I hope they never will."

狼

The beginning of the journey to Norfolk was quiet for the three in the coach and on the ferry. Reuben didn't speak much at first. He sat opposite from his father and Renee with a thousand mile stare in his eyes as he watched the scenery pass by. It was awkward for both Aaron and Renee not knowing what to say or talk about. Doctor Chelmsford mentioned to both of them not to bring up anything about the war or military, especially Villanueva. They had no intention to bring up any of the last year. As far as they both were concerned, they were happy Reuben was coming home.

"Your mother has a nice dinner planned this evening," said Renee.

"Aye, that she has, son. Both she and Lucy are preparing a feast for your homecoming," added Aaron.

Reuben turned his attention to the two and gently smiled. "I am hungry."

Aaron looked at Renee and smiled and then he turned to Reuben and patted him on his knee. "I bet you are, lad."

"These clothes are comfortable," Reuben said as he raised his arms to inspect the cuffs. "It's been a long time since I wore civilian clothes. They don't itch."

All three began to laugh and the awkwardness was lifted and the journey became more pleasant. Renee moved over next to Reuben and began to talk about their younger days.

Once they arrived at the city house, Coleen, Monroe, and Lucy were waiting outside. When Reuben stepped off the carriage, he went to his mother right away and embraced her.

"I'm sorry I haven't come home sooner, Mama."

"That's all right," replied Coleen as she caressed her son's face. "You're home now and that's what counts."

He turned to Monroe. Monroe held out his hand, but was surprised when Reuben took him into his arms. "I love you, Monroe and never forget that." Monroe was not familiar with this type of affection from his younger brother.

Reuben turned his attention to his younger sister. Lucy didn't wait for him to come to her. She leaped into his arms and began to cry tears of joy and happiness. She missed Reuben probably the most of all and thinking of him while he was away always brought tears to her eyes.

"Come on now. I'm hungry," said Aaron and began to walk into the house.

The others followed except for Coleen who gently took Renee's arm. Surprised, Renee turned to face Coleen who now had taken both of her hands most affectionately. "I don't know how you did it, but thank you so very much for bringing my Reuben back home to us. I knew you would be able to convince him."

Renee embraced Coleen and held her in the way a daughter would hug her mother. "It's wonderful to have him home."

As they walked into the house, Coleen thought it such a waste for Renee to be married off like a Negro sold off into slavery, and denied the love of her son.

狼

Dinner was placed on the table. All of everyone's favorite dishes, including Renee's, had been served. It was a real feast. Everyone seated at the table all commented at the wonderful spread.

As Aaron sat down, everyone lowered their head and reached out to take each other's hands, except for Reuben.

"Reuben, take my hand," said Renee.

He looked at her hand and then looked at his mother's hand waiting for him to take hold. He looked at the palms of his hands and took up his linen napkin, roughly wiped his hands, and timidly took both of their hands. He didn't bow his head or didn't recite the blessing as his father took the lead. This was very noticeable to Aaron, but he didn't want to make an issue about it and figured he would address it later.

However it was all forgotten when the bread was broken by Reuben himself and he began to pass it around. Soon the dining room was filled with sounds of spoons scooping, knives carving, and forks scraping, as well as happy conversation and laughter. Happiness once again returned to the Duran home and Renee was so happy to be a part of it.

Once dinner was finished, everyone helped to clear the table and clean. After the chores were finished, they all entered the parlor where Lucy sat at the piano and began to play. Aaron took his wife in his arms and danced. Monroe asked Renee for a dance and she gladly accepted. Reuben sat on the bench next to Lucy and watched with amusement.

Lucy finished her first song and began to play another. Monroe requested a dance from his mother who accepted. Renee came to Reuben and stood next to him.

"Please dance with me, Reuben," she asked.

"No thank you. You know I don't dance well. I would much rather watch you dance with Da."

"Come on, Son," said Aaron. "The evening is young and I have plenty of time to dance with Renee."

"No, really, I'm fine here sitting next to Lucy."

Renee placed her hand on Reuben's shoulder, "Please."

"I said NO!" responded Reuben very sternly, as if giving orders to troops.

Lucy stopped playing and had a frightened look on her face. Monroe and Coleen stopped dancing and Renee pulled her hand away as if Reuben's shoulder bit it. Aaron came to his side.

Reuben closed his eyes and took in a deep breath and let it out slowly. His eyes opened to see Renee kneeling in front of him, her hands on his knees. He gently placed his hands over hers.

"I'm sorry, very sorry. I'm just a bit overwhelmed, I guess," he said looking at Renee with regret in his eyes.

She stood and lightly kissed him on his cheek, which in turn made him smile and relax.

"Of course you are, lad," said Aaron. "You've had a long day."

"And also a grand meal," Lucy added.

"Yes indeed. I'm still full," replied Monroe rubbing his stomach in a circular motion.

Reuben began to laugh, "Of course, you always ate more than your share," he said as he rose and placed his hand on top of Monroe's.

Laughter replaced the tension and as soon as the awkward stillness was started, it was over. Reuben came over to Renee and took her by the hand.

Renee took him in her arms and motioned Lucy to start playing and once again music and laughter was being heard from outside the house. For an hour to follow, the atmosphere in the Duran home was joyful, until a knock was heard at the door. Renee looked at the clock above the mantle. "That will be my father," she said, regretfully.

狼

Reuben walked Renee to the coach where her parents awaited. As he helped Renee up, her father looked down at him. "It's good to have you back home," he said in a matter-of-fact tone rather than with sincerity. "Renee was worried you would miss her wedding," he added with a formal tone in his voice.

"Goodnight, Reuben," said Renee's mother, much to her father's and Renee's surprise.

"Yes, Reuben, goodnight, I'll come by and see you tomorrow," said Renee.

"I'm afraid you can't, my daughter," responded her father fearing Reuben's return may cause a rift between Renee and William Sinclair. "Young William will be arriving the day after tomorrow and you have much to do prior to your move to Charleston after the wedding," he emphasized.

"Yes, of course. I forgot. I'm sorry, Reuben, but I'll be by as soon as I can."

"I'll be fine, Renee. Goodnight," said Reuben.

Renee's father tapped his walking stick to the floor board signaling the coachman to leave. The coachman snapped the reins and the coach began rolling away, Renee's eyes not leaving Reuben. Once they were out of sight, Reuben turned and went back into the house.

"Has Renee left, son?" asked Coleen.

"Yes Mama."

"Will you be off to bed then?"

Reuben stopped and turned to his mother. He walked up to and hugged her. She took him in her arms and felt him whimper. "Goodnight, Mama," he whispered in her ear, kissed her on the cheek, and climbed the stairs.

Monroe was already in bed when Reuben walked into the room. He took off his shoes, vest, and removed the braces from his shoulders. He sat on the bed, rested his face in his hands, and fell asleep in that position.

狼

The next couple of days were not as pleasant in the Duran home. Every night, Reuben would wake in cold sweats, screaming waking everyone in the house. The first night, Monroe jumped out of his bed and went to console Reuben by taking hold of his shoulders. Furiously, Reuben rose and grabbed Monroe by the collar of his night shirt and nearly shook him unconscious. The following nights, Monroe took to sleeping in the parlor.

Even Lucy was victim to Reuben's rage. Seeing her brother crying in the kitchen, she came to console him. As she began to speak, Reuben rose to his feet and yelled for her to leave him alone, making her run away afraid and crying.

He spent most of his days walking along the riverfront and sitting out on the jetty alone. Renee had not been by since the day he came home, and he missed her. He figured her father had something to do with her not being by for a visit. Probably keeping her busy with the fiancé now that he is in town, he thought.

Walking home, he passed a second hand store and an item in the window caught his eye. He walked in and had the storekeeper retrieve the item for a closer look.

"That's not of much use except for a conversation piece," said the clerk.

"It's perfect. Do you have ammunition for it?"

"Yes I do, at no cost."

"I'll have it then."

Reuben paid the clerk three dollars for the small single shot pocket pistol and placed it in his jacket pocket. It fits just fine, he thought.

He started to leave the store when the clerk said, "Excuse me sir, the ammunition?"

"Oh yes, I forgot. I'll take one round."

"Only one round, sir?" asked the clerk.

"That's all I need." Reuben looked at his reflection in the large mirror hanging behind the clerk. "I'm a good shot."

狼

When Reuben returned home from his walk, Renee was waiting for him. As he crossed the doorway and heard her laughter from the parlor, he hastened his pace. Upon entering the parlor, his face brightened up.

"Renee! Where have you been?" he asked with delight.

Renee rose and stepped quickly into his open arms and they hugged. "I'm so sorry I haven't been by to visit sooner. My parents have been keeping me busy with the wed... jobs around the house and other things."

"I understand. Is your fiancé still in town?"

Renee felt uncomfortable for the moment. She looked around and saw Coleen motion for Lucy to follow her into the kitchen to give Renee and Reuben some privacy.

"Yes, he's still here," she said, non-enthusiastically. "The truth is I snuck away from him to come and visit with you. You know how easy it is to sneak out of that huge house I live in," she continued and giggled after.

Reuben followed with a laugh. "I've been a bad influence on you. Heaven help that poor man."

Instead of laughing along with Reuben, she looked out the window.

"Can we go for a walk, Reuben? I've been cooped up inside houses, churches, and shops for the past few days. I could really use some open space right now."

"Of course we can. I can always use a walk."

The two made their way out of the house and onto the walkway toward the riverfront. They walked in silence. As they made their way through the downtown streets of Norfolk, Renee could not help but watch Reuben as he walked. Although he looked content, she could tell inside he was falling apart and was struggling to be as happy as he once was. She thought to herself, if only he could see what I'm thinking and perhaps both of us could be at peace and less lonely.

And so they continued to walk until they reached the river and stood by the gated walkway watching the ships in the harbor.

"I don't want to get married, Reuben," said Renee, breaking the silence.

"I know."

Renee was taken by surprise. "You do?"

"Of course, it shows. You don't want to be married any more than Negro's want to be slaves, but you have obligations." Reuben turned his attention from the ships to Renee. "I don't want you to get married either, but sometimes we can't always get what we want. Your father is a very powerful man and for him to be successful, he must have a successful business and powerful family ties. My family doesn't fit his mold."

"That's rubbish, Reuben, and you know it!" Renee said with anger in her voice.

"Rubbish? Did you learn that from Wickham?"

"Oh, shut up, Reuben! I'm being serious."

"I know you are, Renee. Listen, family traditions are strong, especially in this region and you know that. But always remember this secret of mine, Renee, I will always love you, and forever be yours." Reuben turned his attention back to the ships. "Perhaps, I should have joined the navy."

Renee smiled and suddenly felt less lonely. "I love you also, Reuben."

Reuben looked to Renee and smiled back. "I better get you home. It's getting late and no doubt your father will be wondering where you snuck off to, that's if he finds out you're missing at all."

As Reuben walked Renee back to her neighborhood, she brought up the autumn ball.

"Will you be coming to the ball this season? I'll be there with my parents, and of course, William Sinclair. I can introduce you to him if you like." She cringed in regret the moment that escaped her mouth and was about to apologize until Reuben began to speak.

"My family is going so I'll go... for you," he said getting the impression Renee's invitation was more of a plea for Reuben to come so she would have some moral support rather than an inquiry.

Renee smiled and wrapped her arms around him. "Thank you. You have no idea how much this means to me."

Still feeling what she had said about meeting her fiancé was inappropriate, she said, "You don't have to meet William Sinclair. Trust me, he and his family are nowhere as enjoyable as yours. I would rather be showing you off than him."

Taken by surprise, he responded, "That's a bit overdoing it, Renee, but thanks. Not as enjoyable, huh? Oh, that poor bastard. You're going to make his life hell with your shenanigans. I give that marriage about a year before he winds up in an insane asylum after you drive him crazy."

Giggling at his remark, Renee asked, "And how is it I haven't driven you crazy, Reuben Duran?"

"Because I'm just as crazy as you are, Renee Wallace, you adorable Wickham girl," he answered and commenced to playfully try to slap her face.

"What do I have to do to get you to stop calling me that, you shoddy farm boy?"

Renee followed and tried to land some hits of her own on Reuben's face as they both laughed and giggled like children, rather than adults. Their shenanigans caught the eyes of onlookers causing them to stop in mid slaps. They brought their hands down, cleared their throats, and began acting appropriately. Once the onlookers shook their heads and went on about their business, Renee and Reuben looked at each other and snickered.

They turned the corner onto Renee's street and stopped.

"Well, I better let you go on your own from here," said Reuben, looking down the street. He hoped no one would see Renee with him, knowing her father would give her a difficult time if he found out she had snuck off to visit him.

"This was a nice walk, Reuben, thank you. I really needed it. Well, until the ball I guess. Give your family my best, okay?"

"You bet," he said as he stared into her eyes. He smiled, turned, and began his walk back home.

Renee stood at the corner, watching and hoping he would turn for a final look and wave, but he didn't. With his hands in his pockets and his head slumped low, he walked as if the world of joy he was just in turned into one of gloom.

Feeling emotional, Renee brought her hand to her forehead and found herself in deep concentration, the way she always felt when she had a need to write.

She quickly made her way to the house, up the main pathway, in through the front door, and was on her way up the stairs when her father called to her in a polite manner.

"Renee, where have you been?"

William Sinclair stepped up next to him. "We didn't know you were gone," he said.

Thinking quickly, she answered, "Really? I mentioned to mother I was going with some friends to the shops and look for floral patterns. Maybe she didn't hear me."

Doing her best to keep a straight face, she thought to herself, ah geez, floral patterns? What am I thinking? They're going to see right through that lie.

"Good, I hope you found something pretty for our future home," replied William Sinclair.

Franklin Wallace slapped William Sinclair on the shoulders. "See young man, she is going to be one fine domestic. Come, daughter, you are just in time. Refreshments are about to be served on the back terrace."

"Please allow me some time to freshen up," said Renee.

"Okay, my pet, but don't keep me waiting," answered William Sinclair as he and her father made their way through the hall.

Quickly, Renee raced to her room, closed the door behind her, and leaned against it. Bringing her hands to her head, she said, "Heaven's sakes, they actually bought that? Good lord. Reuben is right. I'm going to drive that poor bastard crazy. Pet... I can't stand it when he calls me pet. Where in the world did he ever learn to call me that?"

Looking toward her bureau, she shook off the recent exchange with her father and fiancé and went to open the bottom drawer. She retrieved her writing utensils, a sheet of parchment, and sat at the small desk in the corner of her large room. Reaching behind the desk, she pulled out the image case containing Reuben's picture from its hiding place. She reached down the middle of her camisole where she had sewn a small pocket concealing a shiny VMI button close to her cleavage where she knew no one, not even Reuben himself, would dare go looking. She pulled it out and placed it next to the picture.

Looking out the window for a few moments, she nodded, picked up her pen, dipped it in the ink bottle, and put her day's thoughts on paper...

> *You wear a smile of joy*
> *But it's in your eyes I see your true struggle*
> *Sadness, despair, and gloom*
> *What has war done to you my love?*
> *I wear a smile of joy*
> *But it's in my heart I feel our true struggle*
> *Sadness, despair, and gloom*
> *This is what obligation has done to me.*
> *I grieve for you*
> *I grieve for me*
> *I grieve for us*
> *With hands in your pockets, you walk away*
> *Another place, another time*
> *Perhaps someday I will be your Wickham girl*
> *And you will be my shoddy farm boy*

狼

The ballroom was decorated in rich autumn colors and the orchestra was playing wonderfully as always.

Renee was standing along the draped wall with other girls her age, including Cynthia Garrett, her finishing school nemesis. Her intention of standing with these other girls was to be away from her own family and fiancé.

However, when she saw the Duran family enter the room, she left the group of girls without uttering a farewell. She walked up behind Aaron, tapped his right shoulder, and moved to his left. Aaron looked to his right and heard a familiar giggle.

"Renee Wallace, you troublemaker, come here and give me a hug."

She did so and went on to give Coleen, Lucy, and even Monroe a hug in greeting.

Reuben stepped up behind her and tapped her left shoulder as he moved to her right. As she looked to her left, she heard him say, "Ha! That's for my Da."

"You jackass…"

The entire Duran family began laughing except for Reuben who said, "Jackass? Now that's not a very nice term of endearment."

"Oh, shut up you adorable jackass, and give me a hug," said Renee with affection.

Reuben did so and he expressed how beautiful she looked.

"You really think I look beautiful?"

"Well, yeah. Except your hair. You know I like it down-flowing free."

"Of course, but you know I have to wear it this way because I am, of course, the great Franklin Wallace's *elegant* daughter," she said in a snooty, mocking manner.

Reuben snickered, "You, elegant? Don't forget, I've seen you eat a worm."

"Why you shoddy farm boy," she said, turning red with embarrassment and laughing.

"Wickham girl," said Reuben as he mockingly curtseyed.

"Okay you two," said Coleen. "Good heavens, after you graduating from Wickham and you from VMI, I thought you two would have finally matured by now."

Renee wrapped her arm around Reuben's shoulders and said, "Who us?"

"Never!" added Reuben as he looked at Renee and wrapped his arm around her shoulders.

It was like old times before Reuben went off to Mexico, laughter and talking over good memories at their usual table. Of course, it was in a dignified manner, especially for the sake of Renee whose family and fiancé were within sight and sound of their table.

Both Aaron and Coleen were concerned Renee's father would be angered with her spending so much time at their table, but they soon noticed Franklin Wallace was too busy introducing Renee's fiancé to his business associates and gloating over him.

One of Coleen's favorite waltzes was being played by the orchestra so Aaron took her on the dance floor leaving the others at the table.

Although Reuben seemed to be having a good time, he still felt very awkward at the ball, even with Renee at his side, but was very glad to have her close by.

"Okay, Reuben, like it or not, you're going to dance with me this evening. Now remember what I taught you about dancing," said Renee. "Place your hands in the leading position, but let me lead. That way you won't be stepping on both of our feet," said Renee, followed by a laugh.

"You're going to dance with me, right brother?" asked Lucy.

"Of course I will." Reuben turned his attention to Monroe. "But not until after Monroe. He's our older brother and that gives him first dances with you and Mama."

Reuben patted his brother on the shoulder as Monroe smiled back.

"So that means you can dance with me now," said Renee.

"I guess it…"

Reuben was interrupted as William Sinclair strolled up to the table loudly clearing his throat. "Excuse me. Are you going to introduce me to your friends, my darling?"

Taken by complete surprise by William Sinclair's presence, Renee looked up and stood along with Reuben holding onto his arm. Monroe and Lucy also stood and stepped next to Reuben and Renee.

"Of course, William, may I introduce you to Monroe and Reuben Duran and their sister Lucy."

"Indeed." William Sinclair walked past Monroe ignoring his offered hand and stepped up to Reuben. Reuben's peaceful face suddenly turned cold and fierce. He didn't care for the rudeness William Sinclair showed Monroe.

Renee quickly released her hold on Reuben's arm as William Sinclair noticed.

"So you are the war hero I have heard so much about," said William Sinclair with contempt, and giving Renee a look of dominance. "I understand you are quite the soldier."

"Perhaps before, but no longer," replied Reuben.

"Ah, I see." William Sinclair took Renee by the hand. "Come my pet, your father has an early wedding gift for us." Looking at Reuben in a manner of warning, he said, "If you will please excuse us."

"Gladly," replied Monroe rather coldly.

Reuben's hands turned into fists when he heard William Sinclair call Renee, pet. Lucy noticed and quickly took hold of his left hand causing it to relax.

As William Sinclair and Renee walked off, she glanced back. The look on her face was of regret.

"Are you okay, Reuben?" asked Lucy, still holding his hand.

"Sure he is, right brother?" answered Monroe as he sat back down.

"I'm fine. I'm going for some punch," said Reuben as he began to walk off. Lucy let go of his hand and began to follow until Monroe caught her by the wrist. She looked at her older brother as he motioned her to sit.

"Let him have some time to himself. Trust me."

101

狼

Reuben walked past the refreshment table to find a dark corner to fade away into the darkness. Two gentlemen were standing near the table. One was no other than Doctor Lawrence Chelmsford and the other, an unfamiliar man to this land. His head was shaven and he had very exotic features on his face. The doctor was discussing his recent study of war effects on individuals as the other gentleman was listening very intently.

When Reuben strolled past the table, Doctor Chelmsford noticed and called to him, "Reuben, it's good to see you. How have you been?"

When Reuben saw Doctor Chelmsford he felt glad, but also tense. The sight of the doctor caused Reuben to quickly see visions of Villanueva in his mind. His first instinct was to flee and duck for cover. He wanted to turn and leave, but his feet seemed rooted to the floor.

"Come, Reuben, I want you to meet a very distinguished visitor. Mr. Akagi, I would like to introduce you to Reuben Duran. Reuben, this is Mr. Genda Akagi."

Mr. Akagi formally bowed and offered his hand in greeting. Reuben took his hand and began to greet him until a door slammed shut loudly, causing Reuben to flinch and grasp Mr. Akagi's hand tighter. Mr. Akagi took notice of Reuben's reaction and felt a shocking sensation as Reuben's hand tightened.

When Reuben regained his composure, he looked directly into Mr. Akagi's eyes and gazed upon them for a moment that seemed like an eternity.

"My goodness. Reuben, are you okay?" asked Doctor Chelmsford.

Reuben nodded and released Mr. Akagi's hand and walked away. When he was halfway to the table where Monroe and Lucy sat, the music started. He saw William Sinclair take Renee in his arms and they began to dance. He watched the two until he was asked to make room for those who wanted to dance. He walked off the dance floor, past his table, and out the door.

"Excuse me, Doctor," asked Mr. Akagi with broken English. "That young man, how do you know of him?"

"He and I served together in the same regiment. You met his father, Aaron Duran."

"That is his son? I do not see a resemblance. The army you say, that explains it."

"Explains what, Mr. Akagi?"

"His eyes... he has warrior's eyes. And his ki, it flows."

"Reuben?" asked Doctor Chelmsford questionably. "He did fight in Mexico, but it took a lot out of him and he had to leave the army. He's the man I was describing in my study of warfare's effects on a soldier's psyche. He fought very strong and honorably. However, it had a horrible effect on him."

"Nonetheless, but he has the look of a warrior, a lost warrior, but still... a warrior. One that needs to learn the meaning of... the code," he said more to himself than to Doctor Chelmsford. He turned his attention to the doctor. "Please excuse me. I would want to meet that man some more. I will return."

Without waiting for Doctor Chelmsford's reply, Mr. Akagi began walking toward the door to look for Reuben.

狼

Without looking back, Reuben walked to the riverfront at a quick pace, fighting tears. As he came up to Saint Mary's church, he stopped at the steps. He began to think of God and wondered why such a being would allow such pain and sadness happen to good people. He began to think God was the devil himself, or at least a sadist playing his own sadistic game with the people on this world.

He picked up a rock and was about to hurl it at the front door. He lowered and dropped it thinking, what's the point. He turned his back to the church and continued his walk.

Once on the riverfront, he headed to the jetty where he would sit for hours since returning home. He traversed the stony jetty to the edge where he stood looking out over the ripples of the river.

Thoughts of Renee entered his mind intertwined with images of his family and the horrors of Villanueva. He reached into his inside jacket breast pocket and retrieved the small single shot pistol he had purchased. It had been loaded.

"Please forgive me, Renee," he said as he placed the muzzle of the pistol under his chin. He cocked back the hammer and began to squeeze the trigger.

As the pressure began to take hold, he heard a voice coming from a man standing mere inches next to him looking across the river reciting what sounded like a poetic passage in a foreign language.

Reuben released the pressure on the trigger and jumped back with surprise. His heart was pounding. He was frightened from the surprise of this man standing very calmly. How could he have snuck up so close to me without uttering a sound, thought Reuben.

Reuben regained his composure and stepped up closer to this man with curiosity and recognized it was Mr. Akagi. "What did you say?" he asked.

"Please forgive me. Allow me to translate. I said... one's path is filled with many obstacles to keep one from their just rewards, and may cause one to retreat, but dark shadows of the past will never let you. In your case, Reuben-San, life itself seems to be your dark shadows of the past."

Reuben felt calm listening Mr. Akagi, the only other person to do that besides Renee. "What's that, a prayer of some sort?"

Akagi Genda-San turned to Reuben and smiled widely, his grin shinning. "Ah, inquisitive, I like that. You have the makings of a great student."

Reuben shook his head in confusion, trying to understand. "Who are you? Where did you come from?"

"Very inquisitive, allow me to further introduce myself. I am Akagi Genda. I am from the island nation of Nippon."

"Ak... Gend... What are you doing here?"

"You may call me Genda, and I am here doing what you are doing this very moment."

Reuben again shook his head and asked, "What am I doing?"

"Learning," answered Akagi Genda-San.

"And that... prayer?" asked Reuben.

"Not a prayer, young Reuben-San, but a lesson, a lesson for warriors such as yourself. You were a warrior in your army, were you not, Reuben-San?"

"Not anymore!" replied Reuben, angrily. "I was only a soldier."

"You must open your heart to the lesson I recited and you will see you are more than just a soldier."

Reuben thought about the words of the lesson Akagi Genda-San recited. "What does it mean... the lesson?"

Akagi Genda-San perked up even higher and gently tapped Reuben on his chest with his finger tips. "That is for you to figure out. What that lesson means to you may mean something entirely different to another... warrior."

Akagi Genda-San turned away and walked off the jetty leaving Reuben behind. Reuben looked at the pistol in his hand with the hammer still cocked. He gently squeezed the trigger and with his thumb, replaced the hammer back to its home and tossed it into the river. "Hey, wait!" Reuben yelled out as he fumbled his way off the jetty following Akagi Genda-San.

"Tell me more of this lesson. Where does it come from? Are there any more like it?"

Akagi Genda-San turned to face Reuben. "That is one of thousands of lessons you have yet to learn. It is an old samurai lesson passed down from the time when the gods dipped their swords in the water and shook off the droplets forming the islands of my homeland. It is a lesson for warriors... warriors like you, Reuben-San."

"I told you, I'm not a warrior!" Reuben replied, perturbed. "I was a soldier in a wicked war, nothing more, nothing less."

Although Reuben had anger in his tone, Akagi Genda-San remained pleasant and calm. "Warriors come in many forms. The simplest of warriors are... cruel, wicked, evil, and filled with hatred. But the true warriors of heart are the ones who are loyal, honest, and benevolent. They can defend with deadly accuracy one moment, and become a poet, the next."

Akagi Genda-San slowly walked around Reuben, looking him up and down as Reuben stood still, watching. Stopping in front of Reuben, he said, "You are a lost warrior, Reuben-San, and it is not too late to find yourself. That is if you take heed of the lesson I recited to you. If you accept my challenge to follow me, you will become a most valuable man to the ones who love you, and live the path with the one love has chosen for you."

Reuben nodded, thinking deeply. Not the thoughts like those of the past months, but thoughts of a future. A future he thought was over moments ago on the jetty with the pistol he tossed into the river.

"Do any of these thousands of lessons help deal with dark memories?"

Akagi Genda-San smiled and gently stroked his chin. "Memories in one's mind is like grains of sand on a tranquil beach, numerous, but small, even the worst of memories. They can be dealt with and even used if you become one with the code."

With a most questionable look in Reuben's face, he asked with severe sincerity, "What code is that?"

Akagi Genda-San brought his hands together as if he were praying and responded, "Bushido. Way of the Warrior."

石
水

In the year of our Lord, 1847, a romantic tale continues.
New philosophies from a different land, and precious gifts from the heart…

Stones and Water

Reuben and Akagi Genda-San arrived by foot at the farm close to midnight. After Akagi Genda-San explained the Bushido code to Reuben near the jetty, Reuben was eager to learn as much about the code as possible. Akagi Genda-San, invited by Reuben to stay at the farm, was just as eager to teach Reuben. During the walk, Akagi Genda-San told Reuben about his home and how honor is such a distinct element in his culture. Reuben was raised on honor principles by his parents and further learned at VMI, but to hear how honor plays a vital part in Akagi Genda-San's culture took honor to a level exceeding anything he learned from his parents or instructors.

Upon arriving at the farm, they entered the house startling May who came out of her room scared out of her wits until she saw Reuben.

"Reuben, what in the world is you doing here at this late hour, and who is that man with you?" she asked rather upset.

Reuben didn't answer but filled a pail with bread and a large bottle filled with water. He opened the back door and left. Akagi Genda-San silently faced May, bowed in greeting, smiling, and followed Reuben at a quick pace.

May went to the door and watched as they entered the stable. Reuben lit a lantern and she saw the two rummaging around. The noise they were making gained the attention of Noah and Henry, who came out of their cabin. They came to the house where May was watching very concerned.

"Is that Reuben in the stable making all that racket?" asked Henry.

"Yes, and he's with a strange looking man I've never seen before."

"What's he doing?" asked Noah

"I don't know. They entered the house, got some food and water, and headed to the stable."

"Suppose Mr. and Mrs. Duran knows he's here?"

"I doubt it, Noah, but you better ride out early in the morning to let them know."

In the stable, Reuben opened a long wooden chest and nearly dove in. He rose with an old broken rake. "Here, Genda-San, how's this?"

"Perfect, Reuben-San, give that to me and see if you can find another."

Returning back, head first into the chest, Reuben rummaged some more and came up with another handle with no tool head attached.

"Excellent, now we must cut these to about chest level."

Reuben retrieved a handsaw hanging on the wall, took the broken rake and measured it against his body. Akagi Genda-San pointed to a point on the handle and said, "Right there, Reuben-San. Cut it there and make the other the same length."

Reuben did as instructed and handed both tool handles to Akagi Genda-San who closely inspected them. "Good, they will serve our purpose. Come, Reuben-San, where can we begin?"

"I know the perfect place. Follow me."

Reuben led Akagi Genda-San to the oak tree by the creek.

"Now, Reuben-San, I am going to teach you the practice of misogi-no-jo, the practice of purification," said Akagi Genda-San in a serious manner. "It is done in many forms, most common with the use of water. As a warrior, I find my purification most enlightening with the jo."

Reuben stood straight and ridged as if he were being instructed by one of his past VMI instructors.

"Is that what the sticks are for?"

"Think of them not as sticks, Reuben-San, but as extensions of your body."

"Extensions?" asked Reuben curiously.

Akagi Genda-San elegantly twirled the stick he had in his left hand, passing it to his right behind his back and in a high arc swung it down toward Reuben's head stopping less than an inch away from his forehead. Ever so impressive, Reuben didn't flinch, of which Akagi Genda-San took serious note.

"That was incredible!" said Reuben.

"What is even more incredible, Reuben-San, is you did not move. Tell me, Reuben-San, do you fear death?"

Dropping his head shamefully, he feared his answer of no would be wrong.

"Reuben-San, you must answer the question and you must answer honestly. Do you fear death?"

Reuben lifted his head and looking straight into Akagi Genda-San's eyes as he answered, "No. At times I welcome it."

Akagi Genda-San lowered the stick and asked, "Why?"

"I don't know if this will make any sense, but when I was in Mexico and about to go on an assignment, I assumed I was already dead. It allowed me not to think of my family and Renee, and gave me full focus on those who relied on me to keep them alive. By assuming I was already dead, I felt as if I had nothing to lose if I were killed."

"Very interesting, Reuben-San, much like Musashi. You have just described one of the most important traits of a samurai, to accept death as a consequence to your actions. That in itself makes you a survivor."

"Samurai? Genda-San, what's a samurai?" asked Reuben.

"Samurai are those who serve their master."

"Like slaves?"

"No, Reuben-San, they are warriors who live, breathe, and bleed the Bushido code. Tell me, Reuben-San, do you still welcome death?"

"Yes."

"And why is this, Reuben-San?"

"Because I'm tired and see no point of my existence."

"Well then, Reuben-San, we must wake you, and find your purpose of existence. We will start our search with this deadly weapon."

Looking curiously at the stick, Reuben replied, "Deadly weapon? This old broken rake handle?"

"This *old broken rake handle* is the only weapon the great swordsman, Musashi himself, could not defeat. This deadly weapon is called the jo, the short staff, and it will become your extension to the heavens and life itself."

"Musashi. You mentioned that name before. Is he one of these samurai?"

"Ah, Miyamoto Musashi, he was the greatest swordsman in all of Japan, and master of the two sword technique. Long before you told me your theory of death, he once said, *'To win any battle, you must fight as if you are already dead.'* You have already learned one of his most valuable lessons."

The quoted words of Miyamoto Musashi spoken by Akagi Genda-San had a profound effect on Reuben. The night before Adam's death, Reuben had a deep feeling of déjà vu, and said something similar when Adam asked how Reuben could continue to fight the way he did.

"Reuben-San, with this weapon, a weapon Musashi valued as much as the sword, you will learn the ways of Bushido in physical and spiritual elements. Now take the jo in your hand and assume the first position. I am about to teach you the twenty three jo kata."

狼

Making her way up the large path leading to the front of Renee's house, Lucy sprinted the last few steps to the front door. She pounded on the large carved oak doors with her small fists calling out Renee's name.

The door opened by a servant with a perturbed look on his face. "Excuse me, may I help you?" he said in an angered tone.

"Is Renee here? I need to speak to her. It's very important. Renee!" yelled Lucy, excitedly and rushed past the servant.

"Hey, get back here!" called the servant, and began giving chase.

Lucy raced through the huge house calling Renee's name.

In a large room, Margret Wallace and several ladies were admiring china patterns that were to be used for Renee's upcoming wedding reception. Renee sat off in the corner very uninterested. She heard her name being called as did the others in the room.

Suddenly Renee spotted Lucy running through the hall past the room they were in with the servant still chasing after her.

Renee rose and ran to the archway and called out to Lucy. When Lucy heard her name, she made a dead stop, turned and ran in the opposite direction causing the servant to trip over his own feet and fall to the floor.

"Renee, Renee! Have you seen my brother?! He never came home after the ball last night and Mama is sick with worry! Please tell me if you know where he is!" cried out Lucy, distraughtly.

"You are coming with me, Miss! I'm so sorry, Miss Wallace. I'll make sure this girl is seen to," said the servant as he forcefully took hold of Lucy by the shoulder.

"No! Let her go, Ramie!" said Renee as she took Lucy by her hands. "What's this about Reuben being missing, Lucy?"

"That's right, Renee, he never came home last night. Mama sent me here to see if you might know where he is. I ran past the jetty where he usually goes to sit, and I also checked the room at the school. Da is arranging a carriage. We're going to the farm to see if he's there. Unless you know where he is?"

"Well, come on then, let's go!" said Renee as she pulled on Lucy's hands and started running down the hall.

"Renee! Just what do you think you are doing?!" called out Margret Wallace.

Renee stopped, turned, and with a determined look she said, "I'm going to help Lucy's family find Reuben. I'll be back when we know he's safe. Is that all right with you, mother?"

Without waiting for a response, she turned and continued running out of the house leaving her mother and the other ladies speechless.

Monique Wilcox came to Margret and said, "The sooner you and Franklin marry off that daughter of yours to the Sinclair boy, the better. That Duran family has been a bad influence on her."

Together Renee and Lucy ran back to the Duran home quickly stopping at the school one more time to see if Reuben might be in the secret room he had found several years back. He wasn't there, so they continued to the house. As the two girls turned the corner onto Lucy's street, they saw Aaron, Coleen, and Monroe standing next to a carriage. There was no sign of Reuben and Coleen was being consoled by Monroe.

"Here comes Lucy and Renee, Mama. Hey, you two, did you find him?" called out Monroe.

Coleen stepped quickly to meet the two. "Please tell me you have seen him!"

Renee took hold of Coleen's hands saying, "No, Mrs. Duran. Lucy and I even stopped at a couple of places on the way here to look. Are you going to the farm to look for him now?"

"That we are," said Aaron as he was double checking the harnesses to the carriage team.

"Please may I come along?" asked Renee, pleading.

"Of course you can. Quickly everyone, get onboard!" said Aaron as he motioned for them to board the carriage.

The moment Aaron made sure everyone was safely seated, he snapped the reins of the carriage team, and they were off at a quick trot to the farm. During the ride, everyone was discussing the last time each one had seen Reuben. No one could guess where he may have gone off to, but one thing was for certain, the last time anyone saw him was at the ball. That caused Aaron to stop the carriage.

"Why are you stopping, Aaron?" asked Coleen.

Having a moment of thought, Aaron answered, "What if he never left the ballroom? Maybe we should go back and check there before we go any further."

"That's a good idea, Da," Monroe replied.

"With respect, Mr. Duran," said Renee, "If Reuben wanted to be alone, and isn't in the city, he would have gone to the farm away from everyone. I'm sure of it."

"Renee's right, Da, I think we should continue to the farm," agreed Lucy. "She and Reuben practically think alike."

"Hey look! Is that Noah coming this way?" asked Monroe, pointing toward a horse and rider.

Riding at a quick gallop, Noah saw the Duran family sitting in the stopped carriage. He heeled his mount causing the horse to quicken its pace. Within several yards, he pulled back the reins bringing the horse to a stop, but still twisting in circles.

"Quick, come with me! It's Reuben. He's at the farm with this other man!"

"Good lord, Noah, is he okay?!" called out Coleen.

"He's fine but, but... but come quickly!"

Noah turned the horse back in the direction he came from and heeled the horse to go. Aaron reined the team to follow.

"See, I knew Renee was right!" exclaimed Lucy.

狼

May heard Noah and the carriage coming up the lane from the side of the house where she and Henry were watching Akagi Genda-San direct Reuben in practice. She turned and hurried to meet them as they came to a stop in front of the house.

Lucy leaped off the carriage followed by Renee.

"Is he here, May?! Is Reuben here?!" called out Lucy, running toward her.

May stopped just short of running into Lucy. She waited and watched Aaron help Coleen off the carriage and very soon, everyone was standing around May with questionable looks on their faces.

May finally answered Lucy's question. "Reuben arrived here very late last night with a strange man. One thing for sure, he's not from around these here parts. He and Reuben have been together ever since they got here. Right down yonder by the oak tree. Come, I'll show you."

"Why didn't you come tell us when he got here?" asked Coleen rather upset.

"As May said, Mrs. Duran, they arrived very late last night, close to midnight if it wasn't a minute more. They've been under the tree doing strange things all night long," answered

Noah. "Since he seemed to be safe, we thought it be best I head out first thing this morning to tell you."

As they passed Henry and Noah's cabin, the barn, and the large planting field, they came to a stop when they saw a strange man standing and watching Reuben at a distance. Coleen began to step forward until Aaron held her back.

"Hold on, I think I know that man," said Aaron. "Wait here."

Aaron moved forward slowly. He was about ten yards away when Akagi Genda-San said, "Ohayo gozaimas, Mr. Duran."

Aaron stopped in his tracks, startled. He was very curious how this man could know who he was without looking back at him.

Akagi Genda-San peered to the side looking for Aaron. He noticed Aaron stopped so he motioned to Aaron, "Please, Mr. Duran, come look at this, quickly."

Aaron looked back to the family and motioned them to stay put as he advanced toward Akagi Genda-San.

When he reached him, Akagi Genda-San said, "Look at your boy, Aaron-San. May I call you Aaron-San? It has only been several hours and he has already fully learned the twenty three jo kata, and he does not even know the basic suburi techniques!" he exclaimed, enthusiastically.

He looked at Aaron, "Your boy is most inquisitive and easy to train. Ah, I see you are curious. Please forgive me. We have met, at the ball last evening."

"Yes, we have. What's he doing?" asked Aaron watching Reuben as he restarted the kata.

"He is finding focus," answered Akagi Genda-San as he motioned the others to come forward.

"Please forgive Reuben-San for his absence. It is entirely my doing. I told him of his needs and how he could obtain peace over his shadows. He became so eager to learn, he could not wait to arrive at this peaceful setting to start training."

There was wide-eyed silence from everyone. "Ah, I see introductions are in order. I will do so myself. I do not want to interrupt Reuben-San."

In a very pleasant manner Akagi Genda-San bowed in a most formal fashion, the likes they had never seen before. "My name is Genda, Genda Akagi. I am a visitor to your country from the islands of Nippon, or Japan as you know of it. I have come to learn the ways of the western world, and see how my region of Itosai could benefit from it."

There was still silence and the curious looks increased. Akagi Genda-San continued as he focused on the family. "You must be Coleen-Dono, Reuben-San's precious mother. And you are Monroe-San, Reuben-San's very intelligent brother and you, you are Lucy-Dono, his very pretty and creative sister. He described you all with much love and affection."

Looking at May, he again bowed toward her. "May-Dono, we met briefly. Reuben-San says you are a wonderful cook. Henry-San, you have been described as the best craftsman in, how does Reuben-San put it... the county, and of course, Noah-San, Reuben-San's friend who he has known since his youth. He also described you three with much love and affection."

112

He turned and looked to Renee, took a step closer to her, bowed and rose. "And you, you are the most beautiful Renee-Dono. Reuben-San described you so beautifully, it caused me to picture the precious, freshly bloomed cherry blossoms in my gardens back in Itosai."

Renee felt flush. Never has she ever been so complemented. "What did he say, Mr. Akagi."

"Ah, that I cannot say because I cannot express Reuben-San's affection in the manner he can. It would not be the same coming from myself."

Speaking for the first time, Coleen said quite perturbed, "What are you having my son do over there with that stick?"

"Please, Coleen-Dono, do not be alarmed. Your son is making the first steps of rediscovering spirituality."

"What's this heathen nonsense? My boy is a believer in our Lord God and Jesus Christ. How dare you try to convert him into some, some strange pagan religion!" cried Coleen, taking steps closer to Akagi Genda-San. Aaron took hold of her.

Akagi Genda-San, in a very solemn manner, replied to Coleen, "Rest assured, there is no conversion taking place. Reuben-San has long lost his faith in such a deity. During my visit, I have come to learn warfare is most barbaric in your western world. Many brave, strong men are thrust into situations causing them to question the existence of a deity. These are the ones who take on more than what is asked of them because it is within their nature. They are... protectors. The ones who do not want to fight, but do so for the sake of their brethren who are unable to care for themselves. These are the most honorable of men and your son is one of these warriors, yet he does not realize it. He has yet to find his balance. What you see him doing now, he is taking his first steps to once again becoming your son..." Akagi Genda-San turned his focus from Coleen to Renee and continued, "And to you, Renee-Dono, becoming the loved one you have lost."

Akagi Genda-San then commenced to tell of how he and Reuben met and how they came to the farm. He spoke of when he first saw him at the ball, he saw in Reuben, a lost honorable man who needed guidance to regain his path. He told them how he followed Reuben as he left the ball in distress, and how he stopped him from taking his life on the jetty.

Until the moment when Akagi Genda-San mentioned Reuben's suicide attempt, they had no idea how desperate and lost he was. Although they had no understanding of Akagi Genda-San's methods, they, especially Coleen and Renee, expressed their gratitude for him being with Reuben to stop him.

"What I can't understand is, why the stick? What help is that supposed to be? He looks like a, a sissy dancing with a mop handle," said Monroe.

"Hmm, I know not what 'sissy' means, but I will show you the purpose of his, dance," answered Akagi Genda-San. He turned his attention to Reuben and with a very deep frightening sound causing the others to startle, he shouted "YAME!"

At the sound of Akagi Genda-San's order, in a very disciplined manner, Reuben ceased his movements and quickly lowered himself to the ground.

"Now stay back and observe. Reuben-San has been doing this kata exercise over and over throughout the night. He can do it flawlessly, but now he, and you as well, will see why."

Akagi Genda-San left the group of onlookers and made his way to where Reuben sat. Reuben was unaware the others were off in the distance observing.

Akagi Genda-San stood in front of Reuben and asked, "Reuben-San, do you know why I made you do this exercise over and over again?"

"No, Genda-San."

"Stand and ready yourself and let's see if you have learned anything."

Reuben stood and took the ready position of the kata while Akagi Genda-San retrieved his jo. He stood directly in front of Reuben, his jo held in a thrust position. Reuben watched curiously, but remained alert.

"EEP!!! Without notice, Akagi Genda-San side stepped off Reuben's path and thrust his jo directly to Reuben's chest. Reuben quickly reacted by raising his jo in the first movement of the kata, a counter strike.

"AIHT-HOOIP-EEP!!!" Akagi Genda-San again continued to thrust, strike, and swing his jo directly at Reuben's body. All the while, Reuben counter struck successfully deflecting Akagi Genda-San's near fatal strikes up until the end of the twenty three step kata.

At the end of the exercise, a final block holding Akagi Genda-San's jo in check, Reuben looked amazed at what he had accomplished. He stepped back and looked at his jo in awe.

"AEAT!!!"

Suddenly Reuben found himself flat on his back looking up at the oak tree having his legs taken out from underneath him by Akagi Genda-San.

"Never take your focus away from your opponent either, in victory or defeat, Reuben-San. When you win a victory, keep you sword clean and your armor near."

"Hai, Genda-San!"

狼

"That was amazing! I never knew you can move like that, Reuben!" called out Lucy as she ran to her brother and kneeled next to him as he still lay on his back. "That was so incredible... well, up until that man knocked you on your backside. Can I learn how to do that?!"

"Don't even think about it, Lucy Duran!" said Coleen, also coming closer. "It's one thing for Reuben to do such things, but no daughter of mine is going to engage in such unladylike activities."

Reuben struggled to get to his feet when he heard his mother's voice. "Mama, Da. What are you doing here?"

"Looking for you," said Renee coming out from behind Aaron and Monroe.

"Renee, I... I.... Why are you here?"

She didn't answer, but instead walked up to Reuben and wrapped her arms around him tightly. After a few moments of silence, she spoke, "Mr. Akagi... he told us what you almost did to yourself. Geez, Reuben, do you have any idea what you would be putting me… your, your family through if you, you….”

She couldn't finish putting her thoughts into words, but instead held him tighter, buried her face into his shoulder, and began weeping. He raised his arms and held her.

“I'm sorry, Renee.”

“Ah, Reuben-San. I believe it is time to rest from training. I believe it is time for, all of us, to take time to rest. May-Dono, I understand you make wonderful meals. I would enjoy to sample one,” said Akagi Genda-San in an attempt to ease the tension beneath the oak tree. It worked.

May, feeling flushed, said, “Ah, sure. Have you ever had dumplings?”

“Not dumplings from America.”

“Well, you are in for a treat, foreign man. Come on then. Come on all of you.”

“Excellent, I have a great hunger. I can eat as you say in your land, a donkey, I believe.”

Everyone began laughing, except for Renee and Reuben who were still in each other's arms.

“Not exactly, Mr. Akagi, but we get your jest. I'm so hungry myself, I can also eat a, donkey,” said Aaron as he began to lead everyone to the house until he saw Coleen watching Renee and Reuben. He stepped up to her and placed his arm around her shoulder guiding her away.

“Come dear. Let's let those two alone. I think our son is safe now, especially with Renee here.”

Swallowing hard and holding back a cry, she nodded. “Oh, Aaron, will our son ever be the same as he was before he went off to Mexico?”

“I don't know, my love. But there is one thing for certain. Let's be grateful Mr. Akagi found him just in time.”

狼

Renee and Reuben didn't realize they were alone until she looked up from his shoulder.

“Hey, where did everyone go?”

“To the house, probably,” replied Reuben.

“Then we better go join them,” she said, releasing her hold and slowly starting to walk toward the house.

Sensing he was not following, she looked back to see Reuben facing the creek. She stopped and said, “Reuben, please come with me.”

“What do you mean by that, Renee?” he asked, still facing toward the creek.

“I don't understand.”

“Neither do I.”

“Reuben…” she began to talk, but not exactly knowing what her thoughts were. She knew Reuben directed that question toward her upcoming wedding.

“I'm sorry Renee, that was… out of line of me.”

Stepping closer to Reuben, she asked, "What's this man teaching you, Reuben? Is it... safe?"

"He calls it Bushido. A warrior's code in his country."

"I thought you hated being a soldier?"

Turning to face Renee, he answered her, "Genda-San says wars fought in his country are much different than the ones we fight here. They have meaning and honor. They have a code so disciplined, it's too incredible to comprehend. Genda-San says he sees that code in me. It's a code used to suppress... emotions, both in combat and in peace. It seems to bind the two together to give a simple meaning of the universe. At least that's what he gets from it. He says its meaning differs from one individual to another. I don't understand what it means to me, but what little I have learned has enlightened me. He explains things to me in ways I would have never thought of, and it makes my horrors seem so... small. Even your marriage, it's getting somewhat easier to accept."

Renee took in what he was saying as best she could until his last word. It made her sad thinking Reuben could finally come to terms she was getting married. Deep within herself, selfishly she didn't want him to come to terms with it. She didn't want to come to terms with it herself, and to have him feel the same way made her feel less lonely.

Reuben continued, interrupting Renee's thoughts. "Take this creek for example. All we see is water, but Genda-San sees a powerful force of nature. Although it takes a long time, it carves up the earth and even moves mountains. I never saw it like that before, but I remember when we first came here, the creek was thinner. Now it's wider and deeper. Genda-San is right and I think he's right about me."

"For our sake, I hope you are right and he can help you come back to me," replied Renee with a sudden fear of what she said.

He looked at her in wonder. Instead of questioning her, he decided to derail the same thought that seemed to be going through both their minds and said, "How in the world did your father allow you to come here? I bet he didn't, did he? Yeah, you're in trouble."

"You don't know the half of it. I ran out with Lucy during some wedding planning with my mother and other ladies."

"Ah, Renee, I'm going to miss you when you move to Charleston," he said as he took her hand and began leading her to the house.

She lagged a step behind so she could hide her emotional pain of what Reuben said about her moving away.

狼

The rest of the morning was spent at the house. After a meal that Akagi Genda-San praised May as one of the best cooks he has ever had the pleasure and honor of being in the presence of, they all moved to the front porch to enjoy the fresh warm autumn day.

Akagi Genda-San entertained with stories of his homeland, which everyone found fascinating. The more he spoke, the more they began to accept him as a new friend of the family, including Coleen who was beginning to see how much he wanted to help her son.

However, for reasons unknown to her, Renee still had her doubts of his presence. She feared Reuben might be replacing her friendship with his. Feeling incredibly selfish, she didn't want to lose Reuben to anyone, not to Akagi Genda-San or because of William Sinclair.

With midafternoon approaching, Coleen, out of concern for Renee, felt they had better take her back home to which even Akagi Genda-San agreed after hearing of Franklin Wallace's strictness over her.

Renee wanted to hate Akagi Genda-San, but found it difficult because she saw the old cheerful Reuben he once was because of him and also, he made it very difficult to dislike him. She kept reminding herself that he's helping her... special friend.

"I have to go now, Reuben, but I'll be back to visit," she said as Reuben was about to help her onto the carriage.

"Not to worry, Renee. I know you are kept busy. But it was wonderful seeing you today and knowing you still... care."

"Reuben, I have never stopped caring and never will." She hugged him tightly and kissed him lightly on the cheek. As the carriage rode away, they both stared at one another until the carriage turned onto the road.

Akagi Genda-San stepped up to Reuben. He watched their exchange at a distance. Thinking of his marriage, he could not help but feel compassion for the two.

"You know, Reuben-San, the situation between you two is not uncommon. Stones and water, Reuben-San, stones and water."

"What does that mean, Genda-San?" asked Reuben, looking to where Akagi Genda-San had once been standing, but he had moved toward the oak tree.

After hearing Reuben's question, he turned and in a cheerful voice he replied, "You will know in time, Reuben-San. Now come! I have much to teach you and no time to do so. Come, Reuben-San, we have training to do!" he said as he raised his arms and face to the sky.

狼

Aaron stopped the carriage in front of the Duran home in the city. Monroe stepped down and helped his sister to the ground. He was about to help Renee when Aaron told Renee to stay.

"That's all right, Mr. Duran, I can walk home. I could use the walk."

"No, sweetheart, Aaron and I won't allow you to face your parents alone, not after you ran off to help us find our son."

"Then we want to come too," said Lucy.

"No, Lucy, you stay here with Monroe, and the both of you, pack your mother a bag." Aaron looked at Coleen. "I believe I'll be taking her back to the farm when we return from taking Renee home."

Aaron snapped the reins and the carriage was underway. As they rode to Renee's house, not much was said. For the most part, all three had the same thoughts going through their heads, how much help is Akagi Genda-San actually being?

As they neared the house, Aaron spoke to Renee. "I don't know if you'll be allowed to visit the house, but we'll get word to you somehow about Reuben's progress."

117

"I appreciate that, Mr. and Mrs. Duran, but I believe my father owes me something after all these years of... suppression. There's only five weeks until I'm married and he has forced me from the things I love most. Well, if he wants me to make his business great, then he owes me," she said in such a manner Aaron and Coleen found both admirable and frightening.

"Well said, my dear. Just don't go and do anything... desperate. Promise us, Renee. Promise to both Aaron and myself you won't do anything that will do you any harm."

Renee embraced Coleen and said, "I promise not only to you two, but to Reuben as well."

Aaron placed his hand on Renee's shoulder. "In that case, I'll leave this carriage in the care of the stable and feel free to use it."

She let go of Coleen and gave Aaron a hug saying, "Thank you very much, Mr. Duran. I love you both."

They were nearing the house when they saw Franklin and Margret Wallace standing outside the main gate leading to the house. Aaron pulled the team to stop, set the brake, and began to step off the carriage to assist Renee.

"Never you mind, Duran. I will help my daughter," Franklin said with harshness in his voice.

Coleen, in a very calm and motherly manner, said, "We can't thank Renee enough for helping us find our son. She was very helpful."

"Your boy is well then?" asked Margret Wallace. Her concern received a stern look from her husband.

"Yes he is. He's back at the farm where we think it's best for him."

"Good, good. Now come, Renee. Your absence has delayed your mother's plans. Farewell, Duran," said Franklin Wallace without looking toward Aaron and Coleen and taking Renee by the arm leading her toward the house.

Coleen motioned Aaron to leave, which he did, and they began the ride back to the city house.

There was silence as Renee walked with her parents to the house. Upon entering the front door, Franklin Wallace turned Renee to look at him.

"That is it, young lady! What you did was inexcusable to your mother!"

Feeling the frustrations of the last five years since her father arranged her marriage swirling in her head, Renee spoke forcefully. "No father! What I did was help find my friend who was on the verge of killing himself! His parents needed my help! You remember what it's like to be parents, don't you?!" said Renee surprising her parents, and herself as well.

"How dare you speak to us in such a manner! You are no longer to see anyone in that Duran family, do you understand me?!" replied her father.

"No!"

"No? What do you mean, no?"

Renee had to suppress a laugh, let alone a smile, of thoughts of what Reuben would say at a moment like this. *'What word did you not understand'* is what he would be saying right about now, she thought.

She took in a deep breath and let it out to calm herself down, and in a most diplomatic manner she could conjure up she said, "Look, father, you and mother have kept me on a short leash for the last five years. At thirteen you arranged this upcoming wedding without my consent, not that having my consent would have mattered to you. In five weeks' time, I will be married to William Sinclair, move away to Charleston, never to return to Norfolk, and your precious business will double in size."

Renee's parents were still in shock. Renee began to wonder if this is the longest conversation she ever had with the both of them. Not losing this opportunity of still having their attention, she continued to speak.

"I'm eighteen now, father, old enough to be married as you arranged. You are a businessman, so let's talk business. I have five weeks before I'm married. During that time, I will help mother with the wedding and when the day comes, I will marry William Sinclair and be his wife so your business can thrive and I will be... happy."

Rubbing his chin the same way he does when discussing business ventures with others, Renee's father looked down upon her, even feeling a small form of admiration for what seemed to be a business negotiation. "I see, continue."

"I'm allowed to visit with the Durans to help see to their son's health. After the wedding, I will no longer see them ever again. You don't even have to invite them to the wedding."

"And there will be no more of this Reuben nonsense?"

"Never. I will be the wife of William Sinclair and live... happily ever after."

Franklin Wallace crossed his arms across his chest and breathed in, making himself look imposing, the way he does when he completes a successful business deal with other shippers and merchants. Feeling like he finally overcame his daughter's nine year foolish friendship with what he considered an unworthy citizen of Norfolk's society, he nodded in agreement. He held out his hand and said, "Done."

Renee looked at his hand and timidly took hold of it. It was cold and icy, so unlike Reuben's father. Giving a forceful shake with a sly grin Renee could see as a victory smile, he said, "Deal."

狼

Good to his word, Franklin Wallace allowed his daughter some leeway in what remained of her time before the wedding. And equally good to her word, Renee assisted her mother with the wedding plans, going as far as taking interest in the actual plans herself. To Renee's belief, if this was going to be her life from now on, she better begin the transition to a world where the Durans no longer exist, especially once she moves away to Charleston, South Carolina.

It been four days since Renee and Reuben's family found him and Akagi Genda-San on the farm. During those days, she visited the Duran house each day as agreed by her parents to hear of Reuben's progress. Aaron provided her with details of what sounded like good progress. She so dearly wanted to go to the farm to see for herself, but wedding plans with her mother didn't allow the time for the ride to the farm.

On the fifth day, Renee received a special package from across the Atlantic on board the ocean steamer, the *Morning Star*, one of Franklin Wallace's vessels. It carried Renee's wedding dress from Paris, France.

It was early in the morning when the dress was revealed to Renee and her mother for the first time. Margret Wallace was in total fascination and even Renee could not help but admire how beautiful the dress looked. She even stepped behind the display mannequin in front of a full length mirror to get an idea of how she would look in it. She also went as far as pulling her hair tight against her scalp and behind her head.

"You are going to make the most beautiful bride this city has ever known, my daughter," said Franklin Wallace. "What do you think, Margret?"

"Oh yes. We must have a fitting at the dressmakers this afternoon."

Looking at his daughter as she enthusiastically admired the dress, he felt good about how she had gotten involved in her wedding planning the past week. At first he was skeptical about her end of the deal they made, but she showed signs of actually becoming a proper future wife of social stature. However, he still had his doubts. He wanted to put her to the test.

"No, Margret, I have a better idea. Being that our daughter has been so very helpful to you, I believe we owe her some time to herself, to visit the Duran boy to see his progress perhaps."

Renee made no reaction to what her father said. Instead she maintained her proper mannerism as was taught to her at Wickham. However, as she seemed to be admiring the lace work of the dress, inside her heart rate was rising and she was thinking to herself, stay calm and don't show them any happiness. Just act like it's more of an inconvenience than a reward.

"Do you think that is such a good idea, Franklin?" asked Margret very concerned.

"I believe it is my dear. Renee has been keeping up her end of the bargain, haven't you, my dear daughter?"

Moving her attention from the dress to her father, Renee replied, "I suppose so, father, but I have a better idea for mother."

Looking inquisitive, her father asked, "Oh really, and what would that be?"

Stepping up to her mother, Renee took her hands. "Instead of going to the dressmakers, how about we have a formal fitting here, in the garden parlor, say about three in the afternoon? We can serve tea."

Renee's parents were taken by surprise. Her mother became very happy and gently gave Renee a hug, void of emotion, so unlike the hugs she receives from Coleen.

"My, that is a capital idea!" exclaimed Franklin Wallace. "Well then, it's settled. Come then, I will get the coachman to take you to the Duran house. I suppose you can get on from there?"

"Yes father, and thank you. Not to worry either, I will not stay long and I will be back long before our fitting," she said, as she looked into her mother's eyes.

狼

The door to the Duran house was opened by Monroe. "I wish you would just come in for crying out loud. You practically live here," he joked as he welcomed Renee. "You interrupted Mama as she was telling us about Reuben."

"Mrs. Duran is here? How's he doing?" she asked, excitedly.

"She got here a little while ago to get some more clothes. Come in."

Renee entered the Duran parlor and practically leaped into Coleen's open arms. Coleen's hug was so very warm and inviting and she felt so very content in her arms like a true daughter.

"How's he doing?" asked Renee.

"He's doing wonderfully, Renee. Mr. Akagi has been doing wonders. Reuben is a little different, but still, he's almost back to his old self. When can you come to see him? He asks for you every day."

"I can come see him today! You have no idea what I had to go through to get this chance, but I have to be back at my house no later than two o'clock this afternoon."

"Then what are we waiting for?!" cried out Aaron, coming from the hallway as he overheard the conversation. "Come, Monroe and Lucy, off your arse and into the carriage. Let's go have lunch at the farm!"

The ride to the farm was much more pleasant than the last time when the same group made this trip in search of Reuben. Coleen, in detail, brought Renee up to date on Reuben's progress. She told her of how Akagi Genda-San's unusual assistance has been bringing back the old Reuben.

"It's so strange, sometimes it looks like they're fighting and dancing at the same time. What those two have been doing is so unbelievable. You'll see what I mean when we get there."

When they arrived, Aaron and Coleen, with Monroe and Lucy, went into the house while Renee, in such a hurry to see Reuben, went to where she knew he would be, under the large oak tree. As she cleared the large crop field, she saw Reuben. He was preforming the misogi-no-jo exercises. His movements were so mesmerizing. She couldn't believe he could move in such a manner.

"Ah, good morning, Renee-Dono, it is most pleasant for you to visit. Have you come to see how Reuben-San is progressing?" asked Akagi Genda-San, without looking back to see Renee approach.

Again, she was awed at how this man can easily sense out a person's presence without the need to look and see who is coming near him. It was rather frightening to her.

"Hello, Mr. Akagi. How's he doing?"

"Take a look, young one," he said very approvingly. "It is uncanny how he picks up on techniques. Look, he has barely learned that kata and has already incorporated his unique personality into it. Very impressive."

Renee watched admiringly as Reuben practiced the misogi-no-jo katas Akagi Genda-San taught him. She was seeing a different Reuben and didn't know what to make of it. He did seem to be more at peace and calmer. For that she was grateful, but the method for him to regain what he lost was still odd.

"Will he be his old self, with no bad memories and dreams of the war?" asked Renee, hopeful.

Akagi Genda-San continued to watch Reuben and let out a sigh. "You care much for Reuben-San?"

"Yes, I do. Very much," she answered as she also continued to watch.

"You love him perhaps?"

Taken by surprise, she turned her attention to Akagi Genda-San, as he watched Reuben. "Of course I love him. Reuben is my... best friend."

"Best friend, nothing more?"

Renee looked down and lowered herself to the ground, sat, picked a blade of grass, and held it close to her face watching it bend and twist in the breeze.

"It can't be anything more. My father has already determined my future. His arrangement, remember?"

Akagi Genda-San looked down toward Renee. She continued to watch the blade of grass. A feeling of sympathy entered his mind. Watching her, he saw her eyes water, but noticed how desperately she was keeping her sorrowful emotion locked up inside. He lowered himself next to her and also picked a blade of grass.

"I too was a... victim of an arranged marriage."

Renee turned her attention to Akagi Genda-San. "You were, Mr. Akagi? Did your parents arrange your marriage also?"

Akagi Genda-San chuckled, "No, young Renee-Dono, it was I who arranged it with another Daimyo, or Regional Lord. What you would call a governor in this country."

"Really, how come? Was it to merge your business, like my father?"

Keeping his focus on the blade of grass, Akagi Genda-San answered, "No, nothing trivial as that. It was to prevent war."

Renee expression was of shock. Her mouth and jaw dropped open, eyes opened wide in disbelief. "War, are you serious?! How did your arranged marriage stop a war?"

Akagi Genda-San's turned his attention from the blade of grass to Renee. "You see, Renee-Dono, arranged marriages are more than tradition in my land. The Daimyo of the region north of Itosai, had his eyes on my lands in the mountains, rich in many resources including precious metals. He harassed my border villages causing me to send out my samurai to ward his off."

Renee was in total fascination and turned her seated position to face Akagi Genda-San to give him her full attention to his story.

He continued. "The Daimyo's name was Kano. Kano had an army, but it was mostly made up of ronin, masterless samurai. What you would call, roaming warriors for hire. Not totally loyal except to themselves, but nonetheless, they were a nuisance. So much so, I had decided to invade Kano's region and take it for myself. I made my intentions clear and in turn, he offered his daughter to be my wife if I would not invade his region."

He lowered his eyes in sorrow. "I was to be wed to Yanna, a woman I loved dearly and she loved me also, but to avoid bloodshed, I had to set aside Yanna to marry Azami, Kano's daughter."

Looking toward Reuben and watching for a few moments, he nodded in an approving manner and continued his story. "And so, for two years, Azami and I were husband and wife and there was peace between Kano's clan and mine."

"What happened after two years?" asked Renee with much interest.

"Azami died of a terminal illness which she and Kano kept a secret from me."

"I'm so sorry. You must have been devastated," said Renee very sympathetically.

Akagi Genda-San let out a grunt. "There is no need to be sorry, Renee-Dono. Kano was very crafty and cold hearted."

"What do you mean?"

"Knowing his daughter was going to die, he used that time to secretly build his army and defenses. When Azami died, he felt the treaty died with her and he began invading my upper region by attacking my border villages and outposts and acquiring a great deal of my land."

Completely in awe at Akagi Genda-San's story, Renee found it difficult to comprehend such conflicts occur in other countries of the world, all over an arranged marriage. "That's horrible, Mr. Akagi. What happened next?"

"The only thing I could do. I led my samurai to Kano's region, and conquered it, laying waste and devastation to his lands. They now belong to me."

"And Kano? What happened to him?"

"I had him appear in my presence, in his own home to commit seppuku for his dishonor and the dishonor of his daughter for her marriage under false pretenses."

"Sep, seppu..."

"Seppuku, ritual suicide by disemboweling for one's dishonor."

Bringing her hands to her mouth to hide her gasp, Renee was horrified at the thought of a person cutting open their own stomach because they have done wrong. Lowering her hands, she timidly asked Akagi Genda-San, "May I ask what ever happened to... Yanna?"

Akagi Genda-San smiled at the sound of her name. He turned and looked at Renee. "I took her as my bride soon after and have been happy ever since. You see, Renee-Dono, one should marry for love, not to avert war, or gain business."

He turned his attention back to Reuben, stood, and walked in that direction.

As Renee watched Akagi Genda-San walk away, she said to herself, "If it were only that easy with my father."

Renee remained sitting, deep in thought, about her past and future. Thoughts about the wedding dress and how nice it would look on her standing next to Reuben instead of William

Sinclair. She thought how wonderful it would be to have a wedding under the large oak tree and not in a huge impartial church.

As she thought of the oak tree, she looked up toward it, but Reuben was no longer there, and neither was Akagi Genda-San. She was about to stand when suddenly hands covered her eyes from behind, and a happy familiar voice she had not heard in a very long time since Reuben went away to Mexico said, "Guess who?"

Pulling his hands away, Renee stood and turned to see Reuben looking ever so happy.

"It's you, you little sneak. Please don't tell me Mr. Akagi taught you how to sneak up on people without them knowing? That's just so wrong," she said joyfully and playfully slapped him on his shoulder.

"Hey, why so violent? Aren't you happy to see me?"

Elated, seeing Reuben so happy and playful, Renee could not help but become playful herself.

"Oh, that's nothing you shoddy farm boy!"

"Let's see what you got, Wickham girl!"

"Hey! You're going to pay for that! Stop calling me Wickham girl!" she said as she reached to grab his shoulder, but he quickly turned and disappeared from her view only to be tapped on the back of her head.

"How did you get behind me like that?" she asked, turning to face him.

Reuben leaned forward, gently tapped her nose with his fingertip, the way he did to get her to chase him and said, "Magic."

"I'll show you magic," she called out as she reached to grab his shoulder again but this time, in a graceful sweeping manner and without grabbing her wrist, Reuben used the back of his hand and in a low circle brought her arm downward and back up causing her to bend over forward. He held her in that position for a moment and gently pushed her forward making her roll onto the ground and land on her backside in the soft grass.

Sitting in the grass dumbfounded for a moment, Renee looked back at Reuben as she started rubbing her rear end. "Just what in the heck was that?!" she said to him rather perturbed.

Reuben came and knelt next to her and with a cheerful look, he said as he tweaked her nose, "That's kaiten-nage. Want me to teach you how to do it?"

"YES!" Renee said excitedly as her beautiful, bright, brown eyes opened wide and a huge smile came to her face.

For the rest of the visit, Renee and Reuben were inseparable. They talked, walked, and as young adults, played childhood games with Lucy and Noah just as they did when they were children.

Akagi Genda-San took Renee off to the side to provide her in detail how Reuben's training has been helping him, but pointed out he still had much to learn and a long time before he will be completely content. This had a concerning effect on Renee, but was still happy to see him as he was before Mexico and VMI. He still did not provide Renee an answer to the question she had asked earlier about Reuben being his old self, with no bad memories and dreams of the war.

She could have stayed all day with Reuben if it were not for Aaron who was keeping strict watch of time for her sake. When he informed Renee it was time to start heading back, she wanted to cry, and felt like a child who was being denied her favorite treat. But she knew the deal she made with her father was binding, so she woefully accepted the fact this visit had to come to an end.

As everyone gathered near the carriage, Akagi Genda-San said to Renee, "In a week's time, I must leave to journey back to my country. It would be my most honored and humble request that you, Renee-Dono, accompany this wonderful family to bid me farewell."

The manner in which he made his request was for Renee to understand she must hold her pact with her father true so she would be allowed not only to see Akagi Genda-San off, but to also have another visit with Reuben.

Sensing his meaning, she formally bowed to him as he did when they first met saying, "I'll be there, Mr. Akagi."

Reuben stepped up to Renee and took her hands into his. "I had a great time with you today, Renee."

She wrapped her arms around him saying, "So did I. I don't know when I'll see you again, but just know I always keep you in my thoughts."

"So do I."

With that said, he helped her into the carriage, and as the carriage rode away, Renee and Reuben watched each other until the carriage turned onto the road.

The ride back to the city was quiet, but everyone was cheerful. To see Reuben in his old happy state did everyone good, especially Renee who couldn't see him as often as she wished.

The Durans delivered Renee back to her house and true to her word she was home long before the scheduled formal dress fitting and tea.

Compared to the day she spent with Reuben, the afternoon formal affair was horribly dull and a bore, but Renee played it off as if she was having the time of her life.

It was early in the evening, shortly after dinner, when Renee announced she was retiring for the night. She asked her mother if it would be all right for her to take the mannequin, which was clad with the wedding dress to her room.

"Why would you care to do that?" asked her father before her mother could reply.

"Anticipation, father, anticipation of what I have to look forward to," she answered thinking of how Akagi Genda-San sensed for her to get her way, she had to improvise.

Expressing a gloating smile, he nodded his approval and had a couple of the house servants take the mannequin to her room.

Sitting alone in her room, staring at the dress which she no longer found appealing, she thought to herself she was going to need courage to wear the garment. She retrieved a small sewing basket from her closet, lifted the large hooped skirt, and saw a perfect part underneath the dress no one would notice if it had been cut off.

During the night, Renee cut, snipped, and carefully stitched two pockets into the dress. She stitched a small pocket on the bodice that could fit a button from a VMI cadet's uniform tunic, and a larger pocket hidden in the pleats of the skirt, large enough to hold an image case.

狼

"OPP-ETHE-OYI!" shouted Reuben as he completed all twenty two suburi's for the short staff, known as the jo, flawlessly, a feat that impressed Akagi Genda-San very much.

Akagi Genda-San was amazed at how quickly Reuben picked up his lessons with little or no repetition of instruction. He found Reuben very attentive and eager to learn even if he showed signs of doubt.

"If it can be done, I want to learn how to do it," Reuben said many times, a response Akagi Genda-San found refreshing.

"YAME! Come, Reuben-San, I have a question I wish to ask you."

Reuben switched the jo from his left hand to his right, as instructed by Akagi Genda-San, a sign of non-aggression. He stepped to him and lowered himself to the ground to the seiza position and bowed. Akagi Genda-San nodded approvingly.

"Tell me, Reuben-San, why is it you learn my teachings so quickly?"

Reuben rose with a thoughtful look in his eyes. "Luck I guess."

"Luck you say? Tell me, Reuben-San. Are you a believer in fate?"

"Fate? I never gave it much thought," answered Reuben, intrigued knowing a valuable lesson was about to be taught.

"Ah, fate, Reuben-San, fate is an awesome power filled with irony. Answer me this, Reuben-San, why did you grasp my hand tightly when the door slammed that evening at the ball?"

"Reflex."

"Reflex for what?"

"From gun fire," answered Reuben, embarrassingly.

Akagi Genda-San lowered himself into the seiza position in front of Reuben.

"Ah, as I suspected. If it were not for that door to cause that reflex, I would have never taken notice of you, our meeting on the jetty would not have happened, and your family and Renee-Dono would be grieving your death. However, because of fate, that door caused you to react in such a way a samurai would if he were on eternal alert. An acquired trait you possess. A trait which may have gone unnoticed by others, except for myself who, through the teachings of the Bushido code, saw as a sign of alertness. Because of fate, we are here now having this discussion about fate itself."

"So you have no belief in luck, Genda-San?"

"Luck, Reuben-San, is for those who do not believe in fate, and how often are those people lucky?"

Remembering all the officers in Mexico who trusted in luck and got his platoon killed because of it, Reuben snorted, "Hardly ever."

"Correct, Reuben-San, those who believe in fate, make their own luck. But enough lecture. It is time to begin our training of the relationship between kendo and taijutsu."

Akagi Genda-San rose and took hold of his jo as Reuben did the same.

In an instructive manner, Akagi Genda-San began his lesson. "Kendo is the way of the sword and taijutsu is the practice of hand-to-hand combat with no weapons. Two very different forms of combat, but still closely related."

Inquisitive as ever, Reuben asked, "In what way?"

Carefully laying down his jo, Akagi Genda-San held out his arm. "Take my wrist, Reuben-San, tightly."

Reuben laid down his jo and did as instructed.

In a swift movement, Akagi Genda-San took hold of Reuben's wrist of the hand holding Akagi Genda-San's wrist. He stepped in front of Reuben at an angle twisting Reuben off balance. Akagi Genda-San turned counterclockwise and ducked under Reuben's arm bringing his hand to the back of his shoulder and threw him as if casting a fishing line. Reuben laid flat on his back. He rose with a look of understanding.

"What did you see, Reuben-San?"

"You used my arm as if it were a sword."

"Hai, hai, Reuben-San, what else?"

"Then as you turned, it looked as if you err... cut off my head."

"Excellent, Reuben-San, when it comes to hand-to-hand combat, one must practice as though one has a sword, and when it comes to sword combat, one must practice as though one has no sword. So now, let us practice the four directional throw."

For the next two hours, Akagi Genda-San and Reuben trained in the four directional throw in various holds and attacks. As with Akagi Genda-San's other lessons, Reuben soon became proficient in this technique even going as far as learning how to reverse himself out of the technique.

As they were taking turns throwing one another from the technique, Renee and Lucy quietly made their way to where the two were training. Both girls were in awe watching the two as they threw each other and quickly rose for another turn.

They stopped and lowered themselves to the ground and continued to watch.

"I wish Mama would let me learn some of that stuff Mr. Akagi is teaching Reuben," said Lucy.

Renee didn't respond. Her focus was on Reuben. She could not take her eyes off him and was amazed at how he could move and use his body in such ways Akagi Genda-San was teaching. She began to vision Reuben taking hold of her in such swift gentle turns in his arms.

"Gosh, Renee, if your mouth opens any wider, your brain is going to fall out," said Lucy, following by making kissing noises.

"Shut up, Lucy!"

"Renee and Reuben sitting in the oak tree..." sang Lucy as she rose and started running from Renee who was giving chase.

"Better not let me catch you, you brat!"

Lucy ran up to and behind Reuben using him as a shield from Renee's grasps completely surprising Akagi Genda-San and Reuben.

Akagi Genda-San began laughing hard at the two girls chasing each other while Reuben was caught in the middle.

"It looks like you have a visitor, Reuben-San. What do you say we stop training for now so you can have a pleasant visit? I am going to see if May-Dono will make me some of her wonderful dumplings."

He turned and made his way to the house as he continued laughing at Reuben's predicament.

Eventually Reuben joined in on the chasing game with Renee and Lucy. It wasn't long before Reuben was the one being chased and tackled by Renee, falling to the ground and rolling down a slope laughing. When they reached the bottom, they continued to lay on the ground in each other's arms.

"Yuck, if you two are going to start playing lovey dovey, then I'm going to see if Mr. Akagi will teach me something!" called out Lucy at the top of the slope.

Reuben began to get up to run after his sister, but was held back by Renee as she was laughing.

"Stay here, Reuben, and tell me what you and Mr. Akagi have been doing," she said.

Reuben sat next to her. "You're wearing the dress from your picture. That's my favorite."

"I've kept it at your house in the city after I had that picture taken. I changed before we left the house. I knew we would end up goofing around. That was fun. We haven't done that in years."

"You don't think we're too old for such shenanigans, do you?" asked Reuben, laughing.

"Never too old for shenanigans," answered Renee.

"Too bad Monroe missed out. Where is he and Da?"

"Da... I mean your dad had lots of work at his office and Monroe went to help, thinking it would be helpful for his upcoming law exams."

"I can't believe he's going to be an attorney like Da," he said, impressed and proud of his brother.

"Yeah, so what were you and Mr. Akagi doing when Lucy and I came?"

For the next half hour, Renee and Reuben talked about what he and Akagi Genda-San had been doing for the past few days since Renee's last visit. She was impressed on how much Reuben regained of his old self. He was happier and more relaxed. He even tried to ask her about the upcoming wedding, but not wanting to discuss it, she changed the topic by asking him about his plans of becoming a teacher.

"Yes, I still want to be a teacher like Mama. She's the best."

"That she is. There was no teacher at Wickham that came close to her. When do you think you might start looking into getting a teaching certificate?"

Reuben didn't answer, but had a hundred acre look in his face.

"I'm sorry, Reuben, I didn't mean to…"

"No, Renee, don't be sorry. I could use a kick in the ass to get me in line and who else better to kick me than you," he said smiling at her.

He cupped her face with his hand and continued, "Let's just see how things go when Genda-San leaves."

"I suppose you're right. But in the meantime, will you teach me something Mr. Akagi has taught you?"

With a huge smile on his face, Reuben rose and assisted Renee to her feet and said, "Are you serious?"

"Yes."

"Great! Grab my wrist."

狼

After another thirty minutes, Lucy came to fetch Renee and Reuben for lunch. As they entered the house through the kitchen door and made their way to the dining room, everyone began laughing including Akagi Genda-San.

"What's so funny," asked Renee.

"Look at you two. You look like two children who have been playing at recess for far too long," answered Coleen.

More laugher ensued at Renee and Reuben's expense, including their own after they took the time to look at each other.

"I have not seen you two that messy since we last played at the creek when we were growing up," said Noah.

"Why didn't you come and join us," asked Renee as both she and Reuben started taking sips of lemonade Lucy had just poured.

"Well, the type of 'games' you two were playing, I don't think I would have been invited to join in on, if you catch my meaning," replied Noah.

Both Renee and Reuben spit out mouths full of lemonade and turned beet red at Noah's response as more laughter followed.

For the rest of the day Akagi Genda-San entertained everyone with more stories of his homeland as he did during the last visits and as midafternoon came along, it was time for Coleen and Lucy to take Renee back home. Before leaving, Coleen helped Renee transform her back into Franklin and Margret Wallace's image of the perfect daughter.

When Coleen finished pinning Renee's hair back up, she took her face into her hands and said, "There, sweetheart, your parents will never know the shenanigans you got into today."

Renee took Coleen into her arms and held her as a daughter would hold her mother. "Thank you, Mrs. Duran. Thank you very much," she said with a hint of a whimper.

Coleen returned Renee's hug and rocked her saying, "That's all right, my dear. Anytime, and I do mean anytime."

Once Coleen, Renee, and Lucy were onboard the carriage and goodbyes were said, they were off and as usual, Renee and Reuben watched each other until the carriage turned onto the road.

Akagi Genda-San came up and placed his arm around Reuben's shoulders. Reuben looked at him and asked, "Stones and water, Genda-San?"

Akagi Genda-San let out a hardy laugh, slapped Reuben on the back and said joyfully, "Come, Reuben-San, we still have many hours of daylight for training."

That would be the last visit Renee would make to the farm before Akagi Genda-San would depart back to his homeland.

狼

The day for Akagi Genda-San to depart finally arrived. The day before, after one last training session lasting nearly the entire day, Reuben, Akagi Genda-San, May, and Noah rode to the city house where a great meal was prepared by Coleen, Lucy, and Renee all supervised by May. After the meal, everyone reflected on the past two weeks Akagi Genda-San spent with Reuben instead of his original plans of touring Washington, and then to Baltimore where he would depart for home by way around South America and San Francisco.

Aaron and Coleen took Akagi Genda-San aside to express their sincere appreciation for his sacrifice to spend all this time with their son.

"It is entirely my honor to have spent this rewarding time with Reuben-San. I do not intend to speak disrespectful toward your culture and rich history, but in my travels within your country, it is your son who has provided me with hope true honor, which exists in my land, exists in yours. For that, I felt compelled and honor bound to stay, and nurture what little he displayed so he could grow into becoming a most wonderful man you desire in a son who has had more than his share of hardship."

The next morning, a hired coach containing the Duran family along with May, Noah, and their guest, Akagi Genda-San, rode to Renee's house. Upon arrival, Renee was waiting outside with her father standing behind her like a stone guardian. He was also intrigued to see this foreigner his daughter admired as a great man of wisdom.

The coach came to a stop and the door was opened by Reuben who stepped off followed by Aaron.

"A very good morning to you, Franklin. Thank you very much for allowing Renee to accompany us to the train station with Mr. Akagi," Aaron said very cordially.

"Good morning, Duran. It is nice to see you. Where is this visitor my daughter has told me about? I would like to meet him," said Franklin Wallace both in an interested and mocking manner.

"I am Genda Akagi. I am most honored to make your acquaintance, Mr. Wallace," said Akagi Genda-San who appeared next to Franklin Wallace without his knowledge.

Franklin Wallace stepped to the side startled as Renee suppressed a smile. "He does that all the time father."

Looking at his daughter and then to Akagi Genda-San, he nodded in greeting.

Akagi Genda-San formally bowed in greeting and offered his hand. Upon taking his offered hand in his, Franklin Wallace immediately felt a warm radiating pulse come from Akagi Genda-San's hand.

"It is an honor to meet the father of such a well-mannered and delightfully intelligent daughter. You no doubt have excellent skills, not only in business, but in raising such a wonderful person as Renee-Dono. You are to be commended."

Completely taken off his guard, Akagi Genda-San made Franklin Wallace speechless. Never had he been so complemented before. Renee was amused at how Akagi Genda-San stymied her father.

Akagi Genda-San continued. "Renee-Dono has described your successful business and it is with sincere wishes and hopes that in time, my country's ocean boarders will open to western trade, and your vessels will be amongst the first."

"Why, thank you. Thank you very much, Mr. ah…"

"It is my pleasure and I must also thank you for allowing Renee-Dono to come and bid me farewell on my journey back home. She has been a delight to visit with and learn from."

"Oh, say no more, Mr. ah… it is all my pleasure," said Franklin Wallace with much enthusiasm seeing the possible future business opportunities. "Are you sure you cannot stay longer? We must discuss a future business portfolio."

"As much intriguing as that sounds, I am afraid I must return to my provincial region. My regional lands have been without its Daimyo for far too long."

"Da… pardon me?" asked Franklin Wallace, questionably.

"Daimyo, father, Mr. Akagi is a regional lord in his province, what we would call our state governor," said Renee very proudly.

Franklin Wallace's eyes widened and his demeanor became humbled. "Indeed, oh my, well in that case, come Renee, we must not keep, Mr. ah, eh… this very distinguished gentleman from his travels. Here, let me help you," said Franklin Wallace as he delicately assisted Renee onto the coach.

The rest of the group, including the coachman who was acquainted with Franklin Wallace, was amazed. As Renee boarded the coach, she looked to Akagi Genda-San. With his hands together in front of his chest as if praying, he bowed his head to her, raised it, and winked. Renee had to again hide a giggle.

The ride to the depot was pleasant. Reuben pointed out points of interest to Akagi Genda-San who never actually had a chance to tour the city. They rode by the school where Coleen taught her children and Renee, Aaron's law office, and what Renee referred to as her personal prison, Wickham Finishing School for Girls.

When they arrived at the depot, Reuben and Monroe carried Akagi Genda-San's baggage to be checked in.

May and Noah said their farewells at the coach since it was prohibited for persons of color be permitted entrance into the depot.

"Mr. Akagi, I have made you something for your journey, just in case you have the hungers."

May presented him with a red checkered sack.

Akagi Genda-San opened the sack and his eyes widened with delight. "Ah, May-Dono, you honor me with your glorious dumplings. I shall make these last as long as I possibly can." Accepting the dumplings, he formally bowed to her causing her to feel proud and very happy.

"And you, Noah-San, you must try to assist Reuben-San in his training. Perhaps too, you may be good enough to be called upon to be his obedient retainer."

"Retainer, Mr. Akagi, What's that?" asked Noah.

"His attendant and loyal bodyguard. I foresee he will be in need of one in the distant future."

The Duran family entered the depot with Akagi Genda-San, Renee, and Reuben following behind. Lucy became inquisitive of the train schedules and Monroe went to assist her on how to read them. Aaron and Coleen also went to the schedule boards discussing plans on taking a train ride to Richmond for a visit.

Reuben strolled off by himself onto the platform. He was staring in the direction the train had taken him away to the Virginia Military Institute several years prior.

"Hello, Genda-San," he said without looking back to see Akagi Genda-San approach.

"Looking through windows of the past, Reuben-San?"

"It was in that direction where my nightmares began. It's where my time ended," said Reuben as he looked at the watch his parents had given him the day he boarded that train.

He turned to face Akagi Genda-San, and with watery eyes he said, "Genda-San, I have two special treasures in my life. One is a picture of Renee I will never part with, and the other is this pocket watch my parents gave me when I left to VMI. When I came back from Mexico, I had no need for time anymore. I dearly treasure the time you have spent with me. Perhaps someday I will accept your challenge, but for now, I wish to give you this watch to show my everlasting gratitude."

Akagi Genda-San looked at the watch being presented to him. He was moved far beyond he had ever expected. "Reuben-San, I cannot accept such a valuable gift. It is far to meaning to you to be giving it away."

Trying to hold back his emotions, Reuben replied, "I don't consider it, 'giving it away,' Genda-San. I consider it a token of my friendship to you and for the enlightenment you have shown me."

He held it in both hands as if he were presenting a jo for training, and formally bowed just as Akagi Genda-San did the first time they met. Akagi Genda-San took the watch from Reuben's hands and returned the formal bow.

"Domo Arigato Gozaimashita, Reuben-San, you have so honored me. I will treasure this gift for as long as Itosai stands as a sovereign region under my rule." He rose, took Reuben into his arms, and embraced him tightly.

Renee had been standing watching their exchange at a distance. When she saw Akagi Genda-San take Reuben into his arms, she came forward and placed her hand gently on Reuben's shoulder. It startled him and he released his embrace and looked down.

Using his sleeve to wipe his eyes, he walked toward the inside of the station. "Please excuse me, I got train soot in my eyes, I'll be back." he said desperately hiding his emotional state.

Renee was about to follow, but Akagi Genda-San held her back. "Give Reuben-San some time to gather himself, Renee-Dono. He has just opened himself, making him most vulnerable and I suspect he does not wish you to see him in this state. He will be back soon with joy in his face."

Renee took this opportunity to ask Akagi Genda-San a question she asked before, but never received a definite answer. "Mr. Akagi, you never did answer me. Will Reuben be his old self again, with no bad memories and dreams of the war?"

Akagi Genda-San stood admiring the watch Reuben gave him. He accepted it as a symbolic gesture of Reuben's friendship.

"I wonder if even the Emperor himself has a watch such as this. I am most fortunate to have received this gift. It is truly a gift from the heart is it not, Renee-Dono?" he asked not requiring an answer.

Renee became confused. Did he not hear my question, she wondered. She was about to ask again just as Akagi Genda-San began to speak.

"You see, Renee-Dono, gifts from the heart are the most precious. Love is one such gift. Ah, love, now that is a puzzling gift. It can be the most joyful gift one can ever receive. Or it can be the most painful."

Akagi Genda-San placed the watch in his vest pocket, turned his attention to Renee, and offered her a seat on the platform bench. They both took a seat. Renee didn't know Akagi Genda-San well at all, but she did know from her infrequent visits with him, he spoke in a very philosophical manner, very deep in meaning, much like her poetry. He may lecture on about something, but it will be moments, or even days later until one would realize he provided one with the most enlightening conversation one has ever had. She began to listen closely.

"Reuben-San has received that gift of love from his family, the gift of joy. He has also received it from someone else. You, Renee-Dono, and to him, that gift of love is the most meaningful."

"And the most painful," said Renee looking down.

Akagi Genda-San placed his arm around Renee's shoulder and gently squeezed. She raised her head and looked at his hand. She felt it radiating with energy. It was amazing. She turned to face Akagi Genda-San.

He removed his arm from her shoulder and picked up his personal travel bag. He opened it and pulled out an object. He looked at Renee and with a most charming look, he said, "I have a gift for you, Renee-Dono, a gift from my heart, if you will. Please, hold out your hand."

Renee did as she was asked and Akagi Genda-San placed a very smooth stone which fit perfectly in the palm of her hand. She looked at it oddly.

"A stone?" she asked, sounding very puzzled.

"This is no ordinary stone, Renee-Dono. This too is a clock, or rather, it is time itself. I give you the gift of time, time Reuben-San needs desperately."

Pointing to the stones on the rail bed, he began to explain, "Look at those stones on the ground. See how rough and jagged they are?"

She nodded knowing the answer to her question is somehow in this explanation.

He brought his hands together as though he were praying. "If you take one of those stones and toss it into the water, the water will make that jagged stone smooth, smooth, just as the one in your hand which used to be just as jagged. But it will take time."

Renee looked at the smooth stone Akagi Genda-San placed in her hand. She brought up her other hand and began to cradle the stone as if it suddenly became a precious gem.

"Reuben-San is a jagged stone, Renee-Dono, and you are his water. You must flow over him as the water flows over stones, and use the gift of time I give you so he too will become smooth. If you do not flow, he will never be the Reuben-San you knew... and love. He will continue to use his memories of war against his love for you. You cannot allow him to do so. Reuben-San is a warrior of good, not a warrior of hate. Only the good warrior will come from you, Renee-Dono, but it will take time."

"I'll do anything to make Reuben the same as he was, Mr. Akagi," said Renee in a pleading manner.

Akagi Genda-San closed his eyes and breathed in slowly. He opened them and turned to face Renee. "Unbeknownst to his family, and until now, you, I offered Reuben-San a challenge he must decide on his own if he is worthy to accept. I challenged him to seek me out to continue his growth in the ways of Bushido. That is if he is serious in his quest to achieve true victory not only for himself, but for you as well, Renee-Dono."

He placed his hand over the smooth stone in Renee's hands and looked down on it. "He is willing and wants to accept this challenge to smooth his jagged edges, but to do so, water must allow him to go and tumble in its waves to become smooth. There will be a time, very soon, my young Renee-Dono, when you will have to be strong. Stronger than Reuben-San himself. It is then when you must sacrifice most of what you have for both of you to achieve victory. It is only you that can wash away the jagged edges of his stone. In doing so, then and only then, will he become well, and then both of you will achieve your own self victories.

"Why can't he leave with you now, Mr. Akagi?" she asked.

"Why indeed. If he were to leave with me now, he would be doing so for the wrong reasons, and you and he will not bond as love and fate intends. This is the moment in your young lives where you both must make that decisive sacrifice together. You see, my young precious Renee-Dono, there is a time and place for you and Reuben-San. Stones and water, Renee-Dono, stones and water."

Renee looked upon the stone with heartfelt sorrow and also, faith and love. Instead of seeing a puzzling gift as before, she now saw a vision of love. Next to Reuben's image case and his button, the stone now became one of her favored treasures.

石
水

In the year of our Lord, 1847, a romantic tale continues.
Plans, schemes, and sacrifices...

Let Us Be One Under Our Tree

The days following Akagi Genda-San's departure, life in the Duran home and farm returned back to normal. Reuben stayed at the city house for several days. During that time, he and Renee were able to have several short visits. The first couple were pleasant, but the next few were awkward. Renee found Reuben to be somewhat confused and his joyful demeanor was dissipating. When she came by the house one week after Akagi Genda-San left, Reuben was no longer at the house. He returned to the farm with no spoken word, except for a note left on the mantle in the parlor that read...

> *Dear all,*
> *I have gone back to the farm.*
> *Reuben*

Renee began to fear what Akagi Genda-San warned her about on the station platform. There was no doubt in her mind she had to see Reuben to make sure he was all right, so she spent the next few days at her house being cooperative with her parents. This indeed had the desired effect Renee hoped for because her father allowed her a full day to herself. She asked and was granted permission to visit with the Durans for the entire day.

She walked to the Duran home early in the morning. She stepped up to the front door and knocked. As usual, Monroe answered the door.

"Oh, it's you. Come in," he said, plainly.

"Well, hello to you too, Monroe. Wake up on the wrong side of the morning today?"

"I'm sorry, Renee. Please come in. It's Reuben."

"Is he okay? What's wrong?"

"He's going back to his melancholic ways, I'm afraid," answered Coleen coming to greet Renee.

"I'm on my way back to the farm if you have time to come along."

Renee brightened up saying, "Of course, gladly."

A week and a few days after Akagi Genda-San departed, Reuben found himself back on the farm feeling lost. Trying hard as possible, he could not replicate the same effects of the training Akagi Genda-San taught him. It was as if one who had been drinking liquor their entire life suddenly stopped. Reuben had no outlet, no guidance, and no help. He was all alone once again and began to see the blood of the past return to the palms of his hands, and the limp body of Adam Stanns lay across his lap every time he sat.

Every little thing seemed to make him angry and he would take out his frustrations on Henry, Noah, and even May. That itself caused him even more anger, so rather than cause them any emotional trauma, he would spend all his time under the oak tree by the creek doing his best to practice the katas Akagi Genda-San taught him, but to no effect.

On this one particular day when Renee came with Coleen to visit, she found Reuben lying on the ground under the oak tree, asleep but twitching. He was talking in his restless sleep, calling out orders.

"Mr. Evans, tell the boys to fall back... fall back! There's too much fire! We can't stay here any longer! Adam, for god sakes keep your head down..."

Not knowing what to do, Renee kneeled down and took hold of Reuben gently by the shoulder and shook him.

"Reuben, wake up. It's me, Renee."

She shook a little harder causing Reuben to wake. He roughly pushed her away as he rolled in the opposite direction. The look on his face terrified her. She had never seen him look so angry.

"You! What are you doing here!" shouted Reuben harshly, causing birds to fly off startled. Besides the day Reuben came home from Fort Monroe when he bluntly said no when Renee asked Reuben to dance, he had never raised his voice in anger toward Renee like this.

"Please, Reuben. Come sit and talk with me."

"About what? What's so damned important you had to come all this way to talk to me about?"

Renee began sobbing. It was horrible to see Reuben like this, but she didn't give up. She rose and took a few steps toward him holding out her hand. He slapped it away.

"Damn it, Renee, why do you keep tormenting me? Why do you keep me hanging on a rope? Just tie it into a noose, string it around my neck, and yank? I don't belong to you. I never will."

Reuben took hold of her wrist and started walking toward the house pulling her along.

"Please, Reuben, stop!" she cried as she struggled to free herself.

Reuben kept walking at a quick pace causing Renee to trip and stumble behind him. When they arrived at the house, Reuben's mother came out after seeing him pulling Renee along. May and the others stayed inside the house watching through the window.

"Mama, take Renee home and never bring her back again!" he shouted.

"Reuben, please stop and listen," pleaded Renee.

"No, you listen! You don't belong to me! You belong to William Sinclair! You're better off with him! I'm broken, damn it, can't you see that?! Go to your William, get married, and have lots of children. Forget about me Renee. It's for your own good!"

Reuben turned and walked off toward the oak tree, not looking back.

Coleen quickly took hold of Renee, who was now crying uncontrollably and was about to follow after him. Holding her in a motherly fashion, Coleen held Renee close as Renee held on tightly in return.

May and the others came out to help console Renee.

"May, Henry, Noah, perhaps you should go stay at the Wilcox's while Reuben is in this state."

"No, Mrs. Duran," answered Noah. "Even though he may want to be alone, I think it's best we stay. It might keep him from feeling lonely."

"Perhaps you're right, Noah," said Coleen. She led Renee to the carriage.

As they rode back into the city, they were both quiet. Tears were still coming down from Renee's eyes and Coleen had her sit close.

Nearing the city limits, Coleen finally spoke, "Renee, I know my Reuben didn't mean any of those things he said. I think he's trying to make you hate him so you can be happier when you get married next week."

"I could never hate Reuben, Mrs. Duran, and do you know why?"

"Why is that, my dear?"

"Because I have never forgotten what you told me when you first read one of my poems, never give up faith and love. Mr. Akagi kind of told me the same thing before he left. And also, I could never hate Reuben because… I love him."

"And I know he loves you."

Mentioning Akagi Genda-San caused Renee to have a fascinating idea come to mind. She sat up straight, wiped her face with her hands, and began to compose herself back into the so called perfect daughter of a successful Southern aristocratic business man.

"Please, Mrs. Duran, instead of taking me to my house, can you please drop me off at one of my father's wharves?"

"Why sure my dear, but whatever for?" asked Coleen.

Not wanting to lie to one of the two people who ever treated her like a true daughter, Renee answered, "A couple of weeks ago, one of my father's ocean steamers came home and I would like to visit with the ship's master, James Forrest. I want to ask him some questions Mr. Akagi told me about the ocean. Plus, I don't want to go to my house and face my parents yet." Not exactly a lie, and not exactly the truth either, but Coleen agreed.

After Coleen left Renee at the wharf where the *Morning Star* was tied up, she called upon James Forrest, who was extremely happy to see her. He and Renee's father sailed together in their younger years on wind driven schooners delivering goods up and down the coast. They had become good friends in those days and when Franklin Wallace started his own shipping company, James Forrest was his first ship's master. After the birth of Renee, Franklin Wallace asked James Forrest to become her Godfather. However, as years progressed, their friendship became that as an employer and employee, with the exception of Renee with whom James Forest always maintained his Godfather position. To Renee, next to Reuben, his father, and Martin

Doogan, James Forrest was the only other man she could trust. For the rest of that day and the next, both Renee and James Forrest visited and discussed ocean travel.

狼

It was late in the evening. Earlier that day, Renee had another productive visit with her Godfather and master of the *Morning Star*, James Forrest. Renee snuck out of her house, and using the carriage Aaron kept in the stable, she rode to the Duran farm. It had been a couple of days since she last seen Reuben. During that visit, Reuben had gotten worse. It had been almost three weeks since Akagi Genda-San departed back to his homeland. Try as hard as he could, Reuben could not capture the true essence of Akagi Genda-San's teachings, thus causing frustrations and the return of his memories and night terrors. The fact Renee's wedding was almost a week away also caused him emotional trauma.

It was also during that last visit Reuben raised his voice in anger to Renee for the first time in that type of manner. With his war memories and Renee's wedding both playing havoc in his mind, he ranted at her to leave him alone. Angrily he told her she was better off with William Sinclair because he could offer her a stable life. Reuben practically ordered Renee, in a way an Army officer would order a private, she was to forget about him. There was no stopping Reuben's rage.

Renee was heartbroken to see him like this. So much so, Coleen took her away and did her best to console her. Renee wanted to see Reuben well. She remembered what Coleen had told her many years ago, never give up faith and love. And she also remembered what Akagi Genda-San said about both her and Reuben making that decisive sacrifice together for him to find his personal victory that will serve as hers as well. It was this faith and love, and decisive sacrifice that gave Renee an idea she hoped Reuben would accept.

She arrived at the farm a little after nine. The sound of the carriage attracted May's attention and she went outside to meet Renee.

"Miss Renee! God almighty, it's late. What in the world are you doing here?"

"Please, Miss May, I need to speak to Reuben. It's very important. About something Mr. Akagi said to me. He hasn't gone off to bed yet, has he?"

"Why no, child. Actually, he took a stroll down to the creek, to, as he said, *'pay for dishonor?'* whatever that means. I think he just wanted to clear his head like he has been doing every night since that Mr. Akagi man left."

Renee took what May said very curiously. It didn't make sense, but there was something that sounded familiar about it.

"Do you mind if I go find him?"

"Not at all, child. If fact, if you can get him to come back in to get some sleep, I would appreciate it. He's been working very hard these past several days and I think it's getting to him. It worries me."

"Thank you, Miss May, I'll tell him," said Renee as she was making her way around the house toward the creek. She knew he would be sitting under the oak tree, so she headed in that direction thinking of what May said.

"Pay for dishonor," Renee said to herself. She wondered what that meant. "And where did I hear something like that before?"

Suddenly she stopped as horror overcame her when she remembered what Akagi Genda-San told her about the suicide ritual called seppuku.

"Geez oh geez oh geez Reuben, no!" she exclaimed, and began running to the tree.

She was nearing the tree and saw Reuben in the moonlight sitting in the position Akagi Genda-San called seiza. She slowed down her pace until she saw Reuben raise a knife in front of his abdomen. At full speed, she sprinted and shouted "NO, REUBEN!" as he was making a downward motion.

She leaped and tackled Reuben to the ground just as the knife was about to enter his stomach. The tackle caused Reuben to drop the knife. Renee rolled over and saw the knife next to him. She reached, grasped it, and with all her strength, threw it toward the creek. A few seconds later, a splash was heard.

Reuben lay face down on the ground sobbing and pounding his fist in the grass.

"Why, why, why, why did you stop me?! Can't you see this is the only way?"

Renee crawled to Reuben, forced him onto his back, grabbed his shirt with both hands, and raised him into a seated position.

He desperately tried to look away, ashamed. He began to push at Renee, trying to break free from her grip, but she held on tight.

"Never scare me like that ever again, do you hear me, Reuben Duran!" she cried in anger, the first time she raised her voice in anger toward Reuben. She wrapped her arms around him and pulled him tight into her. Reuben just sat there, his arms hanging limp.

Silent sobs came from Reuben and again he asked, "Why did you stop me?"

"Because... I love you."

"But we cannot be. We can never be and even if we can, my mind is broken and I'll never be the same. I still see Adam's dead limp body laying across my lap every time I sit. That's why I always stand. Every time I look at my hands, I see blood from the dead I couldn't protect. That's why I can't bring myself to touch you."

Reuben dropped his head onto her shoulder. He silently sobbed in her arms, and she ran her fingers through his hair as she began to speak softly.

"You're right, Reuben. We cannot be, at least not now. Timing is wrong for both of us. But what we do need now is time. We need lots of it, especially you. It breaks my heart to see you like this and to watch you almost take your own life.... Oh geez, Reuben, can you even imagine what you would be putting me through if I wasn't here to stop you?"

With his head still resting on her shoulder, Reuben sighed heavily. She was right and he knew it. Renee was always right.

"I'm so sorry, Renee. I'm sorry for being awful to you the last time you were here. I'm sorry for this evening. But I hurt for myself, I hurt for you, and I hurt for us. I can't see how I can go on without you."

Reaching deep within, searching for as much strength she can summon, Renee closed her eyes tightly and said, "I know how you can go on without me, Reuben. You must... go away."

Lifting his head from her shoulder, he looked upon her with amazement. He saw her eyes closed tight, fighting back tears.

"What do you mean, I *'must go away'*?"

Without opening her eyes, she placed her head on his shoulder this time and replied, "You must take time to get better and the only way you can do that is to go... go away after Mr. Akagi. He told me about his challenge to you. You must accept his challenge and follow him, for both our sakes."

Feeling as though an icicle had been thrust into his heart, he said as if stating a fact, "You really mean that."

With confusion running though his mind, he stood, leaving Renee sitting on the ground. He paced several steps thinking of what she said. *"Go away after Mr. Akagi."*

Again Renee was right, but how could she so easily say that? Reuben looked down at her. Renee was now crying with her face in her hands. He came and knelt down in front of her. At first, he was about to question how she could say such a thing, but the closer he looked upon her, he realized it wasn't easy at all for her to tell him he must go away. Rather than question her reasoning, he moved away her hands and raised her face. Renee's eyes opened releasing tears down her cheeks. Her beautiful, marvelous eyes, the eyes Reuben could stare into for the rest of his life. Looking into Renee's eyes, he said, "I love you too."

They both stood up, and Renee took Reuben into her arms and replied as she rested her head on his shoulder, "I love you so much, I have to let you go to become... smooth."

Under the oak tree, the tree where they became friends, they held on to each other in silence for several moments. They didn't want it to end.

Reuben finally broke the silence, "How? How in the world am I supposed to go find Genda-San? He's on his way somewhere on the other side of the world. I know you mean well, but it's impossible, Renee, impossible."

Renee lifted her head from Reuben's shoulder. Her eyes brightened up as she placed her hand softly on his face and said, "I know someone who can help *us*."

Reuben had a look of deep curiosity, placed his hand over hers and asked, "Who?"

Renee gave an impish smile and answered, "My father... and he'll never know he helped us."

狼

For the next half hour, Renee told Reuben about her visits with the master of the *Morning Star*, James Forrest, and her idea of him helping Reuben to journey to Japan to seek out Akagi Genda-San.

Reuben listened intently and was in complete awe with her idea. "You mean to tell me, this Mr. Forrest will take me to Japan?" he asked very interested.

"Well, no, or maybe. Even he doesn't know for sure, but what he does know is next Friday, his vessel sails to San Francisco, where Mr. Akagi went to continue on to Japan. When

Mr. Forrest gets you to San Francisco, he will help you find another vessel to take you the rest of the way."

"What's the, *'maybe'*?"

"If Mr. Forrest cannot find you a ship to take you the rest of the way, he will do it himself."

Reuben paced around the trunk of the oak tree deep in thought. "Why will this Mr. Forrest do this for me... *us*?" he asked, coming to a stop in front of Renee.

"Next to you, your father, and Mr. Doogan, he's the only other man I trust."

"That doesn't answer the why," said Reuben, looking very sternly at Renee.

"Mr. Forrest is my Godfather."

"Come on, that can't be the only reason."

"Okay, he hates my father! Almost everyone hates my father, you know that. And I'm using that to our advantage," she said as she took hold of his shirt roughly with both hands.

"All right, all right, calm down. Why does he hate your father, and why haven't you mentioned him before?"

She released her hold on Reuben's shirt and took his hands. "I've never mentioned him because he spends most of his time at sea. As for him hating my father, I'm not certain, but it has something to do with the way he treats his ship's crews, and also my wedding arrangement. Being my Godfather, he was upset he wasn't involved in that decision which he should have been and if he had, I probably wouldn't be getting married."

Reuben's eyes widened as Renee mentioned her getting married.

"What is it, Reuben?"

"You realize, the day the ship leaves is the day you get married, right?"

The moment he mentioned that, her hands gripped his tighter. For both their sakes, she did what she could to distract that topic by saying, "That's right, so we have less than a week to get the details settled."

The distraction worked as Reuben looked up to the sky and noticed the position of the moon.

"It's very late. I better get you back home. We can discuss this further on the way," he said as he took her by the hand and began walking to the house quickly.

As the two entered the house through the kitchen door, May was seated at the table. She was a bit startled because she didn't know in what state Reuben would be in. However, when she saw him, he was cheerful for the first time since before Akagi Genda-San left.

Reuben took May by the hands and said, "I'm taking Renee back home. She shouldn't be on the roads at night by herself. I'll be staying in the city for a few of days."

He took her into his arms. "I'm very sorry for my behavior, Aunty May. I hope you can forgive me."

Reuben never called her that before and it touched her deeply. Returning his embrace, she answered, "There's nothing to forgive, boy. I know what you're going through isn't personal toward any of us. Now go and get Renee back home before her father realizes she's missing."

He kissed May on the cheek, took hold of Renee's hand, and led her to the carriage. As they rode back to the city, Renee sat very close to Reuben with her arms wrapped around his waist. They both discussed all the details and plans on how to get Reuben to Japan. One thing they both had to agree on is all these schemes needed to be kept secret from Reuben's family, and especially Franklin Wallace, the one who was providing the initial transportation for Reuben's journey.

Reuben brought the carriage to a stop a few streets away from Renee's house, and from there he walked her the rest of the way home. They reached the alley gate leading to the large backyard of the Wallace's house. From there, she could scale the ivy covered rails to the terrace below the balcony of her room located on the far side of the house, opposite her parent's room. Even if she made any noise, it would go unheard.

Just before Renee was about to make her assent up the rail, she said, "Okay, what time will you meet me and Mr. Forrest at the wharf?"

"9 o'clock."

"Right, I'll tell my parents I'm going to meet some girls for breakfast to invite them to the wedding. Will you have any troubles getting into your house?"

"No, I have a key. Everyone should be asleep by now so I'll just sleep in the parlor. I'll try to be out of the house before everyone wakes up. But if not, I'll just be my pleasant self and excuse myself for a morning walk."

Renee chuckled, "You're anything but pleasant, Reuben Duran."

"And you, Renee Wallace, with all your secret planning, scheming, and sneaking around, are starting to remind me of your father," replied Reuben with a grin.

Renee sternly said, "You need to take that back right now."

"Ouch, struck a nerve, did I?"

"You think?"

"Okay, okay, I take it back. Now get inside and I'll see you tomorrow."

Reuben began to walk backwards toward the alley gate as he watched Renee begin climbing the rails. She stopped for a moment and looked back at Reuben. She jumped down and ran to Reuben, wrapped her arms around him, kissed his lips, and went back to climb the rails to her room. Once safely inside, Reuben turned and ran back to the carriage.

After Reuben saw to the carriage and team at the stable, he went to his house. It was well after midnight and the house was dark and quiet. He unlocked the door and silently made his way through the house and into the parlor. He retrieved a blanket from the sofa, removed his shoes, and laid back.

He lay on his back staring at the ceiling, thinking of Renee's idea and plans. He couldn't believe she would go through so much just so he could put all his horrors to rest. She had much to lose if her father found out what she was up to, all for him. Little did Reuben know, Renee was doing it for both of them.

Eventually his eyes felt heavy, and he fell asleep. For the first time since Akagi Genda-San left, he didn't dream.

狼

"Reuben is home, Reuben is home!" called out Lucy as she saw him sleeping in the parlor. Her call startled Reuben awake causing him to fall off the sofa and onto the floor.

Lucy ran and kneeled next to her brother and gave him a hug. "What are you doing here? When did you get home?" she asked.

Before he could answer, Aaron and Coleen entered the parlor.

"Lucy, help your brother off the floor. Good heavens, son, it's great to see you," said Coleen, pushing Lucy aside and taking Reuben into her arms.

"Isn't anyone going to help me up?"

"Of course, come, let me help you," said Aaron as he offered his hand to Reuben and assisted him to his feet. He then took him into his arms and held him tightly saying, "It's good to see you, my boy. How are you feeling?"

Reuben stepped back from his father's arms and began to wipe the sleep from his face as he answered. "Renee came by the farm last evening to visit."

Coleen took hold of Reuben's hands and moved them away from his face and in a concerned manner asked, "Renee... oh my, is everything all right..."

Before she could finish, he smiled and nodded saying, "Everything is fine between us, Mama. She was just worried about me, that's all. We talked. I apologized for my horrible behavior toward her and she forgave me. Yes, Mama, we are still best friends."

"Oh thank heavens," said Coleen.

"Since it was dark, I didn't want her to travel the roads alone, so I escorted her home," Reuben continued. "It was after midnight when I got here so I let myself in and slept in here so as not to cause a scare, especially with Lucy."

"Hey, I don't scare easily," commented Lucy.

Aaron smiled and patted Reuben on the shoulder. "Good son. That's mighty good of you to see her safely home. I'm assuming you quietly escorted her home? No doubt she went to visit you without her parent's permission."

"Of course," replied Reuben as he chuckled.

It had been a while since Reuben's family heard any type of laughter come from him and it brought joy to everyone to hear.

Reuben again began to rub his eyes awake and continued to say, "I was wondering, would it be all right if I stay here for a while, for a change of scenery?"

Lucy hopped a couple of times out of sheer joy. Coleen brought her hands to her mouth as she let out a gasp of joy herself, and Aaron placed his arm around Reuben's shoulder.

"Of course you can, my boy! Of course you can! This is still your home," said Aaron. "Monroe is back off to school so it will only be you in your old room."

"That's okay," Reuben said. He chuckled again causing more happiness with his family. "It wouldn't matter if he was here anyway. I think Monroe is too scared to sleep in the same room with me."

"Well, I'm not," said Lucy, cheerfully. "We can have bedroom sleepovers like the old days."

Reuben hugged his sister and said, "You bet Lucy. We can tell spooky stories like we used to."

Coleen placed her hands on each side of Reuben's face and kissed him on his forehead. "How about I make us all some breakfast? I suppose Lucy and I can be a little late for school this morning."

Reuben's eyes widened when his mother said 'breakfast.' Not because he was hungry, but because of the time. He took a quick glance at the clock above the mantle. It was almost 8 o'clock.

Thinking quickly, he said, "That's okay, Mama. I would like to freshen up and take a morning walk and besides, I can't keep the students of Norfolk from their best teacher."

"Well, if that's what you want. How about I at least lay out some of your old clothes for you?"

"That would be great, Mama," Reuben answered, as he made his way to the stairs.

At the top of the stairs, he entered the wash room and as he poured water into the basin, he caught a glimpse of himself in the mirror. Staring at his image, he began to feel anger toward himself. After what he had just experienced with his family in the parlor this morning, he could not help wondering, what if Renee hadn't come to see him last night. She wouldn't have been there to stop him from thrusting the knife into his belly. All of his family's joy he had just witnessed would be replaced with sorrow and grief. And Renee, she would be devastated and might have even done something just as drastic to herself, he thought.

Is this what Genda-San meant when he discussed the wonders of fate, Reuben thought. *"Fate Reuben-San, it is an awesome power filled with irony."* Is everything that seems to be happening to him and Renee all because of the power of fate, he continued to wonder. From Genda-San standing next to Reuben when he first attempted to kill himself, to Renee tackling him to the ground last night when he attempted a second time. *"Always go with fate Reuben-San and never with luck. Luck is for those who have no faith in fate. Those who go with fate will be the ones who create their own luck."*

狼

All freshened up and freshly dressed in clean clothes, Reuben accompanied his mother and Lucy to school, a pleasant treat for all three. It had been years since all three made this walk together. Being this was Lucy's last year of school, it was an extremely special occasion for her.

He watched as they entered the school building and asked the closest person if they had the time.

"Sure, it's twenty minutes to nine."

Excellent, he thought. He had enough time to make it to the wharf. At a quick pace, he made his way to meet with Renee and her Godfather, James Forrest.

He made good time arriving to where the *Morning Star* was tied up. At first, the sight of the ships gave him a frightful feeling. Memories of the journey on the *USS Rigel* to its destination in Mexico began to enter his mind. He closed his eyes and breathed in deeply allowing air to fill his lungs. Breathing out slowly from his center while uttering a low sounding kiai as Akagi Genda-San instructed, caused the thoughts to dissipate. Feeling much better, he opened his eyes and continued on.

He came to a stop at the prow of the *Morning Star* and stood staring.

"You must be Mr. Duran."

Reuben turned to see a well-dressed man standing before him. He wore a dark, blue frock coat with the insignia of a ship's captain, and atop his head was a peaked cap tilted to the right. He was about the same height as Reuben and he had a friendly look about his face which was covered with a neatly trimmed, dark mustache and beard.

"Yes, sir," answered Reuben, who immediately came to attention at the sight of the uniform. "Are you Mr. Forrest?"

"Come, come, son, no need to be formal. Yes I am. James Forrest, Master of the ocean steam vessel, the *Morning Star*, at your service. Please, please. Stand down, son. You're going to make my crew think I have turned all by the book," said James Forrest, humorously.

"Sorry, sir, it's the uniform. Habit I guess."

"Ah yes, Renee did tell me you were in the army."

"Oh, great, you two have met," said Renee as she came upon them quickly. She stepped past her Godfather and took Reuben into her arms and gave him a warm, tight hug.

Reuben was taken by surprise by her gesture, but still smiled at her.

"You look great, Reuben. Looks like your family saw you before you had a chance to leave this morning, otherwise your mother wouldn't have let you out of the house the way you were looking yesterday," she said with laughter.

"Ah, so there's another side to this young man as you described," said James Forrest, followed with a hardy laugh causing Reuben to laugh himself.

Like his family earlier this morning, the sound of Reuben's laughter made Renee feel joyful.

But once the laughter died down, Reuben looked around as if he were a look out. "I'm sorry, but should we be out in the open like this? What if Renee's father…"

"Don't worry about that old sea bass," James Forrest interrupted. "No offense, my dear," he said to Renee. She giggled.

"These may be his wharves and his ships, but that high ole mighty would never be caught dead where real work is being done. But I do suppose we should find a quieter place to conduct our visit, so please, follow me. We can use my office in the warehouse."

147

As they walked to James Forrest's office, Renee took Reuben by the arm. Many of the crew members and wharf workers admired her beauty, and also admired Reuben to have such a pretty girl attached to his arm.

As they entered the office, James Forrest offered the two seats which they took immediately with Renee sitting closely to Reuben and taking his hand. James Forrest removed his frock coat and cap and sat at his desk. He thumped the desk blotter with his fingers.

"Okay, let's get to business. My precious Goddaughter tells me you need passage to Japan. Not a short trip, I tell you. It's practically on the other side of the globe." He stood and walked to the wall and pulled on a string attached to a large map of the world.

Reuben stood and walked to the map and Renee followed.

"As you see, Mr. Duran, the country of Japan is made up of several islands," instructed James Forrest pointing at the location of Japan. "It's made up of four large islands and surrounded by many smaller islands. I assume you know what island you're traveling to?"

Reuben stepped closer to the map and with a very intense look on his face, he pointed to a portion of the map, "Honshu. That's where I must go."

James Forrest nodded. "Hmm, the largest island. How much do you know of Japan, Mr. Duran?"

"Not much at all," he answered, not taking his eyes off the map.

Renee stepped back to observe Reuben. This was a side of Reuben she had never seen. Is this the soldier side of him, she wondered. It was rather impressive, but also frightening for her to watch him in this manner. She also found it both appealing and attractive.

"Unfortunately, my young man, not much is known about this country," said James Forrest, startling Renee from her thoughts. "You see, Japan is a closed country, poised to isolationism. Foreigners have been known to be put to death being caught on its shores. Renee has not told me why you need to go there, but she has stressed it is most important for both of you. You, Reuben Duran, must be a very special man to this girl for her to go through all this trouble to get you this passage."

Reuben looked away from the map to Renee. His intense studious expression was replaced with affection. He reached for her hand and took hold of it. "I'm not special, Mr. Forrest. She's the one who is special."

"Aye, she is that. Okay, let's get to it then. In order for me to take you on, I must know exactly your reason for this journey, honestly," said James Forrest indicating for Renee and Reuben to take their seats. It was his way to test Reuben for his integrity. He knew of the Sinclair's through their shipping company and had met Renee's fiancé several times. He found him to be rather arrogant and self-obsessed, much like many of that class. Although he trusted his Goddaughter, James Forest had to make certain Reuben's intentions toward her were pure and true.

Turning his attention from Renee to James Forrest, Reuben sternly nodded and began from the night Akagi Genda-San found him on the jetty attempting to kill himself. Reuben was severely truthful and honest for his reasoning to make this journey to find his mentor. So much so Renee had no idea what Reuben had been dealing with within his mind. The war, the deaths of his platoon, the death of his friend Adam, and of course, the loss of the girl he loves to another man. She knew some of the circumstances, but not all and not in such detail as he described to Mr. Forrest. When he was finished, James Forrest looked at him wide-eyed and awed for several moments until Reuben spoke up.

"You said to be honest… was that honest enough for you?"

"Indeed, it was. Very honest, maybe too honest," answered James Forrest. Here before him sat what he believed to be an unsung hero struggling to live with the demons plaguing him with everlasting horrific memories. A man willing to do anything he can to assure the girl he loves, and obviously loves him in return, survives for both their sakes. Damn Franklin for keeping these two apart, thought James Forrest as he looked upon the two young adults sitting across his desk, hand-in-hand.

"Mr. Duran…"

Before James Forrest could continue, Reuben interrupted. "I know taking me on this passage is risky for both yourself and Renee, especially Renee, and there's no way I can ever repay this tremendous gesture to either of you. But know this, Captain Forrest, if you take me on this passage, I don't intend to travel as a passenger. I intend to earn my way as a member of your crew. I don't require any pay for my service. I'll consider the passage my pay. I may not know much about seamanship, but in the remaining time there is before your vessel embarks, I'll work and learn as much as possible to be a productive member of your crew."

James Forrest nodded approvingly. He glanced at Renee and watched as she took Reuben by his arm. Thinking how wrong it was for her father to separate these two in such an archaic manner, and Reuben's demeanor and love for his Goddaughter gave him the sense he was a true man of honor and worthy of his assistance.

Coming out from behind his desk, Captain James Forrest, Master of the *Morning Star*, presented his hand. "Very well, Mr. Duran, welcome aboard the *Morning Star* as a member of its crew."

狼

Upon the completion of the meeting, Renee had to leave, but assured Reuben she would come by the house later in the day. In the meantime, James Forrest took Reuben aboard the *Morning Star* for a tour of the ship. Reuben was introduced to the ship's mates as a new crew member.

"And this, Reuben, is Mr. Donny Sullivan, my ships bosun. Mr. Sullivan, this is Reuben Duran. He'll be joining us on our next trip to San Francisco. He's a novice, but learns quickly."

Donny Sullivan was a veteran seaman recently discharged from the navy, serving a year in the Mexican campaign. He looked rough and able, just as Reuben pictured a veteran mariner to be. Reuben didn't intend to stay, but he ended up spending the entire work day aboard the ship training in the ways of seamanship. As with soldiering, and misogi-no-jo, he picked up the basics of the job naturally.

"Are you sure you never worked a ship before, Mr. Duran?" asked Donny Sullivan, as the crew was about to secure from the day's work activities.

"Never. The only ship I was on was the *USS Rigel* to and from Mexico."

"You don't say!? I was on the *Sirius* myself, sailing alongside the *Rigel* during the voyage to Mexico. You and I are practically brothers."

"I was actually in the army."

"Army, navy... we all did our share for our flag, did we not?"

Reuben solemnly looked toward the river with momentary thoughts of the day his ship pulled away from Fort Monroe. "That we did, Mr. Sullivan."

Donny Sullivan took note of Reuben's manner. He felt Reuben had a past regarding the Mexican campaign. He patted him on the shoulder saying, "Donny, Reuben. Call me Donny. See you tomorrow morning?"

Coming back to the present, Reuben looked at Donny Sullivan and said, "You bet, bright and early."

Reuben didn't realize how late it was. Nearly dinner time and he told his family he would only be out for a morning walk. They must be worried out of their minds, he thought as he practically sprinted home.

He opened the door running through the hall shouting, "I'm home! I'm home! Sorry for not coming back sooner!"

He reached the dining room where everyone was seated, including Renee.

"Hey, it's about time you got here," she said standing up to greet him. "I told your parents we met earlier at the jetty and as we were walking you met up with an old VMI classmate," she continued, her facial expressions telling him to play along. "I said you and he must have ended up spending the day together." She felt horrible lying to Reuben's family.

"Ah, yeah... we sure did. Talked over old school days we did," replied Reuben, nervously.

Aaron asked, "Why didn't you invite him over? We would've liked to have met him."

Reuben felt a bit of panic come over him, but kept a straight face. He was about to come up with an answer, but Renee came to his rescue.

"Didn't he say he had to catch a train back to Richmond?" she said.

"Yep," he responded quickly with a rush of relief washing over him. It didn't last long.

"What did you do for the rest of the day?" asked Lucy.

This time both Renee and Reuben felt a bit of panic. "Ah, I got a job," he said taking a seat at the table. His response surprised Renee.

"A job, where?" asked Coleen.

"On the docks, loading cargo."

Aaron, with a questionable look replied, "A dock worker, son, really?"

"I don't like the idea of you working down there. It sounds dangerous," said Coleen.

Reuben reached across the table and filled a glass with water as he responded to his mother, "Come on, Mama, I spent a year in Mexico with thousands of angry Mexicans trying to kill me. Compared to that, loading cargo onto ships is child's play. Besides, it's only temporary. I still have aspirations of becoming a teacher like you. I thought this is a good opportunity to, hmm, distract myself from the past..." he glanced to Renee standing next to him, "and present."

"I still think it sounds dangerous," said Coleen.

"Well, I think it sound fantastic," said Renee joyfully, as she stepped behind Reuben's seat and placed her hands on his shoulders and gave them a gentle, affectionate squeeze.

"Yes, yes, it does sound fantastic," said Aaron, nodding approvingly. "Well done, my boy, very well done."

Perturbed, Coleen said, "Why is everyone against me on this?"

"I'm not against you, Mama," spoke up Lucy. "Everyone in this family is crazy and those two," she continued as she pointed to Renee and Reuben, "are the craziest of us all."

Laughter broke out and with Reuben included in the humor, all seemed to be as it was in the old days.

After dinner, Reuben walked Renee home. As they walked, he told her the events of his day. They arrived at the back alley gate and took a moment to have a final chat.

"I can't believe you can lie so easily," said Reuben.

Renee chuckled, "If you had to live with my parents, you'd find it comes naturally. Besides, what about your, *'I got myself a job on the docks.'* Where did you learn to lie like that?"

"From you of course. Have you ever lied to me, Renee?" asked Reuben.

"Who me?" answered Renee, humorously. Then, she suddenly turned serious.

"Listen, Reuben, this is going to be the last week we'll be able to visit. It's going to be hard to say goodbye, forever. How do you think we should do that?"

Reuben looked down and paced around her a couple of time before coming to a stop. "I suppose we should say goodbye on Wednesday. I have to go back to the farm to get a few things before Friday when the ship leaves, and I suspect you'll be too busy on Thursday to get away to see me."

Feeling very emotional, Renee took Reuben into her arms. "Wednesday is only two days away. That's not a lot of time."

"I know, but I think it's for the best... for both of us," he replied as he wrapped his arms around her and pulled her tighter into his body.

She raised her face and as she stared into his eyes, she said, "I love you, Reuben."

"Is that a lie, Renee?"

She moved in closer and her lips met his as she began to kiss him deeply and he kissed her in return. She kept staring into his eyes as she pulled her lips away and answered, "No."

She released Reuben and entered the yard. Reuben watched as she made her way up the rails to the terrace and onto the balcony to her room.

狼

The following morning, Reuben made himself a quick breakfast and lunch, and was out the door before anyone came downstairs. He practically ran to the wharves and boarded the *Morning Star* to continue his shipboard training and work. Donny Sullivan was pleased to see him back and so eager. For the entire morning, Donny trained Reuben on all the duties that were going to be expected of him on the upcoming journey, including emergencies such as man overboard and abandoning ship, all of which Reuben picked up quickly, with little or no repetition.

"Where on earth did you find this man, Captain? He's a natural." asked Donny.

"Pure luck, Mr. Sullivan, but don't get too excited about his services, he's only temporary until we get to San Francisco," answered James Forrest.

"Damn shame, he would make an excellent member of the crew."

The ships bell sounded noon time. Crew members and dock workers began to lay down their tools and bundles, and make their way off the ship to the tavern across the avenue for lunch time meals and breaks. All, that is, except for Reuben who sat on the bow of the *Morning Star*. He was about take a bite out of the sandwich he made until he heard Donny call his name from the wharf.

"Hey, Reuben, you got a visitor and it looks like she has lunch for you! Shall I tell her to go away so you can eat that pathetic looking sandwich you're about to bite into, or are you going to see what she has here for you!"

Renee stood beside Donny holding a covered basket. Her hair untied cascading over her shoulders just as Reuben liked it and she also had a bright smile. Reuben tossed his sandwich over the side and nearly tripped several times running off the ship to meet her.

"Excellent, Reuben, my man! I wish I had a pretty lady to bring me a lunch," said Donny, as Reuben finally made his way to them.

Donny bid them goodbye and Renee and Reuben walked into the warehouse and found a quiet corner. Reuben shifted a large crate to use as a table and as he searched for smaller crates to use for seats, Renee laid out a cloth and started pulling out lunch from the basket.

"This is great. I didn't expect this at all," Reuben said.

"Well, my working man needs to eat you know," she answered with a giggle.

The two had a very pleasant visit. As he ate, Reuben told Renee what he had been doing all morning. She could not help but watch him as he ate the lunch she brought him. It made her feel as if she was caring for a husband, a husband she actually loves. During the visit, they both caught themselves calling each other *dear* several times and would chuckle.

Although Renee was joyful, Reuben felt she had something difficult to say. He moved his seat closer to her, took her hands, and looked at her deeply. "Renee, there's something you need to tell me, isn't there?" She tried to pull her hands away, but he didn't let her. "Please Renee, now isn't the time to avoid anything, pleasant or not, so tell me."

She took a deep breath and said, "I won't be able to see you tomorrow to say goodbye like we planned. William Sinclair and his family will be arriving late this evening and my

152

parents have me on a tight schedule for tomorrow. Can you come by the alley gate early this evening?"

Reuben released her hands and took her into his arms. "Yes, my dear. I'll be there."

The ship's bell rang announcing time to commence afternoon duties. Reuben helped Renee pack the basket and walked her to the avenue and watched as she disappeared into the crowd.

"Okay, lover boy, time to turn to now," said Donny coming up behind Reuben. Reuben chuckled. "What's so funny?"

"There was a friend of mine at VMI. He went on and on about his girl and we all called him 'lover boy.' I never thought anyone would ever call me that. So, Donny, what does the afternoon look like today?"

狼

Evening finally fell upon the city of Norfolk. Reuben excused himself for an evening walk. Lucy wanted to accompany him, and as much as he wanted her to come, he had to tell her no. It broke his heart seeing her wanting to walk with him, but this was one walk he had to make on his own. He assured her he would walk with her tomorrow evening, the last evening he would ever see her, his mother and father. He wished Monroe was home from school. The last time he saw his brother, he was full of anger. Not like now he was filled with anticipation for his voyage to seek Akagi Genda-San, and to see Renee one last time.

He arrived at the alley gate waiting for Renee to show herself on her balcony. He noticed the doors open and saw her step out.

"Psst!"

Renee looked to the alley gate where she heard the noise. She didn't see Reuben, but knew it had to be him. She went to her desk and picked up the small chest she kept her written passages and began her climb down to the terrace and onto the rails. She made her way across the yard and through the gate where Reuben awaited on the other side. She ran to him, carefully placed the chest on the ground, and wrapped her arms around his neck bringing his face down close to hers and their lips met. They kissed deeply.

When they finished, she stood in his arms as he asked what was in the chest.

"Personal memoirs I can't take with me. I want to give them to you for safe keeping. I know you will protect them for me."

"With my life."

Renee again gave Reuben another deep passionate kiss. When finished, they stood arm-in-arm in the moonlight.

"So I assume all of your time is planned out for you starting tomorrow?" Reuben asked.

She let out a sigh. "Tomorrow is a formal brunch with the Sinclair family, followed by a rehearsal. Then tea with the bridesmaids and maid of honor, whom I have never met before, and my mother, future mother-in-law, and other snooty women. Of course there will be a large dinner party. I swear all this is more for them than me. Thursday at noon, we're all heading to the Hotel Grand, where I'll stay for the night. My last night of freedom to spend all alone in a luxury hotel room."

She placed her head on Reuben's shoulder and said. "If it were you and me, I would only want us with your parents, Monroe as you best man, Lucy as my maid of honor, May, Henry, and Noah as witnesses, and the priest under the oak tree."

Wanting to change the topic of the wedding, she quickly asked, "Is everything set for your voyage, Reuben?" with a tremble in her voice.

"I'm ready as I'll ever be. I have a few things at the farm I need to get, so I'll go there Thursday after work. I already told my parents I'll be going to the farm for the weekend to help Noah with some late harvesting. I'll have to wait until May, Henry, and Noah go to sleep before I walk back."

"Walk back? That's a long way, Reuben."

"I know. But considering the journey I'm about to undertake, that walk from the farm to the wharves will be like a walk around the block."

Renee let out a small laugh and raised her hand to cup his face. "Please get well for me, Reuben. The only way I'll be able to go on is if I know you're doing what you can to rid yourself of your anger."

"I promise, Renee, and I also promise I'll someday return. We may not be as love intended and maybe someday, you will learn to love your husband. But always remember my secret I told you, I will always love you, and forever be yours. You will always have my heart, Renee, and if you ever become without a husband for any reason, no matter how young or old you may be, I'll be waiting for you."

That caused Renee to embrace Reuben tighter than ever before and kiss him for as long as she could. Feeling she couldn't leave Reuben with just a spoken farewell she began to pull on his shirt until she heard her father call out her name.

"Renee! Where are you, my dear daughter? I thought she was in her room. Renee, guess who has just arrived?!" she heard him say as he was roaming the house looking for her.

She released the hold on Reuben's shirt.

"I have to go," she said as she began to cry. "I don't want to say goodbye."

"Well, instead," said Reuben, as he wiped the tears from her checks with his thumbs, "say, until we meet again, that way, it's not permanent."

She let out a slight laugh and smile, "You always know how to make things much easier." She reached around her neck and unhooked the chain holding an oval shaped locket and placed it around his neck.

She gave him one last kiss, stepped back and said, "Until we meet again, Reuben Duran, my true love." She turned and ran toward the house.

Reuben watched as she climbed back into her room, picked up her chest of written passages, and made his way back to the main avenue. Under a bright street lamp, he opened the locket to see the image of Renee she given him during his first year at VMI on one side, and the image of him he given her before he went off to Mexico on the other.

154

狼

Wednesday morning came, and Reuben went to work on the *Morning Star*. He wasn't as talkative, but still very attentive to his duties.

"So, Reuben, is your lady friend going to be bringing you lunch again today?" asked Donny, gleefully.

"No," replied Reuben, flat out plainly.

Hearing his response and seeing the manner in which it was said caused Donny concern. "Why not?" he asked.

Continuing with his task of coiling up lines, Reuben said, "She's getting married."

Donny suddenly felt shock. He began to have an understanding why Reuben was here on the ship that was to take him far away from this place. He patted him on the back. "Well, not to worry, Reuben, soon we will be underway and your troubles will be behind you."

Reuben looked up at Donny with a scowl on his face that made Donny step back. Reuben's scowl changed into an emotionless face as he looked toward the river leading to the bay. He looked back to Donny and nodded, then back to the lines and continued his work.

At the dinner table, everyone ate quietly. Renee's wedding was on everyone's mind, but no one dared to speak of it. When dinner was finished, Reuben and Lucy cleaned and put away the dishes.

"Hey, Lucy, how about that walk now?" asked Reuben.

Lucy's face shined and she took hold of his hand and led him to the front door.

They walked up the street in silence. Lucy wanted to talk, but was afraid because of the closeness of the wedding and remembering how easily Reuben could be set off by something said wrong, so she waited until he spoke. It didn't come until they found themselves in front of the school building.

Reuben noticed Lucy looking sad. He wanted to tell her so much what he and Renee had been up to the last several days, but he knew she would insist for him to tell their parents and if Reuben wouldn't, Lucy would out of concern.

He turned to face her and asked, "Lucy, can you keep a secret for me?"

"Of course I can, brother. You can trust me."

"Good. I want you to know, no matter what happens to Renee, I will always love her, and forever be hers."

Looking at him curiously, she asked him, "Why are you telling me this and not her?"

"I have, but as time goes by and if she ever has any doubt, I want you to remind her."

"Me, why?"

"Because, I trust you the most with this secret and you will use it when it's needed."

"How will I know when it's needed?"

Cupping his sister's face with one of his hands, he said, "You will know when."

Lucy nodded and wrapped her arms around her brother.

Reuben remembered the small chest Renee gave him to care for. I can't take that with me, he thought and looked to Lucy.

"One more thing Lucy, Renee gave me a small chest she can't take with her to Charleston and asked if I could hold onto it for her. I really don't want to take it to the farm, so I was wondering if you can keep it safe in your room."

"Why can't you keep it in your room, Reuben?"

"Because I'll be staying at the farm for most of the time helping Noah and Henry and I trust you to keep it safe."

Lucy looked up to her brother in puzzlement and asked, "What's in it?"

"Renee said its personal memoirs she can't take with her. So what do you say, can I count on you for these two requests?"

"Yes, I give you my word."

Again, Thursday morning, Reuben was back on the *Morning Star* assisting with final preparation for getting underway. All duties were completed shortly after noon and Captain James Forrest gave the crew the rest of the day to themselves.

Reuben went back home and spent the rest of the afternoon at his house he grew up in when not on the farm. He roamed each room wondering if he would ever see this place again. Entering the room he shared with Monroe, he sat at the small desk next to the window. He would look out watching for Renee to come and visit when they were children. Visions of them playing on the street came to his mind.

Shaking the visions from his mind, he picked up a pen, dipped it in the ink bottle and began to write. When his task was finished, he pressed the letter he drafted against another page of paper to dry off the ink, folded the written page, and placed it in an envelope.

It was nearly time for his mother and sister to be home from school, so he quickly placed the letter on the mantel in the parlor and left. He had no reason to stay since he told his family he would be going to the farm after he was let out from work.

He stepped outside the front door and made his way to the street where he took one last look at the front of the house. As taught by Akagi Genda-San, he formally bowed to it, raised himself, and walked off in the direction of the farm.

狼

Reuben arrived at the farm to find May, Henry, and Noah sitting on the porch. He sat with them for a while, talking about the upcoming winter and what was needed to get things in order for the onset of the colder weather that was soon to come. After supper, Reuben went to the oak tree to enjoy the unusual warm autumn evening, and looked up to the clouds beginning to form in the sky thinking of Akagi Genda-San and what he would be telling him at a time like this. He would probably say something very meaningful, like how the sky rests above both him and the girl he loves at the same time meaning they are never alone.

He saw a flash of lightning in the distance. "Looks like I'll be walking in the rain tonight," he said to himself before he headed back to the house.

Reuben was tying a small bundle to the rake handle Akagi Genda-San had him turn into a jo in his room when he heard the sounds of a carriage making its way up the lane to the front of the house. He walked out of his room to the stairs and came down with the tied bundle in his hands. May was already at the large parlor window looking out to see who was riding up to the house.

"Who is it, Aunty May?" asked Reuben as he leaned the jo against the mantle.

"It looks like Miss Renee. What could she be doing here at this time, and of all evenings?"

Reuben's stomach began to feel as if he did actually commit seppuku. He thought their goodbyes had been said Tuesday and May was right Reuben thought, of all evenings, why this one, the one before her wedding. That was seriously risky on her part.

"Not sure, but it looks like I'll have to take her back to the city. Why does that girl insist on riding out here on her own knowing it'll be late when she has to go back," he said, trying to mask his true feelings of seeing her. Either way, he had an excuse to leave the farm instead of waiting for May, Henry, and Noah to turn in for the night, and also a ride. Fate, he wondered.

"I'll go out to see what's going on," Reuben said as he went outside.

"Well don't dally, it looks like rain this evening," said Henry.

Reuben walked out the front door, off the porch, and up to the carriage as Renee was hopping off. She turned and saw Reuben walking to her and she ran and leaped into his arms. She didn't utter a word, but held on to him tightly and he returned her embrace.

"Is everything okay, Renee?"

With her head on his shoulder and face turned away to hide her tears, she said, "Everything is fine. I was looking at the weather and didn't want you to walk back to the city if it started raining."

"And another reason to see me?" he asked.

"Yes. Can we go somewhere and have a talk?"

"Sure, let me get Noah to take the team and carriage into the barn in case it begins to rain."

The two entered the house to find May, Henry, and Noah sitting at the dining room table. They all stood when they entered.

"Good evening, Miss Renee, how nice it is to see you," greeted May.

"Hello, everyone. If it's all right, I would like to speak to Reuben."

May motioned to the others to give them some privacy. "Of course you can, we'll get out of your way."

"No, please stay," said Renee. She looked at Reuben. "Can we go to the oak tree?"

Reuben nodded and asked for Noah to move the carriage into the barn. He held the door open for Renee. Renee gave May a long meaningful look. May nodded and watched the two walk out of the kitchen door and told Noah to see to the carriage and return inside the house quickly.

"Now what do you think those two are up to?" asked Henry.

May sighed compassionately and said, "If you have to ask, then you have no clue about romance."

狼

Renee led the way to the oak tree holding Reuben's hand. They walked in silence until they reached the tree.

"Are you all packed and ready to go?" asked Renee rather awkwardly.

"All my things are on the ship already, you know that. Why are you here, Renee? This is very risky for you. You're supposed to be at the Hotel Grand. What if someone finds you're missing?"

"I made an excuse I was sick so I could leave the reception to come and be with you."

Reuben stepped up closer behind Renee and wrapped his arms around her and as he did so, she took hold of them and leaned her head back and turned to face him. She brought up one of her hands to caress his face.

"Tuesday we said our farewells as friends and it was hard." She turned around within his arms. "Tomorrow you will be sailing off and I'll be married to a man who I'm not intended to be with."

Reuben pulled her closer into his body and held her lovingly. He took a deep breath and began speaking, "I have never been good putting my thoughts together as beautifully as you do on pages, but know this, no matter where I end up, I will love you always and forever. To me there will be no other. You hold my heart and soul, Renee, and it's for us I make this journey. I guess the best way for me to put this is, the same sun, moon, and sky that covers you, also covers me. When I look up to them, my thoughts will be of you, and you of all people know I always keep my eyes toward the heavens."

Renee raised her face to look at his. "For someone who can't put his thoughts together beautifully, you just did wonders."

A gentle rain began to fall upon the branches of the oak tree. As it did, they remained in each other's arms. Renee stepped back out of Reuben's arms and took his hands. This time, it was she who took in a deep breath.

"Reuben, I have a very special request to ask of you. Tomorrow, I'll belong to William Sinclair as his wife, and I'll never know love the way I know it with you. So for this one evening, for this one moment we have right here, right now, I want to be yours and I want you to be mine. For at least one time in our lives, let us be one under our tree."

She stepped closer releasing his hands and slid off the braces from his shoulders and unbuttoned his shirt. She placed her hands underneath his unbuttoned shirt against his bare chest and slid his shirt from his shoulders. For the first time, she saw the scar from the bullet that penetrated through his shoulder. She gently caressed it with her fingertips, lowered her head and kissed it, rose and kissed his lips.

Reuben, in turn, unbuttoned the bodice of Renee's dress as she allowed it to fall from her body. She reached up and grasped the ribbon tied in a bow holding her camisole in place and pulled the bow apart as that also fell from her body exposing her soft skin.

Her hair, wet from the gentle falling rain, rested against her bare shoulders and chest as Reuben began running his fingers through the wet, silky strands.

Staring into each other's eyes, they took hold of one another and slowly began to lower themselves to the soft grass below. Reuben lay on his back as Renee lay on top of him as their lips met and they kissed deeply.

For this one, warm autumn evening, under the oak tree where they first met, where they played as children, and where they would talk and laugh, Renee and Reuben were at last one, as love intended.

狼

Once they were dressed, Renee and Reuben sat in each other's arms against the trunk of their oak tree. They both felt joyful and filled with love for one another.

"I need to get you back to the hotel," said Reuben as he stood and assisted her to her bare feet.

Holding her shoes, he carried Renee in his arms rather than having her walk by his side. She held onto him and rested her head against his shoulder the entire way until they reached the carriage in the barn where he lifted her onto it. He quickly went into the house and retrieved the jo with the tied bundle and returned to the barn and onto the carriage.

As they rode back into the city, Renee sat closely to Reuben with her arms around his waist as she did the other night he brought her back to the city. Along the way they continued to kiss and hold one another as the carriage team stayed to the road.

Once in the downtown area of the city, Reuben pulled the carriage into an alley close to the Hotel Grand where Renee and the rest of the wedding party were staying. He walked her to the rear of the hotel and held her closely. He began to speak, but she placed her fingers against his lips as she looked deeply into his eyes.

Renee kissed him one last time, stepped out of his arms, and entered the hotel through the back service door where earlier that evening she had made her escape to give Reuben the farewell she felt they both deserved.

狼

Early Friday morning, Coleen noticed an envelope on the mantle. She took the envelope and looked at it curiously. It was addressed to *'My Family.'* She opened it and took out the letter folded within. She unfolded the page and began to read its contents.

"To my Dearest Family,

It is with a heavy heart I write you this letter to inform you of my departure, not only from this home of mine, but the country as well. With the help of Renee, I have received passage aboard a vessel that will take me to San Francisco where I will begin my search for Genda-San. Before he left, he offered me a challenge that if I were not able to ease my demons of the past, I am to search for him and continue what he started. You may not understand, but both Renee and I believe this is the better way for me to deal with my illnesses other than the alternative.

Please don't feel anger toward Renee for helping me. She did so for the caring love she has, not only for me, but for you as well. What she did to assist me, she did in the best interests of the Duran Family, and for that, I love her with all my heart.

For my brother Monroe, you have proven you're much smarter and intelligent than I am. I ask that you use that intelligence to help Mama and Da in any way you can. I may not have been as close to you as I have been with Lucy, but my love for you has always been true.

For my sister Lucy, you have proven to be more creative than your two brothers in your music and the games you have invented we played at the farm and in the city. Use that creativity to help Mama and Da to let them know what I do is what is best for our family. Remember my secret well and don't forget to use it when the time comes. I am counting on you.

Mama and Da, you have raised me to be an honest and true person. Admittedly for the past several days, I have not been honest and I will never forgive myself for that sin, but it was a sin to spare you of my pain I deal with constantly. I will never forget the lessons you have taught me and I will carry your love always.

Please don't think of this as a farewell, but as a greeting. A greeting for the son plagued with horrors and anger of the past who will return as he once was.

Your Loving and Obedient Son,
Reuben

When Coleen finished reading the letter, she let out a loud scream and began crying endlessly as she fell to her knees. Aaron and Lucy came quickly to her side kneeling.

"What is it, my dear, what's wrong?"

Coleen took hold of her husband and held him tightly, "He's gone! Our son, he's gone!"

狼

The bells of Saint Mary's church were chiming as the congregation inside were waiting for what was to be the grand wedding of the season. All the planning in which Renee had little participation was being played out in front of the upper society of Norfolk. Franklin and Margret Wallace invited everyone of importance to the city and it looked as if they all were in attendance. Everyone from the mayor of the city to top executives of politics and business were seated amongst the pews of the large church.

The pipes of the church organ were playing solemn psalm melodies while the groom with his best man made their way down the aisle. William Sinclair, very smartly dressed, had a very smug confident look as he stepped to shake hands of the guests along the way.

In the vestibule of the church, the bridesmaids were giddy and joyful as Renee's mother and other ladies tried to keep them quiet. Her maid of honor, who Renee still had no idea who she was, began to see to the last minute details on Renee's dress. When she attempted to even out the pleats on the skirt, Renee stepped back and lightly pushed her away, an action that cause a confused look from the maid.

Renee stepped to the doorway of the church for some air as she put her hand on the hidden pocket concealing the image case of Reuben and the stone Akagi Genda-San gave her.

Once she was dressed at the hotel, she asked for a moment to be alone. That moment, she retrieved the image case, button, and stone from her travel trunk and placed them in the pockets she had stitched into the dress. These items were more than objects. To Renee, they were talismans to provide her courage to go through what was to happen this day.

Startled from her thoughts, her mother took her by the hand saying, "It is time, my daughter."

My daughter, even on this day she still can't call me by my name, Renee thought as she was being led to her waiting father to walk her down the aisle.

"Let me have a look at you," said Franklin Wallace, beaming with pride. "Yes, indeed you make a lovely bride."

All Renee could do in response is force a smile.

The organ music died down to a low hush, then all of a sudden the music selected for the wedding procession began playing.

At the sound of the first note of the music, Renee felt a very sharp stabbing pain in her stomach. Oh geez, is this what seppuku feels like, she wondered.

Her feet began to feel like stone as she saw her mother walk down the aisle in step with the music followed by her bridesmaids, girls who she also didn't know. The maid of honor began her march as two little flower girls followed dropping rose petals onto the aisle.

Taking his daughter's arm and placing it in the crook of his, Franklin Wallace said to Renee, "Now it is our turn."

The music of the bride's march down the aisle began playing and Franklin Wallace stepped off. Renee didn't step off as her father did, causing him to stumble. She looked up to him and gave an apologetic smile and began stepping forward.

As the music played, father and daughter made their way down the aisle, and the congregation stood. Renee looked to her left and to her right. She didn't know almost any of these people. They're not here for me, they're here for my father, she was thinking. Where's Mr. and Mrs. Duran? Where's Lucy and Monroe? Where's May, Henry, and Noah? Those are the people I need to be here.

That sharp stabbing pain in her stomach began to feel as if it were twisting. Where's Reuben? Oh please, Reuben, come and rescue me from this walk. Damn it, he can't, Renee thought, feeling panic as visions of the evening she spent with Reuben before this day were flashing in her mind.

Renee suddenly stopped as she and her father reached halfway down the aisle, again causing her father to stumble. He looked back to her, but this time there was no apologetic smile, only a look of despair.

She let go of her father's arm and dropped the bouquet of flowers to the floor. "Geez oh geez oh geez what have I done? I let him go," she said as she took a couple of steps away from her father.

"Renee, what are you doing?" asked Franklin Wallace in a perturbed manner.

"I can't do this, father. I can't let him go," she answered as she turned and began making her way out of the church.

Renee's father reached and took hold of his daughter's wrist and pulled her back. "Remember our deal?" he told her in a low angered tone.

Renee tried with all her strength to pull away, but her father's grip was firm. Realizing she could not free her wrist, in a graceful sweeping manner, Renee used her father's strength against him. She relaxed her arm and in a low circle, brought her arm downward and back up causing her father to bend over forward. Instead of holding that position as Reuben did with her, she flung her father's arm forward flipping him in the air. He landed hard on his back on the floor of the aisle.

Not believing what she had just done, in a low whisper she said, "Kaiten-nage." She began to sprint out of the church pulling hair pins out of her hair letting it fall over her shoulders, the way Reuben likes it. The stunned congregation looked on with shock and awe.

Renee was attracting strange glances and stares from the people on the streets as she sprinted to the wharves. She noticed the time on the clock on city hall. It was half an hour before the *Morning Star* was to set sail. She had enough time to get to the pier and stop Reuben from leaving her. Somehow we'll get you better, Reuben, you and I together. We will do it together, she kept thinking to herself as she ran.

She made the final turn onto Waterside Avenue and stood before the wharf where the *Morning Star* used to be tied up. There she stood and stared in disbelief. Before her eyes was the empty slit where the *Morning Star* had once been. The ship had been given its all clear prior to its scheduled departure.

She fell to her knees and bowed her head down in despair as she began to cry. Suddenly she heard the sound of Akagi Genda-San's voice appear in her mind, *"There will be a time, very soon, my young Renee-Dono, when you will have to be strong. Stronger than Reuben-San himself. It is then when you must sacrifice most of what you have for both of you to achieve victory. It is only you that can wash away the jagged edges of his stone. In doing so, then and only then, will he become well, and then both of you will achieve your own self victories."* She lifted her head to look at the empty slit. *"You see, my young precious Renee-Dono, there is a time and place for you and Reuben-San. Stones and water, Renee-Dono, stones and water."*

"Faith and love, this is where our time and place begin," Renee said to herself.

石
水

In the year of our Lord, 1847, a destiny continues of a romantic tale.
One's family's hate becomes another family's love…

You're One of Us

Renee laid down her pen and covered the ink bottle. She looked over her newest passage, closed her eyes and held the page to her heart. She reopened her eyes, placed the page next to the picture of Reuben, stood, and walked over to the sofa in the hidden room of the city schoolhouse where she attended before she was forced, by her father, to attend Wickham Finishing School for Girls.

She was still wearing her wedding gown, the only garment her father allowed her to keep when he threw her out of his house. Utterly exhausted, she lay down and covered herself with the only blanket available, a large burlap sack. Her future was now very uncertain, but her past, especially this day, was clear. She was homeless and alone, yet she had a profound sense a presence was within her.

The day before, she arrived at the wharf after running out on her wedding to stop Reuben from leaving the country. She was too late. It felt like an iron spike had been driven through her heart when she saw the empty slit where the *Morning Star* had once been moored. Falling to her knees, she wept as onlookers walked by.

"Miss Wallace? Is that you?" asked Jacob Curtis, one of her father's dock workers, and a good friend.

She looked up with tears rolling down her cheeks. Jacob knelt down and helped her up.

"The *Morning Star*, when did it leave?"

"Less than 20 minutes ago. Why?

She couldn't answer, only able to slump over to cry. Jacob walked her out of the public's view, trying very hard to comfort her. After a few moments, Renee settled down and told Jacob why she had come to the pier. When her story was done, Jacob felt very sympathetic.

"I don't know what I'm going to do now. The man I love is gone and my father is going to be furious with me," she said, whimpering.

Knowing what type of man Franklin Wallace was, Jacob wished he could do more to help Renee than lend a sympathetic ear.

Without saying a word, Renee walked away, heading to her house, a walk she knew was going to be unpleasant at its end. Jacob Curtis shook his head in despair as he watched her disappear in the crowd of dock workers and loads of cargo lined along the wharves.

She took the long way to her house, prolonging the inevitable wrath from her father. Onlookers pointed and spoke in hushed tones as she roamed the paths and streets. Wearing the

163

wedding gown that now was not in its best condition caused many stares. Renee was oblivious to the onlookers. She was deep in thought. If she ran away sooner, she could have stopped Reuben. If she was brave enough to stand up to her father, none of this would have happened. So what if he would have given me nothing? I was never happy with what he and mother gave me, she thought. Wishing for the best, she hoped her father realized she was unhappy all along and would forgive her. After all, she was his only daughter. Maybe he came to his senses his flesh and blood came before his business or social standing.

That thought ended as she finally made it to the path of her front doorstep. She walked the path which seemed to grow two steps for every one she took.

She opened the door to see the receiving room vacant. She didn't realize how much she hated her house until this moment. The furniture she wasn't allowed to sit on. The portraits of people she never knew if they were relatives. It was like living in a museum. It was so unlike Reuben's home in the city and the farm. To her, those were not houses, they were homes always filled with laughter.

A cough was heard coming from her father's den, a room she was forbidden to enter without his permission. She made her way to the archway and made her presence known by clearing her throat.

Inside the room sat her mother on an elaborate leather sofa, handkerchief in hand wiping away tears. Her father was standing looking out the huge picture window with crumpled documents in his hands. At the sound of Renee's entrance, he turned to face her.

"What do you have to say for yourself?" he asked in a neutral tone.

"Father…"

"Shut up!" he screamed as he quickly closed the distance between them. He was within arm's reach when he presented the crumpled documents in his hands to her.

"Do you know what these are? Well do you?" he insisted.

Renee shook her head, keeping quiet, too scared to utter a sound.

"These are the contracts no longer in effect with Sinclair Southeast Shipping! Because of your little stunt today, Steven Sinclair has rejected the merger of my company and has set my financial stability back six years! Now where the hell did you run off to and what were you thinking?!" he said angrily as he threw the documents at her.

Renee cringed, her mouth quivering trying to speak.

"Well answer me, damn you!"

"I, I went to stop Reuben from leaving."

"You what?!" he yelled, causing Renee's mother to shudder. He raised his arm and struck his daughter in the face with the back side of his hand sending her across the hall, falling to the floor.

"You threw away a great marriage to chase after a… psychotic army has-been?! What were you thinking, you ungrateful little whore?!" Franklin Wallace's face was red with anger as he stepped closer to his daughter on the floor. He swung his leg back and kicked her as Renee instinctively rolled over and curled up to protect her front.

164

"Father, how could you?!" cried out Renee in pain. "Mother please!" she begged, looking to her mother for help.

Margret stood from the sofa and came to Franklin's side. She looked down to the girl she gave birth to eighteen years ago. She shook her head, turned, and walked away, going up the staircase not saying a single word.

"Mother…" Renee cried out again.

Franklin reached down and grabbed a handful of Renee's beautiful, dark, brown hair and began dragging her down the hallway. Renee took hold of his hand, trying to ease the pain.

"Please stop, Father, you're hurting me!"

Franklin Wallace stopped, turned to face Renee and again with the backside of his hand, struck her.

"Never call me *'father'* again! You are no longer any daughter of mine!" He continued to drag her to the rear of the house, her legs kicking against the floor and walls.

The house servants, hearing Franklin Wallace's rage, made haste to other rooms, closing the doors behind them. For many of them, they would have to be sold off as field hands to make up a fraction of his loses, a notion that wasn't well received, and caused hatred toward Renee for her actions.

Franklin Wallace made it to the servant's rear entrance of the house, let go of Renee's hair, and kicked open the door. He reached and grabbed Renee by her shoulders, stood her up, and spit in her face. He threw her out onto the dirt path leading to the alley.

"I never want to see your whorish face anywhere near this house ever again. You understand me, you filthy bitch? You are no longer a part of my lineage! Now get the hell out of here before I call the law to have you hauled away for trespassing!" Franklin Wallace yelled, and slammed the door shut.

Renee lay on the path, crying and sore from Franklin Wallace's strikes. Slowly she began to crawl on her hands and knees toward the back gate. She heard the door open and looked back, but her father was not at its opening. There were three female house servants, each holding a switch taken from one of the garden trees. They came closer and circled her.

"Because of you, our sons are going to be sold off as field hands in Tennessee, and we'll never see them again," said the oldest of the three and swung down the switch hitting Renee on her shoulder. The other two commenced to also start swinging their switches at Renee.

Renee quickly stood and ran as fast as her legs could carry her to the gate with the three women giving chase. She opened the gate and continued running, not looking back.

She ran not knowing where she was going. Her eyes were filled with tears and her heart with despair not of losing her home, but of losing Reuben.

She had nowhere to go and was all alone with nothing except the wedding gown she was wearing and her three precious treasures in hidden pockets.

It was getting late and she was frightened and hungry. She wondered about going to Reuben's home to ask for help.

"No, I can't do that," she said to herself. "It's because of me, Reuben left. They probably hate me just as much as... my parents."

Her thoughts turned to Reuben, wondering if he was safe, wondering if he was thinking of her. Suddenly she said, "Reuben's hidden room at the schoolhouse. There's probably some food there also."

With a shimmer of hope, Renee began to run to the schoolhouse to the hidden room Reuben had found many years ago.

狼

The Durans were still recovering after they found Reuben's letter. The family was devastated and the house was unusually quiet.

They were not invited to the wedding, so they didn't know of the events that happened at the church. It was late in the afternoon when a knock was heard at the front door. Monroe arrived to spend the weekend at home and was the first one to answer it with the rest of the family quickly coming to the door. It was Mrs. O'Neal, a neighbor from down and across the street, who came from the church where the wedding was supposed to be held. She informed the Duran family of what happened and said Renee had gone missing.

After Mrs. O'Neal left, Aaron and Coleen left the house to go to the Wallace home leaving Monroe and Lucy behind in case either Renee or Reuben would show.

Early in the evening, they arrived at the front doorstep of the Wallace house. Aaron rapped on the door. It was answered by a female servant. Not giving her a chance to greet them, Aaron quickly asked, "Is Mr. Wallace at home? We've come to see if Renee is all right."

The servant started to shudder, not knowing what to say. She was about to reply when Franklin Wallace let loose a yell from atop the stairs.

"What the hell do you want, Duran?! Get the hell out of my house!"

"Franklin, what about Renee?" asked Coleen.

"That bitch no longer lives here," replied Franklin Wallace as he came down the stairs and walked dangerously close to Aaron causing him to back up a few steps.

His response caused Coleen to raise her hands to her mouth and gasp in horror.

"That whore ruined my business because of that bastard son of yours! Now get..."

Aaron didn't allow Franklin Wallace a chance to finish his statement. Blacking out and laying flat on his back with blood trickling from his nose, Franklin Wallace found himself looking up at Aaron who was standing above him with his hands in fists.

Aaron grabbed Franklin Wallace by his lapels and raised him in a sitting position on the floor.

"What did you do to your daughter, Franklin? What did you do to Renee?!"

"I threw that little bitch out!"

Aaron, filled with rage, raised his fist to strike. Franklin Wallace cringed awaiting the next blow. It never came. Aaron, seeing the pathetic look of Renee's father, lowered his fist and released his grip on Franklin Wallace's lapel causing him to fall to the floor. Aaron stood up, took Coleen by the hand, and led her to the front door.

Coleen stopped and took a look back into the house. She saw Margret running to her husband. Coleen's and Margret's eyes met. Margret's concern for Franklin Wallace, instead of her daughter, nearly made her reenter the house and confront Renee's mother. Aaron regained her attention by tugging at her hand.

"Come on, we have no time to waste on the likes of them. We have to go look for Renee. She's all alone and may be scared to death."

Coleen nodded, "You're right. Let's go get Monroe and Lucy to help."

For the rest of the evening and late into the night, the Duran family searched for Renee. It was nearing midnight when they came back home with hopes she would be waiting for them inside the house. They left the door unlocked and a note pinned to the door telling her to come in if she happened to come by while they were searching, but there was no sign of her.

They all decided to get some sleep and start another search early. Although everyone was in their beds, not a wink of sleep was had in the Duran home that night.

狼

The second day for the search of Renee, Lucy struck out on her own very early. The day before, the Duran family searched all the obvious places where Renee might be, such as friends of the Wallaces, churches, and of course, her house where Aaron and Coleen learned the awful truth about Renee's father disowning and throwing her out of his family and life. Although Coleen was distraught about Reuben's departure to the unknown, she could not help but feel anger and hatred toward Renee's mother for allowing her husband to act in such a despicable manner.

As Lucy roamed the city streets in the early morning hours, rather than searching, she was deep in thought.

"If I were Renee, where would I run off to?" she asked herself.

An idea came to her and she thought she might find some clues if she started her search from the doorsteps of Renee's house, or at least the front of the house.

Lucy made her way to Renee's neighborhood and walked up to the path leading to the front door of the house. She faced the street and began to think hard.

"Now if that mean old Mr. Wallace was my Da and kicked me out of the house, I'd probably be very sad, crying even," said Lucy to herself. Using her creative intellect, Lucy looked at the street as if a clue would leap into her hands. She continued to think out loud again, "Nothing in the street that I can see." She looked in both directions up and down the street. As she scanned the neighborhood, she began to reminisce of the happier times when Reuben would walk Renee home from school and Lucy would walk behind the two, teasing them that they should hold hands. Suddenly Lucy's eyes opened wide as if someone slapped her face and her hands came to her mouth as she gasped for air.

"Now why did I not think of this before? I know where she is! She's got to be there," Lucy shouted as she began to run in the direction of the schoolhouse.

Several years back, when Reuben was nearing his last year of school, he found an old abandoned room in the school, hidden by a large heavy oak bookcase. The bookcase had been placed in front of the door, and as the years went by, the door was forgotten. Reuben turned the room into his personal space of solitude. It was in this room where Reuben would escape when he was feeling low about his future without Renee.

Reuben rigged the bookcase to the door and attached a lock inside the room. He also cut a hole into the wall that led to the back side of the school hidden by shrubs, and fashioned a small hidden door so the room could be accessed from the outside. On several dark nights, he would sneak out of his house, enter the school through his secret room, and furnish the room with furniture from the main part of the school. He moved in a student desk, a medium sized table, chairs, and even a comfortable couch from the superintendent's office. The couch was the only item ever questioned of its whereabouts.

It was on an October day when Lucy secretly followed Reuben and learned of his hidden space of solitude. Of course, Reuben was angry when he found Lucy followed him, but as always, he could never stay mad at her for long and Reuben made her promise to keep his secret. As she loved her brother so dearly and understood his need for peace, she promised and, good to her word, kept his secret until Reuben left for VMI.

Knowing how Renee felt about attending Wickham Finishing School for Girls, she told her about Reuben's room.

"That little sneak, how could he keep this room a secret from me?" asked Renee, once Lucy showed it to her. "I'm surprised you didn't tell me either, Lucy. Why are you telling me about this room now?"

"I know how much you hate Wickham, and I know you have jumped the wall to ditch school and have nearly gotten caught. Well, now you have a place to go and hide. You can do your writing in peace and quiet in here."

Ever since then, Renee would leave the walls of Wickham at least once a week for a couple of hours at a time and escape to Reuben's personal space of solitude.

Gasping for breath, Lucy found her way to the hidden door. Since neither Reuben nor Renee had use for the room any longer, it had been undisturbed for almost a year. However, when Lucy glanced at the small door, she saw fresh marks on the ground and hand prints on the door. She grasped the door, lifted it open, slid it aside, and noticed the oil lamp was lit. Quickly Lucy crawled into the room, rose and looked from one end of the room to the other. When she looked to the couch, there was Renee, covered with a burlap sack, still wearing the torn and dirty wedding dress.

On the table, Lucy saw bread crusts, a tin cup half filled with water, and the image case Reuben had given her before he left to Mexico and a VMI button resting on a very smooth stone. She slowly walked to where Renee was lying. She timidly grabbed her shoulder and gently shook her.

"Renee? Are you okay?" Lucy asked. There was no response so Lucy shook harder. "Renee, wake up. It's me, Lucy!"

Lucy's call startled Renee awake. She reared herself into a fetal position and started to scream. Lucy grabbed hold of her and cradled her tightly.

"It's me, Lucy. Don't be scared! I've come to find you. My whole family has been looking for you."

Renee began to calm down. She looked up to see the concerned look of Lucy staring down at her. She wiped her eyes with her shaking hands.

"My gosh, Renee, you look a fright. Are you all right?"

Renee didn't respond right away. Instead she ran her fingers through her unkept hair and started pulling on it.

"Geez oh geez oh geez I did it, I did it, I made him go. I tried to stop him, but I was too late. It's my fault," she said as she began sobbing. She finally recognized Lucy and continued.

"Oh, Lucy, I'm so sorry. You must hate me."

"Why would you say such a thing, Renee? Why?"

"Because I convinced your brother to leave and follow Mr. Akagi. I couldn't marry William Sinclair because I love your brother. Mr. Akagi made me realize there is a future with Reuben, but I was too late to understand his meaning and now I don't have Reuben anymore."

Lucy pulled Renee into her arms and held her tightly to comfort her, just as Renee did the day Reuben's train left for VMI. "You still have Reuben. He left a letter explaining why he was leaving to look for Mr. Akagi. It's not your fault he had to leave. I don't understand it too well, but I do know it was his decision. He said in his letter he had to continue what Mr. Akagi was teaching him or he would kill himself. He said he was doing this for him and for you. He loves you too, Renee, that much I know. We have always known, but your father kept us from seeing it."

Renee gently pulled away from Lucy's embrace and looked up at her. A hint of a smile peaked out and she glanced at the table. She stood and began to make her way to the table but stumbled. Lucy rose to catch her. Renee steadied herself and leaned against the table. There was a piece of parchment on the surface. Renee picked up the parchment and handed it to Lucy. As Lucy was looking it over, Renee picked up the tin cup and began to take a sip of water. It made her gag and she started to heave. She quickly stumbled across the floor where a bucket was in the far corner of the room. As she made it to the bucket, she lowered her head just as she began to vomit. Lucy quickly folded up the page and slipped it into her skirt pocket, ran to Renee, and steadied her as she continued to be sick.

After a few minutes, Renee moved to a chair with Lucy's help.

"Have you been sick all this time, Renee? Come on, you're coming home with me right now."

"No! No! I can't face anyone. I won't be a burden!"

"You can't stay here! You're sick and you need food."

"No please, Lucy, don't tell anyone where I am. Everyone hates me. Please promise me..."

Before she could finish, Renee passed out and fell from the chair onto the floor. Lucy knelt down and rolled her over and shook her by the shoulders. "Renee! Wake up!"

Lucy began to panic and cry. With all her strength, she lifted Renee and dragged her across the floor to the couch. She labored to lay Renee onto the couch and covered her with the burlap sack. "I didn't promise, Renee," she said as she made her way to the small door leading outside.

Once outside, she closed the door and ran back home hoping her parents had not left the house to continue their search for Renee.

狼

Aaron, Coleen, and Monroe were emerging from the house to continue their search. Since Lucy wasn't home, they assumed she had gone off to search on her own. Aaron handed some money to Monroe. "Here, son, take this money and hire a horse for the day and ride out to the farm to see if Renee showed up there."

Monroe took the money and was about to head off in the opposite direction when he heard the loud cries of his sister.

"Wait! I found her, I found her!" Lucy yelled as she came closer to the house.

Lucy came to a stop and doubled over out of breath. Aaron assisted her as she began to sit on the front doorsteps.

"Where, child, where is she?" asked Coleen, anxiously.

Talking between breaths, Lucy said, "She's in Reuben's secret room at the school and she's very sick. We need to go get her now. She fainted and I think she has a fever."

"What secret room at the school?" Coleen asked.

Aaron rose and said, "Never mind about that now." He turned to Monroe and ordered, "Go fetch Doctor Weldon and bring him to the house." Then he said to Lucy, "Come, girl, take us to her quickly."

The family broke into their respective treks in quick haste. As they were running to the school, Coleen shouted, "Should we inform Franklin and Margret Wallace?"

"After yesterday, I wouldn't count on those two giving a damn about their daughter. Renee is the closest we have to Reuben and we must see to her safety. If not for the Wallace's sake, at least for our son's," answered Aaron very determined.

Lucy began to stumble. She was exhausted making this run twice. Both her parents took hold of her and helped. She led them to the rear of the school near the shrubs hiding the door to Reuben's secret room. When they arrived, Lucy dropped to her knees and pointed.

"There, between those two bushes is the door. Lift up and pull to the side," she instructed as she was catching her breath.

Aaron dove between the bushes and did as Lucy directed and the hidden door easily popped open causing Coleen to gasp in surprise.

"Why that little sneak! How could he keep this room a secret from me?" asked Coleen.

"That's what Renee said when I showed it to her," answered Lucy.

Aaron crawled through the opening and raised himself on his knees. He looked all around the room. It was darker now because the oil lamp was flickering in and out. He heard a gentle moan, rose to his feet, and looked to the direction of the moan.

He saw the limp form of Renee on the couch looking pathetically ill and dirty. With tears forming in his eyes, he moved over to her. Without saying a word, he scooped her up in his arms and carried her to the small portal.

"Coleen, quick, come and help me!"

Coleen dropped to her knees and saw Renee's bare feet coming out of the opening. She grabbed hold and pulled. When Lucy saw Renee's feet, she crawled to help her mother. Aaron finished handing Renee's limp form to Coleen and Lucy and quickly crawled out of the room and watched as Coleen looked her over as a mother looking over her own sick child.

"She's cold, but doesn't have a fever. Oh my dear, Aaron, look at these bruises on her face. Did she tell you how she got these, Lucy?"

"No, Mama. I didn't notice them until we got her into the light just now."

"We need to get her back to the house. Monroe should be arriving with Doctor Weldon any time now," said Coleen.

Renee gained consciousness enough to recognize Coleen and Aaron looking down upon her. She reached up and Aaron took her hand in his and gripped it tightly. She focused on Coleen, who was cradling her as she was kneeling on the ground.

"Mrs. Duran? No," she said, weakly. "I'm horrible. Reuben ran away because of me. You must hate me. I don't deserve your pity, just leave me to die."

She quickly told them of how she stopped Reuben from trying to kill himself under the oak tree and Akagi Genda-San's challenge for Reuben to find him and continue what he started.

Coleen caressed Renee's face, "No, child, we could never hate you. You alone may have saved our son from his own hands and besides, you're practically a part of our family."

Renee revealed a hint of a smile before she drifted back out of consciousness.

"Come on, we need to get our Renee back home so the doctor can look her over!" said Aaron.

Lucy began to follow, but quickly stopped and looked back to the uncovered opening of the room. She stepped back and crawled into the room, looked to the table, and scooped up the image case and button in both hands. She was about to leave until the strange smooth stone caught her eyes. She glanced at it wondering if it had any significance, and snatched it up as well. She crawled outside and ran to catch up with her parents.

狼

"Come now, Monroe, how much longer must I wait? I have other patients I need to visit before I start my day at the clinic."

Monroe was able to locate Doctor Richard Weldon as he was leaving his home to make early morning rounds and convinced him to come to the Duran home. On the way, Monroe told Doctor Weldon of the events from the past couple of days. He found it unbelievable Franklin

Wallace would abandon his daughter. He nearly didn't come with Monroe except for the mere fact Aaron Duran was a good friend and besides, the story Monroe told the doctor raised his interest and concern since he was present at Renee's wedding when she ran out of the church. Monroe and Doctor Weldon arrived at the house nearly thirty minutes after the family split on their assignments. Monroe made sure the doctor was comfortable, not knowing how long it would be when the others would arrive with Renee, if she was where Lucy said she was.

Doctor Weldon's patience was beginning to wear thin as he thumbed at his pocket watch looking at the time. He finally rose and made his way to the front door saying, "I'm sorry, Monroe, but I can't wait any longer. I'll come back this afternoon…"

Before he could finish, the door burst open and in ran Aaron with Renee in his arms. He momentarily stopped at the archway of the parlor where Monroe and Doctor Weldon were standing.

"Quick, Richard, she's very ill!" Aaron called out, and ran upstairs to Lucy's room.

Doctor Weldon quickly grabbed his bag and followed Aaron.

Once inside Lucy's bedroom, Aaron gently laid Renee down and was pushed away by Doctor Weldon. He quickly gave her a visual examination. While doing so, Coleen entered the room. Aaron placed his arm around Coleen as they watched the doctor work. Lucy and Monroe stood silently at the door.

"Good, good, she has no fever, but is very weak. Who found her?" asked the doctor.

"I did," said Lucy.

"How long had she been in this condition?"

"At least since yesterday," answered Coleen.

"It looks like she has been sick. You know, vomiting," added Lucy.

"What about these bruises on her face?" the doctor asked very concerned.

"We didn't notice them until we got her into the day light," answered Coleen.

"Okay, let's clear this room out. Coleen, will you please stay? Aaron, Monroe, and Lucy, bring some warm water and some towels. You may also want to start drawing a bath so we can get her cleaned up."

"Right away, Richard. Come on you two," said Aaron.

"Please, Coleen, help me undress her. Have you contacted her parents?"

Coleen breathed out hard, "Her parents won't have anything to do with her," she said in a tone of irritation.

"Shame, she's in a bad way."

With Coleen's aid, Renee was undressed. In doing so, they noticed more bruises on her upper arms, as if someone had taken hold of her roughly, a bruise on her hip as a result of a kick, and welts on her back from being hit with a switch. Coleen covered her with one of Lucy's robes and stood close by as the doctor did a more detailed examination. The look of concern on his face caused Coleen to worry.

"Please, Richard, how is she?"

172

"She's well… just, let me see." Doctor Weldon finished his examination in about 10 minutes and then covered Renee with a blanket he retrieved from the back of a chair.

At that moment came a knock on the door. "Mama, I have warm water and towels," said Lucy. "Is it okay for me to come in?"

Coleen looked at the doctor and he nodded his head. She stepped to the door and opened it. Lucy stood in the hall with a basin in her hands and towels draped over her arms.

"Come in, sweetheart. Put that on the desk and continue helping your Da and Monroe."

"Yes, Mama."

"No, wait," said the doctor. "Please, Lucy, you said Renee had been sick? Vomiting you say? How do you know this?"

Lucy timidly looked at her mother and Coleen moved next to her and placed her arm around her shoulders. "Go ahead, tell the doctor what he needs to know."

Lucy started to shudder and her eyes began to water. "I saw her vomit when I found her. There was a bucket in the far end of the room and it looked like she had been using it often because she ran straight to it, like she knew where it was."

"Indeed," answered the doctor. "That's very observant, Lucy. Then what happened?"

"When she was done, I helped her to the table and then she collapsed. I had to drag her back to the couch. She didn't want me to tell anyone she was hiding, tried to make me promise, but she passed out before I could. But even if I did, I would've still come and got Mama and Da."

Doctor Weldon nodded in approval. "Well done, Lucy. You did right and maybe because of your quick thinking, you may have spared Renee a very severe illness."

Lucy looked up at her mother and asked, "Is she going to be okay, Mama?"

Coleen looked to the doctor and he nodded yes, then back to Lucy. "Yes, my dear child. She's going to be just fine. Now please go back and help your father and Monroe."

Renee rose to her elbows and moaned. Doctor Weldon quickly sat at her side and eased her back down. "There, there, child. You just lay back and relax. You've had quite an episode and you need rest."

Renee strained to look around Doctor Weldon. "Lucy! You promised you wouldn't tell anyone," she said as she began to sob.

Lucy broke away from Coleen's arm and knelt next to the bed. "Renee, you're sick. You didn't give me a chance to promise and besides, if I did, I would've still told my parents. We love you, Renee. We want to take care of you."

Renee looked away as tears began to fall from her eyes. "Go away, Lucy," she said.

Looking distraught, Lucy rose to her feet and started walking out of the room. She stopped at the door, turned, and walked back to the bed and knelt. She reached under her bed to retrieve Renee's small chest containing her written passages Reuben asked her to watch over. She placed it on the nightstand, stood and slid her hand into her skirt pocket and pulled out the contents. She opened the image case with Reuben's picture and placed it on the chest, set the

VMI button in the center of the image case, and then the stone. The parchment, she placed back in her pocket.

Renee turned her head as Lucy placed the stone down and momentarily looked at Reuben's image and said, "Lucy, wait!" She reached out her left hand toward her. "I'm sorry, please forgive me."

Lucy quickly moved back to Renee's side and embraced her. As she held Renee in her arms, she said, "There's nothing to be sorry about. Just don't... be sick in my bed, or you will have something to be sorry about."

Renee smiled and let out a small laugh, the first since the last time she was with Reuben.

"Now do as Doctor Weldon and Mama tell you. I'm going to go fix you a bath and something to eat."

Doctor Weldon placed his hand on Lucy's shoulder and again nodded his approval to her. As she stood to leave the room, Coleen gave Lucy a quick hug and walked her to the door.

"Now listen, Renee, you need to rest and do as the Durans tell you. You're very lucky to have such wonderful people to look over your welfare," said Doctor Weldon.

Renee made no response. She reached and took Reuben's picture from the nightstand, and continued to stare at the image.

The doctor took a closer look at the bruise on her face. "Tell me, young lady, how did you get these bruises?"

Without looking away from Reuben's picture, Renee replied, "My father."

Coleen grunted in anger. Doctor Weldon looked up at her and nodded. He brought his attention back to Renee and gently gave her forehead a caress. "You're safe now. I'll be back later this afternoon to see how you're doing, okay?"

Renee nodded.

As the doctor stood, Coleen took his place and took Renee's free hand. "I'm going to walk Doctor Weldon out, but I'll be back to help you get cleaned up. You just lay here and rest."

"I will, Mrs. Duran. Thank you."

Coleen smiled and kissed Renee on her forehead. She stood and both she and the doctor left the room.

When they reached the top of the stairs, Doctor Weldon said to Coleen, "I must speak to you and Aaron privately."

"Of course, Richard."

They walked to the kitchen where Aaron and the two siblings were at work heating water for Renee's bath. "Aaron, dear, Richard needs to have a chat with us."

"Yes, definitely. You two continue warming this water."

Aaron, Coleen, and Doctor Weldon made their way to the parlor out of earshot of Monroe and Lucy.

"How is she?" asked Aaron.

"Tired and in need of liquids, nothing too serious. Suffering of exposure and dehydration more than anything, but it was very fortunate Lucy found her when she did or she could have gotten worse. I would however, still like to look in on her if that's all right?"

"Of course, Richard," replied Aaron.

Doctor Weldon sighed and began to speak frankly, "Aaron, Coleen, I do know of Franklin Wallace's arrangement of his daughter's wedding to that boy from Charleston. It has been the talk of the town, of course. I was there when we all saw Renee run out of the church, but were not given details. I assume by Renee's state and from what Monroe told me, it's quite obvious, Franklin, being the proud man he is, was despicable by disowning his daughter as evidence from her bruises." He shook his head in anger and continued.

"A man with such prestige, money, and influence. It's sinful for him to act in such a way. Being a doctor, it's difficult not to get emotional about such things. In this day and age for parents to still place tradition higher than family is appalling." Again, he shook his head in frustration.

Thinking of how Renee quickly took interest in the picture of Reuben, he took a serious tone with Aaron and Coleen. "Where's Reuben?"

Coleen began to sob and Aaron held her tight. As he comforted his wife, he began to tell Doctor Weldon of the events leading to Reuben's departure to seek out Akagi Genda-San. He spoke of how Reuben and Akagi Genda-San met and how he was providing good advice to Reuben aiding him to cope with his memories of Mexico. He mentioned how Reuben was making great progress, until Akagi Genda-San had to leave, and then Reuben reverted back to his melancholic ways.

Coleen added it was at this point when Renee's upcoming wedding was also making it difficult for Reuben and he became suicidal. She told the doctor of how Renee stopped Reuben in time just before he was going to stab himself in his stomach, some sort of 'ritual' suicide method Akagi Genda-San spoke of.

Aaron added it wasn't until they found Reuben's letter they learned he and Renee secretly planned for him to travel to Japan to seek out Akagi Genda-San to continue his teachings so Reuben would get well. Renee couldn't live knowing Reuben, at any time, would take his life. They made a pact they would both live, even if it was at a great distance apart from each other.

At the end of Aaron and Coleen's story, Doctor Weldon could not help but feel emotional. Renee's reaction to the Durans, especially how she took special notice when Lucy placed the image of Reuben on the nightstand roused his suspicions. "That has the makings of a tragic love story, and I do mean love," said Doctor Weldon. He cleared his throat and continued.

"Your Reuben and Renee, they are good friends?"

Aaron replied, "The best."

"They grew up together," added Coleen.

"And to your knowledge, they were nothing more than just friends?"

Coleen answered, "It was obvious they wanted to be more, but because of Renee's father and his arranging her to be married to the Sinclair boy, they couldn't." Coleen got a very puzzled look on her face. "What are you getting at, Richard?"

"Oh, nothing, I find it very comforting the poor girl has good people such as you to care for her. Considering her predicament, you may be the only family she has right now," he replied, yet he was becoming curious if Renee and Reuben were, by chance, more than just friends.

"She has probably spent more time with us than her real family," said Coleen with a hint of a smile on her face.

Doctor Weldon nodded in approval and picked up his medical bag, "Well, I must take my leave, but I would like to come back this afternoon to see how she's doing."

"Yes, of course, thank you, Richard," said Aaron, as he walked Doctor Weldon to the door. When he returned to the parlor, he found Coleen sitting on the sofa with Reuben's picture in her lap. He came and sat next to her.

They sat in silence staring at the picture. After a long, quiet moment, Aaron, using his fingertips, turned Coleen's face toward his. Aaron said softly to his wife, "We must care for Renee as if she is one of our own. Having her with us is like Reuben never left. I sense his presence in her."

Coleen nodded in agreement and replied, "She can stay as long as she wants and more."

狼

The rest of the day was quiet and peaceful. Once Aaron was satisfied all was well with Renee, he departed to his law office to rearrange appointments for the past couple days he missed in order to search for Renee with his family.

Monroe went to the livery stable to hire a mount to ride out to the farm to tell May and the others about Renee and Reuben and how Renee was safe living in the city home. When he finished that task, he returned the horse and went to Aaron's law office to continue his studies for his upcoming law exams.

In the Duran home, Coleen and Lucy helped Renee bathe and arranged living space in Lucy's room for her. As much as she wanted to help, Coleen would not allow Renee to lift a finger. "You heard the doctor, you need to rest. You're still weak and desperately need to regain all of your strength," Coleen told Renee.

"Yeah, Renee. Now that you'll be living with us, I've got someone to share my chores with," said Lucy, gleefully.

"Mrs. Duran, I sincerely don't expect to be a burden..."

Coleen cut Renee off, "Now stop right there, child. You're not a burden of any kind. You're the closest thing we have to Reuben being here and we are not going to give that up, do you understand?"

Renee nodded and replied, "As long as you allow me to contribute... when I'm well."

Throughout the day, Coleen and Lucy rearranged Lucy's room. Coleen had the idea when Monroe departs for school, Renee could use that room which he shared with Reuben.

However, Lucy pleaded with Renee to stay in her room. She was excited to share her room with Renee and Renee also liked the idea. All her life, Renee felt so alone living in the big house where she once was a resident. Now she had a companion with whom she could share a living space. With that settled, Coleen and Lucy went as far as taking apart Reuben's bed and moved it into what was now Lucy and Renee's room. Renee immediately made use of Reuben's bed.

As the clock in the parlor chimed 4 o'clock in the afternoon, a knock was heard at the door. Coleen answered the door and true to his word, Doctor Weldon came by to check in on Renee. After a cordial greeting and a quick update from Coleen on Renee's welfare, they made their way up to see Renee.

Doctor Weldon was pleased to see Renee looking very radiant after the state she looked earlier this day. She was sitting on Reuben's bed, covered with a quilt that didn't fit the décor of the room, but it had belonged to Reuben so it had to be a part of the bed Renee could now call hers.

"So my dear lass, how are you feeling? I hope you have been resting. By the looks of this room it looks like a lot of work has been done. I certainly hope you were not part of it," said Doctor Weldon pleasantly, as he looked at Coleen.

"No, Richard, as much as she wanted to lend a hand, Lucy and I didn't allow her to help."

"Good, good. And have you had anything to eat?"

Renee nodded as she answered, "I did have a little soup Lucy made, but I couldn't eat too much. I got nauseous." She quickly looked at Lucy and added, "But it wasn't the soup, Lucy. It was delicious from what I could eat."

"I see," replied Doctor Weldon. "This nausea, how often does it bother you?"

"Not much, I think I was eating too fast."

Doctor Weldon nodded, "That makes sense, you were a bit undernourished and when that's the case, one must take in nourishment slowly."

"I still feel a little weak. That doesn't mean anything serious, does it, Doctor Weldon?" asked Renee in a concerning manner.

"Not at all, Miss Renee, not at all. I believe you will make a full recovery in a day or so. I suspect you suffered from exposure, dehydration, and not enough to eat."

"That doesn't seem too serious. I suppose I'll live," answered Renee as she fondly looked at the picture of Reuben now resting on her own nightstand and picking up the button, bringing it to her lips.

Doctor Weldon gently placed his hand on Renee's head, "That you will. The both of you," he said with a great deal of compassion.

Quickly he cleared his throat to hide his emotion and picked up his medical bag. "Good then. Well, I have to go now. I'll be by again tomorrow and bring some medicine that will help with the nausea. Mind you, it doesn't taste too good, but it will help. In the meantime, try to eat something more solid than soup this evening, take in plenty of liquids, and get some rest and tomorrow we can try to have you walk around to help regain your strength."

"Thank you, Doctor," said Renee, pleasantly.

Doctor Weldon made his way out of the room followed by Coleen.

As Doctor Weldon was exiting the house, Aaron and Monroe arrived at the front door.

"Ah, come to see your patient, did you, Richard?" asked Aaron in greeting the doctor at the doorstep.

"How's she doing?" asked Monroe.

Very cheerfully, the doctor replied, "Very well. She should be back to herself in a day or so. I can tell she is very grateful for what you have done for her. I assume she'll be staying with your family?"

"Of course," Aaron answered without hesitation. "She's practically a part of our family so whatever your fee is, please let me pay."

"No, no, no. That won't be necessary, Aaron. It's the least I can do considering what the poor dear has gone through... with her own family. Listen, I must be off now. I'll be bringing some medicine for Renee to help with the nausea tomorrow, so in the meantime, have a wonderful evening."

"You as well, Richard," replied Aaron.

"I hear you are close to finishing law school, Monroe. Good on you, my boy, good on you."

"One more semester, Doctor Weldon," replied Monroe, proudly.

Doctor Richard Weldon began to make his way home. After several steps, he turned to look at the Duran home. Thinking of the discussion he had with Aaron and Coleen in the parlor earlier this day about Renee and Reuben, and observing how fondly attached she was to his picture and button, he began to wonder if there may be a possibility he would be calling upon the Duran home in a month's time or so.

狼

A day after Renee was taken in by the Durans, she regained her health and became a very active member of the family in every way. She mostly stayed inside the house, occasionally sitting on the doorstep in the early evening hours, always with Reuben's picture next to her.

She ventured out with Coleen and Lucy a few times, but each time, people who knew of the wedding event would, in hush tones, gossip and gawk at her. It made Renee very self-conscious and felt Coleen and Lucy didn't deserve the ridicule of the closed minds of the so called citizens of society. There were many who knew the true nature of Franklin Wallace and commended Aaron and Coleen for taking in Renee. But to her, it was all pity and she didn't want to be known as a girl who could not hold her own.

Aaron felt it was unhealthy for Renee to continually stay in the house. He did have her come to his law office to assist in paperwork, and work alongside Lorena, Aaron's secretary, which she did enjoy and it made her feel useful, but again, she was under the watchful stares of people who both pitied and condemned her. Eventually, Aaron came up with a superb idea.

James Wilcox, the owner of the large plantation up the road from the Duran farm, purchased a larger plantation in North Carolina complete with field hands and servants which meant he didn't have need of the ones he owned now. He began to sell them off and that would include the three Aaron hired to maintain the Duran farm. As much as Aaron despised the institution of slavery, he could not see it in his heart to see May, Henry, and Noah sold off with the possibility of never seeing one another again, especially since all three were blood related.

Noah's mother, June, was May's sister. Several years ago, James sold off June, her husband, and the rest of Noah's siblings one after another until only Noah remained. With Henry being May's uncle and all three being blood family, and after what happened with Renee, Aaron could not allow them to be sold off separately, so he purchased them from James Wilcox.

The whole transaction made Aaron sick to his stomach. That was until Renee was doing some reading in Aaron's law office when there was no work to be done. She read about a legal statute regarding the legality of freed persons of color being paid wages to work as laborers in shops, factories, and agriculture. Since this was not in the realm of law Aaron practiced, it would have gone unknown if it wasn't for Renee. For that, he praised her for the answer to his moral dilemma and immediately filed the proper procedures for the freedom of May, Henry, and Noah for which they were grateful, and agreed to stay on as hired laborers.

As for Renee, she would move out to the farm and serve as the "Duran Agriculture Liaison," a position made up by Aaron, and knowing, by his profession and the realm of law he did practice, merchants psychologically keyed in on fancy titles and that would give Renee an advantage. The title served her well by receiving feed, seed, and other farming needs at lower rates. Her pleasant, adorable personality and beauty may have also aided in the lower rates, after all, she was the only "Agriculture Liaison" in the county, and a woman at that.

Renee thrived at her new role for several reasons, such as being productive and useful, to work, to be away from the city, and most of all, to be on the farm where she and Reuben first met, grew up, and had their farewell moment.

For the next several weeks, the arrangement was proving to be productive. Renee, with the help of May, Henry, and Noah, was able to make use of the farm's resources and earn a little extra money which Aaron allowed them to keep. In the past, all crops and animal products went to James Wilcox in trade for the use of his servants. Now with that arrangement at an end, the farm became self-sustaining.

Lucy was also spending much of her time helping Renee, especially since she was nearing the end of her schooling. They both worked tirelessly with May, Henry, and Noah. When free time was available, Lucy would give Renee lessons on the piano Aaron moved from the Norfolk home to the farm. The same piano Franklin Wallace gave the Duran family many years ago, an irony Renee could not help but find amusing every time she sat on the bench.

All was going well for Renee, except for the fact her love for Reuben grew more each day. She would sit beneath the oak tree, where they had their special farewell moment, almost every evening at twilight. It had been nearly two months since that one evening. Nearly two months since Lucy found her in Reuben's secret room where she hid after her father threw her out of his life. Nearly two months since the Durans took her in as a member of their family. And now she began to have moments of fatigue, nausea and stomach pains, symptoms May had suspicions about, remembering the evening Renee and Reuben went off on their own.

狼

Early in the morning, Noah and Henry hitched up the farm wagon to the horse team for Renee, May, and Lucy. May convinced Renee to travel into the city for Doctor Weldon to have a look at her. Although May had suspicions, she kept them to herself. She could only assume Renee didn't know what was ailing her, but led her to believe it was in her best interest to see to her health, being that she, for all intents and purposes, managed the farm.

Once the wagon was ready, everyone with the exception of Henry, were on the way to the Duran home in the city. The journey took close to half an hour and was always a pleasant ride.

They arrived at the Duran home where Noah left the three women and continued to the livery stable to park the wagon for the day.

Lucy entered the house and called out for her mother.

"Mama, it's me, with Renee and May."

Coleen came around the corner from the parlor and had a bright smile on her face.

"My, this is a surprise! Come on in. What are you doing in town?" she asked, as she walked them all into the Parlor. "May, it's been quite a while. How have you been?"

"I have been very well, Mrs. Duran. How are you and Mr. Duran getting along?"

"We still think of Reuben every day, but I keep my faith and love he's safe and will one day return," said Coleen as she suddenly began to feel emotional. Renee quickly came to her side and took Coleen in her arms to console her. Coleen returned the gesture as she continued. "It would be so much easier if there was at least a small living part of Reuben here."

Coleen then cleared her throat, released her hold of Renee, and said, "Come, let's all have a seat. To what do I owe this pleasure?"

Renee answered, "Well, it's nothing really. I haven't been feeling too well lately and May pointed out I should see Doctor Weldon."

Coleen quickly stood up and sat next to Renee. She placed her hand on Renee's forehead checking for a fever. "Oh my heavens, what is it? What's wrong? Lucy, quick as you can, go to Doctor Weldon's clinic and ask if he could come over as soon as he can, and then fetch your father."

"Yes, Mama," replied Lucy as she was making her way to the door. Before Renee could say anything, she was gone.

"Please, Mrs. Duran, I'm sure it's nothing. I've just been feeling tired and achy lately. Really, I've been working hard and I'm probably over doing it a bit."

"That may be so," said May, "but we can't have you down with… a fever or something."

"May is right. Come and let's go into the dining room. I was about to make some tea."

For the next hour, Coleen, May, and Renee sat at the large family dining room table having a nice visit. Noah eventually arrived from the stable and joined the three ladies. The discussions ranged from how the farm was doing to the weather.

As Coleen was about to start discussing Renee's health, the front door opened and Aaron's voice was heard. "Hello, where is everyone?! Renee, where are you?!"

180

He walked through the hall, glanced into the parlor, and continued until he came to the dining room where he saw the ladies and Noah sitting at the table. He quickly stepped to Renee, kneeled down and placed his hands gently on her shoulders, looking into her face at every angle possible from his position. All Renee could do was sit and stare back at Aaron with her adorable, big bright brown eyes.

"What's wrong, sweetheart? Lucy says you're sick. You haven't been working too hard on the farm getting all worn out now are you?"

"Da, I never said she was sick. I only said she wasn't feeling too well," said Lucy.

"Sick, not well, what's the difference? Where's Richard, damn it? Coleen, why are you having her sit at the table? She should be lying down!"

"Gosh Da, you were never this concerned when me and my brothers were sick."

"See! There goes that word again, sick! Now Renee, get upstairs and into bed until Doctor Weldon gets here."

Renee could not help but giggle. "Please, Mr. Duran, calm down. Here, let me get you some tea. I'm not an invalid you know," she said as she got up to retrieve a cup and saucer from the cabinet. Everyone else around the table all started laughing.

"That's right, laugh it up, Noah, my young lad," said Aaron as he motioned toward him. "The only other man in this room, and he sides with the women. This is a sad affair, I'm telling you, a sad affair indeed."

Once Aaron was served tea by Renee and he began to calm down, she told him of her symptoms and felt she might be over working a little and was quite sure Doctor Weldon would agree.

Coleen and May, on the other hand, looked at one another, as Coleen brought her hand to cover her mouth wondering as she recognized the symptoms.

No sooner did Aaron finish his tea, when a knock was heard at the front door.

"That must be Doctor Weldon," said Lucy. "I'll get it."

As Lucy went to answer the door, everyone else got up from the table and made their way to the parlor.

Lucy escorted Doctor Weldon into the parlor where the others were waiting. Aaron stepped up and presented his hand in greeting as the doctor returned the gesture.

"Richard, it's good to see you, my friend."

"You as well, Aaron. Well, we certainly have quite a gathering now," said Doctor Weldon.

Coleen stepped up to offer her greetings and began the introductions. "Richard, these are two dear friends of the family, May and Noah. They help Renee oversee the farm."

Doctor Weldon greeted May and Noah pleasantly, "Indeed. It's very nice to finally meet you. Aaron and Coleen have told me a great deal about you and, ah… Henry, is that correct? Is he here as well?"

"No sir," answered May.

Doctor Weldon turned his attention to Renee, who was standing off to the side of the room next to Lucy. "So, Miss Renee, Lucy tells me you have not been feeling too well. You look pleasant to me, but what do you say we go to your room and see what's wrong. If there is anything wrong, that is. Have you been keeping up your nourishment? The last time I saw you, you were a bit under nourished. Coleen, will you please join us?"

Coleen nodded and followed the doctor and Renee up the stairs and into the room Lucy and Renee share. Once inside, Doctor Weldon removed his jacket and rolled up his sleeves. The last time he saw Renee, he had a feeling he would be making this visit.

He asked Renee about her symptoms and when they started.

"They started sometime last week," she answered.

Doctor Weldon brought his hand to his chin and began rubbing it in thought. "Hmm, let's see. That has been close to two months since I last saw you, correct?"

Renee nodded in agreement.

"Coleen, can you please help Renee undress. She doesn't have to undress completely, just to her undergarments."

As Coleen assisted Renee, Doctor Weldon opened his medical bag, dug out his stethoscope, and blew on it several times to take the chill off.

Once Renee was prepared, Doctor Weldon said, "Okay, Renee, lay back and relax, I'm going to take a listen and feel around your abdomen. It won't hurt a bit."

As he listened and felt, he nodded. He asked Renee again about her symptoms. "I know this may be redundant, but I just want to be sure of what we have here."

Again she stated the symptoms, "Tiredness, nausea, cramps, and my chest has been sore."

"Hmm, I see. You can get dressed now," he said with no worry in his voice so as not to cause any concern for Renee.

However, as she was dressing, he glanced toward Coleen and gave her a slight nod having the sense she also knew the cause of Renee's symptoms. Upon seeing the doctor's nod, she brought her hand up to her mouth as she did earlier when she asked Renee of her symptoms.

When Renee was dressed, she sat on the edge of Reuben's bed. "Well, Doctor, am I going to live?" she asked in her charming manner.

"For a very long time," replied Doctor Weldon. He turned his attention to Coleen. "Coleen, could I please speak to Renee in private. I'll want to speak to you and Aaron when I'm finished."

"Of course, Richard," replied Coleen and she exited the room, closing the door behind her.

All this began to make Renee feel uneasy and she started to worry. Doctor Weldon noticed and pulled up a chair and sat in front of her. He took her hands and as pleasantly as he could, he began to speak.

"Renee, I have some serious questions to ask you. Will you be honest with me?"

"Oh no, it is serious," Renee said very worried.

"No, no. Not at all. You're perfectly healthy for a girl in your condition."

"What do you mean, *'a girl in your condition'?*"

Trying to muster the best way he could to ask a delicate question, Doctor Weldon looked Renee in her eyes and asked, "Renee, my dear, when was the last time you were with your best friend, Reuben?"

Renee had a questionable look in her expression. She never mentioned her friendship with Reuben to Doctor Weldon. She slowly answered, "The evening before he left to Japan, the same evening before I was supposed to be married, why?"

"Hmm, how can I put this? When you were with Reuben, were you with him in the manner of, the way lovers would be?"

Now it was Renee's turn to bring her hands up to her mouth in concern. She began to gasp for air. Doctor Weldon moved from the chair next to her on the edge of the bed and comforted her by placing his arm around her. Her eyes began to water and she began to silently sob. Doctor Weldon pulled out a handkerchief from his shirt pocket and wiped her eyes and allowed her to take it.

"Geez oh geez oh geez Mr. and Mrs. Duran are going to be furious with me. Not only did I help Reuben leave, but now I have to tell them I have his child in me in sin. Oh geez, I am a horrible person like my father said I was."

Doctor Weldon now wrapped both his arms around Renee and began to speak. "Renee, you have the Durans all wrong. This entire family loves you as if you are one of their own." He released his embrace to look her face-to-face. "I suspect Coleen has had suspicions herself. Now you tell me, would the mother of the son who has blessed you with a living gift have these suspicions and curse you? No, and that's because she, and all of them, love you."

Renee wiped her eyes and nodded, but Doctor Weldon could still see she seemed unconvinced.

"It's going to be all right, Renee," said Doctor Weldon trying his best to reassure her. "Tell you what, you gather yourself up, and I'll go have a word with Aaron and Coleen, all right?"

Renee nodded and handed Doctor Weldon his handkerchief back. He held up his hand and said, "No, you keep that, those are your tears and you'll see what were sad tears will turn into happy tears."

He rose, retrieved his jacket, his bag, and exited the room closing the door behind him.

When he reached the parlor, Aaron and Coleen were sitting with May and Noah. When they saw the doctor enter the room, they all rose. He asked if he could discuss Renee's condition in private with Aaron and Coleen. May and Noah excused themselves and made their way to the kitchen where May, out of habit, began to prepare a meal.

Once they were alone, Coleen spoke first. "Is she, Richard?"

"You have had your suspicions, Coleen?" asked Doctor Weldon.

"Yes I have. May had suspicions as well from the night Renee went to see Reuben."

"But you have not shared them with Aaron?"

Aaron was looking back and forth dumbfounded as Coleen and Doctor Weldon were talking.

"What suspicions? Is anyone going to tell me what's going on here?" asked Aaron quite perturbed.

Doctor Richard Weldon took in a deep breath and began to speak as delicately as he could. "Although it's still a little too soon to be certain, with all my years of experience in this sort of thing, I believe your Reuben and Renee did, shall I say, spend at least one moment together, ah... to say goodbye for instance, considering their individual circumstances."

Coleen's reached and took hold of Aaron's arm as she said, "You mean to say it's true, our Renee is with Reuben's child?"

Aaron looked up toward the stairs and back to his wife.

"Yes, I do. After all, with what you have told me about those two and how they feel toward one another."

Doctor Weldon retrieved his bag and placed his hand on Aaron's shoulder. "Listen, I'm not one who condones children in such a manner without marriage, but... what those two have is love in its purest form, and there's no better way for a child to be conceived."

He gave Aaron's shoulder a gentle squeeze. "Listen, she's very healthy, but very frightened."

"Frightened of what?" asked Aaron.

"Of you two."

Aaron placed his arm around Coleen's waist and said, "Are you joking? This is probably the next best thing to happen to this family since we took in Renee."

"Then I suggest you two go up and reassure her because she thinks she has done a terrible thing."

"Right away, Richard. Can you please...."

"Not to worry, I know the way," said Doctor Weldon with a very pleasant tone. "Listen, I want to see her at least a couple times a month for the next few months, and as time gets closer, I'll want to see her more often," he added as he made his way to the door.

狼

Standing by herself, staring out of the window watching Doctor Weldon get into his carriage and ride away, Renee could not help but feel she let the whole world down. She reached into her skirt pocket and pulled out the image case of Reuben. She opened it and held it with her left hand as she instinctively placed her right hand on her stomach. She looked upon the picture with love as she said, "You never did leave me did you..."

There was a soft knock at the door and it slowly opened. Coleen and Aaron slowly walked in. Renee, standing on the other side of Lucy's bed next to the window, looked at the two, her eyes full of tears as they rolled down her cheeks. She had a sad frown on her face, her lower lip quivering.

Coleen looked at Aaron as he looked back. She stepped forward, widely opened her arms, and motioned Renee to come into them.

184

Renee's shoulders dropped as if a huge weight was released and quickly stepped around Lucy's bed and into Coleen's waiting arms that wrapped tightly around her. Aaron wrapped his arms around the both of them.

Coleen said, "Remember when I said earlier today, it would be so much easier if there was at least a small living part of Reuben here? Well, my precious Renee, you have just provided us with that part of Reuben, and it will grow into a wonderful gift of love both you and Reuben have created."

Renee looked up. She no longer had a sad frown, but instead a reassured looked. She spoke directly to both Coleen and Aaron. "I know it was sinful what Reuben and I did, but I... we, we just had to be with the one we loved at least one time. I'm sorry this baby will be born with us apart and not married. I know there are bad names for children like this..."

Aaron interrupted Renee's thought. "Listen to me, my dear, you have nothing to be sorry about, and as for those names, there's going to be only one name that child is going to have besides its given name and that name will be, Duran."

He took the image case from Renee's hand and opened it. He held it to the side of her face. Renee, with a puzzled look wondered what Aaron was doing. He let out a hefty sigh and said, "I just hope this child won't have Reuben's eyes because yours are much prettier than his."

Renee let out a small laugh, "Oh, Mr. Duran..."

"Hey! I think it's about time you start calling me Da and Coleen here Mama, like our other children."

This time, it was Renee who embraced both Aaron and Coleen.

狼

After several minutes to allow Renee to regain her composure and accept the reality of her condition, Renee, Coleen, and Aaron came downstairs to the kitchen where Lucy, May, and Noah were anxiously waiting to hear what Doctor Weldon's prognosis was for Renee. The three walked into the kitchen with Renee in the middle. She had a blank expression on her face. Although Coleen and Aaron were delighted with the news, Renee was still apprehensive about the other's thoughts of how she and Reuben conceived a child.

There were several moments of silence and questionable looks from the three who had been waiting all this time. It was Lucy who finally broke the silence, "Okay, so what's going on? Are you going to be all right, Renee? What did the doctor say?"

Renee opened her mouth to answer, but she couldn't think of anything to say. She dropped her face into her hands and turned into Coleen who took her into her arms.

"There, there. It's not bad at all, Renee. Aaron, you tell them the wonderful news."

"Wonderful news? What wonderful news?" asked Noah.

Aaron placed his arm around Renee's shoulders and eased her away from Coleen. She turned her face to hide it in Aaron's chest. Aaron gently patted Renee's shoulder and proudly said, "Our Renee is with child. Our Reuben's child."

Renee cringed deeper into Aaron's arms awaiting ridicule, but instead there was a few moments of silence until May finally spoke. "Thank the Lord you two finally proclaimed your love! It's about time! Do you have any idea how nerve-racking it has been watching you two grow up knowing that eventually the both of you would come to your senses! Come here, baby doll!" she exclaimed as she held out open arms.

Aaron released Renee and gently nudged her toward May. Renee slowly moved toward her as May closed the distance and embraced her.

As she was in May's arms, Renee turned her face toward Lucy. Lucy had a bright smile and her eyes were moist. She stepped forward and said, "At last, you're finally and truly a part of our family. You're one of us!"

Renee left May's embrace and went into Lucy's open arms.

When all was said and done, Lucy and Coleen assisted May with the meal she started earlier. There was much discussion. Renee was overwhelmed with the love and support and could not believe how fortunate she was.

"We need to get word to Reuben," remarked Noah. "How in the world do we do that?"

Aaron lightly pounded his fist on the table thinking. "He's been gone for almost two months. I wonder if he's even made it to Japan yet. Did he have any money with him?" he asked Renee.

Renee shook her head no, "He didn't take much."

"Well, how did you two plan his trip?" asked Coleen.

Renee went into detail how a couple weeks prior, she convinced Captain James Forrest, the master of the *Morning Star*, one of her father's ocean steamers, to take on Reuben as a member of his crew to San Francisco. From there, with Captain Forrest's help, they would find a vessel that would take Reuben the rest of the way.

Coleen and Aaron were taken by utter surprise. All this detailed planning taking place right under their noses. Coleen began to feel anxious and started to shudder. Lucy came to her side to comfort her.

"Renee, my dear, how could you let our Reuben be placed in the hands of someone we have never met?" said Coleen rather perturbed, the first time ever toward Renee.

In a very reassuring manner, Renee took hold of Coleen's hands and with a pleading look answered, "Captain Forrest is a very good man. He and my father are not on the best of terms because of the way my father raised me, but he's his best ships master. He's also my Godfather. In many ways, James Forrest is much like Mr. Du... Da, very truthful, honest, and honorable. I trust him. I would never let Reuben travel with anyone else. James Forrest gave me his word he would see to it Reuben would successfully make this journey, even if it meant he had to steal my father's ship and take Reuben to Japan himself."

Renee let go of Coleen's hands and dropped her head and a look of deep sorrow showed. She began to get emotional with tears filling her eyes. She spoke in a soft tone to no one in particular, "He doesn't know I came to stop him. He doesn't know I didn't marry William Sinclair. He doesn't know about our baby." She bit down on her lower lip to stop it from quivering. "He's going to forget about me."

It was now Coleen's turn to reassure Renee. "Renee, my sweetheart, I want you to remember what I told you many years ago when I first read one of your poems. I told you to never give up faith and love. Reuben's farewell letter was filled with his love for you. That son of mine will never stop loving you and he will for damn sure never forget you. As he said in his letter, he made this journey so he can be a better man for your sake."

When Coleen mentioned reading one of Renee's poems, Lucy suddenly remembered the parchment Renee handed her when she first found Renee hiding in the school. She quickly ran out of kitchen startling everyone in the room.

"What has gotten into that girl?" asked May.

Everyone shrugged their shoulders, looking toward the archway of the kitchen.

"Lucy! Is everything all right?" called out Aaron.

There was no response, except for the sounds of frantic footsteps from above. Aaron was about to stand to investigate when Lucy's footsteps were heard on the stairs coming down. She emerged back into the kitchen with the parchment in her hand.

"Good heavens, girl! You are forever running here and there. You need to knock that off!" said Noah.

"Shh, be quiet, Noah," said Lucy. She pulled a chair next to Renee. "Look at this, Renee. Do you remember giving this to me the day I found you in the school?"

"Uh-uh," Renee answered as she shook her head no. Suddenly she gasped in surprise. "Yes, I do remember. I wrote that the day I went to hide."

Lucy handed it to Renee, "Here, read it, out loud."

Renee took the parchment and unfolded it. She looked it over and began to read…

Your presence is etched in my memory
Vividly as the first day we met
My warmth, your touch, our everlasting love
But yet our time and place had not been set

Faith and Love
Stones and Water
Different wisdom, same meaning comes from within
We plunge into our sacrifices for our self-victory
Now our time and place begin

After she read her poem, she folded the page and held it to her heart, just as she did when she first wrote it. Lucy, using her fingertips, lifted Renee's chin, and in a very loving manner said, "Renee, you wrote that about Reuben. My brother told me a secret a couple of nights before he left to keep to myself until I knew when to use it, and this is the time. He told me to tell you, no matter what happens to you, he will always love you, and forever be yours. Renee, it may not be today, it may not be tomorrow, it may not even be next year, but I do know this for certain, you and my brother will be one."

Renee reached into her skirt pocket and again took out the image case of Reuben, opened it and placed it in the middle of the table for all to see. Then she pulled out the stone Akagi Genda-San gave her at the train station and held it gently in one hand as she caressed it with the other.

"What's that?" asked Aaron.

"Time," answered Renee.

"I don't understand," said Coleen.

Renee looked up and presented the stone to Coleen. Coleen took and held it in her hands, looking upon it curiously.

"Mr. Akagi gave that to me before he left and with it he told me, *'You see, my young precious Renee-Dono, there is a time and place for you and Reuben-San.'* He explained to me Reuben is a jagged stone and I'm his water, and in time, the time I give him to tumble in water, he will return just as smooth as this stone. He knew... Mr. Akagi knew Reuben and I would be one, and most importantly, he knows Reuben will return as he once was and much more. I just have to give him time to become smooth."

"We all have to give him time," added Coleen as she took Renee's hand, and placed it over hers holding the stone.

"That Mr. Akagi is one wise man in a strange kind of way," said May. "I should have known he was something special, after all, he did love my dumplings."

石
水

In the year of our Lord, 1847, a romantic tale continues.
A jagged stone tumbling in water, and a new unexpected friend…

That's Just Damn Spooky

It was a cold winter's day when the *Morning Star* made port in San Francisco. The voyage took nearly six weeks and was uneventful with the exception of a few days of rough seas when the *Morning Star* sailed through the Strait of Magellan.

During the voyage, Reuben proved himself to be a great asset as a member of the crew. So much so Donny Sullivan tried to convince Reuben to stay onboard as a crew member rather than travel to uncertainty across the Pacific.

"Come on, Reuben, you're a natural mariner. Just think of the adventures we can have sailing around the world," Donny pleaded as Reuben was disembarking with James Forrest in search for a ship to continue passage for his journey.

"Come now, Mr. Sullivan, none of that. Mr. Duran here has a mission which is most important, not only to himself, but to other special people in his life. Believe me, where he's going, he will have enough adventure to last a lifetime."

Reuben offered his hand to Donny, "And besides, I would hate to think what Franklin Wallace would do to this vessel if he were to find out I sailed on it as crew."

He briefly thought of Renee and how she truly got the better of her father. There was no way he could repay her for all she did to get him this far, with the exception of making it all the way and curing his mentality. She may be married and living another life this very moment, but what he told Lucy held true, no matter what happened to her, he would always love her, and forever be hers.

"Well then, Reuben, farewell and following seas to you. May you find what you are looking for," said Donny taking Reuben's hand and interrupting his thoughts.

The wharves in San Francisco were much busier than those in Norfolk. As he walked the wharves, Reuben kept apologizing to random people he was bumping into since his eyes were roaming, looking at all the wonders he'd never seen before. Mariners from different parts of the globe and ships as well. The cargo being unloaded had items of the likes he'd never seen. He felt so small being subjected to all these wonders and was excited to see more.

"Ah, there it is, Reuben. Our destination," said James Forrest. "The Olden Sword Rest House. There's at least half a dozen ships' captains whom I trust with my life who visit this establishment that may just suit our needs. I see a familiar ship in that dry dock over there, and if luck has it, perhaps the captain and old friend, Sean Aaron will be there."

"Go with luck, Captain, I'll stick to fate," replied Reuben with a smile.

"He-he, still on that fate thing are you? I still think it's absurd, but whatever gets you through the day," said James Forrest, amusingly.

Inside the Olden Sword Rest House, it smelt of salt air and stale ale. It was dark and dank, but it had a relaxing atmosphere, a place where a sailor could come in and unload his troubles away. James Forrest looked throughout the tavern floor until he heard a familiar curse coming from a table at the far end of the bar. He slapped Reuben on the shoulder and with a bright smile he said, "Come along, we're in luck."

"Hey, you old tar, do you kiss your mother with that filthy mouth of yours?" yelled out James Forrest.

"When I'm not kissing yours, you salty bastard!" came the response from an older and heaver set man sitting with a glass of ale in his right hand and a pipe in his left. He slammed them both down, stood up, and took James Forrest's offered hand and shook it vigorously.

"Good lord, James, what the hell are you doing on this side of the country? Is it that time of the year already?"

"Sure is, dropping off precious crap for that greedy old miser."

"Holy shit, don't tell me you're still sailing for that old seahorse's ass, Wallace, are ye?"

Reuben snickered. Even way out here on the Pacific coast, Franklin Wallace's reputation as a hard man is known. He wondered what Renee would think of that, probably wouldn't surprise her, he thought.

"Sit down, man, sit down. Who is this young pup holding on to your coat tails?" blurted out the mariner.

James Forrest took a seat and motioned Reuben to take one as well.

"Sean, I want to introduce you to a good friend of mine, Reuben Duran. Reuben, this here is Sean Aaron, captain of that pirate ship in the dock out yonder."

"Pirate ship! Well at least it's much more sea worthy than that garbage scow you float around in."

"May I remind you, your ship is the one that's in a dry dock and mine is not?"

"Grrr," retorted Sean Aaron through gritted teeth as he took Reuben's offered hand in his and shook it just as vigorously as he did with James Forrest. "Good friend you say? Well, Reuben Duran, any good friend of James' is a good friend of mine and that speaks volumes. So what brings you to my pretty little table?"

"Your ship actually, but what the hell? Why the dry dock?" answered James Forrest.

"Ah, whale shit! Bloody ship's rudder, that's the hell. Just when we were about to set sail to Shanghai two weeks ago."

"How are repairs going?" asked James Forrest, very concerned.

"All done. We slip her into the water tomorrow and the day after, it's off to Shanghai."

James Forrest, with a bright gleam in his face, quickly grasped Reuben's shoulder roughly, causing him to wince, and said, "You don't say?"

"I do say damn it, and what's with that look and the pup? You're up to something, James, don't deny it, I can tell."

"Sean, you and I have been good friends for a long time. I've helped you when you needed it and you've helped me. Both of us had to endure Franklin Wallace's crap in the past, and we know each other too well not to try and put one on the other, correct?"

"Aye, now what's the story?"

James Forrest leaned in further causing Sean Aaron to do so as well. He began to tell of how Reuben became a member of his crew and of his voyage to Japan, including Renee's participation. He mentioned how adaptable Reuben is and would be a great asset for the reminding portion of his passage. When James Forrest was finished, Sean Aaron gave Reuben a long look and nodded.

"Honshu, eh? What's in it for me?"

"Oh come on, Sean," pleaded James Forrest. "Japan is on your way to Shanghai. It'll only take you a few of days out of your way. Besides, I know you always pull in at some secluded cove to pick up Japanese silks you sell to Wallace for way more than he should be paying for."

Taking a puff from his pipe, Sean Aaron began laughing. "You say our little princess, Renee, came up with this caper?"

Reuben looked surprised as he mentioned her name. So much so, Sean Aaron took notice.

"Aye, Reuben, I know of Renee through James here. She is a sweet girl whose only misfortune is being the daughter of a shark prick like Franklin Wallace. If she has gone through all this planning under her father's nose for you, then you must be someone very special to her."

Reuben reached into his haversack and pulled out the image case wrapped with Lucy's ribbon. He untied the ribbon, opened it up, and placed it in the middle of the table. "She's very special to me," he said as all three men looked upon her image.

James Forrest tugged on Sean Aaron's sleeve and asked, "May I, Sean?"

He nodded.

"You see, Reuben, in the old days, all three of us sailed together in the east, myself, Sean, and Franklin. Sean here was to wed Margret Lewis, but Franklin convinced her Sean was not good enough for a woman of 'elegance.' So she married Franklin instead. Sean then came here to San Francisco to sail. Once I told him I became the Godfather of Renee, he in his own way adopted her as a secret Godfather considering the possibility he could have been her father instead of Franklin."

"Yeah, yeah, yeah, I know that's improbable." Sean Aaron interjected. "But considering whom her father is, she deserves way better than who Franklin chose to be her husband, and by the looks of you Reuben, my friend, you are the better man."

191

James Forrest nodded and continued, "Renee is sweet and lovely, but she does share one of Franklin's traits and that's his cunningness. However, unlike her father, she uses it for good, like this journey of yours for example. She knows many people have a harsh dislike for her father, so she is using that for your advantage."

Reuben laughed as he picked up the image case and placed it back in his haversack. "You know, James, she said something similar before we left."

All three men burst out laughing and commenced to drink a toast to Renee Wallace, or as far as Reuben was aware, Renee Sinclair.

狼

For the next hour, Reuben, in detail, just as he did with James Forrest, told Sean Aaron why he's making this journey. Although neither James nor Sean took part in the Mexican campaign, they still felt a bond to a man who ventured out to sample the hardships the world has to offer.

"Okay, so I get you to Honshu. That's the easy part, but what next?" asked Sean. "For crying out loud man, you don't know the language and do you even know where you are going? And when you make it ashore, you won't last long. Have you any idea what those backward heathens do to round-eyes when caught on their land? Hell boy, only the French and Dutch seem to be the only ones allowed to set foot on their shore and that's tolerable at best."

"Oh, don't worry about Reuben, Sean. He has fate on his side," said James Forrest, mockingly.

Tapping his fingers on the table, Reuben was beginning to feel doubt himself, but he had gotten this far. He wasn't about to give up. "I appreciate the concern," he said, "but I have a much bigger reason for completing this journey and I keep her picture in my haversack. I know you find my faith in fate obscure, James, but that's all I have and after Akagi Genda-San told me those who believe in fate make their own luck, well that seems to be working for me right now. I don't know how I'll do it, but somehow, someway, I'll make it to Itosai."

There was silence at the table as James Forrest and Sean Aaron watched Reuben as he rolled his empty glass in his hands.

"Perhaps I may be of assistance," said a young man in broken English sitting at the bar next to their table.

"I don't fancy strangers eavesdropping in on our conversation," said Sean Aaron, harshly.

Reuben, recognizing the accented broken English, stood and walked to the man. "What kind of assistance can you provide?"

"Reuben sit! That man seems like trouble," James Forrest said as he took a hold of Reuben's wrist. Reuben shook off his hand and continued to give the young man his attention.

"I asked, what kind of assistance..."

"You seek apprenticeship with the Akagi, do you not? I happen to owe my life to the Akagi and perhaps by helping you, you can help me repay my debt."

"How do you know Akagi Genda-San?" asked Reuben, completely ignoring James and Sean who became interested in their conversation.

"I was born in Majaul, a village that used to belong to the Kano Clan of the Hisano Provence next to the Itosai region. The Akagi liberated my village from the Kano and provided the village with protection free unlike the Kano. I always wanted to serve the Akagi in return, but was too young."

"So what are you doing here?" asked Reuben.

The young man smiled and raised a long bow, "Came to America seeking glory after my parents died of a fever epidemic."

"Ha, I see you've found it, my slant-eyed friend!" exclaimed Sean Aaron.

Reuben ignored Sean's remark and asked in a concerning manner, "And you didn't find it and are looking for a way back, home?"

"Very perceptive. I can see why you gained the attention of Lord Akagi Genda. And your big friend is right. If caught on the shores of my homeland, you will be executed. But with my assistance, I can get you to Itosai safely."

"And what's in it for you, my little yellow friend?" asked James Forrest as he stood and looked down on the young man.

Taking a casual drink from his glass, the man said, "Assist me to serve the Akagi. Apparently you have good standing with Lord Akagi Genda himself. If so, I'm sure you can arrange that?"

"What's your name?" asked Reuben.

"Sora, Tadashi Sora."

"Loyal huh?"

"You know my language?"

"No, but Genda-San called me that once before he left."

James Forrest walked around Tadashi and placed his hand on Reuben's shoulder. "Fate, Reuben?" he asked.

Reuben nodded and replied, "Fate."

Turning to Sean Aaron, James Forrest said, "Well Sean, you can't beat fate, what do you say?"

"Hey, this is no pleasure craft I'm running like yours James! I can't take on every little pup who needs a ride all over the globe. What the hell do you think I'm running here anyway, a ferry?"

"Come on Sean, one hundred pieces of gold."

Sean Aaron took a puff of his pipe and thought hard. "Make it two hundred. Hell, that's Wallace's gold in the first place you're hoarding. That greedy bastard will never miss it."

"Deal," said James Forrest.

"Damn it, I knew you were using Wallace's money, I should have asked for more!"

Sean Aaron stood and turned Tadashi's stool to face him. "Listen, slant-eye, you got yourself a passage, but only because of that man standing next to you and trust me, if anything happens to him, it's not me or James you'll need to worry about. It'll be the girl who he's doing this for you'll need to keep a watch for over your shoulder."

He turned to Reuben and continued, "And you, I expect you to keep this slant-eye in check or I'll flog you so bad, Renee will never recognize you, understand?"

"Well, Tadashi," said Reuben, "looks like we are dependent upon each other."

狼

After another hour of discussing the arrangements, the group of four departed the Olden Sword Rest House and headed to the dry dock where Sean Aaron's ship had just finished its repairs the day before. James Forrest and Sean Aaron walked ahead discussing the events in the tavern as Reuben and Tadashi followed engrossed in their own conversation.

"What's the story with the bow, Tadashi?"

Tadashi smiled proudly and held the bow in front of him as if it were a trophy.

"I'm a great archer, best in my village. That's why I came to America, but there is no use for archers here in America, unless you are an Indian, Ha! I made some money preforming tricks and winning bets, but not what I expected to be as glory. Don't get me wrong, Reuben, America is great with lots of opportunity, but to serve an honorable samurai lord like Lord Akagi Genda, that's a dream of a great archer such as me."

"You're really that good, huh? How did you learn?" asked Reuben.

"Both my grandfather and father were masters of Kyudo and Yabusame, the Budo Arts of foot and mounted archery. At one time they both served the Kano, but once they acquired firearms, the Kano had no more use of archers so they took away their samurai status and degraded them to peasants."

"You mean to tell me, guns are not common in your country?"

"Oh they are, for many years. But many samurai, such as the Akagi, view them as barbaric weapons. At least with a bow, an archer can see the target he's aiming for. With a firearm, all you do is point and pull a lever. What honor is there in that?"

Indeed, what honor is that, thought Reuben thinking of all the dead, especially four members of his platoon who lost their lives from one cannon shot.

Tadashi noticed Reuben deep in troubled thought. Trying to bring Reuben back into the conversation, Tadashi asked, "What's the story with the stick, Reuben? You carry it as if it were a jo."

Reuben looked up with a changed face. "You know of the jo?" he asked.

"Know of it, but not how to use it. I hear that's Lord Akagi Genda's weapon of choice next to the sword. Did he teach you the ways of the jo?"

As Tadashi did with his bow, Reuben held out his jo as if it were his trophy.

"Genda-San trained me in the ways of misogi-no-jo while he was on my farm."

"Amazing, taught by a master himself. You must show me what he taught you."

"He only taught me for two weeks, so I don't know a lot."

"Two weeks more than I, and in the Budo Arts, that's much to one who has never held a jo."

"Come on, Tadashi, you have had to have held a jo before?"

"I have held sticks and poles, but never a jo."

194

Reuben broke out in laughter.

"What's so funny?" asked Tadashi.

"This is actually an old rake handle Genda-San had me make into a jo."

Tadashi began laughing himself and said, "How do you think the jo was invented? As with many weapons in the Budo Arts, many of them started as common farm tools. You, Reuben, as a farmer with a rake handle, you are the true meaning of a Budo Artist."

"Hey you two, hurry up!" called Sean Aaron. "I want to introduce you to my ship's bosun, the one you'll be working for."

Reuben and Tadashi quickened their pace. At the end of the gangway leading to the dry dock stood a tall, strong, rough looking man standing next to James Forrest and Sean Aaron.

"Bosun, these two will be working for you on our trip across the Pacific. You two, this is the best bosun to sail the Pacific, Gallagher. No need to know his first name since you'll only be with us for the first leg of the trip."

"First leg, Captain?" asked Gallagher.

"Yes, first leg, bosun," replied Sean Aaron, in a manner of authority. "We are dropping these two on the island of Honshu and from there it's onto Shanghai."

"But, Captain, the crew has been preparing for Shanghai for months now."

Sean Aaron took a step closer to the bosun who seemed to cower a bit. "The crew will come to appreciate these two because of their sooner than expected stop on Honshu. You see bosun, we arrive in Honshu, take on silks and other goods we normally have no room for, sail on to Shanghai and sell them there for good profit, and that allows…"

"…the crew at least an extra month's time in Shanghai with more money in their pockets," the bosun finished Sean Aaron's thought.

"Exactly. You see, this is why Gallagher is the best bosun in the Pacific. He thinks as I do. Now bosun, this is Reuben Duran, a good friend of James Forrest who of course is a good friend of mine. That makes Reuben a good friend of mine as well. James here tells me he has proven himself to be an able seaman. That yellow slant standing next to him, his name is ah, Tada… something or other. Anyhow, he's important to Reuben so he comes along. Put them to work as you see fit."

"Aye, Captain, come on you two."

Tadashi began to follow Gallagher while Reuben turned to James Forrest.

"Mr. Forrest, I don't know how to thank you, but somehow I'll find a way," said Reuben, sincerely.

James Forrest took Reuben's offered hand in his. "Listen, Reuben, you can thank both Sean and me by finding what you're looking for, return to Virginia, and rescue Renee from a life she was not destined to live."

Reuben nodded and gave James Forrest a firm shake of his hand. "I know one day she and I will have our time. Remember I have fate on my side."

James Forrest chuckled and shook his head. "Still on about that fate, huh, Reuben?"

"Fate is an awesome power filled with irony, James. I never told you my parent's names, have I?"

James Forrest shook his head no.

"Well my father's name is Aaron, the same as Sean Aaron."

With a look of absurdness on his face, James Forrest said, "That proves nothing, Reuben."

With a childlike hint in his face, Reuben pointed to the aft end of Sean Aaron's ship and said, "Look at the name of the captain's ship. *'Coleen.'* Coleen is my mother's name."

James Forrest's mouth opened and his jaw dropped in awe. "Reuben, that's not luck, and that's not fate. That's just damn spooky. But anyhow, the best to you, my friend."

"And to you."

Reuben was about to walk off, but turned and said, "James, if you happen to see Renee again, please tell her I keep her in my thoughts every day and… I love her."

Without waiting for a response, Reuben turned and followed Sean Aaron onto the dry dock.

James Forrest stayed for several moments watching as his Goddaughter's love walked away. "I will, Reuben Duran, I certainly will," he said to himself. He would never get the opportunity to give Renee Reuben's message, for Franklin Wallace had him remain to sail in the Pacific.

石
水

In the year of our Lord, 1848, a romantic tale continues.
Uncharted land, and a newly awaited treasure about to arrive…

Kare o Korosu

Quickly covering her mouth, Renee rose from her seat and ran to the nearest water closet. Although this day had been one of celebration, Renee was far from the mood to be celebrating. She made the ferry ride between Chesapeake City and Norfolk several times with no problems in the past. However, now in her condition it was a different story.

The family was on their way home from a three day trip to Williamsburg where Monroe recently graduated law school at William and Mary. Renee was very proud and happy for Monroe, but now she wished he attended a school which didn't require a ferry to cross any water.

Watching Renee make a quick dash to the water closet, Coleen quickly followed with an expression of concern. She caught up with Renee just as she entered the closet and shut the door. From outside, Coleen could hear Renee retching. When she sounded as if she was finished, Coleen was about to knock when Renee began to retch again. Coleen could not help but smile at Renee's expense knowing what she must be going through.

Again, when all seemed quiet, Coleen lightly tapped on the door and asked if Renee was all right.

"Yes, I seem to be all right, oops… wait a minute…. BLAAUGH…."

Oh, that poor dear, thought Coleen as she entered the water closet and closed the door behind her. She knelt down to help Renee steady herself and gently rubbed her back.

Believing she was finished, Renee rose, closed the commode, and sat down heavily holding her face in her hands.

"Ugh, geez oh geez oh geez Mama, what has that son of yours done to me?"

Coleen burst out laughing, cradling Renee's head gently. "Don't worry child, in several more months, you'll see what the both of you did and you'll be so amazed none of this will matter."

"Excuse me, but is your sister all right?" asked a young man to Lucy.

Lucy was startled and turned her attention to the young man. He was a good looking man about Lucy's age with wavy light brown hair and hazel eyes. Lucy was awestruck by his eyes and lost in them.

"I'm sorry, I didn't mean to startle you. I'll leave you alone."

"She's not my sister," said Lucy, quickly.

"Oh, I thought…"

"She's almost like a sister. She and my brother are, ah… well, she's my best friend and she's not feeling too well these days. She has my brother's baby in her right now…"

"LUCY!" called out Renee. "What do you think you're doing?"

Cringing from embarrassment, Lucy replied, "Sorry, Renee, but this boy was asking if you were all right."

"Well, Lucy, we do not tell strangers about Renee condition," said Coleen.

"Mama, you too?!" exclaimed Renee, blushing from embarrassment.

Coleen raised her hands to her mouth saying, "Oops, I'm sorry, sweetie."

Monroe began laughing as Aaron said, "You know ladies… everyone on the ferry can hear every word you're saying."

The young man, looking lost, began to back away until Lucy noticed.

"Please don't go away. I'm sorry for this family outburst. Thank you for your concern," she said very apologetic.

Renee caught a glimpse of the look in Lucy's eyes as she spoke to the young man. Renee tapped Coleen on her arm and motioned toward Lucy with her eyes. "Yes, please forgive us. We're not normally like this. It's been a long day. Lucy, are you going to introduce us to your friend?" asked Renee.

Lucy shot Renee a daggered look and looked back to the young man who stepped closer.

"I'm sorry, but I didn't introduce myself to, ah, Lucy, is it? My name is Eric Klaus."

"Hello, Eric Klaus, please have a seat," said Renee.

Eric took a seat directly across from Lucy, looking at her as he did so.

Coleen smiled and began to introduce everyone, starting with Lucy.

Monroe leaned closer to Aaron and asked, "What's going on, Da?"

"Stay out of it son, that poor lad is on his own."

The rest of the ferry ride was pleasant with Eric Klaus accompanying the Duran family. He introduced himself as a son of a merchant who owns a mercantile store in Norfolk, and told of his father having plans on starting another store in Chesapeake City.

"Klaus Mercantile, yes, we go there often," said Lucy.

"I have a feeling we're going to start going more often now, huh, Da," said Monroe to Aaron as both Coleen and Renee shot him an angered look.

"Told you to stay out of it, boy," said Aaron. "Never get involved when women are matchmaking."

When the ferry docked in Norfolk and the luggage was gathered, Monroe went to hire a coach. While the family waited, Lucy stood nervously next to Eric. All the while, Renee, using eye and head motions, tried to get Lucy to talk to him.

Come on Lucy, it's obvious he likes you and you like him so say something, Renee thought as she shot Lucy a stern look. Oh geez, do I have to do everything myself, she continued thinking.

"Lucy, perhaps we could give Eric a ride to where he needs to go," said Renee.

"Yes, Eric, can I take you home… I mean, can we go home with you… grrr," said Lucy in a panic and covered her face with one of her hands after her attempt.

Coleen came to her rescue, "I believe Lucy is asking if we can offer you a ride home," she said, trying desperately to hide her amusement.

Eric smiled brightly, a smile reminding Renee of Reuben back in their younger adolescence days. "I would like to, but my father should be picking me up soon."

Lucy slumped in disappointment.

Renee leaned toward Lucy's ear and whispered, "Dinner, invite him to dinner."

"DINNER?! Ah, would you like to come over for dinner sometime, maybe tomorrow?" Lucy asked, anxiously.

Eric looked at Lucy and tipped his hat and said, "That sounds like fun. Yes, I would like to come for dinner, if that's all right?"

"Splendid," said Coleen.

As the arrangements were being made, Eric's father, Andrew Klaus arrived. After the introductions, followed by a brief conversation, Eric and his father rode away. Lucy and Eric waved as the carriage made its way up the street, a sight that made Renee feel emotional for Reuben, remembering how they used to stare at each other as she rode away from the farm.

"Hey, Renee, didn't you hear me? I did it! I asked him to our house for dinner. Are you okay?"

Renee quickly wiped her eyes with her hand and turned to Lucy and said, "I'm fine. Good, Lucy, very good. Rather awkward, but he said yes."

"Hey, the coach will be coming shortly. What did I miss?" asked Monroe coming up the walkway.

"Guess who's coming to dinner?" asked Aaron to Monroe rather mockingly. His response was answered with a slap on the back of his head by Coleen as Renee and Lucy continued to talk about tomorrow's upcoming dinner.

狼

Lucy anxiously spent the day waiting for dinner time. She went through her closet numerous times looking for the perfect dress to wear for Eric Klaus's visit and pestered her mother about what she was going to be serving.

"Maybe we should go get May to cook, that way I know it'll be a good dinner," recommended Lucy to her mother.

"What are you trying to tell me, Lucy?" asked Coleen, insulted but amused.

Renee was also pestered by Lucy, but didn't mind because she found Lucy's first real interest in a boy refreshing. In the past, Lucy didn't show much interest in boys because she had her music and creativity to keep her occupied. The few times when she did have eyes for a certain boy, she didn't act on it. In a sense, she was fearful of becoming close to a boy because of Renee and Reuben's relationship. Not understanding the feeling of love, she could still see how her brother was in a constant state of hurt knowing he could not be with the one he loved. It was what she saw in him keeping Lucy from becoming interested in pursuing a relationship.

However, now that adolescence turned into young adulthood, Lucy now had endeavors to gain the interest of Eric Klaus.

"Lucy, you've tried that dress three times already and it looks the same as the first time you tried it on," Renee said as Lucy stepped out of the dress to try on another.

"But I have to look just right. Tell me, Renee, how should I greet him, with a simple hand shake or a wave? I know... can you teach me how to curtsey the way you learned at Wickham?"

"WHAT?!" cried Renee disgusted at Lucy's comment. "Lucy, never ever ask me to teach you how to curtsey, never learn how to curtsey, and if you do learn, never curtsey to anyone! That's downright degrading!"

Lucy cowered and sat on her bed. "I'm sorry, Renee, but I just want to make a good impression."

Renee saw she hurt Lucy's feelings and took away her joy this day was bringing. She sighed and sat next to Lucy and took her hands into hers and said, "Don't try to impress him. Remember when we first met you asked me if it was more important to like someone more than loving them?"

Lucy nodded as her hurt look began to fade.

"I told you, I suppose it's important to like someone first because if you didn't, you wouldn't have true love with that person. Do you remember?" asked Renee as Lucy nodded. Renee continued, "Take me and your brother, I never did anything to impress him."

"You ate a worm in front of him," interrupted Lucy.

Bobbling her head, Renee replied, "Yes, okay, I'll give you that one, but sometimes we girls have to do something once in a while to get their attention. Face it, Lucy, boys can be downright stupid. Aside from that worm, which I spit out and didn't eat, your brother and I never felt we had to impress each other. Do you know why Reuben and I got along so well?"

"No, why?" asked Lucy.

With a bright smile, Renee answered, "Because we were ourselves. To us, I was just Renee and he was just Reuben with no expectations. My point is, Lucy, you are a wonderful, fun girl. Very smart, pretty, and creative. You don't need to be any more than you already are. Just be yourself and Eric will like you just as you are. As you told me many years ago, to be able to love someone, you need to like them first."

Lucy reached and embraced Renee tightly as she said, "You're the best sister ever."

Eric arrived promptly at 4 o'clock as planned. He was nicely dressed and brought Lucy some flowers and a large wedge of cheese to offer for the dinner.

"Flowers," whispered Renee to Coleen. "Reuben never gave me flowers. You know, Mama, when your son returns, I'm going to have a serious word with him about this."

Coleen chuckled in response.

Everyone sat in the parlor to have a pleasant visit. Lucy was taking Renee's advice to heart and it showed with her being much more relaxed, and Eric being more open also. They were getting along very well and there was one moment when Lucy's and Renee's eyes met. Renee gave her a reassuring nod and wink to show Lucy was doing just fine.

When it was close to 5 o'clock, Coleen and Renee excused themselves to prepare the dinner to be served and Aaron and Monroe helped by setting the table. Of course this was Coleen's way of giving the two a chance to visit on their own.

"I like your family, Lucy. Everyone is so nice," said Eric very pleasantly.

Lucy smiled shyly, "Thank you. I would like to meet your family sometime," she said, thinking that may be a bit to forward, but she remembered Renee's advice to be herself and Lucy was always a friendly and curious type of person.

"Sure, how would you like to come to my house for dinner this Saturday?"

"Sounds nice, I would like that," she said very politely, but was thinking, fantastic, wait until I tell Renee.

Eric was looking around the parlor until he saw the uniformed picture of Reuben on the mantle. Pointing to the picture, he asked, "Who's he?"

Lucy let out a sorrowful sigh, rose, and took the picture in her hands. Instead of sitting on the opposite end of the sofa as she was before, she took a seat next to Eric.

"This is my brother Reuben. He's the reason why Renee lives with us."

"Are they married? Where is he?"

Lucy's lower lip began to quiver and her eyes began to water. I shouldn't have said anything about him, she thought.

"He's on the other side of the world," said Renee, standing on the threshold of the parlor.

Lucy looked frightened and was about to plead for forgiveness until Renee sat next to her and slowly took Reuben's picture from Lucy's hand and looked at it lovingly.

"This is Lucy's other brother, Eric. He and I are, well, it's difficult to explain, but I trust Lucy will explain it perfectly once she gets to know you much better." Renee placed her hand on Lucy's shoulder and looked at her as a sister and continued, "She's the one who brought Reuben into my life and I'm eternally grateful. Now come you two, dinner is about to be served."

After dinner was served and eaten, the ladies saw to the clearing and cleaning of the dishes as Aaron and Monroe took Eric back into the parlor to have their turn at him. Lucy was watching Renee as she quickly cleaned and put dishes away.

"What's the hurry, Renee?" asked Lucy.

"Are you joking, your father and Monroe alone with Eric?"

A look of fear came to Lucy's face, "Oh, you're right! Come on, Mama, hurry."

"So tell me, young man, what do you have planned for your future?" asked Aaron very friendly.

With a prideful look, Eric said, "My father will be opening a new mercantile store in Chesapeake City and when it's ready to open, I'll be running it on my own. My father has been training me in all aspects of running a general store such as stock, bookkeeping, and special orders. Our plan is to open several stores all over the region."

"That sounds impressive," said Monroe. "Hey, if you ever fall in need of legal advice, we can assist in that avenue."

"Aye, right you are, son," replied Aaron. "Tell me, Eric, since you are becoming a friend of my daughter, perhaps you can provide me some nice warm underwear at a decent price now that the weather is colder these days…"

"DA!" shouted Lucy as she entered the parlor.

For the next hour, before Eric had to leave, dessert was served in the parlor and Lucy played several songs on her tin whistle, which Eric was very impressed to hear. As Lucy played her music, Renee was thinking to herself, see Lucy, you didn't need to do anything like bite a worm in half.

With the evening over, both Lucy and Renee were lying in their beds. Lucy had a warm smile on her face as she was looking at the flowers Eric brought her. She put them in a vase and sat them on her night stand. As she was staring at them, she looked toward Renee who was using the moon light from the window to look at Reuben's picture as she did every night before she fell asleep. She was gently tracing the outline of his face with the tip of her finger.

"Renee, can I ask you a question about my brother?" asked Lucy.

"Always," answered Renee, not taking her eyes away from the picture.

"How did you feel when Reuben looked into your eyes?"

Renee smiled and with her focus remaining on the picture, she said, "When Reuben would look into my eyes, I would feel so special. I felt warm, safe, and tingly. I felt like I was loved. The same way you feel when Eric looks into your eyes, I would guess."

"What? Come on, Renee, you have no idea what you are talking about. Me, in love, that's crazy talk," said Lucy, covering the lower half of her face hiding a grin.

Renee chuckled as she closed the image case, rolled out of bed, and sat on the edge of Lucy's bed. Lucy sat up against the head board.

With a very serious look and tone, but still in a caring manner, Renee spoke to Lucy as an older sister would. "Lucy, please listen to me. Never deny love, not to your family and especially, not to yourself. You will live to regret it if you do. Look at what happened to Reuben and me. We loved each other for years, but because of my father, we denied it to ourselves and we lost out on so much. When we finally had the strength to express our love, it was too late. Never be too late, Lucy. Right now you and Eric are on your way of becoming good friends. If that friendship grows, don't deny your feelings like your brother and I were forced to do. Continue to be yourself and when you feel you are ready to take that next step, don't hesitate. Express your feelings."

"I will, Renee, I promise. Thank you. That makes me feel better."

"Good," replied Renee as she rose and got back into Reuben's bed and snuggled in what used to be his quilt. She smiled and said, "You know, I really need to start looking for things for the baby. Maybe I'll go to the Klaus Mercantile tomorrow and see if they have anything I can use. Perhaps you would like to come along."

Lucy sat up. "Yeah, that's a good idea. I think I can find some time in my busy schedule to go with you."

Renee smiled as she breathed in Reuben's quilt looking at the moon and asked, "Now how busy of a schedule do you actually have, Lucy?"

狼

Reuben stood amidships as he watched the moon slowly rise over the horizon. The *Coleen* was nearing its destination of the island of Honshu. It has been close to three months since he departed Norfolk on his journey to find Akagi Genda-San and Captain Sean Aaron estimated they would be arriving on Honshu within the week.

Just as when he sailed with the *Morning Star*, Reuben proved to be a valuable asset to the crew of the *Coleen*, as did Tadashi. They worked tirelessly and when they had time on their own, Reuben would spend that time learning as much from Tadashi about his homeland as he could.

"Tadashi, I realize guiding me to Itosai is much, but may I bother you for one more favor?" Reuben asked the day the *Coleen* set sail from San Francisco.

"And what would that be, my friend?"

"Teach me your language."

Tadashi looked upon Reuben with admiration. This is truly a spirited individual, thought Tadashi. "Learning my language may be difficult for you, it may take lots of time."

Reuben let out a hint of a laugh. "Time is what we have much of for the next several weeks."

Tadashi nodded in agreement. "I guess you're right, but if I'm to teach you my language and guide you to the Akagi, then you must show me all of what Lord Akagi Genda taught you of the jo staff."

"He only taught me for two weeks, so compared to his knowledge, I didn't even scratch the surface."

"Two weeks is a lifetime compared to what I know."

Reuben nodded and said, "Agreed."

From that moment on, Tadashi spoke to Reuben in his language only with the exception of when he had to clarify translations. Reuben picked up the basics quickly and within days, he was having decent conversations with Tadashi. Now nearing the end of the western passage, Reuben was proving to be quite fluent speaking the Japanese language.

In turn, Reuben taught Tadashi misogi-no-jo just as Akagi Genda-San taught him. They were quite the sight to see on deck training, gaining the attention of the crew who would normally spend their off time playing games of chance or spinning yarns to pass away the time. Some of the younger members of the crew took up sticks and joined in.

Gallagher, the ships bosun, said to Captain Sean Aaron, "I don't know about this activity those two stowaways got some of the crew doing, Captain."

Sean Aaron shrugged it off as he said, "As long as the crew do their duties when required and dance with their sticks on their own time, I have no problem with it. Besides, I have noticed that activity has caused the crew to be just a slight more sharp in their jobs."

Tadashi, grateful for Reuben's jo training, one evening after ships work, set up an old discarded crate and drew a round target on it. With the approval of Gallagher, who was quite interested as well, Tadashi began to show Reuben the way of the bow, Kyudo.

Reuben seen Indians, who served as scouts for his regiment in Mexico, use bows, but not as elegantly disciplined as Tadashi. His bow skills were poetic in his draw and loose. Tadashi amazed Reuben with every draw and loose he made, hitting the target from any angle or position from the ship, even from atop the main mast.

"Ah, that's child's play," said one of the crew. "I've seen Injuns hit hares running at full speed with their bows and arrows."

Looking rather annoyed, Tadashi asked Reuben to retrieve a spool of twine from a pouch attached to his utsubo. He instructed him to tie the end of the twine to one of his arrows and to take hold of the spool tightly.

Reuben, looking very interested, did as instructed. The crew began to gather behind Tadashi as he scanned over the ocean's surface. He lifted his bow and drew its string and held its aim toward the water. Tadashi, at this moment, had the full attention of the entire crew, including Captain Sean Aaron.

In a silent release of the bow string, he let loose his arrow as Reuben held onto the spool tightly. The crew strained to see the unknown target. "Quickly, Reuben, pull in the arrow," Tadashi said lowering his bow.

Reuben pulled and pulled as the crew stepped in closer. As the arrow was nearing the ship, Reuben felt it resisting and he began to smile. During his journey, he'd seen many wonders the ocean had to offer, and one of those wonders was the small silver flying fish skimming across the water's surface. He was amazed, as were the others, to see one of those flying fish on the shaft of the arrow as Reuben took hold of it.

"Ha! That's not child's play in the least. That's art!" exclaimed Reuben as he held the arrow high above his head.

"Thinking of her again, my friend?" asked Tadashi in his native language as he came up behind Reuben.

"Hai, as always," answered Reuben.

Every evening, Reuben stood at this one spot watching the moon slowly rise over the horizon just as the day was about to end. It was a sight that made Tadashi feel sincere pity for Reuben. One of the best ways for Reuben to learn the Japanese language was to tell Tadashi his reason for this journey. It was a tale which made Tadashi see Reuben as a man with strong convictions toward the ones he loves. To travel all this way to bring back what once was for his family and the one he loves, but cannot have was amazing to Tadashi. I never thought I would have sympathy such as this for a round-eye, Tadashi often thought when he would see Reuben watching the horizon every evening during this passage, always holding Renee's image case wrapped with Lucy's purple ribbon.

"I suppose she has had a good night's sleep and about to wake to a new day soon as ours is about to end," said Reuben as the thought of Renee sleeping with the man she was forced to marry ran through his mind. The very thought made his gut twist and would cause him to grasp his jo tightly. He had to constantly remind himself it was not of her doing.

Seeing Reuben's grip on the jo caused Tadashi to lightly place his hand on Reuben's shoulder as he spoke, "Come now, Reuben, once we get to Itosai, perhaps you can find yourself a mountain beauty. I should know, the girls of the mountain region of the Hisano Province are a sight to see. Granted, with your round-eyed looks, you're not much to look at, but I assure you, you'll attract a beauty that will make you forget all about this Renee girl," he said in a considerate manner.

"I can't do that, Tadashi. Renee is not only the love in my life, she's my best friend and I gave her my solemn word I will remain hers for as long as it takes, even if it means until the day I die," said Reuben, not taking his eyes away from the horizon.

Tadashi let loose a small chuckle. "That's crazy talk, Reuben."

Reuben let out a sigh as he kept his eyes on the horizon and handed Tadashi the image case of Renee's picture. Tadashi never seen what was inside the case and he took it gently. He removed Lucy's ribbon and slowly opened the case. Tadashi stood with his eyes wide open and his mouth opened in fascinated awe. "This, this is the girl you speak of, Renee?"

Reuben nodded yes.

"She's beyond beautiful, but what of her personality?"

"It's even more beautiful."

Tadashi took one last look at Renee's image and he closed the case, wrapped Lucy's ribbon around it, and handed it back to Reuben. As Reuben took hold of it, Tadashi didn't let go causing Reuben to look at him.

"Then you must keep your word to this girl," said Tadashi, before he released his hold.

Nightfall came on a cold brisk early January evening as the *Coleen* dropped its anchor in the harbor of the fishing village of Tatao. The evening before, the first mate of the *Coleen*, along with Tadashi and several other crew members, rowed ashore to establish visitation in the means of trade. Tadashi suggested this village to Sean Aaron because of its size, location, and success in its fishing industry. He also knew Tatao had more trade goods to offer other than silks since Edo was a couple day's journey by foot, and Sean Aaron had what the village regent desired from the opposite side of the pacific, coffee and cocoa.

Tatao was one of the largest villages on the east coast of the island of Honshu and more importantly, it was only a few days walk to Itosai. Although punishments were severe for allowing foreign ships to enter the harbor, Tatao, with its high cliffs surrounding the village made it possible for ships to enter unseen. Village officials also looked the other way because they received a large portion of what was being brought into the village. The one thing strictly denied was allowing foreign sailors to leave the visiting ship. All business needed to be conducted in the middle of the harbor with the use of boats.

"All right, so how do we get ashore?" asked Reuben.

Tadashi presented Reuben with a bundle of clothing. "Here, take this. I was able to obtain clothing during our visit to establish trade."

"How?" questioned Reuben.

"Easy. I mentioned I have returned to serve Lord Akagi Genda. He's well known in this region. I simply requested a couple sets of clothes and was given these bundles. I also got you this kasa to cover your face. When the trading commences, you and I will simply board one of the boats."

"That's so incredibly stupid, it could possibly work. My sister would be proud," said Reuben.

As the *Coleen* entered the harbor to commence the trading, all lights on the ship were put out.

"Well, Reuben, my boy, if you ever consider taking to the sea on a more permanent means, you are welcome to be part of my crew. You have proven yourself a true asset just as James said. You as well, slant," said Sean Aaron.

"Mr. Aaron, I must thank you for bringing me this far on my journey."

"You just be careful and make our Renee proud, you understand?"

Reuben nodded as he accepted Sean Aaron's hand.

"And you, my slant-eyed friend. I can't thank you enough for arranging this evening's trade. I had a very lucrative discussion with the village regent. He's quite fond of coffee and cocoa, and it looks like we'll be making this one of our permanent trade stops. You take good care of Reuben here, Tadashi."

"I will, Mr. Sean Aaron, and domo arigato gozaimasu."

There was much activity on deck of the *Coleen* while the trading was underway. So much activity Reuben and Tadashi were able to disembark the ship unnoticed, and onto one of the boats carrying goods to the *Coleen*. They simply carried small kegs of coffee and were easily mistaken as villagers assisting in the trading. No one took notice of Tadashi's bow and utsubo of arrows slung over his shoulder, or Reuben's haversack and jo because of the darkness and the activity.

As the boat was rowed ashore, they simply jumped onto the dock, made their way through the crowd, and up the road leading inland away from the village. They walked for what seemed like hours, but in truth, it was only less than twenty minutes. When they reached the crest of the hill leading away from the village, Reuben stopped and looked back to the *Coleen* still conducting its business. A sudden feeling of emotion overcame him. He felt afraid for the first time since this journey began. He was walking away from his only means of going back home, his only means of returning to his family, and Renee.

Tadashi sensed he was walking alone and turned to see Reuben facing east. He walked back to him and placed his hand on his shoulder. "Come, Reuben. Your family will be there waiting for you when your mission here is complete. And your friend Renee will be there for you also. Maybe not as you and she intended, but still, I'm sure she will be happy to see you when you return."

Reuben dried his eyes with the sleeve of his hanten jacket and nodded. "Let's be off then. The sooner I learn what I can from Genda-San, the sooner I can return."

"That's the spirit, Reuben."

狼

Reuben and Tadashi walked for a few hours in the cold night until they came across an old abandoned hut. Inside the hut was a cooking pit where Reuben made a fire and Tadashi began to prepare a small meal of rice he had taken from the village. He also obtained some vegetables, fruits, and dried fish. Not knowing exactly what lay ahead of them on their hike to Itosai, they both decided to use the food sparingly. After a quick meal, they both settled in next to the fire for warmth and slept for several hours.

Reuben awoke to the sound of horses galloping on the road the two had been following the night before. He rose to take a look out of the window and saw at least fifty to sixty mounted horses with what seemed to be soldiers wearing black armor and helmets. Almost each mounted soldier had a pale blue banner with a white crescent attached to his back. Tadashi, woken by the rumbled din, joined Reuben at the window, took a look, and immediately pulled Reuben down out of view.

"What is it, Tadashi? What's going on?"

"You are on uncharted territory as far as you are concerned, Reuben, so you need to be more careful exposing yourself. That's a troop of mounted samurai, but I don't recognize the banners."

Tadashi rose and took another look. "Nope, I don't know who that banner represents. Perhaps it's a new clan who has claimed stake in the province. I have been away for a long time. But they are definitely on the move for battle. I wonder with whom. We had better stay out of sight until they pass."

Battle? Does this happen often here, Reuben wondered to himself. Reuben took another look, but more cautiously by looking from a lower corner of the window. The sight of the mounted samurai was very impressive to Reuben. Akagi Genda-San described his army of samurai during his visit on Reuben's family farm. The descriptions caused Reuben to think of the tales of King Arthur and the Knights of the Round Table, but these mounted samurai were more than anything beyond what Reuben expected to see. Reuben viewed the mounted men as both inspiring, yet menacing. Tadashi was right, Reuben was on uncharted territory and he had to adapt himself to stay one step ahead while he learned the ways of this new and exciting country he is now a part of.

The column of mounted horses passed, but the two waited another hour until they continued their journey. Before leaving the hut, they looked around for items they could find useful. There wasn't much except for a pair of mino capes to protect them from the elements and keep warm.

Tadashi went out first to see if the road was clear and motioned Reuben to follow. They walked on the side of the road, ready to leap into the brush and forest at the sight or sound of others coming along, but as far as Tadashi was concerned, it was unusually quiet. He knew this was a well-used road and to see it nearly vacant caused him alarm. The display of the mounted samurai only increased his alertness and with Reuben noticing Tadashi's tension, he also enhanced his alertness.

As they walked, Tadashi talked about his home and how the Akagi protected his village. He spoke of the cultural differences between the western world and his homeland. He had less than a couple of days left to prepare Reuben before he would be in the company of Akagi Genda-San, so he crammed as much knowledge into Reuben as possible. He knew even though Reuben had already been in his presence, he instructed Reuben to present himself as if he was meeting Akagi Genda-San for the first time.

They walked the entire day until twilight. They didn't expect to come across any shelter, so they entered deep into the forest where they could make a fire without it being noticed from the road. Tadashi broke out the rations and a rabbit he killed with his bow skills earlier in the day as Reuben gathered wood and made a fire.

After what proved to be a satisfying meal, Reuben and Tadashi continued discussions about what Reuben should expect living in a village under the rule of a samurai lord. Reuben was eager to see Akagi Genda-San, but with all the instruction learned from Tadashi, he had his doubts Akagi Genda-San really meant what he said about Reuben coming to learn from him. Perhaps he only said that not expecting me to follow through, thought Reuben.

"Mr. Akagi did mean it, Reuben. Why else would he have spent his last two weeks with you, my love?" spoke Renee.

Reuben stood leaning with one arm against the oak tree with doubt in his expression. Renee came from underneath and leaned against the tree facing him. She caressed his face, leaned forward and kissed him on the lips.

"Be very careful today, Reuben. If you are drawn to battle, do so to protect others. I can't bear to see you as a bitter warrior. Be my warrior of peace, my love, and protect those who mean the most to you."

"You mean the most to me, Renee, and I couldn't protect you from your father."

"You have protected me in ways beyond your understanding. It may not be clear to you right now, but it will be in time. For now, there are others you need to protect."

Renee again kissed Reuben on the lips after saying, "I love you."

208

"Hey, wake up. It's time to get moving. If we make good time today, we may be in Itosai early this afternoon," said Tadashi, nudging Reuben with his foot waking him from his dream.

Reuben sat up and rubbed his eyes. He looked up to the sky thinking of Renee and how she's somewhere under the same sky. It may be dark, but still the same.

Gathering their belongings, the two made their way back to the road and continued their long walk in discussion. Their talks covered various topics regarding the cultural differences between Japanese and Americans.

"You mean to tell me, Japanese people use rice as currency sometimes? That's so bazaar."

"That's what I thought when I heard how your people barter with colored people in the region you come from."

"Hmm, touché," responded Reuben.

Reuben stopped with an alarming look causing Tadashi to unsling his bow.

"What is it, Reuben?"

He didn't answer but took a couple of steps from the direction they had just come. He stood in silence, turned and ran into the forest grabbing Tadashi by his sleeve pulling him along. They both ran into the woods for several yards and ducked behind some thick shrubs. Reuben removed his kasa and carefully peered over the bush as did Tadashi.

"I hear something," said Tadashi. "Sounds like men running."

Moments later, Reuben and Tadashi witnessed a large number of foot samurai running on the road. It was hard to estimate how many, but Reuben guessed about fifty to seventy and they carried the same banners of pale blue with a crescent as the mounted samurai from the day before.

The sound of a deep horn was heard coming from the opposite direction causing both Reuben and Tadashi to drop behind the bushes and look in the direction of the sound.

"What the hell is that?" asked Reuben, alarmed.

"That's a battle horn. There must be some sort of feud battle happening. Come, follow me quietly and put your hat back on," said Tadashi as he began to string his bow and open the utsubo.

The woods were thick which made Reuben feel safe. No one would send scouts in thickets such as this, he thought.

They traversed the woods carefully for about half a mile until they came to the tree line. There they laid low on the ground as they saw a low laying valley below with two opposing armies facing off at one another. One army, in the black armor with the pale blue banners and white crescent the two had seen the following couple of days, and the other wearing similar armor, but in dark red and black. They carried dark burgundy colored banners.

Not more than a few minutes passed when the two broke free from the thick woods and took cover when they heard the loud holler of "KOGEKI!!!"

209

The two opposing armies charged at each other with swords drawn. They met in the middle of the valley and a brutal battle commenced. Reuben was fascinated by the speed and the lack of firearms. He began to have that familiar feeling of the need to fight he experienced back in Mexico, however, it was somewhat more controlled.

"Geez, that's Genda-San's emblem on the red banners. Is that Genda-San's army, Tadashi?" asked Reuben as he rose off the ground onto his knees.

Tadashi looked up to Reuben and tried to pull him back to the ground. "Hai, it is. Now get down before someone sees you."

Reuben ignored Tadashi and pulled his arm free from his grasp. Reuben frantically started looking to all the samurai in red trying to see if he could recognize Akagi Genda-San. Surely he must be here, he thought.

He heard a single gunshot coming from the line of black armored samurai and saw a cloud of black powder smoke. Reuben looked below the smoke and saw a black armored samurai holding a musket looking toward his target. He saw a mounted samurai in full red armor with a gold Akagi emblem attached to his helmet.

"That's him!" shouted Reuben as he stood up and pointed to the mounted samurai. "We have to do something!"

Reuben started making his way down the slope only to be stopped by Tadashi.

"What the hell, Tadashi?"

"You can't just jump into that fight, Reuben. Look at you. You don't even belong here. Either army will kill you once they get a good look at your face," said Tadashi.

"That gunman was aiming for Genda-San! If we don't do anything, the next shot may hit him! You said you want to serve the Akagi, so now is a good time as any!" said Reuben as he pulled away from Tadashi's grip, slid down the slope, and sprinted toward the mounted horseman Reuben believed to be Akagi Genda-San.

"Reuben, you stupid son of a bitch, get back here!" yelled Tadashi. "Damn it, that idiot round-eye is going to be the death of me." Tadashi followed Reuben while he pulled out several arrows from his utsubo and loaded one.

As Reuben ran toward the horseman, he kept an eye on the gunman loading his musket. He was taking a long time to load causing Reuben to think he was not trained too well with the weapon.

He ran through the black armored samurai, untouched as Tadashi followed at a close distance with his bow drawn ready to clear a path if needed. Reuben was nearing the horseman and saw a black armored samurai raise his sword to strike down one of the Akagi samurai. As the sword was coming down, Reuben swung his jo around his head as Akagi Genda-San shown him using his head as leverage. The jo made contact with the attacker's face causing it to explode as if a musket ball hit it.

The Akagi samurai looked up to see Reuben attack another black armored samurai with his jo, but this samurai avoided Reuben's strike and raised his sword above his head and began swinging it down in an angle for a deadly cut. Reuben parried it downward. The attacker brought his sword back up as Reuben kept contact with the blade and as he swung the sword back for another cut, Reuben blocked the cut and stepped back. Reuben made a thrust toward the attacker's chest as the attacker blocked his thrust. The attacker, with the sword raised, began another downward cut as Reuben brought down his jo after being blocked and parried the cut. Reuben quickly rotated the jo and made another thrust to the attacker's throat. The jo entered the black armored samurai's neck and when Reuben pulled his jo free, blood spewed from the open wound.

The Akagi samurai, lying beneath Reuben, witnessed the contest and recognized his father's jo technique. Before he could rise to his feet, Reuben turned and was about to be cut down by another black armored samurai, but before he could make his strike, an arrow wedged itself in the attacker's face. Reuben looked back to see Tadashi restringing another arrow. He turned and pushed the still standing attacker screaming in agonizing pain out of the way and continued his run to the horseman.

The Akagi samurai got to his feet only to be pushed down again by Tadashi keeping Reuben in his view. He saw another black armored samurai raising his sword to strike at Reuben and he let loose another arrow again hitting the attacker in the face.

Reuben saw the gunman having difficulty placing a cap on the vent of the musket and yelled in English, "GENDA-SAN!!! TAKE COVER. THE GUNMAN IS TAKING AIM AT YOU!!!"

Akagi Genda-San heard his name and the call to him in English. Stunned, he began to look in the direction of where the call came. That sounded like… Reuben-San, Akagi Genda-San thought. Suddenly he saw what appeared to be a ronin run past his horse at a sprint with a jo raised above his head, followed by another ronin clearing a path for the first ronin with his bow skills. The first man ran at a fast pace toward a gunman who was taking aim at Akagi Genda-San and when he saw the gun pointed in his direction, Akagi Genda-San leaped off his horse and lowered himself to one knee, but kept an eye on the mysterious runner. As Reuben neared the gunman, he struck him square in the face just as the black armored samurai was about to fire his gun.

As the gunman was struck in the face, he flung his unfired musket in the air. Reuben caught it and saw two black armored samurai on horseback racing toward Akagi Genda-San with swords raised. Reuben aimed the musket at one horseman and Tadashi aimed his bow at the other as Akagi Genda-San noticed the pending attack and rose to his feet facing the charging samurai. Reuben fired hitting his target in the face causing him to fall off his horse and Tadashi likewise hit his target in the face.

Reuben dropped the musket and ran toward Akagi Genda-San as other Akagi samurai did as well to protect him. A conch shell horn was blown and the black armored samurai began to withdraw toward the road Reuben and Tadashi had been traveling on. When the field was cleared of the pale blue banners, the Akagi samurai began chanting, "AKAGI, AKAGI, AKAGI, AKAGI, SHORI!"

"Father, my Lord, are you unhurt?!" asked the Akagi samurai Reuben protected prior to saving Akagi Genda-San from the gunman.

"Hai, Masaru. All thanks to that man and his companion. Bring them to me."

Reuben stopped when he heard the sound of the conch shell and Tadashi met up with him. "Are you all right, Reuben?" asked Tadashi.

"Yeah, I'm fine. Geez, what is it with you hitting people in the face with your arrows? That's just gruesome."

"I could say the same to you about your jo and the gun, Reuben."

"You two, come with me!" ordered an Akagi samurai.

Reuben and Tadashi looked at each other rather concerned.

"NOW!" shouted the samurai.

Another Akagi samurai grabbed them by the shoulders and moved them along. When they reached Akagi Genda-San and his son, the samurai who had hold of their shoulders pushed them to the ground.

"Keep your head down," whispered Tadashi.

"QUIET YOU!" ordered Masaru.

"Now, now, Masaru, these two saved both our lives. Who are you that I am indebted to?" said Akagi Genda-San.

"I am Sora Tadashi of the Sora Clan from the village of Majaul," answered Tadashi humbly.

"Ah, a Sora archer, the best in the region," replied Akagi Genda-San as he moved in front of Reuben. "And who are you?"

Reuben raised his head and removed his Kasa.

Masaru drew his sword and in anger said, "An off-lander!"

He moved Akagi Genda-San out of the way and kicked Reuben in the chest causing him to fall onto his back. Masaru raised his sword and yelled, "Kare o korosu!"

"YAME!!!" shouted Akagi Genda-San.

Akagi Genda-San came to Reuben's side, knelt down on one knee, took hold of his shoulder, and assisted him to stand. When they rose to their feet, Akagi Genda-San stared hard into Reuben's eyes with an angered glare as Reuben stared back with a neutral look. Akagi Genda-San's expression softened and a smile came to his face as he said, "Hai! Reuben-San, I knew you would come!"

狼

Reuben and Tadashi sat under guard for several hours while the battlefield was being looked over by Akagi Genda-San, his son, and several other samurai Reuben could only assume were Akagi Genda-San's lieutenants. He couldn't ask Tadashi any questions for they were forbidden to speak by the samurai guarding them. Almost every Akagi samurai looked at Reuben oddly causing him to feel as if he were an animal on display in a cage. He didn't quite know what to make of Akagi Genda-San's current treatment of him, but assumed it was the cultural differences Tadashi had instructed him about these past several weeks.

Reuben dozed off and was shaken awake. He looked up, but was blinded by the sun. A figure entered the sunlight and offered a hand. "Rise, Reuben-San."

Reuben took the offered hand and was lifted to his feet. In front of him stood Akagi Genda-San. "Forgive me, my friend, for leaving you like this. I had to survey the results of this day's battle," he said in English.

"I understand. I had to do the same task myself in Mexico," answered Reuben in Japanese.

"Ah, you have learned my language, Reuben-San. Mind you, it is a bit broken, but my English is broken as well," replied Akagi Genda-San, followed by a laugh.

"Tadashi taught me as we traveled across the Pacific."

"I see. Stand Sora Tadashi of Majaul. Tell me of your father, perhaps I know of him."

Tadashi rose and bowed. "My father was Sora Zensa, the son of Sora Kunio."

"Ah, I know of these men. Excellent archers the both of them, and I see you have learned their skills well yourself. Tell me young Tadashi, how did you come to be in the presence of my good friend, Reuben-San."

Tadashi told Akagi Genda-San of his journey to America after the death of his mother and father from a plague causing his village of Majaul to be abandoned. He went on to tell of how he and Reuben met and the deal they struck for Tadashi to guide Reuben to Itosai.

"So you saw your side of the deal through, but what are you to gain in return?" asked Akagi Genda-San.

Reuben spoke up for Tadashi. "Tadashi wishes to serve you as one of your archers, and to pay tribute to you for when you freed his village from the Kano."

"The Kano feuds, I remember them well. That is where I met your father and grandfather. Well, Sora Tadashi-San, you are a good friend of Reuben-San, and you two worked well together on this day of battle. You have taught him our language adequately and trained him on our cultural etiquettes well enough to understand protocols. You are to consider yourself one of my archers to serve under my son, Masaru. Now if you will excuse us, Sora Tadashi-San, I wish to speak to Reuben-San alone."

"I am at your service, my Lord," replied Tadashi as he bowed formally to Akagi Genda-San.

Akagi Genda-San led Reuben away from the samurai guarding him to the shade of a large pine tree. "Here look, I found your jo. I am happy to see you still practice misogi-no-jo. Is this the same rake handle from your farm?" he asked.

Reuben nodded.

Akagi Genda-San did a couple of jo suburi's with Reuben's jo and looked at it approvingly. "You are a true practitioner of the Budo Arts, a farmer who uses his tools as weapons. You make me proud, Reuben-San," he said handing Reuben the jo. Akagi Genda-San continued, "It is not as nice as the oak tree on your farm, but it is away from the others. So, Reuben-San... what are you doing here?"

Reuben smiled as he answered the same question he asked Akagi Genda-San the very night they first met, "Learning."

"Ha! Very good, Reuben-San. I see Renee-Dono understood my meaning of stones and water."

Reuben looked puzzled. "I suppose, if that means why I'm here now. I have to sadly admit I still don't understand what you mean, Genda-San."

Akagi Genda-San let out a laugh. "Do not concern yourself too much on that right now, Reuben-San. Women tend to be much smarter than men in matters of relationships, and your Renee-Dono is very smart. How is she?"

Reuben turned from Akagi Genda-San and looked up to the sky. His emotions began to make him quiver and his eyes to water. Once he got control of his emotions, he said, "She's not my Renee, Genda-San. She's married, as arranged by her father."

Akagi Genda-San placed his arm around Reuben's shoulder feeling sorrow. "To be married off in such a manner is unfortunate, Reuben-San, as I too once traveled the road of arranged marriage. I must tell you, I do feel your hurt and sympathize with you," he said.

He noticed the locket hanging around Reuben's neck and asked, "Is this a gift from Renee-Dono around your neck?"

Reuben nodded.

"May I?"

Reuben removed the locket and handed it to Akagi Genda-San.

Akagi Genda-San took it, gently opened the locket, and peered inside. He saw the two pictures of Renee and Reuben. The sight made him smile and nod. Suddenly he had a puzzled look on his face.

"When did Renee-Dono give this to you?"

"A couple of days before I left. We thought it was our last day together."

"But it was not, was it?"

"No, the night before her wedding day, the same day I left, she came to the farm for one last visit."

"I see. May I ask what happened on this visit, Reuben-San."

Reuben looked at Akagi Genda-San with a look one would view as prying into one's personal business. Akagi Genda-San simply nodded and in a very concerned manner said, "Please, Reuben-San, it is important."

Reuben brought his hands to his face as if he were ashamed. Akagi Genda-San placed his hand on Reuben's shoulder for comfort. Reuben removed his hands and looked at Akagi Genda-San as he described his and Renee's last evening together. From the moment she arrived at the farm, to the moment they shared under the oak tree, and when he took her back to the hotel. When he was finished, his hands returned to his face.

Akagi Genda-San removed them and said, "Reuben-San, you and Renee-Dono have nothing to be ashamed of. What you two shared was a moment of true love for one another in its purest form. That one moment, the two of you left an everlasting mark on each other that will remain for a lifetime." Akagi Genda-San looked to the sky in thought and looked back to Reuben with a cheerful expression. "You will see, Reuben-San. When your mission here is complete and you return home, you will arrive to riches beyond your understanding. I will tell you what I told Renee-Dono at the train station. You see, my friend, there is a time and place for you and Renee-Dono. Stones and water, Reuben-San, stones and water."

狼

The weeks and months that followed, Reuben and Tadashi became closer friends because of the brutal training put on both of them by Masaru and other leading samurai. It was brutal for Ruben because of being an off-lander, and for Tadashi just for being Reuben's friend. However, their spirit was never broken, especially Reuben's.

Akagi Genda-San expressed his apologies he could not see to Reuben's training personally because of the pressing feudal issues. He explained to Reuben while he was away on his tour of America, an ousted samurai from the south named Arata Goro wanted to split the island of Honshu in half, and spread his tyrannical rule both north and south. The Arata army was made up of robbers, thugs, and ronin of questionable backgrounds. In the end, Akagi Genda-San simply referred to them as an army of land pirates. He did express the information Reuben and Tadashi gave him about the mounted and foot samurai traveling the road coming from the east was helpful information. It led alliance scouts to locate villages being used to store supplies for the Arata.

Returning to Itosai several weeks prior to Reuben's arrival, he worked diligently to create an alliance of regional Daimyos of the province. Since Itosai lay in the middle of the regional alliance, Itosai was proclaimed the seat of the alliance, and it was from Akagi Genda-San's home where the alliance was commanded. Reuben offered his service to the alliance, an offer Akagi Genda-San refused.

"I appreciate your offer and your experience," said Akagi Genda-San, "especially with the weapons the Arata have somehow accumulated. But this matter is not of your concern. You are here for another purpose and that purpose is not to get killed. You will be in danger, not only from the Arata, but from the alliance as well."

"Because I'm an off-lander?" Reuben asked.

"Correct."

Reuben's harsh treatment from Akagi Genda-San's son was of no real concern. Frankly, he found it ironically amusing because of how the Negros were treated in America. If they only knew how easy they had it, Reuben thought. He also surmised Akagi Genda-San put him under Masaru's tutelage as part of his training to deal with the harshness of the other samurai after remembering what Akagi Genda-San once said to him, *"Be grateful for harshness, for overcoming it is... victorious."* Knowing Akagi Genda-San was his mentor and friend, Reuben knew he was protected, so to speak.

215

Masaru, on his part, disliked having to see to Reuben's training and expressed his displeasure to his father angrily.

"Why must I take that round-eye under my teaching. I have more important tasks such as defeating the Arata. He will prove himself to be just like any other off-lander, arrogant, prideful, and stupid."

"Ah, everything you just described yourself as being? Listen, my son, Reuben-San is unlike any other off-lander, and you yourself have much to learn from him as well. Trust me, you may not understand it now, but eventually you two will meet in the middle and assist each other in ways neither of you two can do for yourselves."

Nevertheless, Masaru continued his brutality in Reuben's initial training, and unknowingly caused Reuben to learn quicker. His learning ability stemmed from the first day he set foot on Honshu, a theory of staying one step ahead, and in Masaru's training, Reuben was staying two steps ahead causing frustration in Masaru. All the while, Akagi Genda-San watched approvingly at Reuben's progress. He wanted to take part, and he did so as often as he could, but it was the conversations with Reuben he enjoyed most of all. Akagi Genda-San believed the journey to Itosai itself helped Reuben to be one with the code of Bushido, and to begin the smoothing process.

Tadashi was often concerned about Reuben's treatment by Masaru and the other samurai of the village. He was very supportive of Reuben, a sentiment that often got Tadashi some of the same treatment as Reuben. They were both housed in an old abandoned shack where they were not allowed to have bedding or make any type of repairs. But both endured, and the experience made them stronger and smarter, something Masaru was too arrogant to notice.

"I don't understand it father. I train those two long and hard and give them extra chores and yet they end the day with laughter. This Reuben of yours has got to be some sort of imp."

Akagi Genda-San laughed and thought, if you think Reuben-San is an imp, you should meet his Renee-Dono. With those two together, they would drive you insane.

Reuben's days started with early morning chores such as cleaning animal pens and human waste bins, tasks he was used to from working on the family farm, and also in the army when he would assist his platoon. When morning chores were completed, he and Tadashi began their first training session with the samurai of the village. However, they trained with the novices and younger village males. In the afternoons, Reuben was tasked with various chores from gathering wood to again cleaning animal pens and human waste bins. The afternoon training sessions were more intense lasting up to several hours and even afterwards, he and Tadashi continued training on their own. Reuben's day always ended with him looking up at the night's sky with Renee's image case held to his heart.

As time passed, Reuben was surpassing Akagi Genda-San's expectations. Not only was he proficiently learning the Budo techniques, he was adapting his own personality of calmness, with a bit of mischievousness, which in itself was not the Budo way. However, Akagi Genda-San referred to it as, "Reuben's style." It was a style that was quick and low to the ground, like a wolf approaching its prey. As Akagi Genda-San watched Reuben's kumitachi training with Masaru, he noticed Reuben knew Masaru had the upper edge because of his superior sword training, but Reuben used that to his advantage. Unlike taking the usual basic stance, Reuben would make his stance low viewing his opponent upwards making it difficult for the opponent to judge how high to raise their sword. On the farm, Reuben told Akagi Genda-San his methods of capturing cannons by crawling on the ground up to them and striking the most important part of the cannon, the gunner who was the center of the gun operation. It was similar in kumitachi, the most importing part to strike was the opponent's center.

Reuben also never initiated the attacks, advice Akagi Genda-San instilled in him back on the farm. He was very proud Reuben took that advice to heart and proved to be menacing to Masaru. During one kumitachi duel, Reuben and Masaru faced off for over an hour standing and waiting for the other to make the first move. Other such stand-offs, Reuben always lost, but he never initiated the attack and each duel nearly always ended in a close draw. This one particular training duel, Reuben stood his stance lower than usual and to the left side, opposite of normal stance, and his bokken blade was pointing to the rear. This in itself caused confusion in Masaru, thinking Reuben was desperate and reverting to unconventional means of defense and attack, yet, he could not figure a means to lay in a strike.

"Reuben-San, you are a man of unconventional wisdom. One day you will learn to harness that trait and it will become your signature," said Akagi Genda-San back on Reuben's farm.

This was the day Reuben made his signature as the entire village circled around Reuben and Masaru with Akagi Genda-San watching Reuben closely. Masaru had an intense expression of attack on his face, unlike Reuben who had a calm, almost mischievous spark in his eye, much like a wolf cub at play, Akagi Genda-San thought.

Reuben saw Masaru's center expand as he drew in a breath. He slightly slid his right foot back as Masaru raised his bokken to strike. Because of Reuben's low stance, Masaru had difficulties determining how high to raise his weapon. As he began his downward cut, Reuben brought his bokken up and over Masaru's bokken, parrying his cut down and immediately turned the bokken upright cutting upwards, stopping at Masaru's throat. The entire duel lasted less than two seconds.

Masaru stood in silent frustrated awe as the rest of the village inhabitants looked on in amazement, several grumbling because they missed the duel and lost bets of money.

Tadashi looked in both directions and to Akagi Genda-San, who had a proud joyful expression on his face. Tadashi began chanting "REUBEN, REUBEN, REUBEN, REUBEN,

SHOURI!" The audience of villagers and samurai followed suit and also began to chant the same.

In the days to follow, Akagi Genda-San allowed Reuben and Tadashi to train the novices and younger males of the village, allowing the seasoned samurai to concentrate on their training for the defeat of the Arata.

After the duel, Masaru still had bigoted hatred toward Reuben, but began to see him as an equal in skill. However, that too was about to change in the days that were to follow, for Arata Goro was again on the move.

狼

Looking glum, Renee was about to walk into the Klaus Mercantile with Lucy. She'd been going through the usual hormone and mood changes accompanying her condition. Lucy, being Renee's foundation, did her best to keep her spirits up in her own loving, sarcastic way, and it always made Renee end up smiling or laughing.

"What is it now, Renee?"

"Look at me, Lucy," answered Renee as she looked at her reflection in the window of the mercantile. "I look enormous and hideous."

"Oh, please, you don't look enormous and hideous. That's just baby fat and that will go away when the baby is born. The air you let loose in the morning is enormous and hideous."

"LUCY!"

Laughing, Lucy said, "Oh, come on, my handsome Eric awaits me inside."

The two entered the mercantile and were immediately greeted by Annabelle Klaus, Eric's mother. "Hello, Lucy and Renee, come on in. It's so nice to see you!"

Upon hearing Lucy's and Renee's name, two other customers, Mr. Davis and Mr. Lester, two farmers whose farms were near the Duran farm, turned toward the counter and waved. "Good day to you, Miss Renee and Miss Lucy," said Mr. Davis.

"And good day to you, you two handsome farmers," said Renee.

"You see, Jonah, that's why Miss Renee is the best Agricultural Liaison in the county. She knows talent when she sees it," said Mr. Lester.

"I'm the *only* Agricultural Liaison in the county, Mr. Lester," said Renee with a giggle.

"And how is the little one doing?" asked Mr. Davis.

"Getting bigger every day," replied Renee, gleefully as she gently rubbed her tummy.

"Oh, that reminds me," said Mrs. Klaus. "I have something I set aside for you in the back. I'll be but a moment."

As Annabelle entered the back of the store, Andrew and his son came through the same rear entrance. Eric immediately went to Lucy and kissed her on the cheek.

"Hello, Lucy. Hello, Renee. How are Mr. and Mrs. Duran?" asked Eric.

"Just fine, thanks for asking," answered Lucy.

"Hello, Renee, I have some good news and some bad news for you," said Andrew Klaus.

"Oh dear, let me have the good news first, Mr. Klaus."

"Good news is, I received your seed, but the bad news is, instead of receiving two bags, I got six and I can't send back the other four. I don't have the room to store the extra bags."

"Hmm, that is a problem," said Lucy. "We only need one and we got the extra bag to sell to one of our neighbors in case they needed it."

"I know!" Renee said with enthusiasm. "Mr. Davis and Mr. Lester, can you spare one dollar each?"

"For what, my dear lady," answered Mr. Lester.

"Well, you two can buy the four extra bags of seed. You keep one for yourselves and Mr. Davis, you can sell your extra bag to Mr. Elps, and Mr. Lester, you can sell yours to Mr. Foster. I know they need seed. They told me so yesterday, and can't make it into the city until next week. That way, you can get half of your money back and save Mr. Elps and Foster two trips into the city, one to order the seed and another to pick it up, and Mr. Klaus won't have to worry about storing extra seed."

"But I don't need any seed," said Mr. Davis.

"You will in the next few weeks," replied Lucy.

"That's true."

"What about you, Miss Renee? You will have an extra bag yourself," said Mr. Davis.

"Spread the word we have it, and if anyone is in need, they can come and buy it from us. That's what we were going to do in the first place, and if it doesn't sell, we'll at least have it for next season."

"What do you think Fred? That sounds like a good idea, and we'll be doing Jake and Tom a favor."

"Sure, why not. Come on, Andrew, we'll help you load those bags and we'll load yours too, Miss Renee and Miss Lucy," answered Mr. Lester.

"Now that's the farmer's spirit we love so much!" said Lucy.

While Mr. Davis, Mr. Lester, and Andrew went to load the seed, Renee asked Eric about the progress of the Chesapeake City store. Eric said it was coming along nicely and should open on schedule in February of '49. He mentioned he was going to be staying in Chesapeake City to oversee delivery of building materials all of the following week and would not be able to see Lucy until he returned. Lucy was disappointed about his absence until Renee came up with an idea for the both of them.

"How about if Lucy takes the Friday morning ferry to Chesapeake City and you can show her how the store is coming along, then the both of you can come back on the afternoon ferry together? That will give you both something to look forward to and the days will seem to pass quickly."

"That sounds like fun. What do you think, Lucy?"

"Gosh, I've never gone anywhere on my own like that before. You think Mama and Da will let me?"

"I'll have a talk with them," assured Renee.

"Did you and Reuben ever ride the ferry together, Renee?" asked Eric.

"Once," she said thinking of that happy day. "With Lucy's father when we brought Reuben home after he came back from Mexico."

Outside the mercantile, two elegantly dressed ladies peeked in the window.

"Oh my goodness, do you see what I see, Elizabeth?" said Cynthia Garrett, Renee's nemesis from Wickham Finishing School for Girls.

"Is that Renee Wallace?" replied Elizabeth Rogers, one of Cynthia's closest friends. "Look at how fat she is. I heard she was pregnant."

"And unmarried as well, so you know whose baby that is... want to have some fun?"

"Here we go. Sorry it took so long. I misplaced it," said Annabelle, holding up a green work apron. "I saw this in the catalog and when I saw it came in green, I immediately thought of you knowing that's your favorite color."

"This is very smart... look at all those pockets, Lucy," said Renee. "It's large enough to cover my baby belly."

"It's actually for men, but look, it's adjustable so you can still use it when you are no longer carrying the baby, and knowing you, you will have that child with you everywhere so the pockets will come in handy."

"You know me well, Mrs. Klaus," said Renee as she tried it on. "How much is it?"

"It's a gift."

"Really, that's so nice, but I can't accept this."

"Sure she can. That's how she gets by these days is by handouts," said Cynthia Garrett rather vindictively as Elizabeth Rogers snickered.

"Cynthia and Elizabeth, I haven't seen you in over a year. You both look very good," said Renee pleasantly, ignoring Cynthia's rude remark. "How have you two been since school?"

Taken by surprise and expecting Renee to be hurt, Cynthia, in a condescending tone, replied, "I am doing very well, better than the looks of you. I am to be married to Simon Norenham. He is a very talented architect from Richmond. And how about your husband... oh, I forgot, you ran out on your wedding. Oh, what a shame. So that must be Reuben's baby you have there. I heard he ran out on you. How does that feel?"

"You better watch your mouth! That's my brother you're talking about you, Wickham snob!" exclaimed Lucy as she took a step toward Cynthia.

Renee took hold of Lucy's wrist and pulled her back. "Now, now, Lucy, she can't help it," said Renee. "After all, she did go to Wickham."

"But so did you, and you didn't turn out like her."

"Don't forget, I also went to the public school where your mother was my teacher."

"Oh yeah..."

"You do not fool me, Renee Wallace," said Cynthia. "I could always get your blood to boil and I know it is boiling right now. Look at you, abandoned by your parents and living off the handouts of others. And to top it all, getting pregnant and not being married. There is only one type of woman who gets themselves in that sort of mix and they are total social outcasts."

"Hey now, don't be talking in that manner to our Miss Renee!" called out Mr. Lester as he, Mr. Davis, and Andrew entered the store. "Miss Renee is the best lady this city and county has to offer."

"Lady of the night that is," replied Cynthia.

"Okay! That's it! Let me at her!" exclaimed Lucy as she lunged out toward Cynthia as Eric struggled to hold her back.

"Okay, everybody, settle down," said Renee with a hint of humor. "Lucy, untie you knickers will you…"

Renee took a step toward Cynthia and in a most pleasant tone she said, "Listen Cynthia, you're right, my parents disowned me, but I must tell you that was the best thing they ever did for me. Yes, my life isn't as it should be right now, but I have wonderful friends like Mr. Davis and Mr. Lester standing over there who care about me just the way I am. And Mr. and Mrs. Klaus who support our farming community unlike your so called upper crust society. I pity you, Cynthia, because I'm richer in friendship and love than you'll ever be. So keep thinking you're superior because when Reuben returns, we're going to be a very happy family filled with love and joy, while you'll still be an over-privileged, snobby, uptight, horrid Wickham bitch."

"Whoa! Now that's our Miss Renee!" exclaimed Mr. Davis as Mr. Lester whistled in triumph.

"Well I never," said Cynthia.

"And as uptight as you are, Cynthia, you never will," answered Renee.

"YES!!! That's telling her Renee!" said Lucy.

Cynthia stepped closer to Renee and started pointing her right hand finger at her stomach as she said, "You watch yourself, Renee Wallace, you and your bastard child!"

With her finger, she poked at Renee's stomach. In a quick swift move, Renee, with her right hand, reached over and grasped the top of Cynthia's right hand and twisted it clockwise. Renee, with her left hand, cut Cynthia's right elbow from below as she rotated her right hand upward toward Cynthia, causing her to scream out in pain and drop to her knees.

"Ouch, ouch, ouch, ouch, let go, let go, let go, that hurts, that hurts, that hurts! I said let go!"

All in the store were fascinated by Renee's take down of Cynthia and stood in silent awe.

"Come on now, Cynthia, that's not how we were taught at Wickham if we wanted something. Now what do you say?"

"Please, please, please let go, please."

Renee released Cynthia's hand and she fell backwards onto Elizabeth's feet. Elizabeth helped Cynthia to stand and the two made haste out of the store.

"I'm so sorry, Mr. and Mrs. Klaus and Eric, for my language and that display. I'm so ashamed to have acted in that manner. And I apologize to both of you as well, Mr. Davis and

Mr. Lester. How I acted is inexcusable," said Renee looking downward after both Cynthia and Elizabeth ran out of the store.

"Are you joking? That was amazing," said Eric. "Ma could have used that… whatever you did, to a rude customer the other day. Can you teach her how to do that, and me as well?"

"No apology needed, Miss Renee. You made me proud to know you," said Mr. Davis.

"Now that's what I call farmer's spirit," added Mr. Lester.

"Geez, Renee, what in the heck was that?" asked Lucy with pride.

"I believe it's called a reverse wrist twist. It was something Mr. Akagi taught Reuben, and Reuben taught me. By the way, Lucy, when your brother returns, and if he ever asks you to grab his wrist, don't."

狼

"No, Reuben-San! For the last time, you cannot accompany us to fight Arata Goro. You are an outstanding apprentice. Do not ruin your good standing with your insolence," said Akagi Genda-San in frustration.

Reuben had been pleading with Akagi Genda-San to allow him to fight along his side with the rest of the Clan Alliance against the Arata, but Akagi Genda-San denied his request because Reuben had no place in this feud. He was also concerned about Reuben's safety, not only from the Arata, but also from the alliance, many of whom distrust off-landers, especially those with round-eyes.

"Forgive me, Genda-San, but I'm not being insolent. I'm being practical. The Arata are equipped with muskets and I know these weapons. My knowledge is valuable to you in this regard."

"No, Reuben-San, I must ask for your forgiveness for calling you insolent. You are right. Your knowledge would be most helpful, but I cannot risk your life. Although you have been living in this village for close to six months now, and have been accepted by almost all of village…"

"Except for Masaru," added Reuben.

"Hai, and several others of my samurai. Besides, your purpose for being here is not to participate in our feuds. You have a greater purpose, do you understand?"

Grunting in frustration, Reuben nodded in agreement.

"However, perhaps you can tell me all you know about these guns, muskets you call them?" asked Akagi Genda-San.

Reuben's frustrated look faded. "If you wish, at least I'll be doing something to aid you. Do you still have those muskets you took from those Arata men you captured?"

"I had all but one destroyed," said Akagi Genda-San.

"May I see it, and any ammunition captured with it?"

Akagi Genda-San nodded to Tashi, his retainer, who quickly ran off to retrieve the weapon.

"Now, Genda-San, from what I have learned from you, Masaru, and many of the others, you can still rush a musket line as long as you know their firing sequence. And, from how you described Arata Goro, he sounds like a spoiled brat with a new toy who plays with it before knowing its true potential. This is a huge advantage to you."

"Ah, how so, Reuben-San?"

"A trained company of soldiers can load, aim, and fire up to two to three times a minute. A single good soldier can load and fire at a target at least three times, also in one minute, but I seriously doubt Arata Goro's men are trained."

"Three times a minute? That is impossible!" said Masaru, carrying the musket Reuben asked to see with the retainer following. "I took over a minute to load it once."

"See, Genda-San, the untrained will take longer to load, thus giving you time to advance with the support of Masaru and his archers."

"Here then, show me how it's done, round-eye," said Masaru as he threw the musket at Reuben.

Reuben caught it as if he owned the weapon. It was the first time he got a close look at the weapon and his expression showed amazement.

"Oh geez, I don't believe it!"

"What, Reuben-San? What is it you do not believe?" asked Akagi Genda-San very concerned.

"The other muskets, were they just like this one?"

"Hai, hai, what of it?" replied Masaru in anger.

Reuben shook his head in disbelief and said, "What we have here is an 1846 Harper's Ferry smoothbore musket. Genda-San, these are the same muskets we used in Mexico."

"Mexico? You? You were a... soldier?" asked Masaru.

"Hai, I was, now shut up and listen," answered Reuben.

Reuben's response angered Masaru and he began to palm his sword, but Akagi Genda-San placed his hand over his son's as he smiled in amusement of Reuben's forwardness.

"I still can't believe it. This gun came from my home state of Virginia. Genda-San, how ironic would it be if this musket belonged to one of the soldiers in my regiment?"

"I must admit, the irony does amuse me, but what puzzles me is how would such a weapon fall into the hands of Arata Goro?"

"Any number of ways, Genda-San. When my regiment returned from the war, all our weapons were turned over to the armory for repair or replacement. Ones that could not be repaired were either destroyed, used for parts, or simply fell into the hands of thieves who would sell them to anyone. That's probably what happened to this one and all the others Arata Goro has," explained Reuben.

"How can you tell that is what may have happened to this gun?" asked Masaru.

"Here, take a look at the stock. See how cracked it is? A musket in this condition would have been destroyed. If most of Arata Goro's guns are like this one, then he has substandard equipment. I would even think he has all different type of guns making it difficult to get ammunition."

"I have seen them put to use on my visit to your America, Reuben-San, but how exactly do they work?" asked Akagi Genda-San

"This musket fires a .69 caliber musket ball. Do you have the cartridges?"

Akagi Genda-San's retainer handed Reuben half a dozen cartridges mixed with percussion caps.

"Is this how you found these? They weren't in cartridge or cap boxes? How were Arata's men carrying these?"

"In pockets or sacks," said Masaru, now becoming interested.

"Genda-San, Arata's men are not trained at all. They don't have the proper equipment and probably don't know how to care for these weapons," said Reuben as he started to closely inspect the musket in his hands. "Here, look, filthy," said Reuben as he pointed inside the barrel of the musket. "This is probably why it took Masaru over a minute to load one round."

"What do you mean, Reuben?" asked Masaru more politely.

"When the barrel is clean, it's much easier to load. But when you constantly load and shoot without at least giving it a quick field cleaning, carbon accumulates in the barrel and the vent hole making it very hard to load. If this musket was clean, Masaru might have been able to load and shoot it twice in a minute. He may not have been able to hit the broad side of a barn, but he might get two shots off."

"Hai, but what does all this mean, Reuben-San?" asked Akagi Genda-San.

"It means your archers alone can take out Arata's men who have muskets. I guarantee at least close to half of them would misfire on a volley."

"What is misfire?"

Reuben began to instruct how the musket he had is loaded and the proper firing sequences in full and individual volleys. He made it clear the procedures he discussed were for well-trained disciplined soldiers and pointed out, by the looks of the condition of the weapon and how ammunition was carried, Arata Goro's men had no adequate training. He also described the faults of badly cared for muskets and the causes of misfires. He suggested by the use of well-trained disciplined alliance archers, they could easily defeat the Arata armed with firearms.

"So you see, Genda-San, if you concentrate the alliance archers on Arata Goro's gunmen, your mounted samurai can overrun their firing line and take on the Arata army on your own terms."

Akagi Genda-San nodded approvingly. "This strategy sounds excellent. I will confer with the other alliance leaders on this matter. Thank you, Reuben-San. This was most helpful."

"Father, you are going to listen to this man?"

"Hai," said Akagi Genda-San, looking at Reuben with confidence. "He is an expert on western tactics."

"But what does this round-eye know of our battles of honor? Western battles are barbaric."

"And Arata Goro is bringing that barbaric style of warfare here and it must be stopped," said Reuben, in a passionate manner. His expression formed into a hard angered look causing

Masaru to take concern. "Samurai warfare and western warfare may differ significantly, but there is one thing both have in common."

"And what is that?" asked Masaru, smugly.

"In combat, ninety seven percent is nerve-racking boredom… the other three percent is a bitch."

"HA! Very good, Reuben-San! I do not think Musashi could have put it better himself," said Akagi Genda-San.

Masaru grunted and said, "I still do not believe one can fire one of these weapons three times in one minute."

Reuben shook his head and took the water bottle from his obi and commenced to do a quick field cleaning of the musket. When he was finished, he gave it a quick inspection, nodded, and asked Akagi Genda-San if he had his watch Reuben had given him as a gift.

"Hai, Reuben-San."

"Good, when the second hand reaches twelve, tell me to start. Keep your eye on that post Masaru," said Reuben.

"Now, Reuben-San," said Akagi Genda-San, looking at his watch.

Reuben commenced to load his first round. Rather than return the ram rod in its housing, he held it in his left hand, aimed and fired his first shot hitting the post in less than fifteen seconds as Masaru watched in awe. In less than another fifteen seconds, Reuben fired off his second shot hitting the post. The third shot was fired, and just as the second hand on Akagi Genda-San's watch hit twelve, Reuben fired off a fourth shot, also hitting the post.

"That was four shots. You said soldiers could only shoot three in a minute," said Masaru, looking at Reuben rather respectfully.

"I said good soldiers could get off three shots. I was an exceptional soldier."

"You still are, Reuben-San," said Akagi Genda-San with pride. "Now go with Tashi and return that gun to storage. I believe I will want to keep that one a while longer."

"Hai, Genda-San," replied Reuben, as he bowed to Akagi Genda-San and then to Masaru and ran off with Tashi to secure the gun.

"Father, how come I know nothing of that round… Reuben's background of warfare?"

"He requested it not to be known."

"And you believe his advice is sound?"

"You dislike him because he is a quick learner and not of our kind. In the short amount of time he has been here, he has quickly learned the ways of Budo and that frustrates you that a man such as he can learn our ways so quickly. And do you know why he has learned so quickly?"

Masaru shook his head no.

"It is because of your bigotry, your hatred toward him. The way you and the others brutally train him. He knows he is in constant danger from you and many others and he uses that to stay one, even two steps ahead of you. That is why he is so quick in his movements, his thoughts, and how he adapts his own personality into our form. You see, my son, we Akagi fight for honor, but Reuben-San fights for something much more meaningful."

"What can be more meaningful than honor, my Lord?"

"Love."

狼

Sitting under the oak tree, Renee was surrounded with all her treasures. The image case with Reuben's picture, the stone Akagi Genda-San gave her, the chest of her written passages, and hanging from her neck, the VMI button Reuben plucked off his cadet tunic and gave to her as a Christmas gift. She sat with her hands caressing her stomach and feeling the baby within. A hand gently rested on her shoulder and she leaned her head toward it.

"Do you know what awaits you?" asked Renee.

The hand lifted from her shoulder and Reuben walked around Renee. He sat down in seiza in front of her and placed his hand on her stomach. He was dressed very odd in what resembled a long, dark brown skirt with a dark red robe-like jacket covering his upper body tucked into the skirt-like garment. His hair was unkempt, just the way she liked it, and his eyes had that childlike mischievous look she so dearly missed.

"No, my dearest, but whatever this day brings to us both, I want you to remember what I told Lucy to tell you. I will always love you and forever be yours, and I mean that long after I die."

"You're not going to die, are you, Reuben?"

"Never, my love. I still need to tumble in water and I will return to you, and what awaits me."

In the distance, the sound of a conch shell was heard followed by chants of "AKAGI, AKAGI, AKAGI, AKAGI, SHOURI!"

Reuben looked to the direction of the chants and back to Renee.

"I have to go now, my precious Renee. I may not be with you, but very soon, you will be able to hold a part of me, just as I keep a hold of you in my heart."

Reuben lifted his hand off of Renee's stomach, rose, put on his kasa, and began walking away.

"I love you, Reuben!"

Reuben stopped, faced Renee, and smiled adoringly to her as he said, "Aishite'ru yo, Renee!"

Again, he began walking away and the further he walked, the more he faded away, leaving the view of the creek in his place.

Renee awoke from her nap in a state of delight, but quickly felt a sharp cramp like pain. She removed Reuben's blanket and sat on the edge of the bed feeling her stomach. She felt another pain, stronger than the first causing her to softly cry out. Rising off the bed, Renee went downstairs into the parlor where Coleen and May were sitting having a chat. She entered and said, "I had a dream about Reuben. I think our baby is about to be born very soon." Just then, her water broke.

石
水

In the year of our Lord, 1848, a romantic tale continues.
Her eyes, his nose, one bundle of love...

It's a Girl

Seven o'clock in the morning, July 18, 1848, and the signal was given for morning chores in the village dojo to commence. This day was to be as any day in the halls of the dojo although it was filled with less activity. Akagi Genda-San, the previous day, had taken all samurai to accompany the other province clans to halt Arata Goro's army less than two hundred miles away. This could have been Reuben's chance to witness samurai warfare for the second time since his arrival to Japan, the first being a feudal battle also against Arata Goro. But being an off-lander, Akagi Genda-San denied him the opportunity.

"I know you are skilled in warfare from your country's war with Mexico, but in this dispute, you are not welcome, Reuben-San."
"Am I not a citizen of this village?"
"That you are, Reuben-San, but still, I cannot risk your loss to your family in a dispute you are not a part of. Remember, there are clans in the alliance who are unacceptable to off-landers, so your risk is still much greater than if it were just Akagi against Arata."
"With respect, Master, my experience is valuable here. Arata Goro's army is equipped with muskets. I value the code of the sword, but it will be no match with a musket, even with the support of archers."
Akagi Genda-San wished for Reuben to accompany him. His knowledge in such weapons would be valuable. However, other samurai of the Clan Alliance would put him to death, even with his allegiance to Akagi Genda-San. Still, Reuben was willing to take the risk for the man who filled his life with the desire to live after the horrors he witnessed in Mexico.

"Your life would be in danger from either side. You are an apprentice with great promise and have learned much," Akagi Genda-San said. "As much help as you would be, I have more important tasks. Reuben-San, I would consider it a great favor if you would care for my family while we march." With dire sincerity, Akagi Genda-San placed his hand on Reuben's shoulder. "It may not be battle, but if defeated, Arata Goro will devour private lands. It will be up to you to lead the rest of the village and protect my family."

Reuben knew it was an empty task to make him feel needed, but nonetheless, he bowed before Akagi Genda-San. "I'll protect your family as if they were my own."

狼

Five o'clock in the evening, July 17, 1848, Renee lay in her and Lucy's room with Coleen, Lucy, and May at her side. Aaron and Monroe went to retrieve the doctor, for Renee had gone into labor earlier, the same day when Akagi Genda-San marched his samurai along with the provincial alliance to stop Arata Goro.

The time for the arrival of the baby Renee and Reuben had conceived back on that warm autumn evening was at hand. For Renee, that moment nine months ago seemed to have happened as if it were yesterday. Laying on Reuben's bed, with Coleen at her side, she began to reminisce of those past nine months she had been living with Reuben's family to help ease her mind of the contractions. Although her own parents knew Renee had been living with the Durans, and of her condition, Franklin and Margret Wallace still had no desire to have anything to do with her.

"For goodness sakes, Coleen, why do you even bother sending word to her parents?" asked Aaron in frustration. "They have no heart for our Renee."

"That may be true, but still, like it or not, Renee is their flesh and blood. In the Lord's eyes, they have the right to know. Just like we have the right to know what's happening to our Reuben."

"But we don't know what's happening to Reuben, or if he's even alive."

"True, but we have the means to let the Wallaces know of their daughter's welfare, whether they care or not."

Renee was grateful beyond any means to the Durans. For the past nine months, she truly felt she was part of a family. During the rare moments when she felt alone because of her parents disowning her, it was always Aaron who would take Renee in his arms and reassure her she was never alone.

"You have Duran flesh and blood growing in your womb, my lass, and that does not make you just a part of our family. No, my beautiful daughter, that *makes* you family. Just as much family as your Reuben."

Aaron boasted to everyone about his future grandchild, and how proud he was of Renee's strength over the closed-minded who had the nerve to ridicule her for how she conceived. Not only was she carrying his grandchild, but also successfully managing the farm into self-sufficiency at the same time, no easy task for either a man or woman.

Aaron, hiring Renee as his Agricultural Liaison, made her very popular among the farming community and its suppliers. Her charm, wit, and of course, beauty, made it easy for her farming associates to provide her with help, materials, and advice. Of course, these associates knew of her relationship with the Duran family through Reuben and their story of woe. They admired her strength to continue and never give up faith and love her Reuben would someday return. Those who knew of Franklin Wallace, because of business practices, could not believe Renee was his daughter. She was nothing like him, thus causing a loss of business for Franklin

Wallace, not only because of how he abandoned her, but also because Renee had proven herself to be a delightfully caring woman.

There was no doubt of Coleen's love and affection toward Renee. She felt Reuben's presence in Renee, and not because of the unborn baby, but because of the unconditional love Renee had for her son. Not once did Renee concern herself of being denied her belongings when she was abandoned by her parents. She only had four precious treasures that mattered to her, the image case of Reuben, the stone Akagi Genda-San gave her, her written passages about her love for Reuben, and the VMI button she now wore around her neck with pride on a gold chain Coleen gave her specifically for that purpose.

Monroe was also a pillar of strength for Renee. Through her job of managing the farm, she earned money to purchase her own basic needs. At first, Lucy shared her clothes, but as Renee found other means of making the farm profitable, and not to mention her growth because of the baby, she was able to purchase her own clothing. But it was Monroe who, by legal loopholes, which seemed to be his specialty like his father, gained extra funds to purchase items for the baby's needs.

On the farm, May, Henry, and Noah were fantastic in caring for Renee as she lived there before her move to the city home as her time to deliver neared. Renee still worked the farm with the three, but May kept a strict eye on her, and once she saw a slightest sign of fatigue in Renee, she made her stop and rest. Henry built two cribs for the baby, one for the farm and the other for the city home. Noah built a cradle to be used to carry the baby to and from the city home.

But it was Lucy who was Renee's foundation. Shadowing Renee almost always, she was the true definition of a loyal sister. With her relationship with Eric growing, all because of Renee's advice, both Lucy and Eric saw to all of Renee's needs and comforts, especially where the baby was concerned. Eric and his parents helped Renee by finding baby necessities at cost, while also selling Duran farm products in the Klaus Mercantile, along with some handcrafted tools and furniture made by Henry and Noah. Lucy worked by her side with the farm management, but it was her companionship Renee found to be the most rewarding. In the city home, Lucy taught Renee how to play the tin whistle and on the farm, the piano. Renee did well with the two, but her talent was her written passages and it was Lucy's creative idea to put them to music. Lucy would carry her whistle everywhere and they would put Renee's words to Lucy's music. Renee proved to have a beautiful voice for song, however, because of Renee's passionate words, the songs they made were much ahead of the time, so it was only an activity the two did on their own, as sisters.

狼

The dojo banners were raised after morning chores. The main mast, however, was empty for Masaru had taken the large banner to fly along with the other samurai clans aligned with the Clan Alliance.

What was left of the village males, mostly young adolescents, began to arrive for morning training. The hall became busy with activities of pre-training exercises. Reuben clapped his hands as he entered and bowed. All the students ran to their positions and sat in seiza to await the beginning of training. Akagi Genda-San entrusted Reuben and Tadashi to hold small training sessions with the younger males of the village.

The wind picked up and distant thunder could be heard. A storm is coming, Reuben thought as he looked beyond the pillars to the east. For no reason, he began to think of Renee. One of the youths cleared his throat bringing Reuben back to the present. He nodded and faced the others. He turned to face the empty mast where the Akagi banner flew, bowed, raised, and clapped his hands. He turned to face the others, bowed as they bowed back, and began the first of many exercises. Drops of rain began to wet the grounds around the training hall and the thunder was getting louder.

狼

Renee held onto Coleen's hand tightly as another contraction came while Reuben was commencing the morning training session. Breathing hard and sweat beading at her brow, she tried not to show pain. May wiped her brow. "You're doing fine, Renee," said May as she smiled.

The contraction began to fade and Renee's breathing slowed. "Mama, I didn't expect it to be like this. I don't know if I can go on."

Coleen gave her a reassuring smile. "May's right, you're doing fine. Much better than myself when Reuben was being born."

Renee smiled and looked out the window to the west. "I'm thinking of him now. He doesn't know of his baby being born this evening. I don't know where he is, but the memories of our friendship keep me happy. It's like Mr. Doogan said, memories bind friendships."

Lucy took a seat at the foot of the bed. "You do realize if he did know, my brother would never have left and would be with you now."

"I know, but if he didn't go find Mr. Akagi, both of us would be miserable. He with his memories of the war, and me married to a man like my father. And even if I stopped him at the wharf, Reuben's mind would still be in need of help we couldn't provide." Renee frowned for a moment with the thought of her father disowning her. But she looked up at Coleen, Lucy, and May. "Mr. Akagi may have saved me and Reuben in more ways than any of us can imagine."

Coleen tilted her head with happiness and embraced Renee. "I don't know what it is with you two."

The door opened and in walked Doctor Weldon with Aaron. Coleen and Lucy made room for Doctor Weldon to examine Renee.

"Ah, my dear lass, looks like you are having a baby this evening," he said, smiling as he sat next to her.

Coleen advised the doctor of Renee's condition. The doctor cleared the room of everyone except for Coleen and May. Before he left, Aaron came to Renee's side, took her hand and kissed her on the forehead. "That's for Reuben."

狼

A group of thirty thuggish ronin made their way down the hillside toward the village of Itosai masked by tall trees as Aaron kissed Renee on the forehead. They were loyal to Arata

Goro who sent them to assassinate Akagi Genda-San's family and lay waste to Itosai while he was away with his samurai. Arata Goro sent many groups such as this to other Clan Alliance villages to perform the same horrible task.

At the foot of the hill, they stopped and looked over the home of Akagi Genda-San. The apparent leader nodded to the others. Three, armed with muskets, began loading them. A flash of lightning overhead followed by a loud crack of thunder startled one of the men loading, causing him to fire his weapon.

In the dojo, Reuben was training with Tadashi. Loud thunder sounded followed by a peculiar smaller sound of thunder caused Reuben to halt the training. He went to the open window and glanced to where the strange thunder came from. The other students stopped their practice in puzzlement and watched Reuben.

His innocent look he had regained turned back into that cold angered distant stare. The noise was familiar, but not for this land. The wind finally caught up and brought with it a familiar scent, gunpowder. He glanced to the house, to the others, and back to the hills where the sound came from and saw smoke. He caught a glance of a figure ducking into thick brush.

Tadashi stepped to Reuben's side. "What is it?" he asked and noticed a look in Reuben's eyes that frightened him.

"Put away the bokkens and pass out katanas and naginatas, and you, grab your bow. Arata Goro is cheating."

狼

A loud cry came from Lucy's and Renee's room as Tadashi made his way to the edged weapons closet. Aaron paced up and down the hall in the same manner he did when his own children were born. Monroe and Lucy occupied themselves with an unmotivated game of checkers as Eric watched. He arrived moments after the doctor and Lucy was ecstatic he came to share in this family moment. Lucy and Eric had become very close these past several months all due to Renee's advice to Lucy. Eric so wanted to meet Reuben upon hearing of his deeds in Mexico, but mostly because of how Renee kept him nearby even though he was on the far side of the globe. For a man to have such a beautiful woman to remain faithful must be incredible. However, for now, as they were doing different tasks to pass the time, they all had the same thought, where is Reuben and what is he doing at this very moment.

狼

"Open the katana case," Reuben ordered as Lucy jumped three of Monroe's checkers. The others responded without haste. While the weapons were being passed out, Reuben quickly assigned the village defenders posts around the Akagi home and village.

"Stay in pairs of two, but separate into equal distances never losing sight from the other."

Tadashi and the others looked puzzled at the directions Reuben stated. It was a form of alignment never taught. They stood there shrugging their shoulders at one another.

"Quickly, standard skirmish drill except with no muskets." The village defenders continued to wonder. "For heaven sakes, pair up and keep each other in view at all times and if

233

anyone sees any movement, give warning." With that said, they understood and did as Reuben instructed. The defenders soon formed a parameter around the village grounds.

"Tadashi, come with me. We need to get Genda-San's family to the safety of the dojo."

Together they ran to the house, Reuben with a katana in his hand and Tadashi with his bow and utsubo of arrows in his, all while the rain began to come down faster.

Reuben ran on the beaten path to the Akagi home and saw three of the ronin about to enter the house. He yelled, gaining the attention of the intruders. One turned and was met with an arrow in his chest from Tadashi's bow. Reuben raised his sword and sprinted to the nearest intruder. The intruder also raised his sword and made a full cut downward leaving his upper body exposed to Reuben's side cut. After Reuben's swift cut, the intruder's head fell to the ground in one direction as his body fell to the other.

Whipping his sword around, Reuben continued to the house ignoring the other attacker who was about to strike a cut to him. Reuben's faith and trust in Tadashi paid off as the attacker was hit when one of Tadashi's arrows found its mark in the temple of the attacker's head.

狼

"Mama, please don't be offended, but when I see your son, I'm going to slap him so hard, he will have an imprint of my hand on his face for nine months!" Renee said, finishing another long contraction.

Coleen, May, and Doctor Weldon laughed. "That's it lass, that's the way to keep up your spirits," said Doctor Weldon.

"You two would fight and wrestle several times a week for one reason or another," remarked May.

"I remember I had to reset his shoulder after you dislocated it when he put a frog down the back of your dress at school," said Doctor Weldon.

"Dislocating Reuben's shoulder is going to feel like a tickle compared to what he's in store for when he comes home."

"When he comes home," Coleen enjoyed the sound of that. Renee hasn't given up faith and love in him, she thought. However, Coleen continued to wonder, as far as Reuben is aware, Renee is married to William Sinclair, but she knew her son's love for Renee was very strong and unfaltering. Her thought was interrupted when she felt Renee squeeze her hand tightly and began to breathe harder.

"Geez oh geez oh geez Reuben Duran, you shoddy farm boy, I'm going to give you a swift kick in your plums when you return..."

More laughter ensued.

With Renee's breathing slowing, Doctor Weldon said, "It's almost time."

"No, not yet, please, I must speak to Da," moaned Renee.

The others looked puzzled. Coleen nodded to May and she quickly walked to the door. Aaron, still pacing, saw the door open and stopped. "Mr. Duran, sir. Renee wants you. Come quick."

Aaron quickly walked in. He sat at Renee's side. "I'm here, sweet girl."

Renee looked to him with tears in her eyes. They were not tears of pain, but regret. Although she had this conversation with Aaron before, in her state, she felt she needed to express her regret for how she came to live with Reuben's family. "Da, I apologize for bringing this burden to you," she whispered. "My parents abandoned me, and of all times, I need a family now."

Coleen walked around and stood by Aaron's side. "I'm ashamed of how this child is coming into this world," she said. "With no real mother and father," she admitted.

Tears came to May's eyes and Doctor Weldon also felt moved.

"But please know this, what Reuben and I have is true love for each other."

Aaron retrieved his handkerchief and wiped tears coming down Renee's cheeks. "My sweet girl, we have gone through this all before and there's no doubt what you and our Reuben have is love, and you do have a family, see," said Aaron as he motioned to Coleen and May. "And, there is more of your family in the hall waiting for you to bring one more into this family of ours."

"I talked him into going," Renee said, feeling regret. "I feel like I sent him away and will never know if he still loves me."

Aaron smiled sincerely. "We all know how kind and gentle Reuben is. The war took that innocence away, but that kind and gentleness is still deep within him and of all people in the world, you were the only one who could make it surface. It was you who made him leave Fort Monroe. Our son has nothing but love for you and it will always be with him. It's like Mr. Akagi told you, *'there is a time and place for you and Reuben-San.'* And don't forget the secret Reuben told Lucy, he will always love you and forever be yours."

Aaron looked toward the window and frowned. For a brief moment, he felt anger toward Reuben for not being here, but then Akagi Genda-San's words made more sense. If he had stayed, Renee would be married into a life she would dread and Reuben probably would have killed himself like he tried before, and possibly Renee would have done the same. Could this Mr. Akagi be a prophet, Aaron thought. He looked back at Renee and took her hand in his.

"Renee, my dear," Aaron spoke in his deep Scots accent, "Ya have McDurand flesh and blood growing in ye," he said, proudly proclaiming the original family name. "This child you are about to bring into this world is of the McDurand Clan of old Scotland and will forever be a true McDurand just as you are, my daughter." Aaron leaned down and kissed Renee on the forehead.

Renee felt joy. "Thank you. I do love you so very much."

"Hey now, you need to now stop your sulking. My grandchild is waiting to be born!"

狼

Reuben and Tadashi were about to enter the Akagi home as Aaron kissed Renee on her forehead after his comforting words. Every several steps, Reuben looked back toward the village and listened for any warnings from the other defenders. They ran to the rear entrance and ignored protocol for entering a samurai home.

"Yanna-Dono," Reuben hollered as he and Tadashi entered the house.

Akagi Genda-San's wife, Yanna, entered the room followed by her two daughters, Sukuri and Kaoru. "What is the meaning of this intrusion?" she asked, perturbed.

"A thousand pardons, Yanna-Dono, but there is danger and we must get you and your daughters to the safety of the dojo," Reuben explained.

"Nonsense, the danger is miles away," replied Yanna. She didn't speak to Reuben very often and when she did, he was very pleasant, but now, his look was so hard and piercing, it frightened her.

"There's no time to explain," Reuben insisted as a loud bang sounded from the woods. A thud was heard hitting the house. Everyone, except Reuben, hunched down. "Please, Yanna-Dono, take your daughters and follow Tadashi."

Yanna nodded and pulled Sukuri toward the exit of the house as Kaoru rushed back into the inner portion of the house.

"Where are you going? We need to get to the dojo," shouted Reuben.

"I have to get Katsuo, my son," cried Kaoru. "Katsuo is sleeping."

"I'll get him. You go with your mother and sister and follow Tadashi."

Reuben went through the larger portion of the house to the child's room. Katsuo was in a crib-like bed. Reuben gently reached in and picked up the child. Reuben never held a child before. He looked at Katsuo's face and suddenly began to think about Renee. It was odd for thoughts of her to enter his mind while the house and village were under attack. This never happened to Reuben during the Mexican campaign. Back in those days, Reuben went into a fight believing he was already dead. But this time, it was as if he had a reason not only to fight, but also survive.

"Renee, my darling, where are you and what are you doing to me?" he asked softly out loud.

Another musket shot caused Reuben to regain his composure and his face returned back to fierce anger. He covered the child with a blanket and ran out of the house, shielding Katsuo with his body. Yanna and the others were waiting for him.

Another shot was heard and the bullet impacted on the gate. They ran across the village square and made it to the dojo's inner hall. Reuben handed Katsuo to Kaoru. "Taiki, take Yanna-Dono and the others inside the main hall and protect them."

"Hai!" replied Taiki and ushered Akagi Genda-San's wife, daughters, and grandson to the inner hall.

Reuben and Tadashi ran to the entrance where Kenta was taking cover. "What do you see, Kenta?" asked Tadashi.

"It's Arata Goro's men all right. Not Ninjas, but thugs, nonetheless," answered Kenta.

Tadashi, still armed with his bow, looked up to the tower. He was the best archer Reuben had ever seen, even better than Masaru. Reuben looked to the tower above the entrance as well.

"Tadashi, climb into the tower and take out those muskets," Reuben ordered.

Both Kenta and Tadashi looked at Reuben as if he went crazy. "How can I defeat muskets with a bow?" Tadashi asked.

"Yes, they are armed with muskets, but there's only three and they're not well trained. I can tell by the time it takes for them to reload. What you need to do is listen for the musket shot, spot the flash and smoke, and release your arrow below it and trust in fate that you hit the bastard. It can be done. I've seen Indians kill using that technique in Mexico. You are the best archer I have seen. Now go!"

"Hai, Reuben," Tadashi replied, and began to climb the tower.

"REUBEN, LOOK OUT!"

狼

"That's it, Renee, push," said Doctor Weldon, calmly. Renee was panting quickly and holding onto Aaron's hand as her other hand was beating on the mattress. Coleen quickly went to the other side of the bed and grabbed hold of it.

Her breathing slowed down and she stopped pushing. "I'm sorry. I couldn't go on."

"That's okay, lass. Sometimes it takes more than one. Let's rest for a minute and try again."

"This isn't fun, Mama," Renee said.

Coleen smiled. "Don't worry about a thing, Renee. We won't leave you. You have a house full of love supporting you."

"That's nice to hear, but it doesn't make it any easier." Renee started to chuckle.

"What's so funny?" asked May.

"Here I am about to push something the size of a melon out of me and Reuben is somewhere in Japan, probably having the time of his life."

狼

Reuben turned and raised his sword in time to block a thrust from one of the attackers. Kenta was about to thrust his sword, but with his free hand, Reuben quickly grabbed his attacker by the right wrist, twisting it to his left and threw him to the ground. Reuben raised his sword and cut downward. He thrust his blade in the attacker's chest and twisted the blade. He pulled his sword free of the attacker and whipped his sword as he casually tossed the severed arm of the attacker over the hedge. Reuben faced Kenta and instructed him to assist the others.

Above, Tadashi didn't see the altercation, for he was searching and waiting for musket fire. A shot was heard and the bullet struck the post next to him. Tadashi didn't need to search. He saw the muzzle flash right away and instantly raised his bow taking aim as he pulled the string, and let loose his arrow.

One of Arata Goro's gunmen fired his musket missing Tadashi. He began to reload until an arrow pierced his throat. Coughing up blood, he fell back into the bush keeping him hidden. Another gunman leaped to avoid the other falling and was shocked to see the arrow in the man's neck. Angered, he rose to take aim at the tower where he saw Tadashi pulling back his string. He was about to pull the trigger, but Tadashi was quicker and the gunman fell with an arrow wedged into his forehead.

Some of the defenders left to protect the Akagi home. Reuben and Kenta broke up their pairing to help others.

Inside the dojo, two intruders were searching the hall. As one of them entered the main hall, Taiki cut downward, but the attacker rolled out of the way and was back on his feet in less than a second. The other attacker entered, bringing his sword down as Taiki brought his up in time to block. The first attacker was about to thrust his sword into Taiki's back when it was diverted off by a jo staff coming from the side. Standing at the ready was Yanna, with staff in hand.

With both attackers off guard, Taiki rotated with sword raised and cutting at the same time, sliced through the front of one intruder, dropping him down in a single stroke.

Yanna raised her staff with a wide, quick, sweeping motion hitting the other attacker squarely in the face knocking him down to the floor as he coughed up teeth and passed out.

狼

Renee grunted as she pushed. The doctor urged her on while Aaron and Coleen held her hands. May kept wiping her brow and fanned her down.

"That's it, lass, you are doing great. I can see the baby's head," said Doctor Weldon.

"You're almost finished darling," Coleen replied.

Renee kept pushing and closed her eyes. A vibrant image of Reuben came to her mind. His back was facing her and he wore a strange burgundy robe tucked into large, dark brown trousers resembling a skirt. He was standing on a roof in the rain, the hills and distant mountains behind him were deep green, her favorite color. Reuben's face turned to the side and Renee saw a fierce angered look, the same look he had when he raised his voice in anger to her, and told his mother never to bring her to the farm ever again. A strange feeling overcame her as if being touched by a thousand needles. For a moment she thought it was from the pressure of the birthing, but the feeling was coming from deep inside. Something Akagi Genda-San called *"Hara,"* or one's center. The one place every human being has that provides energy to the body, mind, and spirit. While pushing, she let go of Coleen's hand and began to reach out as if trying to grab the image of Reuben in her mind and pull him away from what she believed was danger.

"REUBEN!" Renee cried out, startling everyone in the room, including Monroe, Lucy, and Eric sitting in the hall outside the room. She began to push harder.

狼

Standing on the roof, Reuben fended off another attacker cutting across his abdomen as rain mixed with sweat on his face. He killed far more than he wanted. Although killing the attackers was needed to protect the village and Akagi Genda-San's family, he still had a regret taking those he had stricken down, but this was not how he felt when he took the lives of the enemy in Mexico.

He glanced around to survey the situation. Kenta run his sword through the middle of an assailant as other village defenders were successfully defeating the invaders.

A musket shot was fired and Reuben looked to the tower and saw Tadashi take aim with his bow and let loose an arrow into the brush. A scream came from the woods and a man fell from the bushes with a musket in his hands. With the third gunman down, Tadashi faced the grounds to assist the other defenders with his bow.

Suddenly Reuben, for some strange instinct, began to think of Renee very deeply. He felt warmth overcome him and a feeling of a thousand needles gently touching his *hara*. Very distinctly he heard Renee calling to him in his mind.

"RENEE!" he shouted and faced toward the East in time to see the leader of the gang swing a sword down cutting through Reuben's hanten jacket and gashing his chest. Reuben ducked, ignoring the wound, and rolled on the roof and was back on his feet behind the leader. He made a cut straight downward, but missed and raised his sword for a cut that was sure to follow.

The leader turned and cut again, but Reuben, with his sword, blocked the cut and rotated the leader's arm and weapon in one motion causing his sword to fly from his hand.

Reuben centered himself quickly for the kill and raised his sword as the leader reached into his robe and pulled out a pistol Reuben recognized immediately, a Colt revolver.

As the leader pulled the hammer back, he got a good look at Reuben for the first time. He showed surprise and began to laugh. "A round-eye, I should have known! Only a round-eye would fight like an okami 狼 leading a mangy pack. Being a round-eye, you must know what is going to happen to your head when I pull this trigger."

狼

"You've done it! You did wonderfully!" exclaimed Doctor Weldon as he raised the crying newborn.

Aaron and Coleen in turn gave Renee a hug, but her eyes were still closed as if searching her mind for something. The doctor snipped the umbilical cord and began to wrap the baby in a blanket.

Coleen had a look of panic on her face. "My lord, is she okay?" she asked as she looked from Renee to the doctor.

Still holding the infant, the doctor came to Renee's side as Coleen made room. He put his hand on her heart and felt it beating quickly. He handed the newborn to Coleen and began to examine Renee. She seemed perfectly fine, but in deep concentration, as if she were in a trance. Doctor Weldon was afraid to shake her out of it not knowing the cause of this peculiar condition. The only thing those in the room with Renee could do was helplessly watch her.

狼

With sword raised, Reuben was looking at the leader's center instead of the pistol. The attacker's smug grin turned to an angered frown as he began to squeeze the trigger.

Reuben dropped his sword and quickly stepped off center from the pistol's path. He grasped the leader's pistol hand, and in a circular motion, Reuben cut the attacker's elbow with his other hand. With the pistol still firmly in the leader's hand, Reuben had it pointed upside down to the leader's face. Reuben began to squeeze, but stopped as images filtered into his

239

mind, images of his platoon and Adam Stanns dying in Mexico, followed by joyful images of Renee with looks of relief, happiness, and love surrounded by his family.

The blood on his hands from the attack was washed away by the rain and the village defenders began to gather as what was left of the attackers were fleeing back into the hills.

"I swore to Renee I would never kill needlessly again. You have her to thank for your life being spared," Reuben said, out loud in English as he held the leader's hand with the Colt revolver aimed to his face. He glanced at the rain running off the pistol cylinder and its unsealed chambers, and back to the leader. His fierce angered look disappeared and was replaced with a mischievous boyish look, the same look that attracted Renee the first time they met.

Reuben smiled and squeezed the man's finger on the trigger. The man hollered with horror, but nothing happened except for the sound of a loud click as the hammer sparked the cap.

"As a round-eye, I also know these weapons don't work too well unsealed in the rain."

狼

As her eyes opened, Renee took in a huge, satisfying breath, began to smile, and laughed a little as she saw in her mind Reuben with his mischievous boyish look. She looked at everyone in the room next to her bed and to the bundle in Coleen's arms. "Is Reuben's baby okay?" she asked.

Everyone in the room began to smile and laugh. Coleen placed the infant in Renee's arms. "You and Reuben have given us a beautiful granddaughter."

Renee looked upon the baby with tears of joy running down her cheeks and a very happy smile on her face. She lowered her head and kissed her daughter on the forehead.

The door opened and Lucy and Monroe looked in. "Is it okay to come in now?" Monroe asked.

"Yes it is," said Renee. "Come and meet your niece."

Monroe entered the room followed by Lucy and Eric.

For a long moment, Renee looked up to Aaron and Coleen standing arm-in-arm next to the bed, and to Monroe and Lucy. Renee had a sparkle in her eyes and with a cheerful smile, she said proudly, "Come and meet... Aarleen Moncy Duran."

As the family came closer to see the baby, Renee reached over to the nightstand and took up Reuben's picture and held it in front of Aarleen and said, "This is your Da, Aarleen."

Renee looked at the picture herself and silently said, "Aishite'ru yo, Reuben."

狼

Akagi Genda-San and Masaru returned later that afternoon after hearing of the attacks on defenseless samurai homes and villages by Arata Goro's army of thugs. There was no battle. It was a ruse to pull as many samurai away from their homes to kill their families. Other villages along the Clan Alliance borders were similarly attacked with Akagi Genda-San's village, the only one deep in the Hisano Province cowardly attacked.

When Akagi Genda-San first saw the ransacked house, he feared the worst until he and Masaru met up with his wife, daughters, grandson, and other villagers cleaning up and seeing to captives, including the leader of this particular clique. Tadashi and Yanna described the attack and how Reuben protected the family and property.

"Reuben defeated these animals?" asked Masaru with disbelief.

"Like an okami protecting the pack," said Tadashi, proudly.

"Where is he?" Akagi Genda-San demanded.

"He is in the dojo somewhere. He went there after he was bandaged."

"He is wounded? How badly?" he asked, not waiting for an answer as he quickly ran off to the dojo followed by Masaru.

Akagi Genda-San ran into the hall where he found Reuben sitting on the floor with a bandage wrapped around his back and chest. He silently stepped up and around Reuben, who began to stand, wincing in pain. Akagi Genda-San reached to help.

"Tadashi and my wife told me what happened here today."

"I'm sorry for the damage to the house and village."

"It all can be rebuilt, but the lives you protected today will live on knowing my gratitude to you. You have protected my family and village. For that I am grateful and eternally in your debt, Reuben-San," Akagi Genda-San said, bowing to display honor and respect to Reuben. "I feel this day, you have redeemed yourself of your past sins of war, and have been blessed with life... in many ways."

Akagi Genda-San embraced Reuben carefully, and silently stepped back as he noticed Masaru step before Reuben.

Masaru faced Reuben with a stern look. Reuben's fierce angered wolf-like look he worn earlier this day returned. Masaru felt intimidation for the first time as he looked upon Reuben's face and realized he is a man who has seen his share of death, and now understood why his father welcomed him.

Masaru smartly bowed in respect and rose. Reuben's cheerful face returned and he held out his hand. Masaru took it and embraced Reuben as his father did.

"Thank you for my mother, sisters, and nephew... Reuben-San."

Still with Masaru's hand in his, Reuben asked, "What's this, *okami*, the others have been calling me?"

Akagi Genda-San began laughing and nodded to his son to answer.

Masaru breathed in and stood proudly and said, "Apparently you have been proclaimed as the leader of a pack of who fought like okami today. Okami is like a wild dog."

"Do you mean, like a *wolf* as we say in my language?"

Masaru nodded with a thoughtful look and said, "Hai."

Reuben released Masaru's hand and winced in pain as he let out a little laugh.

"What is so amusing, Reuben?" asked Masaru.

"That is what the other platoons in my company back in Mexico used to call my platoon, a mangy pack of wolves."

Akagi Genda-San came back to Reuben and looked at him with a look reminding him of how his father would when he was about to express his pride. "Reuben-San, today you have become what you are destined to be, a protector of a pack and that pack includes your family back home where new life awaits you. However, you still have much more tumbling in water to do."

"Stones and water, Genda-San?" asked Reuben, cheerfully.

"Hai, Reuben-San! Stones and water. Now go and rest, your picture of Renee-Dono awaits you."

Reuben began to step quickly toward the entrance, but winced in pain and slowed his pace. Once he was gone, Masaru asked his father, "Stones and water, father?"

"Masaru, my son, if you knew of Reuben-San's Renee-Dono, you would understand why he has come so far to rid himself of inner demons and become one with the code," answered Akagi Genda-San.

"He is really that good, father?"

"He is frightening. You just now saw the look in his eyes, did you not?"

Masaru nodded yes.

"My son, if you only knew what Reuben-San has been through with his country's war in Mexico. In a sense, the worst day of your life could be comparable to one of his best days. Now he is on the correct path of becoming one with the code and he will take back what he has learned from us to care for his own family," said Akagi Genda-San as he looked toward the eastern horizon. "May the gods and elements bless you dearly this day, Renee-Dono."

狼

It was late this eventful evening as Renee sat in the parlor, gently rocking Aarleen in her arms with her eyes set on the baby with a loving, motherly smile on her face. Lucy was playing a soothing Scottish tune on her tin whistle while Coleen and May were also relaxing in the parlor.

"Ah, there they are, my son, the five most beautiful ladies in the city of Norfolk, and all are in the same room," said Aaron as he and Monroe entered the parlor after taking Eric back home.

Aaron placed a chair in front of Renee and the baby, and sat as he took a peak at Aarleen. "So how's my precious little angel doing, my lovely daughter?" he asked with focused eyes on the infant.

"I suppose you want to hold her, Da?" asked Renee with amusement.

"Oh may I?" answered Aaron as he was already reaching for Aarleen.

Renee had a huge smile as she handed Aaron his granddaughter. She sat back and relaxed her arms and watched him make silly faces at Aarleen. Geez oh geez oh geez I'm a mother, she thought feeling all warm and tingly inside.

She noticed Monroe holding a package and asked, "What do you have there, Monroe?"

"It's a gift from Mr. and Mrs. Klaus. It's a blanket for Aarleen. Mrs. Klaus said you probably have enough blankets, but when it comes to newborn babies, there is no such thing as enough of anything."

"Lucy, next time you see Eric, please tell him I dearly appreciate him being here with us while Aarleen came into our lives."

"I already have, Renee. Oh, and I forgot, this is from me and Eric for the baby," said Lucy as she retrieved a leather bound book and handed it to Renee.

"A book?" she asked.

"We didn't know if it was going to be a boy or a girl, so since Eric knew how fond you are about writing passages, we thought you can start a diary for Aarleen until she is old enough to keep it up herself."

"Oh, my dear, that's the sweetest thing I have ever heard," said May.

Renee rose from the sofa and made her way slowly out of the parlor saying, "I'll be right back."

Monroe asked if he could hold his newly born niece. Aaron gently gave her to Monroe and he slowly rocked her in his arms. For all the animosity Monroe felt toward Reuben in the past, it disappeared when he looked into the sleeping face of Aarleen.

"Of all things Reuben ever did for me, I never thought he would make me an uncle," he said, proudly. "It's a shame Reuben isn't here now. Whether he's healed or not, the sight of Aarleen would make him forget all about his time in the army."

"I think we shouldn't talk about Reuben in front of Renee right now. At least for a couple of days," said Coleen.

"Why not?" replied Renee startling everyone as she entered the parlor with her writing utensils. "This little sweetheart needs to learn from whom she got her cute little nose, and also when Reuben does return, she will know of the man who is her Da."

"Aye, that she does," said Aaron.

Coleen let out a small laugh and asked, "Does that mean you have forgiven Reuben for the nine months of aches, pains, and sickness?"

"OH NO, Mama," replied Renee. "He's still going to get kicked… you know where when he returns so he can feel some of my pain."

Laughter broke out, but was suddenly silenced when the baby stirred in Monroe's arms.

"Well don't kick him too hard. This little darling will need to have a little brother or sister of her own," said Aaron in good humor.

Renee took her seat on the sofa and picked up the diary. "Da, can you please hold this ink bottle while I write something for Reuben in Aarleen's diary?"

"Of course, my dear, it would be my honor."

Renee opened her image case of Reuben, and placed it on the left side of the diary. She dipped her pen in the ink bottle Aaron was holding and closed her eyes in deep thought for several moments. A smile came to her face as she opened her eyes and began writing. When she was done she said, "Listen to this…"

Monday July 17, 1848
My eyes, your nose, upon the face of this little bundle of love
How I so desire your presence holding what we have created
Beneath our oak tree that warm autumn eve
When we became one in love, far too long we had waited

I long for my love and our bundle longs for her Da
If you could only see such beauty we have brought into this world
Adorable is this bundle and longs to know from where she got her little nose
Stones and Water, Faith and Love, my dearest darling Reuben, it's a girl

石
水

In the year of our Lord, 1849, a romantic tale continues.
A daughter's redemption and smoothing begins...

<u>Will You Marry Me</u>

Saturday, August 26, 1848, the day of the city public school pie auction attracted many participants and spectators. It was always a popular annual charitable event to help augment allocated city funds to the city school for the upcoming year, and it always had a carnival atmosphere. There were games, music, performers, arts and crafts, and of course the main event, the auctioning of the pies.

Coleen, along with the rest of the school teachers and administrators, always planned and put on a successful event each year. However, this year was special for Coleen because not only was she the head chairman of the event, she had a granddaughter to show off.

This was a big day for the Duran family because today, two new members of the family were making their official public debut, Renee and her and Reuben's daughter, Aarleen. Renee sat beneath one of the school yard trees with Aarleen on her lap and Lucy by her side. Renee had not attended a pie auction since the year her father pulled her out of the public school to attend Wickham, so she was excited to help be a part of the event and to have Aarleen with her. The entire Duran family took turns holding Aarleen so they could lend their hands to the event. However, when Renee had Aarleen in her arms that seemed to be the time when people would flock to see and pay respects to the new mother and her child.

"Oh, my goodness, will you look at the sweet angel, bless her little heart. What's her name, my dear?" asked Miss Tilly, one of the city's school teachers.

"Aarleen Moncy Duran," proclaimed Renee proudly as she looked at her daughter so lovingly.

Many would think the display of an unwed mother at a venue such as this would be deemed inappropriate. However, once the true nature of Renee's circumstance came to light, she and the Duran family gained much regard and support. In the time the Durans took Renee in, she proved herself to be a well-rounded citizen with the admiration of the merchants and neighboring farmers as the "Duran Agricultural Liaison."

In retrospect, Renee's redemption is what ironically caused the demise of her father's successful business. Not once did Renee utter any negative remarks about her parents, or felt the need to justify her situation. That alone gained her much respect. When the true details came to light regarding Franklin Wallace's daughter's arranged marriage to increase his business and keep Renee from her true love, the citizens and merchants he did business with began to do

245

business elsewhere. Once the truth was exposed of the disgraceful means by which he abandoned Renee when she stood up for herself, and the one she loved, what was left of his clients eventually abandoned Franklin Wallace, one by one.

Franklin Wallace was deep in debt as he spent money he didn't have before the day Renee was to wed William Sinclair. He was forced to sell off over half his assets to break out close to even. In the end, he had enough money to leave Norfolk and move to Mobile, Alabama to make a new start with one of only two ships he had left, the other being the *Morning Star* still underway in the Pacific.

Because of his social and financial demise, Franklin Wallace had intense hatred toward his daughter and did not care to know of her welfare in the letters Coleen would send to him and his wife.

"Read them if you wish, I have no desire or care for that stupid bitch and her bastard child inside her wretched womb!" Franklin Wallace would say when his wife would receive a letter from Coleen.

The day Franklin Wallace abandoned Renee, her mother was just as furious and carried just as much anger and hatred toward her daughter. She felt disgraced and many of her acquaintances snubbed her at social gatherings. Not only was Franklin Wallace's business failing, so was their social status.

It wasn't until one day in Renee's sixth month of pregnancy when Margret Wallace, by chance, happened to see Renee walking out of the Klaus Mercantile with Lucy and Eric when her anger and hatred began to fade. She saw Renee from behind with her hair unpinned. Margret detested when Renee would wear her hair in such a common fashion. Seeing her daughter coming out, as what her class would consider a, "common shop," dressed in common clothing, and unpinned hair, caused her blood to boil and her stomach to twist in hate. That was until Renee turned sideways and Margret viewed her daughter's protruding belly. Suddenly that hate faded into shame, not toward Renee, but toward herself.

She watched her daughter, hiding herself behind her parasol. Renee was smiling, laughing, and greeting people passing by as others pleasantly greeted her back. Margret Wallace found herself smiling as she watched Renee, Lucy, and Eric walk away joyfully, arm-in-arm.

When the three moved on, Margret Wallace did the unthinkable of her social class and entered the Klaus Mercantile to discreetly ask questions about her daughter.

"I noticed that lovely girl with the long, dark, brown hair with child outside your shop just a while ago. She looked familiar. May I ask if you know of her?" asked Margret Wallace.

"Oh, she's a dear," replied Annabelle. "Her name is Renee Duran... actually its Wallace, but she both lives with and works for the Durans. She manages their farm and she and Lucy Duran come in almost every day at this time to deliver eggs for us to sell."

Looking surprised Margret Wallace said, "That young girl? She manages a farm?"

"Yes and very successfully also. She has the honor of being the only '*Agricultural Liaison*' in the county, and a woman at that. She has the admiration of her farming neighbors and many of the city merchants as well," answered Annabelle. "Do you know her?"

Desperately hiding her emotions, Margret Wallace replied, "No, I am afraid not. I must have been mistaken. She looked so familiar and very... lovely. Thank you for your time."

"You're welcome."

Margret Wallace exited the mercantile and for the many days to follow, she would spend time standing at a distance, at this particular time of day, with hopes of catching a glimpse of her daughter. She did this almost daily, watching Renee and feeling regret for the part she played in her daughter's adolescent dilemma. For the next three months, Margret Wallace tried to gain the courage to step forward and speak to her daughter. Just when she felt she had enough courage to do so, Renee's visits to the mercantile stopped. Margret Wallace became concerned as each day passed with no sign of her daughter. How come she has not been coming by, she thought. After several days, Margret Wallace decided she was going to enter the mercantile and inquire as to Renee's whereabouts. She was about to cross the street when she saw Renee walking up the street with Lucy. Lucy was carrying a large egg basket and Renee was carrying Margret Wallace's grandchild.

"She surely has your precious eyes, but I must say, that nose looks like Reuben's," said Miss Tilly.

"Yes! That's what I keep telling everyone," said Renee with a giggle.

"What does a guy got to do to get some help around here, put on a baby bonnet?" asked Eric holding a box filled with pies for the auction.

"Hello, Eric. Sorry, but I can't help," said Renee. "I already have a sweetie pie in my arms."

"Hello, Renee," greeted Eric. He knelt down to look at Aarleen. "Hello to you as well, Aarleen."

"Come on, Eric, I'll help you," said Lucy. "Where's your mother? I thought she was coming."

"She's at the pie tables with your parents. She has another box of pies to display."

"We'll be right back, Renee. Bye, bye, Aarleen."

"Hey, tell Da, it's his turn to hold Aarleen," said Renee, watching Eric and Lucy make their way to the pie tables.

Lucy and Eric arrived at the pie display tables and began to assist placing the pies Eric and his mother delivered.

"Oh, my goodness, Coleen, there has got to be almost a hundred pies here. Are you sure they all will be auctioned off?" asked Annabelle.

"Just you wait, Annabelle. Especially when there are but a dozen left, that's when the real money starts coming in."

"Hey, Da, Renee said it's your turn to hold Aarleen."

"Oh goodie, goodie, goodie, goodie I'm off to hold my precious little angel. Now make sure you keep this apple crumb pie safe for me, my love."

"Greetings, I have a couple of sweet potato pies here for y'all," said May, strolling up to the table with Noah in tow.

"Hello, May and Noah, I was hoping you could make it today," greeted Coleen. "Is Henry here also."

"Sure is. He's keeping Mr. Duran from holding baby Aarleen," said Noah with a laugh.

Everyone looked to where Renee was seated and saw Henry holding Aarleen while Aaron was standing next to him pointing his finger in a mocking manner.

"Come on, Henry, it's my turn to hold my precious little angel."

"I'm sorry, Mr. Aaron, but I was here first and you missed out, so now you have to wait."

"Come on, Henry! Renee, this is your doing!"

"Hey, am I going to have to take Aarleen back and sit you two in separate corners of the school yard?"

Everyone at the table started laughing at the banter between Aaron and Henry with Renee and Aarleen caught in the middle. Everyone that is until Coleen caught the sight of a woman looking out of place wearing a lovely hooped day dress across the street.

"Excuse me, Lucy, please take over for me. There is someone I need to speak with."

"Sure, Mama, come on, Eric, you can help me."

Watching from across the street, Margret Wallace had a smile on her face as she watched her daughter protecting her grandchild from the overzealous Aaron and Henry arguing about whose turn it was to hold the baby.

"That baby must be very precious to cause two grown men to argue over holding it," Renee's mother said to herself.

"Not only is she precious, she is beautiful," said Coleen as she silently strolled up to Margret.

"Oh, my, pardon me, Coleen, I was just passing by," said Margret, startled and began to walk away.

Coleen gently took hold of her elbow causing Margret to stop. "You really should go and see our granddaughter, Margret," she said, sincerely.

"Granddaughter, a girl?" asked Margret with a proud smile.

Coleen nodded and motioned Margret to follow her.

"I cannot, Coleen. My daughter must hate me, and I cannot bear to put her through any more pain her father and I already put her through. The sight of me would only bring back that horrible day. Look at her. Look at how happy she is. I cannot take that away from her." Margret looked at Coleen and asked, "She is happy? I mean sincerely happy?"

"She is very happy, Margret, and well taken care of."

"I cannot thank you enough for all you and your family have done for her. I dearly appreciated the letters you sent. My husband would not have anything to do with them, but I took them to heart. He does not know I have been watching our daughter from a distance. My daughter must think of me as an evil, horrible mother. But I just had to see her and my grandchild one last time before we depart to Mobile tomorrow."

"Then it's a must you should go and see them both, and by the way, Margret, your daughter has a name. A name you gave her when you held her in your arms the way Renee held her daughter and named her Aarleen. It would probably be very helpful if you call her by her name."

"I appreciate your concern, Coleen, I really do, but I cannot face her."

"Well, I guess I understand, Margret. Tell you what, when you get settled, send me your address in Mobile. I'll continue to send you letters about Renee and Aarleen's progress."

"That would be lovely." Margret took one last look and saw Renee standing over Aaron, who finally got his turn to hold her granddaughter.

Margret looked back to Coleen and asked, "Your son, Reuben, do you know where he is, and if he is well?"

"He's on an island called Honshu on the other side of the world. We have faith and love he is well and will return," replied Coleen, watching Aaron holding Aarleen.

"Does he know my daugh... Renee has been living with your family, or of Aarleen?"

Coleen shook her head no and added, "He doesn't even know Renee didn't get married."

"She really did love your son?"

"She still does, Margret, more and more as each day passes."

Margret nodded and placed a consoling hand on Coleen's arm. "I will pray for his safety and his return, Coleen. I was blind to it before, and after these past few months I have watched Renee from a distance, I have realized your son, my Renee's Reuben, was the better choice for her to have."

"Thank you, Margret."

"I really must go now. My husband will be wondering about my absence. May I ask a favor of you please?"

"Yes, of course."

"If the opportunity ever feels right, can you please tell my Renee of this day and our conversation?"

"Indeed, I will."

Margret nodded and took one last look at her daughter. She was standing with her granddaughter in her arms with the most joyful face Margret had ever seen on Renee's face. Margret turned and began walking away.

狼

Margret walked to the end of the block and crossed the street to continue her walk home via the front of the school. Before she walked in front of the building, she took one last look behind her, but could not see Renee or her granddaughter, so she kept walking with her head lowered in sorrow. How I wish I could make amends with Renee and hold my granddaughter, Aarleen, she thought as she strolled on the walkway oblivious to her surroundings.

She was completely startled when she heard the soft angelic voice of Renee say, "Hello, mother."

Margret stopped dead in her tracks, her feet rooted to the spot, and she felt stress in her belly. She began to panic. Should I run away, she thought.

Renee, with Aarleen in her arms, was sitting on the brick steps leading to the main entrance of the school. When Margret realized Renee was not looking at her, she started to calm down. She timidly took a couple of steps closer to gain a better look at the baby. When she was but a few feet away, Renee looked up to her. She stopped and the stress feeling returned to her belly.

"Would you like to hold your granddaughter, mother?" asked Renee, softly and cheerfully.

How could my daughter speak to me in such a happy manner after all I did to her? Surely there is no chance of forgiveness, Margret thought.

"Well, mother, do you want to hold her?"

Margret nodded silently and lifted her arms.

Renee rose and carefully placed Aarleen in Margret's arms. Margret brought Aarleen closer to her and peered into her face.

"Everyone says she has my eyes, but of course I got my eyes from you. So I guess you can say she has your eyes, mother."

"Oh, Renee, she is so adorable," said Margret as her eyes moistened.

Renee stepped back and gasped raising her hands to her mouth.

Margret looked to Renee and asked, "What is the matter, Renee?"

Renee gasped again, lowered her hands, and smiled. "You hardly ever called me by my name, mother."

"I hardly did anything with you that I should have, Renee," replied Margret with regret and returned her gaze upon Aarleen.

Feeling more curious than angry, Renee asked, "Why, mother? Why did you let father treat me the way he did, and why did you let him drag me out of the house and your life?"

Margret let out a sorrowful sigh as she kept looking into Aarleen's face. "I am not going to insult you by giving you an excuse, Renee, because I have no excuse. Because of your father's past success and the riches that came along with it, I lost sight of motherhood and I am ashamed." She turned her attention to Renee and continued, "You have every right to hate me and never forgive me, Renee. As for myself, all I have to offer is my sincerest apologies and to say I am so very sorry for not being the mother I should have been to you."

Renee wrapped her arms around her mother and said, "I should be furious with you, but I'm not. After seeing the emptiness in Reuben's eyes when he came home from the war, and the pain he was going through, I don't think I could ever compare my hardships to what he had to endure. I saw in him a transformation of an innocent caring boy, into a hollow bitter man who left everything he loves to find the one man who can make him the way he was for his family, and also for me."

"And is this why he has traveled to the far side of the world? To cure himself for you even though he believes you are married to another man?"

Renee released her embrace and looked down as though she was ashamed. Margret placed her hand on Renee's chin and gently lifted her head. Looking into her eyes, she said, "That is the most romantic thing I have ever heard, Renee. We must try to get him back."

Renee showed surprise at her mother's response. "Mother, do you really mean that?"

"Of course I do. I was blind to your love for your Reuben, but no longer. This child in my arms is a living legacy that represents that love you two share. Have you tried to contact him?"

"Yes we have. We have sent letters with any outgoing ship that will take one. Of course it's only a chance. The place Reuben went is isolated from foreign visitors."

Margret nodded and said, "Well, when your father begins his business in Mobile, I will do the same."

"Mobile?"

"Yes, we depart for Alabama tomorrow. That is why I had to come and have one last look at you. I have been watching you from a distance for about three months," she said as she looked down to Aarleen in her arms, "and my granddaughter, Aarleen."

"Oh mother, it's so unfair, now that we are getting reacquainted."

"Listen my darling, Renee, I will send Coleen our address. She said she will keep me up on your and Aarleen's progress. Perhaps you can do that for yourself?"

"I will, mother. What about father?"

Margret let out a grunt, "I am afraid his feelings toward you have not changed."

"Perhaps one day," replied Renee with sincere hope.

"You have a lot of faith and love, but do not waste it on your father, use it for your Reuben. Here, take Aarleen, I really must go."

Renee took Aarleen in her arms and slowly rocked her as she set her eyes upon her daughter's face.

Margret let out a little gasp and said, "Look at you, Renee! You are a mother, a very beautiful mother. Please be to our Aarleen everything I never was to you."

Margret leaned down and kissed Aarleen on her forehead and then kissed Renee on her forehead, as well, and started to walk away.

"Bye, bye, Mama," said Renee.

狼

In the wake of the cowardly July attacks by Arata Goro on the defenseless Clan Alliance villages in the province regions, the alliance went on the offensive, giving chase after the Arata. As Akagi Genda-San predicted, once the alliance gave chase, Arata Goro's undisciplined army scattered. Now, three months after the attack on Itosai, Arata Goro had reformed his army. But rather than trying to conquer the large center province of Hisano as he hoped, he was attacking the smaller, less organized provinces to the east which were quickly falling. The first to fall was the province of Ute. Ute, with its vast shoreline, primarily relied on its fishing villages to sustain its existence. It was from the Ute province through the fishing village of Tatao where Reuben and Tadashi entered Japan. Although the two regions of Ute both had samurai to serve their two

Daimyos, the province never experienced the brute and belligerent type of warfare Arata Goro was introducing to this country.

As for the province of Hisano, there was no significant threat due to the Clan Alliance and previous defeats of the Arata. However, they were still considered a nuisance because small groups from Arata Goro's army still crossed into the province, raiding outlying villages and outposts.

The July attack also prompted Akagi Genda-San to gain permission from the Shogun to begin his dream project, to build a castle to honor the Akagi Clan and protect the village of Itosai. It had always been a desire of his to build such a fortress as a permanent memorial for his village, and spent many hours drawing plans and surveying his region for the best location to build this structure. The Shogun granted Akagi Genda-San permission because of the growing concern of Arata Goro's exploits so near Edo. During his tour of America, Akagi Genda-San took notice of the few forts he happened to see and was fascinated by the star like shaped feature they resembled. He didn't fully understand the purpose of the architecture, but now he had Reuben who served duty in such a structure, Fort Monroe.

"Reuben-San, what is the purpose of the odd, star shaped feature of your American forts?"

Since the day of the attack, Reuben had proven himself a valued and worthy Akagi warrior. He was granted the status of samurai and Akagi Genda-San's retainer for the troop of villagers he lead during that attack. It was Reuben's suggestion he and Tadashi form those specific villagers who defended the village into a home guard, much like the militia units in Reuben's state of Virginia. He described to Akagi Genda-San and Masaru the importance of the militias in his country, and stressed how much of an advantage his army would have by installing such a unit in his village. The novices and youth would be trained by Reuben and Tadashi as first line defenders if the village and future castle would ever come under attack. Meanwhile Akagi Genda-San, Masaru, and their lieutenants could concentrate on the vastly experienced and seasoned samurai army of the Itosai region. It was a suggestion highly praised by Akagi Genda-San who believed the training of this "home guard" would prove useful. Especially when the novices and the youth would eventually fall into the ranks of the "Itosai Regional Army" as he named it.

Reuben's suggestion was also highly praised by Masaru. Since the July attack, Masaru's attitude toward Reuben changed significantly. He saw Reuben as an honorable warrior and his equal. He even went as far as relocating Reuben and Tadashi to more accommodating individual living quarters within the village. Masaru also began to mimic Reuben's low sword technique. It was Masaru who referred to Reuben's style as "Okami no Michi," Way of the Wolf, taking on the description of how he led and fought against Arata Goro's assassins. As the home guard was being established, Masaru christened it "Okami no Mure," The Wolf Pack. "It is they who will defend our den while we take on our enemies elsewhere," Masaru proclaimed.

At first Reuben felt uneasy about being referred to once again as "wolf," stemming from when he was called, "the leader of a pack of wolves" in Mexico. However, the home guard, as well as the entire village, and the Akagi samurai, adopted the title proudly. Reuben began to have a sense of redemption for being the lone survivor of his platoon and embraced the title as a tribute to his fallen comrades of the fifth platoon of Company B in the 9th U.S. Regular Infantry Regiment.

"Star shaped forts are designed to ward off attacks by using the many angles of the walls. In other words, if one wall is attacked, defenders in another wall can repel the attack. Also, with the use of heavy guns, angled walls take on less damage, and with an obstacle surrounding the fort, such as a moat or trench, taking a fort is nearly impossible," answered Reuben.

"Hmm, I see. Do you recommend such a structure for our castle, Reuben-San?"

"If you want to guarantee the safety and protection of the village, then yes, I do."

"But I do not see that as traditional, my Lord," commented Masaru.

Reuben nodded in agreement. He had seen the plans drawn up by Akagi Genda-San and many illustrations of traditional samurai castles, and he found them inspiring works of architecture. "I agree, your country's castles are magnificent. However, all you will be doing is building a star shaped wall around the architectural stronghold design. The traditional structure of the castle will still be the same. And although you deny the truth, Masaru, modern warfare has been introduced to your beautiful country by Arata Goro and I guarantee, we have not seen the last of him. Heaven forbid Itosai will ever be attacked again, but if it is, the star shaped structured wall will be your best defense."

"It's not only the huge stone forts in America that take on that shape, but also the wooden forts in the frontier regions of America, my Lord," said Tadashi, adding his observations. "I took refuge in one such fort as it was attacked by Indians. Try as hard as they could, they could not get any closer than fifty to a hundred yards because of the angled range of fire, and there was no moat or trench surrounding the fort."

"That is fascinating, Tadashi-San. What do you think, Masaru?"

"As much as it pains me to admit, western barbaric warfare has reared its ugly head and we must do what we can to defend against it. I agree, my Lord. We should take such a structure under consideration."

Reuben walked away from the other three as they began to discuss where the castle was to be built. He walked in the direction toward the mountain slope and studied its structure as he moved toward it.

"We have all this space to build it here, my Lord," said Masaru.

"But this is prime farming soil," answered Tadashi.

"Well, it cannot be built to the east of the village because of the downward slope causing the village to be higher than the castle. That would be defeating the whole idea of building a stronghold to protect the village," said Akagi Genda-San. "If not east of the village and not here, then where?"

"How about over there?" asked Reuben, pointing to the mouth of the gorge leading to the slope of the mountain-pass north of the village.

The others joined Reuben and looked in the direction he was pointing.

"What do you mean, Reuben?" asked Masaru in a condescending tone. "Building the castle that far north of the village will leave it completely unprotected. What would be the point?"

Reuben looked to Akagi Genda-San with those mischievous eyes of his and a sly smile on his face.

"No, Reuben-San… you are not thinking what I think you are thinking, the entire village?"

Reuben nodded. "Tadashi and I have explored that gorge many times. It has a natural water source from the falls of the water runoff from the high mountains. The falls themselves could be used to generate forms of power such as steam for various uses. There is no back way in, and the gorge provides a natural barrier from the rear and sides because of the one hundred to one hundred fifty feet high walls of the gorge. It will also provide protection from natural elements especially during the winter."

"What exactly are you proposing, Reuben?" asked Masaru.

"If I may, my son, I believe Reuben-San is proposing we move the entire village into the gorge. Am I correct, Reuben-San?"

"Exactly, and the gorge with the village inside can serve as a fortified portion of the castle as well. The gorge itself becomes the fortress with the castle serving as the entrance."

"That is absurd!" exclaimed Masaru.

"Why? Why is that absurd?" asked Tadashi, coming to Reuben's side to show support of his proposal. "Like Reuben said, he and I have explored that gorge many times. There is more than enough room to build a new and secure village in there and to have it well protected from the sides and rear."

"And the castle serves as the front door to the village so to speak?" questioned Masaru, seeing the potential advantage with the use of the gorge.

"That's right," said Reuben. "By moving the village into the gorge and freeing all that land for farming, also provides a wide defensive frontal view, and will cut construction time significantly."

Akagi Genda-San looked harder at the gorge and nodded approvingly. "Masaru, call a meeting of all retainers and senior warriors. We need to march on the Arata."

"For what purpose, my Lord?" asked Masaru.

"Labor."

狼

Christmas day 1848 had been one of the best ever celebrated by the Duran family. It was celebrated on the farm, and as the day wore on, Andrew and Annabelle arrived to join in on the Christmas day celebration.

A huge feast was served and everything prepared, from the Christmas ham to the handmade table cloth and napkins by May, were provided entirely from the Duran farm. It was a tribute to how successful Renee ran the farm with the assistance of May, Henry, Noah, and Lucy. It was truly a prideful event for everyone, including Andrew and Annabelle Klaus and their son Eric, who helped in the success by selling products produced by the farm.

Lucy and Eric were hand-in-hand most of the day. For the entire month of December, Eric had been spending the weekdays in Chesapeake City overseeing and assisting in the building of the new Klaus Mercantile. The planned grand opening of the store was set for Monday, February 5.

Lucy found it difficult to be apart from Eric during the weekdays, so every Friday, as suggested by Renee several months prior, she would take the ferry to Chesapeake City where Eric would proudly give her a tour of the store's progress. Afterwards, they would enjoy the ferry ride back to Norfolk together. It was a relationship truly sparked by Renee, who enjoyed seeing Lucy and Eric together. Watching their relationship blossom gave her a feeling of redemption for all the years she and Reuben could not truly express their love for each other. She adored the honesty of their relationship and how they could freely express their love by holding hands, something she and Reuben could never do in public.

After Christmas dinner, as everyone was about to help with the cleaning, Renee suggested Lucy and Eric be excused from the chores to watch over Aarleen in the parlor.

"Are you sure, Renee? There are a lot of dishes to be washed."

"I'm sure. There are plenty of people to help. Too many for that matter and Aarleen needs to be watched over."

Lucy gave Renee a hug, took Aarleen from Renee, and led Eric by the hand to the parlor as Eric said, "Thanks, Renee. We will take good care of Aarleen."

Lucy and Eric made themselves comfortable on the sofa as Aarleen lay napping on her front atop a quilt on the floor. Lucy took out her tin whistle and began to play Silent Night.

"That was very pretty," said Eric when she finished. "I put in an order for some of those whistles to sell at the store."

"Did you really? I'm going to have to buy one then. Of course GrandDa's will be my favorite though."

Eric laughed and then he let out a sigh and he had a concerned look.

"What's the matter, Eric?"

"Lucy, starting next month, I'm not going to be able to come back to Norfolk on the weekends. Since January is the last month of building and stocking, I'm going to have to put in some work on the weekends."

"Hmm, that is bad news. I often wonder what will happen to us when the store opens. How often will you and I be able to see each other? It worries me, but then I think of Renee and my brother. They have been apart for over a year, and this is not the first time either, with the war in Mexico, and when he went to VMI. When I worry about not seeing you, I feel selfish because we still have opportunities to see each other. Renee and Reuben don't, and, and…"

Lucy began to get emotional and Eric put his arm around her for consoling and finished her thought by saying, "she does not know if he's alive, right?"

Unable to speak, Lucy nodded yes.

"I'm sure Reuben is still alive, Lucy. Based on all the stories you, Renee, and your family have told me. And I'm also sure he will return, and just imagine to his surprise when he sees Renee is not married. Oh, and what about Aarleen? Boy, is he going to be really surprised!"

Lucy let out a little chuckle as she wiped her eyes with her fingertips and when her eyes were clear, she rose in amazement.

"RENEE, QUICK COME IN HERE!!!" called out Lucy.

"What's wrong, Lucy?" asked Eric, and looked at Aarleen. He rose alongside Lucy and took hold of her.

Renee came into the parlor quickly. "What is it? Is Aarleen okay?" she asked in a panic, and then looked at Aarleen. "Geez oh geez oh geez Aarleen is crawling!"

"Look at what she is crawling to, Renee! Do you see that?"

"What's all the commotion going on in here?" asked Monroe as he and the rest of the family and friends entered the parlor.

"My little Aarleen crawled to the end table and is reaching for my picture of Reuben," cried Renee.

She lifted Aarleen off the floor, picked up the image of Reuben, and held it in front of Aarleen, who took hold of it with her little hands and began to coo at the picture.

"Eric and I were talking about Reuben, and Aarleen began crawling to his picture. She knows he's her Da."

"Well she should," said Noah, chuckling. "Renee constantly shows baby Aarleen that picture all the time. So much so I sometimes think Reuben is my Pa."

Laughter broke out from everyone at Noah's remark.

"Put her back down, Renee, and let's see her crawl again. I don't think everyone got to see," said Monroe.

"Okay," said Renee as she placed Aarleen gently on the quilt.

Aarleen laid kicking out her little legs.

"Renee, put Reuben's picture on the floor," suggested Coleen.

Renee did so and she said, "Come on, Aarleen, go to Reuben, go to your Da."

There was total silence in the parlor as all eyes were on Aarleen. She got up on her hands and knees and began to rock back and forth. There were sounds of gasps and aw's as she began to crawl toward Reuben's image.

When she reached the image case, everyone began to cheer in delight as Renee picked up Aarleen and her picture of Reuben.

"That was fantastic," said Aaron. "Please, Renee, you need to say something about Aarleen's first crawl."

Renee cradled Aarleen close and as she looked upon her little face she said, "Merry Christmas, Reuben, my love."

狼

It was grand opening day for the Chesapeake City Klaus Mercantile. Although there was a chill in the air, a large crowd who had been anticipating its opening stood outside and waited for the ribbon to be cut by Eric Klaus.

The whole Duran family was present, as well as May and Noah. As much as Henry wanted to attend, he had a great fear of crossing the bay so he stayed behind, sending his best wishes along with May. They all stood outside along with Eric and his father while Coleen and Annabelle were inside with Aarleen.

"Ladies and Gentlemen, it's so grand to see all of you here on this cold, but beautiful day for our grand opening," said Eric. "I won't make any speeches because you all being here shows tribute of how much you all have anticipated the opening of the store, and besides, it's too darn cold."

There was laughter from the crowd and as it died down, Lucy called out, "Cut the ribbon, Eric!"

"Okay, without further ado, I welcome each and every one of you to the Chesapeake City Klaus Mercantile!"

Eric cut the yellow ribbon Lucy strung up earlier and applause erupted from the crowd.

"Come on in and enjoy what we have to offer. There is hot coffee and cocoa waiting for you all!"

One-by-one, the customers filed into the store. Everyone on both the Duran and Klaus side of the families each pitched in their hands to assist in the running of the store this day, and it was much needed. It was a full day of business and nearly the entire stock that was on display was sold.

Renee, Lucy, and May assisted customers on the store floor as Aaron, Monroe, and Noah restocked shelves. Eric and Andrew both saw to the till while Annabelle and Coleen tended to the refreshments for the customers. Even baby Aarleen assisted by sitting in one of the baby chairs Henry made, and wearing clothes, both offered as merchandise.

Many of the customers made more than one visit to the store on this day bringing friends and family with them. In the end, it had been a very successful day. Word of the success attracted the Mayor of Chesapeake City, who came by before the store's closing to offer his congratulations. He purchased one of the baby chairs Aarleen was "displaying" for his grandson.

When the last of the customers left and Lucy placed the closed sign in the door, everyone gathered around the till for the day's tally. It was huge. It caused Aaron to take a cup of hot cocoa and say, "Everyone, find a cup of something, anything, coffee, cocoa, water, and join me in a toast."

There was enough hot cocoa to fill cups for everyone and once they had cups in hand, Aaron cleared his throat and said, "To Eric Klaus, who put in many hours and days to make this day a success. May the customers always be welcome and the till flourish!"

"Here, here!" exclaimed Eric's father. "To my son!"

Everyone took sips of their cups and placed them on the counter and started to applaud.

Renee, holding Aarleen, said, "Come on, Eric, now that we're inside and warm, make a speech."

"Yes, speech, speech, speech!" cried out Lucy.

Feeling flush, Eric came out from behind the counter, removed his shop apron, and took Lucy's hands. "I want to thank everyone for all your help and support, especially today. But I want to especially thank Lucy for her support. I know the last couple of months have been difficult because I had to stay here to work, and I had good reason for it."

Eric, still holding Lucy's hands, turned his focus to everyone at the counter. "This past Christmas day, Lucy had worries about what would happen to us once the store opened," said Eric. He turned his full attention to Lucy once again. "You see, Lucy, the reason I have not been able to come back to Norfolk on the weekends is because I have been preparing living space behind the store. It's a part of the store I have not showed you or anyone. Lucy, my sweetheart, I don't want you to worry about us anymore..." Eric, still holding Lucy's hands, lowered down on one knee, and continued, "Lucy Duran, with your father's permission of course, will you marry me?"

Renee smiled brightly and cradled Aarleen closely. Both Coleen and Annabelle gasped in joy. May and Noah both showed silent surprise. Monroe brought his hand to his forehead in sheer disbelief. Andrew and Aaron stood rooted to the spot, mouths gaping open.

"Geez oh geez oh geez," said Lucy.

She looked to her mother and father, and to Renee. "Mama, Da, what do I do?"

Aaron stepped up next to Lucy and took one of her hands from Eric and looked his daughter in the eyes, "My wee lass, this is one decision we cannot make for you. As for you Eric, my fine young lad," said Aaron without looking away from Lucy, "you have my permission for my daughter's hand in marriage. That is, as long as I get all my warm underwear at a discount."

Lucy reached out and embraced Aaron tightly and said, "Yes, Eric, I'll marry you!"

"Excuse me, Lucy, but you are supposed to be hugging Eric," said Renee with a cheerful laugh.

Eric rose from the floor as Lucy jumped into his arms.

There was more applause and cheers for the young couple coming from everyone. Except for Renee, who discreetly backed herself to the shop window and began to peer outside. She looked down to Aarleen in her arms smiling. She was startled when she felt Lucy's hand on her shoulder.

"Are you okay, Renee?"

"Yes, Lucy, I'm just thinking of your brother."

"I'm sorry, Renee. Is this awkward for you?"

Renee turned to face Lucy. "Of course not, Lucy. I'm probably the one who is the happiest for you. You did what I told you to do when you and Eric first started seeing each other and I'm proud of you. I know Reuben would be proud also."

"Want to hear something Eric said to me Christmas day?"

Renee nodded.

"We were talking about how selfish I was worrying about not being able to see Eric on the weekends, when you and Reuben have not seen each other for over a year, and I included when he went to VMI and Mexico. He said to me when Reuben returns, *'just imagine to his surprise when he sees Renee is not married.'* I know my brother will want to marry you on the spot. My point is Renee, it's because of you and Reuben I have Eric in my life, and one of these days your wait will be over."

Renee's eyes began to water and she cradled Aarleen even closer. "I have to admit, Lucy, I sometimes wonder if Reuben will find someone else wherever he is."

Lucy placed both her hands on Renee's face and looked to her eyes as she said, "Listen to me, Renee. You didn't see my brother the night he and I took a walk before he left. There was nothing in this world that would keep him from loving you, Renee. He made me promise to tell you his dearest secret and to use it when it's needed, like now. I told you once before, but I believe my brother intended for me to tell you his secret if you ever began to have doubts about him. His secret was for me to tell you, no matter what happens to you, he will always love you and forever be yours."

Tears began to fall from Renee's eyes. She took a hold of the button hanging around her neck. Lucy used her thumbs to wipe the tears away from Renee's face and took a step back.

"I remember what I said after the first time you told me his secret. It was something Mr. Akagi told me. *'There is a time and place for you and Reuben-San.'* Thank you Lucy, thank you for reminding me." Renee looked down to Aarleen and said to her, "And thank you, my precious daughter. Thank you for being a part of the love your father and I share."

狼

"The entire village, in the gorge, my Lord?"

"Hai, Nobu, the entire village. And it will be guarded by the castle blocking the gorge."

A meeting of the leading warriors of Akagi samurai, Akagi Genda-San's and Masaru's retainers, village elders, and Shinto priests was called to discuss the future plans of the village and castle of Itosai. Unlike meeting in the great hall of the village dojo as usual, this meeting was held at the mouth of the gorge where Reuben suggested the village be relocated for better protection. Before the meeting, Akagi Genda-San took Reuben aside to discuss his idea, in a rather delicate manner.

"Reuben-San, I acknowledge the idea of moving the village is yours. However, it may not be well received by my samurai and villagers if they knew the idea came from, if you will pardon me, an off-lander. Although you have earned the status of samurai and the respect of my warriors and villagers, they still have that stubborn pride and prejudice that off-landers are too ignorant to understand Japanese traditions.

"I have personally spent the last couple of days exploring the gorge with Masaru, village elders, and priests, and one day with my wife and daughters. They also see the benefits of moving the village to the gorge and the acquired farming land. Granted, it will be more land than we need, but it is better to have more of than less, and as you pointed out, a greater view of the land for defense."

Reuben chuckled as he placed his hand on Akagi Genda-San's shoulder and said, "Genda-San, my Lord, my friend. Never in my life I ever thought I would be in this part of the world, using jo's and swords as weapons. You have introduced me to a way of life that has balanced out my light and dark sides, and as you have mentioned when I first arrived, that was my purpose of coming here. Genda-San, this is your village, I only made a suggestion. A suggestion you could have laughed at, almost like Masaru did, but you didn't. In fact, you took that suggestion further. I believe eventually you would have come to the conclusion the gorge is a good natural barrier for the protection of the village and using the castle as its stronghold."

Reuben's eyes began to take on his mischievous spark, the spark gaining the attention of Renee so many years ago under their oak tree. "Besides, Genda-San, when I was a child, we would build forts by the creek under the oak tree, myself, Renee, Noah, Lucy, and sometimes Monroe, and we had fun building them. We would pretend the fort was to protect our farm from invading pirates. If it was that much fun building a fort for play, I can only imagine what fun we will have building a full scale castle, and that's all I want to do."

Akagi Genda-San laughed so hard he began coughing. "Well said, Reuben-San. I believe the smoothing of your stone is taking shape."

"There's one thing that deeply concerns me though, my Lord," said Reuben, returning to a serious manner.

"What is that, my friend?"

"The use of Arata captives as labor, that troubles me. Being raised in a part of my country having the institution of slavery, it makes me uneasy. My family never believed it was right to own another person because of race, as it is in my country."

"Ah, I see, Reuben-San, and I understand. While touring America, I did witness the slavery there, and I too found it most distasteful. But, Reuben-San, our views of 'slavery' differ in many ways. I will try to explain what my purpose is to march on the Arata.

"I have ordered only opposing samurai and the ronin of high standards are to be taken. Being captured by the Akagi will put them in the position to be bound to serve the Akagi, and in this case, the relocating of the village and building of the castle. When the task is complete, the captured samurai will have their status reinstated and will be allowed to return to their homes with honor intact. As for the ronin, they will have the choice to leave or to stay on as citizens of the village, and to serve the Akagi as samurai.

"That, Reuben-San, sounds much more pleasant than to be one of the Negros in your country who find it virtually impossible to gain their freedom."

Reuben nodded. "I suppose that's much better than serving an entire life of servitude. It may take me time to adjust to it, mind you."

"The way I see it, Reuben-San, we will be too busy to even notice who is a captive or who is a citizen."

As Nobu and the other leading warriors looked at the gorge, its steep cliff walls, and the water falls to the end, they began to understand the meaning of the endeavor being discussed.

"Very well, my Lord," said a tall, imposing samurai named Ryo. "When and how many Arata captives do we need?"

"We will need many, but not as much as we cannot care for. For this matter, we will strictly abide by the Bushido code. Although they may be captive labor, we will treat them as skilled workmen. Is that understood?"

"Hai, my Lord!" said all present.

"Very well, I have already dispatched pages to inform the Takumi, Sho, and Satoshi of our march and invited them along if they so desire, but made it clear it was not necessary. Along with the pages, I have invited them for a banquet to inform them of Itosai's relocation and the building of the castle to which they have already known of my plans of building such a structure.

"This will be a major undertaking for every one of our region. From farmer to samurai, from young to old, from male to female, from each and everyone in this region to Daimyo, myself. This enterprise may take many years to complete so we need to encourage pride to build an Itosai and castle we all will be proud and honor bound to defend."

When Akagi Genda-San finished, all present began chanting, "AKAGI, AKAGI, AKAGI!!!"

狼

Two days later, a grand banquet was held in honor of the other Daimyos of the Hisano Province to advise them of Akagi Genda-San's plans for his region. They all embraced the plan. They believed with Itosai located almost in the center of the province, and having it fortified, the entire province would be protected. They also offered man power and materials to the project.

"Akagi Genda-San, I offer stone from the quarries of the Yuna region and my finest stone cutters," said Takumi Sadao-San.

"You will have timber from the high mountains of Itto and ax men for your needs, Akagi Genda-San," added Sho Masaki-San.

"Majaul understands the massive undertaking needed for moving an entire village because of the plague causing Majaul to be relocated. I will dispatch my surveyors and those most key in our relocation process to assist," said Satoshi Kei-San of the Majaul region.

"Excellent, my provincial brothers," said Akagi Genda-San. "With all of you contributing to the relocation of Itosai and building of the castle, I motion the castle be called, Hisano Castle in honor of all four regions making up the Hisano Province,"

"I second the motion," said Satoshi Kei-San.

"I agree."

"I, too, agree. Long live the Hisano Province!"

Within a week, preparations were made to begin making temporary living quarters in the gorge. The entire village population took hold of the relocation proudly. Many of the villagers never felt secure with the village out in the open the way it stood now, especially with the attempted attack of Arata Goro's assassins still fresh in their minds.

While the Akagi were about to march on the Arata to capture manpower, Akagi Genda-San left Reuben's and Tadashi's Okami no Mure to see to the initial start of the relocation process.

Akagi Genda-San and Masaru rode on horseback to where Reuben and Tadashi were erecting a sign. The two dismounted to bid the two good fortune in their task.

"What is it you are doing, Okami?" asked Masaru.

"You can't start building a new village without first placing a sign with the village name. That's asking for all sorts of problems," answered Reuben.

"Hai, very good, Reuben-San. Reuben-San and Tadashi-San, I leave the Okami no Mure in your capable hands. We will return in no more than a weeks' time."

"We'll be here. Don't take too long. Tadashi and I don't want to have this village and castle built before you come back," said Reuben as he began to strike a nail and hit his thumb instead.

"Ouch, son of a bitch!" said Reuben in English.

Masaru looked at Reuben puzzled. "What was that you said, Reuben?"

Looking ashamed, he answered, "I'm very sorry. That was not appropriate. Please forgive me, my Lord."

Akagi Genda-San chuckled, but Masaru stepped closer to Reuben with a look of inquiry.

"Reuben, can you teach me your language?" asked Masaru, sincerely.

Reuben, with a look of surprise, shrugged his shoulders and looked to Akagi Genda-San.

"That is a fantastic idea, my son! Can you do that, Reuben-San? Teach not only Masaru how to speak English, but the village as well? Tadashi-San can assist since he also speaks English."

Feeling overwhelmed with Akagi Genda-San's confidence, Reuben nodded and said, "I don't see why not. I always aspired to become a teacher one day, like my mother, and Renee says I do have the ability to teach. Yes, why not. With Tadashi's help, we can teach the village English, if you wish it, my Lord."

"I wish it. We will discuss this at length when we return. I believe the learning of English will be beneficial, especially for what the future may have in store for our country."

狼

"We are here today on this beautiful Sunday, the first of April in the year of our Lord, 1849 to join Eric and Lucy in a life of commitment. It is fitting and appropriate that the family and friends of Eric and Lucy be here to witness and participate in their union. For the ideals, understanding, and mutual respect which they bring to their life together, had their roots in love and friendship and guidance you have given them. The union of two people makes us aware of the changes wrought by time. But the new relationship will continue to draw much of its beauty and meaning from the intimate associations of their past."

The Duran's and Klaus' family and friends all assembled in a small chapel in Chesapeake City as Lucy Duran was wed to Eric Klaus. Even Henry braved the ferry ride across the bay to attend, all due to Renee. It was her idea to blindfold Henry and keep him below decks of the ferry. She also had Lucy accompany them with her tin whistle so she could play tunes while Renee lead Henry into dancing to mask the effects of the ferry's movement in the water. When they arrived at the opposite side of the bay, Henry had no clue the ferry ever left the Norfolk side.

"Eric and Lucy, you are surrounded by your friends and family, all of whom have gathered here to witness your marriage and share in the joy of this special occasion. Today, as you join yourselves in marriage, there is a vast and unknown future that awaits you. Possibilities and potentials of your newly married life will be great and now fall upon your shoulders. Through your commitment to each other, may you grow and nurture a love that makes both of you better people, a love that continues to give the joy and passion for living, and provides you with patience to face the responsibilities of life."

As the reverend was presiding over the ceremony, Renee sat with Aarleen sitting on her lap. Renee was so very happy and proud of the young couple. She took a hold of the VMI button hanging from her neck, and thought of the day when Reuben will return and that will be them. The day when Eric proposed to Lucy was both joyful and sorrowful for Renee. But Lucy's sympathy and comforting, and her reminder of Reuben's secret, eased Renee of any doubts about Reuben's love for her.

"Lucy, I know this is your wedding, but take it from me, keep it simple and sweet. Not like that behemoth of a wedding my parents had planned."

"Like the way you want to marry my brother under the oak tree?"

"Exactly, but you can't have the tree, I already called dibs."

"Do you, Eric, take Lucy to be your lawfully wedded wife, promising to love and cherish, through joy and sorrow, sickness and health, and whatever challenges you may face, for as long as you both shall live?"

"I do," said Eric, looking into Lucy's eyes.

"Do you, Lucy, take Eric, to be your lawfully wedded husband to be your partner in life and sharing your path, equal in love, promising to honor and cherish, through good times and bad, until death do you part?"

"I do," responded Lucy, gazing into Eric's eyes.

Renee gripped the button tighter and pulled Aarleen closer to her with anticipation of the final portion of the ceremony after the rings were exchanged.

"And now, by the power vested in me, by the Commonwealth of Virginia, I hereby pronounce you husband and wife. Eric, you may kiss your bride."

Eric lifted Lucy's veil and leaned in, as did she, and their lips met. They kissed for a few seconds and when they finished, the reverend announced, "Ladies and gentlemen, family and friends, I present to you Mr. and Mrs. Eric and Lucy Klaus."

Everyone stood and began to applaud, except for Renee who remained seated with Aarleen on her lap. Renee released her hold of the button and applauded. She had a very proud grin on her face as she watched Eric and Lucy hug before the altar.

Renee felt a tug at her neck and looked down to see Aarleen take a hold of the button. Renee watched her closely while still applauding, but suddenly stopped when she heard Aarleen say her first words, "Ooban, Da."

Renee's eyes widened and her jaw dropped. She quickly looked around to everyone who still had their focus on Eric and Lucy. She returned her focus back to Aarleen, lifted her, and said, "What did you say, sweetheart? Can you say that again for me?"

Still with the button in her little hand, Aarleen said, "Ooban, Da."

Renee stood and hugged Aarleen with loving, motherly affection and pride as she said, "I have to remember to write this in your diary."

"I'll remind you if you forget," said Coleen with joyful tears in her eyes from behind, as she also heard Aarleen's first words.

狼

Reuben awoke feeling unusually joyful at this early hour of the morning on the second of April. Unbeknownst to him, his sister Lucy had just been introduced as the wife of Eric Klaus, and the daughter he knows nothing about uttered her first words.

He rose out of his futon in his temporary quarters of the newly relocated village of Itosai and lit a lantern. He retrieved his image case of Renee off the floor next to his futon, untied Lucy's ribbon, and opened the case. He gazed upon Renee's image joyfully.

Reuben could not understand why he felt so joyful at this moment, but rather question the feeling, he chose to enjoy it. He lay back down with Renee's picture still open laying on his scared chest. He closed his eyes, but could not go back to sleep. It was close to four in the morning. He would be getting up in less than an hour to have a quick breakfast of rice and fruit, and lead the Okami no Mure for the early morning training session all before formal breakfast.

Rather than waste this joyful feeling, he rose, closed the image case and retied the ribbon around it. He got dressed quickly and made his breakfast. After he ate, he grabbed his jo, and ran to the training grounds to get in some personal training before the others arrived.

He was in the midst of practicing the suburi of the jo when he heard Akagi Genda-San speak to him, "Ohayo gozaimas, Reuben-San. I had a feeling you would be here early this day."

"How so, my Lord?" asked Reuben, cheerfully.

"I had a fascinating dream. A dream about you and Renee-Dono. I cannot remember what it was about, but I do recall you two were happy together in the dream. It woke me to wonder if you may have had a dream yourself."

"I didn't have any dreams of Renee, but I did wake unusually happy.

"Ah, perhaps this will be a good day for work to be done on the village. But first, in the meantime... onegai shimasu, will you please train with me?"

"Hai, Sensei!"

The relocation of Itosai progressed smoothly, even during the winter months. The gorge was devoid of any snowfall, so work continued on the clearing of the land. A huge help in that endeavor came from the Sho Clan's ax men who hacked away trees and brush as if it were child's play.

Akagi Genda-San returned within a week, as he mentioned, with one hundred seventeen Arata captives from the Ute province. They consisted of 79 samurai with their families, and 38 ronin, all pressed into serving Arata Goro.

There was virtually no battle when the captives were taken. Masaru lead the Akagi samurai numbering three times larger than the outpost from where the captives were taken. The Akagi surrounded the outpost. With fifty mounted samurai, Masaru entered the outpost with Akagi Genda-San and demanded to speak to the warrior in charge. The samurai of the Ute province were on the youthful side with hardly any battle experience and in a sorry state. When they pressed their regional lords to fight the Arata, like the regions of the Hisano Province, their lords refused and cowered under the belligerent forces lead by Arata Goro. When the warrior in charge appeared before Masaru on foot, Masaru looked down upon him and drew his sword.

"You and your men are now prisoners of the Akagi! Grab your belongings, including your swords, and fall into line! We march back into Hisano in an hour's time!"

"If we do not comply?"

"You will all be bound by the code to commit seppuku for joining forces with a marauder and committing treason to your own province of Ute."

"What is to be done with us?"

"You are to be sentenced to labor. Once your sentence is completed, you will be allowed to return to your province with your honor fully intact."

"What of those of us with families. If the Arata come and we are not here, our families will be slaughtered."

Masaru looked to his father. The two confided in hushed tones. Masaru asked, "How many families?"

"Over a dozen, but no more than 20."

Masaru looked back to Akagi Genda-San who nodded. Masaru turned his focus back to the Ute samurai and said, "They will be permitted to come along, but with minimum belongings. Now quickly, we permit you an extra thirty minutes before we march back to Hisano!"

The leader of the outpost turned to his subordinates and discussed their situation. When the Ute Province fell to the Arata, Arata Goro plundered the two regions of all their wealth. The samurai of the province were pressed to serve the Arata, divided up, and sent to outposts such as

265

this one to fend for themselves, with no support from Arata Goro or their regional lords. They were, however, expected to march with the Arata when needed. The leader and subordinates agreed the Akagi offer was more promising.

"Akagi warrior, we agree to lay down our swords, but not as defeated warriors, but as samurai who have been betrayed by their regional lords who subjugated themselves without a fight to the Arata."

"Agreed! You have the right to wear your swords," replied Masaru to the samurai leader. Masaru looked to the group of men standing off to the side who clearly were ronin. "And you as well, ronin," he added with his focus upon them.

These captives and their families proved to be extraordinarily useful and cooperative. Akagi Genda-San addressed them upon their arrival to discuss what was expected. Upon the completion of the project, the samurai and their families would be allowed to return to their province with Akagi allegiance. The allegiance would ultimately result in the allegiances of the Takumi, Sho, and Satoshi.

As for the ronin, they would have a choice to leave or become citizens of Itosai and serve the Akagi.

Reuben was fascinated by this form of "servitude," and admired Akagi Genda-San's leadership in this matter.

"You have had my respect since the day we first met on that jetty, Genda-San, but what you proposed to the captives is very impressive."

"Ah, Reuben-San. All I am doing is practicing three virtues of the Bushido code. Duty, honor, and benevolence. It is my hope these men will align themselves with us against the Arata. As you said yourself, Reuben-San, we have not seen the last of him."

It had been four months since the relocation had begun. The temporary quarters were being quickly replaced by permanent cottages built from stone supplied from the Yuna region and a smaller gorge less than a mile to the Northeast. The captives and their families were being housed in the old village quarters so the transition was moving smoothly. Although the foundation of the castle was not to be built until the relocation of the village was completed, Akagi Genda-San, along with surveyors and advisors sent by Satoshi Kei-San, and Reuben began to outline the position of the walls for the fortress.

The surveyors and advisors questioned Reuben's knowledge, but once he, with Akagi Genda-San's support, provided drawn plans and a small scaled model of the star shaped feature of the walls, they embraced the concept.

Akagi Genda-San became prideful each day of Reuben's emotional progress. His focus was much more intact than when he stopped Reuben from taking his life on the jetty that one autumn evening. His training in the Budo Arts flourished and his sword style, Okami no Michi, was being adopted by several of the Akagi samurai, particularly the ones of shorter stature.

But what earned Reuben the most respect was when he began his school to teach the English language to the citizens of Itosai. Along with Tadashi, they operated a very successful class schedule that didn't impede the work of the massive relocation project. Reuben taught a one hour session in the midmorning while Tadashi taught a one hour session in the midafternoon. Reuben recommended to Akagi Genda-San the classes should start off small with ten to twelve students, and of course, one of the first students to attend was Masaru. The first two classes would learn the rudimental basics of the language and once they learned those basics, Reuben and Tadashi would evaluate and create a structured curriculum. Reuben's idea was to create both a basic and advance class with Tadashi teaching the basics, and Reuben the advanced. Within two and a half months, four classes had been cycled through the basics. Both Reuben and Tadashi used the method Tadashi used to teach Reuben Japanese, but in reverse. It was an endeavor Akagi Genda-San was proud of and he participated on his part by speaking English to the students who attended the school to aid them in their learning.

It was a concept well received by the villagers. However, Reuben confided with Akagi Genda-San about a dilemma he faced when he returns home.

"What is that dilemma, Reuben-San?"

"I have been speaking Japanese ever since Tadashi began teaching me, and now, when I speak my language to the classes, I found I have acquired an odd accent. How am I going to explain that to my mother? Geez oh geez oh geez how will I explain it to Renee? She will never let me live it down."

Akagi Genda-San let out a hardy laugh as he placed his arm around Reuben's shoulder and said, "There is only one thing to do about that, Reuben-San. Grab your jo and onegai shimasu!"

Although there was much activity in Itosai, Akagi Genda-San made time to dedicate toward Reuben's training in the Budo Arts. With the Arata threat neutralized for the time being, Akagi Genda-San felt honor bound to spend time with Reuben considering he challenged him in the first place to come to Itosai. The time they spent together was as if they were back on Reuben's farm training under the oak tree.

It was during these individual training sessions with Akagi Genda-San when Reuben began to understand his meaning of stones and water. Although Renee is married, one day we will be as love intended, just as we were the night before I left, Reuben thought to himself often.

And so the year of our Lord 1849 continued, as did the years to follow. Although separated by half a world apart, both Renee and Reuben grew together with their love for each other never faltering, both unaware of each other's path that would eventually end up meeting in the distant future. A future filled with wonders, treasures, and challenges beyond both of their understanding.

Part Two

I Hear You're a Father

Now These Days …

石
水

In the year of our Lord, 1854, a romantic tale continues.
A soldier's redemption and a little girl's favor for her GrandDa…

My First Entry

Treaty of Kanagawa, March, 31, 1854

> *"The United States of America and the empire of Japan, desiring to establish firm, lasting and sincere friendship between the two nations, have resolved to fix, in a manner clear and positive by means of a treaty or general convention of peace and amity, the rules which shall in future be mutually observed in the intercourse of their respective countries; for which most desirable object the President of the United States has conferred full powers on his commissioner, Matthew Calbraith Perry, special ambassador of the United States to Japan and the august sovereign of Japan has given similar full powers to his commissioners, Hayashi-Dai-gaku-no-kami, Ido, Prince of Tsushima, Izawa, Prince of Mimasaka, and Udono, member of the Board of Revenue."*

With the signing of this treaty, The Empire of Japan opened its ocean boarders with the United States for three primary purposes. The first was for Japan to be used so steamships could restock their coal supply in the Far East. Second, was for shipwrecked sailors to be provided humanitarian treatment, whereas in the past, they were either treated inhumanely and or executed. The third primary purpose of the treaty was for trade.

Once Akagi Genda-San heard the news of the treaty, he became fearful the end of the samurai was drawing near. This premonition of his was what prompted his journey to America so many years ago. When he first arrived and saw all the wonders before his eyes, he knew the sacred way of Bushido would be coming to an end in his beloved country. *"It may take many years, decades even, but the truth of the matter is, the world is growing at a quick pace and for Japan to keep up, it would eventually either elect to join, or be forced to adopt the new age era,"* he wrote in his journal of his travels.

The news of the American fleet dropping anchor 26 miles away from Edo was a warning in Akagi Genda-San's eyes, for these ships didn't carry merchants for trade. They carried soldiers that would be mobilized to man harbor forts and batteries. It was the beginning of the end of the samurai.

狼

It was after midday on a warm summer day in July as Akagi Genda-San arrived to visit Isamu Gorou, a good friend and fifth generation of sword makers. The Isamu Clan lived alongside the Akagi and furnished all edged weapons for all four regions of the Hisano Province.

Isamu Gorou also served Akagi Genda-San's father as one of his samurai before he dedicated his life in the footsteps of his forefathers to the art of sword making. Well into his 70's, Isamu Gorou still forged some of the best swords and naginatas in Japan.

"Ah, Lord Genda-San, welcome! What do I owe this honored visit to my humble workshop?"

"Isamu Gorou-San, it has been far too long since I last stepped into this place where art is forged! How are you, my friend?"

"I am well and still breathing, thank the forefathers. And you and your family?"

"They are also well, thank you for asking."

"The castle, it is nearly finished, is it not?"

"That it is. In about 40 days, a celebration will be held after to honor its completion. I do hope you and your family can attend."

"We will be there for I once served the Akagi as a samurai."

"That you did, and still serve by providing marvelous weapons."

Isamu Gorou motioned Akagi Genda-San to have a seat as one of his granddaughters brought them a bottle of sake and cups.

"Perhaps I can forge some ceremonial naginatas for the occasion, Lord Genda-San."

"That would be wonderful, but as I said, completion will be within several weeks. That is not enough time."

Isamu Gorou laughed and slapped Akagi Genda-San on his knee. "My Lord, I began forging a pair of naginatas for the castle the day you placed the first stone in the ground. They have been awaiting this day for six years."

"Ha! Very good, my friend, very good indeed!" exclaimed Akagi Genda-San, joyfully.

The two discussed the old days when Isamu Gorou served Akagi Genda-San's father and how he was impressed with the relocation of Itosai and the building of Hisano Castle. They went on for close to half an hour when Isamu Gorou asked, "So, Lord Genda-San, I sense you have need of my craft. Perhaps you wish for me to make you a new sword?"

"Hai, my friend. I do need you to forge me a sword, but not just any sword. I have a special sword in mind for a special friend. A friend who I believe will be leaving our community in the near future."

"You speak of the English sensei?"

Akagi Genda-San nodded in silence.

"He is the one many of the villagers call, Okami. My granddaughter's children have learned his language by attending his school. They have very high regard for him. What is so special about this sword you desire for me to forge for him?

Akagi Genda-San began to tell Isamu Gorou the story of how he and Reuben met. He told of how Reuben was a lost warrior and needed the code of Bushido to find his way. He spoke of how in the seven years he served the Akagi, Reuben's jagged rock had been turned into a smooth stone, and the time has come for him to return to the one who let him go. The water has washed away the jagged edges and it was time for her wait to come to an end.

In Akagi Genda-San's personal thoughts, he believed Renee didn't follow through with her arranged marriage because of what Reuben told him of the night they spent under the oak tree before her wedding and his departure. Akagi Genda-San remembered his warning to Renee about how she would have to sacrifice nearly all she had for love, a sacrifice that would have its rewards, but required patience. He also believed the one night beneath the oak tree spawned new life awaiting Reuben's return. They were thoughts he never shared with Reuben, but used them to sharpen Reuben's focus and his purpose in all his training.

Akagi Genda-San told Isamu Gorou he believed Reuben's purpose is to defend the ones he loves, and a warrior who fights for love, is one who needs a special sword. A sword that is non-lethal, yet still lethal. A sword that has not been forged since over one thousand years, and then, only in myth.

"That type of sword you speak of only exists in the written texts of the Kojiki and Nihon Shoki. To reproduce such a sword from those texts would be... blasphemous I would think," said Isamu Gorou with a provoking look.

"Then you refuse to make such a sword?" asked Akagi Genda-San, concerned he may have offended his friend.

Isamu Gorou looked up to the wall of his workshop where unfinished swords hung. He took a sip of sake and looked at the cup.

"This may be the sake speaking, Lord Genda-San, but to make such a sword for your friend, a man who has proven his worth to our community, and who has shed blood for your family would be... an honor. It will be my best work yet! No, not work... art! Yes, it will be a piece of art! My Lord, I still have metal I used to forge your grandson's birth sword, so with your permission, I would like to use what is left of it for this blade."

"Of course my friend, as much as you need. All of it, if necessary."

"Very good. I will take it to the Shinto priests at the monastery this evening to have it blessed and have the priests purify me. I will begin work on this sword in the early dawn of the day's first light. The beginning of a new day sparks the beginning of a new life. A new life for your friend, and a friend of Itosai, Reuben-San... Okami."

The beginning of 1854 started off with Renee writing in the diary Lucy and Eric gave her the day Aarleen was born.

Farewell 1853, and hello 1854. Will this be the year of my Da's return? Mama asks, what will it take? Please Da, come home soon.

The Duran family entered the house in a sad and solemn manner, much like many homes in the Norfolk and surrounding counties. They just returned from Aaron Duran's funeral. Like many in the region, Aaron contracted yellow fever and lost his fight shortly after Aarleen's sixth birthday.

"GrandDa, GrandMama says you will be leaving us soon. Why do you have to go?" asked Aarleen to Aaron as he lay in bed.

"Sometimes we must leave before we are ready. I don't want to leave you, my precious little angel, but the lord is calling for me."

"Can't we tell him you're too busy to go?"

Aaron let out a weak laugh and said, "It doesn't work like that, my wee lass. I wish it did, but it doesn't. I want you to do me a big favor."

"What's that, GrandDa?"

"I want you to be a good girl. Always mind your Mama, GrandMama, Mr. and Mrs. Klaus, your Uncles Monroe and Eric, and Aunty Lucy. Will you do that for me?"

"If you do a favor for me."

"What's that my precious little angel?"

"Find my Da and keep him safe for Mama, and see if you can make him come home."

Aaron let out a smile. "I'll do my very best, my precious Aarleen."

Several hours after, Aaron died in his home with all his family, with the exception of Reuben, near his side. It was heartbreaking for Renee and Coleen to watch Aarleen's last talk with Aaron. Aaron was the only father figure in Aarleen's life and they had a special relationship Renee was so very proud of. It was a relationship she never had with her own father and felt blessed she could be a part of it.

The entire family, including May, Henry, and Noah, all quietly gathered around the dining room table and sat looking at the food with no appetites. Renee, with Aarleen on her lap leaning against her mother's chest, sat in the chair next to the end where Aaron would sit.

Aarleen glanced at everyone in turn seated around the table. She gently bit on her lower lip, just as her mother does when nervous, and asked, "Do you think GrandDa is watching us right now?"

Renee ran her fingers through Aarleen's hair and replied, "He might very well be doing so, sweetie."

"Then won't we be making him sad if he's watching us be sad?"

Coleen let out a little laugh and motioned for Aarleen to come to her.

Aarleen leaped off Renee's lap and went to Coleen's open arms. Coleen hugged her and lifted Aarleen onto her lap. "You are so right, Aarleen. Sometimes it takes the wisdom of a little child to make a good point. Tell me, Aarleen, my little darling, what was your favorite time with GrandDa?"

"Hmm, that's a hard question, GrandMama, because I always had fun with GrandDa. Let me think," said Aarleen as she put a finger to her chin in thought. "I know, I liked it when he would take me to his office and let me welcome people who would come in. He said I did a good job and would always take me to get ice cream after... oops, I wasn't supposed to say that. That was a secret I couldn't tell Mama."

Renee laughed and said, "That's all right, sweetie. That's a wonderful secret you shared with your GrandDa and I never want you to forget that, okay?"

"Renee is right, Aarleen. You need to cherish all your good times with GrandDa," said Monroe with an adoring look to both Renee and Aarleen.

"What was your favorite good time with GrandDa, Uncle Monroe?"

"When he handed my diploma to me when I graduated from law school."

"Hmm, I don't know what a diploma is, but if it's anything like an ice cream, then it must be really good."

Aarleen's comment created joyful remembrances of Aaron's life filled with family adventure, fun, and most of all, love.

Like Aarleen, Aaron was the only true father figure in Renee's life, even before she was abandoned by her own father. Under Aaron's roof, Renee flourished in love for family and friends. The years she had been a part of the Duran family had been the best of her life. Not only were they a comfort for the difficult separation from Reuben, it was a closeness she never had with her own family.

Renee grew into a beautiful person, not only on the outside, but on the inside as well. Her unfaltering love for Reuben made her a strong devoted woman to the Duran family she now was a part of. She was also an extraordinary dedicated mother. In a time when unwed mothers were looked down upon, Renee, because of her proud Duran demeanor and her dedication to the father of her daughter, gained her a great deal of regard.

As the years went by, so did many men who tried to woo Renee's affections. There were those who saw her as a wonderful and respectful person who they cared to have a solid relationship with. And there were those who thought because of her unwed motherhood situation, believed she was an easy target for a fun time. For the first type of men, she showed kindness and appreciation for their candid sincere gestures, and offered respect by informing them of her dedication to Reuben. However, it was the second type she admittedly enjoyed turning down. There were two particular instances most memorable for her and Aarleen.

Charles Jefferson, a regular customer to the Chesapeake City Klaus Mercantile, crudely tried several times to gain Renee's affections when she would visit with Lucy and Eric. Lucy and Eric always forced Charles Jefferson out of their store when he made unwelcomed forward advances on Renee, even going as far as banning him from entering the store. However, every time Renee came for a visit, Charles Jefferson made his presence known. It finally came to a halt one April day, after a heavy rain fall, while Lucy and her son Andy were walking Renee and Aarleen to the ferry station, when Charles Jefferson once again tried to gain Renee's attention.

"Hello, Miss Renee. I see you have again come to show your beauty to me. Oh, and I see you have with you the result of one of your encounters. My, she's just as beautiful as you, a smaller version of yourself."

"Charles Jefferson, you vulgar ass cretin! How many times do I have to tell you to leave Renee alone?!" called out Lucy.

"Come now, Lucy, how many times do I have to tell you to watch your language in front of our children," said Renee, calmly.

"Renee?!" questioned Lucy.

Renee looked at Lucy with her sideways smirk and winked her eye. Lucy nodded and took Aarleen's hand from Renee and stepped back several steps.

"Charles, I must admit I admire your bold advances, but how many times must I tell you, I belong to another? But of course, it has been such a long time since I have been held by a man. Tell me, Charles, have you ever heard of the four directional throw?" asked Renee, seductively.

"I can't say that I have, Miss Renee, but it sounds very interesting. Perhaps you can tell me about it."

"Oh, I can do better, Charles. I can show you," said Renee as she offered her left hand to Charles.

With a huge, sly grin, Charles moved to take Renee by the hand, but before he could take hold, Renee swiftly grasped his wrist with her right hand and using her left, took hold of his hand. She crossed his front and rotated her body to the right under his arm bringing it over her head and back to his shoulder. She held this position for a moment as she told him, "Leave me alone, Charles Jefferson, or next time, I won't be so gentle."

Renee extended her arms just as Reuben had shown her when he taught her the technique of the four directional throw, as taught to him by Akagi Genda-San, and let go throwing Charles Jefferson off the raised walkway into a huge puddle of rain water and mud. Charles Jefferson never bothered Renee again, or entered the Chesapeake City Klaus Mercantile.

The second memorable instance happened outside the Norfolk Klaus Mercantile while Renee and Coleen were taking Aarleen shopping for her first set of school supplies. Exiting the store, they were met by Jack Corbin, a Chandler Academy alum, and cousin of Cynthia Garrett. As a prank, Cynthia crudely described Renee as a woman who would offer herself as entertainment to previous graduates of Chandler Academy. Jack Corbin was just as over-privileged as Cynthia and believed he was owed everything that came his way, and that included Renee.

"Why hello there, Miss Wallace, you do look rather breathtaking today."

"Excuse me, do I know you?" asked Renee.

"Not exactly, but you do know my cousin, Cynthia Norenham. You two went to Wickham together."

"You mean Cynthia Garrett?"

"Yes, that's her. She told me you owed her a favor and I'm here to collect, if you know what I mean," said Jack Corbin with an over confident grin and crudely winking his left eye.

Coleen was about to step forward, but Renee got in her way. "Oh she did, did she? Well you tell your cousin…"

Renee was interrupted when Aarleen tugged at the pant leg of Jack Corbin. He looked down at her as she asked, "Excuse me, mister, but have you ever heard of the four direction toss?"

Jack Corbin looked at her oddly, as did Renee and Coleen. "What did you say, child?"

"I said, have you ever heard of the four direction toss? Mama has not showed me how to do it yet, but I do know the two direction kick. Here let me show you."

Aarleen swung her left leg back and kicked Jack Corbin hard on the shin, causing him to curse and double over grabbing his lower leg in pain trying to maintain his balance on his left leg.

"Oh-oh, here comes the other direction!" said Aarleen as she swung back her right leg and kicked him on the shin of his other leg, causing him to fall hard on his knees in agonizing pain.

With his eyes at Aarleen's level, she pointed her little finger in his face and said, "Now stay away from my Mama or next time I won't be so gentle, you vulgar ass cretin!"

On his hands and knees in pain, Jack Corbin said in anger, "I demand you punish this little... OUCH! Get off my hand!"

"Oh my, I'm sorry young man," said Coleen, removing the heel of her foot from Jack Corbin's hand.

He rose to his knees with tears in his eyes. "Aren't you going to say anything to your brat about her behavior?"

"You're right," said Renee.

Renee lifted Aarleen in her arms and said, "GrandMama and I really need to talk to Aunty Lucy about watching her language around you and Cousin Andy."

Aarleen was the spark in Aaron's eyes. To him, she was the perfect granddaughter who could do no wrong. When she wasn't with Renee, he had her on his shoulders or in his lap. Since the day she was born, Aaron called her his precious little angel. He told her about her father and how brave he was going off to war.

"Is that why he's not here now, GrandDa?"

"In a way, my precious little angel. You see, remember my lessons about good and bad?"

"Yes GrandDa."

"Well, war is bad, but sometimes it's unavoidable. Your father had to fight and that made him angry, so he found a friend who helped him to stop being angry, but the friend left. When he left, your Da returned to being angry, and with the help of your Mama, he went to find that friend to make him better. That's where he is now, getting better for you and your Mama, so he can take care of you."

"Does my Da know about me?"

"I'm afraid not, but just imagine how happy he will be when he sees you."

"Why will he be happy if he doesn't know about me, GrandDa?"

"Because you are a precious little angel created from the love both he and your Mama share."

Aarleen was very bright. She understood why she didn't have a married mother, but it didn't bother her because like Renee, she had faith and love that one day her father would return, and they would be a real family like Cousin Andy and his parents, Uncle Eric and Aunty Lucy.

To see Aarleen was like looking at Renee as a child. She had the same long, dark, brown hair and adorable, big, brown eyes. Of course, everyone told her she had her father's nose and every morning when Renee would wash her face, she would wiggle her nose and stare at it in the mirror. Besides the pictures of Reuben, her nose was the most real thing she had to have a sense of touching him.

"Gosh, Mama, Da must be really cute."

"Why do you say so, sweetie?" asked Renee, amused.

"Because everyone says I have his nose, and my nose is cute, so he must be cute too."

Aarleen was just as attached to Coleen as she was to Aaron. Coleen did with Aarleen as she did with her own children. When she was old enough to hold a pencil, Coleen started to teach Aarleen how to read and write. Coleen always gave her children a head start to learning and Aarleen wasn't any different. She began reading very basic words and could write small sentences by the time she was three. Now at six, she was excited to start her first year of school.

For the most part, Renee and Aarleen lived on the farm so May, Henry, and Noah played a huge part of her growth. Aarleen would help May in the kitchen and keeping the house clean, Noah played with her when the field work and chores were finished, and Aarleen would spend hours watching and helping Henry and Noah make furniture to be sold in both the Klaus' stores. All the diverseness exposed to Aarleen aided in her being well grounded and open-minded.

Renee's relationship with Aarleen was far beyond mother and daughter. Renee took to heart the advice her mother gave her the last time they were together during the school pie auction shortly after Aarleen was born. *"Please be to our Aarleen everything I wasn't to you,"* Margret Wallace told Renee. It was close to six months until Renee received a letter from her mother asking for their progress. Since then, Renee would write her mother letters, sending them to the address Margret provided, which happened to be a neighbor's address. Franklin Wallace's anger toward Renee was still stronger than ever, and he forbade his wife any correspondence with her so all this correspondence was done without his knowing.

Renee and Aarleen's relationship was one of warmth and dedicated love to one another. Not only were they mother and daughter, they were also best friends. They went everywhere and did everything together. On the farm, although there was a spare room, they shared the same room as they did when they stayed in the city home.

When work on the farm was done for the day, they always spent at least some amount of time together under the oak tree. Renee would write poetic passages while Aarleen would either draw or listen to Renee read passages to her. Every night before bedtime, Renee would tell Aarleen bedtime stories with Reuben's picture lying open between them. When Aarleen began learning to read, Renee would have Aarleen read stories out of old fairy tale books, but eventually, Aarleen began making them up once she mentioned one of the heroes in one story reminded her of her Da. From then on, instead of reading stories, they would create and write their own stories with Reuben being the hero, Renee being his queen, and Aarleen the princess. They were wonderful stories filled with action and adventure. The stories included everyone in the family, and once a month, during a monthly family get together, Renee and Aarleen would recite their story of the month after the family dinner. Aarleen was becoming quite a story teller. On her fifth birthday, she began a birthday tradition by reciting an original story to her guests as her way of thanking them for attending her birthday party. These stories were adored by both the children and adults.

Renee continued to write short entries in Aarleen's diary Lucy and Eric gave her when she was born. They were quick entries of what Aarleen did that day worth remembering which was difficult because Renee wanted to remember it all. Eventually she knew Aarleen would one day want to start writing in her own diary, but Renee wanted to hold off on that as long as possible. To Renee, it was her way of telling Reuben the progress of their daughter.

Renee thrived in writing her own personal poetic passages. She no longer had to write them in secret. That alone allowed her to freely open up, and many of her passages were filled with such emotion it was difficult for anyone, even someone such as Monroe, to be able to finish reading them without sheading a tear. Most of her passages were cheerful and there were some one could realize Renee was missing Reuben very much at the time she wrote the passage.

She also thrived as the "Duran Agricultural Liaison." Renee, with the help of May, organized a yearly harvest festival held on the Duran farm where all the farmers of the area came and shared some of their harvest with everyone. The first one was rather awkward to start, but once Tom Foster broke out his fiddle, it began to liven up. After that, the festivals became somewhat of a huge pot luck lunch, including music, games, and cook offs.

These festivals were also showcases for the carpentry work by Henry and Noah who had been making dining tables and chairs that were sold in both of the Klaus' mercantile stores. Their work gained them much notoriety of excellent quality and eventually they were asked to do custom work other than dining room furniture.

The Chesapeake City Klaus Mercantile was doing great business. Since it first opened, the store did so well Eric and Lucy expanded its width for more display space. Every few months, Renee and Aarleen would come to spend a week with Lucy and Eric to help in the store and to visit.

One of those weeks was when Lucy gave birth to their son Andrew, named after his grandfather.

"Holy mother of God, it hurts, Renee! Is this what it felt like when Aarleen was born?" cried out Lucy.

"Oh yeah, that reminds me, I'll be right back, Mama. I need to speak to Eric real quick," said Renee to Coleen as she walked out of the room.

Eric saw Renee emerge from the bedroom and came to her quickly. "How is she, Renee? Can I go in and see her?"

"She's doing fine. It should be any time now, but trust me, you don't want to be in there right now."

"Why? I should be by her side."

"Well, let me put it to you this way. When Reuben returns, I still intend to kick him in his yams to give him a sense of what I went through when Aarleen was born. Don't be surprised if Lucy does the same to you."

Andrew Klaus, or Andy as everyone called him, was born on January 12, 1850. Aarleen and Andy became close cousins and both parents did their best to have them visit as often as possible.

For the last six years, with the exception of Reuben's absence and the recent death of his father, the Duran and Klaus family thrived together. It was a great family bond filled with love and affection for every member of the family, a legacy Aaron Duran could be proud to leave behind. In a sense, it was a bond that would not have been possible had Reuben not left to accept Akagi Genda-San's challenge. Perhaps it was fate. As Aaron lay taking his last breaths, he kept hearing the voice of his precious little angel, *"Find my Da and keep him safe for Mama and see if you can make him come home."*

In his last moments of life, he motioned for his loving wife, Coleen, to come closer to speak to her.

"What is it, my dear husband?"

"I'm going now, my love. Tell my precious little angel, Aarleen, I'll do my best."

Aaron Duran passed away in his home, surrounded by family and friends on Thursday July 20, 1854.

狼

It had been six years since the corner stone of Hisano Castle was planted and now it was completed. It was a grand affair attended by all four clans of the Hisano Province. When the village of Itosai was nearly complete, construction of the castle began. The construction project was monumental and prideful, not only for the Akagi, but also the Takumi, Sho, and Satoshi. All clans provided manpower to the project, and in record time, the new relocated village of Itosai was inhabited with its original community. A nearby smaller gorge provided stone that the Takumi stone cutters made use of which contributed to the accelerated progress of the massive project.

The Ute captives were just as jubilant as the citizens of the Hisano Province and desired permanent citizenship of the region, and to serve the Akagi, as did the ronin captives. Akagi Genda-San agreed to their desire, provided they would build their own portion of the village south of the castle. The portion of their village would not be in the gorge but still in a well-protected position. The structures would have to resemble those located in the gorge and they would have to build their portion of the village themselves. Until then, they remained in the original village. However, as the work was progressing at an astonishing rate, and because of the support of the entire province, there was plenty of manpower to assist the Ute captives in the building of their portion of the village.

Just as Renee thrived with motherhood, Reuben thrived in his training and his involvement in the relocation of the village and construction of the castle. He also had the English school making great progress. Nearly every citizen of Itosai could speak Basic English with several Akagi leaders, including Masaru, speaking in more advanced forms of English. It wasn't until Reuben's fifth year in Itosai, he began to teach some of the Akagi leaders how to write in English, including Akagi Genda-San.

Akagi Genda-San was very proud of Reuben's progress and as each day passed, he knew his time in Itosai was drawing to a close. He knew Reuben would not leave until the castle was complete or at least nearly completed. It was during one of these advanced English writing classes when Akagi Genda-San expressed to Reuben the time was drawing near for him to return to his family.

"Reuben-San, six years is a long time for you to be away from your family. What I ask is difficult, but you must begin to prepare for your return very soon."

"I want to return and I feel I'm ready, but there's one more thing I must do for you before I leave Itosai. I don't know what it is, but it's enough to keep me here for a little while longer."

"Well, my friend, I must admit, there is something in the air that requires my use of your skill. You are right, but nonetheless, you have done great wonders here not only for yourself, but for my region."

Reuben seldom socialized with Akagi Genda-San's family, with the exception of Masaru. Although he was welcome into their home as an adopted member of the family, Reuben was often too busy, but never too busy if Akagi Genda-San's wife or daughters needed his assistance. He did spare some time once a week to attend an evening dinner with Akagi Genda-San's family and these dinners were very much looked forward to, not only by Reuben, but the family as well, especially Akagi Genda-San's daughter, Kaoru, who felt affections for Reuben.

Kaoru was the first daughter of Akagi Genda-San and his wife Yanna. She was a widow of an Akagi samurai named Takeo Takashi who was killed by the Arata shortly after Akagi Genda-San returned from America. She had one child from her marriage, Katsuo, who Reuben protected from the Arata attack the day Aarleen was born. Since that day, she felt affection toward Reuben. This caused great concern for Akagi Genda-San because he knew of Reuben's dedicated love for Renee, who he believed was waiting for him back home with his own child.

"But he is so lonely, father, and I feel for him."

"Kaoru, my daughter, Reuben-San is not as lonely as you may think. His heart is dedicated to another from where he comes. It is her who is one of the reasons he is here."

It was during one of Reuben's individual training sessions with Akagi Genda-San when he mentioned his daughter's affections for Reuben. Reuben showed genuine concern and expressed his appreciation and respect toward Kaoru to Akagi Genda-San, but he emphasized his love could belong to no one other than Renee.

"Kaoru is kind and a beautiful woman, Genda-San, and I feel grateful she appreciates me, but I believe her attraction only lays because I protected her son when Arata Goro's men attacked the village. I do enjoy her presence in friendship, but for me, it can't be anything more. Please forgive me, my friend, if I have offended you."

"No apologies are necessary, Reuben-San. You do honor me with your honesty. I must apologize to you for it was I who wished to know how you stood on this complicated situation."

"Although Renee belongs to another man, I still feel we are destined to one day be together as love intended. I must maintain my focus and dedication to her. It's she who drives me to become the man I once was before Mexico, and the man she deserves. During the days when I first arrived, and Masaru drove me hard, I must admit to you now, I did have desires to leave, but Renee's confidence in me is what caused me to endure the brutality."

"And she is most fortunate to have a man such as you to be dedicated to her. I will discuss this with Kaoru and help her to understand, Reuben-San."

"If it's all the same to you, Genda-San, allow me to talk with her. I believe I should be the one to tell her why we can't be more than friends."

"Very well, Reuben-San. You never cease to amaze me. Once again, you have eased me of a difficult burden to bear."

Reuben's situation with Kaoru differed very much from those Renee faced back in Virginia. For those with pure intentions toward Renee, she simply thanked them for their respect and informed them of her dedication to Reuben. As for those with impure intentions, they were either introduced to the four directional throw or the two direction kick.

It was the following afternoon after Akagi Genda-San spoke with Reuben when he invited Kaoru for a walk. Kaoru was very beautiful with long, straight brown hair and eyes of jade. Her skin was of soft olive tone, unblemished and smooth. She had a pleasant personality nearly mirroring that of Renee's.

They reached one of the many bridges crossing over the river connecting the village from one side of the gorge to the other. They talked about many topics, but Kaoru sensed Reuben's discomfort and as Renee would do when he found it difficult to speak his mind, she placed her hand on his resting on the rail of the bridge.

"I know you have something difficult to tell me, Reuben, and I believe I know what it is, so allow me to help you. It is about the girl from where you come, correct?"

"I'm sorry, Kaoru. You are a wonderful woman, and I adore Katsuo, and I value your friendship as well as Sukuri."

He went on to tell Kaoru of his and Renee's story from when they met, to the night under the oak tree before he left.

"One of these days, I'll have to return to my home and face the truth of my life, and the truth is, I love a girl who belongs to another. I know that's very difficult to understand."

"No, Reuben, it is not. I guess you can say, I am going through the same thing you are. This girl, Renee. She must be someone very special."

Reuben reached into his haversack and pulled out the image case wrapped with Lucy's ribbon. He removed the ribbon and opened the case. When Kaoru saw the image of Renee, she could not help but feel sorrow for the both of them.

Kaoru looked up from the image of Renee to Reuben's face. His eyes were focused on the image and a tear rolled down his cheek. She gently wiped it from his face with her soft hand and said, "I truly have never felt love the way you do for your Renee, Reuben. Not even with my departed husband. I do hope we can remain friends and continue our walks."

"Of course," said Reuben, nodding. "Katsuo says he has been making something for me and I'm looking forward to what it is. I have ten fingers on my hands, Kaoru, and I can count all my special friends on them and still have fingers left over. You are counted on one of those remaining fingers."

Tadashi became quite respected with the Akagi, thanks to Reuben. He assisted Reuben with the English lessons and like Reuben, he tirelessly worked on the Itosai project. With Reuben, he trained the Okami no Mure in Kyudo, while Reuben trained them in the ways of the jo and Okami no Michi, Reuben's personal sword technique. They were quite the team together and their opinions were either welcomed or requested.

In Reuben's third year in Itosai, Tadashi and Sukuri, Akagi Genda-San's second daughter, began to show affections toward one another. Because of Sukuri being his daughter, Tadashi was intimated to show bold affection toward her, however it was Reuben who came to his rescue, much like how Renee did for Lucy and Eric.

"Genda-San, I have a rather delicate matter to discuss with you and your wife."

"Is it about Tadashi-San and Sukuri? If so, speak frankly, Reuben-San," said Akagi Genda-San in a formal tone of voice as he sat next to Yanna.

"Okay, yes it's about Tadashi and your daughter. How do you feel about them?"

Being surprised by Reuben reversing his question back at him, he began to laugh. "Ah, Reuben-San, there is no deceiving you is there? Listen, Yanna and I both know of the affections Tadashi-San and Sukuri have for one another, but they are afraid to speak open about them. Perhaps you can tell us why this is."

"Sure, I have seen it before, with Renee and me. For years it was Renee's father who kept us from our love, even from ourselves. It is heartbreaking, not only for the two in love, but for those around them."

"Hmm, what do you suggest, Reuben-San?" asked Yanna.

"Well, if you approve of the relationship, then express your approval to both of them."

"And if we do not approve?"

"Doesn't matter, they will still continue to defy your disapproval and eventually tear your family apart, as it has with Renee and me," Reuben said, strongly.

This was the closest moment Akagi Genda-San wanted to tell Reuben of his thoughts about Renee waiting for him, however he fought the urge, and instead said, "Well, Reuben-San, it is fortunate for both Tadashi-San and Sukuri, Yanna and I approve. Go and summon both of them here so we can express our approval, as you recommended."

283

狼

September 4, 1854, a week of celebration was to begin by releasing the waters from the river flowing from the high falls of the cliffs from the rear of the gorge surrounding the village of Itosai. The waters to be soon released would fill the moat surrounding the castle of Hisano Province. Villagers and citizens from all over Hisano Province lined the river and around the castle as Akagi Genda-San rose the conch shell to his lips and blew the bellowing signal to release the waters.

It was Masaru, Tadashi, and Reuben who had the honor of opening the floodgates. Using all their strength, they grunted as the large turn wheel resisted their efforts. Reuben motioned the other two to stop and he nodded as he said, "Once more, together, ichi-ni-san!"

All three yelled out, "AKAGI!!!" and pulled the turn wheel. It began to budge. Seeing it begin to move, Katsuo jumped alongside Reuben and also pulled.

With a loud crack, the wheel gave way and it started to turn smoothly. The three and little Katsuo were able to turn the wheel with little effort as the gate lifted and the river waters began to flood into the moat. The cheers roared and echoed against the walls of the gorge. With the waters flowing, the four who opened the flood gate embraced one another in jubilation and Reuben raised Katsuo onto his shoulders.

It took over two hours for the moat to fill as everyone watched and discussed in remembrance of all the work and effort it took to finish this huge task, much ahead of schedule.

With the moat filled, Akagi Genda-San stood atop the forward parapet and again blew into the conch shell, giving the signal to lower the draw bridge, a feature suggested by Reuben. For at first, the original plans called for a permanent stone bridge to cross over the moat. As the bridge was lowered, a loud thud was heard once it hit the ground. Isamu Gorou, the fifth generation sword maker, marched ahead of his son and grandson, the sixth and seventh generation sword makers. He carried the two blessed naginatas he begun forging the day the first stone was set for the castle. They were covered in red and black satin cloths and presented to Akagi Genda-San. As Akagi Genda-San revealed the naginatas, he motioned the three other clan leaders to come forward. Akagi Genda-San, with Takumi Sadao-San, took one naginata and Sho Masaki-San and Satoshi Kei-San took the other. At the same time they placed them in their honored place above the main entrance of the castle.

Akagi Genda-San stood before the other three clan leaders and motioned Masaru to reveal a bronze plaque covered with a red and black silken cloth. As the cloth fell to the ground, the plaque had molded into it, all four clan crests of the Hisano Province.

"Forever live the Hisano Alliance!" cried out the four regional Daimyos of the province. Loud cheers followed along with a celebration that was supposed to last an entire week. However, within several hours into the celebration, a mounted Sho samurai rode across the bridge bringing dire news to the regional Daimyos.

狼

Tadashi and Sukuri watched Reuben playfully teaching Katsuo some jo techniques while Kaoru cheered on her son. Their fun was interrupted when they saw Masaru and several other leading Akagi samurai warriors run past them in alertness.

"What is going on?" asked Kaoru.

"Don't know, what you say we try and find out, Tadashi?" answered Reuben as he handed his jo to Katsuo.

They entered the great hall of the castle to see the Sho samurai rider on his knees giving the four leaders his report. When he was finished, a look of concern and alarm was present in everyone's faces.

Reuben and Tadashi looked at each other and both shrugged their shoulders. "Whatever it is, it can't be good," said Reuben.

The four leaders made their way out of the main hall in concerned discussion as Reuben and Tadashi stepped aside against the wall moving out of their way.

"This is incredible. From where could Arata Goro have gotten them?" asked Satoshi Kei-San.

"That does not matter. What does matter is he has them now and intends to use them on Hisano Castle. You, rider, how many did you say you saw?" asked Akagi Genda-San to the Sho samurai who delivered the report.

"I saw five, my Lord. Huge guns on wheels being rolled up the Bakko road from Ute."

"Cannons!" said Reuben, standing with his back against the wall. All present who heard looked his way.

"Reuben-San," said Akagi Genda-San as he looked at Reuben, and noticed the wolf-like look in his eyes.

"If Arata Goro has cannons, I must see them, my Lord... now!" said Reuben.

狼

It was 8 o'clock in the evening, September 3, 1854 and Aarleen was getting ready for bed as Reuben, Tadashi, Masaru, and Katsuo opened the flood gates to fill the moat of Hasano Castle. It was going to be a big day for Aarleen the following day, her first day of school.

"School sounds like fun, Mama," said Aarleen as she was being tucked into bed by Renee.

She was excited causing concern for Renee hoping Aarleen would be able to sleep for her big day. For the great event, Renee and Aarleen made plans to stay in the city home with Coleen and Monroe for the week.

"Will GrandMama be my teacher, Mama?"

"Hmm, I don't think so, sweetie, but she'll still be a part of your schooling."

"Was she your teacher?"

"Yes, she was before I had to go to another school. Are you scared?" asked Renee, hoping to keep Aarleen from asking questions about her other school she was forced to attend. It worked.

"No, Mama, I only wished Andy and I could go to school together."

"He won't be starting school until next year, so I'm counting on you to pay attention this year so you can give him some good advice when he does start."

"Don't worry, Mama, I'm going to learn all I can."

It was going to be difficult for Aarleen to attend school with Renee and Aarleen living on the farm. Coleen suggested Aarleen live with her in the city during the week, and on the farm for the weekends, but Renee flatly said no, not after what her own mother told her about being the mother she never was to Renee.

"We'll stay with you the first week so I can get a feel of what I can accomplish and we'll go from there."

"It's going to be difficult, my dear, but I admire your dedication to Aarleen. If only we can open an outreach school in your area, like in Princess Anne County. That would solve a lot of problems educating the children out your way."

狼

The following morning, as Renee and Coleen were walking to school with Aarleen between them carrying her school books and lunch pail, Reuben and Tadashi were returning from the Arata camp. They went to scout out the cannons the Sho samurai reported earlier this day. As soon as Reuben told Akagi Genda-San he needed to see the guns, a small detachment of mounted samurai, including Akagi Genda-San, Masaru, the three other clan leaders, and their retainers, left the celebration to where the Sho warrior saw the Arata marching.

At first, Masaru said it was too late to scout the Arata camp and they would have to wait until the morning.

"No time, Masaru. Genda-San, if Arata Goro has cannons, I must see what kind and how many. Tadashi and I can easily infiltrate their camp, take a look around and return without being noticed."

Akagi Genda-San agreed and allowed the two to scout the Arata camp, much to Tadashi's discomfort.

"Something is wrong, Tadashi-San?" asked Akagi Genda-San.

"Of all people to go with him to spy around, he had to choose me. I said this once before and I'll say it again, my Lord, that idiot round-eye is going to be the death of me."

The two returned a little over an hour later unscathed and with disconcerting news. Reuben had with him a rifled musket with ammunition and caps he snatched as they left the camp.

They immediately went to Akagi Genda-San and the rest of the clan leaders to give their report. "What did you see, Reuben-San?" asked Akagi Genda-San.

"Arata Goro has five, six pound cannons. Similar to the ones we used in Mexico."

Akagi Genda-San grunted and paced around the small camp fire. "What do you suggest, Reuben-San?"

"We take them out as soon as possible. We must not let them cross over the Shun Bridge. Once they do, they could blast smaller villages and outposts along the way to Itosai."

"I have seen what those type of guns can do. I do not see how we can stop them," said Satoshi Kei-San. "I say let them come. We will make our stand at Hisano Castle and defeat them there behind our walls."

"Here, here!" replied Takumi Sadao-San

"I disagree. We should stop them as Genda-San's adviser suggests," said Sho Masaki-San

Akagi Genda-San nodded, taking in everyone's input. "Reuben-San, do you think Arata Goro has trained men to use those cannons?"

"For Arata Goro to purchase such weaponry, I would assume he has trained gunners to man them."

"And you believe we must, as you say, 'take them out' before they reach Itosai?"

"Tadashi and I heard men in the Arata camp talk about seeing how strong the castle and village are and want to put them to the test. With all respect, my Lords, a castle isn't designed to attack, only to defend. I personally don't want to see the castle and village we have worked so hard on these past six years to be marred by a war mongering thug with no honor. We need to put a stop to Arata Goro here and now, for good, my Lords."

Akagi Genda-San and the other three regional lords looked at Reuben with admiration.

"So, do you have any recommendation on how to defeat those cannons, Reuben-San," asked Akagi Genda-San.

In the flickering light of the camp fire, Akagi Genda-San could still see the fierce wolf-like look in Reuben's eyes. It was a look he had not seen since he first met Reuben back in America.

"There's only one way I know of to take out those cannons, my Lord, and I'm going to need the alliance to help me."

狼

Aarleen came running out of the school building and into Renee's waiting arms laughing.

"How was your first day of school, sweetie?" asked Renee.

"It was fun. Some of the other children didn't want to be there, but I sure did. I learned a lot today and I can't wait to tell you."

Renee took Aarleen by the hand and began walking home. Along the way, she saw Aaron's law office, now being run by Monroe. She thought about the ice cream memory Aarleen mentioned in the dining room after Aaron's funeral.

Renee stopped and knelt down and said, "How would you like to tell me what you learned over ice cream, just like GrandDa used to get you after a hard day's work in his office?"

"That would be fantastic," said Aarleen. "That's one of the new words I learned today. It means, ah… fantastic."

Renee hugged her daughter and laughed as they entered the diner across the street from the law office to have a bowl of ice cream. As they ate their treat, Aarleen told Renee all about her first day in school.

As Renee was hearing about Aarleen's first day of school over a bowl of ice cream, Reuben, Masaru, and Tadashi stood at the foot of the Shun Bridge. It would be a few hours before the sun would rise. Reuben discussed his plan with Akagi Genda-San, Masaru, and Tadashi, along with the other regional lords listening with great interest.

The evening before, they sent four samurai back to Itosai to mobilize the Clan Alliance and move on toward the Shun Bridge after Reuben's and Tadashi's report. With any luck, the samurai from all four clans would arrive shortly after day break. There was a small contingency of six dozen alliance warriors left to defend the bridge, something both Reuben and Akagi Genda-San hoped it wouldn't come to.

After Reuben finished describing his plan for taking control of the guns, everyone looked at him as if he gone insane.

"That is absolutely idiotic! You have got to be mad!" said Satoshi Kei-San.

"That's what my friend Adam told me the first time I pulled it off."

"First time?! You have done this more than once?" replied Masaru. "How many?"

"Too many to remember, but under the correct conditions, it can be done," said Reuben. "If the alliance makes haste and arrives before the midmorning sun burns off this low fog, we can do it today."

"Reuben, were you successful every time?" asked Tadashi with concern.

Reuben let out a sigh and looked to Akagi Genda-San. "All but once," he answered. "That one time I failed is the reason I came to Akagi Genda-San for his guidance to learn the way of Bushido."

"Good heavens, where have you two been?" asked Coleen as Renee and Aarleen entered the house giggling. "Monroe and I have been waiting for you two to have dinner."

Aarleen looked up to Renee who had her finger to her lips and a smile.

"We were taking our time walking home, talking about my sweetie's first day of school."

"Well it's about time, let's eat," said Monroe walking in from the parlor.

Aarleen told Coleen and Monroe about her first day of school with pride and enthusiasm.

"I'm sorry I didn't get a chance to come and visit you, Aarleen. I have my own class to look over, but I'm glad you have Miss Gaines for your teacher. She's very nice."

"Yes she is," said Aarleen, just before she let out a big yawn.

"My goodness, sweetie, you look exhausted," said Renee. "No surprise since you were so excited last night about today. Perhaps you should lay down for a little nap."

Aarleen reluctantly agreed and Renee carried her up to their room.

"Now take a little nap and I'll come get you in about an hour and we can read your assignment before your real bedtime, okay?"

"Okay, Mama. Mama, can I sleep with Da's picture on my night table next to me?"

"Sure you can, sweetie."

Renee reached over to her night table and placed her picture of Reuben on Aarleen's night table. She gave her a kiss on the cheek and covered her with a quilt.

Aarleen rolled over toward the picture, looked at it for several moments, closed her eyes, and dozed off to sleep as her long, dark, brown hair fell over her face.

Aarleen stood on a hard, well used dirt road in a strange land she never seen the likes of before. The land was covered with green foliage so different from her home in Virginia. She looked to her left and saw hills resembling huge stairs filled with water and strange grass growing from within the water. To her right were high snowcapped mountains. She was frightened. She was about to call for Renee until she heard the sound of a strange bellowing horn. She wanted to turn and run away, but she couldn't.

She began to feel the ground beneath her little feet vibrate. She looked down and saw dirt and tiny pebbles move. The sound of heavy footsteps caused her to look up. Before her, on both sides of the road, marched men dressed in strange looking armor. It wasn't shiny armor like the stories Renee and she would create about knights like King Arthur. This armor was red and black and made the men resemble turtles, and each man had a long, dark red banner attached to their back.

As the men passed, she looked at their faces. They were faces of a people she never seen before. They had narrow eyes. She got the attention of one of the men by timidly walking up to him. "I'm looking for my Da. Do you know someone who can help me find him?" she asked, frightened.

The man looked down to Aarleen, pointed to a column of horse mounted men in strange colorful armor, and continued marching away. Aarleen looked toward the column. Her lower lip began to quiver. She wanted to move out of the way, but her little feet wouldn't move. As the column neared she cringed, waiting for it to trample her to the ground, but the entire column stopped mere yards ahead of her.

Aarleen looked up and saw a large, tall gray horse standing before her with a rider wearing beautifully, bright red colored armor lined with silk, and two swords at his side. He wore a large red helmet atop his head with a gold round emblem attached to it. Covering his face was a mask of black and silver. The rider dismounted and as his feet hit the ground, it shook.

The rider walked to Aarleen and lowered himself down to one knee. He removed his face mask to reveal a man with a friendly face. He smiled and asked, "Anata wa, chīsana ichi daredesuka?"

"I, I don't understand, mister. I'm looking for my Da, do you know him? His name is Reuben Duran."

"Ah, Reuben-San, he is your father?! You have his nose. What is your name, little one?"

"Aarleen," she answered in a frightened manner.

"Ah, Aarleen-Dono, your father is well and he will be returning to you soon, little one, but he still has one more task to do for me this day. You must wake and tell Renee-Dono you three will be a whole family in the near future."

The rider rose, replaced his face mask, remounted his horse, and rode around Aarleen. She turned and watched him ride away. The further he rode, the more he and the men faded away, leaving the familiar scenery of the Duran family farm.

"Mama! Mama! Mama!" cried out Aarleen, waking from her nap. She rose out of Lucy's bed and ran out of the room crying.

Renee and Coleen had just finished putting away the dinner dishes when they heard Aarleen crying out for Renee. Renee ran out of the kitchen, followed closely by Coleen and met Aarleen at the foot of the stairs.

"What's going on?" called out Monroe, coming in from the parlor.

Renee picked up Aarleen, who was now crying uncontrollably. Renee held her tightly and cradled her as Coleen was rubbing Aarleen's back.

"What's the matter, sweetie?" asked Renee.

"I had a bad dream. It was about Da, but he wasn't in it."

Aarleen, with her face buried in Renee's shoulder, went into detail about the dream. She described it so vividly, especially about the man riding the horse. Renee told Aarleen about Akagi Genda-San, but never how he looked. It was disturbing to both Renee and Coleen to hear Aarleen describe Akagi Genda-San, a man she never seen, so accurately.

The most concerning part of Aarleen's dream she described was the rider's message for Renee, *"Tell Renee-Dono you three will be a whole family in the near future."*

Coleen had an emotional look and Monroe felt an empty discomfort in his stomach as Aarleen mentioned the rider's message.

Renee was more concerned about what the rider said of Reuben having one more task to do for him, *"this day."*

Still with Aarleen in her arms, Renee walked into the parlor. She stepped up to the mantle where the uniformed image of Reuben stood. She looked at it with a very worried heart. "What in the world are you doing, my love?"

狼

The sun was peeking over the horizon as an Akagi mounted samurai came riding up the road to the bridge.

"They are on the march with the big guns leading the way!"

"Geez oh geez oh geez," said Reuben in English. "I hope our reinforcements are nearby."

"Quickly, continue to ride until you reach the reinforcements and tell them to make haste to our position! Tell them once they arrive to cross the river and deploy along the river bank with the rest of us!" ordered Akagi Genda-San to the rider.

"Hai, my Lord!"

"What do we do now?" asked Masaru.

"We do what Reuben-San instructed. We hold this bridge. Spread the men across the bank of the river. Try to make it look like we are many," ordered Akagi Genda-San.

With the small contingency of warriors deployed along the bank of the river, Reuben stood on the road facing the hill at the foot of the bridge with the rifled musket slung over his shoulder. Tadashi came forward and stood with him, his bow strung and arrows at the ready.

The ground was covered with a low, misty fog. Reuben hoped the reinforcements would have arrived by now. This fog would be perfect cover for his plan.

His plan, as described in detail, was for the Clan Alliance to make a stand at the bridge forcing Arata Goro to deploy his cannons. Reuben hoped his gunners were trained in battery tactics. Once the cannons were deployed, he, with Masaru, Tadashi, and Shigo Seiji, a superb archer of the Satoshi Clan, would crawl up to the far left cannon and capture it, just like his platoon did many times in Mexico. Reuben decided on only the four to creep on the cannon because of the lack of experience of the other three.

"Why do you get to use a gun and we bows, Reuben," asked Masaru.

"Because I can't shoot a bow to save my life, but I can shoot one of these, and you three are the best archers in the province. My job is to take out the gunner before he fires the cannon. You three take out your targets and we run like mad wolves and turn our cannon to the limber of the next cannon."

"And that will take care of all the guns?"

"No, but it will raise a whole lot of confusion, and that is when the archers cover the mounted warriors attack across the field. It will be up to us to take out the rest of the crews so have your arrows at the ready. I'll have my sword."

As the sun rose higher and sunlight was filling the sky, a conch shell horn was heard from the rear. The reinforcements arrived as the Arata were cresting the ridge from the opposite direction.

Quickly, the Clan Alliance samurai deployed as instructed by the rider who met them on the way.

"Genda-San, get the men to make noise. We got to get Arata Goro to deploy his guns quickly!"

"Hai, Reuben-San!"

Akagi Genda-San did as instructed and the alliance samurai began to yell and chant causing the Arata to halt their advance.

Reuben noticed a rider wearing all black armor atop a black horse. He was surrounded by other samurai on horseback. Reuben also saw what he thought to look like a soldier dressed in a French army officer's uniform with red piping standing next to the man atop the black horse.

"Genda-San, that man on the black horse, is that Arata Goro?"

"Hai, that is him," answered Akagi Genda-San.

"He has an artillery officer with him, French by the looks of it. Damn it, he's not deploying those guns. Wait here, I have an idea."

Reuben walked further up the road and stood facing the Arata army alone.

"My Lord, look at that lone man. What is he up to?"

"Who cares? Listen to me, Captain Kalet! Do as I order and deploy the cannons!" ordered Arata Goro.

"But, General Arata, for some reason that is what they want you to do. I don't like this situation," said the French officer.

"My Lord, look out!"

Reuben, standing in the open, leveled his rifle, pulled back the hammer, aimed, and pulled the trigger. His bullet shot out of the muzzle and hit Arata Goro's silver crescent off the top of his helmet, causing his head to whip back.

Akagi Genda-San came running up to Reuben after he saw him shoot the crescent off of Arata Goro's helmet.

"That was a fantastic shot, Reuben-San!"

"Are you joking? That was lousy. I was aiming for his forehead. I'm sadly out of practice."

Rearing in his saddle, Arata Goro reached down to the French officer and lifted him off the ground by his collar. "DEPLOY THOSE CANNONS NOW DAMN YOU!!! WE TAKE HISANO HERE TODAY!!!"

"Yep, that did it," said Reuben nodding approvingly.

Reuben and Akagi Genda-San ran back to the bridge to prepare for the oncoming cannon barrage. Reuben instructed the clan leaders to spread out to the right of the bridge for the cannons to angle in that direction.

"For heaven's sake, Genda-San, keep the men low and be careful."

"Reuben-San, I am not the one moving on those cannons. You must take care for yourself and Renee-Dono."

Reuben formally bowed to Akagi Genda-San as he heard the cannon on the far right side fire.

The shot landed far ahead of the river. Reuben shook his head. "Amateurs," he said and turned to meet up with his team for their assault.

Within half an hour, all five of Arata Goro's cannons were in action firing toward the right of the bridge. The shots were landing sporadically across the open field, seldom landing near the alliance samurai. The four clan leaders ordered their long range archers to do what they could to keep the attention of the cannons and their crews away from Reuben's team.

The fog was slowly burning off, but there was still enough of it to cover the four crawling up to the far left cannon.

Unlike the other similar assaults Reuben had done during the Mexican Campaign, he had an overwhelming sense of confidence, but was still very alert as foot-by-foot, inch-by-inch, he and the others crawled to their objective. Seeing Reuben's confidence, Masaru also felt as though success was achievable.

"KASAI!" BAM!

The left cannon fired its round when the four were about twenty yards away. With the gun crew's attention looking the other way and the low fog to cover their assault, this is the closest Reuben had ever gotten to a target cannon.

Reuben stopped and motioned the other three to come up to him. With hand motions, he instructed, just as the gunner was about to fire the cannon, he would take him out. Then Masaru, Tadashi, and Seiji were to take out their targets.

"KASAI!" BAM!

The left cannon fired off another shot and Reuben watched as the crew reloaded the gun. As the number one man pulled the ramrod out of the muzzle, Reuben rose to his knees. "For the boys of the fifth platoon, this is for you," he silently said to himself in English as he took aim and pulled the trigger as the fuse was being inserted.

The ball from Reuben's rifle hit its target, the gunner, dead center in the chest. As soon as Reuben fired the rifle, he rose and sprinted to the gun. Masaru likewise rose, as did Tadashi and Seiji, each three drawing their bows and letting loose their arrows, each one hitting their marks. They also began sprinting to the left gun whose crew had been neutralized.

From the bridge, Akagi Genda-San saw the four sprinting to the cannon. He took hold of Sho Masaki-San's shoulder and pointed in their direction.

"Get ready to move!"

"Hai, Genda-San!"

Reuben lifted the gun trail and begun to turn the gun. The others took hold of the wheels and helped.

"A little more... more... there! Okay, get down, this is going to be loud!"

Reuben took hold of the lanyard and gave it a tug. The cannon fired its shot hitting the limber of the gun next to the one they had taken. The limber exploded blasting the crew of that gun from existence.

"Quickly, take out the rest of the crews! I'm going after the artillery officer!" ordered Reuben.

He ran toward the French captain who was about to give the command to fire the first cannon. Before he could utter his command, Reuben drew his sword he had slid back to his side, raised and cut across, decapitating the officer in one swift stroke. With their arrows, Masaru, Tadashi, and Seiji took out what was left of the gun crews that had not ran away.

Reuben noticed the first cannon had been loaded and ready to be fired. He lifted the trail and motioned the others to help him turn the cannon. He aimed the gun at Arata Goro and his lieutenants, took the lanyard in his hand, and pulled. The cannon fired and its shell landed just to the left side of Arata Goro, blasting several of his lieutenants and knocking him from atop his horse.

A bellowing sound of a conch shell was heard from the river and cries of "AKAGI, TAKUMI, SHO, SATOSHI!!!" were heard as the Clan Alliance samurai charged across the open field toward the confused troops of the Arata.

Reuben, Masaru, Tadashi, and Seiji stood and watched as their warriors crossed the field and gave chase to the retreating Arata.

Reuben fell onto his back and began laughing hysterically as a strong feeling of déjà vu overcame him. The other three stood over him with questionable looks on their faces.

"What's so damned funny, Reuben?" asked Tadashi.

Reuben sat up, still laughing. As he began to stop, he said, "Good god that was fun! You should have seen your face when that limber exploded, Masaru. It looked like you crapped your pants!"

After a few moments, when Reuben started laughing again, the other three also began laughing until a gunshot was heard and Masaru fell over on top of Reuben. The other two ducked low and strung arrows in their bows.

Reuben rolled Masaru over and saw a bullet wound in his shoulder. He quickly pressed down on it with the palm of his hand and dragged him to one of the fallen limbers for cover as Tadashi and Seiji covered them.

More shots came from the left of their position. There were two Arata men with rifles and several others advancing on the four with drawn swords.

"Reuben, leave me. You must get Tadashi and Seiji out of here," said Masaru in pain.

Reuben's fierce angered wolf-like look returned. He tore out a piece of cloth from his inner kosode sleeve and jammed it in Masaru's wound.

"NO, GOD DAMN IT, NOT THIS TIME, YOU WILL NOT DO THIS TO ME AGAIN!!! NOBODY DIES THIS TIME!!!" Reuben yelled in English as he rose and sprinted to the closest attacker.

He raised his sword and motioned a straight cut as the attacker positioned his sword for a block, but Reuben reversed his cut and slashed the Arata man across his face. Using his momentum from that cut, Reuben turned completely clockwise, slashing his blade upwards disemboweling the next attacker. He was about to cut downward on another attacker as an arrow pierced the attacker's throat. Seiji quickly shot the two gunmen before they fully loaded their rifles.

"Quickly, Reuben! We need to get back to the other side of the river!" called out Tadashi, as he was lifting Masaru to his feet.

Reuben ran and took Masaru's other arm and they began to run back toward the river with Seiji covering them from behind.

"I do not think we are going to make it. There is more Arata coming after us!" said Seiji from behind.

Reuben raised his mirror-like blade and saw, in its reflection, a large group of men giving chase. He slowed down and turned to face them as they continued to run to the river backwards.

"Why are we running backwards, Reuben?!" asked Tadashi.

"To face our enemy. If we are to die, we will not die with our backs toward them!"

"HAI, REUBEN-SAN!!!" cried out Masaru, painfully, but with pride.

As the Arata men were nearing, they suddenly slowed down, turned, and began retreating in the opposite direction. The four slowed their pace and were knocked down from behind by alliance mounted samurai giving chase to the attackers.

They all rose to their knees and cheered, "AKAGI, SATOSHI, AKAGI, SATOSHI!!!"

The four rose to their feet, arm-in-arm watching as the Clan Alliance samurai chased the Arata. Over the ridge out of view of Reuben, Masaru, Tadashi, and Seiji, the Arata scattered in all directions. The Arata who remained to defend themselves were either quickly struck down or taken captive only to be beheaded once the battle was over.

Arata Goro and what was left of his lieutenants were captured by Akagi samurai and brought before the four regional Daimyo's of the Hisano Province. They were on their knees pleading for mercy, with the exception of Arata Goro, who showed disgust by their groveling. Each one was beheaded, one right after the other in the audience of the other captives.

"Do you have any last words, Arata Goro, before you are put to death?" asked Akagi Genda-San with his sword drawn, pointed to his chest.

"This is disgraceful! I am a samurai, son of Arata Akira, leader of the Arata Clan of the Kway Province! I demand the honorable right of death by seppuku!"

The four regional Daimyo's of the Hisano Province discussed the request amongst themselves. After several minutes, all were seen nodding in agreement. Akagi Genda-San stepped forward and stood over Arata Goro.

"Arata Goro, your reign of terror comes to an end this day. No longer will you rape and plunder defenseless villages and outposts of the Hisano Province. Since it is in our province you have been captured, we have condemned you to death, but not by seppuku. In accordance with the Bushido code, you are not entitled to that privilege. You have acted, not as a samurai, but as a marauder causing fear in the citizens, not only in the Hisano Province, but the surrounding provinces as well. You will be beheaded, your body drawn and quartered. Each one of your limbs will be displayed in each one of the four regions of the Hisano Province, and your head will forever sit upon a post at the foot of the Shun Bridge to give warning to all who dare to plunder the Hisano Province. The matter of your existence is now put to an end."

"No! I am of samurai stock! I demand seppuku!" cried out Arata Goro as one of Akagi Genda-San's retainers positioned his head.

Akagi Genda-San raised his blade and swiftly cut downward neatly severing Arata Goro's head from his shoulders. Akagi Genda-San's retainer lifted Arata Goro's head by the scalp, it's eyes blinking several times before remaining open.

Once the execution of Arata Goro was completed, Akagi Genda-San came to his son with concern on his face.

Reuben had been seeing to Marasu's wound and dressed it as he remembered Doctor Chelmsford did when he too received a similar wound, many years ago in Mexico.

"How is he, Reuben-San?"

"The bleeding has stopped and his wound cleaned and dressed. He'll be his old grumpy-self again in a few days."

"How can you say that, Reuben? I have a fatal wound. I can feel my life close to the end," said Masaru.

"Come on, you big baby, the bullet went straight through your shoulder. Here, look," said Reuben as he exposed the same wound scar he received back in Mexico. "See, the same thing happened to me and I'm still alive and kicking, just as you will be, so you will not be getting any sympathy from me."

Masaru reached and touched Reuben's scar and let out a little painful chuckle. "We are now truly brothers, Reuben-San."

狼

Aarleen stood on a hard, well used dirt road in a strange land she seen once before in a previous dream. She looked to her right and saw the same hills resembling huge stairs filled with water and strange grass growing from within the water. Now there were people wading in the water tending to the grass. Some of them stopped to wave at Aarleen and she waved back. To her left were the high snowcapped mountains. She wasn't frightened as she had been the first time she visited this land in her previous dream. She wanted to call for Renee, not out of fear, but to share with her how beautiful it was here until she heard the sound of lots of men chanting "AKAGI, AKAGI, AKAGI, AKAGI, SHOURI!!!"

It was the same men in the red and black armor that made them resemble turtles, and had passed in her previous dream. This time, instead of looking angry and fierce, they looked joyous and jubilant. As they passed Aarleen on both sides of the road, they smiled, waved, and would say to her, "kon'nichiwa, chīsana ichi!" cheerfully. Some of them stopped and gave her little field flowers.

She heard the sound of heavy hoof falls from a horse coming her way. She looked around the men greeting her and saw a familiar gray horse with the same rider wearing the armor of red. He wasn't wearing his helmet and he had a very joyful expression on his face as he neared Aarleen. This time she wasn't frightened and didn't feel the need to move.

"Kon'nichiwa, Aarleen-Dono, I bring you a visitor!"

The rider turned his horse sideways and assisted the man seated behind him off the horse. It was Aarleen's Grandfather, Aaron. Once he dismounted the horse, he turned and squatted down and opened his arms. Aarleen let out a laugh and ran to his open arms as he lifted her up.

"How are you, my sweet precious little angel?"

"I'm good, GrandDa. What are you doing here?"

"I'm doing what you asked of me, my wee lass. I'm looking after your Da and keeping him safe."

"Is he safe, GrandDa? Mama is so worried."

"Tell your Mama, he is safe and for both of you to be proud of him, for today, he became a hero."

Aaron gave Aarleen a kiss on the cheek and lowered her to the ground. He was assisted by the rider back onto the horse.

"Wake up, my precious little angel, and go tell your Mama all is well and her Reuben, your Da, will be home before a year's time."

"I will, GrandDa."

"Farewell, my little precious Aarleen, I love you!"

"Bye, bye, GrandDa! I love you too!"

"Sayonara, Aarleen-Dono, you have a brave father!" said the rider in red armor atop the gray horse and trotted away as Aaron looked back and waved farewell to his precious little angel, Aarleen.

Aarleen woke from her sleep and sat up in Lucy's bed. She rubbed the sleep from her eyes, uncovered herself, hopped out of the bed, and went to Renee's bed. She gently tapped Renee on the shoulder saying, "Mama, Mama, wake up, wake up."

Renee's eyes opened and she suddenly sat up worried. "What's wrong, sweetie? Did you have another bad dream?"

"No, Mama, I had a good dream about Da, but he wasn't in it. GrandDa was though," she said in a hushed tone.

Aarleen told Renee about this new dream just as vividly as her previous one. She was even able to pronounce the foreign language nearly perfect.

"What do you think kon'nichiwa means, Mama? Do you suppose it means hello?"

"I don't know, sweetie," said Renee, enthusiastically. "What else happened?"

Aarleen continued telling her dream. She was very energetic when she spoke about the part of Aaron and what he told her and his message to her mother.

"What do you think of that, Mama? GrandDa said Da became a hero today, but that's funny because it's still nighttime."

Renee laughed and lifted Aarleen onto the bed and into the covers. "Sweetie, your Da is on the other side of the world. When it's nighttime here, it's daytime where he is. You'll be learning all about that now that you're in school."

"That's weird, Mama. Mama, you know the diary you have been keeping for me?"

"Yes I do."

"I was wondering if I can write something in it about my dream in the morning."

Renee hugged Aarleen and said, "Why wait until the morning? Let's do it now. When you have the urge to write, you must do it then or you may forget what you want to write about."

Both mother and daughter got out of bed and went to the small desk by the window. Renee lit an oil lamp and got out Aarleen's diary. It was nearly full with all the entries Renee had been adding except for one last page. She had Aarleen sit on her lap and handed her a pencil.

"Why can't I use a pen and ink like you, Mama?"

"You better start off with a pencil. Pen and ink are a little messy."

"Okay, so how do I start?"

"You start with the day and date like I did here and here, and then you write your thought down. It's that simple."

"Hmm, okay. Here I go."

TUESDAY, SEPTEMBER 5, 1854

MY FIRST ENTRY. I HAD SOME DREAMS ABOUT YOU. I LOVE YOU, DA, PLEASE COME HOME SOON.

"There, how's that?"

"That's perfect, sweetie. Looks like we're going to have to go to Mr. and Mrs. Klaus' store and get you a new diary. Now that you are in school, you can start keeping your diary by yourself."

"I still want you to write in it also, Mama."

Both mother and daughter hugged each other. Renee blew out the lamp and carried Aarleen to her bed. For the rest of the night, they shared the same bed, both snuggling under the quilt that had been used by Reuben, both wondering if Aarleen's dream would be coming true about Reuben returning home soon.

石
水

In the year of our Lord, 1855, a romantic tale continues.
A mother's plea, and the Sword of Spiritual Power...

Kutto

For the soldiers of the
9th U.S. Reg. Inf'y Regiment
Company B, 5th Platoon

Sargent Sam Evers
Corporal Darrel Rall
Private Justin Osborn
Private Edward Taylor
Private Christopher Roberts
Private Jonathan Stewart
Private Rand Allen
Private Steven Matthews
Private Jefferson Peters
Private Lane Jesseps
&
My good friend
Second Lieutenant Adam Stanns

This gun for the one we never took.
You can now Rest in Peace.
Second Lieutenant Reuben Duran

After what was to be called, The Battle of Shun Bridge, the four intact cannons were dispersed to all four regions of the Hisano Province. Akagi Genda-San placed the cannon for the Itosai region within the front parapet of Hisano Castle. Reuben burned into the trail of the cannon his own personal memorial to his fallen comrades he lost that one tragic day when their last assault failed. It was a touching and moving memorial Akagi Genda-San thought when he saw the finished passage.

"That is superb closure, Reuben-San. How are your memories now, my friend?"

"Much better, Genda-San. I only remember the sky, the sun, and the moon. The same sky, sun, and moon that covered both me and Renee back then, and the same sky, sun, and moon that covers us now."

"That is very well said, Reuben-San. I believe Renee-Dono would be very proud of you. I also believe it is time for you to prepare for your journey back home."

299

"I don't know, Genda-San. Itosai is part of me now and I'm part of it. I really don't have anything to go back to except wishes that can't come true."

"You should still wish, Reuben-San. Remember my lesson in fate. Fate is what drives us to live our paths we chose to travel. If one looks at wishes and fate as if they are two parallel lines, in the distance they will meet, metaphorically speaking. You must prepare for your wish to meet your fate, Reuben-San."

Reuben gave Akagi Genda-San an inquisitive look. "Do you know something I don't, Genda-San?"

Akagi Genda-San let out a laugh and said, "No, Reuben-San, only what fate has taught me in the past."

"Well, I have made a promise to teach English to the new citizens from Ute. I must honor that promise. That will take several months, but I'll begin to see to my preparations."

Akagi Genda-San nodded and placed his arm around Reuben's shoulders. "You have been my best pupil, Reuben-San, and when you do depart Itosai, I will dearly cherish the years you spent here."

狼

It had been seven months since that one discussion Reuben had with Akagi Genda-San about preparing to return home. During that time, he fulfilled his promise to continue his English lessons to the newest villagers of Itosai. He also continued his training in the Budo Arts and spent most of his free time roaming the village and region on foot and horseback alone recording every inch to memory. This was his way of transitioning to the difficult change awaiting him.

Although Kaoru became involved with one of the leading Sho samurai from the Itto region, she still found it difficult to think Reuben was leaving soon. She dearly admired Renee. She must be a truly wonderful woman to keep the heart of this man, Kaoru often thought.

Tadashi requested Sukuri's hand in marriage from Akagi Genda-San. Both he and his wife granted Tadashi's request and a date in the month of June was set for their wedding. It was then when Reuben decided, after the wedding he would take his leave of Itosai, and return to Virginia.

Akagi Genda-San was both pleased and saddened Reuben finally made a definite date for his departure.

Reuben became very concerned about his return trip. His journey to Itosai was purely a result of fate falling in his lap, but now the question was unanswered until Akagi Genda-San told him of the Treaty of Kanagawa of the previous year. Reuben was unaware of the treaty and its purposes until Akagi Genda-San explained it to him. Instead of working his way back to America, he could actually travel as a passenger, just as Akagi Genda-San did on his journey.

"I will pay your passage home, Reuben-San. It is the least I can do for the warrior who saved and protected every member of my family. I will have no argument about it."

"Fate, Genda-San?" asked Reuben with a smirk.

"Ha! Fate, Reuben-San," replied Akagi Genda-San.

All preparations were made, including a farewell celebration held along with Tadashi and Sukuri's wedding. That was until a messenger from Edo crossed over the draw bridge of Hisano Castle bearing a letter from America addressed to Akagi Genda-San.

Akagi Genda-San and Yanna were in the great hall of Hisano Castle when his retainer presented the messenger. The messenger entered the hall and hastened his pace to Akagi Genda-San, lowered himself to the floor, bowed, and presented the letter in both hands above his head. Akagi Genda-San took the letter and the messenger lowered himself back to the floor.

"Arigato," said Akagi Genda-San to the messenger.

"Domo arigato gozaimasu, my Lord," replied the messenger. He rose and quickly left the hall.

Akagi Genda-San paced the hall looking at the letter. It was wrinkled, creased, folded, and worn along the edges, but still intact. He carefully opened the envelope and pulled out another sealed envelope. The second envelope had Reuben's name written on it.

"Guard!" ordered Akagi Genda-San.

A samurai guard entered the hall quickly, lowered himself to the floor, and bowed.

"Hai, my Lord?"

"Quickly, find Reuben-San and bring him here immediately. He should be teaching lessons this time of day in the English school."

"Hai, my Lord," replied the guard. He rose and sprinted out of the hall.

"What is it, my husband?" asked Yanna.

"I do not know," answered Akagi Genda-San. "It looks like a letter from Reuben-San's family."

The guard ran through the castle, over the rear draw bridge, and into the village. The school where Reuben taught English was located near his cottage near the rear of the gorge. Reuben had chosen this location for his cottage and school for its peaceful setting, along with a beautiful view of the tall waterfalls feeding the huge pond and river flowing through the center of the village.

Reuben was inside the school listening as the small class of ten made up of both children and adults were reciting phrases written on a smooth slate attached to the wall. They were about to finish the last phrase when the castle guard quietly entered the back of the classroom.

"Very good, everyone," said Reuben when the class finished the last phrase. "I will have you reading Shakespeare in no time."

Reuben noticed the castle guard standing in the rear looking anxious. "Class, we have a visitor. Let's turn around and greet Mr. Hayate."

The class turned to face the guard and altogether said in near perfect English, "Good morning, Mr. Hayate."

"Ohayo gozaimasu…"

"Dame, Mr. Hayate. You've taken this class before. What is the response in English?" said Reuben.

"Sorry, Sensei. Good morning everyone."

"Perfect, Mr. Hayate. What can I do for you?" asked Reuben.

"Please, Reuben-San Sensei, Lord Akagi requires your presence in the great hall immediately," said Hayate very urgently.

"Very well, ah... class dismissed. Let's go, Hayate."

Reuben and Hayate both ran out of the classroom and sprinted through the streets of the village and across the draw bridge.

Hayate entered the hall and presented Reuben to Akagi Genda-San and his wife.

Reuben lowered himself to the floor and bowed before Akagi Genda-San saying, "You summoned me, my Lord?"

Akagi Genda-San sat before Reuben in seiza and said, "Reuben-San, I have received a letter from Edo. Inside the letter was another letter and it is addressed to you."

Reuben rose as if he heard a cannon fire nearby. "A letter for me?" he asked quite frightened.

"Hai, here," said Akagi Genda-San as he presented Reuben the letter in both hands.

Reuben took the letter timidly and stared at it. His eyes began to fill with tears and his hand trembled as he saw his mother's handwriting.

"Here, Reuben-San, let me help you," said Akagi Genda-San as he took the letter and carefully opened the envelope. He gently pulled out the letter and handed it to Reuben.

Reuben took the letter and opened it. It had only two sentences...

Dear Reuben,   *20 July 1854*

Your father is no longer with us as of this day. I don't know where you are, but if you can, please come home.

With Much Love, Mama

"It's from Mama. My Da has died," he said with much emotion in his voice. "He died last July."

Akagi Genda-San came around and placed his arm around Reuben's shoulder as did Yanna to comfort him.

"Aaron-San was a noble man. We are very sorry for your loss, Reuben-San," said Akagi Genda-San.

"I wasn't there, Genda-San. Have I been away too long that I no longer care for my family?" asked Reuben, dropping his face into his hands.

"No, Reuben, you must not think as such," said Yanna taking him into her arms and holding him as a mother would hold her child. "You have been away for a long time, but it was for the sake of your family which shows you care deeply for them. But now your mother needs you, and you must return."

"Yanna is correct. You must go see to your family. You have learned much, enough for you to carry on and continue on your path. Now your family is your path. Your stone is now smooth and your water awaits you," said Akagi Genda-San, taking hold of Reuben's hands.

狼

While Reuben left the castle to his cottage to prepare to leave, Akagi Genda-San summoned his senior advisor, Yoru, and sent him to Edo with orders to secure passage for Reuben within the week. Since the Treaty of Kanagawa, Akagi Genda-San, because of his regional position, was kept well informed of travel to and from Japan. He even had standing reservations for any vessel departing Japan for America. It was Akagi Genda-San's intention to escort Reuben to Edo first thing the following morning.

Meanwhile, Reuben gathered what little belongings he had. He had several pairs of fresh clothes both Yanna and Kaoru made for him, a couple of pair of leather sandals, and several pairs of tabi socks given to him by Sukuri. He also packed a bundle of clothes Yanna had made special for Reuben, but they were not for him.

"What are these? This is too much, Yanna-Dono," stated Reuben when Yanna presented him some new clothes.

"These clothes here, I had made for you. These are for the one you call Renee."

"I'm much grateful, but I may never see Renee again."

"You never know, Reuben-San. Remember what my husband told you about fate and wishes in parallel lines, Reuben-San? They tend to meet. I hope you will approve, but after what you have told me about Renee-Dono, she sounds much like you. With that in mind, I had made for her a hakama of green, her favorite color."

On the mantle laid the obi in Akagi burgundy Masaru presented to Reuben the day after the attack on the village many years back. Only those who drew blood from the enemy in the defense of Akagi blood were permitted to be presented and wear this obi. Reuben planned on wearing that on his journey home. He was leaving with more than he arrived with.

He lifted up his old haversack that traveled with him from America and he placed three journals he kept during his stay and, of course, his most precious possession, the image case with Renee's picture inside wrapped with Lucy's purple ribbon. Throughout the day, he checked and rechecked to make sure it was packed safely in his haversack.

Hanging on the wall was the kasa Tadashi gave him to wear to hide his face when they first arrived to Japan. He took it from the wall and gave it a look over. The hat was still in excellent condition. He could not help but smile of the absurdity of hiding his face when he first arrived. Now with all his accomplishments and high regard, not only in the Itosai region, but the regions of Yuna, Itto, and Majaul, he could roam with no fear of being harmed because he was an off-lander. And that was long before the Treaty of Kanagawa. He planned on wearing the kasa home.

There was a knock on the door and it slid opened. Tadashi entered and bowed to Reuben.

"I have just heard of your father, Reuben. I came as quickly as I could to offer my condolences."

"Thank you, my friend," said Reuben still holding the kasa.

"I understand you will be leaving for Edo early tomorrow to gain passage back home. I would consider it an honor if you allow me to accompany you."

"Of course, Tadashi, I wouldn't have it any other way. It's only fitting you see me off since you saw me on," said Reuben holding up the kasa.

Tadashi took the hat from Reuben and chuckled. "There have been many times I said to myself and others, *'that idiot round-eye is going to be the death of me.'*"

"But I didn't, did I?" replied Reuben with a small laugh.

"You and that damn fate of yours."

Reuben took a seat, as he offered one to Tadashi. "I'm sorry I won't be here for the wedding."

"That's all right, I understand and so will Sukuri."

Reuben looked all-round the front room of his cottage. It was a small cottage with four rooms, the front room, a bedroom, cooking room, and a wash room which was unique to all the other cottages in the village. Akagi Genda-San gave Reuben a plot of land of his choosing to build a cottage of his own for all he had done for him and the village, not to mention the entire province. With the help of Tadashi, they built this cottage together with plenty of space left over to add on.

"Listen, Tadashi, I want you and Sukuri to have this cottage. I know it's not much, but I don't know who else to give it to."

"Ah, come on, Reuben, I can't take this from you. Besides, Sukuri and I will need a larger place, but I'll tell you what. We will keep this place in order."

"What for?"

"Knowing you, Reuben, you will return someday. I still believe your round-eyed face is going to be the death of me one of these days."

Reuben looked to his haversack where the image case with Renee's picture was packed safely away for travel. He thought she would dearly love to visit Itosai and even live in this little cottage he and Tadashi built.

狼

In the evening, Reuben was summoned to the castle where Akagi Genda-San's family awaited him to have one last meal together. During the meal, they discussed the travel plans to Edo in the morning.

"I assume you have no western style clothing with you, Reuben-San?" asked Akagi Genda-San.

"No, only the clothes Yanna-Dono and Kaoru-Dono made for me and I have those packed and ready to go."

"Well, that is of no concern. The last time I was in Edo a few months back, many citizens have taken to wearing western style garments. When I sent my senior advisor, Yoru, to Edo earlier this day, I gave him instructions to locate you some clothes for your journey."

"I thank you, Genda-San, but I have no money for such…"

"Never mind about that, Reuben-San," said Akagi Genda-San raising his hand.

For the next hour and a half, there was much discussion about Reuben's stay in Itosai. From the first time Masaru was going to kill him on the battlefield once he saw he was an off-lander, to this morning when he made the castle guard deliver his message in English.

They discussed the upcoming wedding of Sukuri and Tadashi and how it won't be the same with Reuben not being in attendance, and how Tadashi will take over the English classes.

Akagi Genda-San pulled out his pocket watch, the one Reuben gave him when he left Norfolk, and nodded. "Come everyone, it is time."

Looking puzzled, Reuben watched as everyone rose and began walking toward the observation terrace from the castle keep overlooking the village. Reuben rose and followed.

They all stepped onto the huge terrace and Akagi Genda-San motioned Reuben to stand by his side. Suddenly Reuben saw flickering lights along the river's edge on both sides. Floating along the current of the river, hundreds of lighted lanterns were released. From the stone bridge over the river near the temple, the Shinto priests from the monastery stood reciting solemn chants.

"What's going on, Genda-San?" asked Reuben.

"The village, Reuben-San, they are honoring your father this evening," replied Akagi Genda-San.

"I feel... so honored," said Reuben, emotionally.

Akagi Genda-San took hold of Reuben by the shoulders and said in all purity, "To earn the admiration of a community is to blossom in glory and honor. Your father was an honorable man, Reuben-San, and you are as well."

狼

Reuben was escorted by the entire Akagi family to Edo very early the following morning. They didn't arrive until late afternoon where Akagi Genda-San's senior advisor, Yoru, had accommodations arranged.

Yoru advised Akagi Genda-San and Reuben, he arranged passage on the next outgoing steamer leaving for San Francisco the next day. He booked the passage because the next vessel would not be leaving for another two weeks.

"What luck is that, Reuben-San?" said Akagi Genda-San.

"Not luck, Genda-San, fate. The same kind of fate I had when I came here."

After a large meal in a tearoom catering to samurai elite, they retired to a grand inn Yoru also arranged for the night's accommodations.

As Reuben was about to settle in for the evening, there was a knock at the door. He rose to answer it. It was Akagi Genda-San, Yanna, and Yoru who was carrying several packages. Reuben welcomed them into his room.

"Reuben-San, since the vessel departs tomorrow, Yoru took the liberty to purchase some garments for your journey. There may be too many for you to carry, so take your choosing."

Yoru purchased several suit type clothes with shirts, under garments, a pair of shoes, and a pair of knee high leather boots.

"Well, I never liked wearing a suit and I want to travel light, so let's make this simple. I have my hanten jacket and kosodes so I'll take a couple of shirts. Got to have the undergarments for certain, and as for the trousers, I'll take two pair. I came here with much less."

"How about the shoes, Reuben-San?" asked Yoru.

"The boots, definitely the boots."

"And the braces for your trousers?"

"I have the Akagi obi for that."

With his garments chosen, he rearranged his knapsack to fit his new clothes, and still had some space to spare.

Akagi Genda-San excused Yanna and Yoru from the room so he could have a private talk with Reuben.

"Well, Reuben-San. I am proud of you and I know your father is looking down on you this very moment with pride in his soul as well. Come and sit, I have something for you."

Akagi Genda-San motioned Reuben to sit. He withdrew a satin sack of Akagi dark red and placed it on the mat between them.

"Reuben-San, in the seven years you have been in Itosai, you never once asked for anything. Not a morsel of food or a coin of money. Everything you acquired, you either worked for or made yourself. You had a purpose Reuben-San, and that purpose was not to acquire wealth. However, I have not forgotten all you have done. You have shed blood for my family, for which I adopted you as family. You have shed blood for Itosai, for which the village and region adopted you as a citizen." Akagi Genda-San opened the sack and withdrew twenty five Oban coins of gold and a string of smaller coins of gold, silver, and copper. "The Oban is your wages you have earned while serving as a retainer. The string of coins is contributions from the citizens of Itosai to assist you on your journey home. I recommend you keep the Oban safe until you reach your home, and use the string of coins in your travels. There is more than enough to pay your way home. The citizens were honored to contribute, and most charitable."

With wide eyes, Reuben looked at the vast amount of money lying on the mat before him. "Great jumping gosh almighty, I'm speechless, Genda-San! I'm completely without speech! I... I can't accept this. This is too much. As you said, I came here not to make money."

Akagi Genda-San laughed at Reuben's response, and then said firmly, "Reuben-San, I insist, and so does the region of Itosai. You have earned it with hard work, kindness, and most of all, blood."

"Very well, I don't know what I can use that sort of money for. I was a simple man before I came to Itosai, and I have not changed in my means of acquiring wealth. I remain the same... simple, but with focus."

"Perhaps you may have plans in the future that may help your community, Reuben-San, and this will aid in that purpose."

"Maybe so, Genda-San, I do have a plan."

"Excellent. I have two more gold coins to give you, but you must keep them for something special," said Akagi Genda-San. He handed Reuben two smaller gold coins with square holes in the center. "Think of these two coins as your future, a future of bonding."

"I don't understand."

"Ah, Reuben-San, life is not all about understanding, but accepting what is given to you and taking advantage of its resource."

狼

The following morning, after a hardy breakfast, the Akagi family escorted Reuben to the dock where the steamer taking Reuben back to America was berthed. They all stood near the gangway and one by one, each member of the family said farewell to Reuben.

"I never did apologize for wanting to kill you the first time I saw you, my brother," said Masaru.

"That's okay. There were plenty of times I wanted to kill you myself when you first started training me," replied Reuben as he took Masaru in his arms and embraced him tightly.

"Be safe, Reuben."

Tadashi stepped up to Reuben next. "Remember the boat ride here, my friend? Looks like you are going back in style."

"I'll never forget all you have done for me, my friend. I wish the best to both you and Sukuri."

Reuben looked to Sukuri and said, "I'm sorry I won't be here for your big day, Sukuri. I hope you will forgive me."

Sukuri reached to give Reuben a kiss on the cheek and replied, "I know you will be with us in spirit."

Reuben felt a tug on his pant leg. He looked down to see Katsuo holding a package wrapped in a bow.

Reuben knelt down on one knee and asked, "What's this, Katsuo?"

"It is what I have been working on for you. Imue, the wood carver, helped me."

Reuben took the package and unwrapped it. Inside was a wooden turtle with a string attached.

"It is an inrou box. I made it so you can give it to someone as a gift. You cannot return home without giving someone a gift from where you came. That is rude."

"Right you are, Katsuo. I'll be sure to give this to someone very special," said Reuben as he gave Katsuo a hug.

He rose to face Kaoru. Her eyes were glistening with tears. Reuben took her by the hands and said, "I'm sorry we couldn't be more than friends, Kaoru, but I dearly appreciate your understanding."

Kaoru gripped Reuben's hands tightly. "Your Renee, I truly hope one day you and your Renee will be one as love intends the both of you to be." She smiled, leaned forward, and lightly kissed Reuben on his cheek.

Yanna took Reuben's hands from Kaoru and took her place. "As a mother, I embrace and kiss you as your own mother would before a long journey for good fortune," she said as she took Reuben into her arms and hugged him tightly. "Thank you for the safety of my children and grandson, Reuben-San." She kissed him on his forehead and stepped away.

Akagi Genda-San took her place as he nodded to Masaru.

"Reuben-San, do you know your purpose?"

Thinking of his family and Renee, Reuben answered, "To protect those I love, Genda-San."

"Very good, Reuben-San, you have evolved and no longer are you a jagged rock. You are a stone washed smooth by the waters caressing its surface. Reuben-San, you are a warrior, a warrior of peace. Such a warrior needs to wield a weapon of peace. With that in mind, I paid a visit to Isamu Gorou, fifth generation sword maker, to forge a blade that has not been forged for over a thousand years, and then, only in legend."

Masaru stepped up to Akagi Genda-San and bowed as he presented him with a sword in a black satin cover. Akagi Genda-San took the sword in both hands, turned and presented it to Reuben as he bowed.

Reuben took the sword with both hands and bowed in return. He looked at Akagi Genda-San who nodded.

Reuben untied and unwound the cord of the cover and opened the end to expose the black ito of the tsuka. He took hold of the tsuka and drew the sword free of the saya and immediately noticed the uniqueness of the blade.

"Genda-San, it is exquisite. The blade, it is reversed. What type of katana is this?"

"It is a... Kutto, a sword which is non-lethal, yet still lethal. In the ancient writings of the Kojiki and the Nihon Shoki, the Kutto was referred to as the Sword of Spiritual Power. It was a sword used for the protection of loved ones and the innocent. It's deadly side to be used only as a means of last resort. With this sword, you can protect your loved ones and yet, not have to take life unless absolutely necessary."

Reuben returned the blade to its saya and covered it. Once he retied the cord, he looked at Akagi Genda-San and, unable to contain himself any longer, he wrapped his arms around his mentor and savior as Akagi Genda-San also wrapped his arms around Reuben. The two embraced each other tightly for several long moments.

"My last piece of advice to you, Reuben-San... You will not want to fight, but sometimes you have to. Use this Kutto wisely, my friend."

The whistle sounded the signal for final passengers to board. Reuben and Akagi Genda-San stood apart and looked at one another.

"Time to go, Reuben-San. May your journey be a safe one and your wishes come true when you reach your destination," said Akagi Genda-San with hope his thoughts about Renee were true.

Reuben nodded. He tucked the Kutto into his Akagi obi of burgundy, reached for his knapsack and slung it over his shoulder, and took his jo from Katsuo. He gave the Akagi family one last look, turned, and made his way up the gangway. Once onboard the steamer, he stood along the rail and waved as the ship began pulling away from its berth. It was a far better farewell than the one he gave his family when he left Norfolk, Virginia back in '47.

狼

"You be good for GrandMama, and give Aunty Lucy and Uncle Eric a hug and kiss for me, okay?" said Renee as she lifted Aarleen onto the carriage.

"I will, Mama."

Renee watched as her little girl was being seated by Monroe. It was going to be their first time away from each other for more than one day. Monroe had an important law case in Hampton and Coleen was going along to visit with Lucy, Eric, and Andy. With the importance of keeping the two cousins close, Coleen was taking Aarleen along. As much as she wanted to go, Renee couldn't. There was an important order of seed due to arrive at the Klaus Mercantile she had to personally sign for.

"Don't worry, Renee. I'll have Aarleen back before her birthday and I'll be bringing back Lucy and Andy for the party," said Monroe.

Renee, feeling emotional, couldn't answer so she only nodded.

Coleen took Renee in her arms to console her. "I don't know how I'm going to be able to be without my little sweetie, Mama," said Renee.

"You know, my darling, I think you're taking this harder than Aarleen," said Coleen with a little laugh.

"I think you're right, Mama," replied Renee, feeling a little better.

"Come on, Mama, let me help you up," said Monroe

Renee stepped back up to the carriage and motioned for Aarleen to come to the side for one last hug and kiss.

"Don't worry, Mama. I'll be good and I'll help Andy with his reading."

"I love you, sweetie."

"I love you too, Mama. Hey, Mama, I just thought of something. I'm going to be seven next Tuesday. You know what they say about the number seven! It's lucky!"

"That's right, sweetie. I have a feeling this is going to be your best birthday yet."

"Me too, Mama, me too."

石
水

In the year of our Lord, 1855, a romantic tale continues.
A surprising homecoming and the first step on a new path...

Reuben is Home

"Welcome aboard. Please have a pleasant trip to Norfolk," greeted Charlie, the conductor, as he welcomed passengers onto the first class rail coach. With a friendly face he took the tickets from each passenger, checked for authenticity, and welcomed them aboard the 9:30 from Richmond to Norfolk. It looked like it was going to be a full car of passengers.

The first class rail coach was at the head of the train and very plush. The best way to travel from Richmond to Norfolk and only the highest of society could afford to travel in its luxury.

"Ah, welcome aboard, Captain and Mrs. Peters, have another wonderful visit to Richmond, did you?"

"Yes we did, Charley. Thank you for asking," answered Captain Peters as he handed the conductor, his and his young wife's tickets. A young company commander of one of several infantry units out of Fort Monroe, he and his wife traveled to Richmond on a furlough to visit family and the city as often as his duties permitted.

"Looks like you are the last to board, so we'll be getting along shortly."

"Excellent. Come along, dearest."

As the young couple boarded the car and Charley began lifting the step, up walked one more passenger. He cleared his throat, gaining the attention of the conductor. Charley finished placing the step onto the car and turned to see a strange looking man.

Charley looked the man from his feet up. He was dressed in black, knee high leather boots with black trousers tucked into them and held up by a burgundy colored thick cotton sash tied at his waist. Tucked into the sash was a long object incased in black satin. He wore a black shirt with the sleeves rolled up past his elbows and several top buttons undone. On his head he wore a strange, wide conical hat made of Japanese cypress. He had no luggage with the exception of a large knapsack strapped to his back and a haversack resting on his right hip. He carried a chest-length stick with a burgundy colored jacket tied to the end.

Charley snorted at the passenger, went back to securing the step and pointed with his thumb over his shoulder saying, "Third class passengers to the rear of the train."

"Excuse me, my excellent fellow, but I have booked passage on this car for this last leg of my journey," said the passenger with a strange accent as he held out his ticket to Charley.

"You've got to be joking," said the conductor as he rudely snatched the ticket out of the passenger's hand.

He looked it over and his eyes widened when he saw this was indeed a ticket for the first class rail coach. He looked at the passenger in a questionable manner wondering if he had perhaps stolen the ticket.

The passenger, becoming impatient, asked, "Is there a problem? As you can see my passage is bought and paid for. I would appreciate if you allow me to board," he said in a tone of authority.

Feeling intimidated, Charley stepped aside to allow the passenger to climb onto the car without the use of the step. He was about to enter the car, but halted and stepped back. He reached into his pocket and called out to the conductor, "Pardon me. Here, for your trouble." He tossed a shiny object at the conductor who caught it. The passenger then entered the car.

Charley opened his hand, and to his amazement was a large silver coin with a square hole in the center, and an odd looking crest stamped on both sides.

Inside the first class rail coach, all manner of discussions were silenced when the strange looking passenger stepped through the door. He removed his hat and ignored the stares he was attracting as he made his way down the aisle to the only empty seat next to Captain Peters and his wife who boarded just prior.

"Oh my, have you ever seen such an... impressive looking man ever in your life?" whispered a very elegantly dressed woman to her female friend sitting across from her at another table.

"You can't be serious?" she answered as she stared admiringly.

"Excuse me, is this seat taken?" asked the traveler.

"No," answered Mrs. Peters with a crackle in her voice and a lustful look in her eyes.

Her husband elbowed her causing her to jump.

"Arigatō," he replied as he leaned the stick in the corner and removed his knapsack and placed it underneath his seat. He removed the long object from the sash tied at his waist, sat down, and placed it on his lap and faced toward the window.

"Excuse me, what is your name?" asked Mrs. Peters, who received a stern look from her husband.

Without looking away from the window, the traveler answered, "Reuben, Reuben Duran."

"Where are you from and where are your travels taking you?" Mrs. Peters inquired politely, which gained another stern look and elbow from her husband.

Again without looking away from the window, Reuben replied with a relaxing sigh, "I'm from Norfolk and I'm going... home."

The train began to move forward. Reuben looked away from the window and examined the plush chair he was sitting in. He made himself more comfortable.

"May I ask a favor?" Reuben asked.

The couple watching him with fascination nodded.

312

"If it isn't too much trouble, can you please wake me when we get closer to Norfolk? I have been traveling for a long time and now that my journey is almost over, I could really use some sleep before I arrive home to... my family."

The couple both nodded again.

"I appreciate it," Reuben said as he leaned further back into his seat. He took the long object in the satin cover, cradled it in his arms, placed his hat of cypress over his face, and was soon sleeping peacefully to the sounds of the rails beneath the car.

A gentle nudge awoke Reuben from his restful sleep. He removed his hat and saw the smiling face of Mrs. Peters. Her husband was nowhere to be seen.

"We are almost to the station in Norfolk, Mr. Duran."

Reuben yawned and stretched out his arms. In doing so, his shirt opened from the first few undone buttons exposing a large scar across Reuben's chest, and showing a silver oval locket with two gold coins attached to a silver chain.

If there's a woman in this man's life, she has got to be the luckiest woman in the world, thought the young Mrs. Peters as her lustful looks returned.

They quickly disappeared as her husband returned, but not after he caught a glimpse of her and in an act of dominance, he removed his sword from his belt and placed it on the table.

Reuben didn't notice the act as his attention was directed toward the window. Frustrated at his lack of interest, the captain loudly cleared his throat. Reuben still kept his eyes on the scenery of his hometown coming into view.

Once more the captain tried to get Reuben's attention by picking up his sword and lightly dropping it on the table.

"Nice looking sword you have, Captain. I carried one myself many years ago. Found them to be useless, so I carried a gun instead," said Reuben without looking away from the passing scenery.

Startled by his response, the captain looked perplexed.

"You were in the army?" asked Captain Peters.

"Yes, during the Mexican Campaign."

"Is that where you got that scar on your chest?" asked Mrs. Peters.

Reuben looked down from the scenery and buttoned his shirt. He chuckled, "Sorry about that. It's been a while since I wore garments with buttons. No, I didn't receive this scar in Mexico. It's a wound I received from a katana."

"A ka, kat..."

"Katana, Captain, a Japanese sword," Reuben said, looking back toward the passing scenery.

Pointing to the object in the satin cover, Captain Peters asked, "Is that what you are holding, a katana?"

"It's a Kutto, a special katana."

"What is so special about it?" asked Mrs. Peters.

313

Reuben looked away from the window to the covered Kutto. He took hold of the locket and closed his eyes and a vision of Renee came to his mind. He opened his eyes, released his hold of the locket and untied the satin cover and exposed the tsuka and tsuba. Using the back handed technique, Reuben swiftly drew the sword and held it in front of the couple. They were mesmerized at its mirror-like blade.

"As you can see, the blade is reversed. I made a promise to a special person my days of killing are over unless it's only to protect."

As swiftly as he drew the blade, he returned it back to the saya and recovered the sword. For the final moments of the train ride, Reuben briefly told them of his journey to Japan, not in detail, but enough to settle their interests of his mysterious background.

The train began coming to a stop as Reuben was telling the couple his long journey had been comfortable. He mentioned he always wanted to travel on the first class rail car ever since he traveled by train to VMI, and wanted his last leg of his travels to be as comfortable as possible.

"Well, what did you think of the first class rail coach, Mr. Duran?" asked Mrs. Peters.

Reuben looked out the window watching the station slowly pass by with a huge happy grin and he chuckled. "I could have saved some money."

"You didn't like it?"

"It was wonderful, but either by luxury or if I walked, the result would be the same. I'm home," said Reuben with a smile and look one could describe as, longing.

Reuben rose and tucked the Kutto into his burgundy obi, retrieved his knapsack, jo, and hat. He bid the couple good day and made his way off the car as the couple watched in fond respect.

狼

Reuben stepped off the first class rail coach onto the same platform he stood on before he boarded the train taking him to VMI. The same platform he stood on with Akagi Genda-San when he departed before he and Renee made plans for Reuben to follow. As back then, he walked to the edge of the platform and looked out in the direction both trains rode away each time.

The station clock chimed noon time, breaking Reuben's past memories. He turned and made his way into the station. It changed little in the seven years he had been away. He realized no bad memories haunted him and happily made his way to the street. He looked both ways, put on his wide conical cypress kasa attracting odd looks, and was off in the direction of his father's law office.

The walk to the office took a little longer than it should because Reuben stopped to look at the changes of his hometown. When he finally arrived to the office, it was closed with a printed sign in the window.

"Attorney at Law, Monroe Duran is currently on case trial in Hampton and will return Monday."

314

"You did it, brother. You became a lawyer. Well done, Monroe. I knew you could do it," said Reuben out loud startling others as they were walking by.

Giddy like a schoolboy, he quickly walked in the direction of the school where his mother taught. When he reached the front steps, he beamed with delight. Pleasant memories of him sharing lunch and walking Renee home from school entered his mind. "I wonder?" he said, and went to the back of the school and straight to the place where his secret room was. It was overgrown with shrubs, but he still dug through until he saw bricks covering the area where the door used to be.

"Ah, someone found it. Probably Mama. I knew I couldn't keep it a secret from her," he said as he chuckled after.

At a brisk pace and greeting everyone along the way, he finally arrived at his home in the city. Nothing changed. From the same door knocker with the "Duran" name plate above it, to the key scratches on the key hole. He stepped up to the door and tried the door knob but it was locked. He knocked several times.

"Excuse me, but no one is home," said a little girl from the walkway.

Reuben turned and smiled at the child. He took off his kasa and knelt down and asked, "Oh, I see. Do you know where Mrs. Duran may be?"

"She went with her son to Hampton so she could visit Lucy and Eric in Chesapeake City."

"Lucy and Eric?" asked Reuben.

"Yeah, you know, Mr. and Mrs. Klaus. Hey, who are you, mister?"

"Lucy married?! Well I'll be. I would never have guessed," he said, joyfully. "Oh sorry, I am a… an old friend of the family," he said, figuring the little girl wouldn't believe who he was in the first place.

"By any chance will Mrs. Duran be back on Monday?"

"Yes, how did you know?"

"I saw a sign at Da's law off… I mean her son's law office."

He stood and patted the little girl on the shoulder and said, "Thank you very much, little one, you have been most helpful. You have a good day now."

"You too, mister," she replied, and started skipping down the street.

Looking perplexed, but still happy, Reuben said, "Well, to the farm I guess. Hopefully someone is there, if we still own it, that is."

狼

Reuben Duran had not seen the small family farm for seven years. The house and land looked well kept. He was pleased, yet unsure of how he would be welcomed. If indeed he would be welcome at all. For all intents and purposes, he abandoned his family. He left all he loved behind for his journey. His parents, older brother, and younger sister were left behind without him saying goodbye, except in a letter. Renee, he also left, just when she needed him the most. He loved her and she loved him, but it was a love that could not be for she was promised

315

to another. He wondered where she could be now as each foot step brought him closer to the farm house.

Did she find happiness with her husband, William Sinclair? Has she forgotten about him after all these years apart or does she remember the last night they spent with each other under the oak tree, as he often remembered from time-to-time. She must be living in Charleston these days, he thought.

He forced himself back to thinking about his family and the loss of his father almost a year ago. The news hit him very hard. The letter that came from his mother took almost a year's time to reach him had only two sentences…

Dear Reuben,   *20 July 1854*
Your father is no longer with us. I don't know where you are, but if you can, please come home.

With Much Love, Mama

"You must go see to your family. You have learned much, enough for you to carry on and to continue on your path. Now your family needs you. Your stone is now smooth and your water awaits you," said Akagi Genda-san after Reuben read the letter. *"Your water awaits you."* What did that mean? Reuben wondered. Up to the end, Akagi Genda-San continued to speak in puzzles for Reuben to figure out on his own.

狼

Henry and Noah were tending to the railed fence in front of the house when Noah saw a man dressed in dark trousers, boots, and a strange dark red garment resembling a jacket with no buttons. Slung over a shoulder was a knapsack, and a long object in a satin cover was tucked into a burgundy colored belt tied in the front. He was carrying a stick, but not using it as a walking stick, and he wore a strange looking hat.

"Henry, looks like we have a vagabond coming up the road, best let the ladies know," said Noah to Henry.

"Don't go starting anything, boy. Just you ask what his business is and be polite like Renee says so," said Henry as he began to walk to the house.

Inside the house, May and Renee were in the parlor. They had been cleaning the inside of the house, keeping it ready for Coleen and Aarleen's return. Coleen and Aarleen had gone with Monroe to Hampton where he had business to conduct so they could visit with Lucy and Eric and their son, Andy in Chesapeake City.

Renee picked up a vase she wanted to use to put fresh flowers in to place on the dinner table for their return.

Henry came in the parlor through the rear entrance, dust falling from his trousers with every step. "You darn fool!" cried May when she saw the cloud of dust around his shoes. "Can't you see Renee and I are cleaning this here parlor for Mrs. Duran's and Aarleen's return?"

Renee chuckled nearly dropping the vase. "Henry, May is going to make you dress in an apron and finish the dusting."

"I'm sorry, Renee, but a traveler is coming up the lane and I think he may be coming here to ask for a hand out or something."

"Well, I'm sure he means no harm, so let's show him some hospitality, like Mama would," replied Renee.

狼

"Good afternoon, mister, what can I do for you," called out Noah to the stranger walking up the path to the house.

Reuben didn't respond, but kept walking. He didn't know what to say, but he felt joy seeing his childhood friend. He began to slow his pace because he sensed Noah's *ki* with nervousness and saw Noah cautiously start walking backwards away from him. He slowed until he came to a complete stop a few yards away.

"Don't be frightened, Noah," he called gently.

Noah stopped moving backwards and looked at the man in front of him with much curiosity. Although there was an accent, the voice was familiar, but he couldn't recognize him because his hat covered the top half of his face. "Mister, who are you? How do you know my name?" Noah asked.

"I've known you nearly all my life, my friend."

Noah suddenly felt joyful energy coming from this man once he spoke. Noah smiled and realized who he was. "Reuben? Is that you?"

Reuben removed his hat and smiled so wonderfully it looked as if his face actually shined.

Noah couldn't contain himself, ran, and took Reuben in his arms and lifted him off the ground, laughing loudly and embracing him tightly. Reuben had no choice but to let Noah express his joy and he felt joy in doing so.

Noah put Reuben down and it was Reuben's turn to embrace his old friend. "I have missed you, my dear friend."

"I can't believe it! You're here! In person! I just can't believe it! REUBEN IS HOME!" Noah shouted with gleeful happiness.

狼

CRASH!

At the sound of Noah shouting Reuben's name, Renee dropped the vase and stood in the parlor as if she had seen a ghost. May stepped up to her quickly thinking she was about to faint. Henry ran to the window to take a look.

"Great googly-moogly, it is Reuben!" he said, and headed to the front door with a cloud of dust following in his wake.

May held Renee to steady her. She was trembling and trying to look outside the open door to get a glimpse.

"Are you okay, Renee?"

317

Renee breathed in and out a few times to regain her composure. "Yes, May, I'm fine. Is it true? Is that Reuben standing out there?"

May moved to the window and took a good long look, "It sure looks to be him."

"Geez oh geez oh geez is it really him? How long has it been? I must look a fright. I can't let him see me like this."

"Renee, that man has not seen you for over seven years and he might not even expect you to be in this here house. That's the father of Aarleen who he knows nothing about. Just seeing the sight of you will be pure joy to him, no matter if you are dressed in a beautiful gown or coveralls covered in dirt, and if I recall my old Reuben, he would rather see you covered in dirt."

"You go out first please, May?"

"Okay, but you better be close behind."

May walked toward the door and outside as Renee began to gather herself up and slowly followed.

Both Henry and Noah were shaking Reuben's hands and patting his back.

"Reuben, young child," called out May, "how dare you run off without telling me goodbye, young man?! Is that any way to treat the woman who saw to your cuts and scrapes?"

"Aunty May!" Reuben ran up to May and lifted her in the air and embraced her joyfully. May felt cheerful energy coming from Reuben she never felt before, not from anyone. "It's wonderful to see you, all of you. This is so great seeing you all. I see Mr. Wilcox still hires you out to the farm."

"Actually, they live here now," said Renee from atop the house porch.

Reuben slowly and gently lowered May back to the ground, released her, and turned toward Renee. He slowly stepped toward her. He was in delighted shock to see her and she looked just as wonderful as she did the last time they were together. Her long, dark, brown hair was loose, cascading over her shoulders, just the way he liked it. Renee stepped down from the porch and they both walked slowly toward each other. May, Henry, and Noah stood to the side in silence.

"Reuben, is it really you?" asked Renee with a warm, loving, quivering smile as she raised her hand to touch his face.

Reuben didn't answer. Instead, he took Renee into his arms as she did the same. For the first time in many years, Renee and Reuben felt complete happiness and joy and it radiated so dear, it was felt by the others.

"What are you doing here? Are you visiting from Charleston?" asked Reuben, gleefully.

Renee looked puzzled at the question and his accent, and realized she was in the arms of the man she sacrificed so much for. It dawned on her Reuben had no idea how she ended up living with his family, but she was still joyful. She could actually feel love and joy emanating through his arms, the same way joyful energy flowed from Akagi Genda-San's hands when he touched her. It made her tingle. She stepped back out of his arms, but held on tightly to his hands. She looked at him from head to toe. He looks handsome, she thought. She noticed the locket she gave him hanging around his neck as well as the two gold coins Akagi Genda-San gave him. Renee smiled as she opened it to see their two pictures inside. She closed it and re-embraced Reuben again tightly with her face resting on his shoulder. "It's so wonderful to have you back in my arms, Reuben."

Reuben felt just as joyful, but awkward with Renee expressing such affection to him. He cleared his throat and asked, "How's your... husband?"

Renee's eyes opened wide and her smile faded. Her face lifted from his shoulder and she began to gently bite her lower lip, something she always did when she felt very nervous. Reuben liked that about her because she looked adorable when she did it. She did that the last night they spent with each other before they made love under the oak tree by the creek.

May cleared her throat and said to Henry and Noah, "Come on, you two, and let's let these two alone for a while. We have a welcome home dinner to prepare so let's get to it."

May shuffled Henry off into the house as Noah picked up Reuben's knapsack and hat to take into the house. He noticed the stick Reuben had been carrying and picked that up as well. Noah recognized it as the stick Reuben made into a jo and noticed the strange markings on it 狼.

"Excuse me, Noah my friend, can you please carry these into the house for me as well?" asked Reuben as he removed his covered Kutto from his obi and presented it to Noah with both hands.

Noah slung Reuben's knapsack over his shoulder and with his free hand, he carefully took the Kutto, looking at it with caution. Noah admired it for a moment and felt Reuben place the strap of his haversack on his shoulder. Noah nodded and followed Henry and May into the house.

Renee watched as the others walked into the house and looked back to Reuben. "Reuben, we need to have a serious talk."

Arm-in-arm, they walked toward the creek in silence. Reuben was very calm and that effect caused Renee to feel secure, although she was scared of what she was about to tell him. He was looking out over the land with a smile and his eyes were wide and bright. Her frightened frown faded away into a gleeful smile. He looks so much at peace, she thought to herself as she stared at his eyes.

At the end of the planted field, he spotted the oak tree and stopped. He let go of Renee's arm and made a few quick steps ahead of her and stopped again. He turned and with an exultant look, he shouted to Renee, "There it is, Renee! Our tree, just as we left it so many years ago! Come on," he said like a little child as he took hold of her hand and began running to the oak tree with Renee in tow laughing.

When they reached the shade of the tree, Reuben slowed down, let go of Renee's hand, and ran around its trunk several times. Renee was wide-eyed in amazement. She had never seen him showing so much pleasure.

Reuben made one more lap round the trunk of the tree and made three quick wide steps and leaped into the air and rotated his entire body in midair landing on his feet facing the tree. He looked at the wide trunk of the oak tree and ran straight toward the trunk. Renee thought he was going to run into it head on and was about to cover her eyes until Reuben literally ran up the tree three steps, kicked off with his feet, flipping his body backwards, and landing on his feet facing the tree. He wrapped his arms around the trunk and embraced it tightly.

"I have missed this old tree, Renee!"

Renee stood with her eyes still wide open and her lower jaw dropped. Never in her life did she think the human body was capable of such acrobatics, particularly Reuben's body.

Unable to contain herself any longer, she ran up behind him and wrapped her arms around Reuben as he still embraced the trunk.

"Geez oh geez oh geez Reuben, is this really you?" asked Renee as she pressed her face between his shoulders.

Reuben released the trunk and turned to face Renee. Their faces were inches apart. Reuben cleared his throat in the awkwardness of the moment and said, "You had something to talk about."

For the first time since walking away from the house, Renee looked downward. Reuben gently lifted her chin back up so his eyes were looking into hers. His eyes are not lifeless anymore, she thought. They had that childlike mischievous look again. The same look that caught her attention the first time they met. She smiled as a tear rolled down her cheek and began to tell Reuben about what happen the day of her wedding. How she couldn't go through with it, and her father abandoning her. She told him how his family took her in and how May, Henry, and Noah came to live with them. She told him about his father creating her position as the Duran Agriculture Liaison, and with the help of the others and his sister, she managed the farm. Renee spoke of Monroe becoming a successful lawyer taking over his father's law practice and Lucy's marriage to Eric Klaus. She told Reuben how his mother cried so much when he left, and how she has been dealing with the loss of Aaron, who died the year before. And of course, she told Reuben of how she ran to the wharves to try and stop him, but didn't make it in time, and of the smooth stone Akagi Genda-San gave her, and of its meaning. Of all the topics she told Reuben, she left out the one of his daughter. She kept that from him, but couldn't understand why.

When she was finished, she looked back downward. She felt his arms wrap around and pull her close into him. He ran his fingers through her long, dark, brown hair and she began to whimper. Again he lifted her chin, but this time her face was much closer to his. He slowly and gently kissed her on the lips. She smiled and returned the kiss with one of her own.

For the rest of the late afternoon until the sun was above the horizon, Reuben and Renee sat in each other's arms leaning against the trunk of the oak tree talking about their days growing up. Renee wanted to hear so much about Japan, but they were having such a wonderful time remembering the days of playing on and around the oak tree they were sitting under and, of course, the day they met under the tree.

"I have only one word to say about the day we met, Renee."

Renee sighed in wonder as she closed her eyes and relaxed in Reuben's arms and asked, "What's that?"

"Worm…"

Renee's eyes opened, she sat up, and pounded on Reuben's chest. "I can't believe I did that just to get your attention," she said, laughing in embarrassment.

Reuben let out a yelp when Renee hit him and began laughing. "You really didn't have to because you had my attention when you asked me, *'Wha'cha doing?'*" he said.

"You mean to tell me, I put that worm in my mouth for nothing?" Renee answered with a playfully perturbed look.

"Ah, yep."

"Why you shoddy little farm boy," she replied, immediately cringing in regret knowing what Reuben's reply was going to be.

Reuben expressed a mischievous shimmer in his eyes and a boy-like smile as he said, "Wickham girl."

She let out a chuckle as she lightly beat on his chest saying, "I told you never call me that!"

As they lightly wrestled against the trunk of the oak tree, they soon made eye contact and looked at one another both thinking, but not saying a word about the one other time, one warm autumn evening in the rain, spent under the very same tree they first met.

Renee snuggled back into Reuben's arms thinking of that one evening. "When your mother returns on Monday, she'll have something that will be a pleasant surprise for you," Renee said, pulling his arms tighter around her.

"A surprise, what kind of surprise?" he asked.

"You'll see soon enough, shoddy farm boy."

"Wickham girl."

They would have sat all evening and into the night under the tree if it had not been for Noah coming to call them in for dinner. Reuben walked back to the house between Renee and Noah with his arms around both of them. As soon as they got into the house, Reuben excused himself to clean up in the rear room. May brought Reuben's bag to the room along with a pitcher of hot water. He assured May he would be quick and she, in turn, told him to take his time, for she would keep dinner warm and the others from starting without him.

She closed the door behind her and started up to Reuben's old bedroom, the room Renee and Aarleen had been sharing. She gently knocked on the open door catching Renee's attention.

"Reuben is downstairs cleaning up. I told him to take his time."

"Thank you very much, May. I can't believe he is actually downstairs, in this house, home!" said Renee as she twirled in a circle with a huge, radiant smile of delight. "He took the news of my wedding, and how you all took me in, very well."

"Well, believe it, Renee, because I had both Henry and Noah pinch me to make sure I wasn't dreaming. However, I do have a question."

"What's that?"

"Where's he going to sleep tonight? I assume you haven't told him about Aarleen until she arrives so he can see her himself. Suppose he will want to stay in his old room? If he does, he will see Aarleen's clothes and belongings."

Renee's smile went away as she looked to Aarleen's side of the room. "Good heavens, you're right." She quickly thought to herself and was interrupted by May.

"Don't worry girl, your ole Aunty May will come up with something. I also told Henry and Noah not to mention anything about Aarleen until you tell them to."

"Oh, May, you're the best. Thank you. I want both Aarleen and Reuben to be surprised together, especially since she'll be back the day before her birthday."

"That indeed is going to be an early birthday present they both will never forget. Now let's get downstairs."

Henry and Noah were already sitting at the table and stood when the ladies walked into the room. As they were getting ready to sit, Reuben walked into the dining room with a fresh face and shirt. He looked at everyone at the table and smiled brightly. He took the seat next to Renee. "Please, let's sit and eat. I'm about starved and I have missed Aunty May's biscuits."

Everyone sat laughing. Reuben began to reach for a bowl of greens as the others lowered their heads for the blessing.

"Ahem!" said May, startling everyone at the table. "Perhaps Reuben would like to say the blessing since this is his first night home."

He felt awkward all of a sudden. For the last seven years he gained faith in his path and physical elements of the world, and lost the need of a symbolic deity such as God. He was about to decline until Renee said, "Please, Reuben. That would be nice."

Reuben nodded and thought for a moment. "All right, it has been a long time, but I'll do my best," he said, smiling. The others bowed their heads.

He took in a large breath and let it out. He looked upwards, closed his eyes, reached out his arms to each side causing the others at the table to look up. He brought his hands together, clapped loudly two times, bowed his head, and began to recite a short passage in Japanese. When he finished, he raised his head and opened his eyes to see everyone looking at him strangely, except for Renee. She looked at him with sincere affection.

"That's beautiful, Reuben. What does it mean?" asked Renee.

"It's something Genda-San's wife, Yanna-Dono would tell me when she would catch me looking inside my locket. *'Bless the cherry blossoms that fall from their trees and onto your cheek, for they are kisses from the gods.'*"

Not proper, thought May, but it was beautifully said.

"Let's eat!" said Noah to break the silence.

Bowls and plates were passed and everyone began to eat, but stopped when Reuben pulled out two sticks and began to eat with them. He noticed the silence and looked up as he was stuffing his mouth with green beans using the sticks. He chewed once and looked at the sticks. He began to laugh and he placed them down on the table and picked up the fork next to his plate. "I hope I can remember how to use one of these." Laughter broke out and everyone began to enjoy the meal May had prepared.

狼

When dinner was finished and the dining room and kitchen were cleaned, everyone retired to the parlor. Before Reuben made it to the parlor, he went to retrieve his haversack from the washroom. He sat on the sofa and Renee sat next to him, no longer concerned about being discreet.

"Tell us about your travels already," asked Noah, showing impatience and curiosity.

"Where should I start? There's so much to tell about my journey and the years in training I spent."

"Training?" asked Henry, "What sort of training?"

"That's hard to answer Henry so let me start with something easier. I kept a journal and wrote in it every day, but I also became accustomed to sketching." He reached into his bag, pulled out a book with a thin wooden cover and back, and handed it to Renee.

Renee gently took hold of the book and opened it to the first page. The first sketch was one of Reuben holding Renee. "That looks like you and Renee," said Noah.

"It is," replied Reuben, looking at Renee. "I drew a lot of you from my memory."

"These are beautiful," she said, turning page after page until she came to one that looked like Reuben. It was two sketches of him on one page. In the first sketch, he was drawing a katana from its saya and his eyes were drawn hard and lifeless. However, the second was of him looking happy with childlike eyes, much like the ones he had all day.

As they looked at the sketch book, Reuben rolled up his sleeves. Renee passed the sketch book to May so she could have a better look at the drawings and took Reuben's hand in hers. The rest of the evening, Reuben told them about his voyage and the beauty of Japan. He told of his passage on the *Morning Star*, and the irony of the second ship with the name of the captain and the ship. He mentioned how he met his good friend, Sora Tadashi, and how he taught Reuben to speak and write Japanese. And of course, Reuben spoke of the massive relocation of the village of Itosai, the building of Hisano Castle, and the part he played in its construction.

"Come on, Reuben, really, a castle? You built a castle?" asked Noah.

"Yes, Noah, and we could have used both you and Henry to help us. Here, let me show you," replied Reuben as he reached for another journal book.

When he pulled it out, he also had the image case in his grasp. He looked at the case and smiled. "Here, please hold this, Renee," said Reuben as he handed her the case.

"Oh my goodness, is this my picture I gave you when you were at VMI?" asked Renee.

"Yes it is, kept it with me every day, even when we battled the Arata."

"Battled?" asked Renee, turning very concerned.

Reuben ignored Renee's question and thumbed through his journal until he reached a page with a completed drawing of Hisano Castle and the village of Itosai in its background.

"You see, the castle itself is of traditional design, but I recommended the wall around the castle be made into a star shape, like the forts here in America. It was a recommendation Genda-San adopted full heartedly."

"And you built this?" asked Noah.

"The entire Hisano Province built the castle. All four regions worked together on this massive project, sometimes both day and night to get it finished.

"Because of these… Arata people?" Renee asked, still concerned.

Reuben faced Renee and nodded yes. He told them of the feud between the regional lords and Arata Goro. He continued on about how the Arata army terrorized the smaller unprotected villages and outpost in all four regions, and the surrounding smaller provinces. He spoke of his first encounter with Arata Goro's thuggish assassins close to nine months after he left Norfolk.

When Reuben mentioned his first encounter, Renee had a strange feeling of déjà vu, but kept it to herself.

Reuben went on to tell them of how Akagi Genda-San used Arata captives as labor, and compared that form of servitude to the slavery practices here in America. He mentioned in the end the captives became citizens of Itosai and took part in the final battle against Arata Goro.

"What happened to this Goro person?" asked May with a serious look of interest.

Reuben explained to them Arata Goro acquired cannons and it was Reuben's idea on how to stop the Arata from using them.

"Oh geez, Reuben, isn't that what you and your men did in Mexico?" Renee asked with fear in her tone.

Reuben turned his attention to Renee and took hold of her hands as he said, "Yes it is, but this one time was so much different."

"How so, darling?" she said with the fear in her voice fading.

Looking deeply into Renee's eyes, Reuben answered, "Because I had a true focus of what my purpose of life is, Renee. That purpose is to protect those I love. I love Genda-San and his family for helping me gain my prospective and adopting me as one of their own. I love my family for giving me the gift of family love. I love May, Henry, and Noah for their dedication and love for my family. And most of all, Renee, I love you. I always have and always will. And that's what Genda-San meant by washing away my jaggedness and becoming smooth like that stone he gave you."

Renee's eyes filled with moisture, as did May's, and even Henry's and Noah's eyes.

Reuben let go of Renee's hands, stood, and walked to the mantle where he leaned the covered Kutto earlier. "Because of my purpose to protect those I love, Genda-San had this sword made for me," he said as he took hold of the Kutto and returned to his seat next to Renee.

"As Genda-San presented me this katana, moments before I boarded the ship to bring me home, he explained the uniqueness of this sword. It's a sword not meant to take life, but to protect it. It isn't lethal, yet still lethal. Not to kill unless absolutely necessary, and only in the protection of those I love, such as you, Renee."

May cleared her throat trying to regain her composure and asked, "Well, you didn't answer my question about what happened to this Goro person. Did he get captured?"

Reuben, still gazing into Renee's eyes with affection, nodded yes. "He, and most of his leadership, was captured and each one beheaded. Arata Goro was beheaded by Genda-San

324

himself. His body quartered and his head mounted on a post at the foot of the bridge where the battle was fought," answered Reuben as Renee caressed his face, maintaining her look of affection.

"Good lord!" exclaimed May.

The silence at that moment was broken when the clock above the mantle chimed ten o'clock, startling everyone in the room except for Renee and Reuben.

"My goodness, look at the time and we have a trip into the city tomorrow. We had better turn in," said May.

Reuben yawned and covered his mouth. "You're right, Aunty May. I must admit that I have met my days limit."

Renee began to wonder what to say if Reuben were to go to his room to retire, but he took a blanket from the back of Aaron's chair and began to make up the sofa to sleep on. She felt at ease. Henry and Noah said their goodnights and left to their cabin. Renee stayed behind.

"Are you sure you want to sleep on the sofa?" she asked, thinking after that wasn't a good idea to ask.

"I think its best until..." he paused and thought for a moment. "Our future is an open path now, Renee. This day has been both exciting and emotional for both of us. We have an open future free of obstacles, but we still need to proceed carefully. You and I have made a tremendous step this day and it wasn't even a full day. Can you just imagine what tomorrow will bring?"

Renee embraced Reuben and rested her face into his shoulder. "I love you, Reuben."

"I love you too, Renee. In the past seven years, I knew my path lead me to your direction, as if you caused me to tumble in your waves to make me... smooth."

"Well, I didn't make you entirely smooth, Reuben."

"What do you mean?"

"Your accent..."

Reuben dropped his head and slapped his hand to his forehead and said, "Oh the blessed gods of the high mountains, I knew you would say something about that sooner or later."

Renee laughed and raised his head with her hands cradling his face. "I think it's adorable."

They looked at each other and kissed.

"May I take your journal up to bed with me? The one with the picture you drew of us?" asked Renee.

Reuben retrieved the journal from the table and handed it to Renee. She took it in her hands and held it close to her chest. Renee didn't want to leave, but forced herself away and up the stairs looking at Reuben every step of the way as he watched her. She disappeared into his old room, looking at Reuben one last time as he was looking back at her.

Reuben lay on his back with his hands behind his head staring at the ceiling for a while reflecting on the events of the day. Glancing to the end of the sofa, he saw his covered Kutto leaning against the arm. He rose to retrieve it and laid back down cradling it in his arms.

325

Looking toward his old room where the girl he so loved was sleeping in his bed, he smiled and said softly, "It's our time, Renee. It's your time to be loved as you should, and it's my time to provide you with that love."

In the year of our Lord, 1855, a romantic tale continues.
Father and daughter, and a birthday wish come true…

Can We Call Him Riley

Renee awoke bright and fresh considering she hardly slept because of the thought of Reuben sleeping downstairs in the parlor. Yesterday had been one of the best days of her life, and thinking of being in Reuben's arms caused her to toss and turn. Renee eventually got out of bed and spent some late hours putting away some of Aarleen's clothes and belongings along with hers in case Reuben was to come into the room. Renee truly wanted to tell him about Aarleen, but had to wait until she came home. Both Renee and May felt it was the right thing to do.

Wide awake, Renee laid in bed looking at the sketch of her and Reuben which rested on her chest. She cuddled with his journal book during the time she was able to sleep. She thumbed through some of the pages, admiring his writing in kanji. I've got to have him translate this for me, she thought.

She was so happy. She glanced at the clock. It was almost six and since it was Saturday and a trip into the city was planned for the day, everyone took advantage to sleep in later than usual.

Renee rose and reached for her robe. I'm going to make Reuben breakfast, she thought. Of all these years since living with his family, she never made a meal for anyone, except for Aarleen. She stood up and walked to the wash basin. As she was about to pour water, she heard a sharp shout coming from outside. It caught her attention and reminded her of the sounds Reuben and Akagi Genda-San would make when they were training under the oak tree. She walked to the window, pitcher in hand.

Renee looked out the window to see a lovely sun rise and in its glow was Reuben underneath the oak tree. He was wearing a burgundy type of jacket tucked into what resembled a dark brown skirt.

Reuben was performing misogi-no-jo exercises with the jo staff he was carrying yesterday. His movements were hypnotic and she could not help but feel happy watching him. "He looks like he's dancing with the wind," she said, softly.

She watched Reuben train cradling the pitcher of water until water poured onto her bare feet causing her to jump. She quickly went to the basin, washed her face, put on a day dress, tied her hair up with a ribbon, and left the room to go outside.

She walked through the backdoor in bare feet and noticed Reuben was now waving the sword he displayed in its cover last evening. He was moving in such graceful, circular motions causing her to wonder how it was possible for a person to move in such a way. She heard a fumble coming from the barn and noticed Noah was also watching Reuben, trying to mimic his movements and tripping over his own feet. She silently chuckled and looked back toward Reuben.

As she watched on, Noah silently stepped up beside her. "I've never seen anything like that in my life," he said, softly.

"He's truly a changed man. He's so much at..." the sentence lingered until Noah finished it for Renee.

"Peace."

"Yes," she turned to look at Noah and embraced him with joy. "I'm so very happy he's returned to us." She released Noah and both of them continued to watch Reuben perform his training. Soon, Henry came and joined them, as did May. They all watched in silent awe instead of getting ready for the trip into the city.

The sun was fully exposed over the horizon. Reuben did one last thrust technique, returned his Kutto to its saya, bowed toward the sun, and lowered himself to the ground in his seiza position as he put on his kasa, bowing his head down in meditation.

"He must be finished," Renee said.

"Good gracious, look at the time. We had better get going soon," said Henry.

Henry and Noah made their way to the barn to hitch up the wagon while May entered the house to prepare for the day's trip. Renee stayed behind watching Reuben and slowly began moving toward him.

"I hope I won't be disturbing him," she said as she very softly walked toward him.

Renee stopped when she was about fifteen yards away from Reuben thinking he was unaware of her presence. She stood in the shadow of the oak tree.

"Good morning, Renee," Reuben said without moving out of his seated position, startling her.

"Good morning. I'm not disturbing you, am I?"

"Of course not. Please come and sit with me."

She smiled, approached Reuben, and lowered herself beside him trying to copy the way he was sitting, thinking it was the proper thing to do. He didn't move nor lift his head or open his eyes.

"How are you this beautiful morning?" he asked.

"I'm wonderful. I hope you don't mind, but I was watching you from the house. What was it you were doing?"

"Clearing my mind, meditating, touching nature, and letting it touch me back," Reuben responded, keeping his eyes closed and breathing in deeply.

Renee cocked her head, trying to understand. It wasn't an answer she was expecting.

Reuben recited a passage in fluid Japanese causing Renee to look at him in a most adoringly manner.

Reuben opened his eyes and turned to face Renee. He raised his hand to untie the ribbon holding her hair. Her hair cascaded over her shoulders, just the way he liked it. He caressed her cheek with his fingertips and translated what he said for her understanding. "Bridge yourself

328

between heaven and earth and heed the word of the gods, the strong will always defeat their enemies, but it is the powerful that will not only defeat their enemies, but show them compassion as well."

"That's lovely, but I don't understand."

Reuben rose as if he floated rather than using his legs. He turned to face Renee and reached down for her to take his hands. He helped her to her feet and released her hands while gazing into her eyes. A smile came to his face and he kissed her on the cheek and said, "Here, let me show you."

"You're not going to ask me to grab your wrist, are you? I remember all those other times you did and I ended up on my backside," said Renee with a questionable, adorable grin.

"No, my dear Renee, I don't want you to grab my wrist... Wickham girl."

Renee's grin turned into a perturbed frown as she raised her fist to strike Reuben on the shoulder saying, "Stop calling me Wickham girl!"

Renee swung her right fist toward Reuben's shoulder. Swiftly, using his right arm, he blocked her strike from underneath, and trapped it under his arm, rotating his body to the right. At the same time, Reuben gently placed his left hand around her head on her left cheek, pulling her close to his right shoulder. Reuben rotated his body back to the left causing Renee to fall into his left arm facing up to him. Using his right arm, he lifted her off the ground and cradled her in both his arms.

"See, you became my foe and I defeated you. But look at you now, not only did I defeat you... I am now showing you compassion. Now isn't that better than grabbing my wrist?" asked Reuben, gazing into Renee's beautiful brown eyes.

Renee let out a little girlish giggle. She removed his kasa and placed it on her head saying as she did, "I can only assume there's more to that because I didn't wind up on my backside, but I think I understand. So now that you have me in your arms, give me a kiss you shoddy farm boy."

狼

"HEY! Hurry up in there! We're starting half an hour late!" shouted Henry from the wagon, with Noah seated next to him.

May came out the front door carrying a large basket filled with the eggs she gathered earlier for the Klaus Mercantile, and right behind her was Renee, dressed in a lovely day dress of green, her favorite color. As they were about to climb on the wagon, Reuben came out of the house wearing common, black trousers tucked into his knee high boots and a black band collar shirt with the top three buttons undone and the sleeves rolled up to his elbows. With his haversack crossed over his shoulder, he carried his jo as he walked toward the wagon. He had no vest or hat.

May, rather perturbed about his appearance said, "Reuben, what would your Mama say seeing you dressed like that, a grown man and everything? Now get in that house and put on a vest or at least a hat."

Renee looked at him adoringly thinking he looked very handsome just the way he was, and wouldn't want him any other way.

"We don't have time, Aunty May. You heard Henry, we're burning daylight and besides, you look wonderful for both of us. Now give me those eggs before you drop them or toss them at me in frustration."

Reuben took the basket before she had a chance to hand it to him and helped her onto the wagon. He helped Renee onto the wagon and jumped on himself.

Like a lighthearted little boy, Reuben said, not to anyone in particular, "This is great! I haven't ridden in a wagon in over seven years!"

Henry snapped the reins and they were off to the city. Renee told Reuben the purpose of their visit into the city and Reuben couldn't wait to see Renee's "Agricultural Liaison" position in action.

Another purpose for the visit was to purchase birthday related items for Aarleen's birthday party on Tuesday. This caused a delicate dilemma since Reuben was unaware of Aarleen's existence. Renee came up with the excuse that one of the Foster children was having a birthday party and they asked if Renee would pick up the items since they were going to be in the city for the day.

"That's genius, Renee. Oh my, now that Reuben is back, please don't tell me you two are going to get mischievous with your old shenanigans and such?" asked May.

"You never know. He's got that look back in his eyes and I need to step up to his game."

May told Renee she would need to stall Reuben before he entered the mercantile so May could inform Andrew and Annabelle Klaus of Reuben's return and for them not to mention Aarleen. Renee agreed.

Henry asked Reuben if he wanted to visit the city house, but Reuben said he had already been there. Instead he did express a desire to visit his father's resting place in Elmhurst Cemetery.

As they rode into the city, Reuben pointed to this, that, and the other, remembering places as they passed along the road. He was chatting away like a little schoolboy on a school fieldtrip out to the country for the first time, and Renee and the others were enjoying it so much, they could not help but join in with their own memories. It made for a very happy ride. Reuben waved and greeted everyone they passed by along the way.

"Hey! What is going on here with Mr. Wilcox's old barn?" asked Reuben as they were coming up to James Wilcox's old property.

Along the side of the road was a small plot of land for sale with a small barn on its premises. James Wilcox used it mainly for excess crop storage.

"Oh, that's one of the county's stories of woe for Mr. Lester," answered Henry.

"Story of woe?" asked Reuben.

"You see, Reuben," said Renee as she began to explain. "When Mr. Wilcox moved away, he still owed Mr. Lester money he didn't want to pay back. So instead, Mr. Wilcox talked Mr. Lester into taking that small plot of land with the barn included."

"That sounds fair," said Reuben.

"Not really," added Noah. "Mr. Lester found out much later, after Mr. Wilcox left, the plot of land was nowhere worth the amount of money owed to him, and besides, that plot is out of the way of his own property."

"He's been trying to get rid of that plot for years now," said Henry.

"Why doesn't Mr. Davis buy it since it's adjacent to his property?" asked Reuben.

Renee answered, "Because Mr. Davis and Mr. Wilcox had a huge feud and he told me, when I asked him your same question, '*I won't buy anything Wilcox owned for it is probably jinxed,*'" said Renee with a manly impression of Mr. Davis.

"Yeah, I can see that. Mr. Wilcox was kind of a piece of work," said Reuben as he was still eyeing the barn. "How much is Mr. Lester asking for that plot."

"The same amount Mr. Wilcox owed him, $300," answered Renee. "But no one is going to buy it for that price, especially since there's no practical use for that barn."

Reuben nodded and turned his attention back to the ride, but still had the barn on his mind. Renee noticed his concentrated thoughts about the plot of land, and began to wonder what he was conjuring up in his mind.

Both of their thoughts were interrupted when May said, "I have an idea. How about Henry drops you two off at Elmhurst to visit your father, Reuben, and we'll ride on to the mercantile?" May gave Renee a quick little wink.

With a look of relief, Renee said, "That's a wonderful idea, May."

Renee had been wondering how she was going to stall Reuben from entering the mercantile, allowing May to talk with Andrew and Annabelle about not mentioning Aarleen to Reuben.

"But don't you have to sign for a shipment?" asked Reuben.

"Renee can do that after your visit. In the meantime, I can pick up the... Foster's birthday items," said May. "Besides, Reuben, I believe the both of you should visit your father's place of rest together alone after what you two have been through these past years," May added in all sincerity.

"That's very true, Aunty May," said Reuben as he took hold of Renee's hand.

狼

Reuben helped Renee off the wagon by taking her by the waist and lifting her with no effort onto the ground. After a short goodbye, May, Henry, and Noah rode off. Renee and Reuben walked through the cemetery hand-in-hand, something they never did out in the open and they could not help but feel joyous, even in this solemn place. Their joyful feeling faded as Renee mentioned they were close to Aaron's resting place.

They came to the shade of a large elm tree and beneath its low hanging limbs laid Aaron Duran in eternal sleep. Reuben stood at the foot of the grave and read the marble headstone…

Aaron Duran
Loving Husband
And
Father
September 19, 1802
July 20, 1854

Reuben removed his haversack, unbuckled the strap, and retrieved a long wooden box. He placed the haversack on the ground and stepped up to the headstone. Renee picked up his haversack off the ground.

Reuben slid the top of the box open, pulled out a stick of incense and placed it in the ground at the foot of the headstone. He took a match to the incense and lit it. The fragrance was of ginger. Reuben stepped back to the foot of Aaron's grave and lowered himself into the seiza seated position, brought his hands together as if he were praying and closed his eyes. He loudly clapped his hands twice and bowed low to the ground.

"Oh, dear Da, please forgive me for leaving you the way I did. Please forgive me for not being here when you needed me the most," Reuben pleaded, and began to whimper to the ground.

Renee lowered herself next to him and placed her arms around Reuben's shoulders and held him tightly. She so wanted to tell Reuben of Aarleen's dream she had of Aaron riding on the back of Akagi Genda-San's horse. Instead she said, "Your Da was very proud of you, my dear Reuben. He never gave up on you."

Reuben rose and looked at Renee. Tears were trailing from his eyes and she wiped them away with her thumbs. She continued to say, "Your Da, I owe him so much, Reuben. He treated me as one of his own and never felt any shame about you and me."

Reuben placed his hand on Renee's cheek as she leaned into his touch. "You see, Da, it's just as I told you in my meditations, I love this woman with all my heart, and I thank you for keeping her safe for me," he said to his father, but kept his gaze on Renee's face.

Taking one last look at his father's headstone, Reuben rose to his feet, then helped Renee to hers. He nodded in approval and said, "I believe we had better get to the others so you can conduct your business."

狼

It took both Renee and Reuben several minutes for the visit to wear down. It was emotional for both of them, but they felt a sense of closure, especially Reuben. They roamed the streets in silence hand-in-hand and as they were about to cross the street, a German Shepard puppy came running to Reuben. The puppy ran between Renee and Reuben as if it were hiding and nearly caused them both to trip over the rope attached to the puppy's neck.

Reuben looked down and noticed blood coming from welts on the puppy's head and back.

"Hey there pup, what happened to you?" he said picking up the rope and felt it tug out of his hand. The puppy yelped as it was being pulled on its back over the street.

Reuben's eyes went dark and fierce. He rose and walked up to a large man pulling the puppy against its will.

"Hey, can't you see you are hurting that dog?" Reuben hollered out.

The large man known as Dodson, stopped and turned to face Reuben. He kicked the puppy aside, walked up to Reuben, and with his finger, jabbed it into his chest, "Why don't you mind your own business, little man?"

"When innocents are being threatened, it becomes my business," replied Reuben.

A crowd started to gather and Renee began to feel frightened. Dodson was a well-known brutish thug and runaway slave hunter, twice the size of Reuben. She feared he would severely hurt Reuben.

"Listen, little man, this dog belongs to me and I will do with him as I please," he shouted and kicked the puppy again causing it to yelp in pain.

"That may be true, but don't you also belong to the dog? Does he also have the right to do to you what he pleases?"

Reuben knelt down and motioned the puppy to come to him. The puppy timidly came to Reuben's out-reached hands. Dodson reached down and grabbed Reuben by his right shoulder and yanked him to his feet. Some in the crowd began to look away as Dodson balled up his hand into a huge fist, and took a swung at Reuben like Renee did earlier this day, but with intent to do serious damage to Reuben.

Renee started to run to Reuben until she saw him swiftly block Dodson's swing like he done to Renee, trapping Dodson's right arm, and turned to the right. Instead of gently reaching around Dodson's head to place it on Reuben's shoulder, Reuben grasped his collar behind his neck. Taking Dodson's balance, Reuben turned back to the left, bringing his right arm across Dodson's neck with the palm of his hand up. Reuben rotated his arm down and thrust his hip into Dodson's side, causing him to be thrown off his feet and landing hard on his back. A loud snap was heard coming from Dodson's right shoulder. His shoulder had been dislocated when he landed on the street.

Renee stood with hands to her mouth and gasped in amazement.

Reuben walked to Dodson, knelt next to him, and said, "Don't underestimate a smaller being, whether it be man or beast. Size means nothing when injustice is being practiced."

Reuben rose to his feet, walked back to Renee as his boyish cheerful look returned, and took her by the hand. "Well, we should go see if your shipment has arrived," he said as if nothing happened.

As they walked away, Dodson was crying in pain and rolling on the street grasping his hurt shoulder.

Reuben stopped and glanced back at him. He looked at Renee and said, "Remember when I said, 'Bridge yourself between heaven and earth and heed the word of the gods, the strong will always defeat their enemies, but it is the powerful that will not only defeat their

333

enemies, but show them compassion as well?' Well, I guess it's time to show him how powerful I am."

Reuben let go of Renee's hand and walked back to Dodson. He squatted down next to him and put one hand on Dodson's shoulder and the other on his back.

"NO! Don't touch me! You made your point! Get away from me!" shouted Dodson.

Reuben pressed Dodson's back and rotated his shoulder and another loud snap was heard. Dodson shouted out in pain again and rolled away from Reuben. Reuben rose and walked back to Renee taking her hand in his. As he did, Dodson's cries went silent and he sat up rolling his shoulder around, feeling the pain fade away.

"That's right! Walk away you coward!" yelled Dodson as he rose and took a couple of steps toward Reuben.

Reuben stopped and faced Renee causing Dodson to stop, turn, and run away. Reuben said to Renee, "I'm very sorry about that display of violence. Please forgive me."

"You have nothing to apologize for, my dear," Renee said with an adoring look, feeling lustful. "Not only are you powerful, you are... amazing."

Suddenly Renee felt something walk between her and Reuben, and they both looked down. It was the puppy pawing at Reuben's foot and wagging its tail. Reuben knelt down and untied the rope from the puppy's neck. "Looks like you have your own life now, pup," he said as he rose and continued to walk with the puppy following closely at his heels.

"Looks like we made a new friend," said Renee.

"Hey, we can never have enough friends, can we?" replied Reuben, placing his arm around her waist.

狼

"The wagon is outside the mercantile so May, Henry, and Noah must be here. Come on, Reuben, you really must meet Mr. and Mrs. Klaus, Andrew and Annabelle. They're wonderful," Renee said taking Reuben by the hand and pulling him along.

Renee entered the store with a huge smile on her face. She was about to introduce Reuben as hers for the very first time and wanted to enjoy every word of it. "Hey, Andrew and Annabelle, my Reuben is home! Here, look!" she said, presenting Reuben with her arms wrapped around him.

The Klaus' came out from behind the counter to welcome Reuben. Andrew took Reuben's offered hand and shook it vigorously. "Reuben, it's so very grand to meet you," said Andrew.

"Our Renee has told us so much about you. We feel we already know you," added Annabelle. "You're right, Renee. He is a very handsome man."

"Aww shucks," responded Reuben to Annabelle's comment, as he began to blush.

Henry and Noah busted out laughing, as May said, "Well, I'll be, Mrs. Klaus... you got Reuben to turn red. Renee is the only person able to do that."

"Oh come on, Aunty May, I'm ah, ah... flustered by the fight I almost got into a while ago. Yeah, that's it, right, Renee?"

334

"Fight?" asked Noah.

Renee told them of Reuben's encounter with Dodson, the thug and runaway slave hunter, moments before they entered the store and how Reuben, effortlessly, threw him down.

"By the way, what happened to our little friend?" asked Renee.

"Probably enjoying his freedom," answered Reuben. "So I hear my Renee is quite the Agricultural Liaison," he continued.

"That she is, Reuben. As a matter of fact, Renee, that shipment finally came in. I'm sorry it took so long," said Andrew.

"That's okay, Andrew. I know you can't control when orders come in."

"What did you order?" asked Reuben.

"We and several other farms ordered planting seed in bulk. We all pitched in the money and were able to get twice the amount of seed for half the money. Since May and I come into town almost every day, I placed the order and since it's in bulk, I have to sign for it."

"Yeah, this was all Renee's idea," added Henry.

"Your Renee is quite the brain storm'er there, Reuben," said Annabelle.

"So now that you are home, Reuben, are you going to take over as the Duran Agricultural Liaison?" asked Andrew.

Reuben shook his head no. "Why fix something that isn't broken?" he said.

"So I guess that means you'll be working for her then," said Annabelle, humorously.

"Me work for Renee? Are you joking? She's too bossy. I was going to ask if you had a job to offer," answered Reuben, laughing after.

"Reuben!" called out Renee as she slapped him on his shoulder.

For the next hour, they visited. Reuben was feeling pride in Renee hearing from the Klaus' of her accomplishments with the farming community.

We could have used her ingenious cleverness for the relocation of Itosai and building Hisano Castle, he thought. The more Andrew and Annabelle spoke highly of Renee, the more she began to blush in modesty.

"Ha! Look, she's blushing," said Reuben, pointing to Renee.

Renee again slapped Reuben's shoulder and everyone laughed.

When the laugher died down, Reuben took hold of Renee by the shoulders and looked to her with high respect. He said to her the words Akagi Genda-San spoke to Reuben the night the village of Itosai honored his father in Japanese.

Reuben took Renee into his arms and hugged her tightly as he translated, "To earn the admiration of a community is to blossom in glory and honor."

Reuben put his lips to Renee's and kissed her tenderly. "You are a very honorable woman, Renee-Dono, and I feel much pride to call you the one I love."

There was warm emotional silence as Renee kissed Reuben and said, "I love you too."

Everyone stood and watched Renee and Reuben gazing at each other. The happiness they were sharing filled the entire store and was felt by everyone.

"Come on, Noah, how about we get this seed loaded," Reuben said as he and Renee were still in each other's arms.

"Please, follow me and I'll help," said Andrew, clearing his throat masking his emotions.

Reuben and Noah were led to the back by Andrew.

Annabelle took Renee by the hands and said, "That, my dear, Renee, was the most romantic thing I have ever heard and seen." Annabelle looked toward the opening to the back to see if Reuben was out of ear shot and continued, "Once he sees Aarleen, he's going to be the happiest man in the world."

Renee also looked to the opening and replied, "I want to tell him so much."

"Why haven't you?" asked Annabelle.

Renee sighed as she tried to put her thoughts to words. "I want to be certain Reuben will love me because he wants to and not because he has to."

Annabelle said, "I don't know, Renee, from all that I have been told by everyone and what I just witnessed, Reuben has always loved you since the day you two first met, but I can understand your hesitation."

"Thank you, Annabelle. I'm sure of his love also, but I just have to ease this uncertainty," said Renee.

Reuben came out of the back with his first sack of seed.

"Here, let me get the door for you since you seem to be working for me at the moment," said Renee as she opened the door.

"Not for long. I got plans, Wickham girl."

"Don't call me that," said Renee as she kicked Reuben's backside as he passed her by.

"Yep, that's love all right," said May.

Sitting outside was the puppy. As soon as it saw Reuben, it rose and began panting and wagging its tail.

"Whoa, there he is, Renee!" said Reuben.

Once the wagon was loaded Renee, May, Henry, and Noah bid farewell to Andrew and Annabelle. Reuben shook Andrew's hand, thanking him for supporting Renee all these years. As he was about to climb onto the wagon, he heard a bark. Reuben looked down to see the puppy pawing at his foot.

"Yeah, you're coming too, whatever your name is," said Reuben as he lifted the puppy up into the wagon.

During the visit, Annabelle nearly mentioned Aarleen several times and as the wagon was rolling away, she almost did so again by saying, "See you at Aar... ah, Mr. Foster's child's birthday party."

狼

The group, including Renee's and Reuben's new friend, returned to the house late in the afternoon. Reuben helped Henry and Noah unhitch the team from the wagon and unload the seed while May and Renee carried in the other items they brought back. Henry and Noah began to carry out the daily chores, helped by Reuben who had the puppy constantly staying by his side. There wasn't much time to finish all the chores, but with Reuben's help, Henry and Noah got a lot done.

When the clock above the parlor mantle chimed 5 o'clock, they all sat down to supper and, like the night before, Reuben felt awkward as May said the blessing. Reuben ate quickly for he wanted to get in some training under the oak tree before the sun settled. He excused himself, went into the back room, and changed into his black kosode undershirt and hakama. With the satin covered Kutto and jo in hand, he strolled to where he spent the first part of the morning with the puppy following.

Everyone else finished dinner and cleared the table. Henry and Noah went to sit out on the back porch to watch Reuben while Renee and May cleaned the kitchen and dishes. However, Renee wasn't much help. She kept watching Reuben though the back kitchen window. She nearly dropped the same plate she already washed three times.

"For heaven sakes, girl, you are of no use to me in this state," said May, half angry and half amused. "Go on and play with him, like you used to when you were children."

Renee placed the over cleaned plate back into the dirty dishwater, hugged and kissed May on the cheek, and ran out the door. She ran until she was close to the tree and slowed down to a very slow walk. The puppy came up to her and she knelt down to run her fingers through his fur. She walked around Reuben as he was doing exercises with his jo. His eyes were closed and she thought he was in a very deep state of concentration.

"Kon'nichiwa, Renee," he said, startling her.

Renee immediately thought of Aarleen's dream when she asked, *"What do you think kon'nichiwa means, Mama? Do you suppose it means hello?"*

"I said hello, Renee," he repeated in English thinking she didn't understand the first time. "I'm not disturbing you, am I?"

"No, as a matter of fact, I've been thinking of you."

Renee became intrigued. It looked as if he was thinking of nothing except what he was doing. "How could you be thinking of me while you are doing... whatever you are doing?"

Reuben smiled as his eyes remained closed and he continued his movements, coming closer to her. She didn't move and thought this was rather odd. She remembered watching Reuben and Akagi Genda-San train together, but what Reuben was doing now was much more focused, much more advanced, much more... romantic.

Suddenly Reuben flung the jo in the air and elegantly circled around Renee and wrapped his arms around her from behind. He used his left hand to turn her head to face his. She looked into his eyes and felt her body tingle. She noticed his other arm was extended with his hand open wide. Without turning his eyes away from her face, he caught the jo in his hand as it came down. Renee gasped in amazement while Reuben moved around her and with the jo, pulled her close into his arms. She rested her head on his chest and noticed for the first time the large scar running diagonal on his chest. With her fingertips, she touched it.

"Where did you get this scar? You didn't have it before you left," she asked with concern.

"You gave it to me, in a way," he responded.

Renee pulled back, but still had her arms on his shoulders. "What do you mean?"

"Come, let's sit. I must ask you something of the most importance that will affect our lives."

Renee walked toward the trunk of the tree with the puppy following and sat on the soft grass as Reuben retrieved the satin covered Kutto. He sat across from Renee, closely, pulled out the Kutto from the cover, and placed it on her lap gently. She moved her hands away as if it were going to bite her. Reuben took them into his and held them tenderly.

"About nine months after I left Norfolk, I had been training in Genda-San's village dojo. Arata Goro was on the march and Genda-San took command of the Clan Alliance to stop him. He entrusted me and Tadashi to watch over his family, his property, and the village. We thought we were safe until we were attacked by some of the Arata's assassins."

Renee grasped his hands tighter and began to tremble. That's what he had been trying to get away from she thought and began to feel sorrow.

Reuben continued. "That day, I took the lives of seven men." He took a deep breath and sighed with sorrow, but continued. "After I took the life of the fourth man, I forgot where I was and began to think of you."

Suddenly Renee's eyes opened wide with déjà vu. *"Nine months after I left Norfolk."* "Do you remember when this happened?" asked Renee.

"Funny you ask. It will have been exactly seven years ago come Tuesday."

Renee felt as if her body was being pricked by thousands upon thousands of needles. She brought up her right hand to cover her gasp. The same day Aarleen was born, she thought.

Reuben didn't take any notice for he had his eyes closed as he continued, "I knew I should have been thinking of my task given to me by Genda-San, but you were very deep in my thoughts, so much I felt you call to me. I heard you call my name so vividly it caused me to look up and around just in time to see another attacker bringing his sword across. I moved, but not fast enough, for he caught me across my chest." He opened his eyes and looked down to the scar. She moved her hand from covering her mouth and placed it on the scar. "If I would not have felt you call my name and turned around, instead of this scar, the attacker would have taken my head." Reuben placed a hand over hers.

"I didn't take that man's life. I easily could have, but I spared him because I felt I didn't need to, and my understanding of my path was becoming clear. The attack was over and no one from Genda-San's family or the village got seriously injured."

He picked up the Kutto from Renee's lap. "After Genda-San returned and heard I shed blood in the protection of his family and village, he adopted me into his clan and told me of the protector in me. Life is fragile, Renee, more fragile than anyone gives credit. I took lives in Mexico and Japan to protect others, but that weighs heavy on a man, and Genda-San saw that was the root of my darkness. He focused my training in the protection of the ones I love."

Renee sat listening very intently with her whole being. She was fascinated with what he was saying to her. Of all the years they grew up, and even the last night they spent with each other before his journey, Reuben never before spoken such meaningful words to Renee.

As he continued, he gazed deeply into Renee's eyes. "One lesson Genda-San taught me of the protection of loved ones states, *'True victory is having the ability and right to destroy your enemy, but choose not to.'*" His eyes focused on his Kutto. "I told everyone last evening this is a special sword. It's a symbol of protection." For the first time in front of Renee, he unsheathed it. Its blade glimmered in the setting sun's rays and Renee could clearly see her face in the blade as if it were a mirror.

As she looked at the sword, she noticed something strange about the blade. She had seen swords and knives with the sharp edge on the curved side, but the curved side of this sword had no sharp edge. "The blade looks backwards," she said, observantly.

Reuben smiled. "That's what's special about this sword, the Kutto, the Sword of Spiritual Power. It is not lethal, yet it can be. To be used for the protection of loved ones and the innocent." His smile faded and he replaced the sword in its saya, placed it by his side, and took hold of her hands.

"Renee, I ran away seven years ago so my jaggedness could be washed away. Now I'm smooth as a stone that has been caressed by water. Renee, I am that stone and you are my water. Fate has kept us together, even though we were apart. Now that our wishes and fates have met, you and I must cherish each other as love intended. Renee, my love, I wish to cherish you as my wife, if you will cherish me as your husband."

Renee released his hands and brought them to her mouth as she gasped in surprise. Many thoughts went through her head at this very moment. She thought of the night they spent together under this very tree before Reuben left. She thought of how his family took her in when she was abandoned by hers. She thought of giving birth to Aarleen and raising her with the help of his family. Suddenly all thoughts went away, except for the thought of the man she always loved asking her to marry him, and all in the name of unconditional love.

Renee raised her arms and leaped into Reuben's, causing him to fall over backwards and she kissed him on his lips. The puppy started jumping and barking while its tail wagged. She raised herself up and with a bright smile she replied, "YES! I will be your wife!"

They both rose to their feet and embraced one another.

As they held each other, Renee said, "The tree, Reuben, let's get married under our tree."

Reuben looked at Renee and with a very bright smile said "Sugureta aidea... I mean excellent idea!"

"Geez oh geez oh geez!" exclaimed Renee as she skipped around Reuben in joy as the puppy hopped on its four legs, wagging its tail and barking.

Reuben took hold of Renee, held her closely, and said, "Renee, no more hide and seek. All though our adolescence, you and I loved each other, but we could never show it."

"Now we can, and the whole world can see us," Renee said, proudly.

Reuben sighed and stepped back. Renee was curious. "What is it, Reuben?"

"I was just thinking of Genda-San," replied Reuben as he let out a little chuckle. "I just realized that man knew all along about you and me. He knew you and I had to be apart for our love to blossom into what we have, and what we have is each other. We have always had each other."

Reuben took Renee by the hands and said, "I believe Genda-San helped me gather up all my dreams, both good and bad, and merge them together to make me whole again. There was a time I was afraid to touch you because I could see the blood of my comrades and friend on the palms of my hands. But the blood was all in my mind and not real. You, my precious Renee, you are real and I will keep you in my hands forever. You and I must cherish each other and stay together. That's our intended fate."

Gripping Reuben's hands tightly, Renee, with a joyous look said, "I knew Mr. Akagi was wise."

They both began to laugh. Renee still had Reuben's hands in hers. She kissed him deeply on his lips as she let go of his right hand and brought her left hand to caress his face. Renee lifted his left arm as if to place it around her shoulder and as she was about to do so, she gave Reuben a mischievous look and rotated her body to the right under his arm. Renee swiftly swept Reuben's arm down and back up causing him to bend over forward. She pushed Reuben's arm over his back throwing him onto the ground.

Reuben sat up, shaking his head in wonder, with the puppy jumping on his lap yapping joyfully.

Astonished, Reuben looked up to Renee and said, "What kind of cherishing is that?"

Renee knelt next to Reuben and said as she tweaked his nose, "That's kaiten-nagi cherishing, you shoddy farm boy."

Renee rose and began running to the house.

"HEY! Where are you going?" called out Reuben.

"I have to go tell May and the others."

"Wow, Genda-San didn't warn me of painful cherishing," said Reuben to the puppy as he twirled its ears with his fingers. "You know pup, you need a name."

狼

The rest of the evening was filled with joy and laughter. Renee and Reuben were inseparable as the evening passed by until everyone was ready to turn in. Reuben walked Renee to the stairs, hugged, and kissed her goodnight. For the last two days, he still had not set foot on the second floor of the house. He turned to ready the sofa for his night's rest.

"You have grown into such a strong, good man, Reuben," said May helping him spread a quilt.

"Why do you say so, Aunty May?"

"Just look at you. When you came back from Mexico, you were a recluse and the only one who could get you to come out was Renee. Now you are so cheerful with such feelings of love for her. I can't believe it took you seven years to realize you loved her."

Reuben walked to the fireplace where his Kutto leaned. He picked it up and cradled it as if it were an infant. "I didn't need seven years. I loved her long before I left, but I knew… I thought I knew she was already taken, so I had nothing to keep me here. But she never left my mind, soul, and memory. It was as if Renee was within my reach, but like trying to capture the morning mist with my hands. Then I saw her yesterday and learned of her fate. I knew our path began when we first met under the oak tree."

May saw Reuben tremble, and for the first time, noticed a tear fall from his eyes. She placed her arm around his shoulder to comfort him.

"I let her go seven years ago. I can not allow that to happen again. I love her. I always have."

May tightened her embrace for several moments, let go, and stepped in front of Reuben. "Boy, your father would be ever so proud of you. You have done the right thing for all the right reasons and not because you have to, and I know Renee is the happiest girl… woman in the world because of that."

"I'm very happy myself. And I'm very tired. I think all of these seven years is catching up to me, and my… our true life has not yet begun."

"Yes, it has, Reuben, and so far it's wonderful. Now get some sleep. We have to get the house ready for your mother's return. Oh my, we also have to prepare for a wedding." May took the Kutto from Reuben's hands and placed it on top of the mantel rather than leaning it against the fireplace and walked him to the sofa where he laid down. May covered him with the quilt and Reuben was asleep before she had a chance to say goodnight.

From above the stairs, Renee's eyes glistened with tears of joy as she overheard the conversation between Reuben and May. Renee felt a push against her leg and looked down to see the puppy sitting looking up at her wagging its tail. Renee ran her fingers through the puppy's fur and smiled. "We really need to get you a name if you are going to hang around here." She rose and walked into her room. She prepared herself for bed and as she lay down and pulled up the covers, the puppy made a few circles and settled down beneath the bed.

狼

Reuben was up before dawn and under the oak tree training. After his training, he took a walk with his new friend following close at his heels. Although it was Sunday, there were many chores to be done since most of the day before was spent in the city, but he wanted to visit the plot of land for sale he saw yesterday.

Renee awoke and rose out of bed feeling cheerful. She looked to the spot where the puppy laid down last evening, but was gone. Thinking Reuben might be out by the oak tree, she got out of bed and went to the window to take a look, but he was nowhere to be seen. Renee quickly dressed and went down stairs looking for Reuben. She looked all over the house and being unable to find him, she had a horrible thought the last couple of days may have been a dream.

"May, have you seen Reuben?" Renee asked.

"No child, I thought he would be by the tree."

"Whew, it wasn't a dream. He isn't. I looked from my window."

Renee still had panic running through her body and May noticed. She came to her and placed her hands on Renee's shoulders.

"Calm down, Renee. I'm sure he's around here somewhere."

Henry entered through the kitchen door.

"Henry, have you seen Reuben?" asked Renee, quickly.

"Surely, when he finished his... playing by the tree, he and that pooch went walking up the lane to the main road. I don't think he would go too far being he is dressed in that silly get up of his."

Renee thanked Henry and quickly made her way out the front door, off the porch, and up the lane to the road. When Renee reached the road, she looked both ways wondering which way Reuben could have gone. Looking in the direction toward the city, Renee remembered Reuben's interest in Mr. Lester's plot of land. She began to walk in that direction, slowly at first and then picked up her pace to eventually a run.

In the distance, she saw Reuben with the puppy at his side. Just as Henry said, Reuben was, *"Dressed in that silly get up of his."*

Renee slowed her pace and looked at Reuben, feeling déjà vu. Reuben stood in his dark red kosode tucked into his black hakama along with his satin covered Kutto. Sandals with black tabi socks covered his feet and his kasa covered his head. Renee remembered seeing Reuben in a dream wearing similar clothes the day Aarleen was born.

"Reuben!" Renee called out.

Reuben turned and waved. "Renee! Good morning! Come here!" he said, gleefully.

Renee ran to Reuben, took him in her arms, held him tightly, and lightly cried.

"Is everything okay, Renee? What's wrong?" asked Reuben concerned about Renee's tight hug.

"It is now, Reuben. I thought, thought you... a dream."

"You thought I was a dream?" asked Reuben.

Renee looked up and shamefully nodded yes.

"Oh, Renee, my love, I'm real. Here I am and here I'll stay. There's nowhere on earth I'd rather be then by your side," said Reuben, removing his hat letting it hang by its chin strap around his neck. He took her face in his hands and kissed her lovingly on her lips.

Renee let out a little laugh of sheer delight and relief. "I'm sorry to think that, Reuben. What are you doing here?"

"Let me show you, my love. Come," said Reuben, taking Renee's hand.

They walked off the road onto Mr. Lester's plot of land. Reuben motioned with his free hand toward the barn.

"Well, what do you think?" asked Reuben.

"What do I thank about what?"

342

Reuben took both of her hands in his and asked, "Remember yesterday when Mrs. Klaus asked if I was going to be working for you and I said, no because you are too bossy and I have a plan?"

"I remember, but I thought you were joking," replied Renee with a look of curiosity.

"Answer me this, Renee. Do many of the farm children travel into the city to go to school?"

"Only Aar... a few," answered Renee, almost revealing Aarleen by accident. "Once a week on Thursdays, a teacher from the city comes to meet with the children at the county chapel to give lessons and homework. The children turn it in the following week. Sometimes it's Mama who comes. Why?"

"Renee, I have a plan. I've had this plan ever since Tadashi and I started the English school in Itosai. Honesty, Renee, tell me what you think of this, okay?"

"Okay, I guess."

"I'm going to ask Mama to help me get a teaching certificate. Then I'm going to buy this barn from Mr. Lester, donate it to the city school, and make it into a schoolhouse for the children of this area and be its teacher."

Renee looked at Reuben with her big, brown eyes open very wide in fascination.

"Well, Renee, what do you think?"

"THAT'S A FANTASTIC IDEA, REUBEN!!!" shouted Renee as she jumped into Reuben's arms.

"Can you do it, Reuben? Seriously, can you turn this barn into a schoolhouse?"

With a confident look, Reuben said, "I was part of the biggest village relocation and castle construction project in the Hisano Province. I think I can turn this barn into a little schoolhouse."

"And I'll help!" said Renee, enthusiastically.

Reuben removed his kasa from around his neck and placed it on Renee's head and adjusted it. He admired her for a moment and said, "Yep, you'll do for a helper."

"Hey," said Renee, lightly slapping Reuben's shoulder.

"Hmm, brutalizing the boss is it? That will cost you kisses and hugs."

"Only for you, my wonderful husband-to-be," answered Renee.

After a quick look through the barn and the surrounding plot of land, Renee, Reuben, and the pup with no name returned to the farm. Renee and Reuben told the others of Reuben's idea over breakfast, and all thought it was a grand plan. For the longest time, the families had been prompting the city to send out a permanent teacher to the county for the children to be schooled. With all the teachers living in the city, none of them could commit to making the long ride to and from the county to teach school every day. Even Coleen couldn't commit since not only was she teaching classes, she was also becoming involved with school administration. With Reuben living on the farm, he could run an outreach school like the one in Princess Anne County.

"How are you going to pay for that plot of land, Reuben?" asked Noah.

"Let's not worry about that just yet. I need to get certified to teach first," replied Reuben.

"And there should be no difficulties there," added Renee. "Mama has your VMI diploma and ah, military credentials," she added kind of timidly.

"Good, those will come in handy, along with a letter Genda-San gave me when he appointed me English sensei," said Reuben, not concerned about his past military documents.

"What's a... sensei?" asked Henry.

"Teacher," answered Reuben.

When breakfast was finished, the men went to start the chores while May and Renee began seeing to the house.

Rather than change out of his kosode and hakama, Reuben tucked in the legs of his hakama into a pair of habaki leggings. Henry and Noah found it odd, but Reuben assured them this is how he dressed for the last seven years and it was actually more practical. As he did his chores, they tended to agree as he was more active with the roominess of his clothes.

Renee also took notice of Reuben working in his newer style of clothing, but more for lustful reasons causing her to be distracted from her chores.

"Gosh darn it, Renee, will you stop eyeing that boy and see to your work! Coleen and Aarleen will return tomorrow and we have lots to do without you getting all distracted and frisky."

"May!" replied Renee, looking flushed and embarrassed.

The outside chores were being done quickly. Reuben's extra pair of hands was a huge help for Henry and Noah and they were very appreciative. The whole time Reuben was working, the puppy was at his side.

"Okay, pup, if you are going to hang around here, you need to earn your keep," Reuben said to the puppy cradling it in his arms.

Reuben rigged a harness from an old leather tool belt, fit it to the puppy's back and side, and filled it with small tools and materials. Reuben began mending the fencing and got the puppy to recognize the difference between some of the tools and eventually the puppy would give Reuben certain tools when he asked for them. Renee was watching the two and could not help but smile at how adorable they both looked.

"May, come and look at Reuben and the puppy."

"Girl, you are really testing my nerves," May replied as she looked out the window. "Aww... now isn't that the most precious thing you ever did see. For heaven sakes, if Reuben can teach that dog to carry and give him tools, then teaching school will be child's play to him."

Late afternoon came and all the tools were put away. Reuben removed the habaki from his legs allowing his hakama to hang open. He retrieved his jo and began his evening training. Renee came out and sat quietly watching and admiring as she ran her hand over the puppy's fur. She could not get over how graceful Reuben moved and how focused he was. He didn't even flinch when May called out to Renee. She looked toward May and saw her motion to her feverishly to come to the house. She looked back to Reuben. He was still in motion with the jo. She stood up and whispered to the puppy to stay.

She quickly walked back to the house when May ran up to her.

"Coleen, Monroe, and Aarleen are back and Lucy and Andy are with them. They just pulled off the main road onto the lane."

"Good heavens, they're early. What do we do?"

"Well first of all, let's go greet them. You go meet them in the front of the house and I'll go fetch Henry and Noah," said May.

They bumped into each other as they headed off on their assigned tasks and quickly split and ran off in different directions.

Renee made her way through the house to the front door and stepped onto the porch just in time to see Monroe help Coleen down from the carriage.

"Mama!" shouted Aarleen jumping off the carriage, nearly causing Monroe to fall backwards.

Renee ran to Aarleen and opened her arms wide, scooped her up, and hugged her tightly.

"How was your trip, sweetie? Were you a good girl? You didn't give GrandMama any grief now did you?"

"She was a perfect angel," answered Coleen. "How are you, my dear? You look so radiant, more radiant than usual. Anything been going on I should know about?"

"Everything is wonderful, Mama. I have some very exciting news. Come here quick Monroe and Lucy, you have got to hear this too."

Just then, May, Henry, and Noah came to greet Coleen, and the others. "Have you told them yet, Renee?" asked Noah.

"Told us what?" replied Lucy holding Andy anxiously.

Renee held up her hand and shook her head no. She lowered Aarleen to the ground and knelt in front of her. Renee took her little hands in hers. Renee's eyes began to glisten with tears.

"Mama, are you crying?"

"Yes, sweetie, but it's a happy cry."

Coleen was getting very anxious and knelt down also and put her hand on Renee's shoulder. "What's happening?"

Renee kept her focus on Aarleen. "Remember when you told me about the dream you had with GrandDa climbing off a horse with the help of the man in red armor telling you your Da will return soon?"

"Yes Mama."

Coleen felt her heart skip a beat and quickly brought her hands to her mouth as she let out a gasp. Lucy dropped to her knees, her eyes wide open and pulling Andy closer against her body. Monroe brought his hand to his forehead and felt his stomach twist.

"Well, my precious little angel, I have an early birthday present to give you this evening and you will find it out by the oak tree.

"Really, Mama, an early birthday present I can keep?"

"Forever and ever, sweetie, now go see it."

Renee then looked at Coleen and nodded yes. "He's home."

"Okay, Mama. Are you coming too?"

"Yes sweetie. We all are coming, but you must go first."

Aarleen hugged Renee and ran off to the oak tree. Renee, Coleen, and Lucy all stood up.

"Reuben, my Reuben is back?" asked Coleen with glee.

"Yes, Mama, he arrived two days ago, but please... wait. I haven't told him about Aarleen and he asked me to be his wife last evening."

Lucy looked at Andy and said, "Did you hear that, Andy? Your Uncle Reuben is home." Lucy wrapped her free arm around Renee and said to her, "I guess I won't have to keep reminding you of Reuben's secret anymore, sister."

"Listen, I'll wait, but I must at least watch Aarleen meet Reuben from the kitchen window," said Coleen as she made her way into the house. Everyone followed and roamed into the kitchen to peer out of the window with the exception of Monroe who remained behind with a look of dread in his eyes.

狼

Aarleen skipped along the edge of the planting field and came to a stop when she saw a man twirling a stick. He was a handsome man, just as handsome as his picture Renee would show Aarleen every day. He had dark, brown hair, just like hers.

What's he doing? Why is he wearing a dress? Hey, he looks like one of those men in the turtle armor from my dreams. All these thoughts were racing through her mind as she made her way cautiously toward Reuben.

She was afraid to speak to him.

The puppy, seeing Aarleen coming, stood up, and trotted over to her, wagging his tail. She lowered herself and ran her little fingers through the puppy's fur.

"What's your doggie's name?"

Reuben was startled out of his training for the first time ever since he started learning the ways of Bushido, and fell to the ground on his back side. He lifted himself up onto his elbows and in front of him stood a child seven years of age looking at him with familiar eyes. He smiled and walked up to her on his knees.

"Hello, what's your name?" Reuben asked.

"Aarleen," she replied with a smile.

"That's a pretty name."

"My Mama named me after my GrandDa and GrandMama."

Reuben smiled. He had a warm, nice smile and Aarleen continued to smile back at him.

Suddenly Reuben's smiling face turned into a face of question. GrandDa, GrandMama? That's what Monroe, Lucy, and I called our grandparents, thought Reuben as he gazed into Aarleen's adorable smiling face.

"What's your GrandDa's and GrandMama's names, Aarleen?" asked Reuben.

"My GrandDa's name is Aaron and my GrandMama's name is Coleen. Mama put them together like my middle name, Moncy for my Uncle Monroe and Aunty Lucy. Isn't that clever?"

Reuben knelt higher and gently took one of her little hands in his. He looked at it and then looked back at Aarleen's smiling face. Suddenly he realized he was looking into Renee's eyes.

"Mama said you would come back someday, and GrandDa told me he would look for you when he went away and help you come home."

Renee walked up behind Aarleen and was looking down at both of them. Reuben looked up to Renee, his face gleaming with happiness. Renee nodded yes to him.

Reuben stood up and took Aarleen in his hands and lifted her in the air startling her.

"Hey!" said Aarleen giggling.

Reuben lowered Aarleen, but still held onto her. "Do you know who I am?" he asked.

"You're my Da."

With Aarleen in one arm, he took Renee in his other while the rest of the family came running out of the house.

Renee took Reuben's face into her hands, kissed him, and with a bright smile said, "Surprise my love, it's a girl."

He laughed with joy as he held onto Aarleen, determined never to let her go. Aarleen finally had her arms around the man her mother had been telling her about. The puppy was also leaping, barking, and wagging its tail.

"Hey, you still didn't tell me your doggie's name, Da."

Reuben laughed, "You're right, I didn't. He doesn't have a name."

"A boy doggie with no name, that's not right. He has to have a name."

"How about you give him a name," replied Reuben.

Aarleen looked down at the puppy and back to Reuben. "Can we call him Riley?"

"Yes we can." He set Aarleen on the ground. She knelt down and took Riley into her arms.

"Hi, Riley, I'm Aarleen and that's my Da."

Reuben embraced Renee and looked into her eyes. "Blessed gods of the high mountains, Renee, she's beautiful."

Renee smiled and hugged Reuben. She felt his arms release her and looked up to his face. Reuben's attention was focused over Renee's shoulder. She let go of Reuben and turned to see Coleen standing behind her.

Renee stepped aside as Reuben walked to his mother.

"Reuben, my son, is it really you?"

In silence, Reuben took Coleen in his arms and hugged her tightly.

With tears falling from his eyes, he said, "I received your letter. I'm home, Mama."

Coleen and Reuben held each other for several long moments, both with tears in their eyes.

"I hear you're a father now these days," said Coleen, softly in her son's ear.

Reuben let out a soft laugh and said, "Isn't she beautiful, Mama? She looks just like her mother."

347

Renee lifted Aarleen with her left arm and caressed Reuben's back with her right hand. Reuben immediately pulled Renee and Aarleen into his embrace with Coleen.

"I also hear you are taking on a wife. I hope you asked her father for her hand," Coleen said with a hint of amusement.

Both Renee and Reuben laughed at the thought.

"Not likely, but if he did, I would have liked to have seen that discussion," said Monroe.

Reuben let go of Coleen, Renee, and Aarleen. He turned to face Monroe. Reuben took his brother by the shoulders saying, "Monroe, my brother. Look at you! I see you have continued Da's law practice. That is so honorable of you and I am very proud." Reuben embraced Monroe tightly and continued, "I have a feeling I'll be in need of your services in the near future."

"Not home for more than three days and you're already getting yourself into trouble? You haven't changed little brother."

Laughter ensued after Monroe's comment except from Reuben when he caught sight of his little sister, Lucy.

He released his hold on Monroe and stepped toward Lucy. "You must be Mrs. Klaus," said Reuben as he opened his arms to her.

Lucy ran into Reuben's open arms and wrapped hers around him tightly letting out seven years of emotion doing so. "Oh, Reuben…"

"I've missed you so much, baby sister, so very much."

With Aarleen still in her arms, Renee couldn't help bringing her free hand to her mouth as she let out an emotional gasp. The memory of Lucy when she told Renee her secret of Reuben being her favorite brother when they first met came back to Renee so vividly.

"I'm not supposed to pick, but Reuben is my favorite brother. Monroe is great, but I guess since he's the oldest, he's more like a grown up. Reuben is fun and he plays with me all the time. We sometimes play jokes on Monroe. Yep, I love both my brothers very much, but I like Reuben the best. You won't tell anyone will you? Like I said, I'm not supposed to pick."

As Renee watched Lucy and Reuben, it was apparent to her, Lucy was Reuben's favorite sibling as well.

"I never forgot your secret for Renee, my brother. Her love for you never faltered because of your secret you gave me. Did I do good Reuben? Did I?"

Reuben looked to Renee and held out his hand to her. Renee stepped forward, still holding onto Aarleen, and took Reuben's hand tightly. Reuben pulled them into his embrace with Lucy.

"You did wonders, my precious sister, and you honor me."

Together the four stood with their arms holding each other until a small voice came from below.

"Mommy?" said Lucy's son, Andy.

Reuben looked down to see his nephew for the first time. He turned to the little boy. "And you must be my nephew," said Reuben. "What's your name?"

Andy looked up to Reuben. To Andy, his uncle looked menacing in his strange clothes and strong looking features, yet he wasn't afraid. There was something about this man that spread cheer and joy.

"My name is Andrew, but everyone calls me Andy."

Reuben knelt down and took Andy's right hand in his and gave it a shake and said, "Well Andy, my name is Reuben and everyone calls me... Reuben."

Andy laughed and replied, "Because that's your name."

"But in Japan, they call me Okami."

Renee cocked her head sideways in wonder. I'm going to have to ask him about this, she thought.

"Okay, if nobody is going to ask, then I will," said Aarleen. "Why is my Da wearing a dress?" she asked, dropping her hands in a questioning manner.

狼

Eventually the family gathered into the dining room. May conjured up a quick meal for everyone, and they all sat around the large dining room table eating a dish of leftover ham and potatoes from lunch earlier.

Reuben also sat at the table in his usual seat with Aarleen on his lap and Renee standing behind him with her arms resting on his shoulders.

Both Coleen and Renee had concerning looks on their faces when they noticed Monroe took the seat at the head of the table used by Aaron, which he never done before out of respect for his father. Although he showed delight to see Reuben, it was still evident he wasn't as joyous as everyone else.

"Tell us about Japan, Reuben. How is Mr. Akagi?" asked Lucy, wiping Andy's mouth with a napkin.

"Oh this is amazing, Lucy," said Noah. "Tell them about the castle you helped build, Reuben."

Aarleen looked up to Reuben and asked, "Really, Da, you built a castle? Was it like King Arthur's castle in Camelot?"

"Not exactly, little one," answered Reuben. He went on to tell the story of Hisano Castle and all that was involved in the project. Reuben spoke of why Akagi Genda-San wanted to build the castle and how he put Reuben's ideas into action.

"Tell Mama, about the school you and your friend Tadashi started," said Renee.

"School?" asked Coleen very interested.

"That right, Mama. At first Genda-San's son, Masaru, asked if I could teach him English after I smacked my thumb with a hammer and heard me say, son of a..."

Renee quickly smacked Reuben lightly on his cheek to stop him from finishing the phrase.

Reuben flinched and said, "Oh, yeah, sorry. Anyway, Genda-San thought it was a good idea, so he assigned me and Tadashi as English sensei, or teacher. Before I left, we had nearly all of Itosai speaking English."

"Amazing! How on earth were you able to accomplish this task?" asked Coleen.

"Kind of the same way Tadashi taught me Japanese and how samurai train to fight, repetition, repetition, repetition."

"You know how to speak Japanese, Reuben?" asked Lucy.

"Hai, watashi wa nihonjin, rūshī o hanasu hōhō o shitte imasu ka. Yes, I do know how to speak Japanese, Lucy."

"That's amazing," said Lucy.

"So that's why you have a slight accent, Reuben," observed Coleen.

"Darn, I was hoping you wouldn't notice." replied Reuben.

"But isn't it the most adorable accent you have ever heard coming out of your son, Mama?" Renee said as she leaned down and kissed him on the cheek and Aarleen on the forehead.

"Oh, my goodness!" exclaimed Lucy.

Renee looked up and asked, "What's wrong, Lucy?"

"Nothing, it's just so great seeing you and Reuben holding each other freely after all these years, especially, you know, before when you two wanted to so much, but couldn't."

"Oh, Lucy, you have no idea. For the last three days, those two have been holding each other so much it has been... wonderful," said Henry, which got surprised looks from everyone.

Everyone that is, except from Monroe. "So now that you're home, what are you going to do? Run this farm?" asked Monroe rather condescending.

Reuben ignored Monroe's tone, but Renee didn't. Reuben looked to his mother and said, "Well, Mama, this is where you come in."

"Oh yes!" said Renee, excitedly. "Tell them your idea, my dearest."

"What idea?" asked Coleen.

"Well, Mama, I had this idea ever since I started teaching English in Itosai. You know I have aspired to become a teacher and I seem to have a knack for it. Well, I wonder if you can help me acquire a teaching certificate."

"Really, of course I can, Reuben. That's wonderful, but where would you teach? There are no openings for any teachers in the city," said Coleen.

"Tell them about the barn, Reuben," said Henry.

Reuben nodded. "When I receive a teaching certificate, I want to turn the Wilcox barn on that plot of land Mr. Lester has for sale into a schoolhouse for the children in this area, and I'll teach there. That way there will be a full-time teacher here, like in Princess Anne County."

"Isn't that a great idea, Mama?" asked Renee.

"It is indeed, but Reuben, the city school won't buy that plot of land especially for the price Mr. Lester is asking," answered Coleen.

Reuben nodded and said, "I'm going to buy it and donate it to the school. That's where Monroe comes in with the legality portion of the donation."

"You buy it? With what?" asked Monroe in disbelief.

Reuben gave Aarleen a kiss on her cheek and said to her, "Hey, little one, can you do me a favor and bring me my haversack hanging on the hook by the backdoor please?"

Renee noticed when Reuben spoke to Aarleen, and also to Andy, he spoke to them as he would speak to an adult. It concerned her for a moment until she saw how quickly Aarleen responded to Reuben's request.

"Okay, Da, I'll be right back. Save my seat."

As Aarleen hopped off his lap and ran off to retrieve Reuben's haversack, he told everyone in the room his purpose for his journey to Japan wasn't to earn money. He said the entire time he had been living in Itosai, he never touched any form of money, except in the form of rice.

"Rice, they use rice as currency? That's bazaar," said Monroe.

"That's what I told Tadashi when he first told me, but yes, in certain cases, rice is used as a form of payment," answered Reuben.

Reuben went on to explain while he lived in the village, he worked for his meals and clothing and never considered the thought of currency of any type. That was until Akagi Genda-San visited Reuben in his hotel room the evening before he left.

By this time, Aarleen returned with Reuben's haversack.

"Gee, Da, this is heavy," she said, lifting it onto the table and leaping back onto his lap.

"Thank you, my little blossom," Reuben said as he unbuckled the strap and lifted open the flap.

Renee smiled when she heard Reuben call Aarleen, little blossom. She thought that was so adorable.

"Genda-San never discussed with me about any form of wages or allowances for all my work I contributed to the community. Yet, he did have an account for me and he never told me about it until the night before I left."

Reuben pulled out the string of gold, silver, and copper coins. "These were contributions from the villagers to help pay my way back home. As you can see, this is much more than I needed."

Renee pointed to the gold coins on the string saying, "These are like the ones on your locket chain."

Suddenly Reuben took hold of the two gold coins hanging next to the silver locket from his neck and remembered what Akagi Genda-San said to Reuben when he gave them to him.

"I have two more gold coins to give you, but you must keep them for something special. Think of these two coins as your future, a future of bonding."

Reuben turned his attention back to everyone else as he untied the string and removed two gold coins. He pulled out a small ball of string and his tanto dagger. As he continued to talk

351

about Akagi Genda-San's visit to his room, Reuben cut two lengths of string with his tanto and slipped a gold coin on each. He tied one around Aarleen's neck and one around Andy's, and each looked at their coins admiringly.

Monroe looked at the string of coins questionably and said, "Surely there isn't enough there to purchase the plot of land for the price Mr. Lester is asking."

"Probably not with what's left, but there is with what Genda-San paid me," said Reuben.

Reuben pulled out the burgundy silk bag. He untied the cord, opened the bag, and took out the twenty five gold oban coins Akagi Genda-San presented to him. Reuben dropped them one at a time onto the table, each one making a heavy "clank" as they landed on top of one another.

"Good heavens, Reuben! How much is one of these worth?" asked Renee as she picked one up to have a closer look.

"Three should be more than enough to buy that plot of land for the price Mr. Lester is asking. I think Genda-San was a little too generous."

Coleen brought her hands to her face as she said, "Oh my dear, Reuben. I'll certainly discuss your proposal with the superintendent and the board."

"Please, Mama, don't tell them about the plot of land until after I receive a teaching certificate. I don't want to lead the officials into believing I'm trying to buy my way into a position," said Reuben.

"Oh, that's very admirable," commented Monroe rather contemptuously.

Lucy gave Monroe an angered look and replied in a more positive manner, "Yes, Reuben, that is very admirable. A suggestion Mr. Akagi would full heartedly approve."

"Indeed, Lucy," replied Coleen, also giving Monroe an angered look. "You're right, Reuben. We shall wait until we get you certified before moving onto the property issue."

Renee was also angered at Monroe's attitude toward Reuben. The entire time, Monroe had been cold toward his brother, whereas Reuben remained pleasant and respectful in return. She shook off her anger, and added to the conversation by saying enthusiastically, "I told Reuben you have his VMI diploma and military documents."

"Good, I do have those back at the city home, Reuben," said Coleen, but let out a slight sigh after. "If only you had documentation about teaching in Japan."

Reuben reached into his haversack and pulled out a bamboo tube. He lifted Aarleen from his lap, sat her on the table, and rose from his seat. Removing the end cover attached to the tube with a silk cord, Reuben pulled out a rolled document.

"Renee, can you please help me and take this end?" asked Reuben.

Renee took hold of the edge of the document as Reuben unrolled the page and lowered it onto the table. The document was beautifully written in kanji by Akagi Genda-San with his official seal.

"Oh my gracious, this is beautiful. What's it say, Reuben?" asked Coleen.

"This is Genda-San's decree of assigning Tadashi and me as English sensei. It says…

I, Akagi Genda,
Daimyo of the Itosai Region of Hisano Province
Assign Duran Reuben-San and Sora Tadashi-San
As Sensei of English to the citizens of
The Itosai Region
They are hereby granted the title of
Sensei
And be giving full honors and respects.
Akagi Genda, Lord and Master of
Itosai Region.

"Daimyo, what's that?" asked Monroe.

"Regional Lord. Think of him as our state governor, except he isn't elected. Regions are ruled mostly by clan dynasties," answered Reuben.

"I'll take this as well, along with your other documents when I speak with the superintendent and board about your application as soon as I get back to the city after Aarleen's birthday," said Coleen taking one last look at Akagi Genda-San's scroll before Renee carefully rolled it up and placed it back in the tube.

"BIRTHDAY!" exclaimed Reuben as he looked at Aarleen in surprise. "When is your birthday?"

"Tuesday, I'm going to be seven and you are my birthday wish come true!" answered Aarleen.

Reuben's left hand quickly went to his chest as he let out a gasp startling everyone including both Aarleen and Andy.

"Seven years. Seven years. Renee, it was seven years come Tuesday I got this scar. I heard you call my name in my mind."

Renee wrapped her arms around Reuben, placing one of her hands above his hand grasping the scar.

"The day Aarleen was born I called your name because I felt you were in danger. Moments later, I felt as if you were safe," said Renee softly in Reuben's ear.

"You did save my life."

"What are those two gold coins for?" asked Aarleen, pointing to the coins hanging from Reuben's neck next to the locket.

"These are for your Mama and me," answered Reuben.

"For us?" asked Renee taking them in her fingers.

Reuben nodded. "Genda-San said these are to be used for something special. To be thought of as our future, a future of bonding. Does Mr. Elps still do metal work, Renee?"

"Yes he does, why?"

"You and I need to have him melt these down for our future bonding, our wedding rings."

353

Renee had a look of amazement in her face as she said, "Geez oh geez oh geez you were right, Reuben. Mr. Akagi knew the whole time about us."

The emotional moment, felt by nearly everyone was interrupted as Monroe scooted out Aaron's chair and stood up.

"Well, I hate put an end to this touching moment, but I must get back to Norfolk."

"Nonsense, Monroe," said Coleen. "It's too late to ride back to the city."

"Nonetheless, I must be back in Norfolk early. I must file the case I worked on this past week."

"Come on, Monroe, we can share the parlor," said Reuben.

"No thanks brother, I remember the last time I shared a room with you. I ended up with a torn nightshirt and a sore shoulder," said Monroe.

"Monroe…" pleaded Coleen.

"No, really, Mama. I really need to get this case filed, but I'll be back for Aarleen's birthday party. Noah, can you please give me a hand with the luggage?"

"I'll help you, Monroe," said Reuben.

"No thanks, I don't want you to ruin your… fancy clothes."

Monroe bid farewell to everyone and made his way out of the dining room. After a few moments of hesitation, Noah followed.

"It seems like Uncle Monroe is mad at you, Da. Why?" asked Aarleen.

"Sweetie, Uncle Monroe isn't mad…" Renee started to say before Reuben placed his arm around her shoulder and pulled her close to him.

"Your Uncle Monroe is mad because I ran away a long time ago and now I have returned, little blossom."

"But wouldn't that make him happy, Uncle Reuben?" asked Andy, now sitting on Lucy's lap.

"Yeah," agreed Aarleen.

Reuben looked into Renee's eyes and answered, "No, it makes him angrier, I'm afraid."

Reuben let out a sigh and looked to Coleen and continued, "He better get used to it because I'm not going anywhere."

In the year of our Lord, 1855, a romantic tale continues.
As love intended, and a prosperous life…

Here I am and here I'll Stay

Aarleen was woken up by Riley lapping her cheek early Monday morning, the day before her birthday. She giggled as she tried pushing away his snout.

"Be quiet, Riley. You're going to wake Andy."

"AHIT!!!"

A sharp loud yell coming from outside the bedroom window caused Aarleen to rise up in the bed she and her cousin were sharing in Lucy's old room. Riley's ears perked up as he glanced toward the window. His tail started wagging, smacking Aarleen in her face. Riley leaped off the bed and quickly trotted out of the room.

"Riley, where are you going?" whispered Aarleen.

"AHOP!!!"

Aarleen rolled out of bed and tiptoed to the window to peer outside to see what was causing the noise. As she leaned out of the window, she heard the back kitchen door close and saw Riley run toward the oak tree. It was then as she watched Riley when she saw her father dressed as he was the evening before, slashing and cutting the air with a sword.

"He looks like those men in a dream I had," Aarleen said as she continued to watch.

"What did you say, Aarleen?" asked Andy, rousted from his sleep.

"Nothing, Andy, go back to sleep."

"Psst," went Renee from the door, gaining Aarleen's attention.

Aarleen turned to see Renee motioning her to come to the door. She quietly made her way across the room to Renee's open arms. Renee lifted Aarleen and said quietly, "Good morning, sweetie. Were you watching Da?"

"Yes, Mama, what's he doing?"

"How about we go and find out?"

Silently Renee carried Aarleen down the stairs, through the parlor, and out of the kitchen where they were met by May, who greeted them as they went out the kitchen door.

They were nearing the oak tree when they were greeted by Riley. Renee lowered down to rub him between his ears and whispered into Aarleen's ear.

"You want me to say what, Mama?"

"Just what I told you when I give you a wink, okay? It'll make your Da laugh, just you watch."

Hand-in-hand, Renee and Aarleen walked closer to the oak tree. Renee could not help but admire Reuben's movements. It was hard for her to believe such graceful, flowing moves are a means of defending and attacking. He is finally mine, she thought as she and Aarleen stopped next to the huge trunk of the oak tree.

With a mischievous grin, Renee asked in a girlish-like way, "Wha'cha doing?"

Just as Aarleen did the evening before, Renee caused Reuben's concentration to be broken as he dropped his shoulders and began to chuckle and shake his head.

As Reuben turned to face Renee and Aarleen, he said, "I'm practicing draw and return katas."

Renee lifted Aarleen in her arms and gave her a wink, prompting Aarleen to reply, "You're doing it wrong."

Reuben returned his Kutto to its saya and laughed loudly as he remembered the day he and Renee first met under the oak tree.

When his laugher died down, Reuben came to Renee and took Aarleen from her and hugged her. "Good morning, my little cherry blossom. Did your Mama tell you to say that?"

Cherry blossom... that's cute, thought Renee.

"She said it would make you laugh and it did!" she said, grinning ear-to-ear.

"That it did," said Reuben as he hugged Renee with his free arm, and kissed her lips.

"I assume you didn't tell her you ate a worm after?" Reuben added after Renee kissed him back.

"You ate a worm? That's yucky, Mama," said Aarleen making a sour face.

"Hey, I did not eat that worm. I spit that half back into the pail."

"So what are you doing up so early?" Reuben asked Aarleen.

Aarleen pointed her thumb to her chest and with a voice of pride said, "I always get up early. I have assigned chores to do before breakfast."

"Oh, well, we mustn't keep you from them now. Tell me what you have to do," said Reuben, impressed.

"I have to get the hens out of their house and collect the eggs so Mama and I can take them to Mr. and Mrs. Klaus' store. Wanna watch me?"

"Of course," answered Reuben. "And what chores do you have this morning, my bride-to-be?" Reuben added as he looked to Renee.

"May and I will be starting breakfast. We have an early day because we have lots to do. Someone has a birthday tomorrow and we have to get ready for a party."

Coleen was in the kitchen helping May with breakfast and was delighted to see Reuben helping Aarleen with her chore of collecting eggs. After the eggs were collected and brought in to be washed, Renee took Aarleen upstairs to help her get washed and dressed for the day.

Reuben, Henry, and Noah hitched up the team to the wagon. Once the team was hitched, they loaded some finished furniture pieces for delivery to the mercantile, along with some other produce items.

When that was finished, Reuben went into the house to wash up and get dressed. He entered the dining room as everyone was being seated. Every seat was taken with the exception of the chair Aaron would occupy. Rather than take that seat, Reuben went to where Aarleen was seated next to Renee. He lifted Aarleen from her chair, sat down, and sat her on his lap while giving her a hug and kiss on the cheek. She responded with a cheerful, adorable smile and giggle.

Coleen nodded approvingly.

"Now that's the brother I'm used to seeing," laughed Lucy.

Reuben was dressed in his knee high leather boots, black trousers held at the waist with the Akagi obi of burgundy, and a common black band collar shirt with the top three buttons undone.

Lucy added, "I see your taste in dress really hasn't changed, except for what you wore last evening."

"And I wouldn't have him any other way," commented Renee as she took his hand.

Again, the blessing was given, this time by Coleen, especially giving thanks for Reuben's return.

"So when is the big day, you two?" asked Noah once everyone began eating.

"Yeah, Noah's right. We've got to get you two married," added Lucy.

Renee and Reuben looked at each other, shrugging their shoulders and shaking their heads, wondering.

Reuben looked to Coleen and said, "I'm not sure this would be appropriate, but how about Saturday?"

"Why do you think that would not be appropriate, son?" asked Coleen.

"That's the day after Da passed on. I want to marry Renee as soon as possible, but I'm not sure the timing is appropriate because of that solemn day," answered Reuben.

"I think GrandDa would like that," said Aarleen taking a bite out of a biscuit.

Everyone at the table looked at Aarleen with amazed surprise.

"Why do you say that, sweetie?" asked Renee.

"Because Friday we are going to spend the day at GrandDa's resting place and we'll probably be sad. I think GrandDa would want us to be happy the next day to see Mama and Da get married. I know I will. Also, Uncle Eric will be here."

Renee rose out of her seat and came to give Aarleen a hug and looked to Reuben.

Reuben nodded and said, "In that case, we had better go see Mr. Elps today after our trip into the city about getting Genda-San's coins made into rings because Saturday, you, Renee Wallace, are going to become Renee Duran under our oak tree. Does that answer your question, Noah?"

"That's not enough time to put together a wedding!" said Coleen with concern.

"Trust me, Mama, that's more than enough time," replied Renee as she and Reuben gazed into each other's eyes.

After breakfast and the dishes were cleaned and put away, Henry and Noah began their daily routine outside as May did hers on the inside. Coleen wasn't planning on going into the city with the others, but she was eager to discuss Reuben's application for a teaching certificate with the superintendent. The plan was for everyone, other than May, Henry, and Noah, to ride into the city. They would drop off Coleen at the school administrator's office and the rest would go on about their business at the mercantile. Reuben also wanted to visit with Monroe with hopes they could have a more pleasant visit than the one last evening. Renee described her idea of the perfect wedding, including Monroe as Reuben's best man, so Reuben wanted to ease any tensions between him and his brother.

As Coleen and Renee took their seat on the bench of the wagon, Lucy, Aarleen, and Andy sat on some of the stools made by Henry and Noah to be delivered to the mercantile. Reuben did one final check to see if all was secured and when he was satisfied, he slid his jo behind the bench, and climbed aboard the wagon. He looked at Aarleen and he motioned for her to come and sit on his lap, which she did enthusiastically.

With a quick snap of the reins, the team pulled away from the barn and they were on their way to the city. As they neared Mr. Lester's plot of land, Reuben pointed out to Coleen and Lucy how he could convert the barn into a decent schoolhouse. Coleen could see Reuben's descriptions as both he and Renee described what the finished building would look like.

"I bet Henry and Noah can make some teeter totters for recesses," said Aarleen.

"Now that's a good idea, sweetie," replied Renee.

"Once the school is up and going, perhaps Andy can spend a week at the farm and attend school here," added Lucy. "This coming year is going to be his first year."

"Is that right, Andy?" asked Reuben.

"Sure is, Uncle Reuben. Aarleen has been showing me what she learned her first year and I can't wait."

As they rode on, Coleen continued to advise Reuben of what to expect once she arranged an interview. For the time being, Coleen said she would tell the superintendent the plan is to use the county chapel, with the reverend's permission, until a permanent location can be arranged.

"Tell them I'll teach in the front yard if I have to," said Reuben.

Coleen assured Reuben it wouldn't matter as long as there was a permanently located teacher in the county.

In the city, they made their way past the school and on to the superintendent's office where Reuben helped his mother off the wagon. She told Reuben when they were done with their errands to pick her up at the house.

Lucy took Coleen's place on the bench, with Andy on her lap, next to Renee. Reuben took his seat and Aarleen moved from Renee's lap onto Reuben's. With another quick snap of the reins, they were off to the mercantile.

Reuben noticed a familiar landmark which sparked a mischievous idea as Renee and Lucy were discussing the wedding. Since they were not paying attention to Reuben, he whispered into Aarleen's ear. When he was done, Aarleen nodded and said, "Okay, Da."

At the next intersection, Reuben made a right turn onto Wickham Avenue when Lucy said, "Hey, this isn't the way to the store."

"Are you sure? I could be wrong. It's been a long time and my directions may be off," replied Reuben.

Renee narrowed her eyes at Reuben saying, "Wait a minute. You turned down this way on purpose! You know my old school is right there, don't you? Don't you say what I know you're going to say... don't you even think it!"

Lucy laughed as Reuben kept his eyes focused straight ahead trying hard to keep from laughing himself.

"That's right, Reuben Duran. You just keep your mouth shut," warned Renee.

Reuben gave Aarleen a nudge and she said, "Mama is a Wickham girl!"

"Aarleen!" exclaimed Renee as she slapped Reuben on his shoulder. "I know you put her up to this, you shoddy farm boy!"

"Come on, my precious, wave to your alma mater!"

Renee continued to slap Reuben's shoulder a few more times before she wrapped her arms around him and Aarleen, laughing and hugging them both.

After their little detour, they finally made it to the Norfolk Klaus Mercantile. They were met with happy greetings, especially for Lucy and Andy. After Andrew helped Reuben unload the wagon, they all enjoyed a pleasant visit. After half an hour, Reuben excused himself to visit with Monroe. Renee asked if he wanted her to accompany him.

"No, Renee, I think I should see Monroe alone."

Renee nodded and wished him luck after a kiss.

Reuben exited the store, retrieved his jo from the wagon, and made his way to Monroe's law office. It was by sheer habit Reuben had his jo. In Itosai, he earned the right to wear a sword, but he never felt right to do so unless it was standing the guard or when there was a threat. He did, however, always carry his jo. Carrying his jo in the streets of Norfolk didn't get any notice. For all the other citizens, it was just an extra-long walking stick not being used for walking.

The walk to Monroe's law office took less than fifteen minutes. Reuben entered and was greeted by Lorena, Aaron's secretary, who now worked for Monroe. Lorena recognized Reuben as soon as he entered the office and came around her desk to greet him. Upon hearing Lorena say Reuben's name, Monroe, sitting in his office, dropped his head momentarily and then rose from his desk.

"Ah, brother, what can I do for you?" asked Monroe as he emerged from his office.

"Monroe, I was hoping we can talk. I have some wonderful news."

"Please, come into my office," replied Monroe.

"Lorena, it has been a pleasure seeing you," said Reuben to Lorena as he made his way to Monroe's office, previously used by their father.

"You as well, Reuben," replied Lorena.

As Reuben entered the office, Monroe motioned him to have a seat opposite their father's desk, now occupied by Monroe. Before sitting, Reuben walked around the room looking at the old framed documents until he came to Monroe's diploma from William and Mary.

"This is very nice, Monroe. William and Mary, very impressive. I'm sorry I wasn't there for your graduation."

"I'm sure you had your hands full in Japan. Besides, Renee was there and having her there was the same as you being there yourself, in a way."

Reuben nodded, still admiring the document on the wall.

"So, Reuben, what's this wonderful news you mentioned?"

Reuben took the offered seat and said cheerfully, "Saturday, Renee and I are getting married and I want you to be my best man."

Monroe brought his hand to his forehead in disbelief. He also felt a stabbing sensation in his stomach. Letting out a nervous chuckle, he said, "I bet everyone says it's about time, correct?"

"I guess you can say that, but what do you say? Can you be my best man?"

Monroe took in a deep breath and let it out slowly. "I'm sorry, Reuben, I can't. I have to be in Richmond this weekend. I leave Friday on the morning train."

"Morning train? That means you won't be with us to visit Da."

"It can't be helped, Reuben. Last minute notice. Remember when Da told us he couldn't make it to some of our school functions because of one case or another and we thought it wasn't true? Well, it was all true. Da was a very busy man."

"No doubt. Well, I can talk with Renee. I'm sure she'll agree to postpone until you get back."

"No, Reuben. If there's one thing this profession has taught me is never change your set date and time, especially for a wedding. Besides, you and Renee have been waiting for this long before you ran off to Japan."

Reuben's expression went sour the way Monroe said *ran off to Japan*. It made him think of how distant Monroe seemed last evening.

"Monroe, what's the matter?"

"What do you mean?"

"Between us. I know you and I haven't been particularly close, but we always were there for each other."

Monroe took in another deep breath, blew it out, and said, "You haven't been here for the last seven years and it was I who kept Mama, Da, and Lucy together."

"You're right, Monroe, and I have no excuse. You also cared for Renee."

"No, Reuben, that was all Mama and Da, and what they couldn't do for her, she did for herself. Renee is a very strong woman, especially after what you put her through."

"Me?" answered Reuben with a tone of anger.

"Yes, you, Reuben, but don't take that the wrong way. That woman never lost faith and love in you. Yes there may have been once or twice she had her doubts, but Lucy was right there with your little secret to remind her of your unfaltering love. And even in those rare moments of doubt, her love for you never faltered either. Damn it, Reuben! That girl is stronger than any of us in this family of ours, even you."

"I know," said Reuben as he took hold of the locket and gold coins hanging from his neck. "I know, Monroe. When I went to Japan, I gave up my family. She gave up her life. But I intend to give her another one. A life she deserves."

"And that's why you must not postpone your wedding just because I can't be there," said Monroe with sincerity.

Reuben nodded and rose. Monroe did as well.

"I suppose you're right, Monroe. You'll be missed."

"I know."

"You will be at Aarleen's birthday party tomorrow, right?"

"I can't say. I'm still finishing up this last case from last week, but I'll try."

Again Reuben nodded. "Let's hope. I have to pick up Renee and Aarleen. Lucy and Andy will be staying with Andrew and Annabelle for the night. Mama is at the house waiting for us to take her back to the farm."

"Mama came home?"

"Yes, she wanted to arrange an interview for me."

"Ah yes, the teaching idea. Really, Reuben, that's a great idea. Seriously, I wish you the best of luck and not to worry, if there are any legal issues pertaining to donating that property, I'll take care of it for you. Let me just tell you right away, I know you want to get started as soon as possible, but I suggest you hold off on donating that property until you have finished building the schoolhouse."

"Why's that?"

"If it's your property, you can build the schoolhouse the way you want, but if you donate the property before you do, then the city will get involved and they will build it the way they want, more than likely using cheap materials, and they will take their time about it. That's just the way government works. Get the community involved as to what they want, and you will have a schoolhouse that represents your community, and not the city."

"That's great advice. I'll do just that. Thank you, Monroe."

Monroe walked Reuben to the main entrance of the office and shook his hand. He watched Reuben walk off out of sight, and he turned to see Lorena looking at him with an angered look.

"What's this nonsense about you going out of town next weekend? And as for that case, you already filed it away. What's going on, Monroe?" asked Lorena, concerned.

"None of your business, Lorena, but if you must know, I found out about next weekend earlier today. Now if you will excuse me, I have lots of work to do," replied Monroe, sternly.

Monroe entered his office, shut the door, and sat at his desk. He pulled out his scheduler. The weekend of the 21st of July was blank until he picked up a pencil and wrote in "Richmond" on the Friday square, and drew a line through the Saturday and Sunday squares.

Monroe sat back in his chair and rested his chin on his folded knuckles. He thought his discussion with Reuben probably had been the first real heart-to-heart talk he ever had with his brother. Yet, he still couldn't tell Reuben the truth of how he felt about his younger brother. Up until this moment, Monroe didn't realize the turmoil Renee and Reuben had been put through by her father. Monroe knew exactly how the two must have felt all those years because he felt the same way toward a girl he could never possess. After seeing how much Renee's love for Reuben kept her faithful, Monroe could not help falling in love with Renee. And as much shame as it brought him, Monroe hated Reuben for that.

狼

After Reuben returned to the mercantile, Renee and Aarleen bid farewell to Andrew, Annabelle, Lucy, and Andy.

"Are you sure you want to close the store for my birthday, Mr. Klaus? I don't want you to lose any customers," said Aarleen as Andrew handed her to Renee on the bench of the wagon.

"Not to worry, birthday girl. We have had that notice in the window for days that we will be closed for a special family celebration, so everyone knows we won't be open tomorrow," replied Andrew, pointing to the sign in the window.

"Well, I guess that's okay then," said Aarleen as she hugged Renee.

Reuben reined the team and the wagon rolled away. Both Renee and Reuben scooted closer to each other. Holding the reins in his left hand, Reuben placed his right arm around Renee as she leaned into Reuben still holding Aarleen. They looked at each other and began to smile, both knowing it was socially inappropriate to be the way they were in public, but they didn't care. They rode that way until they reached the house. As Reuben set the brake, Coleen came running out of the house.

"Reuben! Get in here quick. We need to find you some decent clothes. You have an interview with the superintendent and the board for Thursday. We have to prepare, young man."

For the next hour and a half, Coleen and Renee were having Reuben trying on his old clothes and some of Aaron's suits while Aarleen provided adorable feedback.

After trying on close to a dozen different combinations of outfits, both Coleen and Renee decided one of Aaron's gray suits was perfect for Reuben to wear for the interview. With that suit picked, Coleen began to go through some of Aaron's black suits.

"Now what are you looking for, Mama?" asked Reuben.

"A suit for you to get married in."

"Whoa, Mama, hold on," said Reuben. "I don't know about wearing a suit for the wedding."

"What? You've got to be kidding? What do you intend to wear?" Coleen asked, hoping Reuben wasn't going to say the outfit he had on last evening.

Renee spoke before Reuben had a chance and said, "Mama, both Reuben and I want our wedding to be as simple as possible. After seeing what my parents put together, I was determined when Reuben and I got married, I didn't want to put much thought into it. As for me, I'm going to wear my soft green day dress. The one I wore during my visits to the farm and kept here after I took that image I gave Reuben, and I want your son to wear what he wore for the image he gave me, simple and meaningful."

"Come here you two," said Coleen as she put her arms around Renee and Reuben. "I have a feeling this wedding is going to be far better than the one your parents were going to have you go through, my dearest Renee."

When Coleen finished her comment, Reuben told Coleen and Renee of his visit with Monroe and how he said he wasn't going to be able to attend the wedding because of a prior commitment. Coleen had a look of anger, but Reuben assured her Monroe told him to not postpone on his account. Still Coleen couldn't understand why she didn't know of this prior commitment.

After Reuben's clothes were selected for his interview, they decided it was time to head back to the farm. Reuben and Renee dropped Coleen and Aarleen off at the farm. They went on to Mr. Elps to discuss making their wedding rings, which Mr. Elps was not only happy to do so, but felt honored as well.

"Don't fret you two. I'll have these casted and polished for you, and I'll even deliver them myself on Thursday and leave them with May since you'll be in town," assured Jake Elps.

On their way back to the farm, Renee wanted to stop at several other farms that provided her support and invite them to the wedding. They all accepted the invitation.

As they were passing the county chapel, Reuben said, "You know, Renee, we've been inviting people to our wedding and we haven't asked the reverend if he can marry us that day."

"Geez oh geez oh geez you're right, Reuben. We better make a stop at his house next." And that's exactly what they did. To their relief, the reverend agreed.

Reverend Michaels knew all too well the story of Renee and Reuben, and was very happy and honored to be asked to finally bond these two who have endured so much.

"The love you two share is a testament to all those who believe they think what true love is," he told the two as they departed back to the farm.

By the time Renee and Reuben arrived, it was nearly supper time. As Reuben jumped off the wagon, he was immediately met by Riley. Reuben helped Renee down and he walked the team and wagon to the stables. Noah came out to help Reuben.

"Your Mama said she got you that interview, Reuben. I'm happy for you."

"Thank you, Noah. You know, when I do get certified, I'm going to need you and Henry to help fix that barn into a schoolhouse."

"You know what, Reuben? With the way so many people have been pleading for a school out these ways, we are going to have more help than we'll know what to do with."

Reuben chuckled as he hung the reins and straps on the wall, stopped for a moment, and looked to Noah as he retrieved his jo.

"You know, Noah, Monroe can't be at the wedding."

"That's too bad. How come?"

"He's going to Richmond on Friday and won't be back until Monday."

"Hmm, that's strange. He usually tells us about these things."

"Listen, Noah, I don't mean for this to sound like you are a second choice, but I was wondering if you would stand in as my best man? I asked Monroe, but he couldn't because of his trip."

"Really, Reuben, you want me to be your best man?"

"Well, yes. Honestly, I asked Monroe out of family obligation, but you and I have been best of friends since we were children, even before I met Renee."

"In that case, Reuben, you have yourself a best man."

狼

After supper was finished and dishes were cleaned and put away, Coleen took Aarleen into the parlor to practice her letters and numbers. Normally Aarleen enjoyed this time with her GrandMama, but this evening she wanted to be with Reuben by the oak tree.

"Come here, my little blossom, and sit on my lap," said Reuben to Aarleen as she was pouting.

Aarleen climbed onto Reuben's lap and rested her head against his chest.

"I'm so happy you want to be with me, but you mustn't neglect others who love you as well. These learning sessions with GrandMama are special and important and you must cherish them."

Coleen took hold of Renee's arm as she watched her son interact with his daughter about the importance of sharing.

"But I'll have to go to bed soon and I want to spend some time with you, Da."

"I know and I will spend time with you. I'll even help Mama put you to bed, okay?"

Aarleen's pouting face faded as she lifted her head and faced Reuben. "Promise?" she asked.

"I promise, my little blossom."

Aarleen gave Reuben a hug and he gave her a kiss on her forehead. She hopped off his lap and took Coleen by the hand and led her to the parlor.

Renee watched Reuben as he took time to wipe his eyes. He looked at her and smiled. Reuben rose and walked to the back room where he had been storing his belongings. Renee followed.

As Reuben began changing into his kosode and hakama, Renee leaned against the wall watching. She was impressed with how he donned on what seemed to be complicated garments with such meticulous attention to details. It looked to Renee as if Reuben was preforming a ritual as he dressed. Each pleat of the hakama he displayed precisely. Even when Reuben tucked the Kutto into his obi, he did so with careful precision. When he was finished, he turned and noticed her watching him.

"Is there anything wrong?" asked Reuben.

Renee shook her head no and replied, "Nothing at all, my love. I was just thinking of how much I missed you."

Reuben took Renee in his arms and kissed her deeply on her lips as she kissed back. He glanced down to her neck and saw the VMI button attached to a gold chain.

Reuben took it in his fingers saying, "I remember when I gave you this button. You said you would cherish it always and it looks like you have done just that."

"Oh, Reuben, it has never been out of my reach since that Christmas ball."

"You know, when I returned to VMI after that Christmas, my classmates were sitting in the dormitory common room coming up with virtues of what each button should stand for. If you can remember, there was so many buttons on that tunic so they narrowed it down to the center row. They were honor, bravery, confidence, dependability, faith, fortitude, perseverance, and loyalty. My departed good friend and roommate, Adam, took notice at my tunic and said *'Your button for loyalty is missing.'* I told him I had given my loyalty to someone very special."

Renee moved herself close to Reuben and held him tightly. "Reuben, if I had only known that story sooner, I would have displayed this button in front of my father," she said resting her face in his neck.

"I have loyalty on my hakama for you also."

Renee lifted her head and looked at him questionably.

"What do you mean?" she asked.

"As with my class' buttons of virtues, samurai applied the same concept for the pleats of our hakamas," Reuben answered.

"Is that why you so precisely placed them?" Renee asked as she stepped back looking at Reuben's hakama.

Reuben nodded and said as he pointed to each pleat, "Gi, rei, yu, meiyo, jin, makoto, and chu. Integrity, respect, courage, honor, benevolence, honesty and sincerity, and loyalty. These are the seven virtues which are the foundation of the Bushido code. The virtues I focused my purpose of being. The virtues that saved me from my darkest memories and dreams, and I want these virtues to be the foundation of our marriage, Renee."

"Oh, Reuben, so do I, very much so."

Reuben smiled and said, "Good, then I have something for you."

He reached inside his knapsack and pulled out a bundle wrapped in a light tan colored kosode tied together with a dark green obi. Reuben turned to Renee and presented the bundle to her.

"Here, a gift from Genda-San's wife, Yanna-Dono. I believe Genda-San told you about her."

The memory of Akagi Genda-San's story of his arranged marriage to another woman other than the one he loved, Yanna, all to avoid war came to Renee so vividly. Renee took the bundle and held it gently.

"Our story touched Yanna-Dono so deeply, she made you this outfit with the hopes our paths would someday rejoin. She apologized to me that the outfit isn't normally worn by women, but she pictured you like me, adventurous," explained Reuben.

Renee looked up from the bundle to Reuben's smiling face and sat on a stool as she began to untie the obi. She removed the kosode as Reuben took it from her to hold. In her lap, she held a dark green folded hakama with habaki leggings of the same shade of green tucked under the himo waist ties, along with a pair of sandals and a couple pair of green tabi socks.

"Geez oh geez oh geez help me put it on please!"

Rather than help Renee, Reuben instructed her as she donned on her new outfit. When she was fully dressed, she twirled around a couple of times in front of Reuben and asked, "Well, how do I look?"

With a sheer look of desire, Reuben said, "You are the most precious girl ever, and I'm the luckiest man to have your love."

Renee took Reuben by the hands and kissed his lips and replied, "And I'm the luckiest girl to have your love."

She looked out the window toward the oak tree and led Reuben outside as she said, "Come on, Reuben, I want to learn that throw you showed me the other day when you lifted me in your arms."

狼

Renee and Reuben spent a little over an hour under the oak tree. Reuben taught Renee the technique she asked for him to teach her from various forms of attack. They were having such a good time, they completely neglected to sit under the oak tree to embrace and enjoy one another as they both intended.

"My dear Reuben, there will be plenty of time to enjoy each other. Perhaps next time you teach me something, you should start off with a more soft romantic way before tossing me to the ground," recommend Renee as Reuben carried her to the house in his arms.

They could have spent the entire evening under the tree, but Reuben had a promise to keep and he had no intention of breaking it.

Renee and Reuben entered the house through the kitchen laughing and giggling, which reminded all who were seated at the table of when they were children.

"So what were you two doing out there?" asked Noah, playfully.

"Not what you're thinking, Noah," answered Renee. "I was tossing Reuben all over the ground."

"Only because I let you," replied Reuben, pouring them both a glass of water from the pitcher on the table.

"Good heavens, Renee, what are you wearing?" asked Coleen, entering the kitchen with Aarleen and Riley.

"Hey! Mama looks just like Da! Do I get a set of clothes like that too?" asked Aarleen, taking a closer look at Renee's green hakama.

Renee knelt down and lifted Aarleen in her arms and said, "Well, if I can get May to help me, I'm sure we can make you a set using mine as a pattern."

"Seriously, Reuben, don't you feel silly wearing that get up?" asked Henry.

Coming to Reuben's defense, Renee answered, "You know, Henry, I can understand why Reuben wears this outfit. It's the most comfortable and practical outfit I have ever worn."

"Even more comfortable than those hooped dresses you wore at Wickham…"

"Don't you say it, Reuben!"

"Wickham girl."

"Aargh… how many times do I have to tell you, don't call me that?"

Aarleen started to giggle, remembering the ride past Renee's old school, as she was about to say, "Mama is a Wick…"

Renee covered Aarleen's mouth with her hand before she finished. "Oh no, not you too?" said Renee, letting out a giggle herself.

Reuben took Aarleen from Renee's arms and asked her, after the laughter died down, "So little blossom, what would you like to do before your bedtime?"

"Hmm, I don't know, Da. What do you want to do?"

Reuben looked at everyone in the room and smiled. "Well, it's such a nice evening so how about all of us go and sit outside on the front porch like we used to do many years ago?" he suggested.

"We do that all the time," said Noah.

"But not since my son returned. That sounds lovely. Come on everyone," replied Coleen as she led the way.

On the front porch, everyone sat in their usual places, except for Reuben who leaned against the porch rail next to Renee with Aarleen on her lap. They discussed Aarleen's upcoming birthday party and what games she wanted to play.

"What games did the children play in Japan, Da?" asked Aarleen.

Reuben, now seated next to Renee after Noah brought him a chair from inside the house, took Renee's hand in his and answered, "The children didn't play too many games. There wasn't much time for the children to be children. You see, my little blossom, Japan isn't like America where we can sit out on our porch and feel safe. In Itosai, and almost every village, there was always a threat of invaders so the children, at a very early age, had to learn how to defend their homes."

Everyone sat very still listening to Reuben with deep interest as he continued. "One of the jobs I had to do with my friend Tadashi was to train the children, some even younger than you, the ways of the Budo Arts, so many of the games that were played revolved around fighting. Every night, everyone in the community took turns guarding the village, even myself, and each time, there was at least one child standing the watch to learn how to defend their homes."

"That is so very interesting, Reuben," said Coleen.

"Also very sad," added May.

"How so?" asked Noah

"It sounds like the children over there grow up too fast and can't enjoy the joys of being a child at play," answered May. "Reminds me when we were still slaves as children. We had no childhood."

Henry cleared his throat before he said, "One thing is for sure, we certainly do take our freedom for granted. It's like Reuben says, we can sit here feeling safe so we tend to fall into a routine. Remember when Mr. Aaron bought us three from Massa Wilcox and because of what Renee read, Mr. Aaron freed us? Remember how joyful we were? But even with that freedom, just because we are Negros, we are still looked upon as slaves and we sometimes forget we are free because of that. That's kind of like taking our freedom for granted, isn't it, Reuben?"

Reuben nodded. "That is well said, Henry."

"After hearing what Reuben said about how the children don't take their freedom for granted in Japan, I'm going to start appreciating my freedom a little more," said Henry. "And I expect you do as well May and Noah. We may be Negros in the eyes of many whites, but we have something special granted to us by Mr. Aaron, God please rest his soul, and that is freedom, something we should be bound to guard and fight for."

Coleen took hold of Henry's hand and gave it a gentle squeeze.

"Now that you're home, why do you still keep learning how to fight, Da?" asked Aarleen.

Reuben smiled as he gently tightened his grip on Renee's hand and answered, "I learn to fight so I don't have to fight."

"If there weren't many games, how about stories? It's almost my bedtime, so tell us a story they tell in Japan, Da," said Aarleen.

Everyone looked to Reuben nodding.

"Yes, my love, how about a story? I'm sure they had fables there," asked Renee.

"I really didn't learn any," answered Reuben.

"Aw, come on, Da, there's got to be one story you can tell?" pleaded Aarleen. "I love reading and making up stories of adventure."

Reuben thought and his head cocked to the side, "Hmm, I guess I can tell you how the Demon of the Western Provinces was defeated by Miyamoto Musashi."

"Ohhh, that sounds good," said Noah. "Yeah, Reuben, tell us that story."

"Actually it isn't a story because this is true. It happened nearly 250 years ago. It was a duel between two of the greatest swordsmen of Japan, Sasaki Kojiro and Miyamoto Musashi."

"Good heavens, those names gave me chills," said May.

Reuben rose from his chair and stepped back to tell his story. "Sasaki Kojiro, also known as the Demon of the Western Provinces, was pure samurai who founded a kenjutsu school for swordsmanship. He was a student of Chujo-ryu style of sword fighting and very skilled in the sword arts. He was taught by some of the greatest kenjutsu teachers. Kojiro was a man of great being, and was also arrogantly self-righteous, a man with a great ego.

"Hmm, sounds like my father," said Renee.

Reuben continued. "Kojiro had prestige, honor, and respect. Then there was Miyamoto Musashi. He was quite the opposite of Kojiro."

Quite the opposite, this is sounding more and more like my father and Reuben, Renee thought.

Using his hands to help tell the story, Reuben continued, "Musashi was a ronin."

"A ronin?" asked Noah, deeply into the story. "What's a ronin?"

"A ronin is a masterless samurai," answered Reuben. "Ronin roamed the country and served no lord or master. They came and went as they pleased, or a samurai became a ronin when his lord or master died, or a samurai lost his master's favor and cast him out.

"Musashi lived his life as a ronin. He served a lord when it suited him. Unlike Kojiro, Musashi didn't attend any schools, and he didn't have a sensei to claim. But he was self-taught and just as great a swordsman as Kojiro. Musashi perfected his own style, the style of two swords. He could wield a sword in each hand and use them as one."

"Wow, can you do that, Da?" asked Aarleen.

"I'm afraid not, little blossom, but that's why I always practice so that one day maybe I can. Anyway, where was I? Oh yes, although Musashi was not socially elite as Kojiro, he was still a strong, quick, and clever man."

"Just like you, Da?" asked Aarleen.

Reuben cocked his head sideways in thought at Aarleen's question and said, "Hmm, yeah, okay, yeah, you can say that."

"Reuben!" said Renee, lightly slapping his shoulder.

"I'm not going to lie to our daughter, darling," said Reuben with a chuckle.

"Go on, Reuben, what happened next?" pleaded Noah.

"Kojiro was known for wielding a nodachi, a sword longer than a normal sized katana, about eight inches longer. Musashi knew of this, so using his intellect, he found a way to combat against Kojiro's long sword. Musashi also was skilled at understanding his opponent's mind, and he used that to his advantage. Knowing of Kojiro's ego, Musashi purposely arrived very late to the appointed time of the duel. This lateness infuriated Kojiro.

"Do you know what it means to be infuriated, little blossom?"

"Uh-uh, Da," answered Aarleen nodding her head no.

"It means to be very angry. You see, Musashi made Kojiro angry on purpose so he wouldn't be able to concentrate and have focus. When Musashi finally arrived by boat, he was about three hours late."

"How was he going to defend himself against that other man's long sword?" asked Coleen.

"While a fisherman rowed Musashi to the island where the duel was to take place, Musashi carved a wooden sword out of a spare oar. He carved it a couple of inches longer than Kojiro's nodachi."

"A wooden sword?" asked Renee.

"Yes, my dear, a wooden sword and when Kojiro saw it, that made him even more furious. He yelled to Musashi, 'MUSASHI WA, ANATA DESU OSOY!!! ANATA MOTTE

IMAS IE MEIYO!!!'" exclaimed Reuben in a deep voice. "Kojiro then drew his long sword and threw his saya to the ground."

"Good heavens, that sounds menacing. What does that mean?" asked May.

"Musashi, you are late. You have no honor."

"That's it? Sounds scarier in Japanese," said May.

Reuben chuckled and continued, "Musashi replied, 'KOJIRO, ANATA MOTTE IMAS MO NAKUSHITA DAKARA ANATA MOTTE IMAS HAIKI SA RETA ANATA NO SAYA, IMI ANATA IE YORI NAGAI MOTTE IMAS IKURAKA SHIYO NO SORE!!!' meaning, 'Kojiro, you have already lost because you have discarded your saya, meaning you no longer have any use of it.'"

Reuben raised his hands as if he were holding a katana and he continued with the story, "Both Kojiro and Musashi had their swords at the ready to strike."

"Reuben, I don't think this is an appropriate story to be telling Aarleen," said Coleen, concerned.

"Shh! What happened next, Reuben?" asked May, now sitting on the edge of her chair.

"The two swordsmen began running along the wide beach until Musashi jumped ahead of Kojiro so the sun would be to Masashi's back. They stood for several long minutes, just staring at each other waiting for the other to make his first move. Musashi stepped forward and caused Kojiro to strike at Masashi. Kojiro's cut was so close it cut Musashi's headband in half. Masashi jumped and struck at Kojiro's head and landed off to the side of Kojiro. The duel was over."

"Over? That quickly? Who won?" asked Henry.

"The two swordsmen stood on the sandy beach staring at each other again, but this time, Musashi had a look of concern when he saw a trickle of blood seep from under Kojiro's headband and drip down his nose. Musashi, with his longer wooden sword, hit Kojiro in a fatal spot on his head and Kojiro fell to the ground. Musashi knelt down to Kojiro and asked for his forgiveness for which Kojiro gave him.

"Kojiro's samurai and students began to give chase to Musashi as he ran to the boat and the fisherman rowed him safely away from the beach."

"Why did Musashi ask for forgiveness, Da?" asked Aarleen.

Reuben knelt down in front of Renee and Aarleen and took Renee's hand in his left and Aarleen's hand in his right and said, "Because, my little cherry blossom, when Musashi defeated Kojiro, in a way he defeated himself."

"I don't understand," said Aarleen.

Looking to Renee, Reuben answered, "The point of Musashi feeling the way he did is because it is noble to achieve greatness, but one mustn't sacrifice one's life to obsess over that achievement."

"I see. We should enjoy other things around us, right, Da?"

"Exactly, my beautiful blossom, exactly."

Coleen nodded with much approval and smiled toward Renee.

Renee pulled her hand from Reuben's and caressed his face lovingly.

"That was a good story with a good moral at the end," said Coleen. "Even with the bloodshed."

"Mama?" asked Aarleen as she looked to Renee, who had her eyes gazing on Reuben's.

"Yes, sweetie,"

"That was a good story wasn't it?"

"Very good, sweetie," Renee answered.

"Ahem! I think it's someone's bedtime," said Coleen, trying to discreetly interrupt Renee and Reuben's moment.

Shaking her head, Renee looked to Aarleen and said, "Goodness, you're right, Mama. Someone has a big day tomorrow and needs her rest."

狼

After Renee got Aarleen ready for bed, Reuben came into their room to help Renee tuck her in. Aarleen crawled under the covers as Riley hopped onto the foot of her bed and laid down. Rubbing Riley's fur between his ears, Reuben sat on the edge of the bed next to Aarleen as Renee stood next to him, putting her arm around his shoulders.

"Did you like that story, my little blossom?"

"Very much."

"Did you learn anything from it besides the main point of the story?"

"I think so. I learned it is important to be one step ahead of other people."

Reuben took his daughter into his arms and hugged her saying, "Excellent, my beautiful Aarleen. That is correct. I'm so proud of you. So proud, I'm going to give you an early birthday present."

"Oh my, what a surprise!" said Renee.

"Really, Da?" asked Aarleen.

Reuben nodded as he reached into the sleeve of his kosode, pulled out a small burgundy bag, and untied the draw cord. He handed it to Aarleen saying, "Go ahead, open it."

Aarleen pulled open the bag, reached in with her little fingers, and pulled out the wooden turtle inrou Katsuo made and gave to Reuben the day he left Japan. He promised Katsuo he would give it to someone special.

"Geez oh geez oh geez this is sooo cute! What is it, Da?" asked Aarleen, cradling it in her little hands.

Riley crawled up for a closer look as well.

"It's an inrou box. Look, it opens," said Reuben as he took it into his hands and showed both Aarleen and Renee. He closed it and handed it back to Aarleen.

"That's clever," said Renee. "What's it used for?"

"Samurai carry these on their obi. They hold valuable trinkets or medicine herbs for healing. A little boy, Katsuo, Genda-San's grandson, made it for me to give to someone very special."

"Hey, I can put my coin in it, huh, Da?"

"If you wish."

Aarleen rose to her knees and wrapped her arms around Reuben and said, "Thank you, Da, and thank you, GrandDa, for bringing my Da home."

Renee brought her hand to her mouth to mask her emotion.

"You're very welcome, my little cherry blossom," said Reuben feeling emotional himself. "Now, little one, you lie down and go to sleep."

Aarleen did as Reuben said and he brought up the covers to her chin and kissed her on the cheek. "Goodnight, my little blossom."

"Goodnight, Da, goodnight, Mama."

After Renee gave Aarleen a hug and kiss goodnight, she walked Reuben downstairs where he was still taking his night's sleep. She helped him arrange the sofa and when she turned, Reuben was in front of her. He took her into his arms and pulled her into him as she held him tightly.

"I love you so very much, my dearest Renee," he said, softly into her ear.

"Oh, Reuben, I love you too. In five days' time, you and I will be husband and wife and will share the same bed. I can't wait."

"Anticipation will make things more pleasant. That's what Genda-San said."

Renee let out a little giggle and said, "That may be true, but I must have you soon."

"And I must have you also, but we must do it right this time."

Renee lifted her head from Reuben's shoulder and said, "What do you mean *'do it right this time?'*"

"You have to admit, Renee, it was our first time ever and we really didn't know what we were doing," answered Reuben with a smirk on his face.

"We must have done something right because we have a beautiful little girl upstairs as a result."

Reuben laughed, as did Renee, while they held each other tighter again.

"By the way, my love, I owe you a very swift kick in your jewels one of these days to give you an idea of what I had to go through to bring your daughter into this world."

"Whoa," said Reuben as he pulled away from Renee and dropped his hands to his groin. "Can you at least wait until after our first night as husband and wife?"

"As long as you don't call me Wickham girl between now and then."

"Ah, so it will be okay after?"

"Why, you shoddy farm boy," said Renee as she acted like she was going to kick Reuben in the groin.

"Okay, okay, okay, take it easy and don't damage the goods."

They both laughed.

"Hey you two, you do realize I can hear you," said May from behind her bedroom door.

Both Renee and Reuben covered their mouths and snickered quietly. Reuben walked Renee to the foot of the stairs. They kissed one last time and went their separate ways to get some sleep before Aarleen's birthday.

The following morning, Reuben woke extra early for training. He trained under the oak tree for an hour without any noise so as not to wake his family. After training, he went inside the house to get cleaned and dressed. He wore his leather boots with black trousers tucked into them, a dark red band collar shirt, and his obi of Akagi burgundy at his waist.

Reuben heard soft noises coming from the kitchen and cleared his throat as he entered so as not to startle May who was up early as usual getting breakfast started.

"Good morning, Aunty May."

"Good morning, Reuben."

"The birthday decorations you and Renee brought for the 'Foster' child, where are they?"

May chuckled and pointed to the broom closet.

Reuben went to the closet, retrieved them, and went out the front door and began to string up the decorations. He wanted the porch to be all decorated before Renee and Aarleen came downstairs. Since the mercantile was closed for this special day, Aarleen didn't have to get up as early to collect eggs and Renee could also get a few minutes extra sleep. However, being that Renee was so used to rising early, she still got out of bed, but let Aarleen sleep.

"And just what do you think you're doing?" asked Renee, coming out of the front door.

"Hey, I wanted to surprise you and Aarleen," answered Reuben.

"Let us surprise Aarleen together then. Here, give me that streamer."

Upstairs, Riley crawled up to Aarleen and started lapping her cheek, waking her as she giggled. She rose and hugged Riley saying, "Happy birthday to me, Riley! This is going to be the best birthday ever!"

Aarleen rolled out of bed and quickly made her way downstairs and looked for anyone in the house.

"Hey? Where is everyone!" Aarleen yelled.

Riley got her attention by pawing at the front door. Aarleen went to open it and as she did, everyone was outside on the porch waiting for her.

"HAPPY BIRTHDAY, AARLEEN!!!"

Breakfast was served on the porch and after the routine of morning chores around the farm was done, everyone began to prepare for the party. It was nearly noon when the first guests, Mr. and Mrs. Klaus and Lucy and Andy, arrived. They greeted the birthday girl and presented her with gifts of books filled with fables. Aarleen took Reuben aside and showed him the pages of parchment filled with stories she and Renee would make up and tell during family events. He was very impressed and fought the urge to sit and take time away from Aarleen's special day to read them.

Aarleen showed the Klaus' and Lucy and Andy the turtle inrou Reuben gave her the evening before.

Other guests began to arrive and Aarleen greeted them with Riley by her side as Renee and Reuben watched. The other farmers were very happy to see Reuben had returned. They could see Renee's spirits were lifted to new levels.

For nearly the entire party, Renee and Reuben were inseparable, even as lunch was being prepared and served. Many of the young ladies had a look of romance when they saw Renee and Reuben together and commented on how such of a lovely couple they made.

"Tell us a story, Aarleen!" called out one of Aarleen's friends.

"Yeah, cousin, a story!" said Andy.

Renee took Reuben by the hand and said, "You have got to watch this. Your little cherry blossom is quite the story teller. Even the older children like to listen to her stories."

"Okay everyone! Gather around!" called out Aarleen as all the other children started forming a circle around her and Riley. Even some of the adults sat in amongst the circle.

"I'm going to tell you a new story. A true story that happened almost 250 years ago. It's the story of how the Demon of the Western Provinces was defeated by Miyamoto Musashi," said Aarleen in all seriousness.

Reuben pulled Renee into his body tighter as he smiled and looked on with pride.

Aarleen recited the story nearly word by word as told by Reuben the evening before, even going as far as pronouncing the names of Kojiro and Musashi flawlessly. She had the eyes and ears of her audience gazing at her with total fascination. As she reached the part of the story when Kojiro tells Musashi he was late, Reuben assisted her by calling out in a deep voice, "MUSASHI WA, ANATA DESU OSOY!!! ANATA MOTTE IMAS IE MEIYO!!!" startling everyone whose eyes were on Aarleen.

Aarleen smiled at Reuben as she translated what he had said. He also assisted Aarleen with Musashi's response.

When Aarleen finished the story, she pointed out the morals of the story and everyone applauded. Reuben knelt down and opened his arms. Aarleen sprinted into Reuben's open arms and he scooped her up and hugged her tightly.

"That was magnificent, my little cherry blossom. You honor me. Happy birthday, my precious Aarleen," said Reuben as Renee wiped away a tear rolling down his cheek.

狼

It was nearly four in the afternoon when the last of Aarleen's party guests departed. Just as she greeted every guest when they arrived, she thanked them for coming and bid them farewell. Everyone expressed to Aarleen how much of a good time they had and how happy they were her father had returned.

When the last wagon rolled away, Aarleen yawned and stretched out her arms.

"Looks like my birthday sweetie needs a nap," said Renee.

"I'm okay, Mama. I can help clean up," responded Aarleen as she began to doze off while Reuben lifted her off the ground.

"Oh yeah, she'll be a big help," said Reuben with a silent chuckle. "I'll lay her down in the parlor, my love."

Renee gave Aarleen a kiss on the cheek and a kiss on Reuben's lips.

It took a little over an hour for the cleaning. After a quick meal of left overs, Andrew and Annabelle said their farewells and departed, but Lucy and Andy stayed for the evening.

When all was quiet, Reuben said to Coleen, "Okay, Mama, the application, let's get to it."

For the next couple of hours, Reuben and his mother went over the application, what to expect, and how to prepare for his interview. The plan was for Henry to take Reuben, Renee, and Aarleen to stay in the city in the morning. That way, Reuben wouldn't have to travel so far for the interview and be well rested. Reuben was going to take along three oban coins. If his interview went well, he would go to the bank and convert the gold oban coins into cash to purchase the plot of land from Mr. Lester.

"This is going to be exciting Reuben. Does Aarleen know you're going to be her teacher?" asked Lucy.

"You know, I don't think she does," replied Reuben.

"I hope it won't be too awkward, but I think she'll be excited," said Renee.

Reuben noticed Coleen looking rather distant. "What's wrong, Mama?" he asked.

Coleen let out a sigh and said, "Your brother. I'm disappointed he didn't come to Aarleen's birthday party."

"Yeah, I'm going to have a word with him about that," said Lucy.

"Please, Lucy, don't," responded Reuben. "There's something bothering Monroe and I think it's me."

"You, Reuben?" asked Renee.

"For seven years, Monroe had to help Da care for you all with no help from me. Now I return and he feels isolated, I guess. Give him some time. I'm sure he'll come around."

"We can give him some time, but he can't totally isolate himself," commented Coleen. "Missing Aarleen's birthday party is one thing, but to miss the wedding?"

"Whoa, he's not coming to the wedding?!" exclaimed Lucy.

"Says he has to be in Richmond," said Reuben.

Coleen shook her head as she said, "That just doesn't make any sense. He always tells me of his out of town trips."

"Said it was last minute notice, Mama," answered Reuben.

"That's a bunch of hogwash. Family should come first," said Lucy.

Renee rose from her seat, stood behind Reuben, and wrapped her arms around him saying, "We can go on and on about what's going on with Monroe and get nowhere when he probably doesn't know himself. However, I do know that look in my Reuben's eyes. That's the same look Aarleen has when she has had enough for one day. My man has a big day to prepare for and we can't get him distracted. If all goes well, and it will, Reuben is going to have his hands full turning that barn into a school."

"Yeah, and after Saturday, he's going to have his hands full of you, huh, Renee?" laughed Lucy.

"Lucy! That is uncalled for," said Coleen.

"But true, Mama," said Renee, giggling after.

Reuben dropped his head to his hands as he laughed. "You know, Da is probably looking down on us right now and having a good laugh," he said.

狼

It was nearly noon as Renee and Lucy paced back and forth outside the front of the city public schoolhouse. They were waiting for Reuben to come out with news the school board approved his application and submitted his certification to teach.

The day before, everyone except May and Noah arrived at the city home. Lucy and Andy stayed with Andrew and Annabelle. The day was spent preparing for the interview. When Monroe came home after work, he too took part. Monroe seemed more pleasant than the last two times Reuben had seen him.

Coleen took some time to discuss his "last minute" trip to Richmond for the weekend and missing the wedding. Monroe was prepared for this line of questioning so he had all the right responses to Coleen's inquires about his trip.

Although Monroe was helpful, he didn't stay to visit after. Instead he went to his and Reuben's old room to retire for the evening, not giving thought as to offering Reuben his bed for the night. It had been many years ago when the Duran family took in Renee, when Coleen and Lucy moved Reuben's bed into Lucy's room for Renee.

"You know, you can sleep in Lucy's and my room, Reuben. Aarleen and I can share Lucy's bed and you can use your old bed," suggested Renee.

Reuben was tempted, but declined. "That's a good idea, but you sleeping next to me would be a distraction, if you take my meaning, and I need a goodnight's sleep."

Renee had a confused look until she understood what Reuben was implying. "Oh... Ohhh, I understand now. I guess I wouldn't be getting much sleep either with you sleeping an arm's reach away too."

"Gee, Lucy! How long does one of these interviews take?" asked Renee, nervously.

"Heaven sakes, Renee, calm down. Reuben has one of the best references he could have... Mama. I'm sure she gave him a good recommendation. Heck, I bet the interview has been over for a while now and they are just sitting and asking Reuben about his time in Japan."

"If that's the case, Lucy, I am going to iriminage him to the ground so hard, it will make his head spin."

"You'll do what? What have you two been doing by the oak tree since he's been back anyway?"

Just then, the front door to the schoolhouse opened and out Reuben came with a scowl on his face. Both Renee and Lucy ran up the steps to meet him, but he walked right past them. Renee and Lucy stopped, looked at each other, shrugged their shoulders, and followed Reuben down the stairs.

"Well, Reuben, how did it go?" asked Renee, excitedly.

"I don't want to talk about it," replied Reuben, sternly.

"Oh come on, Reuben, don't tell me they didn't hire you?" Lucy asked, tapping his shoulder.

"I said I don't want to talk about it. I have other things on my mind right now."

Again, Renee and Lucy shrugged their shoulders as they looked at each other and began walking with Reuben in silence toward the Klaus Mercantile.

Renee timidly took Reuben by the arm and he placed his hand on hers. They came to the end of the city block. Renee and Lucy began to cross the street toward the Klaus Mercantile where everyone was waiting to hear the results of Reuben's interview. Reuben, however, began to cross in the other direction pulling Renee with him.

Startled, Renee asked, "Aren't we going to the store, Reuben?"

"I don't know about you, but I have to go to the bank."

"The bank?" asked Lucy.

"I've got to get these coins converted into cash so I can purchase that plot of land from Mr. Lester to build the school."

"Wait a minute," said Renee, giving Reuben narrow eyes, "Did you get hired or not?"

"Of course I did, my love. I'm Reuben Duran. Who in their right mind would deny me a job, huh?"

"Darn it! What is it with you and your shenanigans all the time?!" shouted Renee, flustered.

Renee raised her arm to strike Reuben's chest as he showed her to get him to block her fist. As he brought his arm up to block, she swiftly took his arm with her other hand and got him in position to throw him to the ground, as he showed her. However, Reuben rotated his body under her arm and reversed the technique on her and lifted her off her feet and cradled her in his arms.

"Hey, I thought I did that right," said Renee, surprised.

"You did," answered Reuben, "but I haven't taught you reversals yet."

Reuben lowered Renee gently to the ground and took her in his arms as they both laughed.

"You know, you two don't need anyone to drive you crazy," said Lucy, standing with her fists on her hips. "You two idiots are doing a damn good job of that yourselves."

The three practically walked at a running pace to the bank like school children released from school.

When they arrived at the bank, Renee introduced Reuben to Alexander Bishop, the bank president. Mr. Bishop had been very helpful and supportive to Renee as the "Duran Agricultural Liaison," and had been good friends with Aaron. After several minutes of pleasantries, Mr. Bishop invited the three into his office to discuss business.

Reuben explained the purpose of his visit and placed three gold oban coins on Mr. Bishop's desk. Mr. Bishop's eyes widened and gently took them in his hands and looked upon them in wonder.

"Mr. Allen, come in here, quickly!"

A slender clerk entered the office and said, "Yes, Mr. Bishop?"

"The daily gold trade, bring it to me quickly!"

"Yes sir, right away."

"You say these are pure gold?" asked Mr. Bishop.

"Feel free to examine them yourself," replied Reuben.

"CARVER, GET IN HERE!!!" shouted Mr. Bishop, startling Reuben, Renee, and Lucy. Another clerk entered the office, "Yes sir?"

"Please take this… ah, coin and have it evaluated quickly."

"Yes sir."

"You say this gold is from Japan, Mr. Duran?"

"Yes."

"Orient gold… very valuable," said Mr. Bishop in wonder, examining the other two coins.

"How so?" asked Renee. "Gold is gold, regardless of where it comes from, isn't it?"

"Well yes, it is. But gold from different parts of the world have different values because of its origins. In this case, because Japan has only recently been open for trade, these coins can be worth top dollar."

Mr. Allen entered the office and handed Mr. Bishop a printed page and excused himself. Mr. Bishop eyed the page very intently. His eyes lit up when he found what he was looking for. He lifted one of the coins and weighed it in his hand. "Hmm, feels to be about eight ounces."

Carver entered the room with an amazed look on his face as he said, "This is pure solid gold, through and through, Mr. Bishop, eight ounces!"

Mr. Bishop took the coin and excused Carver and asked him to close the door as he exited.

"Well, is there enough in these three coins for three hundred dollars?" asked Reuben.

"Mr. Duran, according to this very recent gold trade notice, this one coin alone is worth two hundred dollars."

"Geez oh geez oh geez!" exclaimed both Renee and Reuben at the same time, as Lucy slapped her hands to her mouth to hide a loud gasp.

"You mean to tell me, I have been carrying twenty five of these huge coins worth two hundred dollars each in my haversack halfway around the world! At eight ounces a coin, no wonder my left shoulder was always sore at the end of the day. This has gotta be some sort of sick, Akagi joke!"

"TWENTY FIVE!!!" cried out Mr. Bishop.

After the excitement calmed down, Reuben softly asked if he could convert two of the coins into cash.

"Only two?" asked Mr. Bishop.

"I only need three hundred dollars."

"Are you certain? I can easily convert all three today."

"Yes, I'm certain, only two, but I know now where to come when I need to convert the others."

Try as hard as he could, Mr. Bishop could not get Reuben to cash in all three coins. In the end, Mr. Bishop pulled out a private cash box, counted out four hundred dollars, and exchanged the cash for two coins. As Mr. Bishop took the coins, he eyed them like a child eyeing candy through a candy store window. Reuben got the notion Mr. Bishop was going to keep the coins for himself, considering the cash came from his private cash box.

With their business concluded, Mr. Bishop escorted Reuben, Renee, and Lucy to the front door. Mr. Bishop vigorously shook Reuben's hand and said, "Anytime you want to convert anymore coins, anytime of the day or night, don't hesitate, you hear. Anytime, my fine young man, anytime, anytime."

The three walked in awed silence to the Klaus Mercantile where Coleen and Aarleen were waiting. Once they entered the door, Coleen asked Reuben how the interview went. His response was, "Two hundred dollars each, twenty five coins, haversack, halfway round the world, left shoulder sore, sitting on my hip the entire time, using it as a pillow, gotta be some sort of sick, Akagi joke."

Renee, just as shocked, answered Coleen telling her Reuben was hired and his certification was going to be submitted this afternoon. Then she went on to tell about their trip to the bank.

After the initial shock wore off from everyone who understood how Reuben was feeling, Annabelle asked, "Well, what do we do now?"

"We wait until the store closes, get Monroe, and go to a restaurant and celebrate as others serve us for a change," said Reuben.

"A restaurant? Really, Da? Can I have cake?" asked Aarleen.

Reuben lifted Aarleen and said, "You can have cake and pie!"

"Oh boy, did you hear that, Andy? Cake and pie!"

For the rest of the day, everyone stayed at the store helping until closing time. When the till was counted, cleared, and contents locked away, the entire group walked to Aaron's law office to get Monroe. At first Monroe was hesitant in coming along, but Coleen coaxed him into coming. Reuben invited Lorena as well since she was close to the family as his father's long time secretary.

They entered one of Norfolk's finest restaurants and took a table for ten. They had a grand time and grand meal. Both Aarleen and Andy got slivers of cake and pie as Reuben promised. After their pleasant dining experience, The Klaus', Lucy, and Andy went in their direction home as Coleen, Renee, Reuben, Monroe, and Aarleen went theirs.

When they arrived at the house, they all sat in the parlor and Reuben finally got his chance to tell Coleen about his interview. He told her how the board was impressed with his credentials, especially the document from Akagi Genda-San. Reuben told how he gave the board examples of how he taught English to the villagers of Itosai. He said the board was also impressed of Reuben's knowledge of history, science, and mathematics, all of which is needed for an outreach teacher.

"Of course, I didn't mention my knowledge of all these subjects are a result of war related instances," said Reuben. "I didn't think that would be appropriate to mention."

Coleen expressed her approval.

"I hate to end this lovely celebration, but I have to be at the train station early so I'll be turning in," said Monroe as he rose and made his way to the stairs.

"Are you sure you can't postpone this trip, son?" asked Coleen.

"Mama, I can't. I'm expected."

"We'll miss you at our wedding, Monroe," said Renee as she rose to say goodnight.

Monroe looked at Renee and apologized for not being able to attend. His eyes remained on her as she lowered herself back down next to Reuben, not noticing.

Reuben, on the other hand, noticed Monroe's look toward Renee. It was a look that reminded him of the way he looked at Renee when he thought he could never be hers. Suddenly Monroe's attitude about Reuben's return and their conversation at the law office last Monday was much clearer.

When Monroe left the room and could be heard upstairs, Coleen shook her head saying, "I just don't understand how he could put his job before your wedding."

"I'm sure whatever it is must be very important, Mama," replied Renee.

"It is," said Reuben as he looked at Renee and took her in his arms and hugged her lovingly. He softly said to her, "I love you so very much."

Surprised by this sudden show of affection, Renee hugged Reuben back and felt joyful as she answered, "I love you too."

狼

Saturday, July 21 finally arrived. Renee was in the parlor along with Coleen, May, Annabelle, and Lucy. Unlike the last wedding she was nearly forced into, she wasn't nervous at all. Renee was full of excitement and joy. This time she was surrounded by the ones she treasured as family. The guests awaiting the wonderful event were those of her choosing. Most importantly, she was marrying the man she loved, the man who wasn't arranged for her to be marrying, except in the name of love.

There were no stone feet rooted to the ground, no procrastinating in getting dressed, and no stabbing, twisting, gut wrenching pain in her stomach. Renee felt her body filled with tingles from her head to her toes. This was a walk down an aisle she wanted to run and take the man waiting at the end as her husband.

There was no elaborate confusing wedding dress to tie, hook, and squeeze into. Only Renee's favorite soft, light green, common day dress she wore during her visits to the farm, and when she had her image taken for Reuben, a picture he treasured.

Her beautiful, long, dark hair wasn't tied and pinned tightly against her scalp covered by a gaudy lace wedding veil, but unpinned cascading over her shoulders, just as Reuben liked it.

There was no string of pearls around her slim neck, only a simple gold chain Coleen gave Renee with the shiny VMI button her husband-to-be had given her as a Christmas gift years ago.

One would think she wasn't dressed as a bride, yet she was as radiant as a bride dressed in the most extravagant wedding dress ever worn.

"Here, Mama. Andy and I picked these for you," said Aarleen, entering the parlor with a handful of wildflowers they gathered from the front of the house.

Renee knelt down, took the arranged flowers, and took both Aarleen and Andy in her arms and hugged them lovingly. "Thank you very much. They're beautiful and just what I need," she said joyfully.

"Come on, Andy, we have to go find Mr. Elps and see what you have to do as the ring bearer," Aarleen said as the two cousins exited the parlor.

Renee rose to face the ladies in the room and asked, "Well, how do I look?"

Lucy walked up to Renee and pulled out a single daisy with a spray of green and arranged them in Renee's hair above her left ear. "The finishing touch to the prettiest bride I have ever seen... and I was a very pretty one myself," she said, holding Renee's hands."

Renee stepped to Coleen and said, "The only thing missing is Da to give me away. He was the one I looked up to as my true father. I have never heard of it being done before, but will you give me away, Mama? Although my real mother and I reconciled years ago, like Da, you are the one I look up to as my true mother."

Coleen raised her hands to her mouth to hide a gasp and nodded yes. She took Renee into her arms and said while tearing up, "It will be my pleasure, my beautiful daughter."

Unlike Renee being surrounded by family, Reuben sat alone in the spare room where he had been keeping his belongings. On a small table in front of Reuben, Renee's image case was open with her picture looking at him. He had his Kutto leaning up against his shoulder. He closed his eyes and thought of the joyful times they spent with each other. Suddenly an image of Hisano Castle entered his mind and he could clearly hear Akagi Genda-San say, *"You should still wish, Reuben-San. Remember my lesson in fate. Fate is what drives us to live our paths we chose to travel. If one looks at wishes and fate as if they are two parallel lines, in the distance they will meet, metaphorically speaking. You must prepare to meet your wish with your fate Reuben-San."*

Reuben opened his eyes and lifted the Kutto before his face. He slowly drew the blade from its saya. He turned the sword upward and looked at his image in the mirror-like blade. He smiled, then slowly and elegantly returned the Kutto into its saya. He stood and placed it behind the open image case of Renee, clapped his hands twice, and bowed his head.

There was a knock at the door and it opened. It was Noah.

"It's almost time, Reuben, are you ready?"

Reuben lifted his head, opened his eyes, and with a joyful smile on his face, he answered, "Hai! Noah-San!"

狼

The sight for the wedding was underneath the large oak tree next to the creek. The aisle led from the end of the large planting field to the tree where Reverend Robert Michaels stood. The aisle wasn't a straight path, but one that had a few curves representing the long wavy road Renee and Reuben had taken to arrive to this day. Although Renee and Reuben didn't expect many to attend, it looked as if the entire farming community of the county lined both sides of the aisle and circled around the oak tree.

There was no large organ or choir. Renee and Reuben didn't put any thought into having any form of music. However, during Aarleen's birthday party, Tom Foster, his wife Carol, and Lucy collaborated together, and began practicing an appropriate wedding march. Carol Foster was just as talented with the tin whistle as Lucy. Very early in the day, Lucy, with the help of Reuben, Henry, and Noah, moved the piano from the house to the oak tree. Lucy selected the music for Renee's march down the aisle. She wanted to do more for Renee than stand by her side as her matron of honor. Since Renee enjoyed listening to Lucy play her music on the piano and whistle, Lucy wanted to play music for Renee's and Reuben's special day.

Reuben and Noah made their way down the aisle toward the oak tree and were greeted by everyone as they walked to take their places.

"Are you nervous?" asked Reverend Michaels to Reuben.

"Not in the slightest, Reverend. I have loved Renee for as long as I have known her and love will always defeat nervousness."

Looking impressed, Reverend Michaels replied, "That's a very profound way of looking at it."

Lucy, with the help of Tom Foster on his fiddle and Carol with her tin whistle, began playing on the piano a very soft rendition of Loch Lomond, Aaron's favorite song, while Aarleen and Andy made their way down the aisle.

There were gasps of joy from many ladies as Renee and Coleen walked along the curvy aisle. Renee had a bright smile and her eyes were sparkling. When Renee and Coleen made the last turn in the aisle, Renee saw Reuben for the first time this day. She stopped, causing Coleen to turn and look at Renee.

Renee was gleaming as she saw Reuben waiting for her at the end of the aisle. He was dressed just as she pictured him in a white band collar shirt with the top three buttons undone, black trousers tucked into knee high leather boots, and his obi of Akagi burgundy tied at his waist.

After admiring him for several moments, Renee quickened her pace to reach Reuben and take her place beside him.

When Renee and Coleen reached Reuben and Reverend Michaels, Coleen took both Renee's and Reuben's hands and brought them together. "Reverend Michaels, with love and devotion, it is I, in place of my dear departed Aaron, who gives these two souls in marriage," said Coleen before being asked.

Nodding in approval, Reverend Michaels said, "Very well."

Coleen stepped aside next to May and Henry as Lucy rose from the piano bench to join Renee at her side.

Reverend Michaels cleared his throat and began, "Dear friends and family, we are gathered here today to witness and celebrate the bonding of Renee and Reuben in marriage. The journey they both took to reach this wondrous moment in their lives is a tale of woe that ends in the most happiest of both endings and beginnings, for their woe has finally ended and their happiness begins. That journey has caused them to grow, mature, and truly understand the meaning of unconditional love.

Reuben took hold of Renee's other hand as they both gazed into each other's eyes.

"Renee and Reuben, today you choose each other before your family and friends, to begin your new life. For all the tomorrows that will follow, you will choose each other over and over again, in the privacy of your hearts. Let your love and your friendship guide you, as you learn and grow together. Experience the wonders of what God has to offer. Through the comfort of loving arms, may you always find a safe place to call home."

Lucy looked to Eric with thoughts of their special day. They smiled together anticipating the next portion of the ceremony.

"Do you, Reuben, take Renee to be your lawfully wedded wife, promising to love and cherish, through joy and sorrow, sickness and health, and whatever challenges you may face, for as long as you both shall live?"

Reuben let go of Renee's hands and placed his hands on her waist and said, "Here I am and here I'll stay, by your side, forever and ever, as your husband, my precious Renee."

Reverend Michaels looked confused at Reuben's response. He looked at Renee who had a glorious look. He glanced around and noticed everyone had looks of joy. Reverend Michaels nodded in agreement, smiled, and continued.

"Do you, Renee, take Reuben, to be your lawfully wedded husband, sharing your path, equal in love, promising to honor and cherish, through good times and bad, until death do you part?"

Renee placed her hands on Reuben's shoulders and replied, "Here I am and here I'll stay, by your side, forever and ever, as your wife, my dearest Reuben."

Tears of joy fell from Lucy's eyes, as did from Coleen's and May's, and many other ladies.

Reverend Michaels nodded to Noah, who in turn knelt down to Andy and took the two rings made from the two gold coins Akagi Genda-San gave Reuben the evening before he left Japan. Noah handed them to the reverend. Reverend Michaels placed a ring in Reuben's hand.

Reuben looked at the reverend waiting for instruction. The reverend simply said, "Go ahead, Reuben."

Reuben took Renee's hand and placed her ring on her finger saying, "My precious water, you have washed away the dark spirits and the jaggedness of a rough stone."

The reverend placed the other ring in Renee's hand. She placed it on Reuben's finger saying, "My precious stone, you are as smooth now as the day I first met you under this very oak tree."

Reverend Michaels, in a strong resonating voice said, "By the power vested in me by the Commonwealth of Virginia, I hereby pronounce you husband and wife. Reuben, you may kiss your bride."

Reuben took Renee into his arms, as hers wrapped around Reuben tightly. Their lips met and they kissed as Reverend Michaels proclaimed, "Ladies and gentlemen, family and friends! I present to you, Mr. and Mrs. Reuben and Renee Duran!"

Tom Foster placed his fiddle between his chin and shoulder and began to play a lively Scottish tune, "House on a hill." Carol pulled out her tin whistle and joined in as everyone gathered began to applaud and cheer.

At the same time, both Renee and Reuben looked at Aarleen standing next to Coleen and Riley. Renee and Reuben motioned her to come forward. She sprinted to her mother and father as they both scooped her up and began dancing along with the rest of the guests as Tom and Carol Foster played on with Lucy joining in on the piano, ironically the one given to the Duran family by Renee's father.

石
水

In the year of our lord, 1855, a romantic tale continues.
A new day, and a new adventure…

Well Done, Reuben-San, Well Done

Renee awoke as the sun's rays peeked through the bedroom window and touched her face. Her beautiful, brown eyes blinked a couple of times as they adjusted to the light. She felt Reuben's arm draped over her waist pull her into him as he nuzzled his face into the back of her neck. Renee smiled as she felt the warmth of his naked flesh against hers. She took hold of Reuben's hand and cuddled it against her bare breast as she thought of their first night sharing a bed as husband and wife. Renee could not believe how incredibly happy she was at this very moment.

Closing her eyes, she began to think of the day before, one of the three best days of her life, the other two being the day Aarleen was born and the day Reuben returned from Japan. What was to be a small family wedding turned into a joyous community event filled with friendship and fellowship.

All the farms in the county always seemed to be close, but Renee's and Reuben's wedding brought them even closer. The story of their past was known by many of the guests, and to see the two finally united in the bonds of matrimony was a true happy ending to a sad love story.

After the ceremony, Lucy and the Fosters played several songs together causing others to run home to bring their instruments. Within half an hour, a good sized country band was playing lively Scottish jigs, reels, and songs. Several ladies also joined in and sang beautiful songs of the old countries where many of the families came from.

Noah caught the eye of a recently freed woman of color who was making her way north until she gained employment at the Mason's farm as a housekeeper. Her name was Evergreen, but went by Ever as she was introduced to Noah by Mrs. Mason. Noah and Evergreen spent nearly the entire day getting acquainted with one another. Noah introduced Evergreen to Renee and Reuben and they gave Evergreen the impression of the most perfect couple.

This was also Reuben's first opportunity to meet Eric Klaus, Lucy's husband. They hit it off immediately. Reuben was everything Renee and Lucy had described to Eric, and meeting him in person was a huge privilege.

"Listen to me, Eric," said Reuben. "If my little sister ever gives you any grief, well… you'll just have to live with it. She was born to give nothing but grief."

"REUBEN! YOU BIG BRUTE!!!" yelled out Lucy as she overheard her brother talking to Eric. She started to give chase to Reuben as he began walking away quickly.

As Lucy chased Reuben, Eric said to Renee, "He is not like Monroe at all, is he?"

"That's an understatement, Eric," replied Renee.

Renee and Eric both watched Lucy chase Reuben as they laughed. Suddenly Reuben turned and was running backwards and he extended his arm out to Lucy. Just as Lucy was about to grab Reuben's wrist, Renee shouted, "NO LUCY!!! DON'T GRAB HIS WRIST!!!"

It was too late, for Lucy took a firm hold on Reuben's wrist. He swiftly rotated his body to the left while rotating his wrist over causing Lucy to flip over and land on her backside in the grass.

Reuben knelt down next to Lucy and offered his hand to help her up, but she slapped it away laughing.

Renee and Eric came to Lucy and Reuben also laughing. "Don't blame my husband Lucy. I warned you never to grab his wrist."

"I bet you can't do that again, Reuben," said Lucy.

Reuben offered his other hand to help Lucy up. As she was about to take his hand, Renee again shouted, "NO LUCY!!! NOT HIS HAND EITHER!!!"

As Lucy reached for Reuben's hand, he slightly moved it forward allowing her to take his wrist and when she got a good hold and began to stand, Reuben rotated his hand and wrist to the right making her flip over in the other direction, landing on her backside again.

With handfuls of grass, Lucy threw them at Reuben.

Reuben finally helped Lucy up and showed her the throwing technique he used with her and in several minutes, she was throwing her brother to the ground just as easily.

As the day rolled on, Renee and Reuben met up with Mr. Lester and his wife, Emma. Reuben expressed his desire to purchase the plot of land Mr. Lester had been trying to sell for years.

"Don't get me wrong, Reuben, I'm happy you want to take that land off my hands, but I have to ask… why? I mean you'll have the same problem I had since that property is nowhere near your farm," asked Mr. Lester.

"Actually, I'm buying it to donate to the city public school."

"Whatever for?" asked Emma.

"My husband is going to be certified to become an outreach teacher for the county. He's going to convert that barn into a schoolhouse for the county children," answered Renee proudly holding Reuben's arm.

"Did I hear that correctly, Reuben, my lad? You're going to build a school for the county?" asked Reverend Michaels as he overheard the conversation.

"Yes sir. We may have to use the chapel for a few weeks until I get it completed, but after, the children will have a full-time teacher and a permanent schoolhouse. My brother suggested we convert the barn into a schoolhouse first to make it the way the community wants it, and then donate it to the school. Otherwise, the city will get involved and want to build it the way they want to," answered Reuben.

"Praise the Lord! Do you have any idea how long we have been trying to get a full-time teacher out here in these parts?" asked the reverend.

"Longer than I can remember," said Mr. Lester. "Tell me, Reuben, how soon do you want to buy that plot?"

"Soon as possible. I have the money inside the house as we speak."

"You want to do it today?"

Reuben looked at Renee and smiled. "Perhaps we should wait until Monday. I don't want to conduct business on my wife's special day."

Those gathered laughed at Reuben's comment.

"Quite right, Reuben, quite right. How about bright Monday morning, say about 8 o'clock?" asked Mr. Lester.

"He'll be there," answered Renee.

Mr. Lester offered his hand as Reuben took it to shake on the deal. When Reuben took hold, Mr. Lester felt tingling energy radiating from Reuben's hand. Mr. Lester had a look of thought in his face and said, "Tell you what, Reuben, since what you are doing with that land is for our community and a noble gesture, how about I sell that plot to you for $200 instead of $300? You can use the other $100 for building materials."

Renee's face lit up, as did Reuben's and the reverend's.

"Deal," said Reuben. "I'll see you Monday morning at eight."

"Praise the Lord again! This is magnificent! Would it be all right if I announce this to the congregation at services tomorrow morning?" asked the reverend.

"I don't see why not, but you should say it's only a plan right now," replied Reuben.

"Well, perhaps you could do that yourself, Reuben," said the reverend.

Again Reuben looked to Renee and replied, "I have a feeling Renee and I will probably have a late night and may not be in the best condition to attend services."

"Reuben!" said Renee, blushing from embarrassment as she lightly slapped his arm.

Reverend Michaels and Mr. and Mrs. Lester laughed.

"Understood, Reuben, understood," replied Reverend Michaels.

It was nearly seven in the evening when the last of the guests departed. Renee and Reuben bid each one thanks and farewell as they left.

"Two Duran parties in one week, I can't wait to see what you have planned next, you two," said Mr. Foster after helping return the piano back into the house.

"Just keep your fiddle bow warmed up. Now that I'm home, I suspect there will be plenty of surprises," said Reuben.

When the Fosters left for home, Renee and Reuben stood out in the front holding each other very happily. When they entered the house, everyone was getting ready to leave to the city.

With a questionable look, Renee asked, "Where's everyone going?"

Coleen smiled and replied, "You didn't think we would be staying here on your first weekend as husband and wife, did you? I'll be taking Aarleen and May with me, while Lucy, Eric, and Andy will go home with Annabelle and Andrew. You can pick up Aarleen and May Monday morning when you come into town after your business with Mr. Lester."

"I'm taking Riley too," said Aarleen.

"And don't you worry about Henry and Noah," added May. "I made them two swear they would not enter this house for any reason and that they are to stay in their cabin just in case you two wish to visit the oak tree later on."

Lucy let out a little giggle and said, "Oh, I wouldn't worry about those two making any romance under the oak tree. Knowing them, they will be throwing each other to the ground."

"Lucy!" cried out both Renee and Reuben as they playfully began to slap her on the shoulders.

Renee and Reuben hugged and kissed Aarleen goodbye and told her they would bring her back home Monday.

It wasn't until Renee and Reuben were alone in the house, late into the evening, when Reuben presented Renee a parchment rolled into a scroll tied with a burgundy cord.

"What's this?" Renee asked.

"My first attempt to put my thoughts on paper about how I feel about you on this day," answered Reuben.

Renee slid the cord off and carefully unrolled the parchment. What she saw was a beautifully written passage in kanji. Although she could not read it, she felt very emotional and gently caressed the page with her fingertips.

Reuben took her in his arms from behind and rested his chin on her left shoulder and began to translate...

Forever, I promise you forever
I will be yours no matter where
I will always make you smile
We will have a blessed life we both can share

Our path will be free of any doubt
It will be a path that will not end but continue
I am yours and you are mine
My dearest, most precious Renee, Aishite'ru yo

When Reuben finished translating, Renee carefully rolled the parchment, replaced the cord, and led Reuben by the hand to their bedroom.

Now Renee was looking upon the rolled parchment on the night stand, feeling warm and tingly laying next to her husband with his arm around her as she continued to cuddle his hand against her bare breast.

"Baka Monrō, naze anata wa guntai ni sanka shita nodesu ka," said Reuben clearly in his sleep startling Renee from her thoughts of yesterday. She rolled over to face Reuben and gently nudged him awake.

"Hey you, you overslept your training time. It's... oh geez, it's after 7 o'clock," said Renee as she glanced at a small clock sitting on the night stand on Reuben's side of the bed.

"7 o'clock!" said Reuben as he started to rise, but was held down by Renee.

Reuben laid back down as Renee rested her head on his shoulder. "I have better training for you right here in this bed," she told Reuben as she traced the large katana scar and dotted the bullet scar with her finger tip.

"So in bed you are the sensei?" Reuben asked, amused.

"That's right, and I don't expect to be thrown when I grab your wrist."

After a short laugh, they laid in each other's arms until Renee asked, "Reuben, what does, and I'm not sure I have this right, Baka Monrō... ah, naze anata wa guntai ni sanka... shita nodesu ka... I think that's it. What does that mean?"

Reuben lifted himself on his left elbow facing Renee, "Where did you hear that?"

"You said that in your sleep, just before I woke you."

"Huh, it means... Monroe you idiot, why did you join the army? Are you sure that's what I said?"

"I think so. You said it pretty clearly. Why would you say that?"

With a very concerning look on his face, Reuben answered, "I must have been having a crazy dream. Could you picture Monroe in the army?"

"I can't picture him doing work here on the farm," answered Renee, humorously.

Reuben remained resting on his elbow with a concerned look, trying to remember the dream that would have caused him to say what Renee heard. Renee, looking at Reuben in deep thought, felt he was dwelling too much on the topic. She pulled him down on top of her to get him to stop thinking about it. "Like you said, it was probably a crazy dream. Now for that training I have for you, let's get to it," she said as she wrapped her arms and legs around him.

It would be another hour and a half before they finally emerge from their bedroom.

Renee and Reuben, dressed in their kosodes and hakamas, came down to make themselves a late breakfast. As Renee began cooking, Reuben went to look for Henry and Noah to let them know it was okay to enter the house. He was hoping he could keep a straight face saying that.

He roamed all over the farm, but Henry and Noah were nowhere to be found. Reuben came back into the house telling Renee he couldn't find them.

"Maybe they went to the city with Mama," said Renee.

"No, all the animals have been tended to this morning."

"Hmm, maybe they went fishing or something."

Reuben nodded as he sat down.

Renee served both of them breakfast and after the dishes were washed, they made their way to the oak tree. Renee asked Reuben to show her how to use the jo. Reuben taught her as Akagi Genda-San first taught him many years ago under the same tree by introducing her to the twenty three jo kata. Once Renee understood the basics, she enjoyed training with the jo immensely, especially when Reuben joined in with the two person training exercises with the weapon. As she raised, swung, cut, struck, and thrust the jo, she began to get a sense of how Reuben feels when he is immersed in his individual training.

When Renee completed her first partner session successfully, she stood and looked at the jo Reuben made for her from an old discarded broom and admired it.

"AHIT!!!" With a loud kiai, Reuben side stepped to Renee's right and using his jo, swept her legs out from under her. She landed on her backside with a surprised look on her face.

"WHAT THE HELL, REUBEN!!!" Renee yelled.

Reuben knelt next to her and with his mischievous look Renee found adorable, he said, "Never take your focus away from your opponent, either in victory or defeat, Renee-Dono."

Renee thought for a moment and giggled saying, "That's what Mr. Akagi said when he did the same thing to you."

It was close to noon when they returned to the house. As much as they were enjoying their Sunday alone together, they both wanted to bring Aarleen home sooner than they planned. Reuben changed into his boots, trousers, and a black band collar shirt. Renee decided to wear her kosode and hakama with the matching tabi socks and sandals.

"Are you sure you want to wear that to the city?" asked Reuben.

"Why, don't you think it's appropriate?"

"Oh yes, very much so, but you'll have me distracted knowing I can pull one tie and it will slip off so I can see you in all your glory."

"Well, maybe that's my intention," said Renee with a lustful smile.

"Come on you silly girl, and let's go get our daughter," replied Reuben, giving her a hug after.

They sat arm-in-arm on the bench of the wagon as they rode into the city. Renee had Reuben's jo resting on her lap and was thinking of the earlier practice. She couldn't get over how Reuben was able to teach her how to use the jo and felt pride in herself, and in Reuben.

"Reuben, can I ask you a question, something you said to Andy when you first met him?"

"Of course, you can ask me anything."

"You said they called you Okami in Japan. What does that mean?"

"You haven't figured that out yet?" asked Reuben, glancing toward Renee.

"Of course not or I wouldn't be asking," Renee answered, slapping Reuben's shoulder.

Reuben chuckled and said, "The answer is on that jo you're holding."

Renee released Reuben's arm and studied the jo more closely and at the end, she saw the kanji characters 狼 burned into the wood, surrounded by what appeared to be a wolf, also burned into the wood.

"Hmm, I never noticed that before. Is that a... wolf?" asked Renee.

"Yes, it is." answered Reuben.

"Okami means wolf?"

Reuben nodded yes as he reached and ran his thumb over the wood burning.

With a look of concern, Renee asked, "But Reuben, didn't you say at one time, you and your men in your platoon in Mexico were referred to as wolves? Isn't that kind of a hurtful memory?"

Reuben smiled and he reached over and kissed Renee. He went on to say when the villagers and Masaru first started calling him Okami, it did bother him until he found out why. He explained to Renee how the villagers described, in detail, how Reuben defended the village against Arata's assassins the day Aarleen was born. They described him as a wolf defending its den filled with cubs. He also told Renee how Masaru said Reuben reminded him of an attacking wolf and coined his sword technique, "Okami no Michi." He also told Renee of the "Okami no Mure," the home guard of Itosai.

"With all that positive energy that came with that name, instead of trying to suppress it, I adopted it."

Renee smiled and felt proud of her husband. She reached and kissed him on his cheek and said, "Aww, you're my little wolfy."

"Oh come on, Renee, that's not right!"

They noticed a group of people on the side of the road as they neared the property Reuben was going to buy from Mr. Lester. There were about a dozen people, including Henry, Noah, Mr. Lester, and Reverend Michaels.

"Hey, here they come now!" shouted Noah.

The people gathered on the side of the road began to applaud as Renee and Reuben came near.

Reuben reined the team to a stop and asked, "What's going on here?"

"As I mentioned, Reuben, I told the congregation your idea of turning this barn into an outreach schoolhouse. The people became so joyful, they all came out here to take a glance at your soon-to-be property. We are what's left from the congregation," explained Reverend Michaels.

"Look here, Reuben," said Henry, handing Reuben a sheet of paper. "Noah and I have been out here all morning going through the barn inside and out. This is a list of materials that will be needed. I hope we didn't overstep our bounds."

Reuben looked the list over with Renee looking over his shoulder. Reuben nodded and answered, "Of course not, Henry. You and Noah saved me a whole lot of time. Mr. Lester, how would you feel about conducting business on a Sunday?"

"Well, if the reverend has nothing against it, I don't see why not. Reverend?"

"What do you have in mind, Reuben?" asked Reverend Michaels.

"Renee and I are going into the city to bring back Aarleen and May. How about you and your wife come over for dinner and we can finalize the deal for the plot of land?" asked Reuben.

"Sounds good to me, does 5 o'clock sound okay?"

"Perfect," replied Reuben.

"How about you as well, Reverend Michaels? You can act as a witness," added Renee.

"It will be my pleasure."

After several more minutes of discussion, Renee and Reuben continued on into the city. They asked Henry and Noah if they wanted to come along, but they both said they would rather continue to work on the future schoolhouse.

Renee and Reuben arrived at the house in Norfolk. Their arrival was a surprise since Coleen and May didn't expect them until the next day. Aarleen was especially surprised and was so overcome with joy, she cried. Coleen told Renee and Reuben, Aarleen was so exhausted when they arrived to the house last evening, she went straight to sleep. This morning she woke up refreshed saying she *"Couldn't wait to be picked up by her official Mama and Da."*

Riley was also leaping on all four paws greeting Renee and Reuben and they were happy to hear Riley kept Aarleen good company.

Reuben told Coleen about the gathering they came across on their way to the house and that Mr. Lester, his wife, and Reverend Michaels would be coming for dinner to finalize the purchase of Mr. Lester's plot of land.

"If that's the case, we had better get to the mercantile and say our goodbyes to Lucy, Eric, and Andy so I can get home and get a good dinner going," said May. "They are taking the late afternoon ferry back to Chesapeake City."

With that said, Renee helped Aarleen gather her belongings and they were off to the mercantile. When they arrived, Annabelle admired Renee's outfit. It was to Annabelle's surprise when Renee told her what she was wearing was an outfit worn by men.

"Here, take a closer look, these are actually trousers," said Renee, showing the separate legs of her hakama.

Renee glanced at Aarleen who was playing a game of tag along the store aisles with Andy and asked Annabelle to order the same type of material in blue, Aarleen's favorite color.

Taking Renee aside, Lucy said, "So, how was your first night as husband and wife?"

"Oh, Lucy, it was heavenly. To finally hold Reuben and proclaim he is mine after all these years. I'm still feeling tingly thinking about it."

Lucy nodded and took Renee's hand and pulled her closer as she asked, "That's all fine and dandy, but what about the private time, huh? I'm surprised you're still walking."

"LUCY!!!"

After a short visit, Renee, Reuben, and Aarleen, along with Coleen and May, left the mercantile. They stopped by the house to drop off Coleen and then rode back to the farm. As they were passing the soon-to-be Norfolk County Outreach School, they noticed Henry and Noah were still there. Reuben climbed off the wagon to see what Henry and Noah had accomplished, while Renee and May continued on.

"Can I stay with you, Da? If this is going to be my school, I want to know where my desk is going to be," said Aarleen.

"Sure, my little blossom, but we are not here for fun. We are here to do serious work."

"Oh, I'm all for serious work, Da. After all, if it wasn't for me, the people in the city wouldn't get their eggs. Come on, Riley."

Reuben, Henry, Noah, and Aarleen, with Riley, stayed at the barn for a little over an hour before they headed back home. Reuben was very impressed with all Henry and Noah had gotten accomplished. With the help of several others who had come by earlier, Henry and Noah emptied the barn entirely and sorted out the useful materials. There were a few more items added to the list Henry showed Reuben earlier. Reuben didn't show any concern, for he knew he had more than enough money to cover what materials would be needed.

They arrived at the farm a little before 4 o'clock which gave Reuben and Aarleen a little bit of playtime at the oak tree. He showed her one of the few games he knew the children in Itosai would play, which was actually a training exercise. It was a game the children used to learn how to fall safely and rise up quickly which was needed for hand-to-hand combat. Even Riley got into the game, chasing Aarleen, making her fall, roll, and rise. Their playtime was interrupted by Renee when she came to let Reuben know Mr. and Mrs. Lester had arrived. When Renee, Reuben, and Aarleen made it back to the house, Reverend Michaels arrived.

After a superb dinner of ham, potatoes, and greens, Reuben, Mr. Lester, and Reverend Michaels moved into the parlor to conduct business. Reuben went into detail as to how he wanted the school to look and function, but he made it clear, he was open to any other ideas from the community. He showed them drawn plans for indoors and plans for the use of the outside area.

"My, Reuben, it looks as if you have had some building experience, have you?" asked Reverend Michaels.

Reuben rose and retrieved one of his journals and opened the book to a page of a detailed sketch of Hisano Castle. "This is Hisano Castle, the stronghold of the Hisano Province in Japan. I was a part of building that structure and the relocation of the entire village of Itosai where I lived, trained, and taught for seven years," he explained.

Both Reverend Michaels and Mr. Lester were impressed. With the transfer of the deed and $200 cash, and Reverend Michaels' as witness, Reuben was now the owner of the plot of land where the future Norfolk County Outreach School would be located.

With plans proceeding ahead of schedule, at least one day ahead, Reuben walked out to the oak tree by himself after the dinner guests had departed. He sat alone against the trunk of the oak tree and rested his head against it. He felt a nudge against his hip and looked down to see Riley sitting next to him. Reuben rubbed Riley's fur between his ears and smiled. "I'm sorry I haven't spent much time with you, Riley. I have been very busy, but you have Aarleen to keep you company."

Quietly Renee strolled up to the oak tree and noticed Reuben with Riley laying half way on his lap.

"Hey you, what are you doing here by our tree without me?" asked Renee, smiling.

Reuben held out his hand for her to take, which she did, and sat with him.

"I was catching my breath after such a busy week and thinking our life is going to get much busier. But I wouldn't have it any other way, especially with you by my side. I love you with my entire being, my precious. It's a new world for us, Renee, a new adventure."

"And it's a world and adventure you and I will take on together. I love you with my entire heart and soul, Reuben. I always have and always will."

狼

With a white, lace bordered parasol in her right hand, shielding herself from the mid-morning sun, Cynthia Norenham, dressed in a lavish, hooped gown in soft pastel colors, leisurely walked in high laced shoes from France. Looped in the crook of her right elbow, a superb handbag of black velvet, outlined in lavender lace, hung by her side. She spent a majority of the morning visiting shops, while awaiting her husband, one of the city's most prestigious builders, who was in conference with city planners discussing the widening of Gamby Street to accommodate the city's growth.

She was a woman who enjoyed the life of a true Southern socialite, with all the wealth and prestige her husband's occupation, not to mention his family's background, had to offer. Cynthia Norenham also came from a prestigious family herself. Before becoming the wife of Simon Norenham, she was Cynthia Garrett, the daughter of Albert Garrett, the most successful textile importer and exporter in the Region.

Growing up, she was educated in all forms of social graces, including attending Wickham Finishing School for Girls, where she became the betrothed fiancée to Simon Norenham, an architectural graduate from the University of Virginia. They were married on Cynthia's nineteenth birthday. All her life, Cynthia's needs and wants had been provided for either by her husband or her own parents. For her, it was a truly "blessed" life.

As she strolled along the avenue looking into the windows of various shops, a sight of an oddly dressed female caught her eye. She turned and looked at the woman with contempt.

"My goodness, how revolting to have a woman dressed in such a way to be allowed to walk on our portion of Gamby Street. I will have a word with my husband about this," said an older woman who strolled up next to Cynthia.

"Good morning, Mrs. Noel. Yes, I do agree. At least the Negro women have a sense to wear a bonnet if they must walk on this street for their mistress's errands. I do not even allow our servants to walk on our portion of Gamby Street," replied Cynthia.

Mrs. Sophia Noel, the wife of Jefferson Noel, a successful landowner and developer, and also a city councilman, said, "Indeed, Cynthia. That woman is utterly inappropriate. You have yourself a pleasant day."

"You as well, Sophia," answered Cynthia as Sophia turned and walked in the opposite direction, so as not to get close to the "inappropriately" dressed woman ahead.

Cynthia could not look away from the woman. There was something familiar about her. She couldn't help but feel a sense of déjà vu and some curiosity. She began to slowly walk closer to the woman, and the nearer she got, the woman began to take on the looks of a younger girl, younger than herself.

As Cynthia neared, the girl's attire appeared to look exotically foreign. She wore what appeared to be a light brown robe-like top tucked into what seemed to be a dark green skirt. But with closer scrutiny, Cynthia noticed they were actually large legged trousers with slit vents on the sides at the hips and tied at the waist. She wore open sandals, yet her feet were covered in fitted stockings. She was holding a handled covered basket in both hands. The girl's long, dark, brown hair was untethered, flowing over her shoulders and waving in the gentle breeze, the same way... "Renee? Renee Wallace, is that you?" asked Cynthia as Renee's full profile came into view.

Monday morning, July 23 of '55, Renee, Reuben, and Aarleen came to the city for usual farm business for Renee and Aarleen. As for Reuben, his business was to arrange building materials for the county school project from the city lumber mill. However, he wanted to pay a visit to the law office to see if Monroe had returned from Richmond first.

After their business of delivering Aarleen's eggs was conducted at the mercantile, Renee got Reuben to take Aarleen with him. At first Reuben was hesitant about taking Aarleen thinking his business would be dull for her.

"Don't be too sure, my dearest. That little cherry blossom of yours has a face that will melt the coldest of hearts, and I hear some of those millers have hearts of icebergs," said Renee.

"That's right, Da. I'll get you what you need with my charm," added Aarleen.

Renee leaned closer to whisper into Reuben's ear, "Also, I want to get Aarleen a present for being such a good girl these past several days."

"What kind of present do you have in mind?" Reuben whispered back.

"I'm thinking, since her writing has gotten much better, a pen and ink set. I got my first set about her age. She needs to start transcribing her written stories into a more permanent form of writing," answered Renee.

"That would be good practice. I've read some of her stories. They are magnificent. Hey, what about your passages?" asked Reuben without whispering. "Am I ever going to get a chance to read your poetry one of these days? After all, we are husband and wife."

Renee giggled and said, "Hmm, maybe it is time for you to look in my chest of passages. After all, they're all about you."

Reuben let out a little laugh causing Renee to ask, "What's so funny?"

"Irony," replied Reuben.

"How so?" asked Renee.

"Ever since I left for VMI, you have been writing passages and have a chest full of them. I barely write one passage the day we are married, and you get to read it before I have a chance to read any of yours," said Reuben with affection in his voice.

Renee kissed Reuben and said, "Well, I didn't actually read it. You had to translate it for me."

Cynthia remembered Renee always wore her hair unpinned any chance she got, even during school hours, a habit that constantly got Renee in trouble. Reuben adored how Renee looked with her hair free, even as young children, and as her form of personal revolt against her strict father and rules of Wickham Finishing School for Girls, she would let it cascade over her shoulders with Reuben as her voice of reason.

Back in their school days, Cynthia viewed Renee as unworthy to be attending such a high end school for the "socially elite" daughters of Norfolk. In Cynthia's mind, Renee was ungrateful for the opportunity to attend such a great school, a fact she and other girls would antagonize and torment Renee many times just to witness her be punished by the head mistress of the school, and of course, Renee's father.

At the sound of her name, Renee turned to see Cynthia standing a few yards away. "Cynthia Garrett? Good heavens!" said Renee in a cheerful manner. She placed her basket on the ground and dashed toward Cynthia, those days of torment long forgotten.

However, Cynthia suddenly began to fear for her life. Remembering all the torment she caused Renee back in school, she viewed Renee's approach as hostile and dropped her parasol, held up her hands, turned her face, and shut her eyes tight awaiting Renee's frenzied attack. Instead, she felt arms wrap around her in a gentle embrace. Opening one eye, Cynthia saw Renee, face-to-face, with wide open friendly eyes and a smile to match. Opening her other eye, she began to relax. At that moment, Renee released her embrace and stepped back a few steps.

"Oh! Please forgive me for startling you, Cynthia," Renee said, and reached to retrieve Cynthia's parasol. Renee quickly brushed off the dust and dirt from the edge with her hand and presented it to Cynthia. "There, good as new. Sorry about that, but I couldn't help it. It's been a long time since I last saw you. You look absolutely beautiful. How in the world are you doing?"

Completely dumbfounded by Renee's cheerful greeting, Cynthia stood rooted to the walkway, mouth gaping with a total loss of words. Noticing her uneasy demeanor, Renee calmly extended her right hand and gently took Cynthia's and gave it a smooth shake.

"Just look at you. Cynthia Garrett, the most studious girl in our class, all grown up. Please tell me what you have been doing with yourself all these years."

"Norenham…" answered Cynthia in a stunned state.

"Beg your pardon?" asked Renee.

"My name is now Norenham, Cynthia Norenham."

"Oh, I'm sorry. I remember now. The last time I saw you, you mentioned you were engaged."

That last time came back to Cynthia like a slap in the face. Cynthia, with her friend Elizabeth, saw Renee enter the Klaus Mercantile when Renee was pregnant. Cynthia and Elizabeth attempted to antagonize Renee, but instead, Renee easily dropped Cynthia painfully to her knees from a technique Renee learned from Reuben.

Regaining her composure, Cynthia looked Renee from head to foot and back up. "Renee Wallace, you look… if you will pardon me for saying so, just as, hmmm, unconventional as ever," she said in a surprisingly polite manner. "I do declare, you have not changed at all, except for your, hmmm, attire."

Renee spread her arm out from her sides and twirled around causing her hakama to flow with the breeze. "Thank you, Cynthia. I do assume you mean my being, 'unconventional,' as a complement?" she replied happily.

"Of course, I can honestly say I do admire your ability to, ah, shall I say, be yourself," said Cynthia, sincerely and in her mind, actually meaning it. She suddenly began to feel a sense of envy of Renee being able to express her true nature. As a woman of social graces, Cynthia never had the ability, or even the opportunity, to allow herself to freely express her truest desires. How wonderful it would be, for just a few minutes of the day, to act like a little girl and skip down a path, she thought to herself.

Her thoughts were interrupted when Renee replied, "These are actually men's clothes. My husband gave them to me."

Shocked, Cynthia let out a gasp, "Husband?"

"Yes, I'm no longer Renee Wallace either."

Sincerely intrigued, Cynthia asked very questionably, "William Sinclair?"

Cynthia, as well as all the social daughters of Norfolk, knew of Renee running out on her wedding day of marrying William Sinclair, the man she was promised to by her father. Because of that "despicable" act, Renee had dishonored her father, causing him to leave Norfolk and literally disowning her. Thinking it impossible, Cynthia could only think of William Sinclair as being Renee's husband.

"Oh, heavens no!" replied Renee. "I seriously doubt he would ever give me the time of day. I'm married to Reuben Duran, the one I have always loved," she said with pride.

Shocked even more so, Cynthia began to think Renee was out of her mind. Her strange attire, unconventional personality, and now claiming to have married Reuben Duran, the boy she grew up with and seemed to be the wedge between Renee and her arranged fiancé. It was well known the baby Renee was carrying was from Reuben who it had been said among the out of touch social elite, he had gone insane and committed suicide. Perhaps she is delusional as well, Cynthia thought.

Replying skeptically, she said, "Reuben Duran? If you will beg my pardon, Renee, I was led to believe Reuben Duran died years ago."

"Oh no, he is most assuredly alive and very well. Geez oh geez oh geez is he sooo very well indeed," answered Renee not offended at all, and with a hint of lust in her voice. She continued, "He went away for seven years, but recently returned. We got married this past weekend. We have a beautiful daughter, Aarleen. Reuben fathered her before he departed, but he didn't know until he returned. Now we are a complete family living on our farm in Norfolk County."

Considering Cynthia's upbringing, and their history as rivals, Cynthia could not help but admire Renee's pride in her non-traditional relationship and unwed motherhood. Cynthia continued to listen to Renee with sincere curiosity, but was still doubtful.

Cynthia was about to mention her son, Benjamin, however their visit was interrupted by a call of a man's voice coming from across the street.

"Cynthia, my dear, the meeting went well and I believe I will get the contract," the voice called out as a very well-dressed man crossed the street toward Cynthia and Renee.

"Oh, my, is this your husband?" asked Renee.

"Yes, he is. Simon, if you please, I want to introduce you to an old schoolmate of mine from Wickham. Renee Wallace, um, excuse me, Renee Duran. Renee, my husband, Simon," said Cynthia.

As Simon stepped up onto the walkway, he was met with what he thought was the most intriguing woman he ever had the pleasure of meeting, a manner that didn't escape his own wife.

Simon Norenham was dressed in a very handsome three piece suit, very expensive shoes, and a smart looking derby hat. He carried a walking stick made of black mahogany topped with a head of a golden eagle.

"Indeed, a pleasure to meet you, Mrs. Duran, a pleasant, pleasure indeed," said Simon as he tipped his hat in a most gentlemanly manner. Trying to hide his glances from his wife, he could not help but admire Renee's beauty. Unlike his wife, Renee had a, "wild" form of beauty he could only describe to himself as adorable. A form of beauty he couldn't place on Cynthia. He could not believe Renee, with her adorable looks and friendly pleasant personality, attended such a prestigious school like Wickham that seemed to only turn out girls with vain and self-obsessed personalities. Simon gazed upon Renee for long moments until Cynthia cleared her throat.

"My, *dear*, Simon, We have kept *Mrs.* Duran long enough" she said with an air of authority.

"Simon Norenham... you wouldn't happen to be any relation to Judge Sidney Norenham by any chance?" asked Renee, out of curiosity, not meaning to interrupt Cynthia's attempt to regain her husband's attention.

"Why, yes, I am. He's my father," replied Simon.

Cynthia showed surprise at Renee knowing of Simon's father.

"Judge Sidney, a member of the city public school board?" Renee asked again.

"That's him. He's also a member on the city planning committee, and judge advocate of the region," answered Simon.

"That's incredible!" exclaimed Renee. "He helped my husband get his teaching certificate!"

Cynthia looked upon Renee with extreme interest at the sudden surprising topic. "Teaching certificate?" she said very questionably.

"Indeed, did he now?" asked Simon very surprised. "Is he teaching here in the city school?"

"Oh no, he's going to be the permanent outreach teacher in Norfolk County. He acquired a plot of land he intends to donate to the city school after he converts a barn into a schoolhouse. Now the county children will have a school to call their own," said Renee very proudly.

"Excellent! Did you hear that, Cynthia, my dear? What a grand endeavor, and very commendable as well," said Simon, who was now gently nudging Cynthia aside to give Renee his full attention. Cynthia, looking rather perturbed, but still very curious, tried to step into the conversation to keep her presence known.

"Now that is a great example of what I have been preaching as 'community growth.' not only in the city, but the out-laying county areas as well. Whose grand idea was this?" asked Simon.

"It was hers," Reuben said as he turned the corner with Aarleen on his shoulders and strolled up from behind Renee.

Renee turned toward Reuben and took him into her arms. He, in turn, wrapped his arms around her. They quickly kissed and Renee led Reuben to the Norenhams by the arm to introduce him and their daughter.

Simon and Cynthia were both surprised by the sudden display of affection Renee and Reuben showed in public. Simon saw it as pleasantly refreshing, while Cynthia, who also viewed it as refreshing, had a look of distain. She began to feel very envious Renee found actual true "blessed" happiness.

Unlike Simon, Reuben was dressed in common work clothes. He wore a dark burgundy button band collar shirt, and black trousers with the Akagi obi of burgundy tied at his waist. His feet were covered by his black leather knee high boots. In his right hand, he carried his jo and he wore no hat.

Cynthia vaguely knew of Reuben, and of his family, through Renee from their school years, but never paid him much attention, until this moment. The longer Cynthia Norenham gazed upon Reuben she could not help a feeling of lustfulness come over her she never felt for her own husband. As she witnessed the way Renee held him with affection and her loving looks toward him, Cynthia began to understand how Renee could throw away social status, prestige, and wealth, all for love. Cynthia, for the first time ever, began to admire someone of "lower status," and of all people, the girl she tormented for being socially inadequate.

Simon extended his right hand in greeting as Reuben released Renee, lowered Aarleen from his shoulders, and switched his jo to his left hand and accepted Simon's hand. As they shook hands, Simon was amazed at Reuben's appearance. He didn't look like a teacher, but there was something in his eyes that expressed vast experience and knowledge. Although Simon was much taller, he felt intimidated.

"Reuben, my love, this is Simon Norenham. You may remember his wife Cynthia, an old classmate of mine. Simon is Judge Sidney's son," said Renee cheerfully as she took Aarleen's hand. "And this is our lovely daughter, Aarleen."

"Well hello there, Aarleen. You are so very adorable," said Simon, smiling.

"That's what everybody tells me," said Aarleen with her delightful personality.

"Aarleen! Sorry about that. She's just like her father," said Renee with a giggle.

"Judge Sidney! You don't say?" said Reuben, delighted. "I can't thank your father enough, and neither can my mother. He was instrumental in extending the educational outreach program into the county."

Feeling more at ease and finding Reuben extraordinarily pleasant, much like his wife, Simon replied, "That sounds like a fascinating project, and you say it was your charming wife's idea?"

Reuben returned his Jo to his right hand and in doing so, Cynthia noticed the strange markings 狼 surrounded by what looked like a wolf on the end. Reuben put his left arm around Renee's waist and gently pulled her closer to him. She in turn placed her right arm around Reuben and pulled Aarleen in front of them. Seeing the three huddled together in an affectionate manner caused Cynthia to look upon Renee with both admiration and jealousy. For years, as they went to school together, Cynthia antagonized Renee with hopes of breaking Renee's spirit. By the looks of her happiness, it didn't work. Suddenly Cynthia remembered the last words Renee said to her that day in the Klaus Mercantile when Cynthia tried one last time to break her spirit.

"Listen Cynthia, you're right, my parents disowned me, but I must tell you that was the best thing they ever did for me. Yes, my life isn't as it should be right now, but I have wonderful friends like Mr. Davis and Mr. Lester standing over there who care about me just the way I am, and Mr. and Mrs. Klaus who support our farming community unlike your so called upper crust society. I pity you, Cynthia, because I'm richer in friendship and love than you'll ever be. So keep thinking you are superior because when Reuben returns, we are going to be a very happy family filled with love and joy, while you'll still be an over-privileged, snobby, uptight, horrid Wickham bitch."

After her memory reminded her of that one day, Cynthia began to wonder if she, herself, was happy. After all, she was married to a very successful man, had financial comfort, and a life of luxury, but was she really happy?

Of course I am happy, Cynthia thought. After all, look at them, they are common. How could they be happy, she continued thinking to justify her happiness.

"Renee always had confidence in me that I would one day become a teacher," said Reuben, responding to Simon's question. "And her confidence kept that dream alive, and thus, the Norfolk County Outreach School is being created."

"Well, it cannot be all that popular with the *country folks* out in the sticks," said Cynthia very condescending.

"Cynthia, my dear," said Simon. "That isn't very polite."

Renee felt a sudden emotion of anger that reminded her of Cynthia's torment during their school days and was about to lash out, but felt Reuben's arm tighten around her waist, causing her to look in Reuben's face, which still had a pleasant grin. That sight made her feel warm and calm. She turned her attention back to Cynthia. "On the contrary, many of the county citizens have been very grateful and helpful. Many gathered at the location yesterday to start work on the school, and Reuben hadn't even purchased the plot yet. He purchased it last evening and came to the city to arrange building materials," said Renee very proudly.

"Capital!" exclaimed Simon. "Reuben Duran, you surely are a man of vision. I must ask, with no offense intended, but do you have any building experience?"

Reuben was about to reply, but it was Renee who answered. "He may not be a builder by occupation, but he was part of building Hisano Castle, the stronghold of the Hisano Province and home of the Akagi Samurai Clan in Japan. It was his idea to place the castle in a star shaped foundation which isn't traditionally found in that country."

Both Simon and Cynthia looked at Reuben with awe in their faces. Reuben shrugged his shoulders and replied, "What she said."

"My goodness, I've seen illustrations of such structures in my collage days and found them fascinating. You must tell me all about it, Reuben," said Simon with sincere interest.

Cynthia nudged Simon, gaining his attention. "Dearest, we do not have the time. I must return to mothers for midday tea."

"Oh, quite right dear. Just give me a few more minutes. Reuben, I have just come from a conference with city planners about widening this street because of the new shipping contracts coming to Norfolk. I am the type of man who seeks growth in our community, and that includes the county also. What you have started is a move in that direction," said Simon. "I will do some research on your behalf and see if I have some materials to donate for your endeavor and assist you. Do you happen to have a list of what you need?"

With surprised looks on their faces, Renee and Reuben looked at each other, hugged, and turned back to Simon. Reuben pulled out a folded page from his trouser pocket and handed it to Simon, swapped his jo to his left hand, and extended his right hand to Simon as he in turn accepted the gesture. Renee wrapped her arms around Simon, which surprised him. Cynthia showed only a forced smile.

"That would be wonderful, Simon!" said Renee as she released him and regained her affectionate hold on Reuben.

Reuben, nodding his head in agreement, said, "Any help would be appreciated. If you get a chance, please come visit and see what we have accomplished so far."

"That sounds like a grand idea, doesn't it, Cynthia?" asked Simon very enthusiastically. Cynthia didn't show any emotion at all. "We should make it a family outing, dear. We can bring along Benjamin. I believe we have never taken him out to the country."

"That would be horrible, Simon," said Cynthia, in a distasteful tone. "You know I don't like... the wilderness, and Benjamin might get hurt."

Simon showed embarrassment and was about to scold his wife until Aarleen spoke up.

"Benjamin? Who's Benjamin? Is he your son? I know everything about the country. Hiking, fishing, and other country stuff. I'll make sure he won't get hurt," said Aarleen very adorably.

Cynthia looked at Aarleen with a scowl, but Simon answered. "Yes, he is. He is about your age. It would be nice for him to have a friend who lives in the country," he said pleasantly, and looked at Cynthia with a glare of warning.

"By all means, you must make a family outing to the farm and school. Maybe Benjamin and my little cherry blossom might hit it off and become friends," said Reuben.

Renee covered her mouth to hide a laugh, thinking of Cynthia's son and Aarleen becoming friends. Now that would be some serious irony, Renee thought.

"Oh, I doubt it. I'm sure our children would have absolutely nothing in common," said Cynthia in a matter-of-fact type of tone. Simon was feeling very uncomfortable with the tone his wife was taking toward such a pleasant couple. However, he noticed both Renee and Reuben maintained their pleasant composure. It made him realize how very lucky they were to have one another.

"Aw, come on now, Cindy. Children will be children, and no matter if they are from one side of the tracks or the other, they will always have a common ground... how much they want to get away from their parents and play," Reuben said as if he were a child himself. "After all, Renee and I were from different backgrounds when we first met, and look at us now."

Simon found himself laughing so hard he began to cough and leaned against Cynthia to catch his breath. Renee looked at Reuben as if he committed a horrible sin by calling Cynthia, Cindy, a name she very much despised. Renee began to wonder if the reason Simon was laughing so hard was because of that also, and in turn, she began to giggle.

Very perturbed, Cynthia grabbed hold of Simon's arm and said, "Come, Simon, we have kept the Durans long enough. I must get to that tea."

"Very well, my darling," answered Simon still chuckling, "Mr. Duran, it has been a great honor to meet you," he said as he took hold of Reuben's hand once again and give it a shake. He turned his attention to Renee. "Renee, it has been my pleasure to make your acquaintance. Not to worry, I'll see what I can do for material donations and, 'WE' will come out to visit the school."

"We'll be looking forward to it," answered Reuben. At that moment, Reuben, out of habit, gracefully twirled his jo from his left hand to his right behind his back, and without looking, picked up Renee's basket with the jo's end, lifted it off the ground, and presented it to Renee. "You two have a wonderful and safe day."

"Bye, Cynthia. It was truly wonderful seeing you again," Renee said, cheerfully.

When Simon and Cynthia were gone and around the corner, Renee slapped Reuben on his shoulder as she said with humor, "Reuben Duran, you are an evil man."

"What did I do?" asked Reuben, innocently, as he lifted Aarleen back onto his shoulders and began walking in the opposite direction.

"Calling Cynthia, 'Cindy,' and telling her you and I had nothing in common. Geez oh geez oh geez you have given her something to have nightmares about."

"And what nightmares would that be, my precious?"

Renee leaned in close and whispered into Reuben's ear, "Her little Benjamin and our little Aarleen getting married someday."

Reuben paused and looked at Renee with a sour look saying, "No daughter of mine is going to marry a boy whose mother is a Wickham girl."

"Wickham girl, Wickham girl, my Mama is a Wickham girl!" called out Aarleen.

"Hey, little missy! It's one thing for your Da to call me that, but if you continue to do so, I'll send you to that school," said Renee, playfully warning her as she poked her left side tickling her.

"Ewww, it must really be bad if that's a punishment," replied Aarleen with a giggle.

狼

For the next few weeks, Reuben predicted he would be busy, and he was. Not only did he have a school to build, he also had to attend educator meetings and arrange for teaching materials. Thankfully he had support from all sides, from the farming community with the building of the school, and the support of his mother providing first hand and up to date information regarding the upcoming school year and teaching materials.

Reuben's biggest support came from Renee. If Reuben had to be in two places at the same time, Renee would be in the place where he couldn't be, which was mostly at the school building site. There were a couple of times she picked up teaching materials, but it was overlooked especially when Coleen, with Reuben's consent, finally informed the superintendent and school board what he was doing for the community, and the Norfolk School Outreach Program.

When the superintendent and school board were finally told of Reuben's plan to build a school in the county, both Reuben and Coleen were concerned how the officials would react. However, to their surprise, the school officials showed enthusiasm, especially when they heard the whole farming community was involved.

The day the superintendent and school board went to visit the site of the school, they were amazed by the community involvement. Judge Sidney Norenham noticed labels of his son's building materials, many of his craftsmen, and builders. He asked Reuben of Simon Norenham's involvement.

"My wife, Renee, introduced me to him when she met up with his wife on Gamby Street a few weeks back. He was excited about the project and donated all the building materials. At first I thought it would be a few pieces of lumber and hardware, but it was practically enough materials to build a new building. As you can see, we have put them to good use using the original barn's foundation and frame."

"I knew that son of mine was up to something," said Judge Sidney. "Good on him, and good on you, Reuben Duran."

That day the school officials came to visit, they also got involved for a short while either carrying a plank to where it was needed, or to hammer a nail. They made several other visits throughout the weeks to see the progress and were hopeful, as was Reuben, the school would be ready for the upcoming term starting on the third of September.

It was now close to late August, and it looked as if all that was needed were the desks for the students which the city would supply. Even now, with the bulk of the work done, Henry and Noah found the time to begin building playground equipment.

During the construction of the school, Reuben and Simon Norenham had become good friends, an irony both Renee and Reuben found amusing.

"Who knows, Renee, my darling, perhaps one day your old school nemesis will invite you to one of her tea parties," joked Reuben.

"Not likely, and that's not funny."

"Oh, yes it is."

Bobbing her head back and forth, Renee giggled as she said, "Yeah, okay. I'll admit that is funny."

Simon made several trips to the construction site to see its progress, and also to visit with Reuben to hear all about his years spent in Japan. During one of these visits, Simon brought along his son Benjamin. Benjamin, who was a year younger than Aarleen, had never seen a farm or the country for that matter, and was very timid, shy, and stayed close to his father. That was until he saw Aarleen atop Noah's shoulders enter the house carrying a string of fish.

"Look, Da! Noah and I caught dinner! Oh, hi, Mr. Simon. Remember me?" said Aarleen, very cheerfully.

"That I do, Miss Aarleen. It's wonderful to see you. I didn't know you were good at catching fish."

"Oh yeah, Noah here taught me, and Henry too. Who's that? Is that Benjamin?"

Surprised she remembered, Simon said, "Yes, this is my son. Benjamin, this is Aarleen, Mr. and Mrs. Duran's daughter."

"Hi Benjamin, come with Noah and me, and you can help clean these fish!" said Aarleen as Renee hid a chuckle with her fingertips.

"Go on son. It's okay. Your mother isn't around."

Benjamin slowly followed Noah and Aarleen into the kitchen.

The way Simon had to get his son to follow her daughter by saying, *"Your mother isn't around,"* caused Renee to feel sad for the child. It reminded her the only time she could be a true child was with the Durans, hidden away from her parent's view. Soon she began to hear laughter inside the kitchen from both the children, and her sadness faded. When Renee heard the laughter, she excused herself, and went to the kitchen.

Renee watched Noah help the two children clean the fish. Aarleen and Benjamin were getting along well together. Déjà vu ran through Renee's mind as she watched them. It was like watching her and Reuben when they were children themselves, except the roles were reversed. Aarleen is the shoddy farm girl and Benjamin is the soon to be Chandler boy. Renee had to look away when her thoughts began to wonder, what if this whole scenario is being played all over again with our children.

That same night, when Renee was wrapped in Reuben's arms in bed, he sensed Renee's uneasiness.

"What's wrong, Renee?"

"Nothing is wrong."

"Come on, you're distant. You know you can't keep that from me."

Renee let out a sigh, rose, and leaned on Reuben's chest and asked. "Did you hear Aarleen and Benjamin today?"

"Yes I did. It made me think of us when we first met."

"Then it wasn't just me. I can't help but think…"

"What happened to us will happen to them," said Reuben, finishing Renee's thought.

Renee nodded yes as she lowered her head onto Reuben's chest. Reuben ran his fingers through Renee's hair causing her to smile.

"Renee, if those two become friends, we can't keep them apart, just like your parents couldn't keep you away from me. Love finds a way, just like it found us. Oh geez, what am I saying," Reuben said as he rose and sat on the edge of the bed. "They're only children who cleaned a couple of fish this afternoon. Damn it, Renee, now you got me all worked up and it's too late to go practice katas."

"I'm sorry, Reuben," said Renee with humor.

"It's not funny, Renee."

"I know. We're putting too much thought into this matter. Come now and lay back down."

Reuben remained sitting on the edge of the bed facing away from Renee. She ran her fingers gently down his back causing him to shiver. "Reuben, look at me."

Reuben turned to look at Renee. She removed her nightgown and was beckoning him to come to her. "Come, Reuben, and let us not think of it," she said.

"You think that's going to help, Renee?"

With a sly grin on her face, Renee said, "It couldn't hurt."

"Well, I do need to have something to think about during the teacher's meeting with the superintendent tomorrow afternoon."

狼

September 3, 1855, the first day of school finally arrived. Very early in the morning, Reuben woke and silently rose out of bed. He carefully kissed Renee on her cheek so as not to wake her and left their bedroom. Reuben went downstairs to the spare room where he kept his kosodes and hakamas. He chose the hakama he wore during the last battle the Clan Alliance of Hisano Province had with the Arata.

Carefully and precisely, he donned his garments of Akagi samurai. When he was dressed, he softly walked to the parlor mantle where his Kutto laid next to the smooth stone Akagi Genda-San gave Renee many years ago as a precious gift. With both hands, Reuben lifted his Kutto gently and made his way out of the house to the oak tree.

The sun had not yet peeked over the horizon as Reuben sat in seiza with his Kutto laying in front of him. He bowed low to the ground toward the west, the direction he traveled to learn his purpose and to become smooth as the gift of the stone.

After a few moments in silent meditation, Reuben rose and precisely tucked his Kutto into the obi of Akagi burgundy. In silent swift deliberate movements, Reuben commenced drawing his Kutto in all fifteen basic draw and return katas one at a time.

Upon completion of the final kata, Reuben returned to seiza and continued to meditate. Opening his mind he reached out. Genda-San, if you are in mediation, please send the gods my way, Reuben thought. He bowed low to the ground and rose to his feet. Reuben removed his Kutto from his obi, and with it in his right hand, he made his way back to the house to prepare for the first day of school in the newly constructed Norfolk County Outreach School.

狼

"Heaven help the poor student who leaves an apple on my desk. That's all I have to say," said Reuben at the breakfast table. "I will not have any corny clichés in my schoolhouse."

Laughter followed his comment.

"Well, I'm glad I'm not a student in your class. I'd be spending the entire day sitting in the corner," said Renee.

"Watch it, Renee, that's so cliché," said Coleen as a tease toward Reuben.

Coleen spent the night at the farm so she could accompany Reuben to his first day as the newly appointed outreach teacher of the Norfolk County Outreach School. The week prior, with the help of Renee and Reverend Michaels, Coleen assisted Reuben to prepare the schoolhouse for the first day of school, and the enrollment of students. This year's term is expected to have 22 students of various ages, more than predicted. Of course, the first one to enroll was Miss Aarleen Moncy Duran.

"Don't worry about me, Da. During school, I'll pretend you're not my Da," said Aarleen, as Renee filled out the enrollment form.

Aarleen was very excited to have her father being her teacher. In the short amount of time she knew him, Aarleen learned so much from Reuben. She was very curious how much more she could learn from him as a school teacher.

After breakfast was finished, everyone climbed onto the wagon for the opening ceremony of the first day of school. Renee had to constantly stop Reuben from tugging at his collar. After today, I will not wear a tie to school anymore, Reuben thought.

As they rode up to the school, Reverend Michaels was also arriving. After a cordial greeting, Reuben was about to open the door until Renee stopped him.

"We have to do this properly," she said as she attached a bright red ribbon across the two pillars in front of the front door. "Here, you'll need these when the time comes," said Renee as she handed Reuben a pair of scissors.

Coming from the direction of the city, two carriages rode up containing the school superintendent and school board members.

Another carriage arrived with Simon Norenham, and much to Renee's surprise, Cynthia, although she didn't get out of the carriage.

With the arrival of the school officials, students, along with their parents, began to arrive. It was becoming quite a gathering and once Reuben noticed all the students were present, he called attention by ringing a bell Coleen used when she started teaching. She surprised Reuben with the bell the day before.

"Good morning everyone, I am so very happy to see you here for this joyous event! Now students, as I call roll, please come forward and stand before the steps," said Reuben, cheerfully.

By alphabetical order, Reuben called all the students and they all stepped forward. Once all the students were gathered, Reuben introduced the superintendent. The superintendent made a quick praising speech to the community and wished the students good luck in their studies. Afterwards he officially introduced Reuben as their teacher.

There was loud applause as Reuben took the superintendent's place on the steps. Once the applause died down, Reuben spoke. "What a journey this community has taken these last several weeks. I'm so grateful to so many people that if I started naming them all, these students would be very late for their first day of class. So instead, I want all of you to look upon this schoolhouse every time you pass by and think of it as a monument of the goodwill and pride in our community."

Reuben's comments were followed by more applause and when it died down, he continued. "One thing I was very amazed at was how quickly our community came together, and built this schoolhouse to have it ready in the short amount of time we had. It led me to believe the parents of these students were anxious for them to have an education. However, by the way I saw Mr. Davis hammering away, it dawned on me, many of you thought the quicker this school was up and going, the quicker you would be rid of your children for six hours of the day."

Laughter ensued at Reuben's last comment. Reuben picked up the scissors from the top step and asked the superintendent to do the honors, but he held up his hand. "Mr. Duran, being that this is your classroom and your students, I believe you should do the honors."

"Yeah, Reuben, cut the ribbon!" called out Noah, followed by everyone else.

Reuben stepped up to the ribbon Renee strung up, and cut it in half. More applause followed as Reuben said, "Students of the Norfolk County Outreach School, please enter your schoolhouse and find your desk quietly, they all have been labeled with your names."

狼

After the students entered the schoolhouse, the crowd began to disperse. The school officials bid Reuben good luck and all departed, except for Mrs. Corina Bentley, who remained behind to observe and evaluate Reuben.

"That was a great speech, Reuben. Good luck to you," said Simon Norenham.

"Thank you for coming, Simon, and thank you for all your help."

"Well, Mr. Duran, shall we get started?" asked Mrs. Bentley.

"Sure, I have a desk all set up for you."

With Mrs. Bentley's permission, Renee and Coleen were also permitted to observe for a while. Reuben told Mrs. Bentley they both were his inspiration to become a teacher and would appreciate if they could observe for the opening session.

Renee and Coleen sat quietly in the back of the classroom away from Mrs. Bentley so as not to be a distraction for her or Reuben.

"Good morning, class."

"Good morning, Mr. Duran," answered the class together.

"I have a question. How many of you have attended school? I mean a real school, such as this one, or one like it?"

The only child to raise their hand was Aarleen, but when she noticed she was the only one, she slowly lowered it down.

"Miss Duran, why did you lower your hand?"

"I don't know, Da... Mr. Duran."

"Hmm, is it because you are embarrassed you are the only one who attended a real school?"

"I guess so, Mr. Duran."

Reuben chuckled, "Well, Miss Duran, you have nothing to be embarrassed about and neither do any of you other students. There's nothing embarrassing about wanting to learn and that's what we are here to do."

"Not me. I'm here because my pa told me I have to be here."

"Oh, Tommy Deans, is it? Tell me, Mr. Deans, do you like to learn?"

Tommy Deans, a scruffy boy about the same age as Aarleen, shrugged his shoulders. "Not really. It's boring."

Mrs. Bentley began to wonder where Reuben was going with this and became quite interested.

"Is this your lunchbox, Mr. Deans?" asked Reuben as he picked up Tommy's wooden lunchbox with a carved owl.

"Yes sir."

"Did you do this wood carving into the wood?"

"Yes sir," said Tommy Deans with pride in his work.

"How did you learn to do such good work?"

"My pa taught me."

"Did you have fun when you learned how to wood carve?"

"Lots."

"Ah, see! Learning is fun, and the more you learn about reading, writing, and mathematics, the more fun you will have in this huge world of ours."

"How big is the world, Mr. Duran?" asked a little red headed girl sitting next to Aarleen.

"Well, Miss Lindsey, it took me almost three months to travel from here to the island nation of Japan, and that is only halfway on the other side of this world."

"WOW!" said the class as one.

"Learning is the doorway to this world of ours, and in order to learn, we need to ask questions. So let's have a question to start off a lesson. Anyone?" asked Reuben as he looked around the room. "Yes, Miss Foster, do you have a question?"

"What's the purpose of soap?"

"It makes water wetter. Come on, that was an easy one. I want a real difficult question. One we all can discuss. Yes, Miss Duran."

Aarleen lowered her hand and cleared her throat. "My GrandDa told me you were in the Mexican War. Is that true?"

Renee raised her left hand to hide a gasp while her right hand took hold of Coleen's hand. Geez oh geez oh geez sweetie, how could you ask such a question, Renee thought. Coleen placed her arm around Renee's shoulder.

The war was never spoken of in the Duran home, and Aarleen was never told of her father's involvement in that campaign except that he was there.

Reuben noticed Renee's reaction to Aarleen's question. He tugged at his neck tie and rubbed his chin. "Hmm, a history question. Now those are my favorite."

"History is boring," said Tommy Deans.

"Only if you think of history as dates and places, but history is much more. Who likes stories?"

All the students raised their hands.

"Well, that's what history is, one huge *true* story. Yes, Miss Duran, I was in the Mexican War. Can anyone tell me why our country was involved in that war? Yes, Miss Lindsey."

"My dad told me it was because of magnificent destiny."

Reuben let out a little chuckle and said, "I believe you mean Manifest Destiny, and you are correct. But to understand Manifest Destiny, I'm going to tell you a story of the first people who landed on Plymouth Rock. Does anyone know who they were? Yes, Mr. Lester?"

"They were the Pilgrims. They came in a boat called the Mayflower."

Reuben snapped his fingers on both his hands and pointed to Paul Lester. "Mr. Lester, if I had a cookie, I'd give it to you because you are correct."

Reuben moved from the front of the class to the middle as he said, "Once upon a time, there was a group of people called the Puritans…" He commenced to tell of the voyage of the Puritans starting from the Dutch port of Delfshaven onboard a ship called the Speedwell as he gave his first history lesson.

As he taught, Renee relaxed and felt a huge amount of pride as she watched her husband do what he does best, teach.

After Reuben's history lesson, he gave a quick oral quiz over his lesson of the Pilgrims colonizing the Plymouth colony. Every student answered every question correctly. After the quiz, Reuben excused the class for their first recess.

When the students left the classroom, Reuben went to his wife and said, "Piece of cake."

"That was wonderful, son. I couldn't have done better myself," said Coleen.

"Thanks, Mama, but unfortunately, you're not the one observing me."

Mrs. Bentley came to Reuben. "I must say, Mr. Duran, I was rather concerned of how you were starting off, but the way you led into that history lesson was impressive. Not many people know about the other ship, the Speedwell." commented Mrs. Bentley. "There were a few times I nearly raised my hand to answer a question or two. I'm looking forward to the rest of the day."

"Well then, I guess Renee and I will take our leave and see you after school," said Coleen.

Renee took Reuben by the hands and with a look of admiration, she said, "I'm so proud of you, my dearest husband. I'll be waiting outside for you and Aarleen after school."

Reuben gave Renee a quick kiss and said, "Have your hakama on because after Aarleen's schooling is done, yours begins."

The rest of the school day was just as interesting for the students and Mrs. Bentley. For most of the day, Reuben basically evaluated each student's ability in all the basic subjects. Before the end of school, he rearranged the students seating positions by ages, but most importantly, by abilities. He paired students who had reading skills with students who didn't and the same with math. The logic was the students could help their desk partner, a concept Reuben thought of when he and Adam Stanns helped each other at VMI in their weakest subjects. It was a concept Mrs. Bentley found very interesting.

When two o'clock came, the first day of school ended and as the last of the students exited the classroom, Reuben saw to his desk as Mrs. Bentley finished her notes.

"Well, Mrs. Bentley, how did I do?"

"I have to be honest, Mr. Duran. I was skeptical about you for several reasons. Never teaching a wide range of subjects, not interacting with so many children of various ages at once, and, if you will beg my pardon, a male. There are not many male school teachers, and I believe school teaching is best left to women. But I must say, you have given me something to reconsider. Your methods are unorthodox, but very effective. Mr. Duran, in my opinion, you are one fine educator and it was a pleasure observing you today."

Reuben walked Mrs. Bentley to her waiting carriage and assisted her onboard. He bid her farewell and closed the door.

Reuben turned to see Renee in her kosode and hakama holding Aarleen's hand with Riley sitting next to her. He smiled and quickly walked to them. Reuben lifted Aarleen off the ground with his left arm, and placed his right arm around Renee as Riley rose.

"How did you do, my precious husband?" asked Renee.

"You are looking at a man who is unorthodox, but very effective," answered Reuben.

"Oh really, I could have told you that," replied Renee. She then asked Aarleen, "So how was your first day of school, sweetie?"

"It was fun."

"And did you like your teacher?" asked Renee.

"Mr. Duran is the best and I have something for him. Here you go, Da," said Aarleen as she held out an apple. "See, I didn't put it on your desk."

Reuben laughed, took a bite of the apple, and said as he looked lovingly to Renee and Aarleen, "Come on, my beautiful family, let's go home."

狼

Over 7,000 miles away, Akagi Genda-San woke feeling a soft gentle breeze coming through the open wall from the east, waking him from a pleasant dream of a dear friend. He saw in the dream, his dear friend glimmer with radiant ki as he walked along a hardened dirt road, accompanied by what Akagi Genda-San could only assume was close, immediate family after a day of well-deserved self-victory. He rose from his futon, and noticed the watch he had received as a gift from that same friend many years ago. Akagi Genda-San reached and picked it up as he strolled out onto the room's terrace. He looked over the village of Itosai below his terrace of Hisano Castle, and with the watch in both hands, he brought them close to his face as if he were praying. Smiling, Akagi Genda-San closed his eyes as he said softly, "By the gods of the high mountains... well done, Reuben-San, well done."

Part Three

You're a Civilian, a School Teacher, a Husband, and a Father! Go Home Damn It...

石
水

In the year of our lord, 1861, a romantic tale continues.
A father's journey into adolescence, and the distant drums of war…

RENEE!!! Get out Here! I'm Not Ready for This!

"Reuben-San… It did my heart wonders to receive your letter. You, my friend, have certainly surpassed my expectations of your abilities. I feel honored my document aided in the securing of a teaching position I feel you are no doubt worthy of.

The photograph image you provided of you and your family rests amongst the honored Akagi family. Renee-Dono is just as beautiful as the day I first met her under your magnificent oak tree. As for your daughter, Aarleen-Dono, she is the mirror image of her precious, beautiful mother.

Yanna, my darling wife, sends her warmest regards and you will be surprised to hear Masaru has taken a bride from the Yuna Region. Her name is Tenna. They have one child, a boy, named Ichirou.

Kaoru also became the bride of Chodan, a samurai general of the Itto region. Her son, Katsuo, has become quite the scholar and because of his studious manner, he reminds Kaoru of you, Reuben-San.

Tadashi-San and Sukuri are expecting their third child and live a happy life in the village, which you were so instrumental in its relocation. They both care for your cottage and Tadashi-San has plans to add another room to it once he saw the photograph image of you and your family. Now Aarleen-Dono will have a room of her own.

I have enclosed the seeds you have requested and I hope they will be a most adored gift for which you have planned. May you and your family flourish in good fortune and please express my greetings to your mother, sister, brother, Henry-San, Noah-San, and please tell May-Dono, dumplings have never been the same. Your most humbled Friend, Genda."

狼

She was fast. So fast, Reuben didn't expect her cut to his chest. It would have been a hit if he hadn't stepped off the line of attack and raised his bokken to block her strike.

Reuben went in with a forward thrust and was blocked with a counter strike as Aarleen made a downward cut toward Reuben's head. It was by sheer speed Reuben was able to avoid the cut that could have blacked him out.

Damn, she has gotten quick. How did she get so damn quick without me noticing, thought Reuben as he swiftly shifted his body and two stepped behind Aarleen to strike at her from the rear. However, watching her father's center, as he so many times instructed her to do, Aarleen counter turned and stopped his strike holding Reuben in check.

415

Quickly, Aarleen drew her bokken upward taking Reuben's along with it, exposing his midsection, and swiftly cut downward.

Ah, excellent, she's using one of my draw and strike techniques, Reuben thought as he slid backwards and cut down with his bokken, deflecting her cut.

Although Aarleen was preforming the awase exercise flawlessly, unable to land a strike to her father caused her to become frustrated, and it showed in her eyes. Reuben noticed and set the trap using himself as bait by slightly shifting his bokken off to the side exposing his center.

"AHIT!!!" With a loud kiai, Aarleen took the bait and overreached her cut.

Reuben took advantage of her anxious attack. He took hold of Aarleen's tsuka of her bokken between her hands with his left hand. Reuben slightly turned to the right and quickly rotated back to the left, twisting Aarleen's bokken over, causing her to flip over and land on her back while Reuben disarmed her. He brought down his bokken in a cutting motion stopping inches from Aarleen's throat.

Aarleen looked up at her father in sheer awe, which faded into frustration toward herself and said, "I did it again, didn't I, Da?"

"And what is it you did?" asked Reuben.

"I lost focus by getting too anxious."

"Exactly, my little blossom. What was it that the great swordsman Musashi once said?"

Aarleen let out a sigh and recited, "Never be anxious to attack your opponent. The only way to stop a great swordsman is never initiate the attack."

"You can bet your gold coin in your inrou on that one, my precious cherry blossom," replied Reuben as he offered his right hand to assist Aarleen to her feet.

As he lifted her to her feet, Aarleen asked, "Geez, Da, are you getting quicker with age?"

Reuben laughed and replied, "No, blossom. It's you who is getting quicker and I'm getting luckier to avoid your quickness."

"I thought you didn't believe in luck, Da?"

"When it comes to your quickness, I need a little luck," said Reuben with a hint of humor.

"So you still believe in fate, Da?"

"Of course. If you believe in fate, you make your own luck."

Aarleen expressed an impish smile and said, "Well, Da, in that case, fate has provided me with your hand to help me up."

Reuben eyed Aarleen with a questioning look as he asked, "What do you mean by that?"

Without answering, Aarleen swiftly shifted her body to Reuben's right side and rotated his hand upwards causing his body to shift off balance. With her other arm, she thrust it under Reuben's upturned arm, stepped forward, and using her hips and shoulder, threw her father forward making him flip in midair and land on his side.

Riley, watching from near the trunk of the oak tree, trotted up and started to paw Reuben's back.

"It's a full attack!" exclaimed Reuben as he pulled Riley over onto his back and began rubbing his belly causing his legs to twitch.

Aarleen knelt down and did the same as she said laughing, "I'm sorry, Da."

"Don't be sorry, my little cherry blossom. You had fate land in your hands and with luck... an enormous amount of luck I may add, you got the best of your Da."

"Hey, you two, guests are beginning to arrive! Stop playing around and let's go welcome them birthday girl!" called out Renee.

It was Tuesday, July 17, 1860. Five years earlier, Aarleen received her best birthday gift ever when her father returned from Japan. Now Aarleen was turning twelve and had grown from an adorable, curious little girl into a beautiful, adolescent girl just as curious and fun spirited. Aarleen wore a kosode of light purple and a hakama of her favorite color, dark blue. Hanging from her dark blue obi hung the turtle inrou Reuben gave her on her seventh birthday, which contained the gold coin Reuben also given her the evening they first met. Aarleen was the mirror image of Renee at that age, with the exception of her nose which she had gotten from her father.

Helping each other up, father and daughter, along with Riley, made their way to Renee who was dressed as her husband and daughter in a kosode of sky blue, and a hakama of dark green. Through the years, it became a common sight to see Reuben, his wife, and daughter dressed in such fashion, no one paid any attention anymore. That is with the exception of Cynthia Norenham, who, along with her husband and son, was amongst the first of Aarleen's birthday guests to arrive. It was the first time the Norenham's were attending one of Aarleen's birthday celebrations.

"Ah, I see your best friend has braved a trip into the sticks, my precious Renee," said Reuben sarcastically.

"Reuben... just don't call her Cindy," commented Renee. "Not unless I'm around," she added with a giggle.

"You're an evil woman, Renee Duran," replied Reuben.

Aarleen's birthday parties of the past had always been where all had a good time, and this one was no different. Although Aarleen and her friends had grown, they still enjoyed the same party games consisting of a lot of running and chasing. Games Benjamin Norenham wasn't allowed to participate in as long as his mother was present. Thankfully, Cynthia elected to remain inside the Duran house until it was time to leave.

"You know, Reuben, I just don't understand Simon and Cynthia," said Renee, holding onto Reuben's waist with both arms. Reuben had his arm around her shoulder.

"What is it you don't understand?"

"They are so opposite. Yeah, we were opposite also, but not to the degree they are. Simon is so very friendly and pleasant, and then there's Cynthia. Too good to socialize with others outside her precious social elite circle. What do you make of it?"

Reuben shrugged his shoulders and answered, "Hmm, don't know. She can't be a good cook since they have servants. Maybe she's good in bed."

Renee released her hold on Reuben and slapped his shoulder, "Reuben!"

Reuben cowered against the porch pillar laughing. "What else could it be? Look, there's Simon. I'll go ask him," said Reuben stepping off the porch as Renee chased after him.

"Reuben, don't you dare!" called out Renee, taking hold of Reuben's wrist and swinging it back and over into her favorite technique, kaite-nage, and throwing Reuben to the ground.

"Whoa! Did you see that! Aarleen's ma flipped Mr. Duran to the ground!" shouted out Tommy Deans, one of Aarleen's friends and classmates.

Reuben rolled over on the ground facing Renee who had a mischievous grin on her face.

"Come on you shoddy farm boy, let's see if you have anything left after your training with Aarleen."

Reuben smiled, rolled onto his back, and leaped onto his feet by pushing off from his shoulders. Aarleen's parents commenced to toss each other in turn to the delight of her birthday guests. Ever since Aarleen's eighth birthday, Renee and Reuben, unannounced, would put on a display of Budo Akagi Taijutsu to entertain. This year was going to be different because as Renee threw Reuben to the ground using a wrist twist technique, Aarleen joined in for the first time as each three took turns throwing each other from various forms of attacks and techniques.

The crowd enjoyed the display, cheering each one of the three.

"YAME!!!" yelled Reuben, just as both wife and daughter were about to attack him at the same time.

"Hey, that's not fair! You can't stop now just as Mama and I were about to get you good!" said Aarleen, laughing as applauding and cheering erupted.

The noise caused Cynthia to rise from the sofa to glance out of the window. "I wonder what is going on out there?" she asked herself.

"Probably my brother and his wife throwing each other," said Monroe, startling Cynthia. "Sorry. Didn't mean to bother you. I'm Monroe, Reuben's older brother. What are you doing sitting inside?"

Cynthia introduced herself and said in a curt manner, "No offence, Monroe, but I am here against my will so my son could attend your niece's birthday party. I have never liked your sister-in-law."

Monroe nodded approvingly. "Well, Cynthia, that is something we have in common. I'm here against my will as well," replied Monroe, "I despise my brother."

Monroe and Cynthia spent nearly the entire time inside discussing their common dislikes.

"Story time, Aarleen!" called out her cousin Andy.

"Yeah, Aarleen, tell us one of your stories!" another one of Aarleen's friends called out.

Just as Renee and Reuben's Budo display was a part of Aarleen's birthday celebration, so too was Aarleen's story time. Aarleen's guests seated themselves around her in a circle.

Renee and Reuben always watched Aarleen's story time from atop the porch arm-in-arm.

"What's this?" asked Simon.

"This is Aarleen's gift to her guests. Go and have a seat with Benjamin and have a listen. You'll enjoy this," answered Renee.

As Simon seated himself next to his son, Aarleen began with Riley by her side.

"Once upon a time, in a faraway land of a thousand islands, there was a village, a very humble village called... Itosai."

Renee felt Reuben's arm bring her in tighter. She looked up to him as Reuben watched Aarleen with pride.

"There was this evil lord by the name of Arata Goro who terrorized the region. He had a plan to draw all the warriors, known as samurai, away from the villages so he could plunder the villages unopposed. However, Arata Goro didn't count on one man, who didn't have a name, to be left behind."

As Aarleen recited her story of how the man with no name defended the village, she used her bokken, swinging it in draws and cuts, describing the sword attacks. All the onlookers were in complete fascination with Aarleen's story.

"After the man with no name struck down another attacker, he was momentarily distracted by a vision of his true love who he distinctively heard call out to him. He turned just in time to avoid the leader's sword. He wasn't fast enough, so the attacker's sword cut through his jacket and slashed his chest. Although he was wounded, he still fought like a wolf protecting his den of cubs."

Aarleen went on to recite how the man with no name defeated the leader and explained if it had not been for hearing his true love call out to him, instead of only receiving a wound, he would have lost his head.

"When the lord of Itosai returned with his army, he was told of the attack and how the man with no name rallied the villagers to defend their home and defeat Arata Goro's diabolical plan of destruction. The lord's son, Masaru, disliked the man with no name. But because of his honorable acts of bravery, Masaru was grateful for the man who saved his mother, sisters, and nephew. It was Masaru who named the man Okami... Wolf. The end."

As the audience applauded, Renee turned Reuben to face her. She reached into his burgundy kosode and traced the katana scar lightly with her fingertips and said, "I love you, Okami."

狼

After Aarleen's story, lunch was served. While everyone was enjoying their meal, Reuben snuck away to retrieve Aarleen's birthday present he had been working on for almost three years. It was finally ready to be given to Aarleen. Reuben had it hidden behind the barn in a small wooden box. As he turned the corner of the barn, he found Benjamin leaning against the wall tossing a hand full of pebbles onto the ground one at a time.

"Benjamin? What are you doing here?" asked Reuben.

"Oh nothing. Just waiting until the party is over."

"Why? Aren't you having a good time?" asked Reuben, concerned.

"I was but..."

"But what?" Reuben asked as he gently picked up a small wooden box.

"I don't know."

Reuben nudged Benjamin with his elbow to follow him. "Come on, Ben, you can tell me."

Walking back toward the house with his head down, Benjamin said, "I don't think Aarleen likes me."

"Oh, come now, why do you say that?"

"Well, she plays rough with me."

Reuben smiled, "Aarleen plays rough with everyone. That's probably my fault."

"I know, but she plays with me extra rough. And the slapping, she's always slapping my shoulder and no one else."

Reuben suddenly stopped and looked down to Benjamin. "What do you mean slapping your shoulder?" he asked as a concerned father.

"And Benji, she always calls me Benji when she knows that bothers me."

Benjamin looked up to Reuben and saw his face had a combined look of humor, concern, joy, and especially fear. "Mr. Duran, are you all right?"

"RENEE!!! Get out here! I'm not ready for this!" yelled out Reuben as he kept his glare on Benjamin.

"Mr. Duran? Is everything okay? Did I do something wrong?"

"RENEE!!!"

The kitchen door opened and out ran Renee with Lucy following closely behind. "Good grief, Reuben, what's wrong? You about scared me to death."

Taking a few steps back, Reuben said, "Renee, you need to talk to that daughter of ours. She's flirting with Ben."

It took several minutes for Reuben to calm down. Renee had Lucy take him inside while she had a chat with Benjamin. After Benjamin retold his dilemma to Renee, unlike Reuben's reaction, Renee joyfully laughed and gave Benjamin a warm hug.

Renee reassured Benjamin, Aarleen was fond of him, going as far as saying, "Aarleen may be fonder of you than you might think. But I'll have a talk with her, okay?"

"Okay, Mrs. Duran," replied Benjamin, feeling better.

"Can I tell you a secret, Benjamin?"

"Sure, Mrs. Duran," replied Benjamin.

"Now mind you, I could get into a lot of trouble telling you this because only girls are supposed to know this secret. When a girl seems to be a little meaner to a certain boy, that usually means the girl likes that boy as, shall I say… a special friend. Is it silly? Yes, but us girls tend to be silly when it comes to having boys as, special friends. Do you understand, Benjamin?"

"I think so. I do like Aarleen a lot. She's fun, except when she throws me harder than the other boys."

"That's my husband's fault, and I will have a talk with him about that, trust me. Now come on, Aarleen is about to open some of her birthday gifts."

Out on the front porch, Aarleen spoke to her guests thanking them for coming to celebrate her birthday. She assured them gifts were not necessary because having them over was gift enough. But still there were a few who presented her with a birthday token, mainly family.

Andrew and Annabelle presented Aarleen with the latest book of fables for her collection, which Aarleen adored. She received a leather bound journal book to transcribe her stories from Uncle Eric, Aunty Lucy, and Andy. From Uncle Monroe, she received a fine leather book bag, and from GrandMama Coleen, Aarleen received an exquisite desk box for her to keep her pens and ink.

"Ahem, Miss Duran. Please accept this birthday gift from Mr. Norenham, myself, and our son," said Cynthia, handing Aarleen a long cylinder package.

Aarleen took the gift, opened it, and pulled out a lacy object. She looked at it questionably and said, "Ah, thank you, Mr. and Mrs. Norenham, and Benji... I mean Benjamin. What is it?"

"It is a parasol. One of the best, all the way from France," answered Cynthia with social pride.

Renee had to look away to hide her amusement of the gift. Of course, the parasol was all Cynthia's doing. Renee was proud how Aarleen maintained her composure and showing genuine gratitude for the gift.

"Henry, can you please help me with that table," asked Reuben, relieving the awkwardness.

"Sure thing, Reuben. Is it time?" asked Henry with an excited expression.

"I believe so. I can't keep it hidden any longer, or else she's going to stumble upon it one of these days."

"What's this, Reuben?" asked Renee.

Reuben motioned for Renee to come up onto the porch where Aarleen was opening her gifts.

After Henry helped Reuben place a small table on the porch, Reuben picked up the small wooden box he carried from the barn, and placed it upon the table.

"Come here, my little cherry blossom, and stand next to me."

Aarleen stepped next to Reuben and he placed his hands gently on her shoulders. "I was hoping to give you this gift for your thirteenth birthday, but like I told Henry, I can't keep it hidden any longer. Even your Mama doesn't know about it, so I guess you can say this gift is for both of you."

That comment got a very curious look from Renee.

Reuben continued, "For the last five years, ever since I first became aware of my precious Aarleen, I have called her my little cherry blossom. Now she is growing up and, oh geez, gods from the high mountains help me, flirting with boys."

"Reuben!" said Renee, slapping Reuben on his left shoulder.

421

"Da!" said Aarleen, slapping him on his right.

"I don't know why I started calling Aarleen my little cherry blossom. I believe it's because of what Yanna-Dono, Genda-San's wife, once told me, *'when a cherry blossom lands on your cheek, it's a kiss from the gods'* and to me that's what Aarleen is, a kiss from the gods."

Renee moved closer to Reuben and took him by the arm.

"The year I returned, I taught Aarleen a little song and we still sing it almost every day. It's a song about cherry blossoms and to this day, Aarleen, or Renee for that matter, has never seen a cherry blossom. A few years ago, I mailed a letter to my lord, Genda-San, and he sent me some seeds. I planted one deep in the woods and it spouted. For the last three years, I have tended it."

Reuben faced Aarleen and looked at her with fatherly love. "Look at us now, Aarleen. No longer do I need to kneel down to talk to you face-to-face. Now that you are growing into a beautiful young lady, I don't know what I'll be able to call you anymore because you are getting too big to be called my little cherry blossom."

Aarleen's eyes began to water and Renee had to look away to wipe her eyes, as did many others. Even Cynthia and Monroe were feeling moved.

"Please, Aarleen, my little cherry blossom, will you sing the cherry blossom song with me before I give you your gift?"

Aarleen nodded. She wiped her eyes and both Aarleen and Reuben sang, looking at each other.

"Sakura, sora kara ochi sakura, watashi no hoho ni chakuriku shi, watashi ni kisu o. Sakura, sora kara ochi sakura, anata wa minogasu koto wa dekinainode, watashi wa kichōna hoho o motte iru."

Cherry blossom, cherry blossom falling from the sky, land on my cheek and give me a kiss.
Cherry blossom, cherry blossom falling from the sky, I have a precious cheek so you cannot miss."

When Aarleen and Reuben finished singing, Reuben lifted the box off the table presenting a beautifully pruned little cherry blossom bonsai tree, in full bloom, to Aarleen.

"Happy Birthday, my precious Aarleen," said Reuben.

Aarleen dropped to her knees in front of the little tree, her pretty, brown eyes open wide, and a huge open smile came to her face. Gently she touched the tree with her fingertips. As with everyone, Aarleen was totally speechless as she gazed at the beautiful little tree. She quickly rose and wrapped her arms around Reuben and said loudly, "You can call me your little cherry blossom forever and ever, Da!" and began crying joyfully.

Renee wrapped her arms around both her husband and daughter. "So what else do you have hidden away in the woods," she asked, causing all three of them to laugh together.

狼

It had been a very joyful day and as Aarleen's guests were leaving, as she always did for her previous birthdays, she bid each guest farewell and thanked them for coming to celebrate her birthday with her and her family.

Reuben was helping Henry and Noah carry some chairs to the house when Monroe called him over. He was standing among other men, including Eric and Simon.

"Reuben, as a teacher, what do you think of this anti-slave politician from Illinois, this Lincoln fellow?" asked Monroe.

"Why would me being a teacher have any say in that?" asked Reuben.

"This is history in the making, Reuben," said Mr. Elps. "If this Lincoln becomes our next president, he will completely disrupt our way of life. It might even mean war."

All those gathered nodded their heads in agreement.

"Way of life?" asked Reuben. "What way of life? None of us own any servants or slaves. Even you Simon, your servants belong to your wife's parents. And Eric, you own your own business and have one freed Negro working for you for wages. As for the rest of you, you all own and run your farms just as we do, without the use of slaves."

"Whoa, what about the three Negros you have?" asked Mr. Leeve.

"Oh George, for crying out loud, May, Henry, and Noah have been free for years and own just as much of this farm as Renee and I do. So again I ask you, what way of life? Seems to me, our way of life is taking care of our own without the servitude of others."

"Okay, brother, that's all well said, but what if this Lincoln becomes president and war breaks out between them and us, what side will you choose?" asked Monroe rather harshly.

"Them and us? Do you even know who them and us are, Monroe? For heaven's sake, you're a lawyer yourself, like this Lincoln politician. Where's your logic?"

"So you do know of Lincoln?" asked Monroe.

"Of course I do. Like you said, I'm a teacher. I have to teach this stuff for a living, but that doesn't mean I have to side with one side or the other," replied Reuben.

"I don't know, Reuben. That sounds rather seditious to our way of life. What are you going to do if Lincoln sends Federal troops here to force their Federal ways on us?" asked Eric.

"Again there you say 'way of life.' I just told you we see to our own, so why should I need to get involved? I've done my killing and I don't intend to do any more, no matter if it's for the Federal government or the Commonwealth of Virginia," said Reuben as he continued with his task of taking chairs back inside the house.

"However," said Reuben as he paused and turned with a look of sheer anger causing those gathered to reel back, "heaven help the sorry bastards, Federal or militia, who dares to harm one hair on my wife or daughter," Reuben turned and continued with his task.

"What did he mean, he's done his killing?" asked Simon.

"Reuben never told you?" asked Eric.

Simon shook his head no.

"Simon, Reuben has killed more men in battle in Mexico and Japan than belong to this county's congregation. If war is to come and he decides to take a side, heaven help you if you're on the other side," explained Eric.

狼

"I had a wonderful time at your party Aarleen. Thank you for inviting me," said Benjamin as Aarleen walked him to his parent's carriage. "Sorry about my parent's gift. It wasn't very practical for you. It was all my mother's doing."

"Ah, don't worry about it," replied Aarleen. "I'm sure I'll find a use for it."

Benjamin took a quick look around and said, "Wait here."

He quickly went to the carriage and asked the driver to hand him something. Benjamin came back to Aarleen, took her by the hand, and pulled her out of sight from his parents in case they happen to come by.

"Here, this is from me," said Benjamin as he handed Aarleen a long piece of wood with a blue ribbon tied around it.

"A stick? You're giving me a stick?" said Aarleen offended, remembering hearing Benjamin's mother using the term, "sticks," as an insult to her parents.

"Not just any stick. Look closer. It's hard New England hickory. The same hickory used for the schoolhouse your father built. I remember you said you wished you had some so your father could make you one of those wooden swords. What are they called, bokkens?"

Aarleen took a closer look at the piece of wood Benjamin gave her. "Geez oh geez oh geez this is great! But Benji, that was a long time ago. How come you haven't given it to me sooner?"

Benjamin shyly looked down and said, "My mother would never let me come to visit with my father, and the few times when we did come with him, she would not let me out of her sight. I have wanted to give you that piece of hickory in person ever since you said you wanted some. I'm sorry it has taken me this long."

With her fingertips, Aarleen lifted Benjamin's head up, like she had seen her mother do to her father many times, and said, "Aw, Benji, that's the sweetest thing I have ever heard."

Suddenly Aarleen looked away feeling flushed. Did I just say what I think I said, thought Aarleen. She shook away her thoughts and continued. "Besides my Da's gift, this is the next best gift I received today. Thank you."

Aarleen reached to give Benjamin a hug which made him flinch out of habit. She gave him a quick peck on the cheek. "Thank you, Benji. I'll have my Da help me carve out a bokken right away and show you when it's done. Oops, here come your parents. Bye, Benji."

Again she felt flush once she saw Benjamin's eyes wide open after her little kiss on his cheek. Aarleen let out an adorable, awkward smile and turned on her heels thinking, geez, did I really just kiss an icky boy?

Aarleen ran off and stopped to say farewell to Benjamin's parents as he stood holding his cheek with has hand thinking he liked the way Aarleen called him Benji.

424

"So how did you enjoy your birthday today, sweetie?" asked Renee as she sat on the edge of Aarleen's bed.

"I know I say this every year, but it was the best… well except for my seventh birthday when Da came home. Oh, and this little tree he gave me, next to my little inrou, it's the best," said Aarleen, looking at the little cherry blossom bonsai tree on her night stand.

"You know, your Da says they grow very big. Some as big as our oak tree," said Renee as she delicately touched one of the blooms.

"Do you think Da will take us to Itosai one of these days, Mama?"

"He does have a cottage there and he told me his friend Tadashi and his wife are caring for it. When Tadashi heard about you, he built another room so you would have one to yourself, so who knows. Maybe one day he'll take us there. I know I would like to see where he became smooth."

As both mother and daughter gazed upon the peaceful looking blossoms of the little tree, Aarleen thought about what she overheard some of the men speak of the upcoming election for the next president of the United States.

Aarleen timidly asked Renee, "Mama, I hear talk about war in the future. If there is, would Da have to go?"

Aarleen's sudden question felt like an icicle being thrust into Renee's heart. She turned the little tree to view it from a different angle trying to prolong her answer. "Sweetie, your Da has been through so much. As long as we are safe, he won't go anywhere. Now you mustn't worry yourself about such things," said Renee, more to herself than to Aarleen.

Aarleen nodded and placed the turtle inrou next to her bonsai tree and admired both of them.

Renee smiled, thinking of the perfect topic to change the subject. "Sweetie, what do you think of Benjamin Norenham?" she asked.

"Oh, he's just another icky boy," replied Aarleen as she lowered her head to hide her flush feeling in her cheeks.

Renee gently raised Aarleen's face using her fingers on her chin. "Aarleen, come now. I hear he gave you a special present."

Aarleen smiled as she bit her lower lip and reached under her bed. She showed Renee the piece of New England hickory Benjamin gave her so Reuben could help her carve a bokken out of it. It still had the blue ribbon tied to it.

"This will make a very nice bokken," said Renee. "If I were you, I would wait for a couple of days before you ask Da to help you make a bokken out of it."

"Why, Mama?"

"Well, your Da has a feeling you and Benjamin want to be… special friends."

"Eww, Mama!"

"Come now, sweetie, that's the second time you denied your friendship and blushed at the same time."

Trying her hardest, Aarleen couldn't keep from giggling. "Okay Mama. Benji is cute and I admit I did pay more attention to him than my other friends today."

"Sweetie, throwing Benjamin hard to the ground and slapping his shoulder all the time isn't, *'paying attention'*."

"You do the same thing to Da."

Bobbing her head back and forth, Renee said, "Okay, yes I do, but that's different."

"How so?"

Feeling completely confused and frustrated, Renee lowered her head for a moment to gather her thoughts. "Okay, Aarleen, I'm going to tell you a secret your father told me a long time ago. Now mind you, I can get into big trouble sharing this secret, so you have to promise me you will keep it to yourself."

"I promise, Mama."

"Okay, sweetie, here it is. Boys are stupid."

"All girls know that, Mama."

"Yes, I know, but when it comes to a girl liking a boy, to be a *'special friend'*, they get extra stupid. In other words, they don't have the ability to take a hint. Their brains turn into mush. Do you understand, sweetie?"

"Not sure, Mama," replied Aarleen.

"By you, *'paying more attention'* to Benjamin, you made him feel like you didn't like him."

Aarleen fell backwards onto her pillow and covered her head with her blanket. "Oh no, now it all makes sense! He would run away from me when I would try to talk to him."

Renee pulled the blankets away and lifted Aarleen up and gave her a hug.

"Wow, Mama, I knew boys were stupid, but I didn't realize how stupid. What should I do the next time I see Benji?" asked Aarleen.

"Well, sweetie, that's easy. Just be yourself. That's how Aunty Lucy got Uncle Eric's attention. I get the feeling he likes you just the way you are without the tossing around. Save that for Da."

"Thanks, Mama, I love you."

"I love you too, sweetie."

"Knock, knock," said Reuben. "Can I come in to say goodnight?"

"Of course you can, dear," answered Renee as she put her finger to her lips indicating Aarleen to keep quiet about their conversation. Aarleen nodded.

"Did you have a good day, blossom?"

"One of my best birthdays ever, Da. Thank you for the beautiful tree. I love it."

"And I love you."

"I love you too, Da."

Both Renee and Reuben, in turn, gave Aarleen a hug and kiss goodnight. As Riley entered the room and laid in his bed next to Aarleen's, Reuben blew out the lamp.

Walking hand-in-hand into their bedroom, Renee took Reuben into her arms and kissed him deeply as he returned her affection.

"Come, Reuben," said Renee, seductively as she lay on their bed. "Let's lay down together."

With a serious look on his face, Reuben said, "I don't know, Renee. We boys tend to be pretty stupid about such things."

Renee threw a pillow at Reuben hard and said, "Get in this bed now, you shoddy farm boy."

狼

"Good morning class. Quickly, have a seat. We have much to discuss today," said Reuben as he addressed his students of the Norfolk County Outreach School.

Since its opening five years earlier, the outreach school program in the county proved to be a huge success. Reuben started off with 22 students. Since then, his class size dwindled down to 17 students.

After the first two years, two of his oldest student obtained their graduation certificates and were accepted into the small city college where they were entering their final year. Last year, three of his older students entered their final year of schooling and Reuben proposed an experiment to the superintendent and school board.

He believed students in the outreach school should have the opportunity to attend the Norfolk city school for their final year of learning. It would provide the students the opportunity to be exposed to larger classes with more students their age and prepare them if they wished to attend college. It also provided exposure to current events which was limited in the county.

The school officials found the proposal compelling and worthwhile to try, but the scheme had one flaw, the officials thought. Their concern was how the students were going to be able to travel into the city to attend school.

It was Henry who came up with the solution. The county outreach school started classes at 8 o'clock in the morning, one hour earlier than the city school began lessons. Henry suggested that since Renee traveled to the city every morning to conduct farming business at the mercantile, she could take the students into the city with her. After all, Reuben and Aarleen would ride with her to school. As for bringing the students back home, Henry would ride into the city to bring the students back since a majority of his chores and woodworking were completed prior to 2 o'clock in the afternoon. Since the city school was released at 3 o'clock, Henry had plenty of time to make the ride into the city to pick them up. Both Renee and Henry received a small wage for their transportation which they used for the upkeep of the wagon and team.

The proposal worked magnificently. Last year, Reuben had three final year students who took part in the program, and because of their exposure to the city school, this year those three students are now attending college, two of them at the city college and the other at William and

Mary. The school board extended the program to the counties that had an outreach school, such as Princess Anne County.

Reuben's lessons were challenging for all his students. He pushed them to exceed their abilities. When his proposal was accepted and put into practice, he realized he had to prepare his students to become more efficient and knowledgeable. Although he had his students categorized into grades, he encouraged the senior grades to assist the lower grades, much like how the Akagi dojo was run.

"I'm mad at your father, Aarleen. You and I are seventh grade students and he's making us do eighth grade work. That's not fair," complained Janet Lindsey to Aarleen.

"Listen, Janet, have you ever heard of Miyamoto Musashi?"

"Only from your stories."

"He was a great swordsman, a warrior. You know what made him so great?"

Janet shook her head no.

"Because he did what my Da is doing, keeping us one step ahead of life. The more we learn than we should be learning, the easier life will be for us."

"Fourth and fifth years, your assignments are on the board. Copy them down and go out to the porch and complete the assignment there. Fourth years, extra credit if you do the fifth year assignment also. As for the rest of you, who can tell me what is so important about tomorrow, Tuesday, November 6, 1860? Yes, Mr. John."

"Tomorrow is election day."

"Correct. Today we are going to discuss how we elect the president of our country. Now who can tell me who are the candidates running in this election? This was one of last week's quiz questions."

When the outreach school first opened, Renee and Reuben wondered if it would be awkward for Aarleen to be in the same classroom with her father. It was a concern that quickly ebbed away when it was Aarleen herself who looked upon Reuben as a teacher during school hours. Once she entered the school yard, it was "Mr. Duran" or "teacher" until they both stepped back onto the road. Reuben seldom called on Aarleen and the only time she raised her hand was when other students could not answer a question Reuben would ask, and she always answered correctly.

"Come on, anyone, who are the candidates? There are four of them. Okay, Miss Aarleen, who are they?"

"Abraham Lincoln, Stephen Douglas, John Breckinridge, and John Bell."

"Very good. In this vast world of ours, there are hundreds of countries, each ruled by one form of government. Now look on the board on the easel. I have written five of the most common. They are Anarchy, Monarchy, Republic, Democracy, and Totalitarian. We are going to cover each form of government and how their leaders are elected. Let's start with Anarchy."

Reuben went on to lecture on each form of government by using storytelling and the students to portray forms of governmental leaders. At the end of the lesson, all the students had a clear understanding of each form of government and how the United States elects its leaders in the form of a Republic. As with each group lesson, he quizzed the class and excused them for a recess.

As the students were rising from their desks, a tenth year student asked, "Mr. Duran, is it true if Mr. Lincoln wins the election there might be a war?"

All the students stopped and looked at Reuben. Some of them sat back down. Aarleen, feeling anxious, also sat. She knew discussing war related topics was a delicate matter with her father. The only time he openly discussed the topic was in school lessons.

"How many of you have heard the same thing Mr. Liem just asked?" asked Reuben.

Everyone, including Aarleen, raised their hands.

"That's a difficult question to answer right now, Liem. I certainly hope it does not come to that if Mr. Lincoln is elected. Our country has reached a turning point in its young path. Who can tell me when our country was founded? Yes, Miss Janet."

"1776."

"A mere 84 years ago. Compared to other countries, the United States is an infant child. There are some countries that are thousands of years old. The country I spent many years in, Japan itself, is said to have existed since the year 400 AD. Many of these countries have long done away with slavery. The United States is possibly the only civilized country that still has slavery. It's going to be a difficult decision to make, if Mr. Lincoln is elected, for parts of this country to remain part of this Republic of ours. Liem, I can't answer your question right now because I will be doing the same thing you are doing, learning about what is going to happen. All we can do for the time being is watch and learn because if we do not learn from history, we are bound to repeat our mistakes."

Many of the students nodded. Aarleen felt better and was proud of her father with the way he answered Liem's question. However, her anxious feeling returned when another tenth year student asked, "Mr. Duran, my pa says you were a soldier and killed lots of men. Is that true?"

Aarleen's head fell to her desk making a thump sound.

Reuben looked at Aarleen and walked toward her desk. He placed his hand gently on her back. She raised her head and her eyes were watery showing she was sorry that Jonus, the student who asked the question, asked it in the first place. Reuben smiled and winked his eye letting her know everything was all right.

"Mr. Jonus, yes, I was in the army and yes, I had to… survive both in Mexico and Japan and to survive, sometimes one must… survive."

"If there is a war to come, I'll want to go so I can kill the enemy and become a hero," said Tommy Deans, a seventh year student, and the only troublesome student in the school. Tommy Deans always tried to show up Reuben, but always failed with the same result, embarrassment and having to clean out the school outhouse as his assigned chore.

Other boys nodded in agreement to Tommy Deans' comment.

"Really, Mr. Deans, do you believe you can easily kill the enemy?" asked Reuben.

Aarleen began to wonder where her father was going with this. She noticed everyone was focused on the discussion.

"Well, yeah. Can't be any harder than helping my pa butcher some of our pigs," answered Tommy Deans. "What's it like to kill the enemy, Mr. Duran?"

"Tell me something, Mr. Deans. Do the pigs fight back when you and your father butcher them?" asked Reuben as he slowly made his way to Tommy Deans' desk.

"Of course not."

Upon reaching Tommy Deans' desk, Reuben leaned on it with his fists. With a strong look that caused Tommy Deans and other students who could see his look cower down, he said, "Well, the enemy does fight back. And as for how it feels to kill another man... when you kill another human being, it's like killing yourself, slowly."

Reuben rose and walked back to the blackboard saying, "You all only have ten minutes left for recess so you better get outside and enjoy it." He began to wipe the board clean to write down the next lesson.

When all her classmates exited the classroom, Aarleen walked up to her father.

"What is it, Miss Aarleen?" asked Reuben as he continued to wipe down the board.

Aarleen wrapped her arms around him and hugged him tightly. "I thought you needed that, Da," she said. It was the first time she intentionally called him Da during school hours.

Reuben turned to face her and he hugged her back. "I did, my little cherry blossom. Thank you."

狼

As the students were spending the last ten minutes of the school day conducting chores, Riley entered the classroom and trotted up to Reuben's desk. Every day at this time, Riley would enter the classroom indicating the school day was nearly over and Renee was outside waiting for Reuben and Aarleen.

As the students saw to the cleanliness of the classroom, Reuben was writing the next day's assignment on the board. The wall clock chimed in the back of the classroom. The students quickly took their seats and Reuben addressed them for final comments of the day.

"We did good work today students and, as always, I am proud of your progress. Tomorrow we will continue our discussion on different government systems, and in the subject of English, we will start working on our fall essays. May all of you have a pleasant evening and I'll see you tomorrow. Class is dismissed."

All the students rose from their seats, bid Reuben farewell, and exited the classroom quietly. Aarleen exited more quickly than usual and when she was on the porch, she glanced around looking for her mother. Aarleen saw Renee in her tan kosode and green hakama with matching tabi socks and sandals sitting on a swing twirling around. Seeing her mother playing on a swing always made her smile and this time was no different. However, Aarleen had to shake out the image and ran to Renee to tell her about the war and soldier questions asked today.

"How did your Da react to them, sweetie?" asked Renee, concerned.

"Really well, Mama, but I did give him a hug when all the students were outside. I felt he needed one and he told me he did."

Renee rose from the swing and took her daughter in her arms and hugged her lovingly saying, "Very good, sweetie. Let's not bring this up unless he does, okay?"

"Okay, Mama. Look, here comes Riley."

Riley came out of the schoolhouse with Reuben's jo in his jaws. Reuben taught Riley to carry his jo once he was big enough to carry it by tapping it twice on the ground. Both Renee and Aarleen thought it was adorable.

Riley noticed Renee and Aarleen by the swings and trotted toward them. When he was about five yards away, he dropped the jo and came to greet Aarleen.

"Hey, let's go home!" called out Reuben from the schoolhouse porch heading to the road.

Riley picked up the jo and trotted alongside Renee and Aarleen toward the road where Reuben was waiting.

Renee ran up to Reuben and took him into her arms. He, too, wrapped his arms around her, but Renee could sense by his posture, Reuben was preoccupied with something in his mind.

All four began walking home in silence, which was unusual. Even Riley sensed the tension as he moved closer to Aarleen.

Walking hand-in-hand with her husband, his radiant energy that pulsed through his touch she loved so much seemed to be pulsating more intensely, more so than when they are intimate with each other. It caused her to glance at him every several steps in their walk.

"Aarleen, do you have any schoolwork you haven't finished to do at home?" asked Reuben after about a quarter mile in silence.

"No, Da."

"Good. When we get home, I want you to start your chores right away and when they're done, bring down the piece of hickory Ben gave you for your birthday. We need to start carving it into a bokken. You need to begin getting more serious in your kumitachi training."

Both Renee and Aarleen looked at each other with curiosity.

"Did you hear me, Aarleen?" asked Reuben quite sternly.

"Yes, Da, I will."

"Reuben..." Renee began, but was interrupted by Reuben.

"Renee, until Aarleen is done with her chores, meet me at the oak tree with our jos. I need to you to get more proficient with your jo training as well," Reuben said, just as stern.

"Reuben?" asked Renee.

"Please you two, please do as I ask," said Reuben less sternly, but more concerning and pleading.

Renee and Aarleen agreed, both feeling the seriousness of Reuben's demeanor.

As asked, Aarleen started her chores and Renee waited for Reuben by the oak tree. When he arrived, he was dressed in full Akagi colors with his Kutto tucked into his obi. The look on his face was serious and focused.

"Renee, please sit," said Reuben as he took his usual seiza position on the soft grass.

Renee sat directly in front of him. "Reuben, is everything okay? You're scaring me and Aarleen," she said.

Reuben took her by the hands and said, "I don't mean to. I already know Aarleen told you about the questions asked during one of today's lessons." He put his hand gently to her face and continued, "Please be assured, I am not reverting to my melancholic ways when I returned from Mexico."

Taking Renee by the hands again, Reuben's expression faded from seriously focused to more endearing. "I'm very concerned about your safety. I foresee the upcoming months as being... unpredictable. I have taught you and our daughter several techniques, always in play or fun. Now I need to change that from play and fun to training."

"Reuben, things are not as bad as you may think they are. We are... out of the way," said Renee.

"We thought the same way about the Arata," replied Reuben. Returning back to his serious manner, he continued. "It's like I told the students in school today. Our country has reached a turning point. A turning point I have witnessed many times and every time, that turning point involved conflict, including war. Renee, I don't know what we will face in the upcoming months, but I want us to be prepared. Do you understand?"

"Prepared for what, Reuben?"

Reuben breathed in deeply, slowly let it out, and said, "In case I'm forced to... fight, and I say forced, because that's the only way I will leave you and Aarleen."

"Reuben, do you really think it will come to that?" asked Renee on the verge of tears.

Reuben took her into his arms and whispered into her ear, "Let's hope and pray it doesn't." He kissed her on the lips, rose, and took the jos in his hand and continued to say, "In the meantime, let's train. Now show me the twenty three jo kata."

Renee rose, took the offered jo, and commenced the movements of the kata Reuben taught her a few years ago. When she was finished, Reuben nodded approvingly and had her do it again and again. The last time, he stopped her at each step and corrected her body and weapon position. When that kata was completed, Reuben told Renee the kata wasn't just an exercise to display the jo suburis all at once, but an actual defense technique against an attacker.

"Now prepare yourself. Using the kata, defend against my attack," said Reuben as he began to strike, thrust, and cut at Renee in controlled deliberate movements.

After several runs through the two partner awase, Reuben was impressed with his wife's progress and expressed his approval in the form of a long warming embrace and deep long kiss.

"Ahem, excuse me, but there's a child present," said Aarleen, dressed in her kosode of light purple and hakama of blue holding a piece of New England hickory with a blue ribbon tied around it.

Both Renee and Reuben giggled with their foreheads together.

"Ah, the hickory," said Reuben, attempting to disrupt his and Renee's embarrassment. "The other special birthday gift from young Benji, bring it to me."

For the next couple of hours, mother, father, and daughter sat on the bank of the creek with Riley watching, taking turns using a small wood plane and Reuben's tanto to carve out Aarleen's new bokken.

Renee's and Aarleen's training sessions with Reuben became more structured, whereas before, they were playful. Both mother and daughter understood Reuben's reasoning for the structured change. Although it took several days for Renee and Aarleen to get used to the change, once they saw improvements in themselves, they began to appreciate the new training routine. Renee even found herself training on her own when she wasn't busy while Reuben and Aarleen were at school, and started teaching Noah basic jo and taijutsu techniques.

Reuben's personal training routine also became more structured. Before, he woke an hour before Renee and trained under the oak tree by himself. Now he woke two hours earlier. Using one of Henry's old broken saw horses, he wrapped the center beam with sheep's wool and converted it to be used to practice hard cuts with his bokken. He planted a post, also wrapped with sheep wool to practice side cuts. Both training tools resembled the same tools used in Itosai.

Several times, Renee would wake as Reuben left their bedroom. She would watch Reuben practice in the moonlight from their bedroom window. She very much enjoyed watching Reuben when he trained by himself. His movements were so mesmerizing and calming to watch. However, his newer personal training sessions were fiercer, more deliberate, more frightening. Although he was training by himself, Renee could visualize Reuben defending himself against invisible attackers. Although he was still fascinating to watch, his movements were not as peaceful as before. For several days, even though Reuben told Renee he wasn't becoming melancholic as in the past, she had her doubts. However, her fears faded when after training sessions, Reuben was back to his pleasant fun loving self she adored so much.

CHARLESTON
MERCURY
EXTRA:
Passed unanimously at 1:15 o'clock, P.M., December
20th, 1860

AN ORDINANCE

To dissolve the Union between the State of South Carolina and
other States united with her under compact entitled "The
Constitution of the United States of America."

We, the People of the State of South Carolina, in Convention assembled, do declare and ordain, and ordained,

That the Ordinance adopted by us in Convention, on the twenty-third day of May, in the year of our Lord one thousand seven hundred and eighty-eight, whereby the Constitution of the United States of America was Ratified, and also, all Acts and parts of Acts of the General Assembly of this State, ratifying amendments of the said Constitution, are hereby repealed; and that the union now subsisting between South Carolina and other States, under the name of "The United States of America," is hereby dissolved.

THE

UNION

IS

DISSOLVED!

狼

After it taken Aarleen five weeks to carve the New England hickory down to a raw unfinished bokken, Reuben took hold of it and looked it over approvingly. He took it from this point to make finishing touches by sanding it down to its finished shape and treating the wood. Before Aarleen could use it, Reuben told Aarleen he had to put it to the test. He wanted to be certain it was well balanced and would not crack or break. Reuben did several bokken suburi cuts against the training tools and nodded approvingly. Once he was satisfied the bokken was safe and sturdy, Reuben wood burned the Akagi crest on one side of the tsuka, and a cherry blossom on the other side. On the edge of the tsuka he also wood burned a short passage in kanji.

He tied the blue ribbon Benjamin tied to the raw piece of New England hickory and asked Renee to bring Aarleen to the oak tree where he would meet them both in the morning, Tuesday, December 25, 1860.

On a cool brisk Christmas day, Reuben was seated in his usual seiza position beneath the oak tree with a folded blanket next to him on one side, and Riley on the other when Renee brought Aarleen as requested. May, Henry, and Noah also accompanied them because Renee believed Reuben had something important to tell Aarleen and felt they should be present.

As they approached the oak tree, Renee noticed Reuben was in deep meditation. She had seen him in meditation before, but not to this advanced state of concentrated focus. They stopped several yards away wondering if they should wait until Reuben called them forward.

"Please come closer, all of you, and sit with me. Noah, I have brought chairs for May and Henry, will you please place them close to me so they may sit?" asked Reuben without moving or opening his eyes.

Noah did as Reuben asked while Renee and Aarleen stood before Reuben looking down at him. They all had a look of questionable concern.

Reuben opened his eyes and asked Aarleen to sit in front of him which she did immediately with Riley moving next to her. Renee sat next to Reuben and May, Henry, and Noah also took seats.

"My precious Aarleen, I have a story to tell you. Once upon a time, there was a boy. He was the luckiest boy in the world. He had a wonderful loving family," he looked to May, Henry, and Noah and added, "Beautiful friends that were just as much family as his own." Looking to Renee, he placed his hand gently on her cheek. "And the most wonderful best friend any boy could ever want."

Reuben brought his hand down from Renee's cheek and looked upon Aarleen and continued his story. "This boy had everything he could ever want, except the love of his best friend. Don't get me wrong, because she loved him also, but her father got in the way between the two."

Aarleen realized Reuben was telling her parent's story. For the most part, Aarleen knew this story. It was well known throughout the county. Aarleen's knowledge of her parent's journey came primarily from Renee considering she raised her for the first seven years of her life. However, Aarleen didn't know her father's side. She knew he was a soldier in Mexico and served a regional Daimyo as a retainer and samurai in Japan, but not to the extent of what he actually did. She, as well as the others, was about to find out.

"Because of the boy's best friend's father, the boy chose a path that would make him become a man in the most heinous ways ever known," Reuben continued. "That path took him to a different country where he took away the happiness of other families by killing their husbands, fathers, sons, and brothers. He prayed to his god to forgive him for what he had to do, but as the blood of many more kept staining his hands, he stopped praying for forgiveness. He believed after all the happiness he had taken away from other families, there was no possible way God would forgive him."

Renee, for the first time, began to truly understand Reuben's dark horrors and the effect it had on him when he came home. She moved closer to him and laid her head on his shoulder while wrapping her arms around his waist.

"When the boy came home, he was no longer a boy. He was a man, angry and bitter. The war he fought wreaked havoc in his mind and now with his best friend to be married away, he no longer wanted to be a part of this world. Taking a small pistol he purchased, one night he placed it under his chin and began to pull the trigger. Suddenly he heard calming words in a foreign language coming from a calm soothing voice of a man standing next to him."

"What's did he say, Da?" asked Aarleen.

"One's path is filled with many obstacles to keep one from their just rewards, and may cause one to retreat, but dark shadows of the past will never let you," answered Reuben.

"Da?" Aarleen, knowing the answer to her question asked, "Are you the boy in this story?"

Reuben took Aarleen's hands in his and said, "Yes."

He went on to tell how the man who stopped him from killing himself changed his way of thinking through the Bushido code. Reuben told Aarleen what Renee never told her, how she was conceived on that one warm, rainy, autumn night under the oak tree they were sitting under. Reuben told of how Aarleen's mother helped him journey to Japan and his hardships he encountered because he was not of that land.

Aarleen knew the story of how Reuben fought against Arata Goro's attackers the day she was born, and even recited it at her birthday party. But she didn't know, up until then, he was not accepted or respected until he shed his own blood in the protection of their homes and his lord's family.

"Da, what made killing these men different than the ones you killed in Mexico?" asked Aarleen.

"Yes, Reuben," said Renee raising her head from Reuben's shoulder. "That's a very good question."

"Because, my dearest Renee and precious Aarleen, the day of that attack, Genda-San saw in me what I was destined to become for the both of you, the protector of our family. All of us," said Reuben as he indicated with his hand to May, Henry, and Noah. "To kill because of occupation rips your soul piece by piece as I told Mr. Tommy Deans. But to defend in the protection of loved ones and the innocent, not only do you feel forgiven for good deeds, you achieve self-victory knowing you have done your duty for the special people in your life."

Looking to Renee lovingly, Reuben asked, "Do you understand now?"

Renee caressed Reuben's face gently saying, "I do now, my love."

"Why are you telling us this, Reuben?" asked May.

Renee, and Aarleen, had an idea why and both took each other's hand along with Reuben's.

"Because, Aunty May, all of us have heard the possibilities of conflict now that Mr. Lincoln is our president. And now with southern states starting to leave the Union, it's a matter of time before Virginia follows," answered Reuben.

"But just because there's talk doesn't mean it will actually happen," said Noah.

Reuben shook his head saying, "Ever since I wanted to become a teacher, I have read and studied history. I have learned the history of Japan's past and of its feudal conflicts. If there's one thing I have learned from history, man never learns from it. No matter how factual history is documented, man will always repeat history, especially history of revolution and that's what our country is heading toward, revolution. Whenever the word revolution is spoken, it will happen, and we must be prepared."

Reuben took a tighter hold on Renee's and Aarleen's hands and looked at Renee as he spoke, "I have no intention of becoming involved in whatever is to come our way. I feel we do not benefit from the cause. Our cause is to see to our own. However, because of my past, I foresee the possibilities I may be forced to defend you away from our home. That's why I have been more structured in our training together."

436

Looking at Aarleen, Reuben asked, "Remember the evening before your seventh birthday you asked me what kind of games the children of Japan played, and I told you the games they played were used to train them to defend against invaders?" asked Reuben.

"Yes, Da," answered Aarleen, very focused on her father's question.

"Well, my dear family, we are now playing that game. In the months or years to follow, our family is going to be put to the test, and this is one test where failure is not an option." Turning his attention to Renee, Reuben continued, "We have gone through too much to have our happiness torn apart by a country ruled by leaders who can't learn from history's past."

Looking back to Aarleen, Reuben picked up the folded blanket at his side and placed it between him and Aarleen. "With all I have said, this birthday gift from Benjamin, and Christmas gift from me, is for you, my little cherry blossom," he said as he uncovered the finished hickory bokken. He took it in both hands and bowed to Aarleen as he presented it to her.

Having a feeling of pride she never felt before, she saw her father in a most honorable way. Having her father bow to her caused her to feel honored. She took the bokken with both hands and examined its finished smooth texture, glaring sheen, and the burning into the wood. When she saw the image of the cherry blossom, she smiled.

"Miyamoto Musashi once said, *'The sword has to be more than a simple weapon. It has to be an answer to life's questions,'"* said Reuben as Aarleen admired her bokken.

Placing his hand on Aarleen's cheek, causing her to look up to him, Reuben told her, "Please forgive me, my beautiful precious daughter, but from me you will not receive a special traditional gift to admire on this Christmas day, only a weapon to protect our family, if I am forced to leave."

Aarleen wrapped her arms around Reuben and hugged him tightly. "If there's a test, we will pass with straight A's," she said, strongly.

Renee took hold of Aarleen's new bokken and looked at the kanji on the tsuka. "What does this translate to Reuben?"

With his daughter in his arms, he said, "For my little cherry blossom with fatherly love."

狼

CHARLESTON
MERCURY

The Confederacy's attempt to extend its sovereignty over forts that remained in Union hands received considerable attention, both in the North and the South. When President Lincoln planned to send supplies to Fort Sumter, in Charleston harbor, he informed the state to avoid hostilities. South Carolina, however, asked the commander of the fort to surrender immediately on April 12, 1861. He rejected the offer. Confederate batteries opened fire, firing for 36 straight hours on the fort. The garrison returned fire, but it was ineffective and the fort surrendered. Ft. Sumter rapidly became a symbol of rival definitions of sovereignty and honor.

437

It was a nice, warm April Saturday afternoon when Noah and Evergreen were walking on the road getting ready to make the turn onto the lane leading to the farm. As they reached the lane, several men on horseback galloped by cheering and firing off pistols in the air. News of the surrender of Fort Sumter raced through the city and county of Norfolk like wildfire.

"Them white folk sure is going overboard over the most smallest of news," said Evergreen. "All that activity is far from us so what are they all so worked up about?"

"Reuben says eventually Virginia will do as the other Southern states are doing, and leave the Union," said Noah.

"I don't understand you, Noah. You, May, and Henry is free, but you stay with them white folks."

Noah stopped and took Evergreen by the elbow and turned her to face him. "Listen, Ever, I like you a whole lot, but don't ever talk about Reuben, Renee, and Aarleen like that. Your life may have been troubled before you were freed, but don't blame my family for your troubled past. And yes, I consider them family because they have treated May, Henry, and me as family even when we still belonged to James Wilcox," said Noah, sternly.

"Okay, Noah, I'm sorry. I must admit when it comes to white folk, I tend to be unforgiving and if all this secession talk is about the Southern states wanting to keep their slaves, the sooner the North brings war and wins, the better."

Noah stood looking at the farm with a distant stare thinking of what Evergreen just said.

"Noah? What's wrong?"

"Reuben doesn't want war, but he knows it's unavoidable," answered Noah. "He's very knowledgeable about these things."

"If it does come to that, what side will he choose?" asked Evergreen.

"He will choose the side that will leave us alone," answered Noah, "and may the Lord in heaven have mercy on those who dare harm his family, because Reuben won't."

A carriage turned onto the lane and came to a stop. It was Coleen and Monroe.

"Hello Noah and Miss Ever. Hop aboard, we're heading your way," said Monroe, pleasantly.

As the two climbed on the carriage, Noah noticed Coleen's expression wasn't as pleasant as Monroe's. Her expression was more of concern.

"Are you here to see Reuben, Mrs. Duran?" asked Noah.

"Yes, Noah. How is he?"

Noah knew she was concerned about Reuben's feelings toward the beginning of hostilities.

"Reuben is fine. He's been keeping busy with teaching school and helping me and Henry clear out patches deep in the woods for planting."

"Whatever for?" asked Monroe.

"We asked him that too, even Renee. His answer was, *'just in case.'*"

When the carriage arrived at the front of the house, Renee met Coleen. After a brief greeting, Renee took Coleen to the oak tree where Reuben and Aarleen were training with bokken kumitachi awase techniques. When Reuben saw Renee bringing his mother to him, he halted the training. He told Aarleen to continue on her own and came to speak with Coleen.

"Hello, Mama," greeted Reuben as he hugged her. "How are things in the city?"

"As expected with the news," Coleen replied.

Renee wrapped her arms around Reuben's waist as he placed his left arm around hers. "I take it you're going into Chesapeake City?" Reuben asked his mother.

"I'm taking the afternoon ferry. I desperately want to bring Lucy and Eric back here to Norfolk."

"But Andrew and Annabelle couldn't convince Eric to close the store," said Renee. "Do you think you can convince them?"

"I have to try. Thank God they at least let Andrew and Annabelle bring Andy to Norfolk. They told me Eric is going to try to keep the store open as long as possible and come to Norfolk if Virginia leaves the Union."

"Then I'll go with you, Mama," said Reuben.

"No, Reuben, you have to keep the school open, and that isn't your mother speaking to you, that is a school administrator," said Coleen.

Reuben nodded his head in reluctance and said, "Okay, Mama, but I want you back within a week with Lucy at least. If not, I *will* come and get you."

"Agreed," said Coleen. She called to Aarleen, "Aarleen, sweetheart, come and see me off. I'm going to visit with your Aunty Lucy and Uncle Eric!"

Aarleen twirled her bokken in her right hand and tucked it into her obi and ran to greet Coleen with Riley following close at her heels.

When the four arrived at the carriage, Monroe was coming out of the front door of the house. "Hey, little brother, what do you think of the fall of Fort Sumter? Fabulous, isn't it?" he said climbing onto the bench of the carriage.

Reuben nodded, uninterested, and assisted his mother onto the carriage. Both he and Renee did not want Coleen to make the trip into Chesapeake City.

"Mama, I wish you would reconsider," said Renee. "At least let me go with you."

"NO!" said Reuben sternly, causing Renee and Aarleen to startle. That outburst reminded Renee of the time Reuben first came home from Fort Monroe. When the family was having a good time dancing while Lucy played her piano, and Renee asked Reuben to dance and he blatantly said no the same way he just did.

Reuben closed his eyes and breathed in and out, just as he did back then, turned to Renee, and softly said, "No, my precious, I need you and Aarleen here, okay?"

Renee looked to Coleen who nodded back to her.

"Yes, Reuben," said Renee, taking Aarleen into her arms.

"Remember, Mama, one week. If something happens before then, get back immediately. Fort Monroe is heavily fortified with Federal troops and militia. I'm certain curfews and possibly martial law will be imposed. I'm not concerned about the Federal regulars. It's the militia troops I'm worried about. They're not as well disciplined." said Reuben.

"I will, son. Let's go, Monroe," said Coleen.

Monroe snapped the reins and the carriage pulled away. Coleen turned back and waved to Reuben, Renee, and Aarleen as they waved back. When the carriage turned onto the road, Renee and Aarleen began to walk to the house, but Reuben remained. Renee stopped and told Aarleen to go into the house to see if May needed any help. Aarleen skipped up the porch steps and into the house.

Renee walked back to Reuben and faced him. Although she was in front of him, Reuben's eyes were fixed on the road where his mother rode away. Renee took Reuben's hands and said, "She'll be fine, my love."

"Then why do I feel like I failed her and Da," he replied as tears fell from his eyes.

石
水
In the year of our Lord, 1861, a romantic tale continues.
There are times you don't want to fight, but have to…

<u>Remember the Ribbon</u>

ORDINANCE

To repeal the ratification of the Constitution of the United State of America by the State of Virginia, and to resume all the rights and powers granted under said Constitution.

The people of Virginia in their ratification of the Constitution of the United States of America, adopted by them in convention on the twenty-fifth day of June, in the year of our Lord one thousand seven hundred and eighty-eight, having declared that the powers granted under said Constitution were derived from the people of the United States and might be resumed when so ever the same should be perverted to their injury and oppression, and the Federal Government having perverted said powers not only to the injury of the people of Virginia, but to the oppression of the Southern slave-holding States:

Now, therefore, we, the people of Virginia, do declare and ordain, that the ordinance adopted by the people of this State in convention on the twenty-fifth day of June, in the year of our Lord one thousand seven hundred and eighty-eight, whereby the Constitution of the United States of America was ratified, and all acts of the General Assembly of this State ratifying and adopting amendments to said Constitution, are hereby repealed and abrogated; that the union between the State of Virginia and the other States under the Constitution aforesaid is hereby dissolved, and that the State of Virginia is in the full possession and exercise of all the rights of sovereignty which belong and appertain to a free and independent State.

And they do further declare, that said Constitution of the United States of America is no longer binding on any of the citizens of this State.

This ordinance shall take effect and be an act of this day, when ratified by a majority of the voters of the people of this State cast at a poll to be taken thereon on the fourth Thursday in May next, in pursuance of a schedule hereafter to be enacted.

Done in Convention, in the city of Richmond, on the 17th day of April in the year of our Lord one thousand eight hundred and sixty-one, and in the eighty-fifth year of the Commonwealth of Virginia.

It was as Reuben feared. Martial Law was imposed in Hampton and Chesapeake City and his mother, sister, and brother-in-law were trapped with no way out. Renee returned from

441

the city as Reuben and Aarleen were leaving school. He so wanted to go into the city himself to check on the ferry schedules, but he remained to keep the school open, a duty he was bound by his mother to do.

"What did you find out?" asked Reuben, anxiously.

"I'm sorry, Reuben. All ferries to Chesapeake City have been stopped. Mr. and Mrs. Klaus and Andy were at the station when I arrived. They were going to go across and bring Lucy and Eric back.

"Damn it… damn it, damn it, damn it!" exclaimed Reuben.

He looked to Aarleen who was watching him. Reuben put his hand on her shoulder and said, "I'm sorry, my little blossom. I shouldn't be losing my temper like that. Genda-San would be disappointed."

"That's okay, Da. I'm worried too. Can we go home now?"

"Sure, climb onboard and I'll hand Riley up to you."

Reuben climbed onto the wagon bench and rested his face in his hands.

"Do you want me to drive, my love?" asked Renee.

Reuben only nodded. Renee snapped the reins and scooted closer to Reuben.

Reuben had always been very affectionate with Renee, but with the recent news of Virginia leaving the Union, his affection grew more intense. Renee felt Reuben needed her comfort and warmth even more so as his thoughts were of his mother, sister, and Eric trapped on the other side of the bay. The following weekend, after the ordinance was passed, Renee and Reuben took long walks anywhere and everywhere. When they would come upon a crowd celebrating the ordinance, Reuben would steer away and lead Renee in a different direction. In bed, he would hold Renee throughout the entire night. He even stopped getting out of bed to train so he would be by Renee's side when she woke.

With Aarleen, his structured training fell back to playful sessions. He took her along with him, Henry, and Noah to the patches of land they cleared out deep in the woods and explained the reason for them. The cleared land was for planting crops because he foresaw if Federal troops occupied the city and county, martial law would be imposed, and planting would be prohibited.

Together, Reuben and Aarleen sat under the oak tree and wrote their first story together. It was about an old samurai by the name of Tagoto Hachi. He would roam the countryside bringing peace to all feuds he encountered. Tagoto Hachi carried two swords, but he seldom used them because he used his wisdom and wit to bring peace rather than force and bloodshed. Their first story was fun and exciting to hear, and although both Reuben and Aarleen worked together, it was Aarleen who made up most of the story. Reuben only provided environmental context for Aarleen to use. The following day, he allowed her to recite their story to the class before school was dismissed.

That day after school, Noah and Evergreen came to pick them up from school which was very unusual.

"Where's Mama?" asked Aarleen, very concerned.

"The Norenhams are at the house. They arrived a short while ago so your Mama sent us to come and fetch you," answered Noah.

Both Reuben and Aarleen let out a sigh of relief.

Suddenly Aarleen perked up and said, "Norenhams! Is Benji with them?"

"Why, are you going to hit him with your bokken?" asked Reuben.

Turning beet red, Aarleen slapped Reuben's arm saying, "Knock it off, Da!"

"Did you see that, Noah? What is it with the women in my life and their constant abuse of me?" Reuben asked, amusingly. "Come on, my little blossom. Let's get home before your mother whacks her old classmate, Cindy, with a jo. I sure wouldn't want to miss that."

As the wagon rolled up to the side of the house, Aarleen leaped off when she saw Benjamin sitting with his parents on the porch.

Cynthia was dressed in an elaborate, hooped day dress, very out of place. But it was Simon who was dressed more unusual. He wore a uniform with the insignia of a Confederate major in the Engineering Corps.

"Hello, Mr. and Mrs. Norenham. Hello, Benji. I have something to show you. Wait here," said Aarleen, excitedly as she entered the house, almost running into Renee dressed in a hakama of deep purple and a light gray kosode, carrying out a tray with a pitcher of freshly made lemonade.

Renee laughed and said, "Sorry about that. I think she's a little excited to show Benji, I mean Benjamin, what she made out of his gift."

"Gift, what gift?" asked Cynthia, very sternly as she looked at her son. Benjamin slowly cowered in his chair.

Renee, feeling she caused Benjamin grief, quickly put down the tray and began pouring lemonade into glasses and said, "Well, it really wasn't a gift, was it Benjamin? It was more like a… token. A thank you if you will. It was a piece of leftover wood from when the school was built, a piece Aarleen wanted."

"A piece of wood? Whatever for?" asked Cynthia in a condescending manner, still looking at Benjamin.

"Oh, come on dear, children give the wildest gifts sometimes. I once received a jar of dirt. What's the harm?" asked Simon, amused and trying to help Renee take Cynthia's focus off of Benjamin. It took several more attempts of trying to change the topic until Renee brought up the days she and Cynthia attended Wickham together. That worked since Cynthia always enjoyed talking of her days at Wickham Finishing School for Girls.

Thinking the situation was somewhat defused, along came Aarleen, dressed in her kosode of crimson and hakama of royal blue from the side of the house. She had two bokkens with her, the one made of hickory tucked in her obi and her old bokken.

"Come on, Benji, I want to show you the bokken my Da and I made from that wood you gave me. You can use my old one!"

Benjamin looked questionably to his mother who was sternly looking at him. Simon, however, said, "Go on, son. You don't want to keep Miss Aarleen waiting."

"Simon! I will not have our son rough housing in those clothes!" said Cynthia.

"Oh please, Cynthia, he has more clothes at home to wear so let him go have some fun."

"Really, father?" asked Benjamin with excitement in his eyes.

"Of course, go on and have fun," Simon answered, smiling.

Cynthia had an angry pouting look as she was over ruled by her husband in front of Renee.

Benjamin rose from his chair with a huge smile on his face and made his way off the front porch saying, "Gee, thanks, father."

"Aarleen, sweetie, go easy on Benjamin," said Renee.

"I will, Mama. Don't worry Mr. and Mrs. Norenham, if I do hurt Benji, it won't hurt for long!"

"WHAT?!" yelled Cynthia as Renee slapped her hand against her forehead, shaking her head.

Simon laughed at Aarleen's comment and his wife's reaction then asked, "She is joking, right?"

Watching Simon and Cynthia, Renee began to wonder if those two were a result of an arranged marriage. The thought brought a smile to her face as she saw Reuben coming from the other side of the house with Riley at his side.

"Please excuse me while I go greet my husband," said Renee as she set down the pitcher and made her way off the porch.

Although there were guests watching, Renee skipped like a schoolgirl and greeted Reuben with a hug and kiss.

"What is Cindy doing here with Simon?" asked Reuben, out of earshot of their guests.

"Reuben, be nice. They arrived unexpectedly."

"Oh, I guessed that or you would be wearing a hooped gown with gloves instead of your hakama and serving tea instead of lemonade. Geez oh geez oh geez... Cindy Norenham coming to your house for an unexpected and unannounced visit," said Reuben, amusingly.

Renee, with an impish smile, replied, "I know, doesn't it just boggle your mind?"

Reuben's amused look faded as he noticed Simon's uniform. Renee noticed Reuben's expression and said, "I think that's what he wants to talk to you about."

Renee and Reuben made their way to the porch with Riley at Reuben's side. Reuben looked to see Aarleen showing Benjamin the correct way to hold a bokken. He got Riley's attention by tapping his jo on the ground twice. Riley took hold of Reuben's jo in his jaw and trotted off to Aarleen.

"Simon, how the hell are you? Hello Cindy... ah, I'm sorry, Cynthia. You look very lovely today."

Simon rose and offered his hand as Reuben took it in greeting. Simon took to his seat as Reuben remained standing.

"I hope you don't mind if I stand. I've been sitting all day behind my desk grading essays."

"That's quite all right, Reuben. How is the schoolhouse doing? It looks just as fantastic as the day we finished building it."

"It's well. So let's cut the small talk and tell me about the uniform," said Reuben very bluntly.

"My dear husband is a major in the Confederate Engineer Corps, Mr. Duran. He is going to be doing magnificent engineering projects for our glorious Confederate cause," said Cynthia, proudly.

Renee looked to Reuben with concern.

Reuben took a sip of lemonade and nodded. "Well, good luck to you, Simon. Keep your head down, my friend," he said, unimpressed, placing his arm around Renee's waist and giving her a quick soft kiss on her cheek causing her to grin adorably.

"Keep my head down? What do you mean, Reuben?" asked Simon with concern.

"I mean… if you want to keep that head of yours on your shoulders, and not blasted into goo, then… keep your head down."

Cynthia had a look of repulsiveness, while Simon had one of worry.

Simon cleared his throat and said, "That's exactly why I came to see you."

Reuben took another drink and let Renee sit, but he remained standing. "Really, what exactly do you need from me?" he asked.

"Reuben, when we built the school, we worked very well as a team," Simon began to say. "It became apparent to me your building experience in Japan was a huge influence with the project. I see all the additions to your farm you have made and you can be very useful to me as an aide."

"I'm not an engineer, Simon. I'm a teacher," replied Reuben.

"You are also a soldier, Mr. Duran," said Cynthia, factually.

"*WAS*… a soldier," corrected Renee, rather firmly causing both Simon and Cynthia to startle. "Not anymore," she continued more softly looking at Reuben.

Reuben moved behind Renee and gently placed his hands on her shoulders and said, "Yes Cynthia, I was a soldier, but no longer. I'm more than that now. I'm a warrior with a strict belief in a code simple soldiers cannot comprehend."

"Soldiers, warriors… what's the difference?" asked Cynthia with a cynical tone.

"Look at our daughter, Cynthia. See how detailed she is teaching your son how to use his sword? See the time and patience she has when he needs instruction? Look at how focused she is for her age rather than like most impatient 12 year olds. For over five years I have seen her grow from a talented, curious, loving child, to an even more talented, curious, loving adolescent who yearns to be more than just a simple 12 year old. Our daughter is becoming a warrior. A soldier is the same as an impatient child which Aarleen is not."

Reuben looked to Simon and addressed him directly. "Simon, I have been in the presence of many types of people, so I can tell when someone is not being truthful. Please don't put our friendship at risk because you're afraid to ask me what you really want. You don't want me as an aide, do you Simon? You want me to be a bodyguard."

Simon shamefully looked down and answered, "Yes, Reuben. Please forgive me for trying to deceive you. I'm sorry."

Reuben knelt down next to Simon and placed his hand on his shoulder and said, "I appreciate your confidence very much." With his other hand, Reuben took Renee's hand and continued, "Although I was a retainer in Japan, I wasn't trained for such a duty. My duty and talents are needed elsewhere."

"So you will not help my husband? And here I thought you were brave. Sounds more like cowardice!" said Cynthia, firmly.

Renee rose up to confront Cynthia's accusation, but Reuben quickly stopped her. He stood between Renee and Cynthia and said, "Yes, Cynthia, soldiers and warriors are similar, but there's one tremendous difference. Soldiers are simple warriors, and as a very wise man once told me, the simplest warriors are…cruel, wicked, evil, and filled with hatred. But the true warriors of heart are the ones who are loyal, honest, and benevolent. They can defend with deadly accuracy one moment, and become a poet, the next."

"Please, forgive me, my friend," said Simon again, taking the attention away from Cynthia. "Renee, please forgive me also. My wife may not understand your husband's words, but I do. I choose to be a part of this cause and I have no right to drag your husband into my decision."

Reuben moved back to Simon and placed his hand back on his shoulder, "Spoken like a true warrior of heart, Simon, and those are the warriors who have a better chance to survive."

At that moment, two riders on horseback rode up the lane to the house, both cheering and hollering. One rider wore a gaudy, old style army uniform with gold epilettes and a sword at his waist. The other was Monroe wearing a civilian suit. He also had a sword hanging from his waist.

Renee took Reuben by the arm, Simon rose, and Aarleen and Benjamin came running to the porch.

Seeing Monroe with a sword hanging at his waist caused Reuben to shake his head and mutter silently to Renee, "This day is just full of all sorts of surprises."

May and Henry emerged from the front door at the sound of the commotion, while Noah and Evergreen came from the side of the house.

Monroe and his companion rode up to the front of the house and dismounted. "WOO-HOO!!!" yelled Monroe as he came from around his horse almost tripping on his sword. "Come on brother! Grab that fancy sword of yours and join me and Harvey!"

Reuben moved to the steps of the porch looking down on Monroe. "What the hell did you get yourself into, Monroe?" he asked, disappointedly.

"What did I get myself into, you ask? I got myself into the 66th Virginia Infantry Regiment. That's what I've gotten myself into, and we need experienced men like you to lead our Confederate cause to victory!" said Monroe, excitedly.

"That's right, Reuben Duran. Virginia is calling you!" said Harvey.

Reuben stood at the top of the porch steps shaking his head. "Aarleen, take Ben to the oak tree and train there."

"But, Da…"

"Do as your father says, sweetie," said Renee before Reuben was about to sternly repeat himself.

"Yes Mama. Come on, Benji," replied Aarleen.

She and Benjamin ran around the side of the house, but when they got to the back, Aarleen took hold of Benjamin's hand and pulled him toward the kitchen door. They entered the house through the kitchen and went into the parlor to watch what was happening through the corners of the large parlor window.

Ignoring Harvey's comment, Reuben again asked more firmly, "Again, what in the hell did you get yourself into, Monroe?"

"Come on, little brother. I finally did what you did and joined the army," answered Monroe.

"Monroe, you idiot. Why did you join the army?" asked Reuben. He quickly faced Renee and they both had a sense of déjà vu as they looked at each other. Reuben returned his attention to Monroe.

"Why, you ask? I'll tell you why. Because Virginia is at war and I'm taking up arms to fight for the Confederate cause. You are now addressing *Major* Monroe Duran, aide de camp to the commanding officer of the 66th."

"You're acting like a major pain in the ass, brother," said Reuben, without humor. "It's hard to believe you're the eldest."

"HEY, you can't talk to an aide de camp in that manner," said Harvey. "Are you some sort of Yankee sympathizer?"

"He's not anything of the sort!" retorted Simon, standing next to Reuben trying to figure out the rank of Harvey's ridiculous, gaudy uniform.

Reuben stepped down from the porch and slowly walked to Monroe. "Monroe, do you even know what the Confederate cause is? Do you have any idea what it means to go to war? Do you have any idea what you have done? Didn't you learn anything after the hell and torment I put myself through?!"

"It means to kill Yankees who want to change our way of life!" responded Monroe.

"Simple warriors," commented Renee softly to herself. Cynthia heard Renee's comment and suddenly Reuben's words made sense to her.

"If defending Virginia isn't your cause Reuben, then what is?" Monroe continued, stepping closer to his brother.

"My cause is my wife and daughter. My cause is our mother and sister and her husband trapped on the other side of the bay with no way to get back home. My cause is May, Henry, and Noah who run our farm, the farm given to Da by GrandDa Miles. That's my cause Monroe, an honorable cause. Not a wasted cause that will end in the bloodshed of the innocent."

"You sound like a coward, Reuben! Ha! Maybe it's jealousy. You spent three years at VMI and what did it get you, only second lieutenant. I went to William and Mary, became a successful lawyer like Da, and was made a Major!"

Reuben moved closer to Monroe, causing Renee to come down the steps of the porch. Aarleen left her viewing point from the parlor and came out onto the porch, very worried and frightened. She had seen her father and uncle argue many times. But not like this.

"Seriously, Monroe, is that what you think?" asked Reuben. "Seriously, or is it about someone else? Someone you have always wanted to prove yourself to, but couldn't until now? Someone you can't have because I wouldn't die?"

"You had many times to die, Reuben, a couple by your own hands," replied Monroe, his voice trembling with anger. "Why couldn't you have died one of those times? If you would have died, I wouldn't have had to pry any attention from Da and Mama, and *she* would have forgotten all about you and belong to me now!" said Monroe as he pointed to Renee.

Renee brought her hands to her mouth as she gasped in shock.

Reuben shook his head, "Go, Monroe. Go and fight your war and leave me and my family out of your cause."

"He sounds like a traitor, Major Duran!" called out Harvey. "Traitors need to die. There's your excuse you've been waiting for all these years to get rid of your brother, Monroe!"

"Get off my farm, Monroe, and take your idiot tin soldier with you," said Reuben as he turned and walked to Renee taking her offered hand.

"Don't you turn your back on me, you god damned traitor!" called Monroe as he drew his sword.

Reuben stopped and without turning, he said, "Stop being stupid, Monroe. Put that thing away."

Monroe let out a loud cry, raised his sword, and charged at Reuben. Sensing Monroe's attack, Reuben quickly and instinctively covered Renee with his body to protect her. Reuben shifted Renee out of the way of Monroe's blade as it came down. Protecting his wife, Reuben's shoulder was exposed. Monroe's sword tip made contact tearing through Reuben's shirt and drawing his blood across his right shoulder.

"DA!!!" cried out Aarleen as she tried to make her way off the porch, only to be held back by Henry.

Benjamin came out onto the porch and went to stand in front of his terrified mother, instinctively protecting her as his father made his way off the porch to help Reuben.

"Bully, Major! You can take him! Kill that traitor!" called out Harvey.

Reuben pushed Renee toward the porch into May's arms and held out his hand for Simon to stop. He turned to face Monroe, but he showed no anger. Renee noticed and exclaimed, "Monroe! How could you?!"

"COME ON BROTHER!! LET'S SEE HOW STRONG YOU REALLY ARE!!" yelled Monroe.

"NO, MONROE!!!" cried Renee. "He's your brother!"

"Mama," cried Aarleen, very frightened. For everyone present, especially Aarleen, it was horrifying to see her uncle attack her father with the intent to kill him.

Renee pulled free from May's arms and took Aarleen in hers, and held her tightly.

"Put the sword away, Monroe," said Reuben, calmly. "Let's think about getting Mama, Lucy, and Eric back home, together, you and I. We can't abandon them when they need both of us right now."

"Oh, no, Reuben, I have been waiting to do this for a long time, a very long time."

"It's not in you, brother. Please, Monroe, for Mama and Lucy. Please stop," implored Reuben.

As blood seeped from his wounded shoulder, Reuben remained calm, trying to ease Monroe back from his angered state. "Please, Monroe, our mother and sister and her husband are trapped. We should be working together trying to get them back," he continued to plead softly.

With another loud cry, Monroe raised his sword in his right hand and swung it down toward Reuben's head. Reuben side stepped to Monroe's right side and faced the same direction. With his right hand, Reuben grasped Monroe's sword hand and extended it across his center. Using his left arm, Reuben shot it across Monroe's neck and chest and swiftly swung back, causing Monroe to fall hard onto his back while being disarmed at the same time.

Harvey drew his sword with his right hand, raised it above his head, and began making a downward cut to Reuben's head. Keeping his eyes on Monroe and not looking back, Reuben raised Monroe's sword, now in his hand, and easily blocked Harvey's strike. Harvey stood dumbfounded as Reuben turned to face him. Reuben drew his sword downward bringing Harvey's sword with it. With his left hand, Reuben grasped Harvey's sword hand and easily relieved Harvey of his sword causing him to stumble forward. Harvey regained his balance and turned to face Reuben, only to find his head caught in the middle of the two swords crossed at his throat like a huge pair of scissors. Harvey's expression had a look of terror, while Reuben's face was calm. Reuben lowered the two swords and swiftly kicked Harvey in the groin causing him to squeal out in pain, grab his groin, and fall to the ground.

Turning back to Monroe, who was leaning on his elbows watching, Reuben stepped back to him and shoved him back to the ground with his booted foot. Reuben stood over his brother with a dreadful look of an angered wolf about to attack. He reversed the two swords by twirling them in his hands, and raised them both above his head.

"REUBEN, NO!!!" cried out Renee.

"AHIT!!!" Reuben let out a loud kiai and speared the ground with the sword from his right hand to Monroe's right side of his face, and with another loud kiai, Reuben speared the ground with the other sword to Monroe's left side of his face.

Monroe lay flat on his back with both swords crossed at his face trapping him to the ground.

Reuben knelt next to Monroe and with a neutral look, he said in a calm tone, "War is not a game and neither is petty jealously, Monroe. People die from both. Now see to your comrade and the both of you... get the hell off my farm."

Reuben rose and made his way to the house as everyone watched him in awe. Renee quickly took a towel from May's apron pocket, wadded it, ran to Reuben placing it on his wounded shoulder, and took him in her arms. Aarleen also ran to Reuben and wrapped her arms around his waist.

As the three made their way into the house, Monroe tried to free himself from the swords crossed above his face. There was no way for him to remove them without at least leaving a cut across either side of his face that would leave a scar, reminding him of the day he tried to kill his brother.

狼

"I'm finished with the sweeping, Da," said Aarleen, walking up to Reuben's desk. Once again Aarleen saw to the sweeping of the schoolhouse floors.

"And the outhouse has been cleaned out as well, Mr. Duran," said Tommy Deans, entering the schoolhouse from the side entrance.

Since the day of the ordinance, many of the farm families stopped sending their children to school. Many thought, because Virginia claimed its independence from an oppressive government, sending their children to school that was overseen by the same standards of the Federal government was improper. There were only a few families who still insisted on sending their children to school. One of those students was, surprisingly enough for Reuben, Tommy Deans, his only troublesome student in the school. For all of Tommy Deans' shortcomings, he was still a very bright student and although he wouldn't admit it, he enjoyed school, but only if Reuben was the teacher.

Tommy Deans' interest in school could have also been because of Aarleen. He did, in his own way, take a shine to her, as Renee would put it regarding adolescent relationship tendencies. Reuben's reaction to Renee's evaluation of the matter was, thank the gods of the high mountains my little cherry blossom has eyes for Benji.

For the longest time, when the Norfolk County Outreach School opened, Tommy Deans consistently teased and tormented Aarleen until that beautiful, marvelous day three years ago Reuben felt immensely proud of his daughter when she took matters into her own hands...

The day was cool as the children exited the schoolhouse into the yard for recess. Aarleen, with some other girls her age, made their way to the teeter-totters Henry and Noah had made for the children. Tommy Deans, along with a few of his friends, followed the girls and when they were about to hop on, Tommy Deans and his gang ran and jumped on in front of the girls, laughing.

"You got to be quicker!" yelled out Tommy Deans.

The girls were angered by the display, but Aarleen was furious and about to confront Tommy Deans until she noticed her father watching from the window. She hoped he would come out to tell the boys to allow the girls to play on the teeter-totters, but he just stood there watching. Aarleen got the idea that he was observing to see how she would deal with the situation.

Why does he do that? I'm only a child, she thought to herself expressing one of the very rare moments of frustration toward her father.

Aarleen took in a deep breath and allowed it to circulate through her body as instructed by Reuben. It actually helped and the frustration ebbed away.

"We don't need to play on the teeter-totters. I want to jump rope anyway," said Aarleen cheerfully, and walked off to the shaded part of the schoolyard with her friends following.

"Hey, Aarleen, What's wrong? Your daddy not going to help you?" shouted Tommy Deans, laughing. She looked at him, turned her back, and continued walking.

Tommy Deans, angered by the gesture, hopped off the teeter-totter, letting it fall with one of his followers hitting the ground hard. He ran up to Aarleen and tapped her on the right shoulder.

Aarleen reflected on a lesson Reuben taught her, *"Never initiate the attack, for the one who initiates it, shows their true colors of a coward. Give the attacker the opportunity to gather themselves, but never take the attack twice."*

Aarleen turned to face Tommy Deans. "Don't you turn your back on me when I'm talking to you," he said.

Reuben's full attention was on his daughter now. This was her first confrontation and he was concerned with how she would deal with it. "Renee would kick my ass if she knew I was letting Aarleen handle this on her own," he said to himself.

Aarleen looked at Tommy Deans curiously with her adorable smile and bright eyes.

"I said, your daddy isn't going to help you," repeated Tommy Deans, smugly.

"I'm sorry, but I can't understand what you're saying with those chicken lips of yours," replied Aarleen and turned around to continue to the shaded part of the yard to jump rope.

Her friends, and even some of the other boys, laughed at the comment.

Tommy Deans, frustrated, reached out and grabbed Aarleen's right shoulder rather than tapping it. "Are you saying I have the lips of a chicken, you..."

He didn't get to finish his thought. Aarleen quickly used her left hand to trap Tommy Deans' right hand on her shoulder and swiftly sidestepped out and under his arm, twisting it at the same time. With slight pressure to his wrist, Aarleen had Tommy Deans dancing on his toes in circles around her. She took a step behind him, and using her other arm, cut Tommy Deans at his elbow and twisted him down to the ground like a top with his face landing in a mud puddle. Aarleen had Tommy Deans pinned to the ground using one hand.

Reuben watched on approvingly until the children began to cheer on Aarleen, including Tommy Deans' small gang of boys. "Whoa... geez oh geez oh geez," said Reuben as he tossed the book he was holding onto his desk and ran out into the schoolyard. Being serious, but mostly amused and proud, he gently made his way past the children to reach Aarleen and Tommy Deans.

451

"YAME!!!" shouted Reuben.

At the sound of Reuben's command, Aarleen gently brought Tommy Deans' arm around to his back and released him, moving back, but still maintaining mental contact with her attacker, just as Reuben had taught her.

Tommy Deans quickly stood up. Angry, he made a motion toward Aarleen. Aarleen centered herself in a defensive ready stance and shouted out a loud kiai. Her shout of warning caused Tommy Deans to rear back, holding his hands up as protection.

Reuben stepped in between the two. "All right children, recess is over, so let's get back to work. We still have much to do." He focused on Tommy Deans and Aarleen. "As for you two, grab your readers and the both of you, in the two corners behind my desk."

"But she started it," Tommy Deans began, until he made eye contact with Reuben. His eyes pierced back, causing guilt to flow through Tommy Deans' mind. "Yes sir," he said and walked into the schoolhouse wiping his face.

"Why do I have to sit in the corner, teacher? I was just defending myself, like you, err, my Da, taught me," said Aarleen, very distraughtly as her eyes were tearing up.

"That may be so, but this is a schoolyard, not a dojo. Now do as you are told."

"Yes sir."

A couple of Aarleen's friends walked in with her. "What's a dojo," one of them asked.

Inside the schoolhouse, all the children sat at their desks, taking out their readers, and started reading the assignment written on the blackboard behind Reuben's desk. Tommy Deans sat facing the corner to the left of Reuben, flipping through the pages of his reader instead of reading. Aarleen, to Reuben's right, sat in her corner reading the assignment with tears rolling down her cheeks and onto the pages of her book. Suddenly, she heard Reuben clear his throat and she glanced over to him. He sat at his desk watching her with a smile. He winked his right eye, nodded approvingly to her, and turned to his work. Aarleen's adorable smile replaced her frown, and the tears in her bright eyes dried up as she straightened herself up in the stool. She began to read the assignment with joy in her heart knowing she had pleased her father.

Since then, Tommy Deans kept a respectful relationship, not to mention distance, with Aarleen.

"Well, I'm finished here myself," replied Reuben. "Grab your books and I'll lock up. Thanks for your help, Mr. Deans. Give your parents my best."

"I will, Mr. Duran. See you tomorrow, Aarleen," said Tommy Deans as he raced out the front door of the schoolhouse.

"Bye, Tommy," replied Aarleen as she gathered her school books and lunch pail.

Reuben locked up the schoolhouse and, hand-in-hand, Reuben and Aarleen began walking home.

Because of the unpredictable state in which the city and county were in after the ordinance of secession, Reuben didn't want Renee or Henry riding around in the wagon unless it was absolutely necessary. There had been movement of soldiers, both militia and newly established Confederate troops.

It sure didn't take them long to mobilize a state militia, thought Reuben as a troop of Confederate cavalry troopers trotted by on horseback in the same direction he and his daughter were walking.

Aarleen looked to her father and saw the anguish in his eyes. It had been over two weeks and still, Coleen, Lucy, and Eric were trapped on the other side of the bay.

A few days ago, Andrew came by the farm to inform Reuben and Renee they received a message saying Coleen, Lucy, and Eric were fine, but leaving the city was impossible, especially for those who harbored Confederate sentiment, such as Eric.

"I don't know what it is with that boy of mine," said Andrew. "In the message, your mother says she and Lucy are pleading for him to stop pro-Confederate activity so they can at least leave the city and travel to Williamsburg, catch a ferry across the James, and return by way of Petersburg.

Shaking his head in disappointment, Andrew also said, "My boy, I can't believe he could be a revolutionary. I know you, Reuben... ever since that dreaded ordinance, you have been trying to conjure up a way to get them back home. If you ever figure out a way, I want in, you understand?"

Reuben's only response was a nod of agreement.

Although he walked in silence, Aarleen knew he was thinking hard about how to bring back her GrandMama, Aunty Lucy, and Uncle Eric. She was so very proud to have such a loving, devoted man as her father. With them trapped on the other side of the bay, and the incident between her father and Uncle Monroe, Aarleen began to wonder if this was the test Reuben talked about Christmas day. As she walked with her father, she silently vowed she would be strong for him and her mother, the same way they were strong for each other all those years they were separated.

狼

A young Confederate First Lieutenant knocked on the door, stepped back, and stood waiting with his hands behind his back. The door was answered by Renee, wearing a kosode of sky blue and her dark green hakama. The lieutenant stood, unexpectedly stunned by Renee's beauty as he came to attention and removed his cap.

"Hello, may I help you?" asked Renee, startling the lieutenant out of his trance-like state.

"Good afternoon, ma'am. Allow me to introduce myself. I'm Lieutenant Stevens, Todd Stevens," said the young lieutenant politely and properly. "May I be correct to assume you are Mrs. Duran?"

Renee smiled at the young lieutenant. "Yes I am. Will you please come in?"

"I would be honored," replied Lieutenant Stevens.

He wiped his shoes on the porch and walked over the threshold. Once he was inside the front parlor, he glanced around. "This is a very nice home you have, Mrs. Duran, very nice indeed."

"Thank you, Mr. Stevens. Please have a seat," Renee said, pleasantly.

Lieutenant Stevens could not get over how beautiful Renee was. Her face was radiant and wonderful to look at. He took a seat in the high-backed chair across from the sofa. Renee fetched a glass pitcher of water and a couple of glasses. "May I offer you a glass of cool water?"

"Yes, indeed, please."

Renee poured two glasses full of water and handed one to the Lieutenant. She took the other glass and sat on the sofa. "What may I ask is the purpose of your visit, Mr. Stevens?"

"I was hoping I could speak with your husband. I have a request to ask of him," the lieutenant answered.

Renee's smile faded. What type of request, she wondered. Is this man here to ask Reuben to join the army now that Virginia was mobilizing for war, or was he here to take him away rather than ask? She began to tremble and Lieutenant Stevens noticed. He began to feel some tension, so he quickly smiled as pleasantly as he could.

"I see that you're concerned. Believe me, it's nothing serious. I just need to ask Mr. Duran if I can billet some men across the road over there," he said as he pointed toward the clearing in front of the house.

Renee let out a large sigh and her smile came back. "Oh, is that all? Actually I manage the farm, but under the circumstances, Reuben will have to make the decision."

Impressed that she was the one who ran the farm, Lieutenant Stevens said, "Of course, I understand."

"Your husband, he served in Mexico?" asked Lieutenant Stevens, as a topic of interest.

The smile on Renee's face faded again and an angered look replaced it. "I'm sorry, Mr. Stevens," she said, not very politely, "Mexico isn't discussed in this house. I will tell you, yes he did fight there. He also fought in Japan," she said and motioned with a nod toward the mantel where the Akagi Clan banner Aarleen had made for Reuben hung above his Kutto.

Lieutenant Stevens glanced at the mantel and his eyebrows rose in awe. "I mean no disrespect. On the contrary, Mrs. Duran, your husband is much respected. Yes, his service in Mexico is well known, and so are his travels in Japan. I didn't know about him fighting there however." He saw Renee was still perturbed. "But that's the past and with him teaching here, giving his mother, who was my teacher by the way, full attention to teach in the city is wonderful. I bet he's a very good teacher."

Renee brightened up and her smile returned. "Yes he is. The children enjoy going to school. For many of them, it was their first time when he opened the school," she said, proudly.

"As a matter fact, that's why he's not home now," she said as she turned to the wall clock. "He's probably on his way home now with our daughter, Aarleen."

"I see. Well, I won't take too much of his time away from his family," he said, and finished his glass of water. "May I please have another glass of water?"

Renee filled his glass and noticed Lieutenant Stevens looking at the banner and sword.

"You're curious about that banner?"

"Yes, but if you don't wish to…"

Renee didn't let him finish. "That's all right. Reuben's journey to Japan is much talked about in this house. If it wasn't for that journey, he wouldn't be the man he is today. That's the banner of the Akagi Clan. The circle is the tsuba of a katana sword. The half shaped circles represent the day and night with the sun and moon centered. It represents the region of Itosai is forever on constant vigilance against invaders. He served as a retainer and samurai to the Daimyo of the region of Itosai in the Hisano Province named Akagi Genda. Unlike the war in Mexico, the conflicts Reuben participated in Japan are held with much honor."

Renee continued to tell the lieutenant about Reuben's adventures in Japan as he listened with wide eyes, full of attention and fascination.

狼

Reuben and Aarleen were nearing the farm when he glanced at her. "I'm sorry I'm not too talkative these days, blossom."

"That's okay, Da. I'm worried about them too…" Aarleen said, and hesitated before she continued, "and Uncle Monroe." After saying Monroe's name, she winced slightly.

"I'm worried about him too," replied Reuben, causing Aarleen relief.

Although with the current condition the state of Virginia was in, the farm was still successful. After all these years of being home, Reuben could not get over how fantastic Renee, May, Henry, and Noah kept the farm going. Reuben did his share of the work also, and made many additions to the farm, but he praised them for the overall success of the farm. After all, his primary and full time job was teaching and maintaining the Norfolk County Outreach School.

Again he glanced to Aarleen. Prior to Virginia leaving the Union, Renee and Reuben had discussed the possibilities of having another child. Perhaps a baby brother to pester his big sister as Reuben put it. However, after the secession of Virginia, both Renee and Reuben thought it best to put off such plans until conditions became more stable. Still though, it didn't stop them from being intimate as they always been.

As they neared the lane leading to the house, Aarleen came to an abrupt stop causing Reuben to stumble. "Da, there's soldiers in front of the house," she said, anxiously.

Reuben's pleasant face became stern and fierce. Ever since Virginia joined the Confederacy, there had been troops passing by, but never stopping. He became very curious and pulled Aarleen by the hand closer to his side. "Stay close, blossom, and don't show fear."

The soldiers lining both sides of the road were chatting until Reuben and Aarleen turned down the lane heading toward the house. A few of them tipped their caps in greeting and Reuben nodded in return. A sergeant stood in the middle of the lane. He was a big, strong-looking man, and he had a mocking smirk on his face.

Is this man keeping us from our home, thought Aarleen, fearful but not showing it.

It looked as if he was about to challenge Reuben. Indeed, the sergeant heard Reuben had no intention to fight for the cause and was about to let Reuben know how he felt about his non-involvement.

Reuben gazed through the sergeant as if he wasn't there and kept his pace until Reuben was in front of the sergeant. Reuben stopped. The sergeant looked down on Reuben with that same mocking manner. Reuben's eyes turned from the house to the sergeant's eyes. Reuben's eyes were fierce and piercing with the look of a hungry wolf. The sergeant's mocking look faded and he sensed a form of energy pushing on him. He slowly moved to the side, clearing the lane for Reuben and Aarleen.

"Who's that?" asked a private to the sergeant.

"I don't know, but there's something fierce in him. I actually felt it inside, strange," the sergeant answered, nodding his head in confusion.

"I've never seen you back away from anyone before, Max."

The sergeant sternly looked at the private causing him to wince away. His attention returned to Reuben as he and Aarleen continued to the house.

Just before Reuben and Aarleen reached the porch, Reuben said to Aarleen. "Give me your books and pail and go around the house and see if May needs any chores done. Then we will do some training before dinner."

"Yes, Da," said Aarleen, running to find May.

With Aarleen's books and lunch pail in hand, Reuben walked onto the porch and into the house. Lieutenant Stevens stood up quickly.

Renee walked to Reuben and took him in her arms and greeted him lovingly, as always.

"Mr. Stevens, may I introduce my husband, Reuben Duran. Reuben, this is Todd Stevens."

"This is an honor, Mr. Duran," said Lieutenant Stevens, moving closer and holding out his hand in greeting.

Reuben handed Renee Aarleen's books and lunch pail and took the offered hand. "Thank you, but please, call me Reuben. Why are you here?" he asked, bluntly.

"Mr. Stevens would like to, ah, billet some of his men across the road for the week," Renee answered, realizing the lieutenant was intimidated and hoped to ease the tension.

"Is that so?" asked Reuben. "Please Todd, excuse me, Lieutenant, have a seat. For what purpose do you need this billet?"

"Please call me Todd, sir. The purpose of the billet is to rotate the men from place to place. Colonel McFerrin feels it's good training for the soldiers to be ready to move at a moment's notice. More of a training exercise than anything else," said Lieutenant Stevens.

"That's a good idea. Armies need to move quickly and be prepared at a moment's notice. It builds troop awareness, care of equipment, attention to detail, and most importantly, discipline. Yes, you can billet your men across the road as long as they don't interfere with the working of the farm. The men can have access to the creek as long as they stay to the path. No loud noise or language. We have a twelve year old daughter."

Lieutenant Stevens became somewhat, awed, by Reuben's response. A response filled with the knowledge of the importance of military maneuvers and experience.

Renee herself was also amazed. She never heard her husband speak in such a manner or tone since the day he discussed his passage with her Godfather James Forrest. It frightened her now as it did back then.

"Yes sir. I'll see to it the men will be on the best of behavior. I dearly appreciate this and so does Virginia."

Reuben nodded off that remark and stood up. The lieutenant stood as well, taking the hint to leave. He nervously eyed his sword and glanced to the mantel once again.

"Would you care to see it, Todd?" asked Reuben in a friendly manner and not as formal as the previous discussion.

"Sir, that would be a privilege I would very much appreciate. I have heard of your unique fencing style."

Reuben nodded and walked to the mantel. With both hands, he picked up his Kutto and formally bowed to the banner. He turned and raised the sheathed sword for the lieutenant to view.

"That's a beautiful weapon, Reuben. I would very much like to see how it is used."

Reuben took the sheathed sword into his left hand and tucked it into his obi of Akagi burgundy, tied at his waist. Keeping eye contact with the lieutenant, Reuben swiftly drew the sword with his right hand and brought the blade to rest at the lieutenant's throat in a basic suburi movement. The lieutenant stood stiff as a board, wide-eyed, and breathing hard. Reuben's movement was swift, quick, and quiet. The lieutenant had no idea a human being could move so fast. Without moving his head, he glanced down with his eyes and noticed how the sharpened edge of the sword was on the opposite side. It made him wonder the purpose for such a weapon.

After the incident with Monroe, up until this moment, Renee never saw Reuben raise a sword to anyone, with the exception of training her and Aarleen with wooden bokkens. Watching his demonstration for the lieutenant, done so precisely, caused her to wonder how many times Reuben drawn his sword for real. She turned her head and closed her eyes tightly trying hard to erase that thought from her mind.

Realizing he drew his sword and rested it to the throat of another man in front of his wife, Reuben's concentrated focus turned into concern. He glanced over toward Renee, who now was facing away with her eyes closed. He felt ashamed for such a display in front of the woman he loved. As elegantly and swiftly as Reuben drew the sword, he returned it to its saya.

Trying to defuse the tension, Reuben cleared his throat and said in a pleasant and instructional manner, "This, Todd, is more of a tool rather than a weapon. Weapons are designed to take life, where as tools are designed to build life. It depends on the swordsman how he chooses to use the sword. My lord, Genda-San, would never approve of me to raise this sword to take a life unless innocent lives are being threatened. That's why the blade of this sword is reversed."

Reuben looked back toward Renee who had returned her look to Reuben. He gave her a pleading look of forgiveness. She looked upon him with sorrow, not because of this incident, but of all the pain and sorrow he had to endure on his own in the past. She stepped up to him and took him by the arm. He in turn placed his hand on hers and said to Lieutenant Stevens, "Please feel free to join us for dinner this evening."

"Ah, that would be wonderful. Thank you," replied Lieutenant Stevens in a state of awe.

狼

"Look at that," said a private to the sergeant. "The man of the house is wearing a dress!"

"What are you talking about?" replied the sergeant as he looked toward the front of the house to see Reuben, wearing his burgundy kosode and black hakama, walk off the porch holding what appeared to be a couple of sticks. The sergeant chuckled and slapped the private on the shoulder. "You're right! He is wearing a dress. No wonder he doesn't want to join in the fight for Virginia. Come here, boys, and look at the man the lieutenant respects so much," he continued laughing, forgetting all about his brief meeting earlier.

There were two other privates who came to look. They all began to laugh as Reuben picked up a pail and made his way to the back of the house. "Come on, lets get some water from the creek," said the sergeant, no longer amused but filled with curiosity.

The four soldiers walked on the path, as instructed by the lieutenant, leading to the creek. Once at the creek's edge, they stood watching Reuben pounding what looked like a wedge into the ground holding up a post of stiff thick straw. Next to it, a wooden saw horse stood at waist level thickly wrapped with wool and canvas across the beam, its center concaved. When Reuben finished his task, he lowered himself onto the ground and sat facing the early evening sun with his eyes closed.

"What do you think he's up to, Sergeant?" asked a private.

The sergeant said nothing, but shrugged his shoulders and kept watching. There was no sense of amusement anymore. Sergeant Warren was beginning to have a strange feeling he could not explain. He was tempted to walk to Reuben and ask him what he was doing. Instead he slowly walked closer by way of the creek's edge. As he walked, he glanced to the post and saw horse. He noticed both were worn in certain places as if beaten. Suddenly the sergeant stopped as Reuben, from his sitting position, rolled forward and stood up, and dropped backward rolling onto his feet. Reuben repeated this movement over and over, his hakama flowing with each roll, making him look as if he were floating.

Curiosity began to get the better of Sergeant Warren and he began to step toward Reuben, but quickly stopped, almost tripping forward, when Reuben drew what looked like a curved wooden sword from his obi.

Well centered and balanced, Reuben began his single drills of bokken suburis and thrust technique movements. Upon ending a cut, the sharp loud sound of "KIAI" came out of Reuben's mouth. His movements were very deliberate and defined. Slowly, his movements began to glide and with his hakama flowing with the motions, Reuben looked as if he were hovering over the ground on a black cloud.

Reuben's movements were so calming Sergeant Warren forgot about the other soldiers and knelt down to watch while nodding in amazement. He stood up and picked up a stick and begun to mimic Reuben's thrusts and cuts. Suddenly a loud "CRACK" echoed over the land, causing birds to take flight and startled the sergeant. "CRACK-CRACK-CRACK" echoed loudly again as Reuben's bokken stuck the post. Sergeant Warren stood in awe. He had seen army officers practice duels with their swords, but nothing such as this. The way Reuben was striking the practice post, he could actually injure those army officers with that wooden sword, possibly even kill them, he thought as he watched on.

Reuben went on with his training for thirty minutes non-stop. Sergeant Warren kept watching, forgetting all about the other soldiers. Then he saw Reuben's wife and daughter walking toward Reuben, also dressed the same as him. As Reuben stopped and lowered himself to the ground to rest, Sergeant Warren saw Renee run up behind Reuben, raising the same type of wooden sword over her head, and as she was almost upon Reuben, he rolled forwards and was back on his feet and quickly blocked Renee's strike. She regained her balance and again struck as Reuben easily parried it away, causing her to twist and fall into his arms.

"Almost got you that time!" she said.

"See, I don't have to teach you anything, my love. All you have to do is be sneaky."

They both laughed and embraced each other.

Aarleen came running up and offered Reuben her hand. As he was about to take it, Aarleen quickly took hold of his wrist with her other hand, and swiftly turned her body to the right under his arm and threw him as if she were casting a fishing line. Reuben flipped in the air and landed hard on the ground laughing.

"Who taught you one of the four directional throws?" asked Reuben.

"Mama did! Now it's two against one!"

All three began to laugh with joyful hearts as Renee and Aarleen began to chase Reuben around the tree stopping once in a while to toss one another to the ground. Reuben went from a warrior of heart, training with deadly accuracy one moment, to become a poet the next expressing affection to his family.

Sergeant Warren watched on with respectful amusement. He nodded approvingly and realized what made Reuben so respectful. Lieutenant Stevens told the sergeant of what he knew of Reuben's background and the sergeant found it difficult to believe, until he watched Reuben with his family. At that moment, Sergeant Warren wished there were men like Reuben in the Confederate army.

狼

The next couple of days went on with no incident and as usual for the farm inhabitants, with the exception of the small army camped across the lane, but that was of no concern. On the contrary, the soldiers, especially Sergeant Warren, provided help on the farm when their army duties permitted. They helped Reuben, Henry, and Noah tend to the gardens and field. For the soldiers, it was a pleasant break from the constant drill, drill, drill and more drill.

In the morning, before school, May, Renee, and Aarleen would bring the soldiers fresh biscuits and coffee. When Aarleen returned home from school, she made lemonade for the soldiers and served it before her chores. The soldiers appreciated the treat so much, they would show their gratitude by helping her with her chores so she could have more time with her parents. In the evening, Reuben invited the soldiers to have their meals in the front yard of the house, which was more pleasant than the openness and military atmosphere of the camp.

Aarleen enjoyed having the soldiers around. It made her feel very useful helping her mother and May wash and mend their clothes, a service the soldiers never expected or asked the ladies to do. At one time, Aarleen showed Sergeant Warren the technique she had done on her father, and also the other technique she used on Tommy Deans in the schoolyard.

Reuben and the sergeant also had pleasant conversations and he even taught the sergeant some very basic sword techniques. All was very well indeed. That was until the fires.

狼

The fires across the bay lit up the night's sky. The glow could be seen from the farm and all were in the front of the house watching and praying. Rumors of the Federal militia troops destroying the homes and shops of the residents loyal to the Confederate cause across the bay were all over the city and county. The night sky seemed to be proof the rumors were true. Reuben paced back and forth and the only thing Renee could do was watch. She knew Reuben was scheming of ways to get across the bay. He was the only hope for his mother, Lucy, and Eric. Monroe had long left Norfolk since he joined the 66th Virginia Infantry Regiment. Reuben and Renee both felt Monroe wouldn't be much help anyway.

"Damn it, I don't know how, but I'm going to Chesapeake City and get them out," said Reuben, as he started walking up the path to hitch the team to the wagon.

Renee ran and took him by the arm, pulling him to stop. "You're thinking irrationally, Reuben. You can't just go and swim the bay. I know you want to get them, but we... all of us, have to stop and think this out," she said while caressing his face.

Reuben's breathing started to slow down. Renee's touch was very soothing and comforting, the only thing that could calm Reuben down. "Yes, you're right. You're always right."

"Yes, she is," said Noah. "All of us has got to think this out, isn't that a fact, Henry?"

"All's I know is we isn't going to get across all that water in a row boat," replied Henry.

May slapped the porch rail, "Renee, how about your daddy's old business? Surely there may still be some of his old workers who will have a large boat in the city."

When Franklin Wallace left Norfolk for Alabama, he kept one wharf to be used for his shipping company when he relocated to Mobile. It was overseen by Jacob Curtis, the one who found Renee on her knees wearing an elaborate wedding dress sobbing when she saw the ship taking Reuben on his journey left. Like her Godfather, James Forrest, and many others who worked for Renee's father, Jacob Curtis always showed Renee kindness because she was very kind to them, so unlike her father. From time-to-time, Renee would visit with Jacob Curtis and bring him products produced from the farm. She never forgot his compassion he showed that one day when the *Morning Star* departed for San Francisco taking the boy she loved with it.

"That's a good idea, Aunty May, but I think it's going to take more than Noah and me to row a large boat across the bay," said Reuben, considering the suggestion.

Footsteps coming from the path disrupted the discussion. "Perhaps we can help row that boat," said Sergeant Warren, standing next to Lieutenant Stevens in front of several other soldiers.

狼

The plan was set. Early in the morning Renee and Henry would take the carriage into the city and visit Franklin Wallace's wharf. She would see if Jacob Curtis would be willing to help and find a few others that would take a boat to pick up Reuben, Noah, and the soldiers at the Sewell's Point jetty. Under the cover of darkness, they would row across the bay to Chesapeake City. In the meantime, Reuben, Noah, and Sergeant Warren, with several soldiers, would take the wagon to the jetty and wait, and hopefully Renee would be able to convince Jacob Curtis to help. Lieutenant Stevens would stay behind in case his commanding officer, Colonel McFerrin, came by to inspect. Lieutenant Stevens would cover Sargent Warren's and the other soldiers' absence by saying the sergeant took them on a forced march exercise.

Everyone awoke early the next morning, everyone that is except for Reuben, who tossed and turned all night long. Even Renee's soothing caresses and touches could not settle him down. To Reuben, it was Mexico all over again and the attack on Akagi Genda-San's home by Arata Goro. He had not slept for at least 24 hours, but was still alert and ready to move out with the plan. He figured he could catch some sleep waiting for the boat.

The first ones to leave were Renee and Henry. May and Aarleen stayed behind to make sure the others were fed and had plenty of food to see them through the day and night. Reuben already made it clear this wasn't going to be a quick trip into Chesapeake City to visit relatives.

Reuben walked Renee to the carriage. "Don't worry, my love. I won't let you down. I'm certain Jacob will help somehow. I know he will," said Renee as reassuringly as she could.

"Please be careful, Renee. Even though Norfolk is Confederate territory, it's still tricky to get around."

Reuben took Renee in his arms, held her tightly, kissed her deeply, and helped her onto the carriage.

"I just realized something, dear husband of mine," said Renee as she sat on the carriage bench. "When we grew up together, we played in the creek, but I can never recall you actually swimming like I learned how. You do know how to swim, don't you?"

Reuben looked to the sky thinking and said, "You know, I can't remember."

"Take care, my love. For your mother, Lucy, and Eric," said Renee as Henry snapped the reins and were off to fulfill their portion of the plan.

After a quick breakfast, Reuben stood before the mantel. He looked upon the Akagi Clan banner for several moments, he bowed his head, and silently recited in Japanese the words Akagi Genda-San said to him when he gave Reuben his Kutto. He lifted the sword with both hands and bowed his whole body to the banner Aarleen made with loving care. He placed his Kutto in the black satin cover, wrapped his Akagi burgundy obi around his waist, tied the knot, and turned to see Aarleen watching him with a fearful expression.

"Come here, my little cherry blossom," said Reuben.

Aarleen quickly made her way across the parlor and into Reuben's open arms. She held onto her father tightly and asked, "What was that you just said, Da?"

Reuben released his hold on Aarleen as she did the same. Standing before her, Reuben removed his Kutto from the satin cover and drew the blade. He presented the tsuka to Aarleen. Never did she think her father would ever allow her to touch it, let alone actually hold it.

She took hold of it gently and as Reuben slowly let go, Aarleen gripped it tighter as she started to feel the full weight of the sword. It was much heavier than her bokken.

"This Kutto has never been used in combat, and when it does, it will be used to protect. The last piece of advice Genda-San gave me was, *'You will not want to fight, but sometimes you have to.'* Aarleen, my precious daughter, you are a strong girl, but now I need you to be even stronger. As strong as your Mama," Reuben said with love in his expression.

The fearsome expression on Aarleen's face faded into an expression of strength. "I will, Da," she replied, strong and sure.

Reuben took his Kutto from her and placed it back in its saya. He bowed to Aarleen and she bowed in return.

"Good, my precious cherry blossom. Your Mama will need to count on you while I'm away, so be vigilant. Now go and see if May needs any assistance."

"Hai!"

Aarleen was handing biscuits, lemons, and apples from a basket to the soldiers in the wagon when Reuben walked up behind her. She turned, saw the concern in her father's face, placed the basket on the ground, and wrapped her arms around Reuben. He lifted her off the ground and walked away from the wagon and the others.

"Mama will be back this afternoon and I'll be back late tomorrow or the day after with GrandMama, Aunty Lucy, and Uncle Eric. I promise, sweetheart."

"I know you will, Da. I love you," Aarleen replied, and hugged Reuben tightly.

Reuben kissed her on the cheek and walked off to the wagon. He handed Noah the covered Kutto and pulled himself up. Once on the bench, he took the Kutto and placed it beneath his legs. Noah suddenly realized what it was he held for a moment and felt honored Reuben allowed him to come along. As they rode away, Aarleen and May waved farewell, as did all the occupants in the wagon in return.

狼

The trip to the jetty was slow going as Reuben predicted. There were many stops along the way, but with Sergeant Warren and the other soldiers in the wagon, they met with little opposition.

By late afternoon, they made it to the beach and found a covering near the jetty where they hid the wagon. A young private was selected to stay behind to care for the wagon and team. They waited there until night fall. Reuben and Noah went out to the jetty to wait for the boat Reuben hoped Renee was able to arrange. They sat there quietly in the darkness and waited.

"You know, Reuben, Renee was right," said Noah, breaking the silence.

"About what?" replied Reuben.

"I never did learn how to swim and unless you learned without me, I don't think you know how to either."

Reuben slowly looked at his friend who kept his eyes to the water. "Keep quiet and watch out for the boat, Noah."

"Just trying to ease the tension," replied Noah with a slight laugh.

After an hour of waiting, a form began to emerge on the surface of the water and the sound of a paddle hitting the water could be heard. The form took on the shape of a large whale boat with six men handling the large oars and a heavyset man doing the steering. The boat came right up to the jetty. The heavyset man came to the front of the boat. "You must be Renee's husband, Reuben. Jacob Curtis is the name. Hop in all of you and let's get this adventure underway."

"I can't thank you enough, Mr. Curtis. You have no idea how much I appreciate this," said Reuben.

"Jacob. Young man, please, call me Jacob. Think nothing of it. I always jump at the chance for an overnight adventure to the Yankee side of the water. By the way, Renee wanted me to ask you, do you know how to swim?"

Noah let out a small chuckle while Reuben shook his head and muttered, "Wickham girl."

"Hello, Reuben," said one of the men manning one of the oars.

Reuben took a hard look. "Andrew? What the hell are you doing here?" asked Reuben, quite perturbed.

"I told you, Reuben, if you were to come up with a way to get them back, I wanted in," said Andrew, sternly.

"This isn't going to be easy, Andrew, and it'll be dangerous."

"My son is over there also, Reuben, not only your mother and sister, and don't forget, Lucy is also my daughter-in-law, so I have a stake in this too."

Reuben took in a deep breath and let it out, mainly to clear his tiredness. "Fair enough, Andrew. Let's go bring them back home."

Reuben sat down next to Noah and took up one of the oars. Sergeant Warren and five other privates also boarded and took up oars and followed Jacob Curtis's instruction. Along with the men Jacob Curtis brought with him, there was plenty of muscle to row the large whale boat across the bay. The trip across the bay would take almost the entire night. It took less than an hour with the ferry, but with fourteen men rowing the large boat and Jacob Curtis steering across strong currents, as well as avoiding blockading ships, would take much longer.

They made landfall a couple of hours before sunrise. Jacob directed them to a small out of the way cove where they could hide the boat, but still enabled Reuben to make a quick hike into Chesapeake City. After a quick breakfast of food May had provided, Reuben hopped out of the boat.

"Are you sure I can't come with you?" asked Noah.

"Yes, he's sure, bucko," said Jacob. "Them Yanks catch you walking around with him, they'll nab you for sure, and you'll be sent to what they call a contraband camp.

"He's right, Noah. I'll need you to help with the rowing and you can't do that in one of those camps," replied Reuben.

"Reuben, will you at least let me come along?" asked Sergeant Warren.

Reuben thought it over and nodded in agreement. Reuben looked to Noah. Noah reached below the bench and picked up the satin covered Kutto and handed it to Reuben. Opening the cover, Reuben pulled out his Kutto, tucked it under his obi, and tied the sageo cord next to the knot. He took a few steps away from the boat and swiftly drew the sword and sliced through the air gracefully and slowly brought the blade to his face and held it there in meditation and quickly returned it to the saya.

As Reuben was about to lead the way, Andrew called out with a pleading look, "Reuben… please."

Thinking hard, knowing it wasn't a good idea, Reuben went ahead and nodded his head and said, "Stay close and quiet, Andrew. I'm only letting you come along because of your son."

Andrew nodded and hopped off the boat.

"Let's get to it then," said Reuben, and was off at a quick paced run.

Sergeant Warren took off his jacket and cap and followed.

狼

Reuben had been to Eric's store only a few times and wasn't familiar with Chesapeake City, so he was suddenly grateful for letting Andrew come along. Andrew was very knowledgeable about getting around Chesapeake City and once they made it from the woods to the outskirts, Reuben allowed Andrew to lead the way.

The sun began to come out and the buildings were taking on daylight form. Smoke from the fires filled the air. It reminded him of Colonias from the Mexican campaign, silent, but busy with flickering flames.

It took the three longer than it would have taken to make their way through the town because Reuben kept them to the dark shaded sides of the buildings. Two more blocks and they should be on the street where the store was.

Now on the street, Reuben had the realization there was no one to be seen. In fact he had not seen anyone in the city. This caused both him and Sergeant Warren alarm. It was a given a curfew was in effect, but still there should be people putting out the fires, or even soldiers on patrol. The three backed up against the wall and started to be more cautious. Instead of running through the streets like they had been doing, they started to creep, using the building walls for cover.

Fortunately the store was on the same side of the street they were already on. Reuben did not care too much for the idea of walking out in the open. He began to fear the worst because of all the vandalism. It was utter chaos. The streets were littered with debris and broken furniture. Reuben was within several steps from the corner where the store stood. In front of the store stood a large shade tree and Reuben saw something peek around it. He jumped back against the wall, pulling the sergeant with him. He stretched his head out and saw the form peek again and move back. Reuben realized it was no one peeking around the tree, but someone swinging from it.

Who would be swinging from a tree at a time like this? Reuben thought and slowly walked toward the tree. The figure again swung and Reuben saw it was a man, his arms hung limp from his sides. Sudden horror came over him when he recognized his brother-in-law, Eric, swinging from a limb of the tree. A Confederate National banner lay on the ground beneath him catching the blood coming from the noose around his neck.

"Gods of the high mountains, no!" he cried out in Japanese. He grabbed Andrew by the arm and ran to the store front.

Reuben took hold of Eric's legs and ordered Sergeant Warren to cut him down. Andrew stood in absolute horror as he watched his son being cut down and gently lowered to the ground.

"Andrew, see to your son. I have to find Mama and Lucy," said Reuben as he rose and made his way into the store.

Andrew knelt down next to Eric's broken body. Andrew carefully lifted his son and cradled him close to his chest silently sobbing while Sergeant Warren kept a look out.

Inside the store, Reuben looked all around in a frantic frenzy. The store was looted and torn apart. Reuben jumped over the counter and through the back door into the storeroom leading to the house. The house was still on fire, but that didn't stop Reuben from running into the front parlor. He coughed up smoke and waved his arms around. He completely forgot about Andrew and Sergeant Warren.

"Mama, Lucy! Where are you?!" Reuben yelled, not caring if anyone outside the house heard.

Reuben ducked under the smoke and made his way to the kitchen. He quickly stepped toward the doorway as his heel got caught in a floorboard causing Reuben to fall forward hitting the floor hard enough to cause him to black out for a moment. He raised himself up on his hands and knees, shaking his head. He sat on the floor for a moment to clear his head and wipe his eyes with his sleeve.

When he lowered his arms, he saw the partly charred form of Coleen, his mother. Reuben crawled toward the figure, closed his eyes tightly, lowered his head, and shook it back and forth determining whether what he saw was real. Reuben opened his eyes and raised his head. It was no mistake or dream. It was Reuben's mother, leaning lifeless, half against the wall and on the floor. He fell back on his backside and scooted to the opposite side of the room with a look of horror on his face. His back hit the wall causing him to jump off the floor and onto his feet drawing his Kutto. He turned and touched the wall and turned back to face his mother. He ran back across the floor, kneeled down beside her, and placed his kutto next to his knees.

Reuben took her charred hand in his. "Damn it, Mama! I don't know what to do! What do I do? Tell me, Mama! Wake up and tell me what to do?" With all the death Reuben had seen in Mexico and Japan, nothing could compare to the sight of his mother laying dead and half burned.

Reuben's eyes watered up so much he could not see and the tears started to leave traces on his smoked covered face. "Damn it, Mama. Why couldn't I get here sooner? I could have done it. I'm so sorry. It's entirely my fault. I failed you, Da."

"She's sleeping," a voice said from under the kitchen counter causing Reuben to startle back and pick up his Kutto bringing it up over his head ready to strike. He slowly lowered and replaced it in its saya.

"Lucy? Is that you?"

There was no answer. Reuben moved closer, crawling on the floor. All balled up in a cupboard was Lucy, her clothes torn, half naked, and trembling. Reuben reached for her and touched her bare shoulder. Lucy winced back and tucked herself tighter into a ball.

"Lucy, it's me, Reuben, your brother. Please come out, little sister."

"Reuben?"

"Yes little sister. I've come to take you home. Please come out."

Lucy slowly raised her head. Reuben could see her eyes. They were bruised. She recognized her brother, but still did not want to leave her place of safety.

"Please come out, Lucy." Reuben started to rummage though his pockets and found the ribbon Lucy placed in his hand the day he left to VMI. "Look here, Lucy. I have your ribbon." Reuben held it out to her. "Remember the ribbon?" he asked, pleading.

She reached for the ribbon and took hold of it. Reuben moved closer, very slowly. He gently touched her hand and she touched him back. "Big brother, please hold me," she said as she emerged out of her hiding place. Reuben helped and cradled Lucy in his arms on the floor. She buried her face into his chest and Reuben held her tightly.

"Who did this to you, baby sister? Who hurt you?"

Lucy started sobbing and breathing hard. Not moving her face from Reuben's chest, she cried out, "Yan, Yank, Yankees!"

Reuben closed his eyes tightly and began to tear up again. He loosened his hold on Lucy so he could remove his jacket and place it over Lucy's naked shoulders. "Come, little sister, I want to take you home. Renee needs you. Will you come with me?"

There was no reply, but only a nod of yes. Reuben picked her up in his arms and carried her out of the kitchen, shielding her from the sight of their mother. The fire in the front of the house died down and he made his way into the storeroom when he noticed Andrew still cradling Eric as Sergeant Warren kept guard. He quickly looked around and laid Lucy on the floor in a dark corner.

"You need to sleep, okay, Lucy? Will you sleep for me?" Reuben asked.

There was no reply, but Reuben knew Lucy wasn't going to move anytime soon, so he left her there and went out the front of the store, and ran to Andrew.

Although extremely distraught, Andrew asked, "Did you find Coleen and Lucy?"

Reuben quickly told Andrew and the sergeant about Lucy and his mother. He said they needed to get off the street and into the store. Reuben helped Andrew carry Eric's body into the store and told Sergeant Warren to help Andrew take his son to the backyard. As they did, Reuben checked on Lucy. She was balled up like a baby shivering. Reuben took a blanket from a shelf, covered her, and picked her up and went to the yard. He placed her just inside the doorway so he could keep an eye on her.

"What are we doing here, Reuben? Shouldn't we be getting back?" asked Sergeant Warren.

With a sorrowful look on his face, he said to Andrew as they faintly heard voices coming from a distance, "We can't take Eric and Mama back with us Andrew. They will slow us down."

Cradling his son, Andrew knew Reuben was right. "We must bury them then," said Andrew.

"We can't," replied Reuben.

"What do you mean, we can't? I won't leave my son's body unattended to," replied Andrew with anger.

"Look, Andrew, Federal regulars didn't do this. More than likely it was Federal militia or local citizens sympathetic to the Union. Either way, they'll return and if they find fresh graves, they *will* desecrate them by digging them up looking for valuables," explained Reuben.

"Reuben is right, Andrew. We can't bury them," added Sergeant Warren.

Andrew lowered his head. "What do you suggest?" Andrew asked.

Reuben turned to check on Lucy who was still lying quietly. He noticed his mother in the far end of the kitchen.

"Max, grab those hay bales and make two beds out of them. I'm going to go find some kerosene," said Reuben.

"Wait!" exclaimed Andrew. Although he knew what Reuben had in mind, he hated the idea, but he knew there was no other way. "I know where Eric keeps it. I'll go get it and you stay and help Max."

Reuben placed a reassuring hand on Andrew's shoulder and nodded.

When Andrew returned with the kerosene, he helped Reuben and the sergeant stack the hay bales. When they were done, Andrew laid Eric across one while Reuben went into the kitchen to retrieve his mother. As he lifted her in his arms, he kissed her lips, and cradled her tightly. Again he apologized for failing her. Reuben took her to the yard and laid her next to Eric.

Reuben ran back into the kitchen, and into the parlor where he picked up two blankets. Returning to the yard, he gave one blanket to Andrew and he began to tightly wrap his mother in the other blanket.

Looking at his son, Andrew was about to do the same as Reuben and stopped.

467

"Please wait for a few minutes," he said, and quickly ran into the house.

Moments later, Andrew returned and began wrapping Eric with the Confederate National banner that was beneath his hanging body.

All three began to douse the bodies with kerosene. Reuben made two torches and handed one to Andrew. They looked at each other, nodded, and placed the torches on the bottom of the hay bales. The fires caught quickly and Reuben kneeled on the ground watching the bodies burn. Sergeant Warren stood at attention next to Reuben and raised his hand in a salute. Keeping alert, they remained for the rest of the day as the fires burned. When all that was left was only ashes, Reuben went to retrieve Lucy.

She was still laying in a fetal position, staring at the wall. Reuben picked her up and made their way out of the store and to the hidden boat in the cove with the sergeant following behind keeping a look out. Lucy didn't sleep, but only stared at Reuben's face as he carried her through the town and into the woods. It was getting late, but there was still several hours of daylight left and it was better to cross the bay in the dark to avoid the blockading ships. In the woods Reuben stopped and sat on a fallen tree to hold his sister in his arms while she rested. All along the way, both Andrew and Sergeant Warren offered to carry Lucy, but Reuben refused.

He was only a couple hundred yards away from the others, but sat there spending this time with his little sister, not talking, just sitting and rocking. He sent Andrew and Sergeant Warren on ahead. Reuben and Lucy sat here for a couple of hours in utter silence. Reuben felt Lucy would recover physically, but emotionally she would never be the same. She did not once ask for Eric or her mother, but held onto the ribbon, not letting it go.

With a heavy sigh, Reuben stood up with Lucy in his arms and continued on to the boat. Noah heard the footsteps first and made the sign for the others to take cover. He recognized Reuben carrying Lucy and he ran up to them. "Do you want me to take her from here?" he asked.

Reuben looked at Noah and shook his head no and walked on. Noah never saw such sadness in Reuben's face before. He did not have to ask about Eric and Coleen. Sergeant Warren already told the others of their fate. In complete silence, Reuben boarded the boat and sat at the front on the bottom. Jacob came and offered Reuben a cup of water which he took and swallowed down. He handed the cup back and Jacob refilled it, handed it back, and Reuben tried to give Lucy a drink. She slightly sipped from the cup, but did not drink it all and what she did sip, leaked out of the sides of her lips. Andrew draped a couple of blankets around the brother and sister.

"Well lads, get ready to cast off. It's almost dark enough," said Jacob.

Noah and the others took their places. It was going to be harder on the way back because Reuben would not be helping with the paddling, but attending to Lucy. Andrew was also too worn out from the trip to the store, but mostly from grief. Still they made good time back to the jetty where Reuben, Lucy, Andrew, Noah and the soldiers disembarked. It wasn't light out yet, but they made their way from the jetty to where the young private was still hidden with the wagon.

狼

Renee and Aarleen sat arm-in-arm on the front porch waiting for Reuben and the others to return. Riley sat atop the steps of the porch. It was about noon when he rose on all four legs getting the attention of Renee and Aarleen. Riley glanced at them, back to the lane, and silently ran off in that direction. Renee and Aarleen rose and came to the porch rail.

When they heard the wagon coming down the lane, Renee called out, "They're back!"

Both Renee and Aarleen ran off the porch and out to the lane to meet them as the others filed out quickly. Annabelle held Andy back at the foot of the porch steps and waited for Andrew and Eric to climb off the wagon, but she only saw Andrew.

Noah stopped the wagon in front of the house and Renee ran to Reuben who jumped off the wagon and stumbled under the weight of exhaustion. He regained his balance and turned to meet Renee's face. She never saw such sadness and tiredness in Reuben's face before. It looked like he had aged a couple of years in two days. She realized he had not slept in over three days. He stared at her, gave her a quick hug, turned, and walked to the back of the wagon and retrieved Lucy. Renee, as well as the others, were stunned by the appearance of Lucy cradled in Reuben's arms. He walked past them toward the house.

"What about Mama and Eric?" asked Renee to Noah.

Noah shook his head no.

Sergeant Warren quickly told Renee what they had been through when they arrived at the store, and how they disposed of the bodies.

Renee's only response was a look of deep sadness as she looked up to see the anguish in Andrew's face.

Annabelle screamed sorrowfully as Andy held her tightly. Andrew climbed down from the wagon and went to his wife. As he reached Annabelle, she collapsed into his arms and all three fell to their knees. Aarleen quickly went to them and also dropped to her knees.

Andy rose as Reuben came near holding his mother. Reuben stopped to allow Andy to see his mother, hoping Lucy would break from her emotional state.

"Mom..." said Andy as he took one of her hands.

"Andy... you look so much like your dad," answered Lucy, weakly.

"Come, Reuben, let's get her inside," said Renee, helping him up the steps of the porch.

Aarleen took Andy by his shoulders to console him and led him into the house.

Inside the house, Reuben took Lucy into the room she used as a child, now occupied by Aarleen. He laid her upon her old bed, covered her with a quilt, and sat on the edge holding her hand. Renee stood by Reuben's side and placed her arms around his shoulders while Aarleen led Andy to the other side of the bed where he knelt down beside it, and took one of Lucy's hands.

Lucy's eyes were fixed on Reuben. "Reuben, here, take my ribbon for luck," she said. They were the same exact words Lucy said to Reuben as she reached to give him the ribbon when he was leaving for VMI.

Reuben took the ribbon and kept a tight grasp on her hand.

Lucy asked for Renee. Reuben made room for Renee to sit next to Lucy.

469

"I'm here, Lucy. I'm here."

"Please, Renee, do you remember the secret Reuben told me to tell you if you were ever in doubt?"

Renee nodded. "He told you to remind me, that no matter what happens to me, he will always love me and will forever be mine,"

Lucy weakly nodded and said, "Never forget that secret, Renee. My brother loves you more than anything in the world."

"Reuben," said Lucy, softly.

Renee shifted her position on the edge of the bed so Reuben could move closer.

"I'm still here, Lucy."

"Reuben… Mama and Da don't blame you. They both told me to tell you they know you did your best to bring us back home. They are so very proud of you, and so am I."

"Lucy? What are you saying?" asked Reuben as tears rolled down his cheeks. "Stay with me, Lucy. Don't leave me, my precious baby sister. I need you."

"Reuben, I have to tell you something. Mama told me I was never supposed to choose, but you were my favorite brother."

Lucy took in a deep breath and held it for a few moments. Slowly, her last breath left her lifeless body.

"Lucy? No… Lucy, come back," said Reuben as he lifted her lifeless body and held her tightly.

Renee leaned over and held them both while Aarleen took her cousin in her arms as he began sobbing.

Reuben lowered his sister back down and gently closed her eyes and gave her a kiss.

Reuben rose from the edge of the bed and slowly made his way out of Lucy's room as those gathered cleared a path for him to pass.

"Reuben?" Renee began to ask.

"Please see to her," he said, and walked out of the room.

Renee looked to May who nodded to her, "Go see to you husband, Renee, quickly."

Renee rose and went out of the room, followed by Aarleen.

Reuben went downstairs, crossed the parlor, and went out the front door.

As Renee walked onto the porch, she saw Reuben reach into the wagon and retrieved his Kutto. He removed it from the cover and threw the cover to the ground. Reuben wrapped Lucy's purple ribbon around the tsuka next to the tsuba and tied it tightly.

Tucking his Kutto into his Akagi burgundy obi, he made his way to the side of the house where the soldiers were gathered, listening to Sergeant Warren tell them about the trip into Chesapeake City. They quickly cleared a path for Reuben to pass. Renee and Aarleen followed hand-in-hand at a distance not knowing if they should approach Reuben.

Renee watched her husband as he slowly made his way to the oak tree. His slow walk turned into a quickened pace, and then into a run. Reuben's run turned into a sprint and as he reached the shade of the tree, he made a huge leap rotating his entire body in the air as he drew his Kutto.

Reuben landed on his feet and with a loud, blood curdling, ungodly kiai, swung and thrust his Kutto in the most menacing kata Renee had ever seen him do.

The others, including Lieutenant Stevens, watched from inside the house while Sergeant Warren and the other soldiers watched from the planting field.

Turning in beautiful, deadly circles, and rolling in midair landing on his feet, Reuben danced with his sword. He had the worst look of anger on his face causing Renee and Aarleen to cry as they held each other.

With a very loud kiai causing birds to fly from their perch on the oak tree, Reuben made an elegant circular motion turning the blade exposing its razor sharp edge. In a swift angled cut, he struck and sliced the practice horse in half. He faced the practice post. In another elegant motion, he leaped into the air and as he landed, he waved the sword at the post three times and lowered himself to his knees. The practice post slowly fell apart in three pieces to the ground.

Reuben slowly sheathed his Kutto and fell to the ground. Renee let go of Aarleen, ran to her husband, and held him tightly. He returned her embrace and cried very loudly into Renee's chest. She never knew he could cry so hard.

"Why, Renee, why? I can't let this happen to you and Aarleen. I just can't, and I won't!"

Sudden fear came across Renee's body. The premonition she felt at the edge of the train platform when Reuben went away to VMI came to haunt her. She knew what was going through Reuben's mind. Although Monroe had tried to kill him because of his secret desire for her, Renee knew Reuben would eventually leave to bring Monroe, the last of his family, back home from this war he should not have been involved with.

But for now, she held him as he cried and wept, while Aarleen knelt next to them also weeping. Renee pulled Aarleen into her embrace, and both mother and daughter held Reuben as he fell asleep in their arms out of utter physical and emotional exhaustion.

Renee knew Reuben would again, for the protection of her and their daughter, take on the role of a warrior. And there was nothing she could do about it except maintain her faith and love, and let him go.

石
永

In the year of our Lord, 1862, a romantic tale continues.
Dragged away on one side of the river, helpless on the other...

<u>Go Home and Live a Long Happy Life. That's an Order</u>

Lucy was laid to rest next to Aaron in the plot that would have been occupied by Coleen. Her headstone read...

Lucy Duran-Klaus
Devoted Wife of Eric Klaus,
Mother of Andrew Klaus,
Beloved Daughter & Sister
November 10, 1830
May 2, 1861

The funeral service for Coleen, Lucy, and Eric was expected to be small with only family members and close family friends in attendance. However, there was a large amount of mourners who came to pay their respects. Besides the many in the farming community of Norfolk County, others included were Jacob Curtis and his boat crew who aided in the rescue attempt, First Lieutenant Todd Stevens and Sergeant Max Warren, Doctor Richard Weldon, and the Norenhams along with their son Benjamin.

Renee was the first to pay tribute to Coleen. Although Renee and her real mother reconciled many years prior, Renee praised Coleen as being her true mother in spirit and love.

Andrew paid tribute to his son Eric. Andrew and Annabelle didn't approve of his strong Confederate support and activities, but he still praised his determination for his convictions, the same determination that made the Chesapeake City Klaus Mercantile a successful business.

But it was Reuben who caused the most emotional outcry when he paid tribute to his sister, Lucy. He spoke of her fondness of music and how she never went anywhere without her tin whistle their GrandDa Miles McDurand gave her. May found the whistle in Lucy's skirt pocket shortly after seeing to her body and gave it to Reuben. Reuben placed it next to his Kutto on the mantel beneath the banner of the Akagi Clan. Reuben praised her for her creativity in almost every aspect of life from the music she played to the games she invented. Most of all, Reuben gave full loving credit to Lucy for being the instrumental point of bringing him and Renee together.

"It was my sister who introduced Renee to me under our oak tree. It was my sister who kept Renee's spirits up if she ever had doubts of my love for her. And it was my sister who never gave up hope that one day Renee and I would become husband and wife, long before I made my journey halfway across the world.

"My dearest Lucy, Mama told me the same thing many years ago just after you were born. I was never supposed to choose, but you were also my favorite."

狼

For Aarleen's thirteenth birthday, there was no huge party like in the past. It was her decision to have a small gathering with only the family and close friends. She invited the Norenhams, but Simon had been ordered to Richmond to be assigned to an engineering battalion, and as much as Benjamin wanted to attend, Cynthia wouldn't take him.

Renee and Reuben didn't break out into their Budo routine as with previous parties, but Aarleen still held her traditional story time. When it was time to tell her story, she opened a leather bound journal book and began to read the story she spent many hours under the oak tree writing days before her birthday.

"Once upon a time, there was a man who came across the Atlantic Ocean from Scotland to start a new life for his wife and son, Aaron."

It was a long story that drew everyone listening. It was Aarleen's best story ever told and at its end, nearly everyone in the circle had tears in their eyes, including Evergreen, who didn't know the Duran story in its entirety.

Since Virginia seceded from the Union, the Masons let Evergreen go because of her pro-Union sentiments. It wasn't that the Masons were pro-Confederate themselves, but Evergreen's outspoken sentiments caused them scrutiny. Being that Noah and Evergreen's relationship was developing, she was welcomed to stay on the Duran farm.

The only person who didn't have tears in their eyes after Aarleen's story was Reuben. She included the incident between Reuben and Monroe in her story and that caused Reuben to wonder where his brother could be. Although the two had a major falling out, they were still blood, of which Reuben felt strongly. A few weeks after the incident, Reuben tried to gain information about the 66th Virginia Infantry Regiment's location, but found it difficult, especially since he was adamant in remaining neutral. With his prior military background and neutrality, Reuben was being scrutinized by radical Confederate officials as pro-Union, and any attempts by him trying to gain information about his brother seemed to the officials as an act of espionage.

Although it wasn't a big birthday celebration, it was still pleasant. It was more of a day to reflect on the memories of the family in happier times. Both Renee and Reuben reflected on how difficult it was for them to be best friends knowing each other wanted to be more, but couldn't because of Renee's arranged marriage at the time. Reuben told stories of his ocean travels on the *Morning Star* and the *Coleen*. He told of Tadashi's archery lessons on the *Coleen*, and how he shot a small flying fish to prove his talents to the crew.

Evergreen found Reuben's stories about Japan difficult to believe because of her prior servitude as a slave. She felt there couldn't be any other places in this world as cruel as America, with its handling of people just because they had different color skin.

"At least you could show your face as a slave, Ever," said Reuben in reply to one of her remarks of disbelief. "For the longest time, I had to wear a kasa, that straw conical hat hanging over the mantel, to cover my face. Hell, even when I saved Genda-San from a gunman, his son, Masaru, who I also saved, wanted to kill me because I was an off-lander."

As the day was ending, Andrew and Annabelle asked to have a private discussion with Renee and Reuben. Reuben suggested they walk to the oak tree. As the four made their way toward the tree, Aarleen stayed with Andy.

During the entire gathering, Aarleen's cousin sat by himself, withdrawn from everyone else. Reuben immediately recognized his symptoms of depression and as often as he could, Reuben would sit with Andy and allow him to cry into his shoulder as Reuben would place his arm around Andy for comfort. Renee also comforted Andy as often as she could to reassure him his uncle understood his feelings of loss. When Renee would look at Andy sitting by himself, it reminded her how Reuben looked when he returned from Mexico.

When they reached the oak tree, Renee wrapped her arms around Reuben's waist and he placed his arm around her shoulders.

Both Andrew and Annabelle admired Renee's and Reuben's affection toward one another. They believed it was a pure loving affection, and they were making up for the many years of being denied their true feelings because of Renee's father.

They all stood in silence under the oak tree. It was Reuben who broke the silent tension by saying, "I have a feeling you two have made a decision on Andy's account."

Annabelle replied, "He's getting worse. Today was the first day he had any contact with people, other than us, since the funeral. Everything around here reminds him of his parents. It reminds us also. Oh, Reuben, I don't know how you do it. Sometimes I find myself thinking you're a cold person, but Andrew reminds me of all the horrors you have been exposed to. I guess because of that, you can easily cope with our losses better."

Reuben went to Annabelle and took her into his arms. "Annabelle, I wish I could tell you I have a heart of stone, but I don't. Trust me, I grieve just as much as you, Andrew, and Andy do. Renee can tell you of the restless nights I have because of my grief over our losses."

Renee looked at her husband with admiration as he consoled Annabelle. Many times Renee wondered how Reuben could possibly think of trying to find his brother after Monroe tried to kill him. When her thoughts would wonder in that direction, she quickly went to the mantle where his Kutto laid under the Akagi banner. Right next to the tsuka, Renee placed the stone Akagi Genda-San gave her. Renee would pick up the stone and feel the smoothness against her cheek and think, how could something so hard feel so smooth against my skin. Her thoughts would immediately return to Reuben. After all those years of jaggedness to return smooth, yet remain hard, he was truly a man with true convictions of love, devotion, and self-victory.

"It's because of Andy, Annabelle and I have made a serious decision," said Andrew bringing Renee back from her thoughts.

Returning to Renee's side, Reuben asked, "And what's that decision?"

"We're selling the store and nearly all our belongings, and leaving Virginia," said Andrew very emotionally.

"Geez oh geez oh geez you can't be serious," said Renee bringing her hands to her mouth.

"In time, we may return. Perhaps when this whole Confederate, Union thing is over, but for now, we need to get Andy away from here," Andrew said after he regained his composure.

"Where will you go?" asked Reuben.

"I have relatives in California," said Annabelle.

Renee took hold of Annabelle's hands, grasping them tightly. "Way out there? We will never see you. Are you sure there's no other way we can help Andy?" she asked in a pleading manner.

Reuben placed his hands gently on Renee's shoulders and softly said, "Remember, I had to leave the place of my pain to recover."

"Oh, Reuben," cried Renee as she turned into his arms and held him tightly.

"I don't like it any more than you do, my love, but I believe Andrew and Annabelle have the solution to Andy's welfare," said Reuben, holding Renee.

Keeping a hold on Renee, Reuben asked Andrew, "When do you expect to leave?"

"As soon as possible. We already have a buyer for the store, and listening to you, the sooner we sell the store before the rebellion puts a strain on the economy of the state, the better," answered Andrew.

"Do you need any money?" asked Reuben. "We have plenty to spare."

"That is much appreciated, but we have more than enough assets to get us to California and start a new business," replied Andrew.

"I wish there was a better solution," said Renee, "but Reuben's reassurance is helpful in making me believe your decision is the best for Andy. Can we at least help in any way, such as keeping Andy here on the farm so he will be out of the way as you pack?"

"Actually, he has been very active with that, Renee," said Annabelle. "It takes his mind off his grief. Perhaps when we have a definite date set to leave, you all can come to help us with last minute details."

"We'll be there. Just let us know," said Renee.

Thirty minutes later, after further discussion, all four made their way back to the house. There were several more minutes of farewells, and as Andrew, Annabelle, and Andy rode away, Reuben stayed watching while the others made their way back to the house.

After several steps, Renee realized Reuben wasn't at her side. She stopped and looked back to see him standing in what looked like deep thought. She walked back to him and took him in her arms and asked, "Is everything okay, Reuben?"

"Not really. I think it's our turn to have a discussion of our own."

"About what?" asked Renee, nervously.

"About what to expect in the upcoming days, weeks, months, and maybe years. Let's gather everyone and meet at the dining room table."

Renee nodded and, arm-in-arm, they both walked back to the house.

狼

When Renee and Reuben entered the house, they quickly gathered everyone in the dining room. They all sat around the table as Reuben entered the room. He could never get used to the feeling of being the focal point of the family, an issue Monroe, his older brother, resented. Reuben could never bring himself to sit in Aaron's chair at the head of the table as easily as Monroe could. He either stood or sat between Renee and Aarleen. This time, he reluctantly sat in his father's old chair. He felt uncomfortable and it showed.

"We need to have a serious discussion about our future," Reuben said. He told everyone at the table of the discussion he and Renee had with Andrew and Annabelle. Reuben said the notion to leave Virginia, like Andrew and Annabelle, never entered his mind and he had no intention of leaving the farm his grandfather left to the family. He made it clear both he and Renee support Andrew and Annabelle's decision to leave for Andy's sake.

"But if we're going to stay, it's not going to be easy. We have already seen the changes occurring and the momentum still has not taken to full effect of this rebellion," said Reuben.

"The Yankees will beat down the Confederates in no time, and all this worrying will all be for nothing," said Evergreen with confidence.

Her comment was met with a hard, cold stare from Reuben.

"Quiet, Ever," said Noah, taking note of Reuben's reaction to her comment. "You always go shooting your mouth off before you know all the facts."

"Da, do you believe the rebellion will last longer than everyone thinks?" asked Aarleen, very concerned.

"Even longer. Southern people are proud, spirited, and, along with that, stubborn. The Confederacy doesn't have a chance and do you know why, my little blossom?"

"Because the North has industry and population."

"Exactly, and even though the Confederacy may be acting on gaining its independence, those who succumb to stubbornness would rather fight a losing battle than to admit defeat. I have seen this before. So with that said, I've been taking precautions for our survival."

"Like the plots we've cleared out deep in the woods?" asked Henry.

"Exactly, and starting tomorrow, we plant for ourselves and ourselves only in those plots."

Renee added, "And now with Andrew and Annabelle closing the mercantile, we will be losing our most profitable income so that means we need to save and use everything we have."

"Right," said Reuben. "Along with what Renee said, when South Carolina left the Union, I took five of our oban coins to have Mr. Bishop convert them into cash. Since Virginia was still part of the Union, I got the Federal gold standard. I got those coins converted into $1,000 in cash, all in gold and silver. I know that sounds like a lot of money, but we need to use that as sparingly as we can. In the future, paper money will be next to worthless if the economy gets hit the way I believe it will."

"What about the other coins, Da?" Aarleen asked.

Reuben took in a deep breath and let it out as he looked at Renee and said, "I've hidden them."

"Where?" asked May.

"Only I know where, Aunty May, and unless we need them, I won't say," replied Reuben.

"Oh I see," blurted out Evergreen. "I bet they know," she said, pointing to Renee and Aarleen. "No trust in the colored folk."

"EVER!!!" exclaimed Noah.

"Whoa, Noah, hold on," said Reuben.

Reuben looked at Evergreen with a curious expression, while she had one of disgust. Reuben rose from his father's seat and very slowly made his way around the table to where Evergreen sat.

"Perhaps Evergreen already knows where I hid the gold coins," Reuben said, calmly.

"And just how am I supposed to know where you hid them? I didn't know they existed until you mentioned them just now."

Still using a calm tone, Reuben replied, "I think you know more than you tend to lead on."

Suddenly his tone turned cold and icy, causing the others around the table to feel fear.

"Yes! I think you know exactly where I hid them and have stolen them for yourself!"

"Don't be foolish. I have no idea where you hid that gold, you got to believe me," answered Evergreen, her tone sounding fearful, pleading, and on the verge of tears.

"Reuben, please..." said Renee as she began to rise from her chair.

"DAMN IT!!! I KNOW YOU'RE LYING!!! NOW TELL ME WHERE YOU HAVE HIDDEN OUR GOLD!!!" roared Reuben drawing his tanto as if from nowhere, and stuck it in the table in front of a horrified Evergreen.

Evergreen completely broke down and began wailing as she dropped to her knees pleading, "Please, I swear to God, I never saw you hide the gold or take it! Please, you got to believe me!"

As Evergreen begged on her knees in front of Reuben, the others watched in fear. Aarleen reached out to Renee who took her into her arms and held her tightly.

"Reuben, please stop... you're scaring us," pleaded Renee.

Reuben gently took one of Evergreen's hands from her face and helped her to her feet. His fierce expression changed to an apologetic look and explained not only to Evergreen, but to everyone around the table. "The cruelest of interrogators will know when one is lying. If they know you're lying, they'll stop at nothing, short of death, to get the truth out of you. Not knowing where I hid the gold coins isn't a matter of trust. It's a matter of your safety. The less you know, the safer it is for you. Do you understand, Evergreen?"

Sobbing, Evergreen nodded yes as Reuben took her into his arms to comfort her. "This isn't a game we're playing. This is life in its worst form, war. War brings out the worst of humanity, and all of us around this table needs to learn the two rules of war, and the number one rule is... there are no rules. Rule number two... remember rule number one, especially for this western style of war."

狼

The discussion continued late into the night. They discussed everything from conserving food and clothing to assigning tasks to certain individuals, including Riley. The discussion was long and drawn out, but necessary. The last thing covered was, and it was Renee who brought up the scenario, what would happen if Reuben had to leave for any reason. Reuben assured everyone he wouldn't leave unless it involved finding his brother. He was hoping Monroe's regiment would be assigned to the newly formed Doyle's Brigade, which included the 68th Virginia Infantry Regiment, the same regiment of soldiers who assisted Reuben in his rescue attempt of Coleen, Lucy, and Eric. If that were the case, Monroe's regiment would be part of the home guard brigade kept in the Norfolk and Princess Anne regions to protect its citizens and resources. For the time being, the city and county of Norfolk was out of reach of the Union.

It was minutes after midnight when they finished the discussion and all went off to bed. Renee and Reuben saw Aarleen to bed as they always did every night.

"I'm so very sorry to ruin your special day, my little cherry blossom. I didn't mean for it all to happen this way," pleaded Reuben.

Aarleen reached for her father and took him in her arms. "Oh, Da, the amount of concern you showed all of us this evening is one of the best gifts you have given me. It is a reassurance I have the best Da in the world. It's right up there with my inrou and my little cherry blossom tree. Knowing how very concerned you are for our survival is deep rooted love, and love is all I ask for in a gift."

Renee took both Aarleen and Reuben in her arms saying, "Well said, my little sweetie, very well said."

When they left Aarleen's room, Renee readied herself for bed as Reuben leaned against the wall with one hand, looking out the window toward their oak tree.

"Reuben, please come to bed. It's been a long day and I want your arms to cradle me to sleep," said Renee, softly.

Reuben remained standing staring at the tree.

Renee rolled out of bed, slid under his arm, and sat on the window ledge in front of him. "I think we have everything covered, my love. Aarleen is right you know, your concern is very comforting."

Reuben smiled as he nodded with his look still focused on the oak tree.

"I also believe it was a very good idea to hide the rest of the coins and very wise of you not to tell us where. You're right about knowing when someone is lying. There have been many times I caught Aarleen telling little fibs just by staring her down," said Renee with a little laugh.

Reuben looked down to Renee and also let out a little laugh as he said, "Me, too."

With their eyes locked on each other, Reuben turned serious as he said, "Renee, my precious, I'm sorry I can't tell you where I hid the coins. As I said, it's for your own safety." He chuckled as he continued, "I had a heck of a time trying to figure out where to hide them. Then it finally dawned on me. If Renee had to hide something from me, where would she hide it…" said Reuben, as he focused his eyes from Renee to the oak tree.

Renee turned her head to the oak tree. She smiled. That's exactly where I would have hidden them, Renee thought.

Taking his wife by the hands, Reuben said, "Come, my precious Renee, let's go to bed so I can cradle you in my arms."

狼

Harpers Weekly
August 3, 1861
THE ADVANCE OF THE GRAND ARMY

"The grand advance movement of the Union army into Virginia took place last week. General McDowell, with his staff, left Arlington on the 16th, with nearly his whole force of some 60,000 men, at half past three o'clock. The brigade of General Louis Blenker, comprising the Eighth and Twenty-ninth Regiments New York Volunteers, the Garibaldi Guard, and the Twenty-fourth Regiment Pennsylvania Volunteers, formed the advance column of the grand army.

The rebels evacuated Fairfax Court House and Centerville as our troops advanced, falling back on Bull's Run and Manassas Gap. A reconnaissance by General Tyler of the batteries of the former place, on the 19th, developed the enemy in great strength and on Sunday Morning, 21st, General McDowell attacked them there. These batteries were taken by our troops, and the whole day was spent in hard fighting. At 2 P.M. it seemed that we had carried all the points attacked. But just then General Johnson brought up his army in support of Beauregard, a panic suddenly broke out in our army, and it retreated on Centerville, Fairfax, and lastly on Washington, with considerable loss. Jeff Davis is said to have commanded the enemy in person."

Reuben's predictions about the war came true within a matter of days, four days after Aarleen's birthday and on Renee and Reuben's sixth wedding anniversary.

July 21, 1861, two huge armies met head-to-head on the fields of Manassas, Virginia for the first major battle of what was to be referred to as "The War of The Rebellion."

Evergreen's hopes where shot down hard when the news of the battle was an overwhelming Confederate victory. For the rest of the inhabitants of the Duran farm, the news was met with disregard. For Renee and Reuben, it meant times were going to get worse before they got better, so in the meantime, they and the rest of the family planted in their hidden plots and began to store and stock.

With Noah's help, Aarleen built a small hidden chicken coop to move chickens from the farm if it were needed. They set up small pens and shelters for farm animals to be hidden as well. Aarleen began to train Riley on guarding the hidden plots, coop, pens, and to give early warning of unexpected visitors.

May and Renee did as much food preserving as possible while Henry and Noah dug out hidden root cellars. And of course, Reuben was a part of every preparation project, from helping May and Renee in preserving, to digging out hidden wells for fresh water.

As busy as Reuben was, he always put some time aside to spend with Renee and Aarleen, either in family time or Budo training. Reuben relied on Renee and Aarleen to pass down their training to Noah and even May and Henry.

The only one who didn't seem to be well involved was Evergreen. She spent most of her time in wonder if the Union could defeat the Confederacy. It was May who would threaten to exile her from the farm if she didn't do her part.

"Renee and Reuben, out of the goodness of their hearts, allowed you to come and live with us and this is how you repay their generosity? You praise how grateful you were when you received your freedom, but you haven't shown one ounce of appreciation for it. Henry once said, freedom earned is freedom worth fighting for, and that's exactly what we're doing. Now you had better start getting off your lazy ass and show Noah how strong of a woman you are or he will be the one tossing you out, not me."

There were times when Renee and Evergreen went head-to-head when Renee would ask her to assist or do some task. Evergreen saw it as being forced to work by a white woman rather than helping out with the daily routine of the farm. Their "discussions" always ended up with Evergreen being thrown by one of many throws from Renee when Evergreen attempted to strike at Renee.

"How many times have I told you, never raise a finger to Renee or Aarleen?" Noah would ask Evergreen when she would find herself on the ground after one of her "discussions" with Renee about contributing to the effort of the farm. "You know Renee and Reuben throw each other on a daily basis, both in seriousness and play."

With all of Evergreen's faults, Noah still cared for her and began to build a separate cabin for her and Noah to share. That project is what prompted Evergreen to begin to contribute to the farm's survival during this unstable time. Renee and Reuben believed it was the thought of having something to call her own, such as the cabin, is what caused Evergreen's change in attitude.

"Now she has something to defend, and that will always give someone a sense of worth," said Reuben when Noah asked if he and Evergreen could build the cabin.

When time allowed, everyone would lend a hand to help build the cabin. It turned out to be a welcome project. It provided the diversion everyone needed to forget about the rebellion, and focus on the importance of the farm, family.

On Monday, September 2, the cabin project lost two of it contributors. It was the first day of school of the new session. Although both Reuben and Aarleen were excited for school to begin, there was also a feeling of dread. Last session there were only nine students enrolled because of the secession ordinance and now, only three students enrolled for this new session. It was believed enrollment was low because of Reuben's choice of neutrality toward the rebellion.

Not because many of the farming residents were either pro or anti-Confederate, but because of radical Confederate officials scrutinizing those who associated with others of questionable loyalty.

Throughout the summer months leading up to the start of the school session, Reuben was unsure the school superintendent and board would allow him to continue teaching. Although he'd proven himself to be an excellent educator, his loyalties were a concern. And like with the residents, it was the radicals who prompted the superintendent and board in their decision of whether or not to keep Reuben as a member of the school faculty. In the end, it was Reuben's performance of the past and his statement in response regarding the radical Confederate official's allegations that allowed him to remain in his teaching position.

"I'm not here to choose sides. I'm here to teach, and a teacher's job is to teach and nurture, in an unbiased manner, the young minds that may one day lead our nation, whether it is Confederate or Union. As long as there's one inquisitive young mind who wants to learn, I will teach."

For Renee, it was heartbreaking to see her husband and daughter walk off to school without her taking them as before. Once the ordinance was passed, Reuben didn't want Renee traveling by herself on the roads. Now with Andrew, Annabelle, and Andy gone, there was no reason for Renee to be on the road, and that included taking Reuben and Aarleen to school.

Renee, with Riley, walked Reuben and Aarleen up to the end of the lane and bid them farewell until the end of the school day. She and Riley stood at the end of the lane watching them walk to school until they walked around the bend in the road where Reuben and Aarleen would turn and wave one last time before walking out of sight.

"Okay class, let's have roll and begin our lessons for the day. Tommy Deans."

"Here."

"Aarleen Duran."

"Present."

"Janet Lindsey."

"Present."

"Hmm, okay, I'm glad to see everyone is present today. Well, at least all three of you are eighth year students, so let's get to learning."

As Reuben began to write a lesson on the blackboard, the three students began taking out their books and writing materials.

"What's wrong, teacher?" asked Aarleen as she saw her father standing in front of the board not doing anything.

The other two students also took notice.

Reuben turned and walked to the front of his desk where he leaned comfortably against it.

"Let's cut the formalities for a moment. It's just us four, so you tell me, what do *you* want to learn about today?"

"Not about the war, that's for sure," said Janet Lindsey, while the other two nodded in agreement.

"And why not?" asked Reuben.

"That's all we hear about and it's old and boring," surprisingly replied Tommy Deans.

"I see. But you do realize we're living in what could possibly be one of the most important historical periods of our nation's history."

"Yes, but can we learn about that tomorrow? We want to learn about something else today," said Aarleen in a pleading manner.

Reuben nodded and rubbed his chin in thought. "Okay, I'm up for that. So what's it going to be? Something in science perhaps or maybe literature? I'm not really up for mathematics."

"History," said Tommy Deans, his favorite subject.

The other two students nodded enthusiastically. Of all the subjects Reuben taught, they enjoyed his history lessons the best.

"Okay, history then. What topic shall we discuss?"

Tommy Deans timidly raised his hand causing Reuben to have an odd look. "Mr. Deans, you have a topic to discuss?"

"Well, yes. We all know you've been to Japan, but you never tell us any of its history. I heard of a place there I would like to learn more about."

"Really, what place is that?" asked Reuben very surprised.

The other two students looked very interested, especially Aarleen who was wondering if Tommy Deans might be teasing her father.

Tommy Deans cleared his throat and asked, "What do you know of... let me see if I can pronounce this right... Sek, Seki, Sekiga..."

"SEKIGAHARA!" said Reuben, excitedly.

"Yes, that's the place, Sekigahara."

"How do you know of Sekigahara?" asked Reuben, impressed.

Aarleen was also impressed, while Janet Lindsey looked confused.

"My uncle was in the navy and he sailed to Japan. He's now in the Confederate Navy. He told me about a big battle he heard about in a place called Sekigahara that happened a long time ago. I thought of all people who might know about it, you would."

"I've been there!"

"You have, Da?" asked Aarleen excitedly, completely forgetting they were in school.

"Yes, Genda-San took me along with him on an official visit to Kyoto, and Sekigahara was on the way. You know, what happened in Sekigahara is practically what is happening here now in our country?"

"Really, how so, Mr. Duran?" asked Janet Lindsey.

"Revolution, that's how, Miss Lindsey. You see, up until Sekigahara, Japan was ruled by many regional lords who wanted total control of Japan, so Japan lived in a constant state of civil war for many, many years, such as what we're living in now."

The three young students were wide-eyed in fascination and Reuben had only just begun. He walked behind his desk, grabbed his chair and brought it so he could sit with the three students. Turning the chair around, he sat on it backward, leaned forward against the back, and began to tell them about the largest samurai battle ever fought.

"Toyotomi Hideyoshi took over power from Oda Nobunaga who united one third of Japan until he was assassinated. Soon after, Toyotomi Hideyoshi also died, but he didn't leave a strong enough heir to continue the unification of Japan. That's when another dominating lord named, Tokugawa Ieyasu, made his move to take over.

"In the early morning of October 21, 1600, 262 years ago, 176 years before our country declared its independence from England, on the fields of Sekigahara, Tokugawa Ieyasu's army of 74,000 samurai met with 80,000 Hideyoshi loyalists."

"262 years ago? That's about the same time of Miyamoto Musashi. Was he there, Da?" asked Aarleen.

Reuben nodded as he continued, "As a matter of fact, my little blossom, he was. But he was on the losing side. You see, the battle changed hands three times that day. In the early morning fog, Tokugawa Ieyasu was beating back the loyalists until the loyalists began pushing back. Then something strange happened that would be impossible with the revolution we're going through now."

"What's that, Mr. Duran?" asked Tommy Deans.

"Tokugawa Ieyasu, in the afternoon, made a political move to a faction of the loyalists, and got them to change sides, and then Tokugawa Ieyasu swept the remaining Hideyoshi loyalists from the field, and claimed victory."

Reuben turned his attention to Aarleen and continued, "As for Musashi, he had to flee so as not to be captured because back then, captured enemies were beheaded either on the spot or later when the battle was over."

"Wow, that is brutal," replied Tommy Deans as he was taking notes.

"What happened after, Mr. Duran? Did Japan become a unified country?" asked Janet Lindsey.

"In the end, the Emperor made Tokugawa Ieyasu, Shogun, a title very difficult to gain. To become Shogun one had to be a descendant of the Minamoto Clan of which Tokugawa Ieyasu had documents to make such a claim," answered Reuben.

"What's the difference between the Emperor and the Shogun, Da?" asked Aarleen.

"Ah, good question. You see, the Emperor and his family are the divine leaders of Japan, almost considered like gods, or in our case, the Pope. But it's the Shogun who is the political and military leader of Japan. Once Tokugawa Ieyasu was made Shogun, there has been peace in Japan ever since. That's why in Japan, this is referred to as the, Tokugawa Era. Yes, there are still regional feuds such as the one we had with the Arata, but nothing as horrible as before Sekigahara."

Reuben's lesson of Sekigahara was a much needed distraction for the three young students who were constantly reminded of the war happening in their own country. From

Reuben's lesson of Sekigahara, he went on to teach more history of Japan, such as the first and second Mongol invasions, the second one being diverted by a typhoon known as Kamikaze, the Devine Wind. Much of this history he didn't tell Aarleen at home and she was meticulously taking notes, not because of the lessons, but for future stories to add to her collection. What turned out to be a dreaded first day of school, ended up being a very enlightening day for the students, and their teacher. For one day, the war between the North and the South didn't exist, just the tales of the Land of the Rising Sun.

狼

Report of Lieutenant Jones, executive officer of the ironclad ram CSS *Virginia*, in command during the battle with USS Monitor.

C.S. STEAM BATTERY VIRGINIA,
Off Sewell's Point, March 8, 1862.

FLAG-OFFICER: in consequence of the wound of Flag-Officer Buchanan it becomes my duty to report that the Virginia left the yard this morning at 11 a.m., steamed down the river past our batteries and over to Newport News, where we engaged the frigates Cumberland, Congress, and the batteries ashore, and also two large steam frigates, supposed to be the Minnesota and Roanoke, and a sailing frigate and several small steamers armed with heavy rifled guns. We sank the Cumberland, drove the Congress ashore, where she hauled down her colors and hoisted the white flag, but she fired upon us with the white flag flying, wounding Lieutenant Minor and some of our men. We again opened fire upon her and she is now in flames. The shoal water prevented our reaching the other frigates. This, with approaching night, we think saved them from destruction. Our loss is 2 killed and 8 wounded, two of our guns had the muzzle shot off. The prow was twisted and the armor somewhat damaged; the anchors and all flagstaffs shot away and smokestack and steam pipe were riddled. The bearing of officers and men were all that could be wished, and in fact, it could not have been otherwise after the noble and daring conduct of the flag-officer, whose wound is deeply regretted by all on board, who would gladly have sacrificed themselves in order to save him. We were accompanied from the yard by the Beaufort (Lieutenant Parker) and Raleigh (Lieutenant Alexander), and as soon as it was discovered up the James River that the action had commenced, we were joined by the Patrick Henry (Commander Tucker), the Jamestown (Lieutenant Barney), and the Teaser (Lieutenant Webb), all of which were actively engaged and rendered very efficient service. Enclosed I send the surgeon's report of casualties.

I have the honor to be, sir, very respectfully, your obedient servant,

CATESBY AP R. JONES,
Executive and Ordnance Officer.

Report of Lieutenant Greene, U.S. Navy, executive officer of the [ironclad] USS *Monitor*.

U.S. IRONCLAD STEAMER MONITOR,
Hampton Roads, March 12, 1862.

SIR: Lieutenant Commanding John L. Worden having been disabled in the action of the 9th instant between this vessel and the rebel ironclad frigate Merrimack, I submit to you the following report:

We arrived at Hampton Roads at 9 p.m. on the 8th, instantly and immediately received orders from Captain Marston to proceed to Newport News and protect the Minnesota from the attack of the Merrimack. Acting Master Howard came on board and volunteered to act as pilot.

We left Hampton Roads at 10 p.m. and reached the Minnesota at 11:30 p.m.

The Minnesota, being aground, Captain Worden sent me on board her to enquire if we could render her any assistance, and to state to Captain Van Brunt that we should do all in our power to protect her from the attack of the Merrimack.

I then returned to this vessel and at 1 a. m. on the 9th instantly anchored near the Minnesota. At 4 a.m., supposing the Minnesota to be afloat and coming down upon us, got underway and stood out of the channel. Finding that we were mistaken, anchored at 5:30 a.m. At 8 a.m. perceived the Merrimack underway and standing toward the Minnesota. Hove up the anchor and went to quarters. At 8:45 a.m. we opened fire upon the Merrimack and continued the action until 11:30 a.m., when Captain Worden was injured in the eyes by the explosion of a shell from the Merrimack upon the outside of the eyehole in the pilot house, exactly opposite his eye. Captain Worden then sent for me and told me to take charge of the vessel. We continued the action until 12:15 p.m., when the Merrimack retreated to Sewell's Point and we went to the Minnesota and remained by her until she was afloat.

I am, sir, very respectfully, your obedient servant,

S. D. GREENE,
Lieutenant and Ordnance Officer.

Report of Major-General Huger, C.S. Army, commanding Department of Norfolk, on the impact of ironclad warships in warfare.

HEADQUARTERS DEPARTMENT OF NORFOLK,
Norfolk, Va., March 10, 1862.

SIR: I telegraphed yesterday to the Secretary of War the fact of the naval engagement on the 8th and 9th instants. As the battle was fought by the Navy, Flag-Officer Forrest will no doubt report to the Navy Department the result of the engagement.

The batteries at Sewell's Point opened fire on the steamers Minnesota and Roanoke, which attempted on the 8th to pass to Newport News to the assistance of the frigates attacked by the Virginia. The Minnesota ran aground before reaching there. The Roanoke was struck several times, and for some cause, turned around and went back to Old Point.

The two sailing vessels (Cumberland and Congress) were destroyed--the first sunk and the other burned by the Virginia--and on the 9th the Minnesota, still aground, would probably have been *destroyed but for the ironclad battery of the enemy called, I think, the Monitor. The Virginia and this battery were in actual contact, without inflicting serious injury on either.*

At 2 p.m. on yesterday, the 9th, all our vessels came up to the navy yard for repairs. The Virginia, I understand, has gone into dock for repairs, which will be made at once. This action shows the power and endurance of ironclad vessels. Cannon shot do not harm them, and they can pass batteries or destroy large ships. A vessel like the Virginia or the Monitor, with her two guns, can pass any of our batteries with impunity. The only means of stopping them is by vessels of the same kind. The Virginia, being the most powerful, can stop the Monitor, but a more powerful one would run her down or ashore. As the enemy can build such boats faster than we, they could, when so prepared, overcome any place accessible by water. How these powerful machines are to be stopped is a problem I cannot solve. At present, in Virginia, we have the advantage, but we cannot tell how long this may last.

I remain very respectfully, your obedient servant,

BENJ. HUGER,
Major-General, Commanding.

狼

Throughout the month of April, Confederate troops had been adding more gun batteries along the Sewell's Point area and were being manned both by artillery and infantry troops. Every once in a while, a group of soldiers would stop by the farm asking for water and that prompted Reuben and Noah to dig for a fresh water well in the front of the house. Reuben didn't like the idea of soldiers roaming the farm to get to the creek.

"Why can't we say no when they ask for water?" asked Evergreen, more curious rather than her usual confrontational manner.

"Would you rather them ask or demand water?" asked Reuben.

Evergreen saw Reuben's point and assisted him and Noah with the digging of the well.

As the sounds of the gun batteries could be heard more frequently, it was apparent to Reuben the Federals were preparing an attempt to land troops along Sewell's Point. Both he and Renee watched arm-in-arm as more and more troops were mobilized and heading toward the direction of the Ocean View beaches.

"If the Federals land on the beaches, what will that mean for us, Reuben?" asked Renee, very nervously.

Holding his wife reassuringly, Reuben replied, "Well, thankfully GrandDa Miles chose this location for our farm. We're off the main road leading to the city and very well secluded off the main branch of the river."

"What about the bridge to the main road, Da?" asked Aarleen, just as nervously.

Reuben pulled her into his embrace with Renee and said, "The Federals know our bridge to the main road leads them away from the city and the city is where they would go if they land at all. However, Mr. Davis, Foster, Lester, and I all agreed if that does happen, we're still going to fire the bridge."

"It's a good thing we started all that preparation, huh, Da?"

Reuben didn't reply, but held his wife and daughter tightly hoping his embrace was enough to assure them they were safe.

狼

On May 2, the superintendent paid a visit to Reuben while school was in session. He apologized for his unexpected visit and asked Reuben if he could speak to him in private.

"I believe I know what this is about sir, so let's save some time and let my three, very stable and smart students hear what you have to say," said Reuben.

The superintendent nodded in agreement and addressed everyone in the room. "Children, Reuben, General Huger has issued an order to start removing war materials out of the city and the region of Norfolk. For the safety of your students, I'm going to have you close down the Norfolk County Outreach School. This is only temporary, I promise. Once all military activities are finished, you will commence with studies.

Reuben stood with his arms crossed looking at his three students. "That's a very wise precaution, and I agree. With all the traffic on the roads lately, even I don't feel comfortable allowing my daughter to be on the road with a chance of being trampled by accident," said Reuben.

"Very well, Reuben. Go ahead and finish out this day of study and excuse your students until further notice from myself," instructed the superintendent.

The following week, Renee and Reuben spent most of their time under the oak tree, sometimes with others, but mostly on their own. Reuben never told Renee exactly where on or near the oak tree he hidden the remaining oban coins, but Renee knew if she needed to find them, Reuben would have left a clue.

But the hidden oban coins were not even in her mind these days. These days were spent in Reuben's arms, both in affection and Budo training. They even went fishing together, something they hadn't done since long before Renee's father enrolled her into Wickham Finishing School for Girls.

"Here, Renee," said Reuben as he was handing Renee a worm.

"What's this for? I already have my line baited."

"I know, but this one is too long. I need you to bite it in half for me," answered Reuben in a serious manner.

Renee snatched the worm out of his hand and threw it back at him as he began laughing.

"You're going to pay for that you shoddy farm boy!" she exclaimed as she jumped on top of Reuben.

Reuben took Renee into his arms and they rolled a few times in the soft grass laughing. When they came to a stop, Reuben was on top and looked deeply into Renee's eyes while saying, "Aishite'ru yo, my precious Wickham girl."

"I love you too, my shoddy farm boy."

狼

On Thursday, May 8, Reuben suggested a picnic. Although the sounds of the distant guns could be heard, he wanted a distraction. May thought it was a fantastic idea and began putting together a huge meal with Renee's and Aarleen's help.

The afternoon was spent under the oak tree with food and play.

"I hope you're enjoying this time off from school, my little cherry blossom, because when it's back in session, we're going to be hitting the books hard, little missy," said Reuben as he was chasing Aarleen around the tree.

"I haven't stopped studying, Da, so bring on your best teaching," replied Aarleen with confidence.

Renee watched her husband and daughter chase each other from the bank of the creek with amusement.

"Hello, Ever," said Renee as Evergreen walked up behind her.

"Are you worried about Reuben?" asked Evergreen, surprised Renee knew it was her without looking back.

"Yes, I'm worried. All this seems so familiar."

"What do you mean?" asked Evergreen.

"Separation," answered Renee.

"I'm sorry. I'm sorry for a lot of things. I'm sorry for my previous attitude toward you and your family. You've welcomed me into your home when the Masons let me go and I acted just terrible. I have to admit, I do have a chip on my shoulder, but you and your family are proof there are good people in this world," said Evergreen in all sincerity.

"Oh, Ever, you just have to have faith and love. That's what Reuben's mother told me a long time ago. Faith and love, as long as you have that, anything is possible," replied Renee.

"You know, you're a very lucky woman. Noah spent some time to set me right about you two. I have no right to have this chip after what you and your husband have been through, especially him. I know he has us all in his mind, but it's you and your daughter he will die for, if you don't mind me saying so."

"My Reuben has died so many times inside already, and each time, it makes him stronger and loves us that much more."

Evergreen nodded and timidly asked Renee about Reuben's relationship with God. "I know this is none of my business, but I have often wondered."

"What about, Ever?"

"I never see Reuben pray or attend church services with us. Doesn't he believe in the all mighty Lord God?"

Renee smiled thinking of the first time she came upon Reuben when he returned home from Japan, and was meditating under the oak tree. "He prays all the time, Ever. When he sits by himself under our tree, when he trains with his jo, and especially when he trains with his Kutto. You see, Ever, men like Reuben don't need God... it's God who needs men like Reuben," she replied, and then ran off to join her husband and daughter in their game of chase.

狼

Saturday, May 10, early in the morning, Reuben and Riley were returning after checking on the schoolhouse. He had plans to construct a type of pump used in Itosai to bring water from the creek to the hidden plots in the woods. He had acquired the last of the materials and had it all planned out, but wanted to see if Aarleen could piece it all together as a science project for her education.

As he reached the porch, cannon fire was heard. Much earlier than usual, he thought.

"How's the school?" asked Renee, coming out to greet him.

"Still locked up tight as a drum," said Reuben. "I'm thinking, during this time of no school, maybe we should paint the trim around the windows like you suggested."

"Ooh, that might be fun. We can start this afternoon."

"I checked the paint and it's still fresh and wet, so why not. We can make another picnic out of it."

Just then, several soldiers came running up the lane. "Excuse me sir, but may we fill our canteens from your well, please?"

"Sure, we'll give you a hand. Come on, my precious," said Reuben offering his hand to Renee.

"Why are you men in such a hurry?" asked Renee.

"The entire brigade is being moved to the beaches in case the Yankees make a landing," said a young private.

"Brigade?" asked Reuben. "That wouldn't happen to be Doyle's Brigade would it?"

"Yes sir."

"What regiment are you boys with?"

"The 68th," replied one of the soldiers.

Reuben looked to Renee and said, "That's Lieutenant Stevens' regiment. Do you boys know him?"

"Yes sir. He's now a captain. Captain of Company C. That's our company."

Renee saw Reuben was in deep thought and asked him what was wrong.

He nodded and again asked the soldiers, "When you say the entire brigade, does that mean the 66th as well?"

"Yes sir, many of them are at the beach now."

With a look of hope on his face, Reuben continued his questions. "Have any of you heard of a Major Monroe Duran of the 66th?"

The soldiers looked at each other shaking their heads no. "Sorry sir, but none of us have heard of him, but if he's in the 66th, he might very well be there. There are a lot of high ranking officers on the beaches."

"Can you boys lead me to the 66th?" asked Reuben, excitedly.

"Reuben… no," Renee said in worry.

"Renee, if Monroe is at Sewell's Point or the beach, I can bring him back home. I have to try for Mama's and Da's sake."

Renee began to feel emotional, but she knew this was an opportunity Reuben couldn't pass up. She reluctantly nodded in agreement and took him into her arms.

"Hey, what's going on?" asked Aarleen.

"Quick, sweetie, go and fetch your Da's hanten jacket and jo. Da is going to try to find Uncle Monroe," replied Renee, not letting go of Reuben.

"Mama?" asked Aarleen, concerned and confused.

"Please sweetie, and hurry."

Aarleen ran off to do as Renee asked. Renee took Reuben's face into her hands and said, "Be careful and come home quickly."

"I'll look for Monroe for ah… let's say, a couple of hours, and then come home whether I find him or not. Either way, I'll be home before noon."

"You better," said Renee, pulling Reuben tightly into her arms.

Reuben gave Renee a deep long kiss on her lips.

"Here, Da," said Aarleen, handing Reuben his hanten jacket, tanto, and jo.

Reuben slipped into his jacket and took Aarleen into his arms. "Listen, my little cherry blossom, I'm going to go and try to find Uncle Monroe and bring him home. I'll be back."

"Okay, Da. Be careful and don't dally."

Reuben released his daughter and took a few steps toward the lane with the soldiers. He paused and returned to Renee, took her into his arms, and kissed her once more. "I love you, my precious Renee."

"I love you too, my dearest Reuben."

After one last kiss, Reuben ran off with the soldiers up the lane to the road, and was on his way to look for his brother.

Renee looked to Aarleen and began to cry uncontrollably as Aarleen took her mother into her arms and held her tight.

狼

The gunfire was beginning to sound louder as Reuben and the other soldiers ran across the bridge that connected the road leading from the farm to the main road leading to the city. As he made it across, Reuben saw many high ranking Confederate officers crossing over the main bridge.

"Come on, mister, we got to get across the bridge before it gets too crowded," called out one of the younger soldiers.

Reuben continued running, looking at every officer above the rank of captain hoping he would be able to spot Monroe. The bridge was getting congested and Reuben and the others practically had to fight their way across.

As Reuben made it to the other side, Mr. Davis and Mr. Lester made it across the opposite side and ran to the bridge connecting their homes to the main road. When the two crossed onto their side of the river, Mr. Lester went into to woods to retrieve the hidden canisters of kerosene.

"Fred, what are you doing?!" called out Mr. Davis.

"We got to fire the bridge like Reuben said," replied Mr. Lester.

"Shouldn't we go get Reuben and Tom? We said we would do it together!"

"We don't have time! You saw all those Yankees coming over the beach! We'll stop by their homes and let them know we burned it!"

Reluctantly, Mr. Davis began helping Mr. Lester douse the bridge with kerosene from end-to-end. They used all the canisters and when the last one was emptied, Mr. Lester lit a match and tossed it onto the bridge.

The bridge went up in flames instantly causing the two to quickly step back away from the heat and black smoke.

狼

Reuben and the other soldiers ran almost a mile from the main bridge toward Sewell's Point when he spotted Captain Todd Stevens heading in his direction.

"Hey boys, I see your captain! Stop!" called out Reuben to the soldiers.

They came up behind Reuben, halted, and helped him wave down Captain Stevens.

"Damn it, Reuben, what the hell are you doing here?!" yelled out Captain Stevens.

"I'm looking for my brother! What's going on?!" answered Reuben.

"It's a god damn withdrawal, that's what going on! Damn Yankees over ran the beaches and are heading this way to take the city!"

"Have you seen anyone from the 66th?" asked Reuben.

"Hell, Reuben, I can barely keep track of my own company, let alone an entire other regiment!"

"Where is your company, Todd?"

"There all around us right now, thank heavens!"

"Well, you better rally them back together, or there's going to be hell to pay!"

"Tell me something I don't know! You got to help me, Reuben, please!" pleaded Captain Stevens.

"Me, what the hell are you talking about?! I can't help you! I'm a civilian!"

"Please Reuben, I can't find any of my junior officers and my sergeants have their hands full keeping the boys together!"

"Where's Max... Sergeant Warren?!" asked Reuben.

Captain Stevens pointed to the other side of the road. Reuben saw the sergeant herding a large group of men toward the tree line getting them out of the way of the massive withdrawal of Confederate troops making their way back to the city.

Reuben began thinking hard. Images of his brother flashed through his mind. Suddenly Renee and Aarleen came to his mind vividly. Damn it, damn it... what do I do, Reuben thought franticly.

"Reuben, please! I helped you when you went to get your family out of Chesapeake City! You got to help me now!" called out Captain Stevens, regaining Reuben's attention.

Reuben nodded. "You're right! Gather your company and form them into two long firing lines in that clearing. I'm going to go tell Max to do the same on that side of the road!"

"Hey, you two, just what do you think you're doing standing around?!" called out a colonel on horseback.

"Shut up and get your ass across the bridge!" answered Reuben.

"Reuben! That's Colonel McFerrin of the 68th!" yelled out Captain Stevens.

"Is that so?!" exclaimed Reuben. He then pointed his jo to the colonel and said, "Okay, Colonel McFerrin, sir! How about you use those damn stars on your collar and organize this mess! Get all the men and equipment over the bridge as fast as possible! Captain Stevens and I will slow down the Federals as long as we can!"

Looking confused, Colonel McFerrin eyed Reuben with a combination of anger and awe. "Listen you! I don't know who you are, but we will have words when this is all over!"

"I doubt it! I'm not even in the army! Now move your ass! Colonel, sir!" shouted Reuben.

Colonel McFerrin began to turn his horse when Reuben called out to him once again. "Once you get to the bridge, I suggest you get some engineers to prepare to blow that bridge to slow down the Federals!" said Reuben, thinking more of his family's safety than the survival of the Confederate troops making their way to the city.

"Excellent idea, ah…" replied Colonel McFerrin, not knowing who to address.

"Never mind, as soon as I'm on the other side of the bridge, I'm going home! Come on Todd! Form up those firing lines!"

狼

"Mama, I see black smoke coming from the bridge!" called out Aarleen.

Renee and the others came running out of the house. Renee looked in the direction of the smoke and her gut felt like it had been tied into a knot.

"Do you think Reuben and the others set it on fire?" asked Evergreen.

"I don't know. Reuben has only been gone for little over an hour. Maybe he saw Federal troops coming and turned back," said Renee. "I'm going to walk up to the road."

Renee began to make her way to the lane when Aarleen called out to her. "Wait, Mama!"

Aarleen ran into the house and gathered her bokken and Renee's jo and ran out of the front door. When she was several yards from Renee, Aarleen called out, "Here, Mama," and tossed Renee her jo.

Renee caught it in her right hand and twirled it behind her back to her left hand, just as Reuben does.

"I'm coming with you. Come on, Riley," called Aarleen.

Without hesitation, Renee replied, "Come on, sweetie. Let's go find your Da."

"Renee, Aarleen, get back over here!" called out May.

"I'll look after them," said Noah, and started following Renee and Aarleen.

"What do we do now, May?" asked Evergreen.

"We pray, child. We pray. Henry, we better start taking some of them chickens to the coop and animals to the pen in the woods. Come on, Ever, you can help too."

"READY! AIM! FIRE!" ordered Reuben.

The first volley decimated the unaware Union troops making their way up the road toward the city.

"Fall back behind the last firing line and reload!" ordered Reuben to his firing line.

As the soldiers followed his orders, Reuben stayed behind with Sergeant Warren.

"Whoa, that stopped em' Reuben!" said the sergeant, excitedly.

"But not for long. Right now they're regrouping and they'll be back more organized. I'm heading back with the first line. You got this, Max?"

"I got it, Reuben. I'll see you on the other side of the bridge."

Reuben nodded and made his way to his group of men. On the way he saluted Captain Stevens.

Watching from atop his horse, Colonel McFerrin nodded in approval as Reuben fired off the first volley halting the Union advance.

"Quickly boys, get those guns on the other side!" ordered the colonel as he rode his horse up the road, encouraging the troops to cross the river in an orderly manner.

"Major, how are the engineers coming along with preparing to destroy the bridge?"

"Nearly finished, Colonel," answered the major.

"Good. Now, who in the hell is that man with Captain Stevens?"

"I have no idea sir. I believe he's a local."

"Well, when this is all over, bring him to me."

"Sir, I believe he's a civilian. What if he doesn't want to come?"

"Then arrest him! I need to know his story!"

"Yes sir."

"FIRE!"

Sergeant Warren ordered the second volley once he saw the Union troops advance further than the last wave.

Reuben was right, the sergeant thought, they're getting organized.

He ordered his group of men back behind Reuben to reload.

The Union soldiers were coming quicker and their formations were more solid. Reuben was able to get his group of men to fire off three more volleys until he noticed Union cannons being set up.

"Okay, Todd, my job here is done. I'm not dealing with cannons. I swore after Shun Bridge I was never going to tangle with cannons ever again. Looks like we're the last ones to cross the bridge anyway, so let's get the men across and get the hell out of here," said Reuben.

"Right! Sergeant Warren, get the boys across the river so they can destroy the bridge!"

"You heard the captain, boys, now move it as fast as you can!"

The troops of Company C of the 68th Virginia heeded the order from Sergeant Warren and in an orderly fashion began to run toward the bridge. Several older soldiers were helping the younger ones with frightened looks on their faces.

Although he felt he did all he could do to help Captain Stevens, Reuben still felt he needed to stay back to make sure every man made it across the bridge.

A Union cannon fired and its shell landed on the road knocking a young private off his feet. The soldier tried to stand, but fell under the weight of his body. Reuben ran to him and lifted the soldier over his shoulders and started running toward the bridge. Another cannon fired and its shell landed just ahead of Reuben, but it didn't slow him down.

As Reuben ran across the bridge with the young private over his shoulders, he yelled out, "SOMEONE BLAST THIS DAMN BRIDGE!!!"

As Reuben cleared the bridge, Sergeant Warren came to help him with the young private and they ran and ducked behind an overturned wagon.

Moments later, a large blast was heard causing the ground to shudder, and the main bridge blown from its foundation.

狼

Renee, Aarleen, Noah, and Riley made it as far as the schoolhouse when all of a sudden a loud thunderous blast was heard, shaking the ground beneath their feet. Riley began barking at the sound.

"GEEZ OH PETES, what in the world was that?!" cried out Aarleen, frightened.

"I don't know, but I have a feeling your Da had something to do with it," replied Renee.

Noah pointed and yelled out, "Look, here comes Mr. Davis and Mr. Lester!"

Covering their ears, Mr. Davis and Mr. Lester came running down the road towards Renee, Aarleen, Noah, and Riley.

"Good heavens, Renee, what are you doing here? Quickly, get back to your home! The Yankees are pouring all over the main road!" called out Mr. Davis.

"Yeah, get home quick! We just lit the bridge on fire!" said Mr. Lester.

"Where's my husband? Was he with you when you lit the bridge on fire?!" asked Renee, frantically.

"No, we thought he was at home! We were going to stop at your house to let him know we fired the bridge!"

"GEEZ OH GEEZ OH GEEZ REUBEN IS STILL ON THE OTHER SIDE!!!" cried out Renee, and began sprinting toward the bridge.

"Renee, wait!" yelled out Noah as he and the others followed.

Renee made it to the burning bridge and stumbled down to the edge of the river. She was about to jump in until Mr. Lester held her back. He carried her back to the road as she struggled the entire way.

When Mr. Lester reached the road, he put Renee down. As she was about to start running back to the river's edge, Mr. Lester, Noah, and Aarleen all held her back.

"REUBEN!!!" Renee hollered as loud as she could.

Renee collapsed to her knees holding onto Aarleen. They all watched the chaotic drama before their eyes as soldiers and horses raced toward the city.

Suddenly Aarleen rose and pointed. "There he is, Mama! I see Da!"

狼

With their heads covered, Reuben, Sergeant Warren, and the young private didn't move until the blast was over. Debris from the blast showered them from above. When all was calm, they remained behind the upturned wagon catching their breath. From their position, they heard wheels rolling, horses galloping, and soldiers running.

But throughout that clamor of noise, Reuben distinctively heard Renee's voice call his name from a distance. Reuben rose and peered over the wagon and saw the bridge leading to his farm in flames.

Reuben came out from behind the wagon and saw Renee, Aarleen, Noah, Mr. Davis, Mr. Lester, and Riley on the other side of the river. He removed his jacket and tied it around his waist and said to Sergeant Warren, "Well, Max, I'm going home! If I were you, I'd find another line of work!"

Reuben began walking toward the river waving to those waiting for him on the other side. Suddenly Reuben was tackled to the ground by two Confederate provost marshals causing him to drop his jo.

"That's the one! Bring him to me!" called out Colonel McFerrin.

The two provost marshals lifted Reuben to his feet and began pulling him toward the colonel. Reuben stopped and shifted his weight to the larger of the two, easily taking his balance, and tossed him to his back. Turning his attention to the other marshal, Reuben grasped his wrist and threw him hard using one of the four directional throws. Reuben began running toward the river when another provost came at him with a club. The provost swung down at Reuben. Reuben quickly shifted out of the way of the strike, grabbed the provost wrist's and with his elbow, Reuben jammed it into the provost's face and tossed the provost over his hip.

Watching Reuben fighting off the provosts, Captain Stevens ran up to the colonel and pleaded with him to let Reuben go.

"Please, sir, all he did was help! Just let him go home!"

The colonel ignored the captain and rode his horse toward Reuben.

Reuben had just thrown two other provosts to the ground when one of the first marshals he threw came up behind him and aimed a small carbine rifle at Reuben's head.

"Hold it right there, mister!" yelled the provost.

Reuben turned and instinctively shifted his body away from the muzzle and took hold of the barrel and swung it in a high arch over his head and jammed the butt of the rifle in the provost's face. Reuben began using the carbine as if it were a jo, thrusting and striking at attacking provosts coming from all directions.

"Jesus Christ, who is this man!" called out Colonel McFerrin. "Quick, someone net him before he gets away!"

On the other side of the river Renee watched helplessly as her husband was fighting his way back to her. From her point of view, she saw one soldier after another come at Reuben as he tossed them aside.

"REUBEN!!!" Renee cried, trying to keep her husband's fighting spirit up.

Aarleen also began calling out to her father, as did Noah and the others. Riley also barked and yapped in support.

Renee saw Reuben block a downward strike of a club with the carbine aimed at his head. She saw her husband take hold of the provost's wrist and twist it outward causing him to flip over onto the ground. Once Reuben was free of attackers, he tossed the carbine aside and began sprinting to Renee.

"CRACK!"

The snap of a bullwhip slashed against Reuben's back causing him to stumble and fall.

Upon seeing Reuben fall, Renee again called out to him and began running to the river's edge. Knowing it would have been impossible to swim across in time to come to his aid, Renee still took to the water with the others following.

Renee saw Reuben rise to his feet and begin stumbling forward toward her when another loud crack of another bullwhip was heard, this one catching Reuben around the neck.

"NO!!!" cried Renee as she saw other provosts come at Reuben with a net and irons.

Seeing Reuben netted and being kicked and dragged back to the road, Renee started swimming, but the river was too wide for her to cross on her own and she began sinking under the weight of her soaked hakama.

As she was about to go under, Noah, without hesitation, and learning to swim real quick, pulled her above the water and began dragging her back to the river's edge. Aarleen ran into the water to help Noah bring her mother to the edge as she was calling out Reuben's name.

Reuben saw and heard Renee waving franticly and calling his name from the opposite side of the river's edge. "RENEE!!!" called out Reuben as he was being dragged over the ground. "DON'T WORRY, I'LL BE HOME AS SOON AS I BREAK FREE!!!"

Renee saw one of the provosts raise a club and bring it down on Reuben's back and saw him slump over unconscious.

"Geez oh geez oh geez Reuben, come back," said Renee as she began sobbing in Aarleen's arms.

Reuben awoke in a dark train boxcar filled with other men in chains, some soldiers, and some civilians like him. Pushing himself up from the floor, Reuben felt someone assist him.

"Who's that?" asked Reuben.

"It's me, Max."

"Geez Max, what are you doing here?"

"Got my ass arrested keeping provost from trying to get to you. Jesus, Reuben, you fought off about a dozen men, some twice your size. What the hell are you?"

"I'm just a school teacher trying to get home to my family. Where are we?"

"We're in a boxcar, waiting to head off to Petersburg."

"Petersburg! I can't go to Petersburg! What the hell is in Petersburg?!" exclaimed Reuben in an angered state.

Sergeant Warren patted Reuben on the shoulder showing compassion and said, "All of Doyle's Brigade is evacuating Norfolk. The city has fallen to the Yankees. I hear we're to regroup with General Johnston's army on the Peninsula to stop the Yankees from taking Richmond from the South."

"What does that got to do with me?" asked Reuben, not requiring an answer.

The door of the boxcar slid open bringing forth bright sunlight and causing all inside to shield their eyes.

"Sergeant Warren! Reuben! Where are you two?!" called Captain Stevens.

"Over here, Cap, both of us," said Sergeant Warren.

Captain Stevens entered the car with another soldier. It was the same young soldier Reuben carried back to safety.

"Reuben, please forgive me. I'm doing all I can to get you released," said Captain Stevens.

"Tell you one thing, Todd, this has ruined me for helping you ever again," replied Reuben.

"I don't blame you, Reuben," Captain Stevens replied, chuckling.

"And I don't blame you, Todd," Reuben said, sincerely. "Who's that with you?"

"I'm Private Paul Cutler, sir," quickly answered the young private. "I'm the one you saved from the Yankee cannons. I just had to come and thank you for saving my life. I'm much obliged."

"How old are you, Mr. Cutler?" asked Reuben.

Clearing his throat, trying to make his voice sound deeper, Paul Cutler answered, "18, sir."

"Don't lie to me, boy. I have a 13 year old daughter and I'm a school teacher. I can spot a child lying miles away."

Paul Cutler let out a sigh and replied, "I'm 16."

Reuben shook his head. Geez, three years older than my little cherry blossom, and the same age difference between me and Renee, he thought.

"Where are you from, Paul?" asked Reuben.

"I'm from Princess Anne County, sir."

Reuben looked at Captain Stevens and said, "Listen, Todd, I need young Paul to do me a favor."

"Anything sir, I'm indebted to you for saving me," said Paul Cutler.

Reuben again looked to Captain Stevens who nodded in agreement.

"Listen to me very carefully, Paul Cutler. I want you to go to my home and tell my wife and daughter I'm well, but most importantly, tell them I'll be home as soon as I can. You got that?"

"Yes sir, I'll do that for you, you have my word."

"Good, I'm holding you to that. Captain Stevens will give you detailed directions on how to get to my house."

Paul Cutler looked at Captain Stevens who nodded in return.

"Also, Paul, take off that uniform jacket and cap and put on my jacket. Tell my wife to have it washed and ready for me to use when I get home. Oh, and one more thing, come closer."

Paul Cutler moved closer to Reuben as he whispered something into Paul's ear.

"Think you can remember that, Paul?" asked Reuben.

"Yes sir."

Paul Cutler quickly removed his gray shell jacket and kepi and slipped into Reuben's hanten jacket.

"What do I do when I'm finished with your orders, sir?" Paul Cutler asked Reuben, completely forgetting about Captain Stevens.

Reuben looked to Captain Stevens and let out a long sigh. "Go home and live a long happy life. That's an order."

"Sir?" asked Paul Cutler, questionably.

Reuben shifted to his knees so he could almost look Paul Cutler in the eyes. "Look around you, Paul," said Reuben with sincerity, "you're too young to be a part of this. When this is all over, and if Virginia will be allowed to exist, Virginia is going to need strong, smart, young men like you to get it back on its feet. So go home, go to school, find a nice girl and marry her, and have lots of children. But mostly… live."

"I will, sir. I promise."

"Come on, Mr. Cutler, let's get you started on your orders," said Captain Stevens. "Reuben, I'll see what I can do. And sergeant, keep him company."

Reuben and Sergeant Warren watched Captain Stevens and Paul Cutler exit the car. When they hopped off, the door was closed shut.

"Damn, Reuben, I wished you would have told me that a year ago before I changed sides," said Sergeant Warren.

"Would you have listened?"

"Probably," answered the sergeant.

Captain Stevens walked young Paul Cutler out of the train yard. He sketched out a map with detailed instructions on how to get to Reuben's farm. When Captain Stevens was certain Paul Cutler understood every detail, he sent him on his way.

As Paul Cutler started walking, he paused and asked the captain, "Sir, did Mr. Duran mean it, for me to go home after?"

"Yes he did, and that goes for me too. Go home. You were lucky today, Paul. There aren't many men out there like Reuben Duran, and not enough of them to watch over you. Today you had your one lucky break, so you had better take advantage of it."

"I will, sir."

"Oh, and one more thing, Paul, make sure you carry out Reuben's orders. You don't want to cross men like him."

狼

It was late at night and the house was silent. The lamps in the parlor were still lit in case Reuben came home. Everyone turned in for the evening, but no one was sleeping. Aarleen was lying with Renee in her and Reuben's bed, holding each other. Both were pretending to be asleep, but were listening for Riley who would give a signal if anyone came up the lane to the house.

It took Aarleen, May, and Evergreen to calm Renee down once they returned home after watching Reuben being dragged toward the city. Aarleen helped her mother bathe from her attempt to swim across the river to reach Reuben. Evergreen brought Renee a day dress, but she asked for one of Reuben's kosodes and hakamas. Aarleen brought her his black hakama and Akagi burgundy kosode. Wearing Reuben's clothes comforted her.

Riley began barking, causing Renee and Aarleen to roll out of bed and practically sprint downstairs. By the time Renee opened the front door, everyone else came running to the parlor and out the front door.

Riley looked up to Renee, whined, and looked back to the lane and barked a couple more times.

"There, coming up the lane, Mama! It looks like two boys!" exclaimed Aarleen.

Renee ran, with the others following, toward the two boys coming up the lane.

Aarleen immediately recognized Tommy Deans, but not the other boy he was helping along the way.

"Tommy? Is that you? Who's that with you? Why is he wearing my Da's jacket?" asked Aarleen.

"Says his name is Paul, and he's seriously tuckered out. Says he has a message from your Pa," said Tommy Deans.

"My goodness, he can't be more than 16," said Renee as she took Paul's other arm and helped Tommy Deans carry him to the house.

"Me and my pa were at the river using our boat to help people cross when along comes this guy. Says he was with Mr. Duran during the battle at the big bridge. Said Mr. Duran saved his life and sent him here to deliver you a message, Mrs. Duran."

"Good boy, Tommy. Quick, let's get him inside. May, please fix him something to eat."

"Right away, Renee," said May as she pulled Evergreen along with her.

They brought Paul into the parlor and laid him down on the sofa. Aarleen went to get some water and a damp towel to drape over his forehead.

"Is it okay if I stay, Mrs. Duran? I want to know about Mr. Duran," pleaded Tommy Deans.

"Of course, Tommy, please go help my daughter, will you?"

"Yes Ma'am," Tommy Deans replied as he moved to follow Aarleen.

Paul Cutler awoke, sat up, and looked at Renee. To Paul, she resembled a caring, beautiful angel.

"Whoa, young man, just lay and rest. You're safe now," said Renee, easing him back down.

"Are, are you, Mrs. Duran?" Paul Cutler stammered.

"Yes, I am. My name is Renee. What's yours?"

Aarleen and Tommy Deans returned. Tommy handed Renee a damp towel and immediately Renee applied it to Paul's forehead.

"My name is Paul Cutler. I'm a private in the 68th Virginia Infantry."

"How old are you, Paul?" asked Renee, very concerned.

"16, Ma'am," replied Paul.

"Whoa 16, wow," said Tommy Deans.

"Now don't be getting any ideas, Tommy," said Aarleen. "You heard what my Da said about fighting in a war."

"Don't worry about me, Aarleen. After what I saw today, I'm going to stay as far away from this war as I can," replied Tommy Deans.

Ignoring Aarleen and Tommy Deans, Renee said to Paul, "You have a message from Reuben, my husband? Do you know where he is?"

"The last time I saw him, he was in irons on a train car getting ready to head to Petersburg with the rest of the brigade. The Yankees are taking over the city and all Confederate forces are evacuating the region. Your husband is under arrest, but I don't know why. I don't think he even knows why."

May and Evergreen came in with some bread and ham. Renee and Noah helped Paul sit up. Evergreen offered Paul the food and he grabbed at it and shoved the ham slice in his mouth. He ate so quickly he began to choke. Henry started patting Paul on his back.

"Take it easy, Paul. When was the last time you had a meal?" asked Renee.

"Can't remember, couple of days ago, I think," said Paul between chews.

"Dear lord," commented May.

"Paul, I know you're tired and hungry, but can you tell me what Reuben told you to tell me, please?" asked Renee.

Paul sat up and took in a deep breath. "He said not to worry and he'll be home as soon as he can." Paul glanced at Reuben's jacket he was wearing and began to take it off. "He also said for you to wash this and have it ready for him to use when he returns."

That message caused everyone to lower their shoulders in relief.

"At least he still has his humor," said Henry.

After swallowing a bite of bread, Paul said, "There's one more thing he told me to tell you and Aarleen."

Aarleen moved in closer and said, "I'm Aarleen, Paul. What did he tell you to tell us?"

"He said, just because he's not home, that's no excuse for you not to continue your schoolwork or training, little cherry blossom."

Aarleen let out a whimper as Renee took her into her arms.

"And for you, Mrs. Duran, Mr. Duran said, Aishite'ru yo, my precious Wickham girl."

"Oh, Reuben..." said Renee softly as she brought her hands to her mouth to hide an emotional gasp. Aarleen took Renee into her arms.

"What does that mean?" asked Evergreen.

"It's what Reuben tells me every night before he goes to sleep... I love you."

Renee reached for the VMI button hanging from the gold chain around her neck. She brought it to her lips and said, "I love you too, my shoddy farm boy."

石
水

In the year of our Lord, 1862, a romantic tale continues.
Trading one brother's life, for another brother's life…

<u>Please, let me take Reuben his Kutto</u>

Hudson North Star Headlines:
A BLOODLESS VICTORY!

Norfolk Evacuated!

GENERAL WOOL IN POSSESSION.

THE CITY SURRENDERED BY THE MAYOR.

Gen. Wool's Proclamation.

MERRIMAC BLOWN UP!!

Monitor Gone to Norfolk.

General Viete Military Governor.

Prescott Journal Headlines:
NORFOLK TAKEN.

Navy Yard and Portsmouth in our possession.

THE REBELS FLEE!

HEADQUARTERS DEPARTMENT OF
VIRGINIA, Norfolk, May 10 1862.

The city of Norfolk, having been surrendered to the Government of the United States, military possession of the same is taken in behalf of the national government. Major General John E. Wool, Brigadier General is appointed Military Governor for the time being. He will see that all citizens are carefully protected in all their rights and civil privileges, taking the utmost care to preserve order and to see that no soldiers be permitted to enter the city, except by the written permission of the commanding officer of his brigade or regiment, and he will punish summarily any American soldier who shall infringe upon the rights of any of the inhabitants.

JOHN E. WOOL, Major General… To be promoted to full Major General immediately.

Everyone came to sit at the kitchen table for breakfast. Throughout the night, no one got much sleep except for Paul Cutler. Paul fell right off to sleep once he gave Renee Reuben's message and ate. Renee also insisted Tommy Deans stay the night since it was late. She felt it wasn't safe for him to be roaming around with Federal troops in the area.

Still groggy from the day before, Paul made it to the table. There were still more questions Renee wanted to ask him. All eyes were upon him as he gobbled eggs and hash just as he ate the ham and bread late last night.

It was Tommy Deans who dared to interrupt his eating. "Hey, Paul, tell us what happened yesterday already."

Paul took a long swallow of his breakfast and started with his company's withdrawal from Sewell's Point. "Yankees just poured off of boats and onto the sand. Their Navy gun boats pounded our batteries. As other companies began fleeing, Captain Stevens kept us together along with Sergeant Warren. I don't know what happened to my lieutenant. Although we were not in formation, we kept together double-timing it toward the city. We were about three or four miles ahead of the Yankees when we came to a halt at that big bridge."

Everyone around the table was listening with full attention except for Evergreen. As much as she was grateful Paul Cutler brought news of Reuben's welfare, she still felt contempt toward the boy because of the side he chose to support.

Paul Cutler continued with his story. He told how Reuben met up with Captain Stevens and how he overheard the captain pleading for Reuben's help. Paul stressed he felt it was unusual for an army officer to ask the help of a civilian, but once Reuben nearly took command of the company away from Captain Stevens, Paul thought Reuben was another officer who was wearing civilian clothes. He went on to tell how Reuben formed the company into four long firing lines. Paul said he was in the firing line led by Reuben. "It was our job to hold back the Yankees while the rest of the brigade crossed the river. I thought it was a good idea. Then I heard your husband say to the Sergeant Warren…"

Paul stopped to take a few more bites from his plate.

"What? What? What did he say?!" asked Aarleen, impatiently, causing Paul to cower in his chair with a biscuit in his hand.

"Sweetie, please. There's no need to rush him," said Renee. "Hurry Paul, what did my husband say to Sergeant Warren?"

Taking another long swallow, Paul said, "I overheard Mr. Duran say he was going to get someone to blow up the bridge after we got across and burn the bridge leading to your farm. I think he wanted the bridges destroyed, not to keep the Yankees from catching up with us. I think he wanted to destroy the bridges so they wouldn't get to you."

Everyone sat back in relaxation.

"Wow, Aarleen, your pa really is a hero," said Tommy Deans. "All this time, I thought he was just telling stories."

Aarleen's response was a perturbed glare at Tommy Deans.

"I wonder why he was arrested," said Henry.

Paul shrugged his shoulders and said, "I don't know. I think the colonel wanted to talk to Mr. Duran, but he wanted to get back to y'all as fast as he could. The last thing I remember him saying was to Sergeant Warren, *'Well Max, I'm going home. If I were you, I'd find another line of work.'*"

504

"That sounds like our Reuben, all right," said May with a hint of humor.

Paul had a serious look on his face as he continued. "You know, I was impressed with Mr. Duran and ready to follow him anywhere, but it wasn't until I saw him fighting off all those provosts when I thought your husband wasn't just a soldier... he's a warrior of some sort. I never saw anyone fight that many men at one time.

"Sergeant Warren went to help him and started fighting with the provosts too. He only fought with two before he was tackled down, but Mr. Duran... great Cesar's ghost, I never saw that before. It had to have been almost a dozen men who tried to take him down. If it wouldn't have been for those two with the whips, I believe he could have made it back to this side of the river."

"What happened to Max, I mean, Sergeant Warren?" asked Aarleen.

"He was arrested along with your dad. You didn't see this, but after Mr. Duran came to, he started fighting again, even in arm and leg irons. Using the irons binding his wrists and ankles, he used them as weapons and injured five more guards before they knocked him out again.

"Heaven's ghost, Mrs. Duran, where did you find your husband?" asked Paul in awe.

Renee's lips formed a little smile as she looked out of the kitchen window toward their oak tree.

Outside on the porch, Riley's ears stood erect. He rose to his paws and sniffed in the air. Suddenly he began barking.

Everyone rose from the table, except for Paul who kept eating.

Aarleen went to the front door and opened it letting Riley in so he could run out the back door toward the hidden plots as Aarleen trained him to do.

It was Reuben's idea for Aarleen to train Riley to give warning, and then to run off to guard the hidden plots. It was mainly for Riley's safety knowing if he stayed behind, whoever coming to the farm might hurt, or even kill him.

Coming up the lane, Aarleen saw soldiers, not in Confederate gray, but in Union blue.

"It's Federal troops, Mama," said Aarleen, calm but anxious.

Aarleen's warning caused Paul to stop eating and stand.

"Jumping Jehoshaphat," said Tommy Deans, pointing to Paul's trousers. "If those Yankees see Paul's pants, they'll know he's a soldier."

"Quick, Aarleen, take Paul upstairs and find a pair of your Da's pants for him, and a clean shirt," said Renee.

"Yes, Mama. Come on, Paul," Aarleen replied, pointing Paul to the stairs.

Renee turned to everyone and said, "Okay, remain calm. Remember what Reuben said, don't speak unless they speak to you first, and only short answers as much as possible. It's just another day on the Duran farm."

Everyone nodded in agreement, including Tommy Deans.

Renee exited out the front parlor door onto the porch with her jo in her left hand as a Union officer and a sergeant were about to step onto the porch. There were seven other Union soldiers standing in the front yard with their rifles at the ready.

Startled by Renee's sudden presence on the porch, the Union officer and sergeant stopped from stepping forward any further. One private brought his rifle down and aimed it at Renee. Renee didn't show any concern, although inside she was nervous.

Remember what Reuben said… remain calm and neutral, thought Renee.

"Stand down, soldier!" ordered the sergeant.

The private lowered his rifle toward the ground.

"Sorry about that, ma'am," said the officer, admiring Renee's beauty and her odd attire. "Allow me to introduce myself. I am Captain Oscar Grossman. We mean you no harm as long as you cooperate. May I speak to the man of the house?"

"The man of the house has been arrested by the rebels," said Evergreen, quickly.

Her response received an angered look from Renee, and a tug on the arm by Henry.

"Is that true?" asked Captain Grossman to Renee.

Renee turned her focus back to Captain Grossman and said, "Yes he has. He's my husband."

"I see. Is this his farm?"

"Our farm," answered Renee firmly with short answers just as Reuben instructed her to do.

Captain Grossman eyed everyone who filed out of the house and asked, "Is this everyone from inside the house?"

"No."

"Who else is in the house, if I may ask?"

"My daughter and ah…"

"My cousin Paul," said Tommy Deans quickly. "He's staying with us to help on our farm up the road for the spring planting. He's from Princess Anne County."

"Tommy, why don't you go get Aarleen and Paul and have them come out, please?" asked Renee.

Captain Grossman nodded.

Tommy Deans quickly went back into the house and upstairs to bring Aarleen and Paul outside. When he entered Renee and Reuben's bedroom, Paul just finished putting on his shoes. He was dressed in some of Reuben's old work clothes. Tommy quickly told Paul to pretend to be his cousin visiting from his home to help with spring planting and arrived a couple of days ago.

Back outside, Captain Grossman asked Renee, "Back to your husband, why was he arrested, do you know?"

"No."

Captain Grossman was getting frustrated at Renee's short and simple answers. "Look Mrs… ah, I don't even know your name. May I ask please?"

"Mrs. Duran is fine," answered Renee in a serious tone.

"Ah, Mrs. Duran, very good. All I'm trying to do is compile the population in this area. If your husband has been arrested by the rebels, then perhaps we can help obtain his release. Now, was he arrested because of his sentiment to the Union?"

"No, my husband and I claim neutrality."

"Hmm, I see. Are these four your slaves?"

"WE'RE NOT SLAVES!!!" exclaimed Evergreen.

Again Henry, as well as May, tugged at Evergreen's arm.

"Not slaves?" asked Captain Grossman.

"No Captain. These four are freed persons of color. They live and work this farm as equal partners. They're practically part of the family."

"I see. I assume you can provide proof of their status?"

As soon as the captain finished his statement, May, Henry, Noah, and Evergreen began producing their papers of status.

The captain nodded to the sergeant to retrieve the papers and bring them to him.

As the captain was looking over the papers, Aarleen, Tommy Deans, and Paul Cutler came outside.

The captain noticed Aarleen step next to Renee and gave an odd expression when he saw Aarleen was dressed the same as Renee. He also noticed Aarleen had a stick tucked into the waist line of her skirt, and her right hand grasping the end tightly. The captain also noticed Renee holding what appeared to be a broom stick with no bristles in her left hand. She looked as if she was grasping it tightly as if she was prepared to defend herself.

Captain Grossman turned his attention back to the papers and nodded approvingly. "Here, Sergeant, please return these papers. They look to be in order."

"Listen, Mrs. Duran, I saw a schoolhouse up the road and I noticed the name of the teacher on the plaque, Reuben Duran. Is Reuben Duran your husband?"

"Yes he is," answered Renee, proudly.

"And he's the local school teacher?"

"The best," said Tommy Deans, just as prideful.

Captain Grossman nodded and continued, "And you believe he was arrested because of his neutrality between the Union and rebels?"

"Yes."

Captain Grossman nodded and cleared his throat. "Please answer me this honestly, Mrs. Duran. If the Union can secure your husband's release, would he claim allegiance to the Union?"

Knowing Reuben was probably already in Petersburg against his will by now, Renee stepped down from the porch to speak directly in front of Captain Grossman. "When my husband is released, he will claim allegiance to anyone who will leave us alone, and may God have mercy on those who don't because my Reuben won't."

507

Captain Grossman nodded again, "Very well, Mrs. Duran." His tone turned pleasant as he continued. "I don't see any problems here, but you can expect frequent visits from me as the area inspector. I'll note you have been cooperative and I'll investigate as to why your husband was arrested, and see what we can do to get him released."

"I would appreciate that, Captain. Have a good day."

With that, the captain tipped his hat and nodded to the sergeant.

"Come on you men. On to the next house," said the sergeant.

Everyone remained outside watching the soldiers walk toward the main road.

"What do you make of her?" asked the sergeant to Captain Grossman once they made the turn onto the road.

"Well, she's not lying, but her husband is definitely associated with the military in one way or another. I believe that husband of hers trained her on interrogation tactics. Her answers were short and to the point, not providing anything except what was asked."

"So you believe their claim of neutrality?"

Captain Grossman paused in the walk causing the sergeant to stop the soldiers.

"Did you notice how Mrs. Duran and her daughter were dressed?"

"Yes sir."

"Did you also notice how the two had sticks with them?"

"I did, but figured them to be tools of some sort."

"Sergeant, I was stationed in the Far East before the war broke out. There was only one place where I saw such form of dress the mother and daughter were wearing and that was in Japan. It was the men who wore such clothes."

"Dresses on the men, sir?"

"Not dresses, Sergeant, but soldiers known as samurai. Those 'tools' the mother and daughter had were primitive weapons samurai use. The samurai of Japan are known as some of the fiercest soldiers in the world. I have seen them in training, but I was unimpressed. If Mrs. Duran's husband has had experience with the samurai, I would so dearly enjoy crossing swords with him and making her a widow for my pleasures.

狼

"Okay, you two, come with me," said a Confederate lieutenant with two non-commissioned officers standing behind him.

Since their arrival to Petersburg, Reuben and Sergeant Warren were moved from the rail car into a holding pen with other prisoners. Reuben was the only prisoner shackled with both wrist and leg irons.

"Hold on," said one of the NCOs with a huge bruise on his face and a bandage wrapped around his forehead. He tossed a length of rope to Sergeant Warren and said, "Tie up the slack in his wrist irons."

Reuben chuckled and said, "Oh, I remember you. Sorry about that. Nothing personal, you know. I was only trying to get back home."

The NCO replied by shaking his head and suddenly stopped, wincing in pain.

"Gee, they keeping you in irons, and not me, kind of makes me feel unappreciated," joked Sergeant Warren as he tied up the slack in the chain of Reuben's wrist irons.

"Shut up you and come with me," said the lieutenant.

They made their way out of the holding pen and along the rail tracks. Reuben stumbled with the weight of the leg irons. Sergeant Warren helped him along the way. The rail yard was filled with thousands of Confederate soldiers awaiting transport further up North. Along the way, there were bivouacs set up and separated into branches of service such as infantry, cavalry, artillery, and one for the navy.

The lieutenant led them into the bivouac designated, "infantry." Into a long row of large wall tents, they walked for a quarter of a mile until they reached a tent street designated "Doyle's Brigade." They were halted by two guards. After the lieutenant presented a document, they were allowed to pass. Onward they walked until they reached a large wall tent with Brig. General Doyle's name printed above a large tent fly attached to the tent. The tent flaps were shut.

"Hold them here," said the lieutenant. He made his way into the tent.

The NCO with the bandage eyed Reuben fiercely.

Reuben noticed and said, "You know Sergeant, you really shouldn't be walking around with a head injury. What I did to you was minor, but you not giving it time to heal can cause it to become fatal."

"Shut... ouch. Shut up you!" replied the sergeant.

Moments later, the lieutenant emerged from the tent along with Captain Stevens.

"Reuben, I'm very sorry. I hope you can forgive me. I've done everything I can," said Captain Stevens.

"Deep shit, Todd. Deep shit," replied Reuben.

"Come on Sergeant Warren, you're with me," ordered Captain Stevens.

"Sir, what about Reuben?" asked Sergeant Warren, concerned.

"We'll be seeing him shortly," answered Captain Stevens.

Sergeant Warren nodded and started walking off with Captain Stevens.

"Seeing me shortly? I don't like the sound of that, Todd," said Reuben.

Reuben started humming the cherry blossom song he and Aarleen would sing together until he noticed the bandaged sergeant still eyeing him. "Seriously, Sergeant, you really should be off your feet."

"What do you make of this man, Colonel?" asked General Sidney Doyle.

Inside the general's wall tent, General Doyle sat behind a table, serving as his desk, beside a cot. Standing off to the side of the general's desk stood Colonel David McFerrin, commander of the 68th Virginia Infantry Regiment, the man who had Reuben arrested, and standing near the tent's flaps stood Major Jonathan Lander, the general's adjutant.

Colonel McFerrin cleared his throat, thumbed through his notebook, and said, "He's a mystery. He lacks respect toward authority, yet he has a commanding authority. He used textbook firing line procedures and showed calmness in front of the enemy, as if he had much experience. Maybe even too much experience for what appears to be a simple country school teacher.

"He also showed vast concern about the men's safety. Although he obviously should not have been involved, and escorted along with the other civilians, he stayed behind making sure every man crossed the river. He even carried a wounded soldier across the bridge before it was destroyed.

"And when it was all over, he tried to return home before I had a chance to discuss his actions."

"What do you mean, 'tried to return home,' Colonel?" asked the general.

"Well sir, as I said, I wanted to know more about him so I had a couple of provosts bring him to me, but he fought them off. More provosts went after him and he fought them off just as easily. I sent more to retrieve him and he kept fighting. I never saw anything like that before."

"How many provosts did he fight off?" asked the general, curious.

"Thirteen."

"Thirteen?! Unarmed?" asked Major Lander, moving beside the general's desk.

"He injured five more when he became conscious after they had knocked him out. I still have him in irons."

"Why didn't you just let him go?" asked the major.

"There's something about this man that may be useful."

The general shook his head and let out a little laugh. "How does Captain Stevens know this Mr. Duran?"

"Apparently when he was a lieutenant, his platoon was camped out near Mr. Duran's farm during the initial mobilization. Some of his men, including the sergeant who was arrested with Mr. Duran, rowed a boat across the bay into Chesapeake City to rescue some of his family. By the sounds of it, Yankee militia got to them first and killed his mother and brother-in-law, and raped his sister. The sister later died when he got her back home."

"Jesus Christ," exclaimed the major.

General Doyle picked up a sheet of paper. He asked, as he kept his eyes to the page, "So, you have no idea why he was out there on Gamby Road during the withdrawal, Colonel?"

"None whatsoever, sir."

"Hmm, I just might. You're correct, Colonel. This Mr. Duran has a military background. Graduate from VMI, participated in the Mexican campaign. One of four selected for early commission because of that campaign. Discharged for unknown reasons, and disappears, until now. Did you know he has a brother?"

"No sir."

The general lowered the sheet of paper and continued. "Well, he does, and he's in the Confederate Army. He joined when Virginia left the Union, and signed up with the 66th

Virginia. Highly educated, graduated from William and Mary Law School. He was commissioned a Major for the 66th's staff. Since then, he has been reassigned to the judge advocate department in Richmond. I believe this Reuben Duran is trying to get his brother to come back home, especially after what happened to his kin."

"Desertion, sir?" asked the major.

"Possibly."

"We can't have that! Not now that this war has barely begun," said the colonel in an angered tone.

"Calm down, gentlemen," said General Doyle. "What do we have here now? Two brothers, one civilian, obviously with a military background and a vast amount of experience, and another who is in the army and completely useless."

"Sir, are you thinking..." began Colonel McFerrin before the general interrupted him.

"Yes I am. Call him in and don't speak unless I prompt you... and follow my lead."

"What do you suppose is going to happen to him, Cap," asked Sergeant Warren to Captain Stevens as they made their way to their company.

"I don't know, Max," answered the captain, none too formally. "I still don't know if I saved him from execution. Although, I did have a feeling when I was pleading Reuben's case to the general, the general knew a little more about him than he led on."

"I don't know, Cap. It's very unfair. He practically saved the brigade and now he might get executed for it. What a hell of a way for it to end like this for Reuben Duran."

"REUBEN DURAN!!! Did I hear you say, Reuben Duran?!" said a gentleman in his early to mid-60's wearing a medical apron.

Startled, both Captain Stevens and Sergeant Warren looked at the gentleman with curious looks.

"Yes sir, I said Reuben Duran," said Sergeant Warren. "Do you know him?"

"Reuben Duran, *THE* Reuben Duran, *THE* Reuben Duran from Norfolk, son of Aaron Duran?"

"Yes, that's him," replied Captain Stevens.

"Well, for the love of grits and gravy! I haven't heard of Reuben Duran in over 15 years! Where is that scrappy rascal?!

"He's at General Doyle's headquarters."

"Hot damn and son of a bitch! That boy is still alive thank the maker!" said the older gentleman and made his way toward the command tents in a hurry.

Reuben walked into General Doyle's tent with the two NCOs, one at each side. The general eyed Reuben with a hard look, but Reuben was unimpressed.

"Are those irons necessary?" asked the general.

"Yes, they are," replied Reuben before any of the others could respond.

"And why's that, Mr. Duran?" asked the general, rather amused.

511

"Because I may possibly start ripping heads off, starting with yours," said Reuben, turning his focus toward Colonel McFerrin.

Colonel McFerrin's expression went from stern to worried.

"Now, now, there won't be any of that. What we have here is an interesting dilemma, Mr. Duran."

"What the hell is the dilemma? Just let me go home. I'll even walk from here."

"Why did you help with the withdrawal back in Norfolk?"

"It wasn't my intention. I was looking for someone."

General Doyle nodded and rose from his chair. He walked around his desk and went to the sergeant with the bandaged head.

"Give me the keys, Sergeant," said the general.

The sergeant looked at the general dazed and confused as he handed the general the keys. He began to reel and fell to the ground backwards, blood starting to seep from his nose.

"I told him he shouldn't have been on his feet," said Reuben, looking at him with disregard.

"He's dead," said the other sergeant.

"Did you do this, Mr. Duran?" asked the general.

"I caused his injury, but not his death. That was his stupid-ass mistake."

"Take him out and see to him, Sergeant."

"What about the prisoner, sir?"

General Doyle looked at Reuben with sincere concern. "I'll see to him," he replied.

The sergeant followed the general's order and once out of the tent, the general started to unlock Reuben's wrist irons.

"Sir, I don't think that's a good idea," said Colonel McFerrin as he eyed Reuben with caution and stepped back a few paces.

"As I see it, Mr. Duran is a regrettable detainee, not a prisoner. I trust we can conduct business in a civilized manner."

The general unlocked the irons and let them fall to the ground. Reuben stood rubbing his wrists as the general returned behind his desk and sat down. Once he sat, the general tossed Reuben the keys to unlock the irons around his ankles.

"Tell me, Mr. Duran, was it your brother you were looking for on the road leading to Sewell's Point?" asked the general.

"What of it?" Reuben asked, unlocking the irons from around his ankles.

"Your brother isn't cut out for this type of work, is he?"

"He'll get himself killed and many others with him."

"Yet, you're cut out for this type of work. I see it in your eyes."

Reuben began to laugh at the general's comment.

"What's so funny?" asked the major.

"Tell me, general," asked Reuben, ignoring the major, "do you know of the code?"

"Code? What code?" asked Colonel McFerrin, confused.

"Bushido."

"No, never heard of it. What is it?" asked the general, curiously.

"A warrior's code so intense, it's beyond your understanding. A code neither one of you are capable of understanding with your barbaric form of warfare. It's a code of ultimate honor and loyalty. A code to die for. My brother has no code, just as neither one of you do. What you see in my eyes, you cannot comprehend. What you see isn't a soldier in front of you. What you see is life, an essence capable of taking life away for the protection of others in one moment, and the next, becoming one with harmony."

"That's very profound, Mr. Duran, but find it, shall I say, unattainable in this day and age," said Colonel McFerrin.

"You'll be one of the dead before this war is over," replied Reuben to the colonel's comment.

"Why you over bearing…"

"Let's cut the crap," said Reuben, interrupting the colonel. "What do you want, General, as if I didn't already know?"

"Very well then, straight to the point, I like that. Okay, Mr. Duran, your service to the Confederacy in trade for your brother's. I assume you don't want him to get hurt or killed and we just can't let him go. We need hard fighting men with experience, not men who think just because they went to a fancy university they can lead our way to victory."

Reuben looked around the tent and saw a chair. He brought it in front of the general's desk and sat down. The colonel and major looked at him with contempt. "I've seen graduates from West Point get men slaughtered just as easily as fancy university graduates."

"Granted," said General Doyle, "but still, does your brother have what it takes to go into battle?"

"What if I say no?" asked Reuben.

"I understand you have a family. A wife and child. It could be very easy to sign my name to execution papers for sedition, what you're being accused of now. I can add murder of the sergeant along with that charge. If that were to happen, what will become of them?"

"You have just expressed what Bushido isn't about, General. But my family is my life. My brother is the only remaining blood of my mother and father besides me, so both of us must survive, and I have the best chance to survive in this environment. If it comes down to your despicable sense of dishonor against my honor, I'd be willing to take on your challenge, for my wife and daughter."

Completely discarding Reuben's accusation, General Doyle said, "Then it's a trade, your service for your brother's."

"A trade it is. And after this is all over, you and I, as well as your two minions, will have one hell of a serious discussion. That's if all three of you are still alive after this senseless war is over."

"You're brash, Mr. Duran, but I like you. For now your brother is safe as a baby in a crib in Richmond, but I'll get word to him about our arrangement. Until then, you're now a commissioned captain in the Confederate Army. I'm assigning you to assist Captain Stevens of Company C of the 68th Virginia Infantry. Major Lander, take Captain Duran to get processed."

"Yes sir."

Just then, the tent flaps whipped open and in came the older gentleman who earlier questioned Captain Stevens and Sergeant Warren about Reuben.

"I heard Reuben Duran is here! Where is he?" demanded the older gentleman.

Reuben turned in his seat and his eyes went wide. He rose quickly knocking over the chair onto Major Lander's shins.

"Doc Lawrence Chelmsford! Geez oh geez oh geez, where the hell have you been?!" asked Reuben excitedly, stepping quickly to embrace his old friend.

"I should ask you the same question! Did you fall off the ends of the earth?"

Bobbling his head back and forth, Reuben answered, "Actually, that's not far from the truth."

"Last time I saw you was, ah, let's see, ah yes, autumn ball of '47. That Asian fellow followed after you. His name was, ah…"

"Genda-San, Akagi Genda-San. I followed him to Japan when he left. Stayed there for seven years. He did wonders with me. I blew up my last cannon against rogue samurai over there, believe it or not."

General Doyle, Colonel McFerrin, and Major Lander watched the two dumbfounded. The general tried to get a word in a few times, but Doctor Chelmsford and Reuben wouldn't stop talking.

"That girl you were smitten with, ah… Renee, that's it. She came with your father when you went home from Fort Monroe, what happened to her?"

"Married her, seven years ago come this July. We have a daughter, Aarleen, my little cherry blossom."

"Capital, my boy, grand and capital!"

"What are you doing here, Doc? Being hoodwinked into joining this idiotic cause, like me?"

"Hoodwinked? Oh no, boy, medical advisor for the Confederacy, Sanitary Commission for the Union, a rather unique position you can say. Not trusted by either side, but with still enough pull to keep certain people in line for humanitarian sake. I'm a civilian now these days. Just an old country doctor outside of Petersburg. What's happening to you?" asked Doctor Chelmsford, very concerned.

"I was a civilian also until a few minutes ago when I traded my service to this cause for my brother's."

"Oh no…"

"GENTLEMEN!!!" called out General Doyle. "Mr. Duran, your processing, if you please. You and the doctor can reminisce later. We have a war to win, remember."

"Sorry, Sid. Come, Reuben, I'll go with you," said Doctor Chelmsford.

514

"Actually, Doctor, Mr. Duran will be quite busy for a while, but stay. I wish to talk to you about, ah, the medical supply situation," said General Doyle.

"Of course Sid. Reuben, I'll catch up with you later."

"Doc, the sooner the better. I believe I'm going to be with the 68th, Company C."

With that said, Major Lander pulled Reuben by the sleeve out of the tent.

"Reuben Duran. Good ole Reuben. He looks grand. Married with a daughter, good on him, very good," said Doctor Chelmsford, with pride before he turned his attention to General Doyle. He sat in the chair Reuben occupied. "Okay, Sid, crap on the medical supplies. You want to know how I know Reuben."

"Do you and he share the same mind, Doctor?" asked Colonel McFerrin.

"You can't fool men who have walked in the valley, Colonel. The hell with your elephant, what Reuben has been through would make you shit your drawers and crawl back into your mother's womb even if she is dead and buried."

"You served with him in Mexico?" asked the general.

"He's the reason for my research, the human psyche and the combat soldier. That boy you had in front of you was one of four VMI cadets commissioned after their third year for the Mexican Campaign. He's the lone survivor of his platoon after a botched attack on an artillery battery. His platoon was referred to as *'the lone wolf platoon'* because of the assignments they were given. Reuben has killed more men face-to-face in combat than either of you three could ever imagine.

"What's this about seven years in Japan?" asked General Doyle.

"If that's true, and that Mr. Akagi got his hands on him, then he has had samurai training. Not too certain what that is. Not much information is available about that, but what I learned from Mr. Akagi, the samurai are some of the most fearless warriors in the world. They have the ability to slaughter their enemy with no emotional sense, and then cradle a baby with gentleness when the killing is all over."

"Preposterous!" said Colonel McFerrin. "If this is all true, then how would you suggest we handle this Reuben Duran?"

With a very serious tone, Doctor Lawrence Chelmsford said, "Don't make him your enemy."

狼

It took the remainder of the morning and early part of the afternoon to process Reuben into the Confederate Army. Much of that time was spent on paperwork Reuben found unnecessary and redundant. When it came to outfitting Reuben with a uniform, he refused to wear one except for a plain black shell jacket with his rank on the collar, which he folded over, and he removed all the buttons.

Major Lander led Reuben to the armory to draw arms. The major turned into the gate leading to the armory while Reuben kept walking by.

"Excuse me, Captain Duran," said Major Lander with a hint of distain in his voice. "Don't you want to draw side arms?"

515

"Unless you have a katana made by Isamu Gorou, then there's nothing of any use to me in that armory," replied Reuben, feeling regret about the loss of his jo and tanto.

"Come on now, Captain Duran, not even a sword?"

Reuben turned to the major with that mischievous gleam in his eyes. The same gleam Renee finds so adorable. "You don't like me do you, Major? That's all right, it's probably because I challenged your honor so many times this day and you've yet to show courage to defend it. In Japan, you would be honor bound to commit seppuku... that's ritual suicide by cutting open your belly for your cowardice."

"Are you calling me a coward?!"

"You and your entire family," said Reuben, turning his back to the major.

"That's it! I've had enough of your arrogance!" cried out Major Lander as he drew his sword with his right hand and thrust it at Reuben's back.

Reuben casually sidestepped to his right as the major's blade went past his body. With his left hand, he swiftly grabbed hold of the major's right wrist and raised the major's arm and turned inward and under his arm taking hold of the major's right hand in both hands. With a swift draw upwards on the major's right arm, he easily relieved the major of his sword, and then brought him down to the ground. Reuben released the major's arm and with the tip of the blade, nicked Major Lander's cheek as he rolled over onto his back.

"Pretty cowardly to attack an unarmed man when his back is turned to you, Major Lander, don't you think? And by the way, if I do ever need a sword, I can relieve you of yours, if necessary. Now enough of your processing shenanigans, I need to have a serious discussion with Todd Stevens."

The walk to the 68th's regimental camp was a short walk for Reuben, but a very long one for Major Lander. Reuben still had the major's sword and when they arrived at the regimental camp, Reuben presented the major his sword in the same manner a samurai would present a katana.

Major Lander timidly took his sword and replaced it in its sheath and stood looking at Reuben.

"Well, if you're waiting for me to salute you, Major, the hell with you. You tried to kill me back there. That's twice you and I will have a serious discussion when this is over. That's if the Federals haven't killed you first," said Reuben, and then turned to look for Captain Stevens.

Reuben roamed the camp until he reached the company street labeled "C". He turned down the street and saw a wall tent at the end and made his way toward it. Reuben drew much attention from the soldiers who recognized him from the incident at the bridge.

"That's the one. He's the one who saved our bacon," whispered a young private to his comrades as Reuben strolled by.

"Todd, get your ass out here!" called out Reuben when he reached the company command post.

The tent flap opened and a delighted Sergeant Warren stepped out.

"Reuben! Hey, Cap, it's Reuben!" exclaimed the sergeant.

"Shit, that's what I was afraid of," said Captain Stevens with a combination of relief and fear.

"Good heavens, Reuben, it's good to see you. What happened with the general?" asked Sergeant Warren.

"That's a long story, Max, but to put you at ease, I'm released, so to speak."

Captain Stevens emerged from the tent.

"YOU!!!" exclaimed Reuben.

"Wait, Reuben, before you get all worked up, I have something for you," said Captain Stevens as he reached into his haversack and pulled out Reuben's tanto and handed it to him.

Reuben took it quickly and drew the blade. "You're either very brave or extremely stupid to give this back to me, Todd."

"Hold on," said Captain Stevens quickly and stepped back into the tent and came back out holding Reuben's jo.

Reuben smiled, replaced the blade, and tucked it into his Akagi burgundy obi behind the knot. He motioned for the captain to toss him the jo. The captain obliged and Reuben caught it in his right hand and twirled it behind his back to his left and looked to see the familiar Okami kanji burned into the wood.

"Todd, you have just redeemed yourself."

"What happened, Reuben?" asked Captain Stevens with concern.

"That's captain, Captain," said Reuben, unfolding his collar up to reveal the three captain stripes and folded it back down. "I traded my service for my brother's, and have been assigned to assist you with your company."

Reuben, Captain Stevens, and Sergeant Warren sat beneath the fly of the captain's command tent. Reuben told the two about the discussion he had with General Doyle and Colonel McFerrin, and how he ended up mustering with the Confederate Army. Through a combination of trading his service for Monroe's and the threat of execution for sedition and murder, Reuben found himself in their company.

Reuben felt it rather odd, he being commissioned a captain and assigned to a company already having a captain, until Captain Stevens briefed Reuben of the company's current condition.

"During the withdrawal from Sewell's Point, several of our junior officers were captured leaving only two who led two of the firing lines at the bridge. With the 68th being mustered into service late, our manpower is less than other regiments. Our company has 74 soldiers, 5 NCOs, and 4 officers, including you," briefed Captain Stevens. "We were the last regiment to be put into Doyle's Brigade. We're a part of Major General Hogan's Division. We're currently awaiting the arrival of two more regiments, and then we march to the Northern part of the Peninsula. With General McClellan landing more and more troops at Fort Monroe, General Johnston sees a push by the Yankees to take Richmond from the south."

"We're the only company shorthanded in the regiment," added Sergeant Warren.

"That's an understatement, Sergeant," said a young first lieutenant.

"Ah, gentlemen, come and let me introduce you to our newest member of our staff," said Captain Stevens. "Men, this is Reuben Duran. Reuben, this here is First Lieutenant Matthew Peaks, and that gentleman there is Second Lieutenant Albert Rallins."

The two junior officers immediately recognized Reuben from the incident at the bridge.

"Mr. Duran, it's an honor," said Lieutenant Peaks.

"What do we owe the pleasure of your visit, sir?" asked Lieutenant Rallins.

"Gentlemen, Mr. Duran has been assigned to our company. He's a captain and will be assisting me," stressed Captain Stevens.

The two lieutenants quickly came to attention and saluted.

"Oh, knock it off you two," said Reuben. "You look like idiots. Sit down."

As they took seats, Sergeant Warren rose to leave.

"Where are you going, Max?" asked Reuben.

"I thought y'all would like to be left..."

"Stay, Max," interrupted Reuben. "Sergeants are the backbone of the army, and the company's fists. Besides, I trust Sergeants more than I trust officers."

The captain and two lieutenants looked at each other questionably. Reuben noticed.

"Listen, Todd, I'm not here to take over your company. I have been, for all intents and purposes, blackmailed into this army of yours, so if I have to fight your war, I'm going to fight it my way."

Reuben gave Lieutenant Peaks his attention. "You think we're undermanned. I believe we have too many men. The less men we have, the less we have to be responsible for. The less men we have, the quicker we can mobilize. This company is outfitted for a one hundred head unit, so that means we can draw supplies for one hundred troops. We will be well supplied so make use of that."

"But we don't have enough officers and men to form the amount of platoons we need," replied Lieutenant Rallins.

"The hell with platoons. Split up the men into two units. We have nearly two of everything. Samurai never fought apart. We fought as one and with this type of war, that had better well be the way we fight... as one."

"Fight as one?" asked Captain Stevens. "What do you mean by that?"

Reuben grunted in thought. "Why did you join the Confederacy, Todd?"

"Because my home state left the Union."

"Here, here," replied the two junior officers.

"I take it you all were U.S. Regular before Virginia seceded?" asked Reuben.

All four nodded.

"Loyalty by the sounds of it. Loyalty is noble, but what are you loyal to? Now that's the dilemma. I guarantee you most men carrying a musket in this company, hell, maybe the entire army, on both sides, have no idea what they're fighting for except the sense of adventure and glory. Well, gentlemen, the men of this company got a huge dose of reality at the bridge. War means death, not glory.

"I'm not fighting for Virginia or the Confederate cause. I'm fighting for my survival because as much as you believe in this cause, deep down, you know the Confederacy doesn't have a chance. My survival is my family's survival. My survival depends on your survival and none of us will survive if we don't fight as one. Win or lose, what it all comes down to is being able to walk away with a sane mind, and a family to return to."

Noticing a familiar face walking his way, Reuben rose from his seat and said, "We can talk more about this later, but for now, I need to talk to an old friend."

Without waiting to be dismissed, Reuben walked away to meet Doctor Chelmsford.

As the officers watched Reuben walk away, Sergeant Warren couldn't help notice their looks of disgust in their faces.

"You think he's a traitor, don't you?" asked Sergeant Warren. "Well, after going with him into Chesapeake City to rescue his kin, that man in nothing of the sort. His loyalty is with his family. He may not be a true Confederate, but there's one thing I'm certain of. I'm sure as hell glad he's on our side and in *our* company. Now if you'll excuse me, I need to tell the men there are going to be some serious changes."

狼

"Reuben, my boy, how are you?" asked Doctor Chelmsford as Reuben met up with him. "General Doyle told me all about your… arrangement."

"Bastards. I doubt they'll keep their end of this deal," replied Reuben.

"Come now, lad, it's me, the one who pulled you off that field at Villanueva. You can cut that tough skinned exterior. I didn't know Mr. Akagi too well, but I knew enough he wouldn't want you to lose your focus, and your focus is your family."

Reuben placed his hand on the doctor's shoulder and nodded. He looked and noticed an empty tent and led the doctor to where they could talk out of sight.

"You're right, Doc. Thank you for reminding me. Genda-San would probably be disappointed with me. I've let anger drive my actions. I miss them, Lawrence," said Reuben as his eyes filled with tears, something the doctor never saw Reuben do before.

"The last time I saw them was on the other side of the river watching helplessly as I was being dragged away. Although she knew it was impossible, I saw Renee try to swim across to help me. She nearly drowned. If it wasn't for Noah taking her back to the river's edge… Renee must be going out of her mind from worry, and my little Aarleen is probably using all her strength helping her to be calm," said Reuben, as the doctor noticed a great amount of concern in his expression.

Reuben's reactions were fascinating for Doctor Chelmsford to witness, whereas before, Reuben's reactions were out of the norm, icy and hard. They were still icy and hard he noticed, but there was a spark in his eyes. A spark of happiness, a spark of love, love from the girl he misses so much, and the daughter they both share.

"Tell me, Reuben. Tell me your story. After I last saw you at the autumn ball of '47," pleaded the doctor.

For the next several hours, inside the dark tent with the campfire's glow as their only light, Reuben recited his story to the doctor in vivid detail. There were parts where both laughed, and there were parts where they cried. It was beyond any tale the doctor ever heard and was joyful he played a small part in Reuben's recovery by introducing Reuben to Akagi Genda-San.

"That's an epic story, Reuben," said the doctor when Reuben finished, "Epic, and the best part, a romantic story of love."

Seeing Reuben still emotional thinking of Renee and Aarleen, Doctor Chelmsford moved closer to Reuben and placed his arm around his shoulder. "Tomorrow, I'll leave for Norfolk," he said.

Reuben looked at him curiously, "Norfolk, why?"

"To tell your Renee and Aarleen you're well. To tell them what you're doing for your brother. And to tell them you will survive once again to be in their lives forever. You and I are not like these tin soldiers surrounding us. We have walked the valley. Granted you have walked it more than I have, but I know, Reuben. Seeing tasks and deeds you had to do, I know and understand. That makes us brothers, war brothers. And as your brother, I'll deliver your message to reassure your family you will return."

Feeling guilt, Reuben said, "I can't ask you to do that. You're too…"

"Old? Is that what you're about to say? Well, just hold your tongue right there. You didn't ask me in the first place. Reuben, you have given me something I never thought possible. You gave me insight as to my own father's grief. You have enabled me to understand why he ended his life the way he did, and encouraged me to help others like yourself. No, Reuben, you didn't ask me. This is my crusade… and I'm not as old as I look. I can still kick some ass."

Reuben laughed and his eyes brightened up causing Doctor Chelmsford to show surprise. He was amazed at Reuben's recovery. During the entire time he knew Reuben back during the Mexican Campaign, he could never remember seeing Reuben smile except when he thought of Renee.

"Very well, Doc," said Reuben as he pulled his tanto from his obi. "Give my Renee and my Aarleen my message, and also give them this to know I'm all right."

Reuben removed the extra-long burgundy sageo cord from the saya of his tanto, cut it in half, and handed the two halves to the doctor. Doctor Chelmsford took the two lengths of cord as if they were sacred objects.

"Tell my family, we're going to pass this test."

狼

I see your face when I look in the mirror
The day you were taken from us will not tear us apart
Lived through worse we have and still we survived
Yet there is an emptiness left within my heart.

I see your face when I look in the water
When you last returned you said to respect the gods of above
But your travels say never rely on them
Strong am I outside for our daughter's sake
But come save me on the inside for it is you that we love.

Finding her mother asleep at the kitchen table with her chest of written passages and pages spread before her, Aarleen read Renee's latest page lying next to her ink stained hand.

Renee could not sleep for the past few days, but emotional fatigue took over her body causing her to drift into sleep after writing her passage. It seemed like ages since she and Reuben had been separated for more than a day, but this separation was significantly different. Unlike previous separations which were chosen, such as when Reuben went to VMI and Japan, this separation was not. This time Reuben was stolen from Renee, and she felt violated. She was angry at the Union for causing the entire disturbance having recently ripped their family apart, and she was angry at the Confederacy for stealing her husband away.

After reading her mother's passage, Aarleen cried silently. For the first time, Aarleen had a sense of her mother's pain she felt not knowing if Reuben was alive when he went away to war, and the seven years he spent in Japan. Her precious seventh birthday present had been taken away from her, and she too felt violated and wanted to strike back hard, but didn't know how. Seeing her mother emotionally exhausted, asleep at the table, made her realize she needed to be Renee's pillar of strength. Before it was her Aunty Lucy that was Renee's pillar, but with her gone, it was then, Aarleen realized, that was her means to strike back. To stand by her mother's side, to be her "precious little angel" as her GrandDa used to call her. They were going to get through this separation together and welcome her father home, together.

Aarleen gathered herself up emotionally and gently shook Renee. "Mama. Wake up, Mama, and let me help put you to bed."

Renee woke slowly and looked up to her daughter and gently cupped her face with her left hand and smiled.

"Are you hungry, Mama? Do you want me to make you something?"

"Oh, my sweetie, what are we going to do without him?"

Lifting her mother's head from the table, Aarleen looked into her tired eyes and said, "We're going to survive, Mama. We're going to pass the test Da told us about. That's what he would want us to do. You quoted Musashi in your passage, *'Respect Buddha and the gods without counting on their help.'* We have to rely on ourselves, Mama. You and I, May, Henry,

Noah, and yes, even Ever. Da has trained and prepared us for this test and we must keep going just like he would want us to."

Renee felt pride in her daughter. She straightened up in her seat and cleared her throat. Taking Aarleen's hands in hers, she said, "You may not remember what you said after we came home from GrandDa's funeral because you were very young, but you asked, *'won't we be making GrandDa sad if he's watching us be sad?'* GrandMama said that was the wisest thing she ever heard, and it came from you. What you said now is just as wise and you're right, sweetie. We need to be strong for your Da because I know, in my heart, he's being strong for us right now, wherever he is. Thank you, my precious Aarleen for reminding me we have the strongest and bravest man in our lives, and we must be just as strong and brave as him."

Aarleen took Renee into her arms and they hugged tightly.

"Tell you what, sweetie," said Renee, "let me sleep for a few hours and wake me. Then we'll go to the schoolhouse and paint the window ledges like your Da and I planned so he won't have to do them when he returns."

"Excellent, and we could fix the lose floorboards by the side door too," added Aarleen.

Aarleen told Renee she would see to her pages and chest after she helped her to bed and then start the day, as if it were any other day on the Duran farm. Aarleen let Renee sleep longer than a few hours because she felt her mother needed the rest. When Aarleen woke Renee, they collected materials they needed for painting and loaded them into the wagon.

May was very pleased to see Renee back to her old self, back-boned and with spirit in her face. Everyone wanted to go to the schoolhouse to paint, but someone needed to remain behind in case Federal troops came to inspect as they had been lately. May and Evergreen stayed behind while Henry, Noah, and Paul Cutler went to the schoolhouse. As they were leaving, Tommy Deans was walking up the lane to visit with Paul and Aarleen, and see if he could be of any help to the farm. He immediately climbed into the wagon once Aarleen told him they were going to the school to do some painting and repairs.

"We should stop and pick up Janet Lindsey along the way. I know she would want to help," said Tommy Deans.

Paul Cutler remained on the Duran farm after he delivered Reuben's message. He was severely exhausted from the day on the bridge that included bringing Reuben's message from the rail yards in the city. Renee also felt it was best for him to stay until things became stable for him to travel to his home in Princess Anne County. In the meantime, he provided much needed and appreciated help around the farm, except in the hidden plots deep in the woods. Renee and the others kept the plots a secret remembering what Reuben said about the less people knew, the safer everyone would be.

Captain Grossman and his troopers had come by several more times since the day Reuben was arrested by the Confederates. His visits consisted of visually inspecting the farm, making sure no Confederate activity was present, and tracking the area population. However, Renee felt he had other intentions for his visits since it was the Duran farm he took the most interest in. He questioned Renee about Reuben's travels to the Far East on every visit.

"How do you know my husband has been to Japan?" asked Renee when Captain Grossman first questioned her about his travels.

"Your clothes. Samurai, are they not? Your daughter's wooden sword, what the samurai use to train with. If your husband has been with the samurai, I would enjoy to cross swords with him. I'm quite the swordsman myself, skilled at West Point and fencing champion even in my first year there. I have seen those samurai savages use their fancy swords, but I always felt they wouldn't be a match to our superior blades and skills. Only a real man wields a sword with one hand."

Renee was unimpressed and defiant in his obvious intentions with her husband possibly dead as far as he was concerned. He expressed that sentiment to Renee each time he came by.

"You know, Mrs. Duran, I have investigated every avenue and as far as I can figure, your husband has been executed by the rebels for his non-allegiance. I have seen it many times."

How could you have seen it many times since the war barely started and all you do is ride up and down our road, safe and sound, you pompous jackass, thought Renee.

"Your stand on neutrality could also be harmful, but I can make life much easier for you," he said with a seductive leer. "I'd hate for anything to happen to a beautiful, young widow."

"I'm not a widow, Captain! Now do your job and leave."

"Very well, my pretty, but remember what I said. My services reach far beyond inspecting the population."

"That will not include inspecting me, Captain."

The work they did on the schoolhouse was a welcome diversion. Renee and Aarleen, dressed in kosodes and hakamas, worked on painting the window ledges, while Henry repaired the loose floor boards. Noah and Paul attended to several desks in need of cleaning and sanding, while Tommy Deans and Janet cleared away overgrowth from the backside of the schoolhouse. When Renee was finished with her windows, she began making a list on the blackboard of other items needing attention as Janet came to help Aarleen. These schoolhouse projects, along with the normal farm routine, would be more than enough activity to keep everyone busy rather than sitting and wondering.

It was near late afternoon when they began gathering the tools and cleaning the paint brushes when Riley began barking. Everyone stopped what they were doing and looked at each other. As quickly as Riley started barking, he suddenly stopped.

"Wait here," said Renee.

She walked to the front door and carefully peered outside. Riley was no longer on the porch, so she slowly stepped outside. When she was outside, she saw Riley in the schoolyard being petted by an older gentleman.

"Excuse me, who are you?!" Renee asked in a manner of authority.

"Ah, Miss Renee, or should I say, Mrs. Duran? It sure has been a long time. My, you have grown into a very beautiful woman."

"Do I know you, sir?" asked Renee, but this time more inquisitive.

"I should hope so, my lovely lady. Lawrence Chelmsford, Doctor Lawrence Chelmsford, at your service my lovely lady."

"Geez oh geez oh geez!" exclaimed Renee as though she was looking at a ghost. "Doctor Chelmsford, what are you doing here?!"

At the sound of Renee's tone, everyone began filing out of the schoolhouse, and watched as Renee ran and took the doctor into her arms.

"I'll tell you what I'm doing here, sweetheart. I bring you a message from your husband, Reuben."

Renee brought her hand to her head, and stumbled backwards. She nearly fell over until Aarleen came to her side to steady her.

"Who is this man, Mama?"

"He's a good friend of your Da, sweetie. This is Doctor Chelmsford. He and your Da served in Mexico together. Doctor Chelmsford, this is our precious daughter, Aarleen."

Doctor Chelmsford turned to Aarleen and placed his hands gently on her shoulders and said, "Has anyone ever said you have your father's nose?"

Aarleen giggled and replied, "All the time. Where's my Da, Doctor Chelmsford?"

"Please, call me Lawrence. It's been a long time since I have been formally called Doctor. Your father is safe, well, strong, and causing a lot of hell for those who took him, if you will pardon my language."

"Not at all, Lawrence," said Renee, joyfully. "That sounds like my Reuben, and I wouldn't want him any other way. What have they done with him?"

Doctor Chelmsford went on to tell Renee, Aarleen, and the others of Reuben's predicament from when he first walked in on the discussion General Doyle was having with Reuben, to when the doctor told Reuben he would come and bring this message. He assured Renee her husband was fit and put the fear of an angry wolf into those who have caused his dilemma.

"Ha! I swear that Reuben of yours has told almost every senior officer over him when this war is over, and if any of them survive unscathed, they had better leave Virginia before he gets his hands on them."

Renee felt very reassured, but still violated, and she expressed that to the doctor who sympathized with her. Renee also could not help but feel anger toward Monroe for causing Reuben to go off chasing after him. It wasn't until the day when Monroe tried to kill Reuben in front of everyone when his feelings toward Renee were known. She wondered why he never pursued a relationship with anyone and believed he thought his work was too important and wanting to be a great lawyer as Aaron, he didn't have the time.

No, I won't allow him to make me feel guilty, she thought. He knew my heart only belonged to Reuben.

"Well, I hope his brother appreciates what he's doing for him. After the way he tried to kill Reuben, I doubt it, but I can understand my Reuben's feelings about family," Renee said.

"Kill Reuben, his brother? Whatever for?" asked the doctor.

"Apparently while Reuben was away in Japan, his brother harbored hidden feelings for me and hoped he would never return. When he did, Monroe saw any chance disappear. There was never any chance, Lawrence," replied Renee.

"You have to admire your husband's convictions though. Any other man would have washed their hands at the whole thing and be done with it, but not Reuben. You have a good man, Renee."

Renee looked at Aarleen sitting next to her. She placed her arm around her shoulder and said, "We both have a good man."

"Oh, I nearly forgot," said Doctor Chelmsford as he reached into his haversack. He pulled out the two lengths of sageo cord and handed one each to Renee and Aarleen. "Reuben told me to give these to you to show he's okay and will return. Do you know what they are?"

"He cut his segeo cord from his tanto in half for Mama and me," said Aarleen looking at her piece of cord lovingly.

Renee brought hers to her nose and breathed in. She rose from the step of the porch, and used the cord to tie the sleeves of Reuben's kosode up, just as Reuben does. Feeling proud of her husband, she looked at Doctor Chelmsford and said, "Lawrence, we're already passing this test. Come home and stay with us. As Reuben's war brother, you're welcome in Reuben's home."

狼

The ride back to the farm was filled with Doctor Chelmsford telling everyone about Reuben's defiant attitude. Along the way, they stopped and waited as Tommy Deans walked Janet to her house. Renee thanked her for coming to help and assured Janet she was welcome to help with the other schoolhouse projects. Once Tommy Deans returned, they continued home.

"I swear this is what he said, *'they may be making me fight their war, but I'm going to fight it my way.'* Boy, that husband of yours has them second guessing their decision," continued Doctor Chelmsford, humorously.

He cautioned Renee there may be a possibility Monroe might not be allowed to return right away. Reuben told the doctor he doubts Monroe would go home voluntarily and it would take Reuben himself to force him to go home. Until then, he intended to keep himself away from the fighting as much as possible. Reuben was adamant to his superiors, and the doctor, this wasn't his fight or his cause. His cause was his family.

As they made the turn from the road onto the lane leading to the farm, Riley began barking most furiously causing Henry to stop the wagon.

"What is it, Riley?" asked Aarleen, pulling her bokken out from under the wagon bench.

"Move along, quickly!" came an order from one of Captain Grossman's troopers riding up behind the wagon startling everyone. "I said move!"

Henry snapped the reins and they rolled on toward the house where several dismounted troopers were standing in the front yard. When Henry reined the team to a stop, Aarleen told Riley to run. He did so leaping off the wagon, and made his way toward the creek and to the hidden plots as he was trained to do by Aarleen. The soldiers gave Riley no notice.

May and Evergreen emerged from the front door and ran to the wagon and met Renee as she climbed down.

"It's that Captain Grossman, Renee. I tried stopping him, but he entered the house," said May.

The mounted trooper rode his horse close to Renee.

A sergeant came out of the front door, followed by Captain Grossman with Reuben's Kutto in his hand.

"What the hell do you think you're doing with my husband's Kutto?!" yelled Renee, running to the captain.

Noah, Aarleen, Paul, and Tommy Deans jumped off the wagon and started to follow, but were stopped by the other Federal soldiers in the yard.

"Kutto? I believe this is a katana, poorly made one at that. The idiot who made this sword made the blade backwards," said the captain mockingly.

"Shut up you and give me back my husband's Kutto!"

"Now, now, Mrs. Duran. I'm only doing my duty. No citizens in the occupied area are to have any weapons of any sort and that includes badly made Japanese swords. However, if this sword means that much to you, perhaps you and I can, shall I say, come to some personal terms," said Captain Grossman as he leered at Renee with sexual intent.

"You heard Renee!" called out Noah. "She said give her back Reuben's Kutto, you Union son of a bitch!"

The mounted trooper hit Noah with the butt of his carbine causing Noah to fall hard to the ground. Renee and Evergreen ran to Noah's side as Doctor Chelmsford quickly climbed off the wagon to care for him.

"Bring her to me," ordered Captain Grossman.

One of the soldiers grabbed Renee by the shoulders lifting her to her feet.

Renee stepped off to the side and entered in between his arms, stepped behind him and shifted her hips throwing the soldier off of her.

The mounted trooper heeled his mount to move toward Renee when Aarleen called out as she tossed Renee her jo, "Mama, here, catch!"

Renee caught it in her right hand, twirled it behind her back to her left and swung striking the horse solid in its chest. The horse reeled on its hind legs causing the rider to fall off with his foot stuck in the stirrup. The horse, in pain, started to gallop away toward the road, dragging its rider along with it.

Renee recovered quickly, and without looking behind her, she thrust her jo to the rear striking a soldier in the face. Another soldier came at her from her front and she brought her jo in a downward strike, but the soldier caught the jo under his arm and held it firm. Using the soldier's strength as an anchor, Renee used the jo as leverage, leaped off the ground, and kicked the soldier solid in his face with both her feet, landing well centered ready to strike the next soldier who dared challenge her.

Two soldiers, one drawing his sword, made their way to stop Renee until Aarleen, from out of nowhere, jumped in front of them. She raised her bokken of New England hickory, and made a straight cut hitting the first soldier squarely on the left shoulder. A distinctive snap was heard when the wood met bone.

"You little bitch!" called out the soldier with the drawn sword and swung it at Aarleen. Aarleen easily blocked the blade with the tip of her bokken pointing down. She swiftly rotated her body using her attacker's weight against him while flipping his sword over. She was in perfect striking position to his chest, and she did so. Ribs snapped as her bokken made contact with the soldier's chest.

Renee had just finished striking a soldier in the chest with her jo when Aarleen saw another soldier about to grab her mother from behind. Using the blunt side of the bokken blade, Aarleen shouted out a loud kiai gaining the soldier's attention and using a low up-striking block, she wedged her bokken hard into the soldier's groin. His scream caused birds to take flight from nearby trees.

Renee gave Aarleen a proud, approving nod, twirled her jo behind her back, and faced around. Mother and daughter stood back-to-back with jo and bokken at the ready to fend off more attackers.

The sergeant raised his carbine and took aim at Renee.

BAM!!!

Doctor Chelmsford fired his police-sized colt revolver hitting the sergeant in the thigh causing him to drop his carbine and fall onto the ground grasping his leg as he screamed out in pain.

Paul quickly ran and picked up the carbine and aimed it at the captain as Tommy Deans grabbed a shovel from the wagon, ran, and stood behind Paul covering his back.

"Enough!" yelled Doctor Chelmsford. "Captain, give Mrs. Duran back her husband's sword, now!"

"And just who might you be?" asked Captain Grossman, smugly.

"Doctor Lawrence Chelmsford, U.S. Sanitation Commission. Low on the food chain, but high enough to put your ass in a sling for what you've caused here this afternoon. Now do as I say!"

Captain Grossman let out a smirk and slowly walked to Renee who still had her jo ready to strike.

"Looks like your husband taught you and your daughter a thing or two," he said as he handed Renee Reuben's Kutto.

Maintaining defensive focus, Renee laid down her jo, cautiously took Reuben's Kutto, and quickly tucked it into her obi keeping eye contact with the captain.

527

"If the rebels know of his talents, I'm sure they have him in their ranks and I do hope I'll have the opportunity to meet him on the field of battle," said the captain as he attempted to place his hand on Renee's cheek.

Renee quickly took hold of the captain's wrist and hand and swiftly slid back and downward taking his balance. She rotated his hand and wrist to where his thumb was trapped against her chest. Bowing and dropping her center, she caused the captain to yell out in agonizing pain as she rotated his wrist toward his face bringing him to his knees.

"When and if that day ever happens, may God have mercy on you because my Reuben won't," said Renee and released the captain's wrist. "Now pick up your men and get off my husband's farm."

Renee watched closely as Doctor Chelmsford saw to all the wounded Renee and Aarleen caused. He first tended to Noah, bringing discontent from Captain Grossman.

"I want you to see to my men first, Doctor, and not this darky. After all, it was those two who put these men out of commission," he said motioning toward Renee and Aarleen.

"Really now, Captain," replied Doctor Chelmsford. "Aren't the Negros why you're fighting this war? Are you not their benefactors now?"

The doctor laughed as he looked at Noah.

"What's so funny?" asked the captain, perturbed.

"You do realize Renee could have broken your sword hand and put you out of commission permanently, don't you?"

"Nonsense!"

"I believe she didn't break your wrist with hope you will meet her husband face-to-face, Captain," said Noah. "Why take away his enjoyment of defeating you. That's if you ever find enough courage to actually do any fighting like a real soldier."

"Why you nigger, son of a bitch…"

"Now, now, Captain, remember, you're their saviors. Noah here has hit upon something."

"What's that?"

"In my position, I can easily get word out to Renee's husband about what has happened here today, and when he gets released from being under arrest, Reuben will be out there waiting for you. I believe my position in the commission might allow me to arrange that."

狼

Before Captain Grossman and his bandaged men left the Duran farm, Doctor Chelmsford made it clear to the captain he would file a grievance against his actions. The charges ranged from removal of personal property to assault against innocent civilian citizens. The doctor assured the captain he would have his day on the field, and if irony had any part in it, he would face Reuben just as he hoped.

After a good dinner, the doctor looked over Noah once more. He also checked on Renee and Aarleen and found not even a scratch on them. As he did so, he snickered and chuckled.

"What's so funny, Lawrence?" asked Renee as he was seeing to Aarleen.

"After watching you this afternoon, there's no denying you and Reuben were made for each other. And you Miss Aarleen, you are truly the spawn of your father. Not only do you have his nose, you have his spirit as well."

"Da taught us well, Doctor Lawrence. I can't wait to show him the technique I invented today. I'm going to call it, the Okamikabu nutcracker strike. You should have seen him fight off all those soldiers trying to take him away from us. He would have gotten away if they didn't cheat."

Doctor Chelmsford nodded and thought of what he witnessed of Reuben and his platoon during the Mexican Campaign. "I have seen him in action, my dear, and you need not worry about your father. Not only will he find your uncle, he will return."

At the end of the day, and as everyone was turning in, Renee asked Doctor Chelmsford if she could have a talk with him. He agreed and they sat at the kitchen table.

"Is it true you can get a message to Reuben with your position, Lawrence?" asked Renee.

"It may take some time because I would have to deliver it myself, but yes, I can."

"What is it you actually do?" Renee asked, very inquisitively.

Doctor Chelmsford let out a little laugh. "It's quite interesting actually. By trade I'm a medical physician and when I did my time in the army, I provided detailed research on combat related mental illness which at first was disregarded. Then another medical colleague within the government medical panel of research showed interest in my work, and provided me with, shall I say, a certain amount of clout within the National medical community. That led to a position on the newly formed U.S. Sanitation Commission. As with you and Reuben, I remain neutral in this war and that allows me to serve as a medical advisor to the Confederacy. I like to refer to myself as being an ambassador to both sides in the name of medical health only, and I seem to be accepted by both sides, within limitations of course. One of the functions I can perform without question is the relay of family messages to either side. You see Renee, in this war, there are families fighting against their own members. Brother against brother, father against son, and so on. It's difficult, but I can cross sides to provide only humanitarian aid and comfort."

Renee nodded very interested.

"Yes Renee, I'll take Reuben a message. It's my job. That's what this is all about, isn't it?"

"Yes, Lawrence," said Renee as she began to breakdown and cry.

Doctor Chelmsford scooted his chair next to her and consoled her by placing his arm around her shoulders. "Believe me, Renee, seeing to Reuben, and his family is, how may I put this, my redemption for not doing enough for him when we returned from Mexico. I think its fate that has given me a second chance."

Renee let out a chuckle. "Fate, my husband believes only in fate. It was taught to him by Mr. Akagi."

Doctor Chelmsford smiled and said, "Before I start back to deliver your message, I want to make sure that captain won't bother or interfere with your family. That means I need to go into the city to file a grievance. I'll have to report Reuben is being held as a prisoner of war and not actually in the Confederate Army… which is theoretically correct. For all intents and purposes, Reuben has been illegally coerced and impressed into service. However, if the Federals find out he is in arms against the Union, they could confiscate the farm and have all of you evicted.

"Then I need to start looking for Reuben's regiment. Fortunately I know exactly what regiment and company he belongs to. When I left, they were mobilizing toward Richmond and I can easily travel up the peninsula this time. In the meantime, you and Aarleen get your message together, and any items you think he may want or need. I know he desires your image he had with him in Mexico."

Renee smiled and then she turned serious and asked, "Would you be able to take him his Kutto?"

"That's not possible, Renee. It may be deemed as me being an armed combatant and in my position, I should be unarmed. I'm not supposed to have this small police pistol on my person, but as you saw today, it comes in handy if needed. By the way, what's so special about that sword? What I gather from what the captain said, it's useless," said Doctor Chelmsford.

Renee described the purpose of Reuben's sword and why it was designed in its fashion. She told of how Akagi Genda-San went to a skilled sword maker to have it made and that a sword such as his Kutto had not been made in over a thousand years, and then, only in myth.

"Reuben told me a while back, in the ancient writings of the Kojiki and the Nihon Shoki, the Kutto was referred to as the Sword of Spiritual Power. It was a sword used for the protection of loved ones and the innocent. It's deadly side to be used only as a means of last resort. Besides my image, I know my Reuben desires to have his Kutto tucked in his obi," said Renee with a hint of disappointment. "But I understand, Lawrence, and I don't want you to be put in a position that may get you into any trouble or endanger your life."

Doctor Chelmsford placed his hand on Renee's and with a look of regret he said, "I wish I could, Renee. I'm very sorry."

"How about if I take it to Reuben?" asked Noah, speaking from the doorway of the kitchen. "There's no rule about me just happening to be walking in the same direction as Dr. Lawrence, is there? After all, I'm a free man, free to roam this country."

"No, Noah, I can't ask you to do such a thing," said Renee, startled.

"You isn't asking, I'm saying. A long time ago when we took Mr. Akagi to the train station, he told me one day Reuben would need me to be his retainer. That day has come," said Noah, boldly.

"But Noah, you don't have any idea what happens in war," said Renee.

"Neither do you, Renee, but Reuben needs that Kutto of his and I'm the one who can take it to him. I was his best man at your wedding, and I intend to be his retainer during this time in need."

"What about Evergreen, Noah? She's not going to just let you leave."

"She's going to have to understand family comes first, and you and Reuben have been my family long before she entered my life. She will have to finally decide if she wants to be a member of this family or not."

Noah came and sat on the other side of Renee and looked at her with sincere loyalty. "Reuben's family has provided me with a wonderful life that includes freedom, Renee. Henry, at one time said freedom is worth fighting for. Now is my chance to actually show my gratitude to Reuben's father for making me free, and also to you for finding that law to make me free."

"Oh, Noah, you don't have to do this."

"Renee, how can I truly be free unless I earn it, not only for me, but for May, Henry, and also Evergreen? Please, let me take Reuben his Kutto."

石
水

In the year of our Lord, 1863, a romantic tale continues.
Two brothers, forgiveness, and closure...

Where's Monroe

Hogan's Division linked up with the rest of the Confederate Army under the command of General Joseph E. Johnston in June of '62. Doyle's Brigade was immediately mobilized toward The Chickahominy River where fighting had been continuing for the past several days. For the first time during this campaign, the Union forces under the command of General George B. McClellan seemed to be stymied by the Confederates.

The 68th Virginia was placed into the line along the Chickahominy River to hold a position virtually impossible to defend. It seemed to be a portion of the field neglected by the Confederate commander, and as an afterthought, decided to deploy troops in that area once Union forces were observed crossing the river from the south.

Colonel McFerrin was keeping a close eye on the Union movement and came to the conclusion the position his regiment held could easily be overwhelmed by the vast number of Federal troops. Messenger after messenger arrived telling the colonel to hold and under no circumstance was he to withdraw.

This day of battle seemed to be commencing by the sounds of the guns coming from the south. Colonel McFerrin nervously eyed his pending situation with concern. Knowing if he could not hold this position, Union forces could flank the entire Confederate Army and possibly make an assault on Richmond. His failure could cost the entire Confederate cause to be lost.

Calling a council of all his company commanders and officers, Colonel McFerrin commenced to state the importance of holding this position rather than forming any plan of action. He was praising his company commanders for being good leaders, but not giving any guidance of how to hold this position. The colonel was throwing out one colorful patriotic phrase after another gaining his officers' confidence, and installing them with pride they could hold this position and share in victory with the rest of the army. All his company commanders and nearly all his officers were taking it all in, including Captain Stevens. Yes, all the officers were feeling Colonel McFerrin's momentum, except for one.

While the colonel was addressing the other officers, Reuben watched as the Union troops were slowly crossing the river and constructing earthworks along their encroachment. When the colonel was finished with his speech making, and the officers applauding and cheering silenced, the only sound to be heard was Reuben whistling the cherry blossom song he and Aarleen would sing.

In the short amount of time Reuben had been assigned to Company C of the 68th, his presence had been one of curiosity from both the officers and men. They heard rumors about

Reuben from the men of Company C who told of his deeds at the Gamby Road Bridge, but nothing substantial as to why an extra captain was assigned to the company. He didn't even look like he was in the army with his unmarked shell jacket, and the absence of weapons except for a stick he carried, and a knife tucked into his burgundy belt tied about his waist. He didn't even have a hat.

"Am I boring you, Captain Duran?" asked Colonel McFerrin in a commanding manner.

"Oh no, Colonel, I find you most amusing. So amusing you made me forget you're going to get us all killed as I was watching those Federals crossing the river and inching their way toward our position."

All the officers turned to look toward the river and saw what Reuben was talking about. Many of them silently gasped as the others looked back to the colonel.

Colonel McFerrin looked toward the river himself and nodded with a stern look on his face. The truth in the matter, he was frightened and didn't know how he could stop an assault if one were made. Trying to maintain his commanding manner, he waved them off as if they didn't matter, hoping his officers would see it as of no concern.

The colonel ordered the officers back to their companies to await orders for a pending plan of action. Colonel McFerrin was concerned if the division commander was aware of the pending threat in front of him. He sent Major Lander to relay his concerns.

"Damn it, Reuben, why must you constantly undermine the colonel? Yes, you were practically forced into the army, but that doesn't mean you have to make us all suffer," said Captain Stevens as he, Reuben, and the company's two junior officers returned to their position in the line.

Reuben was the only one walking in a low crouch while the other three walked erect. "I was only pointing out the obvious and, what the hell, you three want your heads blown off your shoulders, get down."

"Come now, Reuben, all the fighting is coming from the south."

"Oh, and those Federals crossing the river in front of us are coming to trade hardtack recipes, I suppose," said Reuben, keeping his eye's on the Union soldiers moving across the river.

For the first time, Captain Stevens and the two lieutenants took a serious look at what Reuben had been trying to point out. Captain Steven's stomach began to turn and the two lieutenants faces turned pale.

"Hey, Max, what's going on?" asked Reuben as he saw Sergeant Warren running toward them in a low crouch.

"Yankees're building earthworks ahead of our position and advancing, that's what's going on. Right now they're about two thirds company strength."

"Todd, we've got to do something now or we're not going to be able to stop them once they reach full company strength. Miyamoto Musashi once said, *'If you do not control the enemy, the enemy will control you.'* We need to take control whether the colonel realizes it or not, and I don't think he does. One who preaches glory rather than directs does not understand the pending doom that's about to fall."

"What are you suggesting, Captain?" asked Lieutenant Rallins.

Reuben rose slightly over the brush to survey the Union's progress of their earthworks. They were high, but weakly put together. He began thinking of the time he and Tadashi rushed into battle when he saved Akagi Genda-San from the Arata gunman. It was an unpredictable move on Reuben's part, completely impetuous and effective. It caught the Arata gunman by surprise, not to mention Akagi Genda-San.

"Oh, Tadashi, I wish you were here now with your bow," said Reuben silently to himself in Japanese.

"What was that, Captain?" asked Lieutenant Peaks.

"We take control of this situation. Todd, if I can distract them for just mere moments, you can charge the men across the gap, take their works, and push them back across the river."

"What about the colonel? Shouldn't we advise him first?"

Looking up toward the sun's position, Reuben said, "There's no time. Besides, he won't do anything because he's scared. I can feel it in his ki. When samurai see an opportunity, we strike and we strike hard. Now, are you with me, or are you going to sit and wait for those Federals to over-take us?"

"I'm with you, Reuben," said Sergeant Warren without hesitation, "and I can guarantee the boys are too. Come on, Cap, we did good at the bridge and we can do good here."

"Very well, we'll probably be thrown in the stockade, but at least we'll be sitting out this war alive." replied Captain Stevens, reluctantly.

"That's the spirit, Todd," exclaimed Reuben.

"Okay, Reuben, what's the plan?" asked Captain Stevens.

"Plan, what plan? I'm just your assistant, remember? This is your company," said Reuben.

Captain Stevens stood with his mouth gapped open in disbelief.

"I'm kidding, you jackass. I'm just trying to ease the tension. Get the men ready to move, Max. Rifles loaded and bayonets fixed. Matt, you take the far left of the line and Albert, you take the right. Position the other NCOs equal distance along the line. Todd, you wait for my signal."

"What will your signal be?"

"Oh, you'll know it when you see it."

Company C was ready within minutes. Reuben's only direction to them was to make it across the gap as fast as possible.

"We may not beat them, but we'll scare the hell out of them, and hopefully that'll be enough for them to fall back to the other side of the river leaving us with a better defensive position."

Within ten minutes, the company was ready to move.

"I still don't know what you mean by waiting for your signal, Reuben," said Captain Stevens, worried.

"Like I said, you'll know it when you see it. When you do, haul ass."

"Okay," said the captain, still uncertain.

Reuben took off his shell jacket and grasped his jo tightly in his left hand. "Okay, Todd, it's showtime. Oh, and Todd, don't leave me hanging out there or I *will* come back and rip your heart out of your throat."

Reuben rose and looked up to the sun once again and noticed it was at his back. Perfect, he thought as he began walking toward the Union troops constructing their earthworks.

"What in the world is he doing?" asked Lieutenant Peaks, astonished at Reuben's actions.

As Reuben casually walked toward the Union works, he silently said to himself, "Well, so much for trying to keep out of this fight. Please forgive me Renee."

狼

A Union corporal saw a lone man walking toward them carrying nothing but a stick. "Hey, Sergeant, what do you make of that?" he asked his NCO.

The sergeant glanced toward the direction the corporal was pointing and gave an odd look. "Hey, Captain! I got something rather strange over here. You'd better come and take a look."

A tall Union captain strolled alongside the sergeant and corporal and looked beyond their earthworks. He used his hand to shade his eyes from the sun and squinted. He was very curious, took a few steps forward, and hollered out to the lone figure, "HALT RIGHT THERE!!!"

After hearing the Union officer call out to him, Reuben raised his free hand and waved. He kept his pace the same. With no jacket, no hat, and sleeves rolled up, he looked like a lost individual out on a morning walk.

"Reuben-San, the enemy is easily surprised, but not easily fooled. When you try to surprise your opponent, do so creatively," is what Akagi Genda-San once told Reuben during training. It worked at the Battle of Shun Bridge when Reuben faced Arata Goro and shot his crescent emblem off his helmet.

Reuben thought there couldn't be any other creative way to surprise his opponent than by just walking up to him to say hello. His creativity was paying off when he saw the Union captain climb over the earthworks and cautiously begin walking toward Reuben. Lucy would be proud, as she was the most creative person in the world, thought Reuben as he kept walking.

Reuben was about ten yards away from the earthworks when the Union captain said, "Hold it right there. Don't come any farther. Who are you and what do you want?"

This odd circumstance got the attention of all the Union soldiers who stopped their work to watch the exchange between their captain and Reuben.

As casually as a stranger saying hello on a city street, Reuben, with his jo in his left hand rested it on the ground in the ready position. He held out his right hand as if offering it in greeting. "My name is Reuben," he said in a friendly manner.

As the captain stepped within striking distance of Reuben's jo, Reuben grasped the top end of his jo with his right hand, thumb down, drew it behind his head, and using his head as leverage, whipped it around and extended his arm. The jo swung around Reuben's head at a tremendous velocity and made contact with the captain's head, crushing in the left side of his skull with blood spewing from severed arteries. The captain didn't have a chance to make a sound before he died.

With the captain down, Reuben sprinted toward the earthworks and leaped off of a grounded branch springing him into the air. Rotating his body in midair, he landed well centered on his feet behind the sergeant. Reuben thrust his jo into the sergeant's back causing him to bend backward. Reuben grabbed him by the face and pulled him down and struck the sergeant with his jo square in the face crushing in the sergeant's nose.

The corporal quickly stepped up to Reuben with his bayonetted rifle and thrust it toward Reuben's midsection. Reuben easily stepped off to the side and grasped the muzzle end of the rifle with his left hand, dropped his jo, and with his right hand, unfixed the bayonet, and thrust it into the corporal's neck.

From his side view, Reuben saw another attacker coming at him from his right side. Reuben pulled out the bayonet from the corporal's neck and thrust it into the abdomen of the attacker. Pulling the bayonet free from the attacker, Reuben threw the bayonet at the nearest Union soldier wedging in deep in the soldier's chest.

Another Union soldier yelled as he charged at Reuben with his rifle. Reuben stepped off to the side, took hold of the rifle barrel, pointed it at an oncoming Union lieutenant, tugged the rifle causing the soldier to pull the trigger and shot the lieutenant in the chest. Reuben took hold of the rifle and slammed the butt end of the rifle into the soldier's chest. The soldier fell back to the ground and Reuben twirled the rifle around and speared the bayonetted rifle into the soldier's groin.

A Union major came at Reuben with a drawn pistol in his right hand and sword in his left. The major fired one shot at Reuben. The shot went wide and hit a Union soldier in the shoulder. Unable to cock back the hammer in time, the major swung his sword sideways toward Reuben's right side. Reuben struck the major's face with the palm of his left hand as he entered in and received the cut of the major's strike with his right hand grasping the major's sword hand. He ducked under the major's arm and swiftly raised it in the air and firmly yanked downward pulling the major's arm out of its socket.

Taking the major's sword, Reuben, in a low wolf-like crouch, sprinted to the nearest Union soldier, in this case a colonel coming from the rear to see what the commotion was all about. Without stopping, Reuben, using his signature Okami no Michi sword style, pounced like a wolf on its pray, decapitating the colonel's head in one swift stroke before he had a chance to ask what was happening.

Landing on his feet, Reuben whipped the sword free of blood and let out a loud blood curdling kiai.

From their vantage point, Captain Stevens and Sergeant Warren watched as Reuben casually walked toward the captain and offered his hand. Moments later, Captain Stevens looked away as Reuben's jo made contact with the captain's head. He looked back in time to see Reuben leaping over the works and landing on the other side taking down the sergeant.

"DAMN!!! That must be the signal, Cap!" exclaimed Sergeant Warren.

"No shit, Sergeant! OKAY BOYS… COMPANY… CHARGE!!!"

The officers and men of Company C raced across the gap toward the Union earthworks virtually unnoticed. It wasn't until Reuben took down the Union major and went after the colonel, when other Union soldiers saw the Confederates charging over the works and attacking the mostly unarmed Union soldiers.

In a panic, the Union troops began to flee back toward and across the river. Seeing Company C making a push, the other companies of the 68th made their own push to drive the Union troops back across the river. In the end, the 68th began using the Union earthworks, fortifying them into their own.

Colonel McFerrin was completely unaware of the assault and was busy pacing in circles deep in thought as to how he was going to defend this portion of the river. Suddenly a musket shot coming from the river caught his attention causing digestive discomfort as he covered his mouth to keep from heaving. He, along with his staff, ran to their vantage point of the river and saw Company C climbing over the Union earthworks and two other companies charging across the field.

Fuming in rage, the colonel heard a frightening familiar yell, a yell he heard at the Gamby Road Bridge. He saw Reuben standing over the decapitated body of a Union officer, sword in hand, and directing Confederate troops toward the river.

Grabbing two of his staff officers by their sleeves, the colonel ran toward the ongoing assault only to arrive as the last of the Union troops crossed back over the river.

"WHAT THE HELL!!! WHAT THE HELL!!! WHAT THE HELL IS GOING ON HERE?!!!" screamed Colonel McFerrin as he rushed toward a group of company officers. "Who the hell ordered this damn assault?"

There was no response except for the shrugging of shoulders. Captain Stevens was about to speak until the colonel said, "Where is he? This has his name written all over it! DURAN!!! Get your ass over her, now!"

"Geez oh geez oh geez Colonel, calm down. Don't you realize there's a battle going on south of our position? All that yelling is going to cause them to come this way, and I don't feel like fighting today," said Reuben with a mischievous glare in his eyes.

Sergeant Warren ducked behind a couple of privates to hide and mask his laughter.

"YOU!!!" cried out Colonel McFerrin as he stomped toward Reuben.

He was about a few yards away when Reuben casually whipped his jo up and rested it over his shoulder. The colonel came to a dead stop nearly toppling over.

The colonel's face was beet red and his nostrils flaring. He was about to speak when one of the colonel's adjutants yelled out, "ATTENTION!!!"

Major General Garvey Hogan rode up along with General Doyle and their staffs on horseback. Major General Hogan rode his horse up along the earthworks surveying the results of the assault and nodded approvingly. He was very pleased and his expression showed a combination of joy and relief, but what pleased him the most was the lack of any casualties of Confederate troops.

Major General Hogan rode back to the gathering of regimental officers and men and asked in a delighted manner, "Who ordered to push those Yankees back across the river?"

Reuben, with an innocent childlike look, casually pointed his thumb toward Colonel McFerrin, suppressing a laugh.

"Is that true, Colonel?" asked General Hogan.

"Ah…"

"Excellent work, Colonel, you may have just saved the entire right flank and Richmond itself! The battle further south is locked in a stalemate, and your action just could have stopped a major shift to the Yankees. Maintain this position along the river and keep them damn Yankees from crossing it again. Outstanding and bully! Let us be off, gentlemen!"

As Major General Hogan and his staff galloped off, General Doyle remained behind. He dismounted and walked to Colonel McFerrin and Reuben.

Captain Stevens and Sergeant Warren, along with the two company junior officers also came and stood side-by-side next to Reuben.

The general had a stern look, but couldn't hold it and chuckled as he shook his head.

"Sir, it was Duran, I swear," pleaded Colonel McFerrin.

"I beg to disagree, General, sir," interrupted Captain Stevens. "It was Company C and ultimately my responsibility as Company Commander. If there are any repercussions for any broken regulations, it is I who must receive them."

"No, Captain, as the General said, excellent job," said General Doyle glancing toward Reuben.

The general remounted and rode off with his staff in tow.

Still breathing hard from anger and beet red, Colonel McFerrin tried to speak, but Reuben held up his hand and said, "You know, Colonel, I hope my wife isn't worrying about me too much because I'm finally starting to have some fun with all this senseless shenanigans."

Reuben turned and walked away singing Aarleen's cherry blossom song.

狼

In their cabin, Noah was packing a haversack as Evergreen watched. She was breathing hard, not in anger, but in fear. For the first time, she felt as if she belonged to a family and the thought of losing the most important part of that family was terrifying for her. It wasn't until this moment as she watched Noah pack she began to have a sense of how Renee must be feeling with her husband being taken away. She must be going through so much turmoil inside, while remaining strong on the outside, Evergreen thought. In Noah's case he chose to go, whereas

539

Reuben was taken away from his wife and child. Evergreen was so happy for Renee and Aarleen when Doctor Chelmsford arrived with the news about Reuben. At least they knew he was well.

"Why, Noah? Why must you go and take that sword to Reuben?" asked Evergreen, trembling.

"He needs it, and a long time ago, Mr. Akagi said Reuben would need me as his retainer."

"What does that mean, retainer? Is that like a slave?"

"No, Ever. Reuben told me it is an honored position to a samurai lord."

"You're talking nonsense, Noah. You have no idea what you are getting yourself into…"
Noah was about to interrupt, but Evergreen continued.

"But in this past year, I have seen how incredible this family has pulled together. Reuben was right, war brings out the worst. Thinking the Yankees were great to fight to free our people, and then see them raise their hands and weapons to Renee and Aarleen, women, that is despicable."

"Not all soldiers are like that, Ever. There are many Union men wishing the best for our people, just as there are many Confederate men also wishing the same. Reuben is one such man, and although he may be on the side keeping our people in bondage, that's not his cause. His cause is that woman and child who defended his family's land."

Noah stopped his packing and walked over to Evergreen and took her hands. He looked deeply into her eyes and said, "One day, Ever, our people will be free, just like us. But until then, we have to see to our own, and seeing to our own includes taking Reuben his Kutto. Renee knows, as I do, he will return, but having his Kutto will guarantee his safe return."

Evergreen took Noah in her arms and held him tightly and said, "As long as it guarantees your return as well."

"Knowing Reuben, he will keep me far away from the fighting as possible," said Noah, to reassure Evergreen.

Renee and Aarleen were sitting under the oak tree with Riley in the middle. Since Reuben had been dragged away, Riley had been staying close to both Renee and Aarleen. He was on constant alert, very seldom wagging his tail in play. He warned everyone when someone was coming up the lane toward the house and kept watch over the hidden chicken coop and animals in the woods.

Mother and daughter were looking over the items to pack in Reuben's haversack for Doctor Chelmsford to deliver to him. They had the items spread out in front of them. They included items he would be in need of such as socks, a couple of shirts, a small sewing kit May had included, a fishing kit Aarleen and Henry put together, some soap and a razor, and even his box of meditating incense.

It would be several weeks until he and Noah would catch up with Reuben. Doctor Chelmsford told Renee it would take time to find him, but assured her he would be found. The

540

doctor also had his reasons to find Reuben. They were brothers of war, and he explained to Renee, that form of brotherhood, to a certain degree, is stronger than blood.

"Remember, sweetie, whatever we send to your Da must be innocent. We don't want to get Lawrence into any trouble," said Renee.

"Right, Mama. I'm going to send him my inrou with the gold coin he gave me when he returned from Japan, so he could wear it on his obi like he said samurai do."

"That's beautiful, sweetie. Let me see it please."

Aarleen handed the inrou to Renee and she opened the little turtle box. She opened her chest of written passages and pulled out the one she written when Aarleen found her asleep at the kitchen table. She began to fold the page over and over and tried to fit it in the little turtle box, but it wouldn't fit. She shook her head and frowned.

"What's wrong, Mama?"

"I wanted to put this passage in your inrou with your coin, but it's too big, even if I keep folding it," said Renee, frustrated.

"I know, rewrite it on a smaller slip of paper and then it will fit."

"I was just thinking that."

"You know what they say, Mama, great minds think alike."

Tearing a piece of paper off of one of her other passages, Renee rewrote the passage and when she finished, she signed her name, something she never did before. She looked at her daughter, and handed her the pen and motioned her to sign it too.

I see your face when I look in the mirror
The day you were taken from us will not tear us apart
Lived through worse we have and still we survived
Yet there is an emptiness left within my heart.

I see your face when I look in the water
When you last returned you said to respect the gods of above
But your travels say never rely on them
Strong am I outside for our daughter's sake
But come save me on the inside for it is you that we love.

With our deepest love,
Renee, your Wickham Girl
&
Aarleen, your Little Cherry Blossom

When they were finished, Renee pressed the paper against another sheet for it to dry. She carefully folded, and inserted it into Aarleen's inrou and closed it. It fit perfectly.

"Well, I guess that's that," said Aarleen.

"Not yet," said Renee as she reached into Reuben's burgundy kosode she was wearing and pulled out his image case Renee sent to him when he was at VMI. The same case with her image he carried to Mexico and Itosai. The case he carried everyday he was away.

She opened it and looked at her picture. She smiled as a tear rolled down her cheek.

"You're very pretty, Mama," said Aarleen as she moved closer to look at the picture also.

"Before your Da went to Mexico, he told me this is his favorite thing in the whole world." Putting her arm around her daughter, Renee pulled Aarleen closer and continued to say, "It's hard to believe this favorite thing of his has traveled to the far side of the world with him. Now he's less than a hundred miles away and is without it. This he must have."

"Oh, Mama, I miss him so much," said Aarleen as she wrapped her arms around Renee and began to cry.

Renee took Aarleen into her arms and cradled her tightly. Riley crawled to the mother and daughter and rested his head on their laps, his ears lowered in sadness.

狼

The evening after the 68th pushed the Union troops back across the river, Reuben went off into the woods. He found a small quiet clearing near a small waterfall feeding into the Chickahominy River. He removed his clothes and sat in seiza underneath the waterfall with his jo in his hands and began to mediate.

He was feeling disappointed with himself. He killed this day. Something he had not done since the Battle of Shun Bridge back in '54. It was a horrible feeling because the deaths he caused this day were not good deaths. He spent the time under the water trying hard to rationalize his actions earlier this day. If the Union troops would have crossed in force, the war could have ended within days, but at what cost? He could have been killed defending an un-defendable position making Renee a widow and Aarleen fatherless. Did I kill today to prevent that, Reuben thought as the water flowed over him.

Water flowing, flowing over stone, I am a smooth stone, smoothed from the water. Renee is my water and, many years ago, she let me go so I could become smooth. A smooth stone is still hard, but smooth against her skin. Please forgive me, my precious Renee, for killing today. I vow I will not kill unless our lives are threatened. Please forgive me, Genda-San, for momentarily losing my way. I am a warrior of good. I am a smooth stone and Renee is my water. She flows over me, keeping me calm, stones and water, my love, stones and water.

Reuben remained under the waterfall for the entire night in penance.

狼

After what was to be known as The Seven Days Battle, the newly named Confederate Army of Northern Virginia began its march north. Although the campaign proved to be a victory for the Union, the Union General in command treated it as a loss. Fighting hard and digging deep, the Confederate Army kept its capital from falling into Union hands. However, a new threat was coming from the northwest.

Under the command of General Robert E. Lee, the Army of Northern Virginia found itself defeating the Union Army around Groveton, Virginia. Unlike the first time the two armies met in this location, this battle lasted more than one day. The result was nearly the same with an overwhelming victory for the Confederate Army.

Doyle's Brigade of Hogan's Division made use of the rail ties as fortifications. Keeping the Union Army from withdrawing in that direction, and nearly caused a full scale retreat like the first time these two armies fought here a little over a year ago.

As promised to his wife, Reuben remained out of this battle. As far as he was concerned, he already done his part by substituting himself for his brother, and pushing back the Federals across the Chickahominy River. Unless his life was threatened within arm's reach, he was determined to keep from killing another man in this war. After all, this isn't my war, he reminded himself time and time again when he saw obvious opportunities to attack and overcome.

Reuben would advise Captain Stevens of his observations and let it go at that. It was Captain Stevens' company and Reuben had no intention to take it over again like he did at the end of the Seven Days Campaign. I'm only acting as an assistant, he kept reminding himself. Besides, he had not heard any news of his brother being discharged from the army. If they were not going to keep their end of the bargain, he felt he should, for all intents and purposes, tag along until they do.

Spending most of his time with Sergeant Warren, Reuben stayed away from the officers for the most part, especially after the second victory on the fields of Manassas. They had become very spirited and confident, over confident as far as Reuben was concerned.

"Remember, Reuben-San, when you win a victory, keep your blade clean and your armor nearby," said Akagi Genda-San many times during Reuben's training.

"They just don't see it, Max," said Reuben. "Forgive me for sounding like a defeatist, but there's no way the Confederacy can last."

"You know, Reuben, there was a time, over a year ago, when we camped near your property, when I would have attacked you for saying such things, not that I would have been able to take you down," replied Sergeant Warren with a chuckle. "But now, I can see it's a lost cause."

"So why are you still here, Max?" asked Reuben.

"Same reason you are, Reuben, obligation."

"Obligation to the Confederacy?" asked Reuben. "Because my obligation is to my family, not the government," he stated.

"No, Reuben, not the Confederacy. The reason I speak of, is them," said Sergeant Warren nodding his head in the direction of the young teenaged soldiers who should be carrying school books instead of rifles. "If not for men like you and me, who's going to look after those boys, definitely not the officers. All they are is wind and smoke. No, Reuben, when I rowed across the bay with you to rescue your kin, I got a huge dose of reality, and the reality is those boys will die if not for men like us who are not stubborn to think we have a chance."

"Want to know the truth about my actions at the bridge and the river, Max?"

"Does it matter?"

"It does to me because I need to be honest with someone and Renee isn't here. The only ones in the army I could trust are sergeants and since you and I have history, the reason I did what I did at the bridge and the river was for my family. I wanted that bridge destroyed so the Federals wouldn't go to my farm and harm my family. If we would have let the Federals cross the river, they would have caved in the flank so I had to take control. I made Todd attack the Federals so that wouldn't happen and I could survive for my family's sake. If that's not selfish, I don't know what is."

"Hey, Reuben, as long as you're selfish, you're keeping me alive too, so remain selfish for that family of yours. That wife and daughter of yours is worth being selfish for."

The deaths of the soldiers at the river still haunted Reuben. All the rationalizing couldn't ease his feelings he had killed unnecessarily. He looked at his jo with disgust. A simple tool handle that used to be a rake was now an instrument of death. The first time he killed with his jo was when he and Tadashi charged into the battle between the Akagi and Arata to save Akagi Genda-San from an Arata gunman. Those deaths were good deaths because it was for the purpose of protecting his friend. The same jo was used to kill a Federal captain, and all for the hopes of creating a diversion. That was not a good death.

He longed for his Kutto. With his Kutto, he could attack and defend without killing. The Kutto was designed for such a purpose. It may maim or cripple, but never kill, unless necessary by the quick rotation of the wrist exposing the razor sharp edge of the blade.

For now the jo will have to do, but Reuben had to make himself aware to use it responsibly, and not like how he did with the Federal captain at the river. The other deaths were also unfortunate, but the captain's death made Reuben feel guilty.

But I understand, thought Reuben. Back in the days of, and after, Mexico, I didn't. That is what makes me smooth and why Renee is my water. Her support has allowed me to understand and live with my actions. I do wish I had my image case with her picture in it.

He longed for the image case, especially now with the spirit of the Confederacy so high. The commander of the army decided to take the war to the North with the hope of gaining foreign recognition to assist in their cause. With the momentum of the Confederacy, Reuben doubted the Union would simply open the doors to their lands and welcome them.

狼

The day the Army of Northern Virginia began its march to cross the boarders into the North was the same day Doctor Chelmsford and Noah departed the farm to look for Reuben. It was a long awaited departure for Renee. For her, the sooner Reuben received his Kutto, the sooner she could feel at ease knowing he had the means to defend himself. Although she knew it would take time for the doctor and Noah to reach Reuben, she still felt a sense of relief his Kutto was on its way.

Before the doctor and Noah departed, Doctor Chelmsford, good to his word, filed a grievance against Captain Oscar Grossman for his actions on the Duran farm. Before he departed, Doctor Chelmsford wanted to be assured the captain would never again step foot on the

544

Duran farm. He had seen the captain's look of lust toward Renee, and although he witnessed firsthand Renee and Aarleen could defend themselves, the doctor wanted to make sure they would be safe from the likes of the captain.

Captain Grossman's defense was weak at best. His overuse of authority was well known, but never brought before the military governor of the region. However, now being addressed by an officer of the U.S. Sanitation Commission, who was an eyewitness of the captain's deeds, made it a serious matter for the governor to deal with.

It was a difficult conclusion for the military governor to come to because Captain Grossman was efficient in his duties, despite his overuse of authority. But with a government official involved in the case, the military governor had no choice but to reprimand the captain, take away his position of area inspector, and assign him to active combat. Within a week, Captain Oscar Grossman found himself assigned to a U.S. militia regiment currently active in the Peninsula Campaign.

Shortly after, the military governor issued an ordinance that all farming and the growing of crops by local farms must cease, and beast of burden confiscated in the occupied areas. It was an ordinance amended from a guidance order from Washington when it was apparent many Southern farms were providing the Confederate Army with food from their harvests.

A week after the passing of the ordinance, the newly assigned military area inspector approached the Duran farm. The inspector was a major recently relieved from combat duty because of a serious injury received during the Peninsula Campaign. A Confederate captain violently pulled his arm out of its socket which had to be amputated. The major, still recovering from his wound, was very strict in his duty, but not to the point of overstepping his bounds. The military governor provided leeway in the ordinance by allowing farms to keep a horse or mule team for transportation, and a small plot of land for self-sufficient farming. The plot consisted of a separate, four square yards of land per individual inhibiting a farm to supplement the allotted food ration each family was authorized on a weekly basis. The major made sure each plot of land was measured out himself, each animal accounted for, and a receipt issued to claim when the rebellion was suppressed.

Henry, Aarleen, and Evergreen quickly hid one more cow and two goats for milking deep in the woods where Aarleen and Noah built the hidden chicken coop and sheltered pens, along with the hidden planting plots. Aarleen and Evergreen brought back nine of the oldest and sickly chickens from the coop for the Federals to confiscate.

When the ordinance went into effect, Paul Cutler decided it was time for him to carry out Reuben's last order for him and go home. He had a small family with just his parents and sister who lived on a much smaller farm than the Duran farm. Not only did he have to carry out Reuben's order, he had to add his number to the allotted land for his family to grow food for their survival. Now that the bridges had been repaired, Henry, along with Tommy Deans, took Paul Cutler back to his home in Princess Anne County in their allotted form of travel, a horse team and wagon.

Tommy Deans had been a huge help to Renee. Not only did he work tirelessly on his own family's farm, he helped with maintaining the schoolhouse as well, often on his own along with Janet Lindsey. He and Paul Cutler became good friends and when it was time for Paul to go home, Tommy Deans asked to accompany Henry.

"Considering Paul is supposed to be my cousin, it would make it easier to get him home with that cover story," said Tommy Deans.

Renee nodded thinking, it's just a type of scheme Reuben would have come up with, and agreed.

As the days rolled into weeks, and the weeks into months, Renee maintained her physical and mental strength by training with Aarleen and Evergreen. Since that one day when Evergreen saw the mother and daughter defend their home against Captain Grossman's troopers, she became involved with their training.

"What seems to look impossible to do is really about finding the right angles, Ever," said Renee when she began teaching Evergreen the first technique Reuben showed her, kaiten-nage.

Try as hard as she could, Evergreen could not do the technique at first. Renee would either escape or reverse the throw and Evergreen would get frustrated to the point she wanted to quit.

"You can't quit, Ever," said Aarleen. "Da never lets us quit and we won't let you quit either. When I would get frustrated, Da would always tell me to close my eyes and breathe out to clear my mind and it works. If you think too much, you can't do it. You have to find that opening no matter how small it is."

Evergreen nodded and again tried to get Renee into the position to throw her, but Renee still kept Evergreen from preforming the technique. Evergreen began stomping around in a circle pounding her head with the palms of her hands. "You two make it look so easy," she said on the verge of tears.

"Come on, Ever. Let's try it once more, but this time don't think about doing the technique, and remember what I said, angles. Reuben says the key is angles," said Renee, grasping Evergreen's wrist.

When Renee emphasized angles, Evergreen's eyes widened.

Evergreen slid in an angle slightly off the center of Renee opening her arm. She saw the opening Aarleen was talking about and entered by stepping in under Renee's arm. Now standing behind Renee, Evergreen raised Renee's arm causing her to bend over and then she saw the angle Renee was emphasizing. Instead of sliding straight back, Evergreen slid back at an angle causing Renee to bend further forward causing no means of escape or reversal. Evergreen stepped forward and using Renee's arm, tossed Renee over and onto the ground.

"YES!!! That's it, Ever! You did it!" shouted Aarleen, coming to Evergreen's side to congratulate her.

Renee came to Evergreen's other side and said, "See, if my sweetie and I can do it, so can you."

"Mama, don't call me sweetie when we are Budo training. That doesn't set the mood," said Aarleen.

"Okay then, what should I call you?" asked Renee with a smirk on her face.

"Okamikabu... wolf cub," answered Aarleen, and then let out a howl which made Riley began to howl too.

Evergreen wanted so much to learn how to use the jo, just as Renee did on the Federals, but Renee told her something she overheard Akagi Genda-San say to Reuben. "Ever, to learn how to fight with a weapon, you must learn to use your hands first. When you fight with your hands, imagine yourself using a weapon, and once you start training with a weapon, train as you don't have a weapon."

狼

HARPERS WEEKLY

OCTOBER 4, 1862

WE illustrate on the preceding page THE ENTHUSLASTIC RECEPTION OF GENERAL McCLLEAN AT FREDRICK, MARYLAND, when he had driven the rebels from the place. A correspondent of the World thus describes the scene:

General McClellan came into the town upon the central road, and such an ovation greeted him! It was very different from Virginia. The people were overjoyed. Flags were displayed upon all the houses. There were all sizes and descriptions; large flags suspended across the streets, and little sixpenny flaglets waved by girls and boys, all of whom had been subject to the general contagion which pervaded everyone.

A PROCLAMATION.

I, ABRAHAM LINCOLN, President of the United States of America, and Commander-in-Chief of the Army and Navy thereof, etc. hereby proclaim and declare, that hereafter, as heretofore, the war will be prosecuted for the object of practically restoring the constitutional relation between the United States and the people thereof in which States that relation is or may be suspended or disturbed; that it is my purpose, upon the next meeting of Congress, to again recommend the adoption of a practical measure tendering pecuniary aid to the free acceptance or rejection of all the Slave States so called, the people whereof may not then be in rebellion against the United States, and which States may then have voluntarily adopted, or thereafter may voluntarily adopt, the immediate or gradual abolishment of Slavery within their respective limits; and that the efforts to colonize persons of African descent with their consent, upon the continent or elsewhere, with the previously obtained consent of the Governments existing there, will be continued.

The campaign into the North came to a halt in Maryland near a town called Sharpsburg. Following the Confederate all-out victory at Manassas in late August, the high spirited troops of the Army of Northern Virginia intended to take the war into enemy territory. General Robert E. Lee's invasion of Maryland was intended to be a dual operation with an invasion of Kentucky by the armies of Generals Braxton Bragg and Kirby Smith.

Logistically, it also served a purpose of taking the war out of Virginia so farms could recover after being stripped bare of food, and possibly gain the support of the Maryland population by being perceived as liberators from their oppressive Union occupiers. However, pro-Union sentiment was overwhelming and civilians generally hid inside their homes or watched in silence as General Lee's army marched through their towns and villages.

Politically, Confederate President, Jefferson Davis, believed foreign recognition and support would increase if the Confederacy won a military victory on Union soil. A victory on Northern soil could possible bring about the recognition and financial support from England and France the South so desperately needed.

However, all hopes of foreign intervention ceased to exist once the campaign was stopped near Sharpsburg. As the Confederate commanders were concerned, the battle proved to be inconclusive. However, it was a strategic victory for the Union causing the end of the Confederate invasion of the North. Although it was not an overwhelming victory for the Union, it was victory enough for Union President, Abraham Lincoln to issue out a proclamation for the freeing of the slaves in states in revolt against the Union. That alone was the last nail hammered into the coffin keeping England and France from entering the war on the side of the Confederacy.

While Hogan's Division was with General Lee's invasion into the North, Doctor Chelmsford and Noah were making their way up north by way of a U.S. Navy warship heading to Baltimore. Besides taking the ferry to Chesapeake City, this was Noah's first real voyage by sea. He was amazed at the vastness of water before his eyes. He felt privileged he was able to experience a view Reuben was able to see many times.

During their travels, Noah assumed the position of Doctor Chelmsford's aide. He carried his haversack along with Reuben's Kutto wrapped tightly in a bedroll Noah kept strapped to his back at all times. So far neither Doctor Chelmsford nor Noah had been seriously searched.

Doctor Chelmsford carried with him his own personal haversack, and the haversack Renee and Aarleen packed for Reuben. They had contingencies if they were ever questioned or searched. Using his position in the U.S. Sanitation Commission, Doctor Chelmsford had the ability to deliver messages and mail to soldiers, thus explaining carrying Reuben's haversack. The one time Doctor Chelmsford was questioned, he simply explained he was bringing the haversack to a soldier. He neglected to mention what side the soldier was on.

Reuben's Kutto was going to be more difficult to explain, but Doctor Chelmsford had an excuse for that as well, if ever confronted. He would simply say it was a specialized medical instrument used for amputations he picked up on one of his travels abroad. This idea came to him after Renee showed Doctor Chelmsford the wooden practice horse and post Reuben sliced through to relieve himself of the stress brought on when he found his mother, sister, and brother-in-law. "You mean to tell me, Reuben did this, with that?" asked Doctor Chelmsford to Renee when she showed him what the sword was capable of. After looking at the sliced practice tools, Doctor Chelmsford shook his head and continued to say, "And that moronic Captain Grossman thought that sword was useless."

Their travels took them to Sharpsburg where they missed the battle by a week, but not the casualties. As a physician, Doctor Chelmsford was obligated to provide any medical assistance he could offer. Noah couldn't understand the delay until the doctor explained to Noah the obligations a physician has when the sick and suffering are in need. He insisted it was a virtue Reuben would appreciate and understand, him being an honorable man himself. Besides, it also aided in their cover story.

As the doctor's aid, Noah had no choice but to assist Doctor Chelmsford in the care of the wounded. It sickened him to the point he had to leave the huge surgical tent where arms and legs were being amputated. Covering his mouth, Noah ran from the tent to vomit. He ran to the end of the tent and dropped to his hands and knees as he heaved. When he finished, he remained on his hands and knees, bringing one hand up to cover his nose and mouth from the foul stench that seemed to be everywhere. He felt something land on his back and drop to the side. He rose to his knees to look at what fell on him. It was a freshly amputated leg. His eyes widened in horror as he tried to quickly rise, only to stumble backwards and fall onto a pile of severed arms and legs causing flies to swarm.

He quickly rose from the pile and stumbled away and ended up in the middle of a temporary recovery area where the wounded awaited transportation for follow up treatment. It was here where Noah heard a conversation causing his sickened stomach to ease.

"I never saw anything like it in all my life. He came from out of nowhere, as if God dropped him in the middle of us armed with only a long stick. He used that stick like it was a part of his body. And fast too, I never saw anyone move so damn fast in my life," said one soldier with two broken legs.

"And none of you could stop him?" asked an orderly.

"No, he had the most terrifying look in his eyes. Those eyes, they were not human eyes. They were the eyes of a…"

"A wolf," answered another wounded soldier with both arms in slings.

"Yes, yes, that's it. That man could have killed us, but he didn't. He held back from that, but he still stopped us cold in our tracks."

"Oh, come on now, you're making up stories. You mean to tell me, one man took on all nine of you armed only with a stick? What really happened to you out there?" asked the orderly with a look of disbelief on his face.

"Listen you sack of shit, Elliot is telling you the truth! That man could have killed us all with his bare hands, but he didn't! He may have crippled us, but he spared our lives!" exclaimed another victim who had all four limbs broken.

"What did he look like?" asked Noah, startling the wounded soldiers having the conversation.

"He was of average size with dark hair and eyes. He wore no form of uniform. I remember a scar across his chest I saw under his unbuttoned shirt. When he was finished, he just looked down upon us, and instead of finishing us off, he left. He could have killed us, but didn't. It was as if he was protecting his men rather than fighting. It's because of him I will never raise my hands in anger toward another man ever again," replied the soldier named Elliot.

"When he was attacking you, did he make any loud noises, you know, like shouts and cries?" inquired Noah.

"Yes, yes he did. Ungodly, blood curdling yells that caused us to cower and run for our lives. Mister, you sound like you know this man. Do you?"

Noah let out a sigh and said, "I hope so. His wife and daughter really need me to find him."

After listening to more of the wounded soldiers' encounters with the man with the long stick, Noah set off to find Doctor Chelmsford.

"Noah, my good fellow, how are you feeling? Better I hope," asked Doctor Chelmsford when he saw Noah from behind.

"Doctor, he was here! Reuben was here! I was listening to some soldiers who had an encounter with him. Reuben made sure they would never fight again."

"Interesting. I overheard a conversation between two officers talking about a man with a so-called broken broom stick dropping men, but not killing them."

"That's Reuben, Doctor! That's what he was trained to do when he went to Japan, only to stop, but not kill. We got to find him."

"Not to worry, my lad. I got us transportation back into Virginia. Apparently the Confederates withdrew back. Two Federal regiments are heading back to Washington to protect the city if the Confederates decide to attack it. There's a medical caravan leaving in half an hour and we ride with them."

Again on the move, back southward, the two messengers traveled with a Union regiment making its way back to Washington. For the month of October, they remained in Washington while Doctor Chelmsford reported to his superiors and provided details of his official assignment only. He was assigned to oversee some of the sanitation conditions of the city, much to both his and Noah's displeasure. It was a task he could not get out of without drawing attention to their desired task of finding Reuben. They had to be very careful with their discussions regarding Reuben and his brother. They were, after all, in the capital of the Union. To have someone hear them speaking about locating Confederates would cause serious suspicion that could land them in detention.

For a while, both Doctor Chelmsford and Noah felt they were trapped until a dispatch called for several regiments to be sent across the Rappahannock River from Fredericksburg, a city between Washington and Richmond. The doctor understood the Federals were planning on taking Fredericksburg.

It was here, Doctor Chelmsford hoped he and Noah would meet up with Reuben. He requested to be released from his duties in Washington to follow the Federal regiments to oversee hospital conditions that were sure to be needed. His request was granted and Doctor Chelmsford and Noah found themselves riding on a medical supply wagon toward Fredericksburg.

The Confederates held the city and heights while the Federals were on the other side of the river awaiting Union engineers to construct pontoon bridges. The Confederates in the city were making a rough going for the engineers with cannon and sharp shooter fire.

This was Noah's first view of actual war and he was both mesmerized and disgusted. To him, it seemed like such a horrible waste of men, no matter what the cause was. He began to think of what Reuben had stressed that one Christmas day when he said his cause was his family, and those who are a part of it. After witnessing the drama before his eyes, that was a cause Noah could agree with.

"I believe I see Reuben's regiment, Noah," said Doctor Chelmsford, looking through a spyglass.

He handed it to Noah and directed him to the location he believed he thought he saw regimental flags of Doyle's brigade.

"One of those regiments has to be Reuben's."

A battle that had begun on Thursday, December 11th, and lasted for several days, ended with the Confederate Army of Northern Virginia striking another victory over the Union Army. And again, Doctor Chelmsford and Noah found themselves stuck on the other side of the river, unable to reach Reuben.

狼

"Oh, did he now?! And just who the hell told him he could replace me? That arrogant…"

Monroe couldn't find the correct word to use to describe his brother without disgracing his mother or father. When word finally reached Monroe about Reuben's agreement to swap Monroe's enlistment for his own, he had a fit. He cursed his brother the entire day when he was given his orders to be discharged.

"Can I fight this? Is this voluntary? Or do I have to cower down to my stupid little brother just because he was in the army before, and I wasn't? You know, he lost his mind after Mexico. Found himself in Japan playing with castles, swords, and sticks. Am I supposed to take this order seriously?"

"Calm down, Major, calm down," said Monroe's superior, Lieutenant Colonel Dempsey, also a well-practiced attorney at law. "You're not the only one to have a self-righteous sibling offer to take their place just because they fired a gun and you didn't. I have two brothers myself, each one saying I shouldn't be in uniform."

"Then you have an idea how embarrassing it is to be told to go home because you're not good enough, but your brother is, especially when he's the youngest," said Monroe with anger, but his tone changed when he remembered overhearing Reuben's stories of the Mexican Campaign when he told them to Akagi Genda-San. "And what's worse, it's true."

Regaining his anger, Monroe began stomping around his desk. "No damn it. I won't go home. I will prove to Renee I'm just as brave a man as my brother and maybe, just maybe, I'll get lucky, and he will finally die leaving her to me."

"Damn it, Monroe. Is this what this is all about, a damn woman?" asked the colonel.

"No! Well, maybe. Hell, I don't know! I'm just so angry to think that little runt of a brother of mine can control my life. Ever since that dreaded day he returned, he became the focal point of the family, and I had to force my presence. Damn it, I became a highly respected attorney graduated from William and Mary, while my stupid little brother went to VMI and became a county outreach school teacher to dimwitted farm children. I have to prove myself not only to him and his wife, but to myself as well, and I can't do that sitting behind this stupid damn desk here in Richmond. Damn it, Colonel, what do I have to do to get into this war?"

"Whoa, hold on, Monroe. What is it we say in our profession about making hasty decisions?"

"Yeah, yeah, be careful what you ask for, you just might get it. But I must at least play a small part in this war. Hell, I was issued that sword and the only person I used it on was my brother."

Colonel Dempsey made a curious look at Monroe after his remark. He shook it off and let out a long sigh and said, "Listen, Monroe, I understand your anger. You're a good attorney, one of the best in this department, and I don't want to lose you. But if you are serious… and out of your mind, I may add, there's a position opening up on General Lee's command staff now in winter quarters near Fredericksburg. Apparently there's need of actual legal work, rather than military justice, regarding the interpretation of military law as it pertains to civilian law, especially if Lee plans another trip back north. The position will not be available until the spring when the army is on the move again."

"I'll take it," said Monroe, not letting the colonel continue.

"Monroe, it isn't going to be like here. You'll be out in the field and possibly near the fighting."

"Don't you understand, Colonel? That's where I want to be. Hell, if my dimwit brother can do it, so can I."

Colonel Dempsey nodded and said, "Very well, Monroe. I'll submit your name to the roster and I'll, 'misplace' these substitute orders."

"Good, Colonel, very good, I appreciate that," said Monroe, feeling good about himself and this decision.

The colonel exited Monroe's office. That brother of yours can't be too dimwitted or stupid if he survived Mexico like my brothers did, thought Colonel Dempsey as he strolled back to his office concerned Monroe's pride might prove his brother right.

狼

As the winter turned into spring, Noah found himself thinking he would never complete Renee's task of delivering Reuben's Kutto to him. He lay on his bedroll with Reuben's Kutto tucked safely under his head between two blankets. Noah began thinking of Evergreen and how her attitude changed from a freed slave with a chip on her shoulder to a contributing caring member of the family. He smiled thinking of the time everyone helped Noah and Evergreen build their cabin. He thought of the day it was finished, just before the winter days turned cold, and they lit the fireplace for the first time.

I'm going to do it. As soon as Reuben and I get back home, I am going to marry Ever, and Reuben is going to be my best man, Noah thought.

Suddenly the tent flap whipped open and Doctor Chelmsford grabbed hold of Noah's foot nearly scaring him to death.

"Quick, lad, the army is on the move! There's complete chaos and confusion around Chancellorsville, west of Fredericksburg. Now is our chance to cross over the lines and find Reuben. Come on, quickly now. Roll up Reuben's fancy sword and let's haul ass. We could go missing without anyone knowing about it."

Noah rose and rolled up his bedroll with Reuben's Kutto tucked into the center tightly. Grabbing his belongings, he and Doctor Chelmsford made their way across a bridge. It was as the doctor said, Federal troops running every which way.

One soldier ran into Noah yelling, "Run for your life! Damn rebels are all over the place!"

Doctor Chelmsford shook his head, grabbed Noah by the shoulder, and pulled him along. He saw an ambulance and asked the teamster if he was heading toward the fighting.

"Not that I have any choice, but yes!"

"Good, I'm a doctor and this is my orderly, take us with you as far as you can, quickly! There's going to be a lot of casualties that will need our help!"

"Hop on then and hold on to your peckers. I got two Virginia quarter horses pulling this wagon!"

Noah helped the doctor onboard and as his right foot cleared the ground, the teamster snapped the reins and off they went. The ride was rough and several times the wagon nearly toppled over, but the teamster kept driving his team, slowing them down once in a while to let them catch their breath.

Although it was late in the day, the sounds of battle were getting louder and it was as the doctor said, chaos and confusion. Federal troops were running in a panic, some fully dressed, some in their drawers and barefooted.

The ambulance stopped in front of a large house and the teamster said, "This is as far as I go, Doc! Hope this is where you wanna be because it's sure as hell where I don't!"

Doctor Chelmsford and Noah jumped off the ambulance and looked all around. "Stay close to me, lad. Both of us could easily get lost in this fray!" called out the doctor to Noah.

Noah grabbed hold of Reuben's haversack strap slung over the doctor's shoulders. He looked toward the large house to see a Union general with his staff looking confused.

"That'll be Hooker!" yelled out Doctor Chelmsford to Noah. "Bet he's going to lose a star over this fiasco! Come on, let's move!"

"Which way, Doctor?" asked Noah.

"The opposite direction all these boys in blue are going! Oh yeah, did Reuben ever tell you about the term, keep your head down?!"

"No, but Renee did!"

"Well, now's the time to keep your head down. Come on, Noah, my lad, hell awaits us!"

狼

"Gentlemen, I have some terrible news to share with you," said General Doyle, solemnly. "Although we have been victorious over the Yankees this day, we did have serious casualties. General Jackson has been severely wounded during the last evening hours."

Nearly all the officers gathered around the command tent were mortified at General Doyle's announcement, many of them gasping and some began to weep silently.

"Apparently, while on a nighttime reconnaissance," General Doyle continued, "General Jackson and several of his staff came upon some Confederate pickets and were mistaken as Yankees and fired upon."

"Ha! That's a shame," commented Reuben with a chuckle from the back of the gathering.

All the officers present looked back at Reuben with utter contempt, as he maintained his look of humor.

"Oh, come on now. Like this hasn't happened before in the past? I know of two instances back in Mexico. What do you expect is going to happen if you go out riding around in the dark in a thick wooded confused battleground? Even Arata Goro, who was a fiend, would never roam in the dark when opposing Akagi samurai were in the vicinity. This isn't the first time this has happened, and I guarantee you this will happen again, and if irony has any part to play in it, probably on this very same battleground."

As much anger the officers felt toward Reuben's lack of condolence toward the news of General Jackson, they could not help but see his point.

Since the incident at the Chickahominy River, many came to view Reuben as an individual cold to the suffering of others, yet sparing the lives of the enemy he came across in battle. Armed with only his jo, he was witnessed by many of his fellow officers as the most aggressive officer they had ever seen, yet he neutralized his opponents by either knocking them unconscious or crippling them. He was one of the few leaders that fought shoulder-to-shoulder with the men, and it was Reuben who seemed to have a keen protective sense when it came to keeping soldiers alive. When one would fall, he took it seriously, more seriously than the loss of a general who carelessly rode in the dark near nervous pickets. Reuben took it as a failure on his part when one of the soldiers under his care fell and he made sure they were well cared for.

Officers of the 68th seemed to give Reuben, as well as the other officers and men of Company C, a wide passage when he or the others happened to walk by. Although Captain Todd Stevens was the company commander, no other officer, junior or senior, dared to cross anyone belonging to Company C because of Reuben. Even the youngest of privates, all they had to say is, *"I'm in Company C,"* and they were either given what they needed or left alone.

There were several officers who wanted to cross and challenge Reuben. After all, he only armed himself with a stick and a knife, he seldom used, tucked in his Akagi burgundy obi behind the knot. However, none of them could summon up the courage to do so, especially once many of them saw he didn't need a weapon to take a man down.

It was during the battle on the Manassas battleground last August when Major Jefferies kept ordering men of his company to charge over their covered position only to be shot down by Federals. Reuben saw the senseless death of the major's men and went to confront him.

"Damn it, you idiot, did you not understand the orders? We are to stand this ground and keep the Federals from withdrawing, not send boys to their death, so knock it off!" yelled Reuben, and turned to return to his part in the line.

As Reuben did so, Major Jefferies ordered another dozen men to charge over their position. Upon hearing the major's orders, Reuben turned around and ordered the men to stand down.

"These are my men, *Captain*! You are out of line, disobedient, and disrespectful to a superior officer!"

"Then court martial me, jackass!" replied Reuben. He turned and again began to make his way back to his position. He heard Major Jefferies pull back the hammer of his Navy Colt revolver.

Very swiftly, Reuben rotated his body to the right and using his left arm to block away the angle of the revolver, he slid it along the major's arm until Reuben's left hand took a grasp of the major's revolver hand. With his right hand, Reuben counter-turned and grasped the revolver and brought it alongside to Major Jefferies right ear. Reuben squeezed the major's revolver hand causing it to fire. Major Jefferies cried out in pain from the blast bursting his eardrum. Reuben extended his arms, throwing the major backward keeping a firm grasp on his hand, which caused Major Jefferies trigger finger and thumb to break, and hang limp from his hand.

"You pull a gun on me ever again, I'll really give you something to cry about, you stupid idiot. Now get off your ass and stop killing your men before they end up killing you."

"Oh yes, by all means, go ahead and cross Captain Duran," warned Sergeant Warren to Captain Rae of Company B. At Sharpsburg, Captain Rae felt he was dishonored by Reuben when he didn't support Reuben's men, and they were nearly overwhelmed by Federal soldiers causing Reuben to take matters into his own hands, bringing embarrassment and shame to Captain Rae. "He won't kill you, but he'll make sure you'll never be able to use your arms or legs ever again."

Regardless of Reuben's lack of confidence in the Confederate cause, its leaders, and the conditions he was serving in its army, every officer in the regiment came to the same conclusion, they were grateful he was on their side.

狼

General Doyle once again called all the officers of his brigade together to inform them of the death of General Jackson from complications of pneumonia. Reuben had no comments to make for his mind was in Norfolk County. Recently, for the past few days after the battle near Chancellorsville, his thoughts of Renee and Aarleen were very strong. He was becoming concerned they may be having difficulties of some sort.

Not my Renee, he thought. She's strong and can take care of herself if she has to, he thought, trying to ease his mind. And my little cherry blossom will stand right next to her mother, he continued to think. However, as much as he tried to put his mind at ease Renee and Aarleen were as safe as they could possibly be, their images were too vivid in his mind with his eyes either open or closed. It was if they were standing in front of him.

General Doyle discussed the pending mobilization northward and the great possibility of another attempt to take the war back onto northern soil. At the mention of that announcement, nearly all the officers gathered began to cheer and holler.

As the general was about to dismiss the officers, Sergeant Warren tapped Reuben on his shoulder interrupting his thoughts of his family, and said, "Hey, Reuben, isn't that the doctor you talked with in Petersburg and your friend Noah, with those guards over there?"

Reuben and Captain Stevens immediately turned to the direction the sergeant was pointing. The images of Renee and Aarleen disappeared as Reuben saw Doctor Chelmsford and Noah being detained by several Confederate guards.

"NOAH!!! DOC!!!" yelled Reuben, startling the officers gathered in front of the general's tent fly.

Both Noah and Doctor Chelmsford easily broke free from their guards and ran to Reuben. They embraced each other joyfully for several moments until Reuben turned very serious.

"What the hell, Noah! You shouldn't be here. This is no place for you. The doc, yes, but not you. Did you bring him with you, Doc?"

"Reuben, please," said Noah, pleading. "Renee, she sent me…"

"What about Renee? Is she all right?! What about Aarleen? Gods of the high mountains, I have had them on my mind lately! What's going on? Why are you here?!"

The three were oblivious to the stares they were receiving from all the officers and men who had been gathered prior to their seeing one another.

"Reuben, my boy, Renee and Aarleen are well. Better than well actually. That wife and daughter of yours took on a Federal inspection team of ten men, and kicked their asses. Renee took on five men and a mounted trooper," said Doctor Chelmsford, excitedly.

"And Aarleen, she broke one soldier's collar bone, another soldier's ribs, and smashed one soldier in the grapes with the bokken you two made," added Noah. "You trained them well, Reuben."

"Well, well. If isn't Doctor Lawrence Chelmsford of the U.S. Sanitation Commission," said General Doyle as he, Colonel McFerrin, and Major Lander walked up on the three.

"And medical advisor to the Confederate Army, may I remind you. Good to see you, Sid," replied Doctor Chelmsford.

"QUIET!!!" called out Reuben, causing the general to look at him with anger. "Noah, you said Renee sent you, why?"

"She sent me to bring you this to guarantee your safety," answered Noah.

Noah unslung his bedroll from his back and lowered himself to his knees. He untied the roll and slowly unrolled the blankets. When it came to the end, Noah retrieved Reuben's Kutto from between the two blankets. He untied the cord and removed the sword from the cover. Reuben's eyes widened in disbelief as Noah presented the Kutto with Lucy's purple ribbon tied to the tsuka in both his hands. Noah bowed his head and said, "Reuben-San, with Renee's love and Aarleen's affection, they send you your Kutto to keep you safe, and to protect those in need of your protection… my Lord."

"Lord?!" called out the brigade chaplain. "What is this pagan ritual going on here?!"

"YAME!!!" exclaimed Reuben, holding his hand up toward the chaplain while keeping his eyes on Noah.

Very delicately, Reuben took his Kutto from Noah's outreached hands. He held it against his heart, closed his eyes, and in a low mellow tone he said, "Hai… Dōmo watashi no kichōna Renī, watashi no saiai no sakura o arigatōgozaimasu. Thank you very much my precious Renee, and my dearest cherry blossom."

Reuben opened his eyes, kneeled down with Noah, placed his hand on Noah's shoulder and said, "And thank you Noah-San, my dear friend. You are truly loyal and I entrust you as my, retainer."

Reuben rose and tucked his Kutto into his obi.

"Y'all better stand back now," said Sergeant Warren with pride. "I've seen that look before."

Reuben lowered himself down in the seiza seated position, closed his eyes, and began breathing in slowly and deeply. Several of the other officers stepped closer, including General Doyle, with curious expressions.

Suddenly Reuben's eyes opened as he leaped from his knees to his feet drawing his Kutto and commenced in the most fearsome, but graceful kata he had done since the last time he held his Kutto under the oak tree with Renee and Aarleen watching.

In hypnotic movements, Reuben twisted and twirled his body as he slashed, cut, and thrust his sword through the air.

The officers and men witnessing Reuben's display were in a state of amazement, many wondering how it's possible for him to move in such a manner.

Closer and closer, Reuben inched his way to the general's tent fly and when he was within striking distance, he made one last thrust, swiftly turned his body, and with a loud kiai, he rotated his wrist exposing the sharpened edge of his sword and looked as if he sliced the center support beam of the fly.

Reuben raised his Kutto over his head and whipped it down to his side and returned the blade to its saya and expressed a childlike grin.

"Noah, Doc, let us go have a talk," said Reuben with happiness as he led them toward Company C's encampment.

With a smug look on his face, Colonel McFerrin said as he and General Doyle walked under the tent fly, "All flash and fancy I tell you. Flash and fancy is worthless."

The general took a closer look at the center beam of the tent fly and noticed a thin cut in the wood. He cautiously touched it, causing the beam to fall apart in half, collapsing the fly on top of both the general and colonel.

狼

Once Reuben, Noah, and Doctor Chelmsford had a chance to have a discussion in private, all of Reuben's fears about his family's welfare were put to rest. Both the doctor and Noah assured Reuben, Renee and Aarleen were quite well. Doctor Chelmsford told Reuben the details of the day Renee and Aarleen defended their home from Captain Grossman, and about the grievance he made in regards of the incident.

Upon hearing of Captain Grossman's attempted advances on Renee, Reuben was near the point of leaving the camp to search out the captain himself. The doctor assured Reuben, Renee didn't allow the captain to lay a finger on her and when he did attempt it, she nearly broke his wrist, but held off.

"Renee had him in that reverse hand trap you've showed me. I told the captain, I believe Renee didn't break his wrist with hope he would meet you out here so you can defeat him yourself," said Noah with amusement.

"What about other Federal inspectors? Surely another officer had to be assigned to that position. What if the next officer is the same as this Grossman, or worse?" asked Reuben, very concerned about his family's safety.

Doctor Chelmsford and Noah looked at each other with humorous amazed expressions. "Well, Reuben, Renee told me about your deep profound belief in fate," said the doctor.

"Yeah, yeah, but what does that have to do with the next officer assigned to that position?" replied Reuben, very anxious.

"Do you happen to remember an incident at the Chickahominy River where you severely wounded a Union major?" asked the doctor.

"That wasn't a good day, Doc. I killed for the first time since the Shun Bridge and they were not good deaths, especially one Federal captain," said Reuben with remorse.

Doctor Chelmsford placed his hand on Reuben's shoulder and said, "Well, Reuben my boy, that major's name is Jonathan MacKay, and he was assigned to Captain Grossman's old position. I'm not going to lie to you, Reuben. When MacKay realized it was you that caused the loss of his arm, he was about to confiscate your farm and evict your family and friends..."

"But?" asked Reuben with a look of worry.

"He became deeply indebted to you when I pointed out, because of an ironic act of fate, you spared his life from further involvement in this war. Although he is still angry at the loss of his arm, he saw my point, even though he wouldn't admit to it," said Doctor Chelmsford very reassuringly.

Reuben's expression somewhat relaxed, but was still concerned as he asked, "This MacKay, he won't take out my actions on Renee and Aarleen or May, Henry, and Ever, will he?"

"I looked into this Major MacKay's background before we left, Reuben," replied the doctor. "He's a decent fellow. Although he's very strict in rules, policies, and regulations, he has taken what I said to heart about you sparing his life when you could have easily taken it. Therefore, he has been giving, shall I say, certain leeway in the way he inspects your farm. He never enters your house or goes beyond the front yard, and he treats Renee with the upmost respect and courtesy," said Doctor Chelmsford.

"Fate is an awesome power filled with irony," said Reuben, to no one in particular.

"Don't worry, Reuben," said Noah as reassuringly as he could. "This Major MacKay is a good man and will not harm Renee, Aarleen, May, Henry, and Ever. Especially after knowing firsthand what you are capable of."

Reuben nodded, still uncertain, but with a better feeling Renee and Aarleen were being watched over somehow. Perhaps it was the way of Bushido they are being looked over. It didn't matter. Reuben still missed his wife and daughter dearly.

After the doctor and Noah brought Reuben up to date with everything that has happened up to the time they departed to find him, Reuben felt somewhat relieved his family was well, able to care for themselves, and had a decent Federal inspector who didn't overstep his authority.

Reuben in turn told them he had not heard anything about Monroe, whether he was discharged or not. He said his superiors seemed to be tight-lipped about the issue. Reuben admitted if Monroe was notified about the substitution order, he would have found a way to avoid it, being that finding loopholes was his specialty, like their father. Either way, he was determined to find Monroe, one way or another, and make him go home even if Reuben had to become a deserter himself and force him to go home.

When all the discussions were over, Doctor Chelmsford put his hand on Reuben's shoulder and said, "With all that said and done, I have saved the best for last."

Doctor Chelmsford unslung Reuben's haversack Renee and Aarleen had packed. All this time, Reuben didn't notice it slung over the doctor's shoulder.

"I believe this belongs to you, my friend," said the doctor as he handed it to Reuben.

Reuben took and quickly opened it. The first thing he grabbed from the haversack was his image case with Renee's picture. Reuben quickly opened it and breathed a long sigh of affection once he saw her image. He closed the case and reached back into the bag and felt another hard object and pulled it out. It was Aarleen's turtle inrou. Joy came to his face as he opened it and saw a folded piece of paper and the gold coin he gave Aarleen, along with Andy. He opened it and read the passage Renee written with both her and Aarleen's signatures on the bottom. I can't believe she signed *'Your Wickham Girl,'* on it, he thought as his eyes began to fill with joyful tears.

Reuben began to feel very emotional and excused himself from the others. With his Kutto at his left hip and his haversack at his right, Reuben made his way down the company street and sat at the edge of the tree line. He retrieved the image case and inrou from his haversack and held them lovingly as he gazed upon the moon.

Elsewhere beneath a large oak tree, a mother and daughter with their four legged guardian also sat, looking up at the same moon.

狼

Within a few days, Reuben, Noah, and Doctor Chelmsford found themselves traveling back northward with the Army of Northern Virginia. After his superb victory at Chancellorsville, General Robert E. Lee led his army in its second invasion into the North. General Lee's army was in very high spirits, and it was his intention to collect supplies from northern farmlands to ease the suffering of war-torn Virginia. He also wanted to gain a major victory on northern soil with hopes it would ease the North's appetite for war and cause more support for the northern appeasement movement.

Although Harrisburg, Pennsylvania seemed to be General Lee's objective, due to a skirmish that would become the largest battle ever fought in the western hemisphere, the Army of Northern Virginia would be battling Union forces defending a small town in south Pennsylvania. It would also be during this battle where two brothers would meet to have a serious discussion regarding their family's future and fate. With all the chaos surrounding him, Reuben's only focus was for his family's survival.

"Move here, move there, I swear, Reuben, my attitude is becoming more like yours each and every day," commented Captain Stevens. "Now suddenly, because some idiot of a general needed a pair of shoes, he diverts his troops to some out of the way shit-burg town and gets his ass put into a sling. Tell me, Reuben and Doctor Chelmsford, was it this bad in Mexico?"

"Boy, it seems to have gotten worse. What say you, Reuben?" replied the doctor.

Reuben nodded in agreement. "Still fighting old war tactics with new war weapons, these inept leaders of ours will never learn. Now you understand why I tell the boys to keep low? It's like Genda-San always told me when he would teach me techniques, *'If you think you look stupid doing it, you are doing it right.'* Yeah, our boys may look stupid crouching low, but we have the least amount of casualties."

"REUBEN, REUBEN!!!" yelled out Sergeant Warren, sprinting down from the head of the column waving a sheet of paper above his head. "YOU GOT TO SEE THIS!!!"

Reuben told Lieutenant Peaks to continue marching the men and stopped as did the doctor, Captain Stevens, and Noah.

"What do you have there, Max?" asked Reuben when the sergeant caught up to them.

Panting and trying to catch his breath, Sergeant Warren spoke between breaths. "My friend, Darrin Frost, you know, the one I keep asking if he has heard anything about your brother? He gave me this copy of the command staff roster. It has a new department listed as Military and Civilian Law Matters Committee. I think your brother is in that department. Here take a look."

Reuben snatched the roster from Sergeant Warren and quickly scanned down the page to where the sergeant mentioned the new department. Noah was the first one to see Monroe's name just below two other names as he looked at the roster also.

"There, Reuben. Major Monroe Duran, Law Adjutant," pointed out Noah.

"You're right, Noah," acknowledged Reuben.

"That's not all. Now that there's a big skirmish going on up ahead, I hear Lee's staff, including all the departments, are heading in that direction. They're probably there now."

Reuben looked up at Sergeant Warren with a look of concern. Geez oh geez oh geez, thought Reuben, the only war Monroe ever saw was when we would play pirates at the creek when we were children.

"Todd, I've got to run ahead and try to find him."

"I understand, Reuben. Go ahead. We can manage."

"I'll come with you," said Noah.

"No," said Doctor Chelmsford before Reuben could say the same. "Noah, what's happening up ahead could be too dangerous for Reuben trying to keep you safe while he looks for Monroe at the same time."

"Doc is right, Noah. I truly appreciate the gesture, but I'll be able to move faster if I go alone," agreed Reuben.

Noah nodded and reluctantly agreed to stay with the doctor. He wanted to do more and Reuben could see it in Noah's expression. Before Reuben ran off, he placed his hand on Noah's shoulder showing brotherly understanding.

Reuben ran past regiment after regiment, brigade after brigade until he reached a portion of the ongoing battle where the Confederates were pushing the Federals through the town to hills known as Cemetery and Culp. He ignored the actual fighting and mayhem, and focused on finding the command staff. Although his goal was to find Monroe, Reuben could not help but appreciate the irony that the Confederate Army was causing the Union Army to retreat and withdraw to the South. He also recognized the pending predicaments of the Union withdrawal. They were retreating toward the higher ground.

"This could be just like Sekigahara where the battle changed hands," said Reuben as he observed the ongoing Confederate push through the town.

It wasn't until late when conditions began to quiet down. This fight isn't over, not by a long shot, Reuben thought as he witnessed brigade after brigade march into town to take up offensive positions in and outside of the town.

He heard General's Lee's command staff and departments were to the west of the town. Reuben headed in that direction playing the role of a messenger. The ruse had the desired effect and got Reuben past many check points and pickets leading him to the command area where he saw several divisional commanders and adjutants.

"You look lost, friend. Can I help you?" asked a sergeant from behind Reuben.

"The Military and Civilian Law Matters Committee, where are they?" he asked.

"Whoa, nobody has ever asked for them before. Are you looking for anyone in particular?" the sergeant asked.

Reuben turned to face the sergeant, a roughly built man who looked as if he had seen his share of fighting.

"Ah, Captain, and who would you be with?" he asked with a delighted tone, noticing Reuben's upturned collar.

"68th Virginia from Norfolk. My name is Reuben, Reuben Duran."

"Jacob Cobb is my name, of Hampton. Me and a few other seasoned men were pulled off the line and assigned to that group of fancy tin soldiers as their assistants. If you ask me, we were meant to be their body guards. Bunch of worthless men in uniform, if you ask me. Hell, we were nowhere near the fighting when the guns began to fire and they all cowered like little schoolgirls. One of them even crapped his pants. Damn, what a hell of a mess."

Oh geez, don't let that one be Monroe, thought Reuben.

"I can imagine," said Reuben. "I'm actually looking for one of them. Where's Monroe?"

"Monroe?" asked the sergeant with a puzzled look and suddenly realized who Reuben was talking about. "Duran, Reuben Duran, you said your name was? You're talking about Major Monroe Duran, right?"

"He's my brother."

With a serious look of amazement, Sergeant Cobb said, "He's your brother? I don't see the resemblance. I mean, you have the look. He doesn't."

Reuben nodded his head. "Yes, I'm his younger brother. I've come to see how he's doing. When he departed over a year ago, it was not the best of goodbyes and I have come to… well, I just want to see him."

"Well, Major Duran is here," the sergeant hesitated for a moment and went on to say, "He's a, ah, fine officer."

"Jacob, veteran to veteran, no brother or relations involved, how is he really doing?"

Sargent Cobb looked Reuben up and down and took a good hard look at his eyes. They were dark with a hint of a troubled past. "You don't sound or act like a younger brother."

Reuben looked around to make sure there was no chance of anyone listening. "The fact is, Jacob, I went to VMI, did my time in the Mexican Campaign, among other places. My brother graduated from William and Mary and never fired a gun in his life."

562

Sergeant Cobb nodded approvingly, "I see. Now I understand why there's no family resemblance."

"What do you mean?" asked Reuben, confused.

"You have the look in your eyes. Your brother doesn't. Don't mistake me, because your brother is a fine gentleman, but as a soldier, I can understand why he and the others were mostly maintained in Richmond." Sergeant Cobb looked away as if ashamed to have put it in those words. He felt a hand on his shoulder. He looked back up to Reuben.

"That's why I'm here, Jacob. I became his substitute, but I knew he wouldn't go home unless I made him. I've got to try and convince him to go back home, or at least to Richmond. He only joined up in spite of me."

"I understand, Cap. You're a good brother," the sergeant said. "Come, I'll take you to him. Follow me."

"Real quick, Jacob. That officer who crapped his pants, that wasn't Monroe, was it?" asked Reuben.

"No, it wasn't, but your brother nearly started balling like a baby when he saw his first casualty."

Reuben and Sergeant Cobb made their way through the camp. They reached the staff area and the sergeant had a few words with the guards to allow Reuben passage to search for Monroe. The sergeant was summoned by a staff officer so he had to let Reuben search for Monroe on his own. He pointed Reuben in the direction of Monroe's encampment and Reuben shook his hand and thanked him for his help.

Reuben roamed the camp looking. Suddenly he saw a few uniforms looking out of place. They were worn uniforms, but fresher than the others he passed. One man in one of those uniforms let out a familiar laugh and Reuben smiled. He quickened his pace and strolled up behind him.

Not exactly knowing how Monroe would react to his presence, Reuben made himself appear proper, as much as he could, considering he had an unmarked uniform except for the captain stripes on his collar he had flipped up.

"Excuse me. Major, may I have a word?" asked Reuben, as he saluted. It felt very odd to salute his brother.

Monroe glanced back quickly enough to notice the rank of a captain and resumed his original form. "Yes, what is it, Captain?"

Perturbed by his brother's contemptuous demeanor after what Sergeant Cobb told Reuben about his cowardly behavior earlier this day, he said, "Sir, I'd like to kick my brother in his ass for not properly greeting his younger brother, sir."

Monroe turned and his face lit up. "Reuben! Is that you?!" Monroe reached out and embraced him. "God in heaven, it's good to see you!" he said with a sound of relief as if he was saved.

Reuben was completely surprised by Monroe's greeting. He was for certain Monroe would have made an angered scene.

563

"How about it, brother? We sure showed them blue bellies how to win a battle today," said Monroe, very high spirited. "Here, Reuben, let me introduce you to my colleagues. This is Major Edwin Norris and Major Gavin Kerby. Gentlemen, this is my brother, Reuben."

The two majors nodded their greetings as they looked Reuben up and down. He didn't look like any of the other officers, or his brother for that matter. They noticed he had no weapons except for a sword-like item in a black cover, and an odd looking knife tucked into his burgundy cotton sash. To them, Reuben had the look of a true hardened soldier.

Reuben nodded back in greeting and asked Monroe if they could speak in private.

"Of course, brother, follow me."

Monroe led Reuben to a shed serving as his department's office. Once inside, Monroe offered Reuben a seat, which he declined. A shell exploded in the distance as Monroe was about to sit and it caused him to duck and cover his head. It had no effect on Reuben. Monroe nervously took a handkerchief from his pocket and wiped his brow with a shaky hand.

Monroe asked nervously, "How's Mama, Lucy, and Eric? Did they get out of Chesapeake City okay?"

"Mama, Lucy, and Eric are dead, Monroe," said Reuben, flatly.

Completely taken by horrified surprise, Monroe asked as he let out a gasp, "How?"

Reuben looked down and untied the cord of the cover of his Kutto. He exposed the tsuka with the purple ribbon tied to it, ran the ribbon through his fingers, and covered it back up. "It really doesn't matter now, Monroe."

Another blast was heard and Monroe again ducked his head and looked up to the ceiling of the shed with fear as dust lightly fell from the ceiling. Again, Reuben showed no effect from the blast.

"Monroe, what are you doing here?" asked Reuben, calmly.

"What do you mean by that?" Monroe asked in an angered tone.

"We both can't be here, Monroe. We're the only ones left from Da and Mama. You and I are what remain from GrandDa Miles. Both of us are the last of the McDurand clan. If we both die in this war we shouldn't have been a part of, our family dies," said Reuben with a serious look.

Monroe looked away. It always frightened him when Reuben had that look. It was a look Reuben returned with from Mexico, and his journey to Japan seemed to enhance it. It was an unnatural look, a look of a wolf on the prowl, of extreme seriousness, despair, and anger. A look only Renee could make disappear. Monroe was getting tense and he realized it was showing. He stood up and pounded his fist against the small table serving as a desk.

"Damn it, Reuben. How dare you substitute yourself for me! I was humiliated when my colonel handed me that order."

Reuben didn't respond, but watched his brother pace from one wall to the other.

"Just because you fought in a war already, you think you're better than me?"

"Cut the crap, Monroe. I know what this is really about. Renee."

Monroe, with anger showing in his face, reached for a tin cup on the desk and threw it at his brother. Without flinching, Reuben caught the cup in his left hand and gently placed it back on the desk.

"You and that girl are meant for each other. I don't know what I ever saw in her!" said Monroe with hatred. He pointed at Reuben and continued, "For seven years she waited for you, not giving me any notice. That girl is just as mad as you are, and then some!"

Reuben grabbed his older brother's outstretched arm, and faster than anything Monroe had ever seen, he rotated his body and tossed Monroe like a rag doll to the far side of the room. "Never speak of Renee in that tone! I may forget you are family," said Reuben with anger in his voice.

Monroe lay on his back, his eyes filled with fear and arms trembling. He knew how awful Reuben could be when angered, especially when it had anything to do with Renee and Aarleen. He began to back up against the wall of the shed as Reuben stepped up to him. He knelt down and wiped his face with his hands and returned his look on Monroe, but it was now a look of concern.

"Monroe, you and I are what is left. Without us, Da and Mama are completely dead. I don't question your bravery, but you are not fit for this type of work. You're too important to be here. When this war is over, Virginia is going to need you desperately. Rebuilding this country when this war is over is your destiny. It's what you have been following Da's example for all your life. You received Da's gift. You are Da's legacy, Monroe, not me. I'm Mama's legacy. I have her gift. You are the one who Da depends on to lead the Duran family into our next generation which includes, Aarleen and Andy. It's you Da chose to guide our family's next generation, not me. Please, Monroe, I beg you, don't compete against me. It's a competition I cannot win. I'm only a teacher. I'm not up for that task as you are."

Reuben offered his hand to Monroe who stared at it for a moment, then pushed it away. "Get out, Captain. Get out before I bring you up on charges for assaulting a superior officer."

Reuben stood up with heart felt sorrow and looked at the floor as he shifted some dirt with the toe of his mud caked boot. He glanced at Monroe's shoes. They looked as if they were just issued. He ran his hand over his Kutto and made his way to the door. Before he exited, he looked back and said, "I'll be on the field tomorrow if you need me," and walked out.

Monroe watched Reuben walk away. A distant shell burst caused him to wince. He looked at his trembling hands and back to the door. He began to remember all the times his younger brother protected him from bullies. With his fingers, Monroe traced the scar on his face as he said, "I need you, Reuben."

Walking through the camp, Reuben heard a familiar voice call out to him, "Hey, Cap. Did you see your brother?"

Reuben turned and saw Sargent Cobb walking up to him. He smiled and felt relieved to see a real soldier.

"So, how did your visit go with the major?" asked the sergeant.

Reuben shook his head and said, "That brother of mine is going to get his ass handed to him full of lead." He silently began to beg for his father's forgiveness for his failures to the Duran family.

狼

Morning came bright and early. Sitting on an overturned keg, Reuben was looking at Renee's image in one hand, and holding Aarleen's inrou in the other. He began to think of the other times they had been separated and two of his most vivid memories began replaying in his mind.

"ADAM, NO!!!"

Reuben covered the wound with his hand and put down pressure.

Adam looked up to his friend who had him cradled in one arm while keeping pressure on the wound with the other.

"I don't want to be here anymore, Reuben. Please take me back to Culpepper."

"I'll have you there before you know it, Adam. Think of Mary, think of her hard."

"Mary Alice, my Mary. She is sweet, she's the best girl in the world."

"That she is, Adam. The best, the very best."

"I need her now. Momma, don't cry. It does not hurt too much."

Reuben began to tremble. Adam told him his mother passed on years before he entered VMI. After these long months of dread, Reuben lost all faith to a god that would let such chaos happen. He began to think of God as a sadist.

"Reuben? I can't see! Are you there?"

"Yes, Adam."

"You must leave me, Reuben. You must go back to your girl, Renee. I always thought she was so beautiful, even more beautiful than my Mary. I will protect you. You must go now and leave me." Adam coughed up blood and gasped a last breath of air and fell silent in Reuben's arms. Reuben closed Adam's eyes shut and cradled him.

Feeling light headed, Reuben fell to his back with Adam still in his arms.

Reuben rolled Masaru over and saw a bullet wound in his shoulder. He quickly pressed down on it with the palm of his hand and dragged him to one of the fallen limbers for cover as Tadashi and Seiji covered them.

More shots came from the left of their position. There were two Arata men with rifles and several others advancing on the four with drawn swords.

"Reuben, leave me. You must get Tadashi and Seiji out of here," said Masaru in pain.

Reuben's fierce, angered, wolf-like look returned. He tore out a piece of cloth from his inner kosode sleeve and jammed it in Masaru's wound.

"NO, GOD DAMN IT, NOT THIS TIME!!! YOU WILL NOT DO THIS TO ME AGAIN!!! NOBODY DIES THIS TIME!!!" Reuben yelled as he rose and sprinted to the closest attacker.

He raised his sword and motioned a straight cut as the attacker positioned his sword for a block, but Reuben reversed his cut and slashed the Arata man across his face. Using his momentum from that cut, Reuben turned completely clockwise slashing his blade upwards disemboweling the next attacker. He was about to cut downward on another attacker as an arrow pierced the attacker's throat. Seiji quickly shot the two gunmen before they fully loaded their rifles.

"Quickly, Reuben! We need to get back to the other side of the river!" called out Tadashi, as he was lifting Masaru to his feet.

Reuben ran and took Masaru's other arm and they began to run back toward the river with Seiji covering them from behind.

"I don't think we are going to make it. There is more Arata coming after us!" said Seiji from behind.

Reuben raised his mirror-like blade and saw a large group of men giving chase in its reflection. He slowed down and turned to face them as they continued to run to the river backwards.

"Why are we running backwards, Reuben?!" asked Tadashi.

"To face our enemy. If we are to die, we will not die with our backs toward them!"

"HAI, REUBEN-SAN!!!" cried out Masaru, painfully, but with pride.

As the Arata men were nearing, they suddenly slowed down, turned, and began retreating in the opposite direction. The four slowed their pace and were knocked down from behind by alliance mounted samurai giving chase to the attackers.

They all rose to their knees and cheered, "AKAGI, SATOSHI, AKAGI, SATOSHI!!!"

"Reuben, are you all right? I said good morning three times already," said Monroe, causing Reuben to come back to the present.

Reuben looked up. A single tear fell from the side of his eye. "Thinking of the past, brother?" Monroe asked. Seeing his brother in this state caused Monroe to feel proud of him for all the hell and torment he put himself through for Renee, and now for Monroe also. Reuben was right he thought.

"Morning, Monroe. What are you doing here?" asked Reuben.

"I've come to apologize. We're family, Reuben. The last ones left, as you said, and you're right. I'm not cut out for this. I've also come to apologize to you for what I said about Renee. When she came to live with us, I had no feelings for her. But her devotion and unfaltering love for you drove me crazy. I actually came to believe she deserved someone better than you. Someone like me, so I fell in love with her even though I knew her love belonged to you."

"Monroe," Reuben started to say, but Monroe held up his hand to stop Reuben's words.

"Please, Reuben, let me finish. I did some serious thinking last night. After I tried to kill you because of how I felt for Renee, you still came looking and substituted yourself to save me from this part of life I am not destined for. That is the family love and devotion Da and Mama installed into you, me, and Lucy. Reuben, my brother, you and Renee are the essence of that love and devotion Da and Mama installed into us and for that, your Renee does have the better man, and I am very proud to be your brother. So, please, forgive me."

Reuben rose and took Monroe into his arms and said, "There's nothing to apologize for, Monroe. It's easy to fall in love with Renee. She is... magical."

The two brothers stepped back from one another, but still held onto each other's arms.

"Once this engagement is over, Reuben, I will honor your order, and let you substitute yourself for me and go back to Norfolk. But first, I will go to Richmond and I'll do what I can to get you relieved from your obligation. From what I understand, the means by which you were coerced into the army are grounds for violating you of your constitutional rights, Confederate or Federal. You know me, Reuben. I'll find a loop hole just like Da would. It's his gift he gave me."

"That would be fantastic, Monroe. You can take Noah back with you."

"Noah? He's here? Why?"

Reuben opened the image case and looked at Renee's picture and said, "Renee sent him to bring my Kutto to guarantee my safety."

Monroe let out a little laugh and said, "See, Reuben, you and Renee are meant for each other. You two are the only ones who can deal with both of your shenanigans."

"Yeah, but we're still trying to determine which one of us is the most crazy," said Reuben.

狼

Thunderous shells blasted the ground with a violent rage. Reuben heard Colonel McFerrin's call to rise and he looked at him as if he suddenly gone mad. The regiment rose and stepped into line within the trees.

"Battalion, forward march!" ordered General Doyle.

Like a behemoth machine, the entire line moved in one motion. Reuben crouched low as did the rest of Company C.

Solid shots were creating great gaps in the line quicker than they could be refilled. An order was given to each wing to close in. Reuben grabbed young boys who should still have been in lower grades of school and moved them as quickly as he could pushing them to hunch down.

One boy from a different company began to wander away from the line.

Reuben ordered Lieutenant Rallins to take over his position as he went off after the young soldier.

"Private, get back over here!" ordered Reuben, but the boy kept wandering away as if mesmerized by the sights and sounds of the battle in front of him.

A loud thunder of musketry sounded causing Reuben to drop to the ground. After the balls fizzed over, he got back to his feet. None of the bullets hit the boy. "Damn Federals can't hit anything today," Reuben said to himself as he continued chasing after the wandering soldier.

Suddenly a huge blast hit the ground tossing Reuben several yards across the field. Dirt and stones rained on top of him and he could barely make out the boy in the dust screaming louder than any other noise on the battlefield. Reuben saw the boy's legs still connected to his hips laying inches away from him. The shell cut the boy in half, his upper body landing straight upward looking as he were standing in a hole. His screaming stopped. His eyes closed. His head slumped down.

Reuben began to rise when another volley of musketry flew above him. He looked for the rest of the brigade, but they had moved on. More muskets were fired and shells were bursting all around him. He realized he was caught in the middle of a vicious crossfire. Bullets and fragments, along with dirt and stones, were beating the ground all around him. He reached for the boys legs and tossed them on his back for cover. He saw another dead body within an arms-reach and pulled it close and used it as a shield, just as he did with Corporal Rall's body back at Villanueva. Reuben could hear and feel bullets hit the corpse. His head was low to the ground and his face in the dirt.

Reuben shut his eyes tightly, wincing as the corpse safely shielded him. As bullets hit the corpse, Reuben began to think of Renee. "She'll die if I don't come home," he said to himself.

Suddenly memories of Monroe entered his thoughts. He shook his head and tried to bring Renee's image back, but the memories of Monroe kept Renee's image away. Memories, happy memories, of his brother in school, on the farm, in the city, and at home kept coming to mind as the crossfire continued. Those memories of Monroe caused Reuben to feel safe as if he was being protected so he could return home to Renee and Aarleen.

The shooting died down and the sound of the battle faded. Reuben cautiously looked over the corpse shielding him and noticed the battle had indeed moved, and the crossfire halted. He pulled the boy's lower body off his back and rose staying low. He looked in all directions, patted the corpse that shielded him on its shoulders in thanks, and ran off to find his company.

As Reuben ran off, the bullet-ridden, lifeless body of Monroe that shielded him rolled onto its back, his dead eyes staring to the heavens above.

石
水

In the year of our Lord, 1864, a romantic tale continues.
Sometimes war brings out the best in some people...

Why Can't You be Like Renee

It was late in the afternoon and with all of her chores done, Aarleen sat on the front porch tending to her little cherry blossom tree Reuben gave her when she turned twelve. Now at fifteen, Aarleen was the splitting image of Renee at that age, with the exception of her nose. In the past twenty three months since her father was taken from her, Aarleen had grown up just as quickly as Renee had at this adolescent age, but under different circumstances.

Aarleen continued her education as best she could under the wartime conditions, all thanks to Major Jonathan MacKay, the Union area inspector who replaced Captain Oscar Grossman. At a time when travel to and from the city was regulated, Aarleen could not attend school. Although Major MacKay was a strict, by-the-book, type of administrator, that deportment of his allowed him to let things happen, so to speak. If a certain issue was not covered in the regulations, orders, directives, or any other form of written instructions, it was open for interpretation. For the case of Aarleen's education, travel to and from the city was strictly regulated keeping her from attending school. However, there was nothing in writing that said education could not come to her, and since education was a regulated issue that stated school must be made available, as a regulation, Major MacKay obligated himself to bring educational materials to Aarleen. She shared her materials and assignments with Tommy Deans and Janet Lindsey who also continued their education along with her under the supervision of Renee. On his weekly tour of his assigned area, he would bring Aarleen educational materials and assignments from the city school as official correspondence. Major MacKay could not bring back the three student's assignments for grading because of a directive that stated government officials could not transport personal correspondence. Their schoolwork was categorized as personal. However, he could act as a mail carrier to deliver mail to the city post office. From there, their schoolwork would be delivered to the school for grading and credit.

Maintaining the schoolhouse also became one of those open for interpretation type of issues. Officially, the schoolhouse belonged to the city and since the city was under a military governorship, it was considered Federal property. However, it needed to be cared for and because of its property status it could only be cared for one day a month. Major MacKay saw a fine line that the schoolhouse also belonged to the community, all due to the fact Reuben's name appeared on the property documents which, open to interpretation, it was Duran property as well. He allowed Renee, Aarleen, and Evergreen, along with Tommy Deans and Janet Lindsey, to see to its upkeep one day a week for Reuben's return.

571

At first, Renee grew wary of Major MacKay's manner by which he conducted his duties with the Duran farm. It seemed it was only with Renee he pushed those open for interpretation issues to the limits. At first she believed he was following in the manner of Captain Grossman of trying to obtain her affections. Although Major MacKay found Renee to be a very beautiful and charming woman, the reasons for his manner were personal.

A week before Doctor Chelmsford and Noah left to find Reuben, Major Jonathan MacKay was assigned his posting of area inspector. When making his initial rounds to view his area of responsibility, he came upon the Duran farm. It was one of those days where everyone spent the day near the creek to unwind, and of course, Renee and Aarleen spent that day training in the Budo Arts. When Major MacKay saw Renee training with her jo, the major immediately had a terrifying memory of the day leading to the loss of his arm.

Flying off into a rage, he stomped down to the oak tree and shouted as he neared, "You! Who showed you how to use that stick in such a manner?!"

Aarleen held back Riley who began barking and was about to charge the major to protect Renee. Renee raised her jo in a ready to strike hasso position while Doctor Chelmsford came and stood between the major and Renee holding his hands up.

"You! That man! That stick! That man with the cold dark eyes of a hungry wolf! He caused the loss of my arm!" said Major MacKay in anger.

"Take another step toward us and I'll cause the loss of your other arm!" retorted Renee.

After several very long tense moments of heated and rather questionable proper dialog between Renee and the major, Doctor Chelmsford led Major MacKay away from the tree for a private discussion.

"I'll see to it this farm is fully confiscated and the inhabitants cleared off never to return!" said the major in a rage loud enough for Renee to hear. "Now that I know the owner of this land is a confirmed rebel officer in arms against the Union, I can legally throw them off and burn this place down to the ground if I wish!"

Taking the major further away from the others, Doctor Chelmsford calmly said, "Come now, Major. You don't want to do such a thing to one of the most respected families in the county."

"Respected hell, they don't have my respect! Only the loss of my arm because of that woman's man! My god, I never saw a man with such fight in him. I'll make him pay and his family will be the first installment."

Doctor Chelmsford laughed as he tried to envision Reuben sparing this man who stood in front of him.

"What's so damned funny?!" yelled the major.

"Seriously, Major. Do you want to make his family suffer after you know what he is capable of? You know men like him will survive, and when he returns to find his family violated, he will undoubtedly seek the ones who did the violating."

A brief look of concern crossed Major MacKay's face, but was quickly replaced again with anger. "The hell with him. He took my arm, so I'm taking his property."

Again the doctor laughed and said, "If you insist, but let me put it to you this way. Reuben may have taken your arm, but he spared your life and got you away from the mayhem. He could have easily taken your life, but he didn't. If you ask me, you owe him, and his family."

As much as he hated to admit, Doctor Chelmsford was right. Major Jonathan MacKay had taken part in the third Seminole war and it left a horrible impression in his mind. As a respected member of his community from Michigan, he felt reluctantly obligated to volunteer his service for his state in this war. He did feel a sense of relief being relieved from active combat duty because of the loss of his arm. It was then when Major Jonathan MacKay began making those issues of interpretation for the Duran farm rather than outwardly apologize for his initial outburst during his first visit. In time, an agreeable and mutual respected relationship was formed between the Duran farm and Major MacKay.

Because of Reuben's position in the Confederate Army, the major could have had his property confiscated and the inhabitants removed with no Federal aid. However, after Doctor Chelmsford described the manner of how Reuben found himself in the Confederate ranks, Major MacKay, after hours of reviewing directives, came to his first issue of interpretation. He viewed this case as a Union citizen, who had his civil rights violated by a malfeasant government, was being held hostage, and impressed into service much like the British did to American sailors leading to the War of 1812. This issue was being pushed to the severe limit. Such an accusation would require a formal investigation, but the major knew such an investigation would root out Reuben's involvement in arms against the Union, thus causing his property to be confiscated and his family evicted, so Major MacKay held off filing his report. To him, this was a civilian matter and since Norfolk and its surrounding counties were under military jurisdiction, military matters had priority. Considering they were operating under wartime conditions, this case would have to wait, possibly until the end of hostilities. All of which was open to interpretation.

The war had many names. The War of the Rebellion, War Between the States, War for Southern Independence, War for the Union, War of Northern and or Southern Aggression were but a few. But for Aarleen, it meant only one thing, separation from her father who she missed so dearly. Many nights she cried herself to sleep bringing back memories for Renee when she did the same at Aarleen's age when Reuben had gone away to VMI, and then to Mexico and Japan.

Renee and Aarleen began using Reuben's and Monroe's old room to sleep in. At first Aarleen slept with Renee in her and Reuben's bed, but Renee felt it was wrong to use their bed while he was detained against his will, so she began using the bed Reuben used in his old room. As for Aarleen's sleeping difficulties with her father gone, Renee had her use Monroe's bed, like when they shared the same room before Reuben returned home from Japan. Many times, one of the two ended up sleeping with the other because of fearful and sad emotions of loneliness.

Evergreen's separation from Noah was also very difficult. All the years she was a slave bore her a thick skin toward others not of her race, including Reuben, Renee, and Aarleen. It wasn't until Reuben's beyond-the-point discussion he and Renee had with the others when Andrew and Annabelle decided to take Andy away from Virginia, when her thick skin began to soften. She truly wanted to believe in liberty and freedom for her people, but it was Reuben's dose of reality that such virtues are not given, they are earned and if not fought for, lost.

She detested the thought of Noah leaving to take Reuben's Kutto to him, but admired the devotion he had to the Duran family. Witnessing Renee's and Aarleen's unfaltering strength and willingness to defend everyone living on the farm caused a shift in her angered attitude toward people not of her race. The stories of how Reuben could have been executed in Japan because of the shape of his eyes and not speaking the language drove the reality deeper into Evergreen. Although slavery in America was a horrid institution, she felt grateful she was in this country considering there were much worse places in the world to be.

Henry being the only man on the farm took that position very seriously. He acted as the father figure toward everyone, including Renee to which she was greatly appreciative. At his age, he still worked tirelessly on all aspects of the farm. From mending tools to planting and harvesting in the allotted family plots to the hidden plots deep in the woods, he did it all. Aarleen and Evergreen saw to the hidden animals allowing Henry to focus on maintaining the wagon team at top condition. Without the team in top condition, life on the farm would be that much more difficult. It was Henry who drove the wagon and was always by Renee's side during their weekly allotted trips into the city for their regulated rations. Although Henry knew Renee and Aarleen were capable of defending themselves, he still presented himself as their guardian.

The glue bonding the entire family together was May. Even with her aging years, she still maintained a motherly strength and spirit needed during these trying times. It was May who constantly reminded everyone about the test Reuben predicted back on that brisk Christmas morning under the oak tree of '60. A test, Reuben said, they must pass, no matter what conditions are tossed their way. May became the designated point of contact with Major MacKay if Renee was absent during his inspection tours. It was through May where the major learned of Renee's and Reuben's troubled past and how he became the man who spared the major's life in battle.

Aarleen become the pillar of Renee's life, just as Lucy had been when Reuben was away in Japan. She shadowed Renee daily, and one could not be found without the other close by. If one was not present, the other knew exactly where the other was. Aarleen and Renee did everything together from tending to the hidden plots and animals, to Aarleen's educational studies. It was under the oak tree where most of their idle time was spent in studies and Budo training. While Renee would sit and write poetic passages, Aarleen would write stories of adventures, her father being her inspiration as the hero figure, and her mother as the strong heroine.

To provide a sense of family togetherness and spirit, Aarleen worked diligently on creating a new story each week to be told every Sunday evening after dinner. These story times were a much anticipated event each week. It was during one of these story events when Major MacKay made a required regulated surprise inspection of the Duran farm. After his inspection, Aarleen invited him and his four other troopers to join the family for the weekly story time. Of course, the major refused because his duties prohibited interaction with civilians unless it was of an official manner. However, he did show interest in the event and ordered his troopers to stand down the horses for a thirty minute rest, within listening distance, as prescribed in the inspection instructions. Major MacKay and his troopers left at the end of the story period not showing any interested attention, but after that one visit, the major and his troopers always seemed to make their surprised inspection on Sunday right around after dinner time.

Renee was the beacon of light for everyone on the farm. After recovering from her initial shock of Reuben being stolen from her, she became a powerhouse of strength. She was determined to keep the family together no matter the cost. Although she deemed it not necessary, nothing was done on the farm without her knowing about it, whether before or after it was done. She was the spearhead of the farm's operation, and conducted all official business with Major MacKay when she was available.

As much as she wanted to provide neighbors with some of the excess food they had from the hidden plots, she maintained a stiff spine. It distressed her to the point of tears and guilt, but it was Aarleen who assured Renee by not sharing their food with the neighbors, it was how they were going to be able to pass the test forced on them.

"Remember what Da said, Mama, before he was taken, *'We plant for ourselves and ourselves only.'* If the Federals found out we've been growing food in secret and hiding it, we could be evicted and the farm confiscated. He also said, the less people know, the safer we are. You're doing exactly what Da said, so you have nothing to feel guilty about. He would be very proud of you. I know I am, Mama."

The only ones receiving a share of extra food were Tommy Deans and Janet Lindsey to share with their families. They were told it came from Noah's portion of the allotted plots and rations and since he was off with Doctor Chelmsford in search for Reuben, it could be spared. After all, Tommy Deans and Janet Lindsey were a huge help to Renee when it came to the care of the schoolhouse.

Every chance she got, Renee would grasp the VMI button hanging from her neck and look up to either the sun or moon and imagine Reuben looking up at the same time. Many times, without either one of them knowing, they were. It was times such as those reminded her of the happiest times of their lives. When she brought him lunch the first day he was working on the *Morning Star* was a very pleasant memory. Although during that visit Renee told Reuben they would have to say their farewell a day sooner than planned, it was still a very special memory. It was the first time Renee made Reuben a meal, and the first time they called each other *'dear'*. And of course, the one memory Renee always treasured was the first time Reuben saw Aarleen and told him, *"Surprise, it's a girl."*

Nearly every day, Renee was dressed in Reuben's black or brown hakama with his black or burgundy kosode and hanten jacket, and when she wasn't, she was in her green or purple hakama and tan or light blue kosode. She and Aarleen wore their hakamas and kosodes everywhere, including their allotted trips into the city. For Renee, it wasn't only a matter of comfort and practicality. Wearing Reuben's clothes made her feel as if Reuben's arms were around her all the time.

Renee was determined not to let Reuben down just as she knew he was not going to let them down by not returning. Knowing he had his Kutto with him reassured her of his safety. In time, Reuben told Renee of the dangerous feats he was a part of in Mexico and Japan. They were too incredible to comprehend, but his eyes held the look of a man who traveled the valley several times and survived. She believed in Reuben, had faith in him, and believed nothing could keep him away from her and his daughter.

Aarleen snipped a tiny branch from her tree when Riley rose to all four legs and let out a growl. Aarleen looked up to the lane, put down her scissors, and reached for her bokken.

Riley's growl turned into a low, grunted woof and remained watchful as Major MacKay and his four troopers trotted down the lane.

"Go get Mama, Riley," said Aarleen as she picked up her scissors and continued pruning her little cherry blossom tree.

The major and his troopers trotted up to the house and dismounted. Major MacKay reached into his saddlebag with his one remaining arm, retrieved a sheet of paper, and walked up to the porch. He stood in front of Aarleen looking up at her as she pruned her little tree with interest.

"Hello, Mr. MacKay. I sent Riley to go fetch Mama. They should be here shortly," greeted Aarleen.

"Fine, Miss Duran, very fine. That's an interesting little plant you have there. It's not food, is it? You know you cannot be growing food unless it's in the allotted plots?" asked the major.

"Oh no, Mr. MacKay, this is my bonsai tree. Da grew and gave it to me when I turned twelve."

"Bon... bonsay..."

"Bonsai. Bonn-sai. Here say it with me... bonsai," instructed Aarleen as she helped the major pronounce bonsai.

"Bonsai."

"There you go, Mr. MacKay, bonsai," said Aarleen, proudly.

"You say that's a tree? Do they grow here in Virginia? I've never seen one before," asked Major MacKay, genuinely interested.

"No, they grow in Japan. My Da's lord in Japan sent him the seeds and he planted it here. It's one of my favorite things in the whole world," said Aarleen, looking at the little tree with affection.

Lord, Japan, favorite thing in the whole world. This Reuben Duran must be a fascinating man, thought Major MacKay. He stepped up to get a closer look at the little tree and watched how delicately Aarleen was tending to it. It was such a graceful little tree and he found comfort looking at it. He found it difficult to believe a man who could exhibit such violence could grow a tree such as this, and raised a beautiful caring daughter who can easily defend herself as violently as her father.

The major was well aware of the incident when Captain Oscar Grossman's troopers tried to subdue Renee and Aarleen, and how they fought and crippled several of them. He saw and spoke to the troopers who the mother and daughter injured, and found it unbelievable until he saw Renee and Aarleen practicing under the oak tree during his initial inspection tour, the day he found out it was Renee's husband who cost him his arm.

Shaking his head in disbelief, Major MacKay said, as he continued to watch Aarleen prune, "Amazing how a man like your father could grow such a beautiful, delicate little tree."

"That's because my Reuben is a warrior true of heart," said Renee, startling Major MacKay as she strolled up behind him.

Watching her mother startle the major caused Aarleen to giggle.

No longer, Reuben my love, will you be able to sneak up on me because I can do it too, thought Renee.

"I beg your pardon?" asked the major as he turned his attention to Renee.

"The simplest of warriors are cruel, wicked, evil, and filled with hatred. But the true warriors of heart are the ones who are loyal, honest, and benevolent. They can defend with deadly accuracy one moment, and become a poet the next. In my husband's case, grow beautiful, delicate little trees and produce a beautiful, precious daughter," explained Renee as she stepped onto the porch and knelt down next to Aarleen and gently caressed one of the blossoms with her fingertip.

Major MacKay nodded his head, actually understanding Renee's explanation. In the amount of time he served as their area inspector, the major learned more about family love and devotion from Renee and Aarleen than his own family. From what he learned from May, and when Doctor Chelmsford first took him aside and told the Duran family story to the major, he found the devotion this family had was much stronger than he had ever seen. Although the major was still bitter about the loss of his arm, he still thought hard about what the doctor told him, *"Reuben may have taken your arm, but he spared your life."*

"To what do we owe this unexpected visit, Mr. MacKay?" asked Renee, interrupting the major's thought.

Clearing his throat, the major said, "I have come to issue you your weekly travel pass to the city for tomorrow."

Looking puzzled, Renee replied, "Tomorrow? We are usually permitted to travel into the city on Thursdays."

The major looked at the permit with a fake questionable look and said, "Ah, you're right. I must have been thinking of the flour and sugar shipment arriving today and being available for rationing out tomorrow only."

"Mr. MacKay, if I didn't know any better, I'd think you're giving us special treatment so we can get flour and sugar," said Aarleen with a giggle.

"Me? Give special treatment?" replied the major, with a hint of humor. "I do my job by the books, Miss Duran, you know that. But if you would rather make your weekly trip into the

577

city on Thursday and miss out on the flour and sugar, I can tear up this permit and make out another."

"No, Mr. MacKay, we will take the permit for tomorrow. I suspect there's paperwork you probably need to do because you have to reissue a new permit, and you are too busy for such tasks. We'll relieve you of that burden," said Renee, nodding at the major's generosity.

Major MacKay grunted a little laugh and said, "You're right, and I do loathe unnecessary paperwork. Here you go and travel safely."

The major handed Renee the travel permit and began walking toward his mount.

"Excuse me, Mr. MacKay, can I ask you a question?" asked Renee.

The major walked back to the porch and said, "As long as it pertains to official business."

"Hmm, okay," said Renee rather stymied. "Well, as it pertains to your official business, how did you become so proficient in your attention to detail in your duties? Perhaps something you did prior to your service in the army?"

Aarleen smiled and the major nodded with a smirk.

"Very good, well played, Mrs. Duran. I worked as a publishing agent before the rebellion, mostly educational textbooks. I did have military experience during the third Seminole War in Florida back in '55. With my educational background, I was commissioned a major when I volunteered for the Union."

"Hey, maybe some of the textbooks my Da uses are some of the ones you published, Mr. MacKay," said Aarleen.

"That is an ironic possibility, Miss Duran," answered the major with a look of irony on his face. Severe fighter and also a school teacher, thought Major MacKay of Reuben. Little delicate trees, precious daughter, beautiful wife, and a school teacher with the ability to fight with deadly accuracy, this Reuben Duran is a true warrior of heart.

"That's very interesting, Mr. MacKay," said Renee interrupting his thoughts again.

"Yes, I suppose. Well, I must be off. I have more permits to issue. I recommend you travel early."

"Thank you, Mr. MacKay. We will," said Renee.

Major MacKay took a couple of steps forward and stopped. He slightly turned and said, "I'm still bitter about the loss of my arm, but I no longer blame your husband, Mrs. Duran. I never told anyone this, but after he injured me and killed my colonel, he kept his men from killing me. When the fight was over and my unit was safely across the river, your husband, a captain, and a sergeant carried me to the river's edge. He told the other two to return and he waved for some of the men from my unit to come and get me. He stayed with me until they were several yards away and ran off. He stopped a short distance away and watched as my men carried me back. It was as if he was making sure I was being cared for safely. And he did apologize to me... like a poet."

"Thank you, Mr. MacKay. Like you, my Reuben carries his duties to the limits."

Major MacKay nodded and mounted his horse. As he was about to heel his mount, Aarleen said to him, "Hey, Mr. MacKay, will you be making one of your surprise inspections this Sunday?"

"If I told you, Miss Duran, then it wouldn't be a surprise, now would it?" he asked with humor. "Why do you ask?"

"Well, I started writing a new story this morning and it features a one armed soldier who is very by-the-book, but fair. He meets up with an enemy soldier, the one who caused the loss of his arm, and end up battling evil soldiers from both sides together, each using their unique capabilities and becoming good friends in the end."

The major nodded with sincere interest and said, "Hmm, I am due for a surprise inspection. Perhaps I should schedule one for Sunday then."

狼

Early Tuesday morning, Henry brought the wagon around to the front of the house. He rechecked all the straps, reins, and the condition of the team while he waited for Renee and Aarleen. Renee retrieved a twenty dollar gold piece out from under the floorboard in her and Reuben's bedroom. She always took some money. Often, extra rations could be purchased. Renee was very picky of how she used the money. Flour and sugar would be some items she wanted to purchase more of, if available. Of the $1000 in cash, in gold and silver, Reuben converted before Virginia seceded, Renee had used it sparingly. Paper money was nearly worthless and much of it was needed for any item needed to be purchased. But solid money in the form of gold or silver was always welcome and much could be purchased with it.

Like Reuben, she didn't tell anyone where she had the money hidden for their safety. As much as Renee wanted to, she kept herself from trying to find the rest of the oban coins Reuben had hidden. She knew he hid them on or near the oak tree, and once in a while when she was sitting under the tree by herself, she would glance up to the tree in various places. One day while training with Aarleen, Renee noticed a small arrow carved into the trunk pointing down with 狼 carved next to it, the kanji characters for wolf. When she saw that marking, she felt all warm and tingly inside. When she was alone, she would always trace the marking with her fingertip, smile, and always sit with her back against it knowing Reuben at one time touched this specific spot on the tree.

"Don't forget your, Janet's, and Tommy's school assignments sweetie," said Renee as she exited the house. "Are we ready to roll, Henry?"

"Yes we are, Renee. Here, let me help you up."

As Henry finished helping Renee onto the wagon, Aarleen came out of the house with May and Evergreen following. Henry helped Aarleen onto the wagon and Evergreen handed Renee her jo and Aarleen's bokken.

"You three be careful now. Do what you need to get done and get right back home," said Evergreen with concern.

"We will, Ever, and I'll get as much flour and sugar as I can. Heaven knows it has been a long time since we had fresh baked bread," said Renee.

"I wish Da was here. He loves fresh baked bread," added Aarleen.

"Are you going to check on the city house and visit Mr. Duran and Lucy?" asked May.

"Yes. I'll give them your regards."

"You do that, and do as Ever says, get home quick."

"We will, May," said Aarleen, waving as Henry snapped the reins.

When they were nearing the schoolhouse, Renee had Henry slow down so they could take a good look at its condition. They could no longer step foot on the schoolhouse property any time they wanted except for the designated day for upkeep, which was an anticipated weekly event like Aarleen's story time after Sunday dinner.

"You should have seen your Da when he first saw this plot of land available for sale, sweetie," said Renee. "He was so excited about building that little school. I'll never forget the day he told me his idea of starting a school. That is when I knew he was home for good."

As she was beginning to feel emotional, she tapped Henry on the shoulder to continue on.

There were several checkpoints along the way to the city, one at each bridge, intersection, and just on the outskirts of the city. Their first stop was at the city house. Although it was still their property, it was locked down by the military. Renee still had the key to the front and back doors, but there was a latch with a huge padlock attached to each door and beam. Major MacKay saw to the condition of the Duran city house because it was listed as property owned by the Duran farm, and made it part of his inspection area of interest and responsibility.

The house may have been sealed tight as a drum, but Aarleen, being just as creative as her Aunty Lucy, knew of a way inside through a grated panel hidden behind a bush in back of the house. Renee and Henry waited out front on the wagon while Aarleen went to check on the inside of the house.

It took less than ten minutes for Aarleen to make a quick walkthrough of the house and leave making sure the grated entry was secure. She returned back to the wagon and assured Renee everything was still in its place.

"It sure is dusty in there, Mama, but everything seems to be undisturbed. I didn't touch anything in case Mr. MacKay enters the house. He won't know I was in there."

"Good, sweetie. I do wish I could take Reuben's VMI picture back to the farm, but if he sees it missing, he'll know we have been inside. I'm quite sure that man has everything inventoried."

"That's right, Renee," said Henry. "It took us a long time to get on his good side and we don't want to spoil that."

With another snap of the reins, they were off to their second stop, the ration depot. Taking Major MacKay's advice by leaving early just as the sun was peeking from the horizon, they arrived to be sixth in line.

When the depot opened, there were four tables set up to service the people. When it was their turn, Renee, Aarleen, and Henry walked up to the third table and presented their ration form. On it was listed six residents of the Duran farm. Noah was still listed as living on the farm even though he left with Doctor Chelmsford over a year ago to deliver Reuben his Kutto. It was a technicality which Major MacKay paid no serious concern. As long as Noah was still on the paperwork, he was considered a resident of the farm.

They were issued their allotted ration of three pounds of flour and one pound of sugar per each member of the residence. Once it was signed for by Renee, the ration officer offered her the opportunity to purchase one more ration for each member of the residence.

"Mind you, Mrs. Duran, it will cost you two dollars for the flour for each member of the residence and one dollar for the sugar."

"Is that paper money cost?" asked Renee.

The officer nodded yes.

Renee reached into the sleeve of her kosode and retrieved the twenty dollar gold piece and displayed it to the officer. "How about cost for coin money?" she asked.

The ration officer eyes widened and nodded approvingly. "Now that's different. The cost will be half of what I quoted. Do you wish to proceed?"

Although still expensive, Renee nodded. For nine dollars, she purchased an additional ration of flour and sugar for each member of the residence.

The officer was about to give Renee her change back in the form of paper script until she held up her hand and said, "No, our Federal area inspector, Major MacKay, told us when receiving change for coin money, it also must be in the form of coin money."

"Ah, Major MacKay is your area inspector, is he?" said the ration officer with a sound of disappointment. "Well, he of all people should know the directives. Very well, please wait here, I need to go to the safe."

Aarleen beamed with pride for her mother. Da would be very proud of Mama, she thought.

"Okay, Mrs. Duran, here is your change, in coin along with your receipt. Take it to the clerk outside and he will issue your ration and excess purchase. There are carts for you to use, don't forget to return them. NEXT!"

With their allotted ration of flour and sugar and excess purchases loaded in the wagon, Henry snapped the reins of the team and began rolling away. Their next stop was Elmhurst Cemetery to visit with Aaron and Lucy.

They spent about an hour in the cemetery pulling out weeds from Aaron's and Lucy's graves and sprucing them up. As Reuben would do, Renee placed an incense stick at the foot of their headstones and lit them.

Renee got down on her knees and leaned her head on Lucy's marker and said with watery eyes, "My dearest sister, I ask you with all my being and love, please look after your brothers and bring them home safely."

Renee rose as Aarleen knelt down and leaned her head against Aaron's marker, just as emotional. She said, "I remember before you left us to go to heaven, I asked you to find Da and make him come home. Please GrandDa, I ask once again, please find Da and make him come home, and to bring Uncle Monroe back with him."

After their emotional visit with Aaron and Lucy, they were once again traveling the streets of Norfolk making their way to Gamby Road. Henry was about to turn onto Gamby Road leading to the school, but Renee told Henry to ride past Andrew and Annabelle's store to see what had become of it. Feeling nostalgic, Henry nodded and steered the team in that direction. The store was closed and dark. It was no longer named the Norfolk Klaus Mercantile. It was renamed the Norfolk General Store by the new owners. By the looks of the condition from the outside, and what they could see of the inside, the store didn't stay in business too long.

As they continued traveling, Aarleen pointed out Monroe's law office. Henry made a quick turn in that direction and slowly rode past the office. They all noticed it also had a huge padlock attached to the door and frame. After they rode past the office, Renee also began to feel nostalgic and asked Henry to take her past the house she lived in before she was taken in by Reuben's family.

The ride to the Wallace house was a mixture of sadness and anger for Renee. When they reached the front of the house, Renee took a long, hard look at the structure. It had been run down and abandoned. No one wanted to live in it after what Franklin Wallace done to his daughter, so it never sold. It was a loss Renee's father had to bear because of his stubborn ego and pride.

Renee never talked to Aarleen about her father. She did tell Aarleen about her mother and how they reconciled before she left for Mobile. For the longest time, Margret corresponded with Renee through the mail using the address of an acquaintance in Mobile because Franklin Wallace continued to forbid his wife to have any dialog with Renee. For a while, Margret's letters showed delight about Aarleen's progress. Then, for no apparent reason, Margret's letters stopped.

Aarleen was curious about her other Grandfather. The short rare moments Franklin Wallace was discussed in front of Aarleen, Renee would not allow Aarleen to refer to him as GrandDa. Renee felt her father was not worthy of that term of endearment.

When Aarleen turned ten, her curiosity got the better of her one day and she timidly asked her father about Franklin Wallace after they finished training under the oak tree.

"How come Mama never talks about my other Grand... father?"

Reuben was sincerely at a complete loss of words and found it very difficult to answer Aarleen's question.

"Please, Da. Mama won't tell me and you always told me you will tell me the truth if I ever have a difficult question."

"You're right, my little blossom. I'll tell you, but you must never tell your Mama unless she brings it up herself, okay?"

"I promise, Da."

"Good. Let me start off by asking you, what did you like about GrandDa Aaron?"

"Oh, Da, he was the best. He called me his precious little angel and treated me like one too. You remind me of GrandDa because he was always kind and loving, just like you. He made me feel very special and I miss him a whole bunch."

Reuben nodded approvingly with a warm smile. Then his smile faded into a neutral look as he said, "Well, my precious blossom, your Mama's father was everything GrandDa was not. He was, and I say this in all honesty, cruel."

Honoring his pledge to be truthful, as Aarleen had asked, Reuben told her how Franklin Wallace treated Renee when she was younger. He described how Franklin tried to keep Renee and Reuben apart and eventually became one of the catalysts causing Reuben to leave the country. But the hardest thing Reuben had to tell Aarleen was how Franklin Wallace brutally threw Renee out of his life. When Reuben was finished, he sat against the trunk of the oak tree, hiding his face with his hands so Aarleen couldn't see the wetness in his eyes.

Aarleen took her father into her arms, hugged him tightly, and said, "Thank you, Da, for telling me. I promise I won't tell Mama you told me unless she asks, like you said."

Aarleen never told her mother about the conversation with her father, but after their talk, Aarleen went to Renee and hugged her as she said, "I'm so very lucky to have had GrandDa Aaron in my life, Mama. I will never forget him."

"Enough, Henry. Take us to the school, and then home," said Renee, with no emotion.

The three traveled up the road, but had to take a detour down Wickham Avenue because the Glent area of the city was being used by the military to house Union officers. Many of the residents had been evicted long ago because of pro-Confederate sentiments, or because some of the families had members fighting against the Union. Those families allowed to remain in their residences had to have them available to quarter Union officers. These residents felt their constitutional rights were being violated with the quartering of the military in their homes. However, as many were told, Virginia was in rebellion against the Union and, therefore, the residents had no constitutional rights.

Renee dreaded riding down Wickham Avenue and said to Aarleen, who had a little adorable smirk on her face, "Don't even think about calling me what you are about to call me, sweetie, or I'll take your bokken away for a week."

"Okay, Mama, I won't call you Wickham girl," she said with a laugh.

Renee could not help but laugh also thinking of when Reuben would say, *"Aishite'ru yo my precious Wickham girl,"* every night before they went to sleep.

As they rode by what used to be the Wickham Finishing School for Girls, Renee noticed it no longer looked in immaculate condition. Renee immediately wondered what happened to Martin Doogan. After she was taken in by Reuben's family, she lost touch with him, the only friend she had in that school.

The building looked run down and the gardens were over grown with weeds. The yards were occupied with people who looked as if they had no place to go. Above the main entrance, the sign had been changed. It now read, "Refugee and Homeless Shelter."

"Geez oh geez oh geez what a fitting end to that place," said Renee with a revengeful giggle. "Did I ever tell you about the time your Aunty Lucy and Mr. Doogan helped me ditch school so I could see your Da before he left to Mexico, sweetie?"

"Yeah, Mama, but tell it again. That's a good story."

As they rode past the old school, Renee began to tell the story, but didn't get too far when Aarleen called out to Henry to stop the wagon.

"WHOA, Henry, stop!"

With a concerned look on her face, Renee asked, "What's wrong, sweetie?"

"Over there, Mama, sitting against the wall! Is it? It is! It is! Benji! HEY, BENJI!!!" yelled out Aarleen as she jumped off the wagon and ran to Benjamin Norenham.

Renee let out a gasp and also jumped off the wagon and followed Aarleen.

When Benjamin heard Aarleen call out his name, he looked at her and began running away, but the state of his shoes caused him to stumble and he fell onto the walkway.

Aarleen ran and knelt by his side and tried to help him, but he desperately tried to push her away.

"Leave me alone, Aarleen. Don't look at me! I'm so ashamed! Go away!" he cried, trying to move away from Aarleen.

Aarleen kept trying to help him. Renee finally caught up and also took hold of Benjamin.

"Benjamin, what happened to you? Where's your mother?" asked Renee, concerned and curious.

"Please, just leave me alone. No one wants to help us. The Yankees evicted us because of father, and mother has lost her mind. We're better off left for dead," said Benjamin, whimpering in both Renee and Aarleen's arms.

Aarleen lifted Benjamin's face and wiped away his tears with the sleeve of her kosode and said, "We'll help you, Benji. Right, Mama?" she asked, not looking away from Benjamin.

"Right, sweetie," said Renee with no hesitation. "Where's your mother, Benjamin? Where's Cynthia?"

"She's in the alley behind the school. They kicked us out of the shelter because mother was causing a ruckus about not being treated properly."

Renee slapped her hand to her forehead and shook her head in wonder. That girl has not changed a bit, Renee thought.

"Henry, over here. Please come and help Aarleen with Benjamin!" called out Renee. "Sweetie, you help Benjamin into the wagon. I'm going to go find his mother."

"Okay, Mama."

"Renee, wait! You may need this," said Henry as he tossed Renee her jo.

"Thank you, Henry! I'll be right back. You two see to Benjamin."

With her jo in hand, Renee made her way to the back of her old school. The memories of this place were flooding her mind. The strict rules, the stupid etiquette lessons, and the torment she received from her old school nemesis, Cynthia, were all becoming too vivid as she ran to find that same nemesis.

"Geez oh geez oh geez I can't believe I'm concerned about Cynthia," said Renee to herself as she made it to the alley. "If only my Reuben could see me now. He would never let me live this moment down."

She made it to the alley and looked down to see several people sitting along the wall of what used to be one of the most prestigious schools in Norfolk. A few looked like they had, at one time, been prosperous people of Norfolk. As Renee walked up the alley, some of the people held up their hands for any type of hand out, but Renee ignored them. Her focus was on finding Cynthia.

Suddenly Renee saw a woman gorging herself on what looked to be some bread. Her blonde hair was stringy and matted, and the dress she wore was now tattered and filthy, but at one time looked to be of high end elegance. Renee slowly approached the woman with a concerned, curious look.

"Cynthia, is that you?" asked Renee, softly.

Cynthia looked up and saw Renee looking down at her. She let out a scream, threw what was left of the bread at Renee, and rose to run away, but fell over the torn skirt portion of her dress.

"Oh good heavens, of all people to find me in this condition, it had to be you," said Cynthia as she lay face down in the dirt.

With no judgment in her mind, Renee knelt down and tried to roll Cynthia over and sit her up. Taking some effort, Renee finally got Cynthia to sit up against the wall of the old school. She was sobbing and hiding her face with her hands.

"Look at what I have been reduced to," said Cynthia in a state of despair. "All because of my husband being a Confederate officer, I have been evicted from my beautiful home and reduced to living in the street. My school, my beautiful Wickham. Look what has become of my school."

Cynthia continued to whine and cry about her personal state while Renee tried caring for her. As Cynthia was going on and on about her welfare, Renee began to lose her feeling of compassion toward Cynthia, then she thought of Aarleen and Henry caring for Benjamin. Renee let out an angered grunt and slapped Cynthia across the face causing Cynthia to wince away from her.

"Shut up, Cynthia! All you are concerned about is you. What about your son, Benjamin? You're his mother, Cynthia! Why are you not caring for your son?! We found him all alone in the front scared out of his mind! Get yourself together for your son, Cynthia!" said Renee grasping Cynthia tightly by the shoulders.

"Benjamin? Oh my son. I forgot all about my son," Cynthia groaned.

"How could you, Cynthia? How could you forget about that wonderful boy of yours? You're reminding me of my father who abandoned me! Now get yourself together and come with me!"

"No, I will not go anywhere with the likes of you, you unappreciative bitch. You never deserved to go to Wickham! You were never of my social class!"

Cynthia awkwardly stood up, pushing Renee away.

"How dare you touch me with your peasant hands! Get away from me!" she yelled as she wiped Renee's hands off her shoulders.

Again, Renee slapped Cynthia, not out of anger, but to stop her shock. However, Renee could not help but think slapping Cynthia hard across her face felt so good after all those years of her torment.

"Get ahold of yourself, Cynthia! Benjamin needs you! Stop acting like an over-privileged, spoiled brat, and start acting like a mother! What would Simon think of you? He's depending on you to care for Benjamin while he's away!"

Feeling shame, Renee's words hit Cynthia as hard as her hand. Cynthia broke down and began crying uncontrollably.

"Good lord, you are right, Renee! What would my Simon think of me? What should I do, Renee? Please help me."

"What about your parents? Where are they?"

"They moved up North, those traitors," she said with a sneer.

Renee ignored Cynthia's absurd comment and continued, "Cynthia, do you have a safe place to take Benjamin? What about family or friends? Your friends like Elizabeth Rodgers?"

"None of them will have anything to do with me because of Simon. They don't want to be evicted for being involved with someone who has a husband in the army," she cried.

Renee let out a long, frustrated sigh and said, "Come on, Cynthia. You're coming with me." She pulled Cynthia by the arm with her to walk back down the alley.

"Where?" asked Cynthia, doubtfully.

"To our farm. You can stay there, provided you and Benjamin contribute," Renee said.

"What? Are you out of your mind? Me live out in the sticks? That is ridiculous!" Cynthia scoffed, stopping and pulling her arm free from Renee's hold.

"Fine, continue living here in the alleys and streets. You don't have to worry about Benjamin. We'll take care of him ourselves."

Renee continued to walk away until Cynthia called out to her.

"Renee, wait! I have reconsidered. I will go with you, but under these conditions."

"Seriously, Cynthia? Oh, please, tell me. This I've got to hear. I haven't had my daily laugh yet." Renee stopped, turned, and looked back at Cynthia with a look of disbelief on her face.

"I must have a room to myself," Cynthia began.

"No," Renee stated.

"I must have at least one servant."

"No."

"I must be able to bring what is left of my wardrobe."

"No."

586

"I will not do any form of domestic or outdoor labor."

"Hmm, okay."

"Really?" replied Cynthia, pleased.

"I was joking. No. Now, are you coming with me or not?" asked Renee, exasperated.

Cynthia's face turned into a sour look. She stomped her foot hard on the ground, nodded yes, and began to walk toward Renee.

"Well, well, well. What do we have here?" asked a rough, dirty, Union soldier coming up the alley. A fellow soldier was behind him.

"Looks like we have ourselves a couple of Southern belles in need of companionship, Nate."

"Oh geez, I don't have time for this boys. I'm so not in the mood to deal with your shenanigans right now," said Renee, picking up her jo off the ground.

"Whoa! I'll have the spirited, dark haired beauty, Nate. You can have that sloppy second blonde."

"Hey, why do I always get stuck with the sloppy seconds, Bert?!" the second soldier complained.

"Because you're sloppy seconds yourself. Now come here you precious, brown eyed beau..."

Before the soldier named Bert could finish his comment, Renee had twirled her jo from her right hand behind her back to her left and struck the soldier in his face. The soldier spat out teeth as he fell to the ground.

"Hey, how dare you strike a Union soldierrrrrrrrrrrrrrrrrrrrr!" said the other soldier as Renee wedged her jo deep and hard into his groin.

Pulling the jo free from the soldier's crotch, Renee twirled it from her left hand to her right and raised it in a defensive position ready to strike.

"Good lord, Renee! That was phenomenal!" exclaimed Cynthia.

"Yes, that certainly was," said Major MacKay, standing off to the side with a corporal.

"Yikes! More Yankees! Quickly, Renee, hit them with your stick!" yelled out Cynthia.

"Oh, be quiet, Cynthia," said Renee as she lowered her jo. "Mr. MacKay, what are you doing here?"

"I saw your daughter and Henry tending to a young boy out front and they told me you might need some assistance back here. By the looks of it, I believe you have the matter well at hand. Corporal, take those two into custody," the major said, pointing towards the two soldiers on the ground.

"Yes sir," replied the corporal, as he quickly escorted the two to the front of the old school.

"And who is this pathetic, looking creature?" asked Major MacKay to Renee as he looked Cynthia up and down.

"Do not tell him anything, Renee! Those heathen Yankees had me and Benjamin evicted from our home!" said Cynthia with hatred.

"I said, be quiet, Cynthia!" stressed Renee to Cynthia. Returning her focus back to the major, "Believe it or not, Mr. MacKay, but Cynthia is an old friend of mine. That boy you saw Henry and Aarleen tending to is her son. She and her son are, ah, refugees."

"We are nothing of the sort! We were evicted by you Yankee sons of bit..." Cynthia began.

"CYNTHIA, WILL YOU PLEASE SHUT UP!!!" shouted Renee, causing Cynthia to cower down and Major MacKay to startle. "Sorry about that, Mr. MacKay. Cynthia isn't used to living outside, and the sun has made her a little off beat."

"Mrs. Duran, you know far more than anyone else how residents are evicted."

"I do."

"And you also know how strict I am with policies."

"Yes, I do as well."

"Good, then may I recommend you advise Miss Cynthia to keep quiet while I conduct this interview."

Renee turned her focus to Cynthia and narrowed her eyes in warning to her. "Did you hear that, Cynthia?"

With a scowl on her face and her arms crossed in front of her chest, looking like a spoiled little brat denied a treat, Cynthia reluctantly nodded yes.

"Very well then. I assume you will be taking this, 'refugee' and her son into your care to live on your farm?" asked the major in an official tone.

"Yes, both of them," answered Renee, keeping her eyes narrowed at Cynthia.

"I see then," replied Major MacKay as he reached into his pocket and pulled out a small notebook. He handed it to Renee and continued. "If you please, Mrs. Duran, write down their names so I can add them to your resident roster so your rations are appropriate."

Renee took the notebook and wrote Cynthia and Benjamin's names down. Saying, "Oops," Renee drew a line across the name Norenham and wrote in Garrett next to it.

"My name is not Garrett anymore it is Norenham..." Cynthia began saying, but again cowered down after seeing Renee shoot her another look of warning.

"Here you go, Mr. MacKay. Cynthia and Benjamin Garrett. My daughter calls Cynthia's son Benji, in case you hear her and wonder."

"Very good. I'll make the necessary amendment to your residence, and be out to measure two plots of land for the two extra mouths you have to feed. This also allows you additional rations of flour and sugar. Being the line is long and your travel permit expires this afternoon, I'll see to it those rations are delivered. Oh yes, and speaking of your travel permit, do you have it on your person? I wouldn't be doing my job if I didn't see it."

Renee nodded and reached into the sleeve of Reuben's kosode, pulled out her travel permit, and handed it to the major. He looked it over and handed it back to Renee, nodding approvingly.

"Thank you for your cooperation, Mrs. Duran. May I suggest you finish your business in town and make your way back home? I don't want to see you detained for being out and about on an expired travel permit." Major MacKay turned his attention to Cynthia and said to her, "You are a very lucky woman to have a friend like Mrs. Duran, Cynthia Garrett. I recommend you listen very carefully to her advice while you are living under her roof. Good day, ladies."

As Major MacKay walked away, Renee began to make her way back to Aarleen, Henry, and Benjamin. Cynthia stumbled on her broken shoes close behind.

"I cannot believe you, Renee, a Yankee collaborator," Cynthia whispered as she walked behind Renee out of the alley.

"Listen, Cynthia. Mr. MacKay did you a huge favor. You had better be grateful. He's one of the few, decent Federal men in this area."

"Oh, I see now. You and him have, shall I say, a certain working relationship? It must be interesting seeing to his needs, being he only has one arm," said Cynthia, rather cynically.

Renee quickly turned on her heels and swung her jo across Cynthia's face and rested it on Cynthia's shoulder. "Listen to me, Cynthia, and listen good. Because of an ironic act of fate, Mr. MacKay treats us decently because he believes he owes us a favor."

"And what favor would that happen to be?" Cynthia asked.

"He feels he owes us because my husband only took his arm, not his life. Now come along. I still have to take Aarleen to the city school so she can turn in her and her friends' schoolwork before our time limit runs out on our travel permit."

狼

Beneath the falls containing water runoff from the snowcapped, high mountains on the far side of the gorge, the Shinto Temple sat beside the large pond that took eons to be created. Inside the temple sat Akagi Genda-San. For the past many months, he had been awakened by disturbing dreams, many of which featured his apprentice and retainer, Reuben-San. In the dreams, Reuben-San displayed great nobility in what one could only think of as trying times.

Knowing of the rebellion currently occurring in Reuben-San's home land, Akagi Genda-San knew all too well, somehow, Reuben-San would be drawn into the conflict either willingly or unwillingly. Considering Reuben-San's path, Akagi Genda-San assumed his involvement would be the latter.

Each and every time Akagi Genda-San was woken by a disturbing dream, the following morning he would make his way from the walls of Hisano Castle, through the paths and bridges of Itosai, past Reuben-San's cottage, the English school, and into the temple to meditate and pray. His meditation and prayers were simple...

"Please ancestors of Akagi past, be with and look after Reuben-San's safety, and for his wife's and daughter's safety as well."

狼

Life on the farm was a huge welcome for Benjamin. Although strictly regulated here in the country, just as in the city, the constant reminder of Union troops everywhere wasn't as apparent like in the city. Occasionally a dust cloud and the sounds of mounted troopers could be seen and heard, but because of the secluded area of the farm, they went unnoticed, with the exception of Riley who would let out a warning bark.

From the day Benjamin arrived on the farm, his spirit rose. He thought the ride back from the city was a welcomed treat. He never rode in a work wagon and laughed every time it hit a bump jarring him out of his seat. Aarleen could not help but feel happy watching Benjamin enjoy the ride and laughed along with him.

As Henry drove the wagon up the lane to the house, Riley let out a welcoming bark and trotted out to meet the wagon as it pulled up to the front of the house. As it came to a stop, Aarleen jumped off and ran to greet Riley with a hug.

"Hey there, Riley, did you miss us? Look, we have two new family members so let's go greet them," said Aarleen, cheerfully.

Renee climbed off the wagon followed by Henry and Benjamin. May and Evergreen came out of the house and noticed the presence of Cynthia and Benjamin right away. As everyone greeted one another, Cynthia remained sitting on the wagon with a sad, puzzled look on her face.

"Is no one going to help me down?" Cynthia asked, pathetically.

"Oh my," commented Evergreen. "I see a lot of potential laughter in the making."

"Be nice, Ever," said Renee as she begin to tell May and Evergreen how they came across Cynthia and her son, and of their plight.

"You have a *big* heart, Renee Duran, a very big heart," said May, well aware of their past history.

"Hey! I am still up here. Renee, have one of your nig…" Cynthia began.

"CYNTHIA, DON'T YOU DARE UTTER ANOTHER WORD YOU WILL BE SORRY FOR!!!" yelled Renee, in anger.

Renee's outburst startled everyone and caused Riley to cower behind Aarleen.

Aarleen came to May and asked, "May, I never heard Mama raise her voice like that before, except when Captain Grossman tried to take Da's Kutto. Please tell me she never raised her voice like that to me when I was too young to remember?"

Both May and Evergreen laughed. "No, child, she never did," replied May.

"Well, how am I supposed to get down from here?" asked Cynthia.

"How did you get up?" asked Renee, exasperated.

"That daughter of yours helped me, and rather rudely I may add," replied Cynthia.

"Calm down, mother. I'll help you," said Benjamin.

Benjamin awkwardly helped his mother down from the wagon and once Cynthia's feet hit the ground, Riley came up to both of them and began sniffing, starting with Benjamin. Riley moved over and began to sniff Cynthia and she started screaming.

"He's attacking us! Someone shoot this mangy beast before it mauls us to death."

"Riley isn't a mangy beast, Mrs. Norenham," said Aarleen. "He's just learning your scent so he won't maul you if he runs into you while he's guarding the farm. Come on, Benji, help me with these sacks of flour and sugar. Then we can go and catch some dinner."

"Catch dinner? You mean fishing?!" asked Benjamin, excitedly.

"Of course, silly, we eat a lot of fish around here. The Federals may control what we grow, but they can't take what we catch."

"OH BOY! I've never been fishing! I remember cleaning fish with you and Noah a long time ago. Will you teach me, Aarleen?" he asked, picking up items from the wagon.

"Of course I will. Henry, you look like you need to relax after driving us to the city. Come with us," Aarleen said, trying to persuade Henry to join them.

"You don't have to ask me twice, lil' missy. Let's get these sacks unloaded and then off to the creek," said Henry.

Evergreen noticed an odd look on Renee's face and asked, "Renee, is there anything wrong?"

"Geez oh geez oh geez my little Aarleen, she has become the shoddy farm girl, and Benjamin is the... oh geez, I can't say it."

"Say it, Renee, say it," urged Evergreen with a hint of humor in her voice.

"Benjamin is the prissy Chandler boy."

May burst out laughing so hard she collapsed into Renee's and Evergreen's arms.

"I'll tell you one thing for certain, Reuben will seriously enjoy this bit of irony," replied May once she regained her composure.

狼

Life on the farm for Cynthia wasn't pleasant, in the beginning. She expected to be catered to, but wasn't. She cried and cried when she never got her way, which was always. Cynthia cried a lot.

If it hadn't been for Benjamin, she wouldn't have been able to cope. He did everything for her, from helping her get dressed in the morning, to covering her up at night. As the days turned into weeks, Cynthia's constant dependence on Benjamin began to take its toll.

"You've got to stop doing everything for your mother, Benji. In this family, we all contribute. She's wearing you down," said Aarleen to Benjamin with compassion as Renee listened.

"I have to see to her, Aarleen. She's my mother. She's had a pampered life and can't cope on her own. She needs me," replied Benjamin, tired after he finished putting his mother down for a nap when she claimed she needed rest after reluctantly helping May fold laundry.

Renee sincerely admired Benjamin's devotion to his mother, but also had contempt toward Cynthia from when she told Renee she forgotten all about her son in the alley behind Wickham.

Unlike Benjamin, Cynthia was unappreciative for her blessings Renee and the others provided for her. Living arrangements for Renee and Aarleen needed to be adjusted to accommodate Cynthia and her son.

Renee moved back into her and Reuben's room and Aarleen moved back into her room. However, Aarleen would still find herself sleeping with Renee. Aarleen was prone to have bad dreams about her father when she did not sleep with or near her mother.

Cynthia and Benjamin were offered Monroe's and Reuben's old room to which Cynthia objected. She demanded to have Aarleen's room to herself.

"And where do you suggest my daughter stay?" Renee asked.

"She can share this room with my son," Cynthia stated.

"That's not going to happen, Cynthia. Even you know that's inappropriate. Now, either you accept this arrangement or I can find you a nice comfy place to sleep out in the barn."

Frowning and stomping her foot, Cynthia agreed. "I will take that bed then," she said, pointing to Reuben's old bed.

"Oh no you won't!" said Renee very sternly with a sense of dominance regarding the bed. "You will use Monroe's bed, and if I ever catch you on Reuben's, I'll hip throw you so hard, you'll wish I left you in that alley where I found you."

Benjamin helped out as much as he could when allowed by his mother. One evening after everyone had gone to bed, Renee caught Benjamin tending to the small allotted crop field.

"Now what in the world do you think you're doing at this late hour, Benjamin?" asked Renee, startling him.

"Oh, hello, Mrs. Duran, I am, ah, doing my part. Mother doesn't allow me enough time to help you and the others, so I sometimes come out here when mother is asleep and tend the crops. It's the least I can do."

Renee felt a great amount of pride in Benjamin. "Come here, Benjamin." He moved to stand near Renee. "You mean to tell me it's you who has been tending the plots all this time? We all thought they were growing well on their own," said Renee as she took him into her arms and gave him a hug.

Benjamin whimpered in Renee's arms. It reminded Renee of all the hugs she received from Aaron and Coleen, real hugs. The type of hugs she never received from her parents.

"Benjamin, you've made me very proud. You're a very strong boy. Now go inside, clean up, and go to bed, okay?"

"Yes, Mrs. Duran," said Benjamin as he started walking to the house. After a few steps, he stopped, turned to Renee, and said, "Thank you very much for taking us in, Mrs. Duran. My mother may not appreciate it, but I sincerely do, very much."

After witnessing Benjamin tending the plots, Renee was determined to have a serious discussion with Cynthia the next day. As it turned out, Renee would not need to have that discussion after the incident which became to be known as, "the day of the shoe."

Although Benjamin went to bed late the night before, he was still up early, even before Aarleen. By the time she woke up, Benjamin already collected eggs, milked the goat, and was assisting Evergreen in preparing breakfast.

Benjamin thrived during the mornings. It was his favorite time of the day. Since his mother slept in late, very late, sometimes past ten o'clock, he took the opportunity to contribute to the farm as much as he could.

He assisted Henry with tending the wagon and its team, and also helped him making repairs to whatever needed fixing. Benjamin helped May and Evergreen with the caring of the house and cabins, but it was Aarleen he enjoyed working with the most. Aarleen taught him everything needed to run the farm. They tended the allotted crop plots and the hidden plots, saw to the animals, and did most of the fishing. They made a good team and Renee could not help but notice a resemblance between them and her and Reuben when they were their age.

Benjamin adored Renee and was always asking if there was anything she needed for him to do. He was grateful to Renee for taking him and his mother in under her care, and felt obligated to contribute as much as he could considering Cynthia took Renee's kindness for granted. It was Benjamin's idea not to tell his mother about the hidden plots and animals.

"How come, Benjamin? Why do you think we shouldn't tell Cynthia about our hidden resources?" asked Renee. She couldn't find it in herself to refer to Cynthia as a mother.

"Well, Mrs. Duran, you know my mother as well as I do, maybe even better. If she knew about the hidden plots and animals, somehow, unknowingly, she will divulge their location to the Yankee area inspector."

"Geez, Benji's right, Mama," said Aarleen.

Renee could not help but chuckle, "No offense to you, Benjamin, but I see your point. Cynthia always had a blabbermouth when we went to school together."

"She still does," replied Benjamin.

Benjamin had a very lively step early in the morning and a cheerful attitude. However, when the whiny voice of his mother called out to him to come help her get out of bed, his lively step and cheerful attitude turned sour. He went from cheerful to depressed at the sound of her voice.

Renee, Aarleen, and Benjamin were outside helping Henry tend to the fishing equipment when Cynthia's high pitched, whiny voice called out to Benjamin to come help her get out of bed. Benjamin let out a sigh of grief, his cheerful face turned into a frown, and his upright squared shoulders dropped and went limp. He turned and started making his way to the house, the same way one who was heading to the gallows would walk.

"Wait, Benjamin, I'm coming with you," said Renee. "This needs to be put to an end."

"No, Mrs. Duran, that's okay. I'm used to it."

"No, Benji, Mama's right. It breaks my heart seeing you tend to your mother's every need."

"Well, okay then, but it's not going to do any good. Mother is just too spoiled."

"We will see. Come on," said Renee, as she put her arm around Benjamin for encouragement.

Benjamin entered the room with Renee following close behind. Aarleen leaned against the door frame. Cynthia was seated on the edge of Monroe's bed with her bare feet dangling down. She was still in the night gown borrowed from Renee.

"Where have you been, Benjamin? I called for you twice. Please fetch me my shoes."

Benjamin was picking up the clothes she had been borrowing from Renee off the floor. She wore Renee's clothes like they were disposable and it angered Benjamin. Out of the goodness of Mrs. Duran's heart, she lends you her clothes and you treat them like trash, Benjamin thought to himself as he picked them off the floor and cared for them gently.

"Cynthia, we need to have a discussion," said Renee.

Cynthia said, "In a moment, Renee." She turned to Benjamin. "Son, I said I need my shoes," she pointed to them resting next to her feet. "Oh my, look at me, I missed breakfast. Oh well, I will have a nice lunch then."

"You always miss breakfast, Mrs. Norenham," said Aarleen, in a discreetly mocking tone.

Although she found Aarleen's comment amusing, Renee looked at her and gave her a combined look of humor and warning. Aarleen responded with a cute little smirk and a shrug of her shoulders causing Renee to shake her head and silently chuckle.

"No, Cynthia, we really need to have a talk," said Renee, turning her attention back to Cynthia. "Benjamin cannot be tending to your every need and work the farm at the…"

"Benjamin, what is for lunch?" asked Cynthia, interrupting Renee. "Make sure you watch that nigra woman who makes my lunch closely."

"DAMN IT, MOTHER! THAT IS ENOUGH!!!" yelled Benjamin, startling Renee and Aarleen while Cynthia brought up the covers to hide behind. "NO MORE! DO YOU UNDERSTAND?! I HAVE HAD ENOUGH!!!" he continued.

"Calm down, Benji," said Aarleen with a worried look, concerned for Benjamin.

"No, Aarleen, I will not calm down! This has been a long time coming and I'm going to enjoy the ride! Mother, ever since Mrs. Duran, Aarleen, and Henry saved our lives, you have been downright ungrateful, mean, and ugly! They have shared their food, clothes, and beds, but you still cannot find it in yourself to be thankful for their kindness! Every night before you go to sleep, you bitch and moan about Mrs. Duran behind her back. *I cannot believe Renee went to Wickham. Renee is not a real lady of social class. How come Renee cannot be like me?'* Well mother, the question should not be… why can't Renee be like you? The question should be… why can't you be like Renee?!"

"Benjamin! Well, I never! My own son talking to me in such a manner," Cynthia replied, shocked.

"Stop it, mother! You are too out of touch to realize how wrong you are and that is going to change today. I honestly don't understand what father see's in you!" Benjamin said, disgusted.

"Whoa…" said Aarleen, ready to warn Benjamin to be careful.

Renee immediately covered both her and Aarleen's mouths with her hands.

Benjamin continued. "I wouldn't be surprised if he joined the army to get away from you! I sure as hell would rather face thousands of angry Yankees than to see to your every little need! So if you want your damn shoes, get off your ass and get them yourself! They are right next to your stupid feet! I'm too busy to fuss over you! I have to go help Aarleen catch today's dinner, and after dinner, Mrs. Duran and Aarleen are going to teach me how to fight just like Mr. Duran taught them!"

Cynthia sat in complete shock with tears forming and starting to roll down her cheeks.

Benjamin stepped up to Renee and with a calm polite voice, he said, "Please forgive me for my outburst and language, Mrs. Duran. I'm ashamed of my behavior. Please don't think badly of me for telling mother the truth." Turning his attention to Aarleen, he continued, "I'm sorry to you also, Aarleen. Please, can we now go fishing, if it's okay with you, Mrs. Duran?"

"Of course," replied Renee, admiring Benjamin for standing up to his mother, something she always wished she could have done to her own father. "Ask Henry to go with you. I believe he wanted to do some fishing himself."

"Thank you, Mama. Come on, Benji."

The two youths left the room leaving Renee alone with Cynthia.

With a face full of tears and a frown on her face, Cynthia said, "What did you need to discuss with me, Renee?"

Feeling slightly awkward, Renee slowly walked backwards out of the room saying, "Oh… never mind."

狼

The days following Benjamin's outburst toward his mother were interesting, to say the least. For the first couple of days, Cynthia did not leave the room, feeling too ashamed to show herself. At first she couldn't understand why she felt that way.

One afternoon, while sitting on Monroe's bed feeling sorry for herself, she heard laughter coming from the oak tree. She went to the window and saw everyone watching Aarleen and Benjamin take turns throwing one another to the ground. When Benjamin was having difficulty doing a technique, Renee would help him by showing him the correct angles.

Cynthia found herself smiling as she watched while tugging a button on the bodice of the dress she was wearing. Suddenly it dawned on her the reason she felt shame was because Benjamin was right. She was selfish and spoiled beyond measure and began to feel anger toward herself.

"Of all people who should hate me, it should be Renee for all the torment I caused her in the past, but she does not. She took us in when our family and friends did not," she said to herself.

Frowning in disappointment, she tugged the button hard and it came off. "Oh no, what have I done? I must fix this, but I don't know how," Cynthia said, on the verge of tears. Suddenly an idea came to her and, for the first time since Benjamin's outburst, she left the room.

Cynthia made her way to the oak tree where everyone was having a good time. Renee noticed Cynthia coming closer and stopped her training with Benjamin to acknowledge her.

"Cynthia, is there anything wrong? Are we being too loud?" asked Renee with full sincerity.

Cynthia walked up to Renee while everyone watched with wide-eyed wonder. Holding out her hand showing the button, she said, "I accidently pulled this button off your dress. I'm sorry. I want to fix it, but I don't know how. Will someone please teach me?"

Benjamin handed Aarleen Reuben's bokken he had been using, walked to his mother, and took her into his arms. Those who were sitting, rose and stepped in closer. Renee took Aarleen in her arms and May put her hand on Cynthia's shoulder.

"Come with me, child, and I'll teach you," said May, moving to take Cynthia to the house.

It took May all of fifteen minutes to teach Cynthia how to sew on the button. May let Cynthia do all the work, including threading the needle. When she was finished, she had a surprised look on her face. "Is that it? Am I finished? Did I really sew on a button?" she asked, surprised at herself.

"Yes you did, Mrs. Norenham," answered May, "and you did a mighty fine job of it."

"Oh goodness, please call me Cynthia. I did it. I actually did it. I sewed on a button. I've got to show Benjamin," said Cynthia as she stood from the kitchen table and ran out the back door calling for her son.

When Benjamin heard his mother calling for him, he didn't have that dreadful feeling from the past. Her call was pleasant. When she arrived back at the oak tree, she proudly showed Benjamin the button she had sewn back onto Renee's dress.

"Renee, I'm sooo very sorry... for everything! Thank you for letting me and Benjamin live here! Please teach me something about the farm, anything! How do you grow food?"

From that day on, Cynthia began to learn more about helping and becoming part of a real family, even going as far as waking up before Benjamin and getting him out of bed to start the day.

狼

It was a nice spring day in May when Major MacKay came by for another inspection tour, but this was the third tour in one week, which was unusual. It was very concerning for Renee and the others.

Renee went to greet the major as he dismounted his horse. He only had one trooper with him, a corporal, the same corporal he had with him the day Cynthia and Benjamin came to the farm.

"Hello, Mr. MacKay, is there anything wrong? You were here just the other day," Renee asked, concerned.

"Oh, there's nothing to concern yourself with, Mrs. Duran. I'm trying to get ahead of my work. The rebellion is going rather nicely for the Union, so I'm finding more time to, ah, make rounds when I feel they are needed."

"And you feel a round is needed to our farm?" Renee asked, suspiciously.

"In your case, yes, I do. Corporal, will you please inspect the front yard and report back to me?"

"Yes, sir," the corporal replied, moving to the front of the house.

"Don't be concerned, Mrs. Duran. This won't take long at all."

With a very puzzled look on her face, she walked back to the house where everyone was gathered on the porch. Aarleen came down to stand by her mother.

"What's going on, Mama?" Aarleen asked, concerned with this unusual inspection from Major MacKay.

With a very worried look, Renee shrugged her shoulders.

The corporal roamed around the front yard in several circles, picked a blade of grass, inspected it, and turned to the major and said, "The front yard looks to be in order, Major."

"Very good, Corporal. Let us be off then," said Major MacKay. He turned his attention to Renee and said, "Sorry to be a bother, Mrs. Duran. We will be on our way."

"That's it?" asked Renee with a look of doubt on her face.

"Yes, Mrs. Duran. I told you it wouldn't take long." answered Major MacKay very pleasantly.

Renee and Aarleen looked at each other with very inquisitive looks. They noticed the major and the corporal taking their time mounting their horses by checking the saddle straps and reins.

"Oh, Corporal, have you heard the latest from Petersburg?" Major MacKay asked.

"Petersburg you say, Major? What's happening in Petersburg?" the corporal replied, pulling out a brush from his saddlebag and began brushing out his horse's mane.

"The rebels are under siege there. I understand *Doyle's* Brigade is there," said Major MacKay, as he adjusted the empty sleeve of his frockcoat.

"*Doyle's* Brigade? My, my, I believe that brigade is made up of regiments from this area."

"That's right, Corporal. One of them is the... *68th*."

"Hey, the owner of this farm is... ah, detained by the *68th* was he not?" asked the corporal, acting as if Renee and the others were not listening to the conversation.

Major MacKay moved next to the corporal and watched as he tended to his horse's mane. "That he was. He was taken from here and impressed into service against his will."

"I hope he is doing okay for his family's sake. They are good people."

"From a letter that somehow got through the lines from a U.S. Sanitation Commission doctor I received yesterday, I understand he is very well. Apparently a messenger took him a special item to keep him safe. That messenger is well also. From what the letter read, the man from this farm is a real pain in the ass to his superiors. A real smart ass from what I understand. He's definitely going to survive his impressment, and the way this rebellion is going our way, all three of them will probably be home soon."

Renee and Aarleen took hold of each other in joyful relief.

"Praise be," Evergreen whispered, as May took her into her arms and Henry took hold of Evergreen's hand.

"What about that rebel engineer battalion in Petersburg Major? I heard several rebels from Norfolk are in that battalion," said the corporal, retuning the brush into the saddlebag.

"Indeed, there's a major, goes by the name... *Simon Norenham,* originally from Richmond but has a wife and son who were refugees and found shelter here in Norfolk County. I understand he was taken prisoner, but will be exchanged."

"I thought General Grant stopped the exchanging of prisoners."

"He did, but this Norenham was wounded in the leg. He is well and still able to walk. The wound he received is good enough to get him exchanged and should be back in Norfolk any day now."

Cynthia and Benjamin both gasped in joy and held onto each other.

"That's good to hear, Major."

"That it is, Corporal. Well, we have other stops to make so let us be on our way."

Major MacKay and the corporal mounted their horses and were about to heel their mounts when Renee called out to the major. "Mr. MacKay, please wait," Renee said while she and Aarleen ran to his horse.

Both Renee and Aarleen looked up to Major MacKay with tears of joy in their eyes. "Thank you very much for such a, ah, wonderful inspection of the front yard today. We do appreciate it very much."

Major Mackay nodded to the corporal to move ahead. As the corporal heeled his mount and slowly trotted away, the major looked down to Renee and Aarleen with a hopeful expression.

"Keep up your faith and love, Renee and Aarleen. Keep up your faith and love."

Major MacKay heeled his horse and quickly galloped away.

狼

It was a warm day late in July of '64, and everyone was relaxing at the creek's edge. Henry, Aarleen, and Benjamin were fishing for the day's dinner. Just prior, Renee, Aarleen, and Benjamin had a very rigorous Budo training session which Aarleen was showing very proficient skill with her bokken.

Renee and Cynthia were sitting with their children watching them fish and talking. Renee was telling Cynthia about Reuben's journey to Japan and all about Akagi Genda-San. Renee told Cynthia she didn't know him too long, but what she did know, she found him to be the wisest man she had ever met, and Reuben was a better man because of him.

Aarleen yawned and asked her mother to watch her line while she took a little nap under the oak tree. Renee took Aarleen's fishing pole and Aarleen walked to the oak tree with Riley following. Aarleen laid down in the soft grass using Riley as a pillow, and slowly drifted off to sleep.

Aarleen stood on a hard, well used dirt road in a strange land she seen twice before in previous dreams many years ago. She looked to her left and saw hills resembling huge stairs filled with water, and strange grass growing from within the water. There were people tending to the grass.

She looked to the right and saw the same snowcapped mountains from her previous dreams. "Hey, I remember this place," Aarleen said out loud with a gleeful feeling.

Slowly, the scenery faded into the war-torn landscape of Virginia. She looked to her left. The hills resembling huge stairs filled with water, and strange grass growing from within the water, faded into trenches with Confederate flags waving in the breeze. The snowcapped mountains to her right faded into Union trenches. Aarleen was standing in the middle of the two opposing armies.

She was beginning to feel terrified and started running down the middle of the shell-torn land. She tripped and fell over what she thought was a log, but saw it was a dead soldier in an undistinguishable uniform. With a look of horror, Aarleen started to crawl as fast as she could with her eyes closed.

She crawled into something solid and fell over. She opened her eyes to see a familiar tall gray horse standing above her.

"Quickly, Aarleen-Dono, rise and climb on, I will help you," said a man in red Akagi samurai armor wearing a large helmet atop his head with the Akagi crest attached.

Aarleen took the samurai's offered hand and was lifted onto the rear of the horse and they galloped toward the Confederate trenches. Aarleen held tight and let out a scream as the samurai's mount leaped over the trench and landed on the other side.

As they rode through the Confederate encampments, she noticed the soldiers were not paying any attention to her and the samurai galloping at a quick pace. They came to a stop and the samurai helped Aarleen off the horse, and then he also dismounted. He removed his facemask of black and silver and looked at Aarleen.

"You're Mr. Akagi," said Aarleen. "I remember you from my other dreams."

"Hai, young one, I am. My, you have grown into a beautiful young woman, Aarleen-Dono. You are the mirror image of your beautiful mother, Renee-Dono, except for your nose. You have your father's nose."

"My Da, are you here because of my Da, like my other dreams I had in the past?! Is he okay? He's not dead, is he?"

"No, Aarleen-Dono, he is very much alive, strong, healthy, and is proving himself worthy to be called an Akagi samurai. He has been doing what he is destined to do, protect those who cannot protect themselves."

"But what about us, Mr. Akagi? We need him home to protect us."

"Ah, my precious Aarleen-Dono, he has protected you."

"How? He was stolen away from us."

"Did he not train you and your mother in the Budo Arts? Did you not use that training to protect your home and persons? And was it not Reuben-San, your father, who foresaw this conflict, and had your family and friends prepare by tilling hidden gardens to grow food so you will not go hungry during these trying times? Was it not your father, by an act of fate, send you a fair and decent man to see to your safety?

"You see, my precious Aarleen-Dono, your father loves you so much, and he prepared you for this family test, which you are passing successfully. He has protected you the best he could under these difficult conditions."

Aarleen began to cry and Akagi Genda-San took her into his armored arms.

"What about *his* protection? Who's protecting my Da?"

"That is why I am here. I, too, have been having dreams about Reuben-San like you, so I have been meditating and praying in the temple for his welfare. Look, there he is," said Akagi Genda-San as he pointed to an open field.

Aarleen looked and saw her father preforming kumitachi katas with his Kutto.

"He's all alone, Mr. Akagi."

"Your heart, young one," said Akagi Genda-San as he covered Aarleen's eyes with his hand. "Look with your heart. Close your eyes and think of nothing except of your mother and your father."

Aarleen did as Akagi Genda-San instructed and thought hard. The memory of the day Renee and Reuben got married under the oak tree came to her mind so vividly. It was the happiest day of her life because that day, they became a true family. The memory made her smile.

Akagi Genda-San moved away his hand and said, "Open your eyes, Aarleen-Dono... and look at your father."

Aarleen opened her eyes and saw her father still preforming katas, but this time he was surrounded by a dozen samurai warriors dressed in full Akagi samurai armor, preforming katas along with him.

"You see, Aarleen-Dono, your father is not alone. I have meditated and called upon some of the greatest Akagi samurai of the past to watch over him so he will return to you and your mother safely. Your father, Reuben-San, is a strong, brave man, Aarleen-Dono, and you must remain just as strong and brave as he. Your father has told you only but a fraction of his deeds. He is more than a sensei, young one. He is a good man. Not only did he devise a plan and help in the defeat of Arata Goro and his army, the rebuilding of Itosai, and the construction of Hisano Castle. Your father stood guard nearly every night he was away from you and your lovely mother. With sword in hand, he protected Itosai and its border outposts and villages from thieves, bandits, and brigands. He has prepared the region of Itosai for the new era that is to come by teaching his language to my citizens. Reuben-San has earned the love and admiration from Itosai's citizens, my family, and I. Your father did all this, and never once did he lose his love and devotion for your mother. He spoke of Renee-Dono and kept her near and dear in his heart every day throughout his absence, even in battle. Your father is a good and righteous man, Aarleen-Dono, a man who deserves your heart, for he has kept your heart in his mind during this time he has been stolen from you. Reuben-San is... Okami. Master of Okami no Michi style of swordsmanship, and General of the Okami no Mure. You, Aarleen-Dono, and your mother, Renee-Dono, have a grand man to cherish, and it is because of that, the Gods of the High Mountains of the Hisano Provence will not allow him to die in this conflict he was forced into for the sake of preserving the Duran Dynasty.

"You know the meaning of stones and water, young Aarleen-Dono. You know the bond of love and devotion between your mother and father is very strong. Have patience, my precious daughter of Reuben-San and Renee-Dono. Your father will return within a year's time. Patience and love, Aarleen-Dono... stones and water.

"Wake now and go tell your mother Reuben-San is not alone and is well protected."

Akagi Genda-San replaced his face mask and remounted his horse.

"Wake up, Aarleen-Dono, wake up, wake up, wake up, sweetie, wake up, sweetie…."

"Wake up, sweetie, wake up!" said Renee with concern in her voice taking Aarleen gently into her arms. "Wake up. You're having another bad dream, sweetie."

Aarleen's eyes opened to see everyone on their knees around her with very concerned faces. She blinked a few times as tears formed in her eyes and began pouring out as she started crying uncontrollably.

Renee rocked and held her tightly.

"Quick, Benjamin, get Aarleen some water," said Cynthia.

"No, wait, Benji," said Aarleen. She looked up into Renee's eyes, "No, Mama. It wasn't a bad dream. It was Mr. Akagi, Mama. He told me to tell you Da is not alone and is well protected. He said Da will be home within a year's time. Oh, Mama, I want my Da!"

"I know, sweetie, I know. I want him also," said Renee as she held Aarleen close to her chest.

Renee took hold of the VMI button hanging from her neck, brought it to her mouth, and kissed it tenderly and said, as she held Aarleen close, "Thank you, Mr. Akagi, for all you have done, and continue to do for my dearest Reuben. Thank you for assuring his little cherry blossom of his care and protection. And I very much thank you for granting me the courage and strength to let him go when he was jagged to become as smooth as the stone you presented to me. Reuben my dear husband, you are my stone, and I will forever be your water. Aishite'ru yo, my shoddy farm boy."

石
水

In the year of our Lord, 1864, a romantic tale continues.
Brothers don't only share blood. They share blood drawn in battle...

<u>Aishite'Ru Yo, My Precious Wickham Girl</u>

Harper's Weekly
August 6, 1864

The army, although no longer marching and fighting day by day, is by no means idle; earth works, of much heavier construction than the temporary rifle-pits thrown up on the march from Culpepper, keep the spade and pick in constant requisition. The enemy's position, in most instances, command ours, giving them the advantage in the constantly renewed artillery firing along the front, and superior protection for their men from the fire of sharp-shooters.

Reuben and Doctor Chelmsford once again found themselves in Petersburg, where Reuben's search for his brother rigorously took shape. The main difference and biggest concern for Reuben during this recent stay in Petersburg, was Noah. Reuben desperately wanted to send him back home ever since Gettysburg. The Federals were not making it easy for Doctor Chelmsford and Noah to cross the lines like they did at Chancellorsville. The new Union General in command was unlike his predecessors who either withdrew from a Confederate victory or didn't follow through with one of their own. This Grant has the drive of a samurai, thought Reuben. Every time he believed the doctor and Noah had a chance to cross the lines and go home, their opportunity would be delayed because of General Grant's instinct to drive his enemy into defeat, no matter the cost to his own army.

The march back to Petersburg was a long drawn out trudge filled with one enemy encounter after another starting after the Confederate defeat in Pennsylvania. After the three day battle where Reuben finally made contact with Monroe, he could not find his brother anywhere. The Army of Northern Virginia was defeated on northern soil once again and was on the run back to Virginia for its survival. The command structure seemed to be in chaos while officers worked diligently to keep their troops together and on the move.

Reuben ran up and down the column of the army looking for any sign of Monroe. Even the Military and Civilian Law Matters Committee Department, of which Monroe was attached, seemed to have disappeared. There was no sign of Sergeant Jacob Cobb, the NCO, who helped Reuben initially locate Monroe.

"I wouldn't be too concerned, Reuben, my boy," said Doctor Chelmsford in a reassuring manner. "Lee may have sent all non-combatant departments back to Virginia ahead of the army. That's common. You know that."

"Yeah, I know, but for Monroe and his department to vanish with no one even hearing of his department. I even asked one of Lee's adjutants and he said he never heard of the Military and Civilian Law Matters Committee Department. That's just too odd."

"Come on, Reuben. I bet Monroe is back on his way to Norfolk right this very minute, especially after what you told us about the talk you had with him the morning of the second day of the battle," said Noah.

"Possibly, but I wanted you to go back with him. I'm going to try a few more times to locate him. Tell Todd and Max I'll be back."

"How about I come along, Reuben?" asked Noah. "Maybe a second pair of eyes might help."

"That's not a bad idea. Okay, come along, but stay close. I don't want you to be mistaken for someone's personal servant and I end up losing you too."

Together, Reuben and Noah headed toward the head of the column where the command staff would be leading the troops back into Virginia. Hopefully, Reuben thought, the department Monroe was in was among what Reuben and many harden veteran soldiers called, rear echelon seat cushions, always in the front marching to and retreating from battle, but nowhere to be found during.

Several times Reuben and Noah passed the presence of a rider atop a light gray blended horse. Its color hue highlighted its rider's uniform. Unlike other generals in the Confederate army whose stars were surrounded with a wreath, this particular general wore the insignia of a full colonel. However, his buttons were arranged in a general's pattern.

This general took notice of Reuben and his companion as they passed him several times. At first, the general ignored the two, but after the third time Reuben and Noah passed, the general became curious about the one carrying such a strange looking sword, the likes he had never seen. Instead of it attached to a leather belt, it was tucked into a burgundy colored, cotton sash tied at the front of the man's waist.

"See any trace of him, Noah?" asked Reuben as they stopped and stepped off the side of the road, both looking up and down the long column of retreating Confederate troops.

"No, Reuben. What now?"

"Let's head back to the company. I hope Doc's right and Monroe's department has been sent on ahead. I'm exhausted."

Reuben and Noah started their long walk back to Company C of the 68th Virginia, miles from the head of the column. Reuben told Noah once they pass the command staff they would find a nice peaceful tree to sit and lean against and wait for the company to catch up to them. They didn't get too far when once again they were seen by the commanding general atop the light gray blended horse.

"Excuse me, Colonel. Those two have crossed before us several times. I believe that one man to be an officer. He appears to have a sword at his side. Please inquire as to who he is and where they belong."

"Yes sir, General, sir," responded the colonel.

The colonel dismounted and stepped lively toward Reuben and Noah and called out to them. "You there, come here!"

Reuben stopped and glanced toward the colonel. Reuben nodded to Noah to step off the road and wait.

"Is there a problem?" asked Reuben in a neutral tone.

"Who are you, ah…"

"Captain," said Reuben, flipping his collar up to display the captain stripes and folded it back down.

"Captain? What regiment are you with?"

"Who wants to know?"

"Excuse me?!" asked the colonel, perturbed. "Do you have any idea how insubordinate you are?! You have passed the commanding general several times, and not once have you rendered a salute!"

"I didn't salute you either, so what's the big deal?" asked Reuben, releasing a yawn and stretching out his arms.

The commanding general looked to his other staff members with a great deal of disbelief as he watched and listened to the colonel's and Reuben's dialog.

"I have a right mind to slap you in irons for your insolence and have you court martialed!"

Reuben stepped closer to the colonel and raised his hands, palms up exposing his wrists. "Go ahead," he said in a calm tone. "It won't be the first time you rear echelon bastards slapped them on to force me to fight for your lost cause."

After his comment, Reuben looked the commanding general eye-to-eye. The general stared back for several seconds and nodded as he saw a hardened warrior in his presence.

"Colonel, allow the captain to be on his way. It is obvious he is a very busy man," said the general.

The colonel nodded and told Reuben to carry on.

"Colonel," said Reuben as he was about to walk away, "You better learn how to use that pistol and sword because things are about to get a lot worse, especially if he continues to sit tall in the saddle," Reuben continued to say as he motioned to the general. "He makes a handsome target I would enjoy seeing in my sights… if I were on the other side." Reuben turned and motioned Noah to his side.

When they were clearly out of ear shot, Noah said to Reuben, "Do you know who that was on that gray horse?"

"Yes."

"I wish Renee could have seen you. Telling off that general's colonel like that. That was amazing."

"Well, I hope you can remember every detail of that conversation and tell me later because I'm so tired, I had no idea what I was saying or who I was saying it to."

"If you will beg my pardon, General, are you sure it's wise to let that, *captain*, be on his way? Clearly he has a problem with authority. Officers like that have no place in this army... sir," asked the colonel, timidly to the commanding general.

As the general atop the light gray blended horse curiously eyed Reuben walking away, he nodded and replied, "Colonel, do you suppose there are any others like him in the ranks?"

"I should hope not. His eyes, they were like..."

"Those of a hungry wolf," said the general, finishing the colonel's statement. "Colonel, if we had more like him, we could end this war within a year's time," said the general with a concerning tone in his voice.

"You say that like it's a bad thing, sir."

"What troubles me is, if we do have more men like him in the ranks and we win this war because of them, heaven help our government if it ever does men like that captain wrong."

狼

The journey to get Noah and the doctor back home was not going to be an easy one. Doctor Chelmsford and Noah could not simply walk away, and as for the doctor, he was obligated to ply his profession to the wounded, which seemed to be everywhere.

Fighting dwindled down to minor battles and skirmishes, but it was apparent the Union intended to drive the Confederates to their breaking point. Much of the war momentum shifted toward the western theater. In mid-September of '63, eight brigades from the Army of Northern Virginia, under the command of Lieutenant General James Longstreet, were instrumental in a Confederate victory in Georgia. It wouldn't be until the spring of '64 when the Army of Northern Virginia would begin the fight for its survival with General Grant locking horns with General Lee in some of the bloodiest fighting this war was yet to see.

In the beginning of May of '64, Reuben found himself, along with the army, near the old Chancellorsville battlefield once again. It was almost a year to the day when Doctor Chelmsford and Noah crossed the lines and eventually found Reuben.

Reuben took this coincidence as fate. As Akagi Genda-San once told Reuben, *"Fate is an awesome power filled with irony."* He was hoping the irony of returning near the same place they crossed over was fate to be taken advantage of. Not only did Reuben instruct Doctor Chelmsford and Noah to be ready at a moment's notice to make their attempt to return to Norfolk, he also instructed Captain Stevens and Sergeant Warren in case a diversion was needed.

Noah tried, many times, to convince Reuben to return with him. As tempted as Reuben was at the notion, he couldn't.

"I don't understand, Reuben. Renee and Aarleen need you. May and Henry need you. And when I get back home, Ever and I will need you. Why can't you come back with me?" pleaded Noah many times.

"Trust me, Noah, my friend. I would leave now if the door was open, but I can't. There are two things keeping me here. My obligation to substitute myself for Monroe is one. The other is them," said Reuben, motioning to Captain Stevens, Sergeant Warren, and the two young lieutenants, Peaks and Rallins. "They and the rest of the company are still alive because of me. Nobody dies this time, Noah, nobody."

As hard as it was to believe, Company C, during the entire time Reuben was assigned to it, never suffered any fatalities. There were several company soldiers wounded, but none of them were fatal. Many of those returned back to duty and a couple were sent home with Reuben's blessing they had served honorably and should never have any regret.

Company C started off undermanned in the beginning, a condition Reuben made clear to Captain Stevens and Sergeant Warren was for the best. There were fewer men to be concerned with and they were able to mobilize quicker than a full sized company. It was easier for the men to look after one another and, as the war wore on, the company became close, and they could function without direction. All this was due to Reuben's experience from Mexico and Japan.

Reuben took a seat on an old powder keg and propped up his booted foot on a human skull left from the last time the two armies met on this field. He took his image case of Renee from his haversack, and untied Aarleen's inrou from his obi. He opened the case and gazed upon Renee's image.

"My place is with Renee and Aarleen, Noah. But for now, I can only give them my love and devotion in spirit. My physical being is needed to protect these men. I have trained my two girls well and I believe, if needed, they can defend themselves. If I only knew Monroe made it back to Richmond or home. Noah, my friend, I failed saving Mama, Lucy, and her husband. I must at least try to save the last two remaining living souls of my parents."

"After your brother tried to kill you before he left Norfolk, and you putting yourself through all of this for him, you have a *big* heart, Reuben Duran, a very big heart," said Noah.

狼

May 5, 1864, a few days over to the year when both armies of the Union and Confederacy met near this same thicket of woods, began with a bang. Mostly musket and rifle fire echoed within the wooded under and overgrowth known by the locals as, The Wilderness. It was too thick for artillery to be put into any effective use. Actually, it was too thick for any man or beast to be put into any effective use, yet cries of battle and horror rose above the sounds of musketry.

Confederate troops were surrounded by Union troops, and those Union troops were surrounded by other Confederate troops. Black powder smoke filled the woods making it impossible to see what soldiers were shooting at, causing many to die from being fired upon by their own comrades.

It was a commander's worse nightmare on both sides. A tactical or strategic impossibility to comprehend any type of advantage both sides hoped to gain against the other. This was no organized course of battle, if there was such a thing. This was an all-out street brawl to be fought to the death. War in its worse form, face-to-face and hand-to-hand, chaos, just the type of war Reuben thrived on. It was just the exact diversion he was hoping for to get Noah and Doctor Chelmsford safely back home.

"This is it, Doc. This is the chance to make a run for home," said Reuben. "It has to be. The gods of the high mountains have blessed us with this diversion."

The sounds of the guns, orders from officers, and cries of the mangled wounded had no effect on Reuben. It was as if he were standing in the middle of a city park enjoying a warm spring day.

Watching Reuben's calm demeanor was very disturbing to Doctor Chelmsford. He remembered how calm Reuben was when he and his platoon took on one of their many dangerous assignments. It was that calmness that drew the doctor's attention to Reuben when they first met at Fort Monroe before mobilizing to Mexico. It was that same calmness he wondered if his own father had when he fought in the second American Revolution of 1812.

While officers, NCOs, and soldiers, were ducking or cowering from the rancid battle all around them, Reuben brushed it aside as one would brush away a pesky gnat. My god, the doctor thought, Mexico brought out the worst of him. Is this what Japan made of him? An unfeeling individual to the suffering of others in their most trying of times, questioned Doctor Chelmsford to himself.

As the doctor was about to confront Reuben about his mental stability, he noticed Reuben clutching Aarleen's inrou hanging from his obi in his left hand and his image case of Renee in his right.

"That's it," Doctor Chelmsford said out loud to himself. "He's fighting for his wife and daughter this very moment. It's Renee who is his pillar of strength and Aarleen who is his focus of what's most important in life. As long as Reuben keeps this chaos away from Norfolk, he's keeping them safe. Is this what my own father felt for us back in his days?"

"Todd, this is it. This is the chance to get Noah and the doc to safety," the doctor heard Reuben say to Captain Stevens.

"Go to it then, Reuben. Take Max with you. Matt, Albert, and I can handle it here, not to worry. We'll do our damnedest to stay out of the fight as much as we can. At least until you return."

Reuben nodded and said to Doctor Chelmsford and Noah, "Okay you two, grab your gear and let's move." Reuben removed Aarleen's inrou from his obi and placed it inside his haversack along with his image case of Renee.

He saw Sergeant Warren loading his rifled musket. "Max, put that down. It'll only slow you down and probably get you killed. Here take this," said Reuben handing the sergeant his jo. "I've showed you how to use this and you've watched me use it. This type of battle is too cumbersome to be loading and firing while on the move."

Reuben had yet to actually put his Kutto to use since the day Akagi Genda-San presented it to him before he boarded the ship bringing him back to Renee and Aarleen. When he saw the other three ready to move, Reuben drew his Kutto in pure samurai fashion, looked toward the direction of home, and hollered out, "Hajime!"

狼

Reuben and the others made their way toward the Southeast. It was no easy task. For every direction they took, there was fighting causing them to make several detours to avoid the two armies locked in combat. Using his Kutto for the first time, Reuben cut a path through fighting soldiers, both Union and Confederate. Not a single soldier was fatally wounded as Reuben struck. If he had the time, Reuben would have stopped to admire the effect the Sword of Spiritual Power had on those who got in his way. The soldiers he struck with the Kutto fell like toy soldiers grasping the areas of their bodies in agonizing pain where the Kutto struck. Those Reuben struck would live, but never fight again. It was truly a weapon to be wielded by a warrior, true of heart, filled with love and devotion for his family.

Fires began to break out everywhere. The linen and paper from the spent musket cartridges, still smoldering from rifle barrels, fell to the ground igniting the dry foliage. Smoke from the fires, along with the black powder smoke, made it impossible to breathe and see. Doctor Chelmsford pulled out bandages and passed them out to Reuben, Noah, and Sergeant Warren to cover their faces. The smoke was so thick, the only way one could see who was Union or Confederate was to drop to the ground and try to determine the color of soldier's trousers.

The noise was terrifying to Noah. It was like nothing he had ever heard before. He truly believed he wasn't going to make it out alive, and prayed for forgiveness for his past sins in case a stray bullet took his life. How in the world can Reuben, the sergeant, and Doctor Chelmsford cope with all this madness, Noah thought as he ran for his life holding onto Reuben's haversack strap. Noah had no idea where he was or where he was going. He held on with a grip of steel being pulled and tugged like a field plow. If Renee only knew what Reuben was going through for his brother, and now for him, she would never let Reuben out of her sight ever again, Noah continued to think.

The smoke began to clear slightly and Reuben stopped to see several Confederate officers on horseback about to be overtaken by Union troops from two sides. The officers were defenseless and oblivious to their pending capture or death. Turning away from the scene, Reuben continued leading the others away from the fighting until his urge to protect those in need got the better of him.

"Max, see to Noah and the doc! I'm going to help those officers back there! I'll catch up!"

"Are you sure, Reuben?! You have that much confidence in me to care for your friends?!" asked Max.

"Max, you're an honorable man and I would trust you with my life. Now go! Like I said, I'll catch up!"

"Reuben!" Noah called out. "Don't leave us!"

"I'm not leaving you, just helping others! But if Max gets you and the doc out of here and back home, tell Renee I'll be home soon!" said Reuben as he was running back toward the surrounded Confederate officers.

Noah began to follow, but was held back by Doctor Chelmsford. "Let him go, Noah! It's in his nature to help others in need. Right now we have Max to care for us. Come on, Max! Get us out of here!"

狼

"General, we will be overtaken if we don't move from this position," said the adjutant to the commanding general atop a light gray blended horse.

The commanding general, who wore the insignia of a full colonel, and his staff officers began to ride toward the southeast only to be stopped by fires blocking their path. To the south, laid thick woods unpassable by either man or horse, and coming from the other directions were Union soldiers inching their way toward the command staff.

Many Confederate troops were fighting the converging soldiers in blue as best they could, but were slowly losing ground. As the last few remaining Confederate defenders were to be overtaken, from out of nowhere, as if the gods of the high mountains placed him, Reuben landed right in the middle of the Union soldiers with his Kutto drawn.

All forms of fighting stopped as Reuben took his Okami no Michi style stance, low to the ground and ready to pounce. A Union lieutenant aimed his revolver at Reuben and before he could pull back the hammer, Reuben's Kutto made contact with the lieutenant's forearm breaking it in three places.

Faster than any human possible, Reuben began cutting and slicing his Kutto taking down Union soldier after Union soldier, sometimes two and three at a time.

All attention moved from the Confederate command officers to the one lone Confederate officer armed only with a sword, moving with the speed of a frenzied demon, but with the grace of a swan skimming over the water. Leaping off of trees and soldiers he had taken down with his Kutto, Reuben attacked with the same accuracy as Tadashi did with his bow.

The Confederate commanding general, along with his staff, watched Reuben with horrific awe as they perceived him as slaughtering every Union soldier with whom he came in contact. The general and his aide immediately recognized Reuben from their encounter on the retreat from Pennsylvania. As they watched Reuben stand his ground, defending them with what appeared to be ease, the staff officers winced away as Reuben would strike an opponent. The commanding general could not help but notice the absence of blood every time Reuben took down a Union soldier.

The momentum of Reuben's attacks did not slow. His attacks seemed to get quicker and quicker after every soldier he crippled. The heated, angry Union shouts went from "Kill that rebel son of a bitch!" to panicked cries of "Run for your life, every man for himself!"

When it was all over, Reuben stood amid a carpet of wounded and crippled Union soldiers. He looked toward the commanding general and his staff and yelled to them, "Get the hell out of here. I don't have time to waste on the likes of you anymore!" and was off in the direction he last left Noah, Doctor Chelmsford, and Sergeant Warren.

The commanding general atop the light gray blended horse looked at the several dozens of Union soldiers lying before him and his staff. Not a single one was dead, but only crippled to the point of not being able to raise their arms in anger toward another human being ever again.

狼

For the rest of the day, Reuben searched for the others with no success. The day's fighting seemed to be dying down and he started making his way back to his company hoping they were still in the same location. It took him several hours of searching, but eventually he found Captain Stevens walking back from an officers meeting.

"Reuben, my god, where have you been?!" asked Captain Stevens.

"Got separated from Max and the others," Reuben replied. "Has Max returned?"

"Not yet. It's a complete mess out there. Can you hear the screams of the wounded being burned alive? It's nauseating. No one seems to know how today's fight went. I have a feeling it's going to start up again tomorrow."

Reuben was hoping the best for the others, but for now he returned back to the company to ready them for the next day. He didn't need Captain Stevens to tell him the fight was going to continue after the amount of ground he covered this day.

As predicted, the battle continued for the next two days. The 68th Virginia did most of its fighting the day Reuben led the doctor and Noah back in the direction of home. After what Reuben witnessed on the first day of battle, he advised Captain Stevens to keep the company as low as possible, and the men within arms distance of each other. Company C was part of a significant Confederate push toward the Union lines protecting the entire left flank on the second day of battle. There were several times Reuben was close enough to take down many Union troops with his Kutto in defense of his company while they did their jobs of fighting the battle. Like in previous engagements, Reuben ran from one side of the company to the other, keeping Union soldiers at bay while the officers and men of Company C could concentrate on fighting. As long as the men of the company knew Reuben was in the vicinity, with either his jo or Kutto, they felt safe and able to perform their duties without worry.

On the evening of the final day of the battle in The Wilderness, General Doyle called upon all his brigade officers. He advised them the recent engagements had no significant advantage to either side. For all intents and purposes, the battle of the last few days proved to be inconclusive. After what Reuben seen on the first day, he didn't need any rear echelon seat cushion to tell him that.

General Doyle made it clear all signs of a Union withdraw or retreat was not evident, unlike the last several times both armies met. There was a big concern for this new Union commanding general whose only goal was to end this war at any cost. A goal Reuben admired.

General Doyle ordered his officers to make haste and prepare to mobilize at a moment's notice, possibly the following day. "The Yankees have the means and the men to make push after push, but we must stand our ground. Have faith in our commanding general, gentlemen. Apparently, the general himself had his own guardian angel saving him and his staff from capture on the first day of this engagement."

The general was about to dismiss his officers when he announced, "Gentlemen, it saddens me to inform you Lieutenant General Longstreet was wounded near the same location Lieutenant General Jackson was wounded about this time last year. Apparently, the general came upon soldiers of Mahone's brigade, and was fired upon mistaking him, and his staff, as Yankee troopers."

All those officers present from the last time General Doyle announced the wounding of General Jackson immediately looked back toward Reuben who stood with his arms across his chest.

Reuben shook his head and let out a silent, grunted laugh and said, "Damn, that's a shame. Sometimes it's a curse to be right all the time."

When Reuben and Captain Stevens returned back to the company, they found Lieutenants Peaks and Rallins tending to Sergeant Warren, Doctor Chelmsford, and Noah.

"What happened, Doc?! Why did you and Noah come back? You should be halfway back to Norfolk by now," said Reuben, rather upset, but relieved to see them safe.

"We couldn't make it through, Reuben," said Sergeant Warren. "I had them away from the fighting and about to send them on their way until..."

"Until what?" asked Reuben anxiously as he took over tending Noah from Lieutenant Peaks.

"Home guard," answered Noah.

"Home guard?" asked Captain Stevens.

"Yeah," said Doctor Chelmsford. "There's a new enemy to contend with for me and Noah to get back to Norfolk, the home guard troops."

"Self-righteous, Confederate radicals claiming they are doing their duty. Cowardly soldiers is what they are, roaming the countryside looking for deserters and shooting them on the spot. We didn't have a chance. They were everywhere just itching to shoot a deserter in defense of the Confederacy," said Sergeant Warren.

"Yes sir. Too coward to shoot a gun at the Federals, but not coward enough to shoot Confederate soldiers running for cover," added Noah.

"It didn't matter if they were soldiers or civilians, they were either rounding them up or shooting them on the spot, like Max said," said Doctor Chelmsford as he finished drinking from a canteen.

Reuben knelt down in front of Noah and the doctor. With a look of despair, he said, "I'm so very sorry. I should have stayed with you. It's my fault. I can't find what happened to Monroe, and I can't get you back home."

Doctor Chelmsford scooted closer to Reuben and placed his hand on Reuben's shoulder saying, "Please don't let it bother you, Reuben. You have been doing all you can under these conditions. Hell, man, there are many who would have quit long before now. We'll have other opportunities to make a chance for Norfolk. What matters is keeping us alive and that's what you've been doing, along with Max, Todd, the lieutenants, and the company. Just keep kicking ass, Reuben. We'll make it back home. All of us."

狼

Doctor Chelmsford was correct. There were plenty of other opportunities to make a chance for Norfolk, but those opportunities turned into one delay after another. For the rest of the month of May and into June, it seemed to be one long drawn out skirmish being fought around Richmond. Like a never ending game of capture the flag, the Union Army of The Potomac kept trying to capture the prize, Richmond, but was repulsed. In a constant battle of trying to get the best of the Confederate Army, a long line of defenses were laid around the city of Petersburg, the last remaining obstacle to the city spires of the Confederate capital. Anchored on the banks of the Appomattox River, the Confederate Army of Northern Virginia dug in for the survival of the Confederacy itself.

Both Reuben and Doctor Chelmsford could not help but be amused by the irony of the North being defended by the South, like in Pennsylvania, but in reverse. While others were looking upon their pending demise with dread, Reuben and the doctor always seemed to be cheerful. When it came to keeping the men of Company C of the 68th Virginia Infantry Regiment spirits up, all they had to do was sit and listen to Reuben and Doctor Chelmsford talk of their involvement in the Mexican Campaign, or Reuben's adventures in Japan.

It was Reuben's stories of Japan that caught their interest the most. The two young lieutenants, Peaks and Rallins, were probably the most grounded junior officers of the entire war, all because of Reuben. After listening to Reuben's descriptions of samurai warfare, and the samurai code of Bushido, they could not help but admire Reuben's coolness toward their past and current dilemmas.

Every day, Reuben looked for opportunities to get the doctor and Noah through the lines, but the task was becoming more and more difficult each day. With the Union Army of The Potomac being supplied and reinforced from City Point, which eventually caused the Confederate defenses to stretch around Petersburg, one could not simply walk across the lines like the doctor and Noah did last year during the battle around Chancellorsville.

It seemed the only way to get past both Confederate and Union pickets was either in a wagon filled with corpses or as a wounded non-combatant, and even in that case, it was by sheer chance. Such was the case of a Confederate major wounded in the leg during the battles around Cold Harbor when his engineering battalion was overtaken.

In a time when the commanding general of the Union Army put a stop to prisoner exchanges, the officer in charge of processing the captured Confederate engineers, either by an act of compassion or laziness, allowed the wounded to be treated and categorized as non-combatant administrators. These so called non-combatants were given a choice of being sent to a Union prisoner of war camp or sent south away from the fighting. After the wounded Confederate engineers witnessed the mass supplies and endless throng of Union soldiers marching before their eyes, they opted for the latter.

One such engineer was Simon Norenham. Once his leg was treated, he was led past the Union lines into the occupied territory of Virginia. Once away from the siege taking place, he was sent to fend on his own. For days he limped, using a broken branch as a crutch, southeast toward home. His journey was difficult, but wasn't without assistance. He found residents willing to provide him with food, clothes, directions, and even transportation for portions of his trek. Just as he thought he would never make it back to Norfolk, he was arrested and detained as a person of questionable interest, and transported into Portsmouth. It was while in custody, his identity as a Confederate officer was known. Immediately he was being processed to be sent to a prisoner of war camp, a journey that would take him across the Elizabeth River into Norfolk, only to be sent on to Fort Monroe to await transportation back north.

Simon found himself city blocks away from his home as he was marched through the city to the ferry station when the column he was in was stopped by a one armed Union officer.

"NORENHAM!! SIMON NORENHAM!! I AM LOOKING FOR A SIMON NORENHAM!!" called the officer, walking down the line of ragged and tattered men who were once the pride of the Confederate Army.

"SIMON NORENHAM, SPEAK UP!! I KNOW YOU'RE IN THIS LINE!!"

As the officer came closer, Simon raised his makeshift crutch and weakly called out, "I'm Simon Norenham!"

The one armed officer had a corporal pull him out of the column. The officer looked him up and down and asked, "Where are you from, Simon Norenham? Are you from Richmond?"

"Yes sir, originally."

"And you have come here to Norfolk to seek refuge from the fighting around Richmond that has forced your family here before you could make your escape?"

Simon had a very questionable look on his face, having no idea what this officer was leading to. He began to shake his head no as the officer was slowly nodding his head yes. Simon's head began to change direction nodding to yes.

"I see," said the officer. "I take it then, you're looking for your family and you've been confused as a Simon *NorGANham*, a known Confederate officer."

"Ah..."

"Captain, there seems to have been a huge mistake," said the one armed officer to the officer in charge of marching the captives to the ferry station. "This man here isn't a prisoner of war. He's a refugee simply looking for his family. I'll take custody of him and escort him to the refugee center."

The captain eyed both the one armed officer and Simon in turn suspiciously.

"Is there a problem, Captain? Because if there is, I can have you investigated for harassing civilians."

"No sir. There's no problem. You will need to sign for his release," said the captain with no hesitation.

Looking as if he was being inconvenienced, the one armed officer said, "Very well," and signed the manifest taking Simon off the list and into his custody.

"Now then, Mr. Norenham, will you please come with us," said the one armed officer, motioning toward the opposite side of the street.

Several hours before Simon was being transported across the Elizabeth River into Norfolk, Major MacKay was standing in for the port manifest officer so he could escort some high profile prisoners to the city jail. Being the by-the-book administrator that he is, Major Mackay reviewed the entire manifest until he came upon the name, Simon Norenham. He immediately thought of Renee taking in Cynthia and her son as refugees onto the Duran farm. The Major clearly remembered when Renee drew a line through the name *Norenham* and wrote *Garrett* next to it. He also remembered the list of Confederate wounded a few weeks back when the name, Simon *Norenham,* stood out. He did some research and learned this is the same Simon Norenham on the wounded list, and is indeed the husband of Cynthia Garrett.

"Ah, this seems like an issue up for interpretation," said the major to no one in particular. "Sergeant, I see an error on this manifest that must be corrected immediately. Stand this post until either the duty officer or I return. Come along, Corporal."

The sergeant nodded his acknowledgement, saluted the major, and took his place behind the desk.

For the rest of the morning, Major MacKay and the corporal awaited the shipment of prisoners and once they arrived, they commenced calling for Simon Norenham.

Simon was taken by the arm by the corporal as Major MacKay led the way toward the homeless and refugee center, formally the Wickham Finishing School for Girls. The major loudly cleared his throat prompting the corporal to say, "Excuse me, Major, we don't have time to take this gentleman to the center. Remember your scheduled inspection this afternoon at the Duran farm?"

"Duran farm?" asked Simon, surprised.

"Quiet you! You're right, Corporal. We have a dilemma here. We can't take Mr. Norenham to the refugee center, and we can't allow him to go on his own. I signed for him. Quickly, commandeer one of those horses from those troopers across the street for Mr. Norenham," the major directed the corporal.

The corporal saluted and crossed the street to a group of Union troopers to commandeer one of their horses for the major's use.

"Very sorry about this, Mr. Norenham, but for the time being, I'm going to have to inconvenience you, possibly for the day. I have an inspection with the Duran farm that must take precedence."

At the major's second mention of the Duran farm, Simon had a hopeful expression that didn't go unnoticed by Major MacKay.

Once the corporal returned with a mount for Simon's use, the three trotted out of the city toward the direction of the Duran farm. During the entire ride, Simon eyed the major and the corporal suspiciously. He tried to ask the major questions as to why he pulled him out of the column to which the major's response was, "My, this is a fine day not to ask any questions that may get one shipped off to a prisoner of war camp now that one is so close to home."

So, quietly Simon rode between the major and corporal, still with unanswered questions running though his mind. As they came to the Norfolk County Outreach School, Simon smiled. As they trotted past it, Simon could not take his eyes off the schoolhouse, admiring how well it looked.

"That schoolhouse has not been used since the school teacher was impressed into service by the rebel government. The wife and daughter of the school teacher have done their best to keep it in order for his return. They are a special family, the Durans are. You would be surprised at the kindness they show toward others," said Major MacKay as he noticed Simon's interest in the school.

As they made the turn from the road onto the lane leading to the Duran farm, Simon began to feel relieved. He heard a sharp bark of a dog and immediately recognized it as being Riley.

"There goes that damned dog again, Major. It's amazing how Miss Aarleen has that beastie trained to know when we're coming."

Renee and Aarleen were sitting on the porch as Riley rose to his four paws and let out his warning bark. Renee and Aarleen looked at each other perplexed.

"This isn't Mr. MacKay's day for a usual inspection, Mama"

"Maybe it's a surprise inspection… or…"

"Or what, Mama?" asked Aarleen, anxiously.

"Or maybe he has some news about your Da he's going to discretely tell us. Pay close attention to what he says, sweetie," said Renee, stepping down from the porch.

Renee began to walk out to the lane to meet up with Major MacKay as Aarleen followed with hopes her mother was right about the major having news about her father.

"CYNTHIA!!! BENJAMIN!!! GET OUT HERE, NOW!!!" yelled Renee, as she sprinted toward the three riders.

"Geez oh geez oh geez it's Benji's dad!" said Aarleen, excitedly.

The front door opened as Cynthia emerged onto the porch and Benjamin came from around the house.

"Mrs. Norenham, it's your husband, come quick! Look Benji! Mr. MacKay has your dad with him!" said Aarleen.

"SIMON!!! LOOK BEN!!! IT'S YOUR FATHER!!!" screamed Cynthia as she sprinted toward her husband.

Benjamin took hold of Aarleen's hand and she ran with him to meet up with his father.

Upon hearing Renee call out for Cynthia, Simon quickly dismounted his horse. He fell to the ground once his wounded leg touched the lane. The corporal dismounted to assist him, but Renee was already at his side helping him up.

Cynthia was within arm's reach of Simon when she stopped and held her hands to her mouth hiding her surprised gasps. Unable to contain herself, she took Simon into her arms and held him tightly. Her touch was much different than he last remembered. It was no longer an embrace of obligation, but of a loving wife.

Benjamin and Aarleen caught up and right away Cynthia motioned for Benjamin to join their family embrace.

"Excuse me, Mrs. Duran, but do you know this gentleman?" asked the major.

"Yes, Mr. MacKay, we do." answered Renee, very jubilantly.

"I can only assume since this gentleman is acquainted with Cynthia and Benjamin Garrett, he's a relative of some sort?"

"That's correct, Mr. MacKay," answered Aarleen, gleefully.

"Well, in that case, I believe you have another refugee I'll be adding to your residence. Corporal, go and measure out another plot for the new mouth for Mrs. Duran to feed."

"What's going on?" asked Simon, confused.

"Be quiet, Simon, my love," said Cynthia, holding her husband and son tightly. "Let Renee handle this. She knows what she's doing."

"Mrs. Duran, I had to sign for this gentleman. He was about to be shipped off to a prisoner of war camp. Since I signed for him, I'll need your signature to take him into your custody."

"Yes, Mr. MacKay, thank you very much," said Renee as she reached for the document being handed to her.

"Now, mind you, Mrs. Duran," instructed the major as his focus was on Simon, "This gentleman must remain on your property until this rebellion is put to an end. He is still viewed as a questionable person of interest and could still very well be sent to prisoner of war camp, and your property seized if he is found off your property without my permission."

"Do you understand that, Simon?" asked Cynthia.

Surprised at Cynthia's pleasant and caring attitude, Simon nodded yes.

"Very well, once the corporal is finished measuring out the plot, we will be on our way. I'm sorry, Mrs. Duran, but I haven't heard anything out of Petersburg lately. Once I do, somehow you'll find out."

"Thank you very much, Mr. MacKay," replied Renee, handing back the document.

"It is I who must thank you for taking this refugee off my hands. Inspections are a pain, but they are a real pain totting around extra baggage."

狼

After Major MacKay and the corporal left, Cynthia and Benjamin helped Simon into the house. While Cynthia tended to Simon, May and Evergreen fixed him something to eat, as Benjamin and Aarleen began drawing warm water for a bath.

Renee went upstairs to get Simon some of Reuben's clothes to wear. With all the boys and men having to use Reuben's clothes, he won't have any to wear himself when he comes home, thought Renee with a smile. Suddenly that smile turned into a frown. She sat on the edge of their bed and brought one of Reuben's shirts up to caress her face. All this time Renee had been wearing Reuben's kosodes and hakamas, and letting Cynthia and Evergreen wear her clothes.

Renee began crying into the shirt.

"Mama, we have the bath ready for Mr. Norenham. Mama, are you all right?" asked Aarleen when she saw her mother crying into Reuben's shirt.

"Your Da doesn't have any more clothes, sweetie. I've given them out for others to wear. First it was Paul, then Benjamin, and now Simon will be wearing his clothes."

Aarleen sat beside Renee and took her mother into her arms tightly.

"It's so hard to see your Da's clothes walking around without him in them. It's like he's here, but invisible."

"Oh, Mama, you know Da will understand. He's more comfortable in his hakama anyway. Of course, you will have to start wearing yours," said Aarleen, causing Renee to giggle.

Renee pulled away from Aarleen's embrace, but kept her arms around her. "Since when did you become the voice of reason around here, sweetie?"

"You're the voice of reason, Mama. I just echo it."

Mother and daughter hugged each other once again, stood, and walked out of the room together. When they reached the top of the stairs, they saw Cynthia tending to Simon very tenderly. Renee never thought she would see the day her old school nemesis would have a caring bone in her body. By the looks of it, Simon was also surprised.

After a quick meal, a bath, and a change of clothes, Simon stretched out on the sofa in the parlor and slept for hours with Cynthia sitting by his side holding his hand the entire time.

"Mrs. Duran, I can't thank you enough," said Benjamin as he watched his mother so lovingly sit by his father's side as he slept.

"Whatever for, Benjamin?" asked Renee.

"For my mother," said Benjamin, "Because of you and Aarleen, and also May, Ever, and Henry, you all showed my mother what a real family is like. Because of you, we are a real family now."

Renee took Benjamin into her arms. "It's like Reuben has said, there's good in everyone. It's just a matter of beating it out of them," she said as both she and Benjamin watched Cynthia.

狼

"Reuben is out there, Renee, and causing all sorts of hell for both the Confederates and Yankees," said Simon at the dinner table.

After a long nap, a late dinner was served. It was a huge dinner to celebrate Simon's return. There was a couple of roasted chickens, potatoes, beans, and of course, fish. Fresh bread was baked by Renee. By the looks of the table, one wouldn't think the Duran farm was living on rations. There was going to actually be left overs for lunch the following day.

"Did you see my Da, Mr. Norenham?" asked Aarleen.

"No, Aarleen, but I heard stories about him."

"Like what?" asked Henry.

Putting down his knife and fork, Simon cleared his throat and said, "I heard the commanding general of the army and his staff was saved by a lone Confederate officer armed only with a strange sword that didn't kill any Yankees trying to capture the general. It was said he left the ground covered with Yankee wounded."

Renee took Aarleen's hand and they looked at each other with joy.

"That's not all. When I was having my leg tended to, I overheard a group of wounded Yankees telling stories of how they had been crippled by a man with a fancy sword who pounced on them like a wolf pouncing on prey. They said he was faster than a tornado's wind, but as graceful as a fawn running through the woods. I also had a chat with a Yankee lieutenant who had his leg broken by a man with a sword that didn't draw blood. He said this man only attacked when his men were threatened and it was as if that Confederate was protecting his soldiers so they could do their jobs without fear of being hurt."

"That sounds like your Reuben, Renee," said May.

Feeling a bit emotional, both Renee and Aarleen held each other. When dinner was finished, Cynthia told Renee to take Aarleen to the oak tree and spend some time together while she helped May and Evergreen clean off the dinner table and kitchen.

While they were cleaning, Evergreen looked sad. It was Cynthia who came to comfort her by saying, "I'm sure Noah is all right. Just because Simon didn't mention him doesn't mean he has come to any harm."

"Cynthia is right, Ever," commented May. "If I know Reuben, he's probably keeping Noah safe, away from the fighting, even trying to get him back home. If he's keeping the fighting boys safe, I can only imagine he has a tight watch on Noah."

Cynthia and May's comments caused Evergreen to feel a little better, but she was still very concerned.

"Mama, is having patience the same as stones and water?" asked Aarleen.

Sitting against the trunk of the oak tree in each other's arms, Renee smiled at Aarleen's question. "Is that what Mr. Akagi told you in your dream, sweetie?"

"Kind of. He told me I know the meaning of stones and water, but I'm still uncertain of the actual meaning. I hear you and Da sometimes. He calls you his water, and you call him your stone. It has something to do with time, huh, Mama?"

"Exactly, sweetie, time, time needed to smooth our rough edges. You know that stone Mr. Akagi gave me that lays on the mantel where your Da keeps his Kutto?"

"Yes, Mama," replied Aarleen.

"That stone, at one time, had been very rough and jagged, much like your Da before he went to Japan. Then that stone was put into the water, and with the motion of the water, time washed away the rough jaggedness and made that stone smooth. Just like what I had to do for your Da. I had to let him go and give him time to become smooth."

Aarleen cuddled closer to Renee as she said, "I don't mean for this to sound horrible, Mama, but I'm glad I didn't know Da before he went to Japan. I'm glad you washed away his rough jaggedness before I met him."

Renee kissed the top of Aarleen's head as she said, "Sweetie, your Da would entirely agree with you."

"He's a strong man, huh, Mama?"

"Sweetie, your Da is the strongest man because, not only can he protect us and others in need, he can love also. That's what's so special about him."

"I miss him, Mama."

"I know you do, sweetie," said Renee, wishing there was a way to ease her daughter's worry. Suddenly she had a thought and said, "Do you know why I always sit here against this one spot of our oak tree?"

"No," replied Aarleen, lifting her head to look at her mother.

"Remember when your Da told us he hidden the remaining gold oban coins, but wouldn't tell us where?"

"Sure I do. He said he didn't want to tell us for our safety," said Aarleen, sitting up with an expression of interest.

"Well, take a close look on the tree where I lean my back," said Renee as she scooted over for Aarleen to take a look. "See, your Da is always thinking of us."

Aarleen saw the small kanji characters for wolf and an arrow pointing down carved into the trunk of the oak tree. She immediately traced them with her fingertip and hugged Renee. "Oh, Mama, I just know Da will be home within a year's time. Mr. Akagi has never lied to me in my dreams."

狼

BOOM!!!

A huge explosion shook the ground and was felt for miles around early in the morning. Nearly every window in Petersburg was shattered. Over 250 Confederate soldiers didn't have a chance to cry out in pain, for they were either incinerated or their bodies were torn apart immediately. Dirt, debris, and human limbs rained down on those who survived the massive blast leaving a crater gouged into the earth 170 feet long, 120 feet wide, and 30 feet deep.

After the blast there was complete silence from both sides of the battlefield. The atmosphere of shock and awe was as thick as the smoke of the blast. Confederate soldiers roamed around in a daze wondering if they were alive or died and arrived in hell.

Bugles and drums sounding the signal of attack were heard coming from the Union side of the huge pit recently carved into the earth by tons of black powder. What started off as a Union attempt to end the siege in Petersburg, would end up as a day filled with the worst nightmares come to life.

The Union troops charged across no man's land and rather than attack around the smoldering pit, they charged into it. With visions of victory in their grasp, the soldiers in blue felt they blasted a front door leading into the city of Petersburg and their next stop would be

Richmond. The only obstacle preventing them from doing so was the 30 foot wall they ran into on the opposite side of the crater.

As the first wave of Union soldiers hit the wall, they were crushed against it by wave after wave of more Union soldiers being funneled into the gigantic hole. Confederate soldiers began converging around the edge of the colossal hole and started raining musket and cannon fire on the Union soldiers trapped in their own engineering disaster.

Union troops who actually survived the 30 foot climb were met by hordes of angry Confederates firing point blank, or were pushed back into the pit. Bayonetted rifles were being thrown into the blue colored pit like spears after they were fired. Eerie blood curdling whistling sounds filled the air as ram rods were being fired out of Confederate muskets entering several Union soldiers at once. Screams filled the air making it sound as if the devil himself was conducting a horrible symphony of sinful music.

It was sheer, utter chaos. This was the worst form of chaos known to man, with no hope of forgiveness from the heavens above. However, for Reuben, it was the perfect type of chaos he hoped for and jumped at the opportunity to get Noah and the doctor back home.

As elements of Doyle's Brigade, including the 68th Virginia, merged with Mahone's Brigade, Reuben grabbed hold of Doctor Chelmsford and Noah by the shoulders and led them toward the far right flank of the crater. As chaotic as it was, the three easily made their way across the field of sinful death and nightmarish hell.

"Reuben, my boy, if we survive this, I'll never set foot on another battlefield for the rest of my life!" shouted the doctor, showing outward fear for the first time ever as he was being pulled through the congested field of battle.

Noah was silent from fear. He wanted to stop, curl up into a ball, and wait until it was all over, but Reuben wouldn't let him. Noah caught a glimpse of Reuben's determined look. There was no fear in his eyes. All Noah could see in Reuben's eyes was years of pain and anguish all balled up into hope to get him safely back home. Dear Lord God, whatever you do, don't send down Jesus because this is no place for children, Noah thought.

As they were nearing the extreme right flank, a cannon blast knocked all three to the ground causing them to take cover while they were thrown into the middle of a furious crossfire.

More and more Union troops were converging into and around the crater. To add insult to an already injured Confederate Army, units of the United States Colored Troops began charging into the battle. For many of the Confederate soldiers, this was the last straw and the momentum of their deadly counterattack increased. Cries of "Spare the white man, kill the nigger!" were heard all along the rim of the crater. White Union soldiers themselves began to bayonet the colored soldiers with hopes they would be spared of reprisals from Confederate troops.

With the crossfire somewhat eased, Reuben rose to find himself alone. He desperately looked for the doctor and Noah. He looked to his right to see Doctor Chelmsford treating a wounded Confederate soldier.

"Doc, we don't have time for that! Get off your ass and help me find Noah!"

Reuben saw the doctor pointing toward the rim of the crater as he was still tending to the soldier. Reuben looked in the direction the doctor was pointing toward and saw Noah crawling away from the fighting dangerously close to the rim of the crater.

"Stay there, Doc! I'm going to get him!"

"Go, Reuben, I'll be okay! I'll wait for you and Noah here!"

Noah stood, trying to find Reuben and the doctor. The cannon blast separated them and Noah never felt so alone in his life.

"There's one of those Yankee niggers! Kill that son of a bitch!" yelled a Confederate soldier, pointing to Noah.

The shout from the Confederate caused Noah to look over his shoulder to see who the soldier was referring to when he realized the soldier was talking about him.

"NO!!! I'm with Captain Duran of the 68th Virginia!" cried Noah to the Confederate soldiers.

A Confederate fired his rifle at Noah, hitting him in his lower left leg.

Noah stumbled backward, lost his footing, and tumbled into the crater.

"NOAH!!!" cried out Reuben as he watched in anger as his childhood friend fall into the pit. He drew his Kutto. Using the reverse draw technique exposing the sharper than razor edge side of his sword, he charged the Confederate who shot Noah.

With a ferocious rabid look, Reuben leaped in front of the soldier, roared out a powerful kiai, and cut the Confederate who caused Noah to fall into the pit diagonally into two from his right shoulder to left hip. The faces of the remaining Confederate soldiers, who were also threating Noah, changed from heroic defenders of the Confederacy to shocked horror as Reuben's sharpen edged Kutto cut each one of them in two as well.

Reuben's attention turned to the rim of the crater as he desperately tried to find Noah on the crowded floor of the hole. Off to the side, lying against the wall of the crater, Reuben spotted him. Reuben let out a loud roaring kiai, and leaped into the crater landing on top of Union soldiers.

When Reuben landed, it seemed like a shock wave as soldiers fell away from him. Reversing his Kutto to the unsharpened curved edge, Reuben cut and hacked his way to Noah, crippling every Union soldier his Kutto came in contact with.

"NOAH!!! HOLD ON, I'LL GET YOU OUT OF HERE!!!" yelled out Reuben as he stuck his Kutto into the wall of the enormous hole. In one swift motion, Reuben raised Noah up onto his shoulders, retrieved his Kutto, and turned to see Union soldiers surrounding him with his back against the wall.

"Leave me Reuben and save yourself! I'm done for…" cried Noah.

"Shut up, Noah! No one dies this time, especially you!" replied Reuben.

One soldier lunged at Reuben with a bayonetted rifle. His shoulder snapped in two with the blunt edge of Reuben's Kutto. As another Union soldier was about to attack, he was shot dead center in the forehead. Other Union soldiers began falling at Reuben's feet as if a path was being cleared for him. Déjà vu ran through Reuben's mind as he remembered how Tadashi and Masaru would clear a path for Reuben with their arrows.

Reuben looked up to the rim of the crater to see Sergeant Warren and several other members of Company C firing their rifles into the pit ahead of Reuben, clearing a path for him and Noah to pass. Reuben quickly nodded toward Sergeant Warren, who yelled, "RUN, REUBEN!!!"

Reuben made his way, holding Noah with his left arm and slashing his Kutto with his right, toward a climbable slope. Reuben glanced back toward Sergeant Warren as the sun broke through the black powder and fire smoke. For a fraction of a second that seemed like long moments, Reuben saw what appeared to be apparitions of samurai in Akagi armor standing behind Sergeant Warren, and each of the Company C men, as if they were directing their fire, clearing a path for Reuben.

"AKAGI!!!" cried out Reuben as he continued his run toward the slope.

Cutting down the last few Union troops in his way, Reuben made his way out of the pit to see throngs of soldiers in blue charging toward him. He turned to his right and began running back to the opposite side of the pit away from its rim. As he ran, Reuben looked at Noah's leg as it was flopping in unnatural ways each step Reuben made. He knew Noah's leg was going to have to be amputated.

Running to a portion of the trenches where there was no fighting, Reuben met up with Doctor Chelmsford and Sergeant Warren. Reuben lowered Noah to the ground where the doctor immediately went to work on Noah's leg.

Reuben knelt by Noah's side, taking his hands and holding them tightly as Noah was fighting the excruciating pain pulsating through his entire body.

"You're safe now, Noah. The doc will fix you up," said Reuben, his face no longer looking like a frenzied wolf, but a saddened, frightened little boy lost in the wilderness.

Doctor Chelmsford splinted Noah's leg as best he could. "We need to get him to the medical tents quickly, Reuben! This is all I can do for Noah now!"

"Right," said Reuben as he lifted Noah back onto his shoulders and began running to the rear with Doctor Chelmsford, Sergeant Warren, and the other boys from Company C in tow.

Without stopping, they ran even when Confederate provosts threatened to shoot them for running away from the battle. One provost came dangerously close to grabbing Reuben, only to be knocked down by Sergeant Warren's rifle butt.

Once they made it to the rear, Doctor Chelmsford led Reuben to the hospital portion. Wounded and dead, both Confederate and Union, littered the ground.

"Reuben, we'll wait over there!" called out Sergeant Warren, pointing to a clearing. Reuben's only response was a nod as he was ushered by the doctor into a huge tent with a sign labeled surgery.

"Find an empty table and lay Noah down so I can go to work on him," said the doctor urgently.

623

"You there! Take that darky out of here!" ordered what appeared to be a doctor wearing a blood soaked apron.

"This man needs attention!" said Reuben.

"I don't care! We don't treat darkies in this tent! Take him elsewhere!"

"Please, doctor," pleaded Doctor Chelmsford. "I'm a doctor. I'll treat him myself. Just give me a space to work."

"I said get out or I'll have the provosts arrest you!"

Reuben looked around the tent and noticed a Confederate major sitting on a table with his left arm in a sling smoking a cigar. Off to the side of the table on the ground, leaned a dead soldier against a tent beam waiting to be taken out.

Walking toward the major, Reuben gently lowered Noah onto the table next to the major. The major looked at both Reuben and Noah with distain.

"What's wrong with you, Major?" asked Reuben.

"That's none of your concern," said the major, angered and shaking.

"Can you stand and walk?"

"I told you that's none of your concern! Now get your nigger off my table!"

"Coward!" said Reuben to the major's face.

The major hopped off the table and reached for his revolver. As he pulled it free from its holster, he aimed it to Reuben's head. Reuben swiftly and easily took hold of the major's hand and twisted it outward, causing the major to flip over onto the ground. Still with the major's hand in his grasp, Reuben drew his Kutto and cut down on the major's uninjured shoulder. A loud crunch was heard when the blade met bone causing those witnessing to turn and look away.

Reuben pushed the screaming major to the side, raised his Kutto, twirling it at the same time, exposing the edged portion of the blade, and sliced the dead soldier in two.

Pointing his Kutto to the doctor who told him to leave, Reuben yelled, "YOU WILL LET THIS DOCTOR SEE TO THIS MAN, OR BY THE GODS OF THE HIGH MOUNTAINS, I WILL SLAUGHTER EVERY MAN IN THIS TENT STARTING WITH YOU!!!"

Cowering down in dreaded fear, the doctor nodded for Doctor Chelmsford to treat Noah.

Doctor Chelmsford gently laid Noah down on the table and began removing the splint.

Reuben lifted the major off the ground and gently placed him next to the dead soldier who moments ago been in one piece.

Reuben moved to the other side of the table and took Noah's hand and held it tightly.

"Reuben, it hurts so bad." said Noah in excruciating pain.

"Not to worry, Noah. Doc will fix you up," said Reuben, as reassuring as he could.

"A saw, I need a saw," called out Doctor Chelmsford.

"What do you mean you need a saw?" asked Reuben. "You're not going to take his leg, are you, Doc?" he continued to ask, knowing it was inevitable.

"I have to, Reuben. There's no bone left to be mended. It's all shattered."

An orderly handed the doctor a bloody, dull bone saw over Noah's chest causing Noah to look at it with horror.

"NO!!! Not that! Please, Reuben, kill me! I would rather die than go through that torture!"

"Doc, isn't there another way?!" asked Reuben, franticly.

"If you have a better idea, now is the time!"

Reuben looked at the tsuka of his Kutto. "As a matter of fact, I do," said Reuben, as he looked back to the doctor.

Doctor Chelmsford understood and nodded. "You there, get me a tourniquet and hold him down."

"Reuben, what are you going to do?" asked Noah, frightened.

"I'm going to help the doc."

"No, Reuben. Just kill me. I can't return to Ever less than a man I was when I left."

"Noah, my friend, my brother, you're more of a man than you know. You're one of the bravest men I have ever had the honor of knowing. It's because of you I will return to Renee and Aarleen. A leg is just a leg, but what counts is what's in your heart, and if what you have told me about Evergreen's transition is true, then it's your heart she loves, not your leg."

Noah grasped Reuben's shoulders and pulled him down. "Really, Reuben, do you mean that?" Noah asked, his eyes full of hope.

"Every word," said Reuben with devotion.

Regaining every ounce of strength and bravery he could muster, Noah nodded and said, "Then go to it and make it quick."

"You won't feel a thing," Reuben told Noah.

Reuben nodded to Doctor Chelmsford as he finished tying the tourniquet. The doctor told Reuben to hold on for a few seconds for the blood to slow its flow to Noah's lower left leg. In the meantime, he scrambled to find some fresh bandages. He was offered some by a very concerned orderly and handed one to Reuben. He asked the orderly for any type of sanitizing agent and was given a bottle of whiskey.

"Quick, Reuben. Your blade, clean it," directed Doctor Chelmsford.

Reuben nodded, drew his Kutto, and did as the doctor instructed.

At this moment, everyone in the tent was drawn to the drama at Noah's table, including the doctor who first told Reuben to get out and the major with the broken right collarbone and left arm in a sling.

Doctor Chelmsford positioned Noah's leg at the edge of the table and instructed Reuben where to make his cut.

"You there, cover his eyes," said the doctor to the orderly as two other orderlies came to assist in holding Noah down.

Doctor Chelmsford took hold of Noah's left leg as Reuben reversed his blade and raised his Kutto in high suburi fashion.

With a sharp kiai, Reuben cut down, slicing through Noah's leg like a hot knife through butter. Noah didn't even wince, and as if by magic, Noah's pain began to ebb away.

Quickly Doctor Chelmsford applied bandages to the open cut to ease the bleeding, but there was none. Reuben's cut was smooth and clean, practically closing vital veins as his blade cut through Noah's leg.

"Hurry, Reuben, cut it off already, I can't wait any longer! Get it over with!" said Noah.

狼

"That's it, Cynthia! Anyone can do it," said Renee as she showed Cynthia how to block an attacking jo and raise her jo into a hasso defending position.

Once Cynthia learned the angles and her footing, she spent the rest of the afternoon twirling an old broken broom stick up and over her head into a hasso position. She thought it was the greatest thing ever.

"I can't thank you enough for enlightening my Cynthia, Renee," said Simon. "She's a much more loving and wonderful person now since you took her and Benjamin in, and I truly appreciate that."

It had been several weeks since Simon was brought to the farm by Major MacKay. In that time, he was amazed at the transformation of his wife. She was no longer a whiny over-privileged snob who looked down on people like Reuben, Renee, and Aarleen.

Renee giggled and said, "Well, I may have taken them in, but it was Benjamin who enlightened Cynthia on the day of the shoe."

"Day of the shoe?" asked Simon with a puzzled look.

Renee told Simon of the first few days when Cynthia and Benjamin came to live on the farm. How Benjamin saw to his mother's every need until the one day she asked for her shoes, which were clearly within her reach, and Benjamin had had enough. Since then, Cynthia could not be kept away from contributing. Her lack of common daily experiences caused her to be rather clumsy, and resulted in humorous mishaps, but at least she was trying and doing her part. If anything, she was contributing by providing laughter, like when Renee was teaching her to bake bread and she opened a sack of flour. Instead of gently opening the sack from the corner, she ripped it open causing the both of them to be covered in a huge poof of flour.

"I have to ask you Simon, and please don't feel offended. Honestly, I don't mean any offense, but I need to know."

"Know what, Renee?"

"Geez oh geez oh geez I can't believe I'm going to ask this. I had to stop Reuben from asking you at one time, but anyway, Cynthia... how and why?"

Simon laughed and answered, "Renee, of all people, you should know."

"Arranged?" asked Renee, assuming that was the case.

"Yep, I'm telling you, if it had not been for Benjamin, that 'for better or for worse' clause would have been tossed out of the window a long time ago."

Renee laughed along with Simon, and kept laughing as he stopped.

"My heavens, you're an amazing woman, Renee."

"How so?"

"After all you and Reuben have been through, and going through now, you can still find time to laugh."

"You can thank Aarleen for that. If it wasn't for her, I would have lost my mind long before Reuben returned from Japan. That little cherry blossom of his is the most precious thing in both our lives. It's because of her, Reuben and I are one, together as love intended. An everlasting mark on our lives as Mr. Akagi once told Reuben."

Taking hold of the button hanging from her neck, Renee took a deep long look at the oak tree. It wasn't until this moment when she realized how much the tree played an important part in their lives. The day they met. The days they played at the foot of its wide trunk. The evening when she stopped Reuben from his attempt to commit suicide a second time. The evening they made love beneath its branches in the soft warm autumn rain. The day he asked her to be his wife. And the day they were married beneath its branches.

"Someday my husband will return and we will be one again. It will be like a whole new do-over," said Renee with a loving look in her eyes. "Until then, I must keep up my spirits for Reuben's little cherry blossom, and she must keep up hers for me. We're a team and have been ever since the day she was born."

Renee looked toward the house as she heard Riley bark. However, his bark was not the usual bark warning of Federal troops. It was a more youthful bark, like when he was a puppy.

The door to the back of the house opened and Aarleen called out, "MAMA!!! IT'S DOCTOR LAWRENCE AND NOAH!!!"

Renee looked at Simon and sprinted to the house. As she came up to Noah and Evergreen's cabin, she stopped and was about to pound on the door as Evergreen opened it quickly.

"Did I hear Aarleen right? Noah is home?" asked Evergreen, full of joy.

"That's what she said. Come on, Ever, come on!" Renee said pulling Evergreen to the house.

Parked out front of the house sat Doctor Chelmsford and Noah in a small carriage being pulled by one horse. Aarleen and Benjamin were standing next to the carriage laughing and greeting the doctor and Noah.

Doctor Chelmsford climbed off the carriage as soon as he saw Renee running to them. He greeted her with a hug while everyone else came and converged around the carriage.

Everyone fell silent when Evergreen came up to the carriage. When she saw Noah, her eyes glistened and tears of joy rolled down her cheeks. She skipped to the carriage and took Noah's offered hands.

"Get down here, you scoundrel," she said, tugging at his hands.

With his mouth beginning to quiver, he said, "I can't get down. Not without any help."

It was then everyone noticed a blanket covering Noah's lap.

"Good heavens, Noah. What's wrong?" asked Evergreen.

"I had a… accident," said Noah as he uncovered his lap revealing the loss of his left leg below the knee.

There was even more silence as Evergreen stepped closer to the carriage. She placed her hand on his leg and said, "I'll help you down, my love."

"You will, Evergreen?" asked Noah with surprise.

"Of course. I'm your woman and you're my man. We take care of our own," said Evergreen as she looked to Renee, "just like Renee's man says."

Noah scooted off the bench of the carriage and set his good leg solid on the ground while Doctor Chelmsford handed Noah his crutches.

Noah and Evergreen embraced each other and kissed. When their lips parted, Evergreen let out a little laugh and said, "Well, at least there's a little less you will have to wash after a hard day's work."

狼

As the entire clan of the farm walked toward the house, the first questions from Noah and Doctor Chelmsford was about Monroe. "Is Monroe here? Have you seen Monroe at all?" they both asked.

When the answer of no was said, Noah and the doctor began to tell of Reuben's desperate attempts to find Monroe, and when he finally did, they had reconciled. Monroe had come to his senses and admitted how right Reuben was, and assured him he would either return back to Richmond or home.

"Reuben came with us when I took Noah to Chimborazo. While there, he scoured Richmond looking for Monroe, even going as far as knocking on the door of the Davis house," said Doctor Chelmsford.

"Yeah, it's as if Monroe has disappeared off the face of the earth," added Noah.

"We tried to convince Reuben to come back with us and he was about to, but his obligation to his brother and the company got the better of him. Although he was torn between coming home and his obligations, he was never without your picture case in one hand and your little turtle box in the other," said Doctor Chelmsford to Renee and Aarleen.

For the second time in less than a year, a huge dinner was served in celebration of Noah and the doctor's return, complete with two hams the doctor picked up in Norfolk before he and Noah came to the farm.

Everyone contributed to the making of the dinner, including Cynthia who was tasked with peeling and mashing potatoes.

"How about I help you make bread, Renee?" asked Cynthia when she finished her task.

"NO!!!" was everyone's humorous cry.

When dinner was finished, everyone remained sitting around the table, listening with fascination to Noah's and the doctor's stories of their journey to find Reuben. They told of how they witnessed Reuben in battle, and how he defended them and his company without killing the enemy, except for when he went after Noah when he fell into the huge pit in Petersburg.

"My lord," said Cynthia. "I cannot believe I thought him a coward before all this happened. I'm sorry, Renee. I was so wrong."

Renee patted Cynthia on her hand and noticed Aarleen and Benjamin looking at Noah's left leg.

"Sweetie, you and Benjamin, stop staring at Noah's… leg. You're being rude."

"We're not staring, Mama. We're thinking," replied Aarleen.

"About what?" asked Doctor Chelmsford with interest.

"Can you bend your knee, Noah?" asked Benjamin.

"Sure can. Here, see," said Noah as he lifted his leg and showed the two youths he could bend his knee. "What's so interesting about that?"

Benjamin nodded his head saying, "I bet with Doctor Lawrence's and Henry's help, Aarleen and I can rig up some sort of fake lower leg so you can walk without crutches. Maybe even run."

"See, Noah. I told you," said the doctor as he slapped the table. "If those two young ones can see it, then it's possible."

"You really think you and Aarleen can do that, Benjamin?" asked Evergreen, enthusiastically.

"I think so, if the doctor and Henry will help us. You might still walk with a limp, but it would be better than using crutches," answered Benjamin.

"Hey, you can walk around with a jo like Da, and use it for a walking stick," added Aarleen.

Renee rose and took Aarleen into her arms saying, "I'm so proud of both of you. What do you say, Noah? Will you let Benjamin and my little sweetie help you?"

Noah looked at everyone sitting around the table. They all had looks of support for him. He nodded and said, "Why not? It will be my goal to walk to Reuben when he comes home."

狼

There were no serious sleeping arrangements needed to be made with the two newest additions to the farm. Actually, only one addition, for all intents and purposes Noah never officially left according to Major MacKay, all up to interpretation of course. Noah had his and Evergreen's cabin and Renee assured the two, no one will come near their cabin until they emerge themselves.

As for Doctor Chelmsford, Benjamin, who had been using Aarleen's room, offered that to the doctor while he would make use of the sofa in the parlor.

As bedtime fell upon the Duran farm, Renee and Aarleen did what they always did before getting into bed. They spent several minutes staring out of the window, up to the moon or the sky, thinking of Reuben. They knew he would be doing the same, wherever he was.

"Goodnight, my shoddy farm boy," said Renee.

"Goodnight, Da," Aarleen said after.

They both got into bed and as Renee was about to turn down the lamp, there was a knock at the door.

"Come in please," said Renee.

The door opened and it was Doctor Chelmsford. "I hope I'm not disturbing you two," he said.

"Oh no, Doctor Lawrence, we were just saying goodnight to Da," said Aarleen.

"Ah, that's what I came to talk to you about. May I come in?"

"Of course. Please have a seat," answered Renee.

Doctor Chelmsford took a chair from the far side of the room and placed it next to the bed. Both Renee and Aarleen moved to sit on the edge of the bed.

The doctor took each one of their hands in his and said, "I came to tell you the last thing Reuben said to me before Noah and I came back to Norfolk. I could not tell you earlier because what he had to say was for you two only, and was meant to be said just before you went to sleep."

He turned his attention to Aarleen and with a warm smile he said, "Your father told me to tell you, you no longer have to worry about having any more bad dreams when you sleep alone. He said he knows he's not alone and well protected with warriors of the past watching over him."

"Oh, Mama! Mr. Akagi *is* watching over Da like he said he would in my dream," said Aarleen as tears fell from her eyes.

Renee took Aarleen into her arms and rocked her a few times until Doctor Chelmsford continued, "Reuben told me to tell you, Renee, he knows you look into the sky every night before you go to sleep, and he does as well. He says you're his water and he's your stone, and he'll be home to hold you once again as love intended, but for now, Aishite'ru yo, my precious Wickham girl."

This time Aarleen was the one who took Renee into her arms.

"Now come, you two," said the doctor clearing his throat trying to hold back his own emotional state, "Lie down and get some sleep. You still have a farm to run."

Renee and Aarleen laid down as the doctor covered them. He leaned down and gave each one a kiss on the forehead and said goodnight before he left the room closing the door behind him.

Renee and Aarleen lay in bed together in each other's arms, both thinking of Reuben's words he told the doctor to tell them.

"You know what, Mama?" asked Aarleen.

"What's that, sweetie."

"With Mr. Norenham, Noah, and Doctor Lawrence home, it's Da's turn to come home."

石
水

In the year of our Lord, 1865, a romantic tale continues.
Just as the living have prayers, so do the dying...

Prayer For The Dying

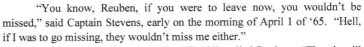

"You know, Reuben, if you were to leave now, you wouldn't be missed," said Captain Stevens, early on the morning of April 1 of '65. "Hell, if I was to go missing, they wouldn't miss me either."

"I was thinking the same thing, Todd," replied Reuben. "There's still fighting going on, but nothing significant where the boys can't take care of themselves."

Captain Stevens moved next to Reuben, placed his hand on his shoulder, and with a most sympathetic tone, he said, "I'm amazed you lasted this long, my friend. Although you refuse to come to terms with it, the fact of the matter is, your brother probably never made it home. So the way I see it, General Doyle and Colonel McFerrin didn't keep their end of the deal."

Reuben shot Captain Stevens a vicious look causing him to reel back and scoot away. Reuben's face softened, accepting the fact the captain was right.

"Damn war. Nothing good ever comes out of it, no matter what side you are on. Even the feudal battles we fought in the Hisano Province. There were always sacrifices we had to contend with. My biggest sacrifice was being separated from Renee for seven years. But, those seven years bonded us with love and devotion so strong, even war can't tear it apart.

"Tell you what, Todd, if nothing happens tomorrow, I'm going home, and I recommend you tell Max, Matthew, Albert, and the rest of the boys, if they have an opportunity, go home too. They've done all they can for this cause that was long lost before it began."

On November 15 of '64, Union Army General William Tecumseh Sherman's troops burned much of the city of Atlanta, Georgia to the ground before continuing their march through the South. General Sherman's Atlanta campaign was turning out to be one of the most decisive victories of the war. With the fall of Atlanta, the one remaining obstacle was Richmond. However, Union Army General Ulysses S. Grant had to break the lines of Petersburg to get to it.

To break the Petersburg lines, a series of battles were fought, which only prolonged the siege causing Confederate Army General Robert E. Lee to stretch his lines to the breaking point. The debacle that caused General Grant to finally break the thin Confederate lines was at Five Forks where General Lee lost his reserves to be used as a fall back fighting force.

With Union Army General Philip Sheridan's infantry supported cavalry, General Lee would thin out his lines dangerously to the breaking point to prevent his army from being completely surrounded. This made General Lee vulnerable to direct assaults all along his lines.

All of this happened shortly after Reuben's and Captain Stevens' discussion. Reuben had to postpone his long walk home when all hell broke out along the Petersburg lines the following day.

Doyle's Brigade was ordered to close up any gaps in the lines as the Federals pounded the Confederates with non-stop artillery and rifle fire. As the Union troops heard of Confederate lines falling apart, it added to their momentum.

Reuben advised Captain Stevens and Lieutenants Peaks and Rallins to keep the company out of the fight as much as possible.

"The end is near, Todd, and this is no time for any of our boys to die needlessly. The way I see it, Lee will probably have us evacuate the trenches and head west before the day is over."

Looking worried, Lieutenant Rallins asked, "Just how are we supposed to keep the entire company out of the fight?"

Without hesitation, Reuben said, "Make them look busy. Have them tote empty boxes, haul crates, dig holes, run in circles, anything to make them look like they're doing something, but keep them close together. If we're to evacuate, it'll be within a moment's notice."

"Right, Captain. Matthew and I will see to it!" exclaimed Lieutenant Rallins, with confidence.

Throughout the day, the men of Company C looked too busy to be put into the lines to fight. It was a successful ruse by Reuben to protect and keep these men alive to go home to their loved ones.

As Reuben predicted, just after dark, General Lee began evacuating the army. It had been a long day, but with Reuben's encouraging attitude, the officers and men of Company C kept their hopes high, any time soon this nightmare would end and everyone would be able to go home.

"Just play along and keep your heads down! I won't let any of you die now that we're so close!" cried out Reuben as he moved the men along.

For the next few days, he watched other Confederates die from Federal skirmishers and felt horrible he couldn't protect them. He had to keep reminding himself the officers and men of Company C were his responsibility. And it was also his responsibility to keep himself alive for Renee and Aarleen.

狼

Noah and Evergreen were taking their morning walk up the lane leading toward the road. From there they would walk toward the Norfolk County Outreach School. It became their morning ritual once Benjamin, with the assistance of Aarleen, Doctor Chelmsford and Henry, fashioned a very serviceable artificial leg for Noah. Every morning after breakfast, Noah and

Evergreen would take this walk. He still needed the use of a cane, but each day he would make progress to the point he only carried and used it if necessary.

Each day they would walk a little further. They hadn't made it as far as the schoolhouse, but it was within view. "In a few more days, I'll make it to that schoolhouse of ours, and that will be the day everyone will come walking with us," said Noah as he and Evergreen were about to turn and walk back to the farm.

As they were heading back to the farm, Major MacKay and a corporal came trotting around the bend heading their way.

Since Noah and Doctor Chelmsford returned, Major MacKay had been by the farm for his usual inspections and noticed the two, but didn't make any mention of it. During one of the major's inspections, Cynthia innocently mentioned their return causing the others to cringe. However, Major MacKay simply said, "Whatever are you talking about, Miss Garrett, Noah has never been taken off the residence list of this farm, and as for the doctor, as a member of the U.S. Sanitation Commission, he comes and goes as he pleases."

As the major and the corporal came nearer, Noah began to feel uneasy. He was concerned about Evergreen's attitude toward the two Federal soldiers. He still had not gotten used to Evergreen's attitude shift. It was surprising for him when she was the one who greeted the two pleasantly as they came near.

"Good morning, Mr. MacKay. Good morning, Corporal."

"And a very fine morning to both of you, Miss Evergreen and Mr. Noah," greeted back Major MacKay just as pleasantly. "My, my, Mr. Noah, you're making wonderful progress."

Not knowing how to respond, Noah simply said, "Thank you."

"Listen you two. I have some important news for Mrs. Duran and the rest of the residents of the farm. You both should be present when I tell this news."

"As a matter of fact, we're making our way back, Mr. MacKay. Is it about Reuben?" asked Evergreen, anxiously.

"Can't really say, but this isn't... bad news. Perhaps Mr. Noah would care to ride my mount."

"If it's not bad news and you're not in a hurry, I would rather walk," replied Noah.

The major chuckled admiringly and said, "Well, then, I'll walk with you. Corporal, please ride ahead and have Mrs. Duran, her daughter, and the others gather in front of the house. Make sure to tell them this isn't bad news."

"Yes, sir," said the corporal as he heeled his mount and trotted on ahead.

Major MacKay dismounted and began walking along with Noah and Evergreen. The major asked Noah how he lost his leg during the crater battle, causing Noah to ask how he knew.

"Oh, in my business, I know almost anything, Mr. Noah. So you say Mr. Duran was the one who assisted Doctor Chelmsford in amputating your leg?"

"He did it himself using his Kutto. One swift stroke, swoosh! I didn't feel a thing. Wait a minute, I shouldn't be telling you this."

"Mr. Noah, I'm not here today as a Federal area inspector. I'm merely out here for a ride to enjoy the countryside. Something I haven't had the pleasure to do because of the rebellion. Now, with it almost over, I have the time to… mingle, if you will. So please, continue your story. It's fascinating."

Noah continued to tell his story about the day he was shot and how Reuben saved his life. When he was finished, the major couldn't believe the irony he shared with Noah. The man who caused the loss of his arm was the same man who amputated Noah's leg. In a sense, Reuben saved both our lives by taking our limbs, thought Major MacKay.

The walk was enjoyable, but Noah and Evergreen were still anxious to know what the major had to say. As they made the turn onto the lane, Riley began to bark. Renee and Aarleen ran to meet the three.

"What's happening, Mr. MacKay?" asked Renee, frantically.

"Please, Mrs. Duran, the news I have isn't bad. In fact, it may be good news for you and your daughter. Please, let's hurry as fast as Mr. Noah can so all can hear this."

Once everyone was gathered, Major MacKay called Renee and Aarleen to his side. "Listen everyone, I'm not here as a Federal administrator. I'm only enjoying a ride through the countryside and came to ask if you have heard the latest news of the rebellion."

Everyone shook their heads no with looks of wonderment in their faces.

"Well, everyone, it seems Richmond has fallen to the Union Army yesterday and the rebels are on the run, heading west. It's believed they are going to try to link up with the rebel army commanded by General Johnston. However, I understand hundreds of rebels have either deserted or have been taken prisoner. Either way, this rebellion is near its end, and hopefully within days, Mr. Duran will be released from his impressment."

Everyone stared at the major in shock.

It was Cynthia who broke the silence by saying, "Did you hear that, Renee? Reuben should be coming home soon! We need to start planning to prepare a feast!"

"Feast?" asked Major MacKay.

"I mean, ah…"

"I don't want to know, Miss Garrett. However, although you didn't hear it from me, you may want to start enlarging your planting field. I believe restrictions will soon be lifted."

When Major MacKay and the corporal departed, Renee and Aarleen went inside to the mantel in the parlor. Renee took hold of the smooth stone Akagi Genda-San gave her many years ago and held it out for Aarleen to hold also. Holding each other's hand with the stone in their grasp, they each laid their heads on each other's shoulders and silently prayed for Reuben's safe and quick return.

狼

Doyle's Brigade, if it was still called Doyle's Brigade, found itself, along with the rest of General Lee's Army of Northern Virginia, making haste toward Lynchburg where much needed ammunition and supplies were supposed to be waiting for them. While the Confederates were making their desperate retreat, Federal cavalry constantly harassed the retreating column with hit and run skirmishes. It was in one of these skirmishes the command staff of Doyle's Brigade was hit, and hit hard. General Doyle was severely injured and Colonel McFerrin went missing. As far as the officers of Company C of the 68th Virginia Infantry Regiment were concerned, they were on their own.

At a winding stream called Sailor's Creek where the two armies clashed, both Captain Stevens and Sergeant Warren caught a glimpse of the massive Union army pounding away at what was left of what used to be the pride of the Confederacy. Reuben, in the meantime, was doing what he could to keep the company together until Captain Stevens took hold of his arm and pulled him aside.

"Reuben, this is it! Max and I are pulling the men from the line and waiting this thing out! It's over, my friend!"

Reuben looked all around and nodded in agreement. "You're right, Todd. I'll have Matthew and Albert start moving the boys to that slope between the thickets! From there we should be able to watch the fight without getting seriously involved!"

Reuben began to step off, but was held back by Captain Stevens.

"What the hell, Todd. Let go of my arm!"

Sergeant Warren took hold of Reuben's other arm while Captain Stevens said, "No, Reuben. It's over for *you*! You've done all you can for us! Now it's your turn to see to your own! As far as I'm concerned, both Doyle and McFerrin are gone, and so is their agreement you made with them! I'm relieving you of your commission, Reuben!"

"You can't do that, Todd! What about the company?!"

"You've taught Todd and me all we need to know to keep them alive until this nightmare is over!" said Max. "It has been an honor to fight by your side, my friend!"

"But…"

"There are no buts about it, Reuben! Now get your ass out of here! You're a civilian, a school teacher, a husband, and a father! Go home damn it!" interrupted Max as he saluted Reuben.

Standing dumbfounded, Reuben, for the first time, winced when a shell hit the ground nearby. Images of Renee standing beneath the oak tree entered his mind, her hair cascading over her shoulders, just the way he always liked it, and her adorable smiling face. Images of Aarleen followed of when he first learned of her, and the day he gave her the bokken made of New England hickory.

"Go, Reuben! You won't have a better diversion than this one right now, and we just might make use of it ourselves!" Todd said, letting go of Reuben's arm and rendering him a salute.

Reuben returned their salutes saying, "When you two return back to Norfolk…"

"We'll bring the whiskey!" finished Todd.

As Reuben was about to step away, Lieutenants Peaks and Rallins called out to him.

"Wait, Reuben!" said Matthew Peaks.

"We have something for you! Here, we've kept this for you since the crater!" added Albert Rallins as he handed Reuben his jo.

"Geez oh geez oh geez I thought I lost this a long time ago. Thank you, Matt. Thank you, Albert. Thank you both."

"Now go! Renee and Aarleen need you!" said Todd.

At the sound of Reuben's wife's and daughter's names, he ran toward the direction of the Union lines.

狼

A Confederate lieutenant colonel stumbled across the battlefield. One of those rear echelon seat cushions Reuben and Max always complained about. However, this seat cushion was far out of place. He was one of the rear echelon officers who barely escaped when Richmond fell. He was an officer whose family's money bought him his rank and a high profile position since the capital of the Confederacy was relocated from Montgomery, Alabama to Richmond, Virginia. Having never seen a shot fired in anger, he suddenly found himself in the middle of a horrific drama filled with fire and blood.

The lieutenant colonel fell to the ground after a thunderous explosion went off several yards away. The concussion of the blast made him dizzy as he tried to return to his feet, but he couldn't regain his balance. Crawling on the ground, he desperately tried to find his way back to his group of officers who also escaped the fall of Richmond, not knowing where they were. He saw Confederates scattering in all directions. He was alone, caught in the middle of a vicious crossfire. With eyes blinded from dirt and dust, and ears ringing from the blast, he could neither see nor make out any type of sounds except for muffled cannon blasts and musketry.

Another cannon shell landed ten yards away throwing him face down to the ground. This time he covered his head with his hands and tried to make himself as flat as he could. As his wits began to return, he thought it would be best to lay and wait until the cannonade subsided and the smoke and dust cleared. At this point, he didn't care if he was on his side of the line or the Union side. He thought, if taken prisoner, he had a better chance of survival as a prisoner of war since the Confederate Army of Northern Virginia was almost out of options to continue.

He chanced a look to his left. Soldiers of both sides were locked in hand-to-hand combat along the creek's edge. He felt he should do his duty and assist his Confederate brethren, but his legs were rooted with fear. He felt shame spending the entire war in luxury enjoying elegant dinners and the company of women both socially proper and not, and never giving any second thoughts to the soldiers who were dying on the fields of battle. Now with the army forced to run for its survival, he found himself in the midst of those soldiers he had never given a second thought.

With hands shaking like leaves and eyes watering, he began to think of such a fool he was encouraging, and sometime threatening, younger men to fight, when he himself never seen the use of rifles, let alone cannons. Feeling deeper shame, he reached for his pistol, pulled it out of the holster, and held it up to his face. He shook his head thinking about how he never fired it at a target for practice. He had to have a sergeant load it for him since he didn't know how.

Mustering as much courage as he could, he thumbed the hammer back and took a quick look in all directions. He said out loud, "I will make my parents proud, and make Renee sorry she didn't keep her father's promise."

Lieutenant Colonel William Sinclair carefully began to stand up. His balance returned, however his legs felt weak from fear. He crouched down and began to make his way to the fighting troops. He raised his pistol and fired off a shot into the group of men, not realizing if he was aiming at troops in Confederate gray or Union blue. He pulled the trigger once again, and again. Every time he pulled the trigger, his courage and steps grew. He was about to fire his last shot when suddenly he was tackled to the ground and pulled into a huge blast hole saving him from a cannon shell ripping the ground apart where he was running.

More shells were landing all around the safety of the hole. Muffled orders of, "fall back," were heard coming from the hand-to-hand fighting he was attempting to reach. The cannon blasts were replaced by musketry. It became silent, and William Sinclair reached to peer over the edge of the hole, but was violently pulled back down. He turned to yell in protest, but was interrupted when horses came running past, and leaping over the hole. He again planted his face back into the earth and waited until the hoof beats could not be heard.

Again he began to raise his head only to feel a heavy weight land across his back. He glanced back to see the headless corpse of a Union soldier lying on top of him. With horror in his eyes, he started to push it off until he saw another battle mutilated corpse was tossed above his head. Lying in a hole full of corpses, nausea swept over his body, gagging him when he noticed the body that lay next to the corpse above his head was moving.

"Put your face down and act dead, now!" said the other soldier in the hole with him.

William Sinclair saw the other soldier was wearing a Confederate shell jacket. The other Confederate soldier laid on his back stretched out in a gruesome manner and with his hand, wiped blood across his face and closed his eyes. William Sinclair laid there in terror and began to hear the sounds of hundreds of shoes marching toward them and it became clear what this soldier was doing. Without thinking, he reached into the wound of the mutilated soldier above his head and smeared the blood across his face as the other soldier did, and planted his face in the mud as he was told.

"FORWARD MEN, WE GOT THEM ON THE RUN!!!"

The marching got louder and it began to turn into the sound of running. William Sinclair began to hear the splashing of footsteps and also the sound of feet landing as Union soldiers were leaping over the hole. Several soldiers, not quite making it fully across, landed in the hole and climbed out to continue the charge. The intense sound of charging soldiers didn't seem like it was ever going to end. What seemed like an eternity finally began to morph into the sounds of stragglers and rear assigned personal leisurely strolling by. William Sinclair stayed completely still and quiet. If I have to, I'll lay here until the end of the war, he thought to himself.

He heard the other soldier stirring around, but he was determined not to move. William Sinclair felt a boot brush against his side as the other soldier began crawling around.

Reuben slowly peered over the edge of the hole in the direction from where the charge came, and then to the direction it went. He saw the stragglers and rear personnel picking up their pace and he peered in all the other directions. Satisfied, he glanced down at the officer he saved. His face was still in the mud, and breathing bubbles could be seen coming from the mud where his face laid. Reuben reached down and hauled the decapitated Union soldier off of the officer's back and moved to the far side of the hole to watch the charge across the creek. "It's safe to come up now, but stay in the hole. We're behind enemy lines now."

William Sinclair rolled onto his back, and with disgust, he kicked and pushed the corpses away from him. He rolled over, heaved a few times, and vomited. He began coughing and gagging and was desperately wiping the blood and mud off his face. He started to sob and suddenly felt something land on his lap. The canteen landing in his lap made him jump and yelp.

"Drink slowly and keep quiet. We're still in serious danger of being caught or killed," said Reuben.

Looking at the Confederate soldier, he noticed the rank of a captain. William Sinclair picked up the canteen, uncorked it, and began to gulp down water disregarding the advice he was given moments ago. The gulping began to make him choke and he coughed up the water.

"I told you to drink slowly," said Reuben, not taking his eyes away from the Union advance. Satisfied it was safe, Reuben finally turned to face William Sinclair, sat back, and began to relax against the wall of the blast hole. "We're safe for the moment, but we really need to get out of here. Here, toss me the canteen."

William Sinclair did as he was told and seeing the captain was somewhat relaxing his guard, he too began to sit back in a more relaxed manner. He watched as the captain began to drink out of the canteen and said, "Thank you, Captain. I am indeed indebted to you. That was a rather macabre, but handy ruse you came up with. I believe I will have nightmares of it until the end of my days, but will be grateful it kept me alive."

William Sinclair began to get a better look at this captain who saved his life. He noticed his uniform was war torn and had seen more than its share of battles. William Sinclair glanced at his own uniform. Although it was filthy from his recent activities, it still had a factory fresh look to it. He realized he still had his pistol in hand and slowly returned the hammer back.

Finished drinking from the canteen, Reuben replaced the cork and slung it over his shoulder. He rested his head back, closed his eyes, and took a few deep breaths. He raised his head back up and opened his eyes. Suddenly he cocked his head to the side as he began to have a deep feeling of déjà vu. "Do I know you from somewhere?" he asked.

William Sinclair also narrowed his eyes and rose to his knees. "You!" he said with anger. "It's you! Of all the people in the world to save my ass, it had to be you! This changes everything you son of a bitch!"

William Sinclair raised the pistol at Reuben and pulled back the hammer. "If you only knew what I had to endure when Renee Wallace ran out leaving me at the altar, and then to find out she was pregnant with your bastard child! I had to endure humiliation! My parents had to endure humiliation! Everyone involved with that wedding endured humiliation! She was supposed to be mine, and then to find out she had feelings for you the entire time, and not for me. If you only knew how much I wished for this day to come, and at last, you're going to see it coming because I'm going to blast your head off!"

Reuben sat unmoved by William Sinclair's threat. Instead, he uncorked the canteen and leisurely began to drink. When he finished, he replaced the cork, wiped his lips on his sleeve, and again peered over the edge of the hole and sat back. He returned his attention to William Sinclair, his name quickly coming back to him. "Do you believe in fate, William Sinclair?" Reuben asked.

Perplexed, William Sinclair, still on his knees and pistol aimed at Reuben's head, could not believe how calm Reuben was with death ready to strike him. William Sinclair looked at Reuben's hands wondering if he had a weapon causing him to be calm, but he noticed he didn't have one. He was surprised to see Reuben didn't wear a pistol. Instead he saw a strange looking handle of a sword tucked into a cloth type of belt tied in the front, and an odd looking knife tucked under the knot.

"What the hell?!" replied William Sinclair at Reuben's response.

"I asked, do you believe in fate?" Reuben glanced at the sky and noticed how blue it looked through the black smoke of the spent black powder. He continued, "Fate is an awesome power filled with irony." He lowered his look, and turned his piercing gaze back at William Sinclair causing fear to settle in.

With the pistol aimed at Reuben's head, William Sinclair said, "I don't know what your game is, but it's not going to work. I heard you married Renee years later, but that's not going to stop me from taking vengeance for all of those who were humiliated because of you. It's because of you no upper class women would take me seriously, so I had to settle for lower class women. It's entirely your fault!"

"Let's examine that, shall we?" replied Reuben, making himself more comfortable and taking on the role of a teacher. He smiled and continued. "Where would we be if Renee did marry you? First of all, I would have been dead for almost 18 years now, and Renee might have learned, or have been forced to love you." Reuben shifted his weight and with a serious look, said, "As it is, I'm still alive and by a sheer act of fate, all due to irony, I saved you from getting your head blown off all these years later. Chances are, if Renee would have married you, you would still be here, but without me to pull you into this hole, and your battle-mutilated corpse would be laying out there rotting into the Virginia soil."

William Sinclair looked down to take in what Reuben said. He shook his head and said, "Nonsense! Utter nonsense!"

Reuben looked up over William Sinclair and back. With a childlike smirk, he said, "Fate between us continues to this very moment. You hate me so much you have your pistol leveled at me, ready to waste your last shot to take vengeance over an incident that happened years ago, or... are you going to use that shot on him," said Reuben as he nodded his head up above William Sinclair.

William Sinclair glanced up in the direction Reuben nodded and saw a Union sergeant aiming a carbine at him. The sergeant looked down at the two with a questionable look on his face wondering why a Confederate officer was pointing his pistol at another Confederate officer.

William Sinclair instinctively twisted around bringing the pistol in a wide arc, leveled it off, closed his eyes, and pulled the trigger. The bullet hit the sergeant in the middle of the face. He made no sound and fell back. William Sinclair remained sitting with the pistol still pointing where the sergeant was standing.

"Fate is an awesome power filled with irony. Now, do you want to get out of here or wait for another Federal to come and see what you did to his buddy? If one does, I doubt fate will save us this time. There's a difference between fate and luck, and I don't happen to believe in luck."

Reuben stood up, adjusted his Kutto, and held out his hand toward William Sinclair.

William Sinclair was dumbfounded and sat in the giant hole holding a now empty pistol. He turned his attention to Reuben standing before him and suddenly saw a different man he first met so many years ago at that autumn ball in '47. This man was radiant with positive energy, considering the predicament they were in. His hatred toward Reuben began to recede and a sensation of trust filled that void. He holstered the pistol and took Reuben's hand. He was startled by his touch for he felt flowing energy through his palm.

Reuben helped him up and placed his other hand on his shoulder and said, "That was a one in a million shot. You probably didn't realize your eyes were shut when you pulled that trigger."

Reuben released his hand and turned his attention to the battle ahead of them.

"My god, what if I missed?" asked William Sinclair in awe of what happened.

"It doesn't matter now. It's done. You just gave us another opportunity to die. Let's hope your faith in luck and mine in fate keeps us alive for another day. Stand tall and dig deep within yourself to find your true pride and follow me. There's only one way back to safety."

"How is that?" questioned William Sinclair.

Reuben placed his hand on the tsuka of his Kutto, turned to face William Sinclair and said, "Right through that line of blue uniforms."

狼

Reuben and William Sinclair both remained standing in the corpse filled blast hole. Reuben removed his tanto, and placed it in his haversack along with Aarleen's inrou attached to his obi. Now isn't the time to lose her precious little trinket box, thought Reuben.

"Okay, Colonel Sinclair, grab hold of my canteen strap and follow me," said Reuben as he reached for his jo leaning against a Confederate corpse.

"Are you serious? We're running toward the Yankees?"

"Not exactly, more parallel. I don't know about you, Colonel, but I'm running toward home."

"Desertion, at a time like this?" asked William Sinclair, rather perturbed.

"What better time? Besides, I was relieved of my commission about an hour ago. I'm only a simple school teacher trying to get home to my wife and daughter. Now, are you coming or not, Colonel?"

William Sinclair's anger ebbed away, replaced by shame. "Please don't call me colonel. I haven't done anything worthy to deserve that title of distinction. Just call me William."

"Colonel. William. Doesn't matter. We're hauling ass. Now come on," said Reuben as he started climbing out of the hole.

William Sinclair followed and stood next to Reuben. Reuben was surveying the battlefield to determine which direction to run.

"Come on, this way!" said Reuben as he ran toward a tree line where the creek was entering.

William Sinclair followed, trying to reach for Reuben's canteen strap.

As they ran, they came upon a hill. Rather than scale it, Reuben steered clear and made their way around the hill. When they cleared the hill, from the opposite side came a platoon of Union soldiers. Reuben and William Sinclair merged with the platoon of Federals and found themselves running along with them in the same direction.

A Union soldier caught a glimpse of the two in Confederate uniforms running with them, and a look of puzzlement overcame him.

Reuben looked at the soldier, smiled, and said "Hey! Nice day for a run in the woods! My name is Reuben. What's yours?"

As the soldier pointed his rifle at Reuben, he grabbed hold of the barrel and stopped as he dropped his center to anchor himself to the ground causing the soldier to flip in the air and land hard on the ground. Reuben pushed William Sinclair down and drew his Kutto.

An officer with a drawn sword slashed toward Reuben, but Reuben blocked his cut easily. Reuben swiftly rotated to the right and struck the officer in the ribs causing several of them to crack.

Another soldier thrust his bayonetted rifle at Reuben. Reuben sidestepped from the attack and struck the soldier in the face dislocating the soldier's jaw with the tsuka of his Kutto.

One soldier took hold of Reuben by the back of his shoulders. Reuben looked back at the soldier and dropped to one side and rose to the rear side of the soldier. Trapping his hand against his shoulder, Reuben pulled the soldier in front of him as another soldier thrusted a bayonetted rifle at Reuben, but impaled the soldier instead.

As he was about to strike the soldier in front of him, a gunshot sounded causing Reuben to turn and see a Union lieutenant holding a pistol at William Sinclair's head.

"Stand fast, Johnny, and drop that sword or I will parole your friend here to hell!"

"Ah, shit," muttered Reuben as he replaced his Kutto to its saya.

狼

A Union soldier took Reuben by the elbow. Immediately Reuben, with his free hand, reached and grabbed the soldier's fingers and stepped under his arm twisting his fingers. Reuben had the soldier standing on his tiptoes and he yanked his fingers down, snapping all four causing the soldier to scream out in pain.

"CLICK!"

The sound of the hammer of the lieutenant's revolver being pulled back caused Reuben to turn toward him.

"I mean it, Johnny! I'll smear this rebel's head all over the place!"

Reuben raised his hands.

"You there. Take his sword and bring it to me," ordered the lieutenant to another soldier. "The major will want this sword. I want his stick. It will become my new walking stick."

The soldier very cautiously approached Reuben and pulled his Kutto free from Reuben's obi, and moved away quickly. While the soldier relieved Reuben of his Kutto, the lieutenant had another soldier disarm William Sinclair.

Quickly snatching Reuben's Kutto from the soldier who relieved him of it, the lieutenant eyed the sword in its sheath curiously. It gave him a feeling of déjà vu.

"Bring them along!" the lieutenant ordered. "And for god sakes, watch that one, but keep your distance from him," he added indicating Reuben.

"That was amazing, Reuben," whispered William Sinclair to Reuben as they were being ushered away. "You beat five men in less than a minute."

"Quiet you!" snapped the lieutenant. "And as for you, my major is going to want to meet you," he added as he turned and began walking with a limp. He tossed away his cane and began using Reuben's jo for a walking stick to aid him.

For what seemed like half an hour, Reuben and William Sinclair were escorted under rifle and bayonet point away from the sounds of the battle. They entered into the woods and alongside the creek to a clearing where other Confederate soldiers were sitting and laying on the ground all being guarded by several Union soldiers. The officers were separated and sitting near a pile of captured swords.

As the newly arrived captives neared, Reuben and William Sinclair were ordered to join the rest of the captured Confederate officers. The lieutenant casually tossed William Sinclair's sword onto the pile, but kept hold of Reuben's Kutto.

As they were being forced to sit on the ground, a loud scream was heard followed by cheers. Both Reuben and William Sinclair looked toward the commotion to see a Union major standing with his sword raised in the air. Below him, a Confederate officer lying at his feet, blood seeping from his back through a piercing sword wound.

"HAZZA!!! Another three cheers for the major and his amazing swordsmanship!" shouted a loud-mouthed sergeant.

As the cheers died down, the major said with confidence, "Sergeant, pick me another sword. I am in excellent form this day."

"With pleasure, Major!"

The lieutenant stepped up to the major and said, "Major, I have someone you would be interested…"

"Not now, Lieutenant!" interrupted the major. "Never bother me when I'm dueling. Whatever it is, can wait. Sergeant, where is that sword?!"

"Here, Major. It's a pretty fancy one at that!"

William Sinclair had a look of fear as he asked one of the captives what was going on.

"Murder. That's what's going on. See that Yank major there? He's some kind of sword dueling expert and has been dueling with us. He has his sergeant pick a sword out of that pile, and the owner of that sword must duel with him to the death."

"Is he any good?" asked William Sinclair.

"See for yourself," answered the fellow captive as he indicated with his head toward a pile of half a dozen dead Confederate officers near the creek.

"Good lord. This is disgraceful. What say you, Reuben?" asked William Sinclair as he looked to Reuben.

Reuben was seated in his usual seiza position, eyes closed, and in meditation.

"Reuben?" asked William Sinclair, only to be answered by Reuben holding up his hand toward him.

"Okay, you bunch of Johnnies, which one of you claims this sword to be yours?" called out the loud-mouthed sergeant.

With a confident look, a colonel rose from the ground, and with a voice of authority said, "That's my sword and I will make you pay for all this murder!"

"Ha! Murder you say," said the major. "How can this be murder when you rebels are the dredge of this marvelous Republic? I'm simply purging away the scum by offering you an honorable way to die. Now please, take your sword, and tell me what school I have the honor of discrediting."

The colonel snagged away his sword from the sergeant. He drew the blade from its scabbard and swiped it in the air a couple of times in anger and said, "I am Colonel Abel Margin of the Military College of South Carolina and commander of the 55th South Carolina Infantry Regiment. I will make you pay for this outrage here today!"

"Ah, a Citadel man. Excellent! I haven't crossed swords with a Citadel man in a while, and a colonel at that. Well, Citadel, may you die with honor today. En Garde!" said the major as he took to his ready stance.

The duel began with Colonel Margin eagerly thrusting his sword at the major. The major easily parried away the colonel's blade on each thrust. It was as if the major was toying in a mocking manner with the colonel causing frustration to build.

This went on for several minutes causing the Confederate captives much anxiety knowing the inevitable outcome. Feeling cheated of a worthy adversary, the major began his own thrusts, his first one entering the colonel's shoulder.

Try as hard as he could, Colonel Margin could not block against the Major's second thrust. The major's blade found its target though the colonel's heart. The major pulled his blade free, smiled, and nodded approvingly with his victory as he wiped his blade free of blood on the colonel's shoulder, a crude and disrespectful act. The colonel looked blankly at the wound, and back to the major for a moment, fell to his knees, and forward to the ground, his eyes still open as he died.

"HAZZA!!! That's one less rebel we have to parole!" shouted the loud-mouthed sergeant raising the major's arm in a victory salute. The other soldiers in blue likewise cheered their superior's win with pride.

Major Oscar Grossman's talent with a sword had been legendary in the ranks of the Union Army. He was fencing champion during his full tenure at West Point, and was even permitted to teach the art to the lower classmen. He never tired of exhibiting his skills, and when the opportunity to use captured Confederate officers as "practice" arose, many soldiers cheered when his blade hit its mark and took down his victims in cold blooded murder.

He took to this gruesome exhibition with the hope he would eventually cross swords with the one man whose wife nearly broke his wrist, and got him relieved of his much desired position as a Federal area inspector in occupied Norfolk County. He was assigned to an active U.S. militia regiment, and promoted to major.

Union solders patted the major on his back congratulating him on his victory, while the Confederate captive officers looked on with fear, with the exception of one. Reuben, like the others, was sitting on the ground being guarded at musket and bayonet point. As his fellow Confederates sat trembling, Reuben calmly remained in his seiza position, his eyes closed, breathing calmly, and meditating on wonderful thoughts of Renee and Aarleen. He thought of the day he returned from Japan and unexpectedly saw Renee emerge from the front door of his childhood home on the farm. How her long, dark, brown hair would flow in the breeze and her beautiful, brown eyes would glisten with joy when he took her into his arms. How he fell out of concentration when Aarleen asked him what his puppy's name was, and learning of his daughter he fathered with Renee the night before his journey seven years prior.

"Reuben, how in the world can you remain so calm when we're about to die most heinously," whispered William Sinclair. But Reuben didn't respond. His thoughts were of him in his wife's arms as they watched their beautiful daughter train with her bokken of New England hickory they made together.

"Time for the next victim, I mean partner," shouted out the loud-mouthed sergeant. The other Union men laughed.

"Major Grossman has already won seven victories, perhaps he needs to rest," responded another soldier.

"Nonsense" said the major. "Sergeant, pick the next sword!"

"With pleasure, sir!" replied the sergeant.

"Wait!" called out the lieutenant. "Major, you need to look at this sword. I believe you will find it quite familiar."

"Bring it to me," said the major.

The lieutenant presented Reuben's Kutto to Major Grossman. Immediately the major's eyes opened wide as he took hold of the sword.

"I know this sword!" proclaimed Major Grossman. "This is the sword that got me reprimanded and relieved of my position in Norfolk! DURAN!!! We meet at last! Show yourself!"

Reuben opened his eyes. He remembered the story Doctor Chelmsford and Noah told him of the over-bearing and abusive Captain Oscar Grossman and how Renee and Aarleen defended their home against his band of Federal troopers. He calmly stood and stepped forward to the major.

Reuben walked up to Major Grossman, dangerously close, causing the sergeant to raise his rifle, aiming it to his head. "That's close enough, Johnny. If that's your sword, take it and let the game begin," he said in a very mocking manner cautiously eyeing Reuben through the sights of his rifle.

The major smirked at Reuben and said, "I hoped I would come across you, and here you are. You do have a very pretty wife. Very spirited, and shall I say... accommodating."

Reuben let out a low grunted laugh. "Musashi you are not, Captain Grossman. You are not one with the code."

William Sinclair rose to his knees, ignoring the guards pushing him back to the ground. My god, Renee. I can understand why you chose him over me, he thought as he admired Reuben's fearlessness in the face of death. This one day alone, William Sinclair witnessed Reuben face death several times, once by William Sinclair himself, and each time he faced it calmly.

"Don't toss that Japanese superstitious bullshit at me Reuben Duran!" exclaimed Major Grossman. "I have been to Japan and wasn't impressed with those backward idiots. They fight like heathens with no style. However, your wife, the lovely Renee, now she does have style."

"Don't talk about Renee in that fashion, you Yankee bastard!" called out William Sinclair. "Come on, Reuben. Do that son of a bitch to his death!"

William Sinclair's comment was met with a rifle butt-end to his back causing him to fall over. Other Confederate captives grumbled and began to move around while their Union guards watched with concern.

"You're correct, Captain Grossman. My Renee does have style," said Reuben, with a mischievous look in his eyes. The same look Renee finds so adorable. "The way I heard of the tale, she spared you from a broken wrist in hopes you will meet me for an actual duel. Perhaps that lame lieutenant of yours is the sorry sod who was dragged when my Renee hit his horse with her jo just before she put several of your men out of commission. Oh, and let us not forget about my precious little cherry blossom, Aarleen, who broke the bones of two of your troopers and mashed the spuds of a third trooper. They did all that damage without killing any of you. Now that *is* style."

The major's face turned red with fury. The exact reaction Reuben wanted.

"Stop calling me captain! I'm a major now, and the best swordsman in the Union Army!"

645

In a very calm voice with a look to match, Reuben responded, "You are nothing more than a fiend, and in the Itosai Region of the Hisano Province, we Akagi behead fiends and place their heads on posts."

Furious, Major Grossman threw Reuben's Kutto at him. Reuben caught it calmly. "You are not going to last long with that poorly made sword with its backward blade. It's going to be a pleasure claiming that sword as a prize, and melting it down to a worthless lump of ore!" said the major, showing an over confident cocky smile.

Reuben raised his Kutto and stepped back a few paces. He held out the sheathed Kutto in both hands, the tsuka pointing to the left, and in a sign of respect, bowed forward to the major, never taking his eyes off of him. Major Grossman's cocky smile faded at the odd gesture from Reuben.

The major took his ready stance with his sword drawn and said, "Before we begin, I must ask from what alma mater you hail? I already know it is the Virginia Military Institute, but for me to claim victory over your school, you must proclaim it yourself."

Reuben stood before the major tucking the sheathed Kutto beneath his obi of Akagi burgundy. He took a basic ready stance with his right arm relaxed at his side, hand open, and fingers extended outward, energy flowing from his fingertips. His left thumb gently pushed the tsuba free from the saya.

"Can't you hear, Johnny? The major asked you what school you attended!" shouted the sergeant. He began to laugh loudly.

Reuben maintained his posture with his eyes fixed on the major's center.

"You will not want to fight, but sometimes you have to, Reuben-San."

Akagi Genda-san words freely entered Reuben's mind. His sword wasn't designed to kill, but in a situation requiring protection and defense, his Kutto could be as deadly as the most razor sharpened katana.

"Now, now, Sergeant, that will do," responded the major with the cocky expression returning to his face. "By the looks of these rebel officers, looks like the Confederate army is promoting anyone these days, school or no school. But I do know you hail from VMI, Captain, so just claim your school."

Reuben kept his focus on the major's center, and waited for his first move.

"Never be anxious to attack your opponent. The only way to stop a great swordsman is never initiate the attack."

Of all the lessons Akagi Genda-San taught Reuben, those of Miyamoto Musashi were his most saving grace.

The major returned his gaze to Reuben and, in a more serious manner, asked again, "From what school do you hail, Reuben Duran? What school do I have the honor of discrediting this afternoon?"

The loud-mouthed sergeant took on the seriousness of the major's question and stepped closer to Reuben. "You heard the major! Answer him, damn it, where did you go to school?!"

As silent as a gentle breeze, and quick as a hurricane wind, Reuben drew his Kutto with a reverse hand technique. He sliced through the air exposing the deadly edge of his Kutto. His blade sliced through the sergeant's neck severing his head from his shoulders so quickly not a drop of blood stained Reuben's blade.

The sergeant's head landed near the feet of Major Grossman while his body remained standing for what seemed like long moments before it collapsed to the ground. The laughter and mocking turned into horrifying silence. The major looked down at the sergeant's head with wide, scared eyes, and swallowed hard.

William Sinclair, as well as the other Confederate captives, was just as awed as their Union captors.

As swift as his previous movement, Reuben raised his Kutto over his head and in a circular motion, whipped it downward to his right side, sheathed his blade, and returned back to the ready stance.

Major Grossman looked back toward Reuben shocked, shaking, and breathing deeply.

"I serve my Lord and Master, Akagi Genda-San. Lord of the Itosai Region in the Hisano Province. Master of Akagi-Jutsu and KenAiDo disciplines. I am... Okami, and it is the banner of the Akagi Clan I represent," answered Reuben in a very calm, relaxed, and proud manner. "Now that I have dispensed with the distraction, shall we begin?"

狼

All eyes were on Major Grossman. His fearful stare at the decapitated head of his sergeant turned angry. He kicked the sergeant's head toward Reuben and lunged.

Reuben simply stepped out of the path of the major's lunge without drawing his Kutto and slapped him in the back of his head.

"Your sergeant may have been a loud-mouthed jackass, but that's no way to treat one who served you," said Reuben calmly as he settled into his signature Okami no Michi style, low, sword undrawn, and right arm and hand extended in front of his body.

The major, confused by Reuben's stance, cautiously began walking around Reuben with his sword pointed at him. Major Grossman slowly made his way around to Reuben's back. When he saw Reuben still facing forward, the major smiled and lunged at Reuben's back toward his right side kidney.

Swiftly, Reuben drew his Kutto as he turned to his right and easily blocked the major's lunge and using his left hand, chopped toward the major's neck causing him to choke and fall hard to the ground.

Major Grossman coughed hard several times and looked up at Reuben who stood before him with his Kutto returned to its saya. The major quickly rose and pointed his sword at Reuben as he stood watching the major unimpressed.

Again the major lunged only to be met with Reuben's palm to his forehead. Reuben rotated his palm swiftly causing the major to fall hard to the ground again.

Watching Reuben as he maneuvered easily around the major's attacks, the Confederate captives began to rise to their knees while the Union guards began to have looks of worry.

Reuben noticed the guards' reaction. It reminded him of when Akagi Genda-San described Arata Goro to him and the other Hisano regional Daimyos.

"Arata Goro is the brain. Take away the brain and you are left with muscle and we all know, muscle has no brain. Take away the brain, you take away the muscle."

Again and again, Major Grossman lunged and sliced toward Reuben. Again and again, Reuben avoided the major's lunges and thrusts, not drawing his Kutto.

"DAMN YOU!!! DRAW YOUR SWORD!!!" yelled Major Grossman.

In a furious attack, the major swung his sword with no apparent skill at Reuben's head. Using a reverse draw, Reuben simply blocked the major's attack and made contact with his head using the tsuka like a club causing Major Grossman to blackout for a second.

When the major regained his balance, Reuben stood before him with his Kutto returned to its saya.

Shaking his head to clear it, Major Grossman regained his composure and stared at Reuben with the look of a furious demon.

Reuben maintained his calm stance with the look of a wolf cub at play.

"This is it, Duran! You can't keep up your calmness much longer! Say goodbye to that pretty little wife of yours! The next time I see her, I'll be between her legs with your daughter tied to a chair waiting her turn!" said Major Grossman.

With a loud grunt, Major Grossman lunged at Reuben with a perfectly executed thrust that would have penetrated any opponent through the heart.

However, Reuben simply sidestepped from the thrust without drawing his Kutto, and took hold of the major's sword hand with his right hand. Raising the major's arm in a low arc, Reuben took hold of Major's Grossman's wrist with his left hand and trapped it against his shoulder as Renee did when she had the major's wrist trapped. This time however, the major had his sword in his hand causing added painful pressure.

"I suppose you remember this trap, Grossman. It's the same trap my Renee had you in. Had she finished the technique, it would have gone like this."

Reuben violently dropped his center and bowed toward Major Grossman causing him to drop to his knees and his wrist to twist and snap away from his lower arm. The major yelled out in horrific pain as he watched his sword slowly slide out of his useless hand while it dangled side-to-side being held to his arm only by skin and muscle.

Reuben drew his Kutto and with a loud kiai, brought it down stopping less than an inch from the major's throat.

"There's no way my Renee would let you near her or our daughter. What I did to your wrist, she could have done back when you tried to take my Kutto away from her. She will be very pleased to hear I finished her technique."

Reuben replaced his Kutto back to its saya and stepped back.

Major Grossman slowly stood, wincing in pain as he cradled his crippled right hand with his left. He took a couple of steps away from Reuben and ordered the watching Union soldiers, "KILL THEM ALL!!!"

There was hesitation from the major's soldiers and he repeated his order, but still they stood fast.

William Sinclair was the first one to move and attacked the nearest Union soldier, disarming him of his rifle and pointing it back at him.

As if on cue, all the Confederate captives rose up and began overpowering their Union captors, while Major Grossman made a sprinting dash into the woods.

Reuben turned to William Sinclair and said, "Take them prisoner and don't kill them, Colonel Sinclair! You are a man of pure Southern honor and principles. Show your honor and don't stoop down to their level!"

Reuben pulled out his tanto from his haversack, tucked it behind the knot of his obi, and ran into the woods after the major.

"As you say, Reuben Duran!" replied William Sinclair as he watched Reuben chase after Major Grossman.

狼

Major Grossman ran through the woods grasping his arm as his limp hand dangled from the end. His face was twisted with anguish as each step he made caused a shock of pain though his entire body. He ran deep into the woods heading toward the sounds of battle in the distance. Suddenly he stopped as he saw a flash of something speed past his path.

He thought he may have seen a deer until he felt a dull thud hit him in his lower back. The major turned, but there was nothing there.

"Still think samurai are backwards heathens, Grossman?" asked Reuben, as he toyed with Major Oscar Grossman.

The major began to tremble. Again, he began to run, sticking close to the trees hoping they would hide his movements. They didn't, for when he ran past two large trees, his feet were taken out from underneath him by a low kick. When he landed on his back, he roared out in agonizing pain from his lame hand.

Major Grossman struggled to rise from the ground and with a limp, began to run, not knowing what direction to run as long as it was away from Reuben. Again, the major saw a flash run before his eyes and stopped. He cautiously looked to his left and to his right. He felt a gentle tap from behind on his shoulder and turned around to see Reuben standing in front of him.

With his palm, Reuben struck Major Grossman in the forehead knocking him hard onto the ground. As the major fell, he used both arms to break his fall. Once his right hand made contact with the ground, the impact tore it off his arm. In horrific agony, the major screamed looking at the stump at the end of his right arm. Using his left arm, he scooted away from Reuben until he backed up against a tree.

Reuben took several steps toward Major Grossman. The major raised his one good arm and pleaded, "Please, no more! I'm sorry. I apologize to you and to your family. You're the better man! Please have mercy!" cried out Major Oscar Grossman, suddenly remembering what Renee told him prior to releasing his wrist, *"May God have mercy on you because my Reuben won't."*

649

Reuben slowly knelt down and gently placed his hand on the major's left shoulder and said, "That wasn't too difficult now, was it? That's all I wanted to hear."

Reuben rose, turned, and began walking away.

Major Grossman's pain laden face slowly turned into fury as he shifted to his knees. With his left hand, he drew his revolver, raised it toward Reuben's back, and pulled back the hammer. Before he had a chance to pull the trigger, Reuben swiftly turned and threw his tanto wedging it in the major's forehead.

Retrieving his tanto from Oscar Grossman's lifeless body, Reuben said, "Using a revolver in a sword duel, how barbaric can you get?"

狼

Reuben emerged from the woods to find the Union soldiers sitting on the ground with the Confederates guarding them under the direction of Lieutenant Colonel William Sinclair.

Upon seeing Reuben entering the clearing, William Sinclair ran to him.

"Where's the major, Reuben?"

"He's gone. But he did apologize, for what it's worth. What's going on here?"

"As you can see, we have taken these blue bellies prisoner."

Reuben let out a silent chuckle. "Good job, Colonel. Today you have earned that distinction. Now, do you want to seriously show your honor to these men, both North and South?"

Looking curious, William Sinclair asked, "How?"

Reuben placed his right hand on William Sinclair's left shoulder and said with sincerity, "Let them go. Let them all go. Not as Union, not as Confederate, but as Americans."

"But the war..." William Sinclair tried to explain.

"The war is over, William. In a matter of hours, if it isn't already, but over nonetheless."

Reuben began walking toward the direction of home.

"Reuben, wait!" said William Sinclair. "I want to thank you."

"Thank me for what?"

"I want to thank you for giving Renee the life I could never have been able to give her myself. She's a very blessed woman."

Reuben offered his hand. William Sinclair grasped it and felt tingling energy emitting from Reuben's palm. "I'm a very blessed man," replied Reuben.

Reuben looked to the Union captives and walked to the lame lieutenant.

"Sorry, Lieutenant, but I believe this belongs to me," said Reuben as he retrieved his jo from the lieutenant's hands. "You may need this more than I do, but quite frankly, I don't care. It's mine. Perhaps you only wanted it because it reminded you of my wife when she struck your horse causing your lame leg. Trust me Lieutenant, living your life with grudges only makes you a bitter man."

Reuben turned and continued to walk home looking toward the sky wondering if Renee and Aarleen were also looking up at this very moment. For the first time since he was dragged away from his family, he began to feel happy.

狼

Reuben walked for several miles ignoring the sounds of the battle. As far as he was concerned, it didn't matter to him anymore. He reattached Aarleen's inrou to his obi and carried the image case containing Renee's picture within wrapped with Lucy's purple ribbon he removed from his Kutto.

He wasn't on any type of road, lane, or beaten path. Only walking in the direction of home. As the sounds of battle faded in the distance, his pace slowed as he suddenly began to feel the fatigue of 35 months start to take hold of him. Reuben entered into the woods and found a nice quiet patch of tall grass beneath a small oak tree. He lowered himself down and looked all around, not in vigilance, but in memory. The memory of when he and Tadashi were walking to Itosai, and entered into the woods off the main road to be out of sight to camp for the night came to him vividly, and he smiled.

Reuben pulled out some morsels of food he'd foraged from the battle dead he passed and began to remember the first time he recklessly ran into his first samurai battle to save Akagi Genda-San from an Arata gunman.

"You can't just go jump into that fight, Reuben. Look at you. You don't even belong here. Either army will kill you once they get a good look at your face," said Tadashi.
"That gunman was aiming for Genda-San! If we don't do anything, his next shot may hit him! You said you want to serve the Akagi, so now is a good time as any!"

"What is it with you hitting people in the face with your arrows? That's gruesome,"
"I could say the same to you about your jo and the gun, Reuben."

Reuben began to name those who shared his most trying times, "Tadashi, Masaru, Max, Todd, Matthew, Albert, Adam, Sam Evers, Doctor Lawrence Chelms…"

Reuben dozed off into a deep, long-needed sleep thinking he failed by not saving those he loved most.

Reuben was asleep beneath the huge oak tree near the creek behind his family's farm. A hand gently nudged him awake.

"Wake up, boy, wake up. There's a good lad," said a very familiar voice.

"Da, is that you?" Reuben asked, confused.

"Aye. It is, my fine lad."

Reuben sat up and saw his father kneeling next to him. "What are you doing here?"

"I'm keeping my promise to my precious little angel and making sure you're going home to her and Renee safely."

"But the sounds of war in the distance…" replied Reuben.

"Are not of any concern to my precious boy," said Coleen as she knelt beside Aaron.

"Mama. Da. I failed you. I couldn't save either you or Lucy," Reuben said, looking at his mother.

"You didn't fail, brother," said Monroe, moving to kneel next to their father.

"No, not you too, Monroe? I saw you alive, in Pennsylvania. You were going to go home. You promised."

"It's not your fault, Reuben. I just wasn't fast enough, but you did save me by your gracious gift of a brother's love, and I did what I could to protect you like you did for me from bullies, and the war."

"I feel so helpless. I tried and tried, but I couldn't keep you alive," said Reuben as tears fell from his eyes.

"You're not helpless, big brother," said Lucy, kneeling next to Reuben taking him into her arms with Eric standing behind her. "I never gave up hope for you. I knew you would come for me, Mama, and Eric, and you did. You did your best and we love you for that. You're a good brother, the best Monroe and I ever had. You didn't fail, Reuben.

"Your support of Andrew and Annabelle's decision to take Andy away was much appreciated by me and Eric. I know one day you will see our son, and when that time comes, please tell him we look upon him with faith and love.

"You see, my precious brother, you saved us all, but most importantly, you saved yourself. You saved yourself for Renee and Aarleen."

"Your sister is right, Reuben," said Adam Stanns.

"Adam! Gods of the high mountains, I couldn't save you either," Reuben groaned.

"You stayed with me Reuben, even when you were blacking out from your own wound. Even in your pain, you still held me, making sure I wouldn't die alone, and that is the essence of a beloved friend."

"What of your Mary Alice? I couldn't save you for her."

"She's well, Reuben. Very well, married and happy, and I approve of her life. You'll see."

"So many lives I couldn't save," said Reuben looking sorrowfully.

"But think of the hundreds of lives you did save, Lieutenant," said Sergeant Sam Evers standing in front of Reuben's platoon from Mexico. "You may not have been able to save us, but you learned how to save others. Because of you, many soldiers will return to their homes and loved ones. You're a good man, Reuben Duran."

"They all speak the truth, Reuben-San. Listen to them. You are a student of Bushido. You are a true warrior of heart and your heart is good. Take the lessons you have learned and keep applying them to your family. Love and cherish Renee-Dono and Aarleen-Dono for they are your legacy, just as you are Aaron-San's and Coleen-Dono's legacy."

"Genda-San, my Lord, my friend, why are you here?" asked Reuben, very worried.

"Put your fears to rest, Reuben-San. I am very much alive, and awaiting the day you and Renee-Dono will introduce me to your daughter. For many days I have meditated for your safety. Now that you are safe, you must honor all those around you in this dream and go home.

You see, Reuben-San, just as the living has prayers, so do the dying. You, Reuben-San, are a prayer for the dying, and the dying prays for you to continue living because you are good."

"We love you, Reuben. All of us who you have touched with your care," said Aaron, as he placed his hand on Reuben's shoulder. "Now sleep a little while longer and go home. Renee and Aarleen are waiting."

As those around him faded, Reuben fell back asleep under the big oak tree where he and Renee first met.

"Hey, fella, are you okay?" asked ragged looking Confederate lieutenant colonel as he gently shook Reuben awake.

Reuben felt his shoulder being touched and immediately grasped the hand touching him and rolled over causing the person to be thrown to the ground. Reuben rose to his knees, drew his Kutto, and raised it to the side of his head in a defending manner.

"Hold on there, fella! The war is over! Besides, I'm on your side... or at least I was," cried the lieutenant colonel.

Reuben slowly lowered his Kutto and asked, "What do you mean it's over? When? Where?"

"Today. At Appomattox Court House."

"Are you paroled?"

"Naw. Once I heard the news, I dismissed my men and walked away. I'm going home. I don't need to be paroled to tell me to go home and that's where I'm going, to Culpepper. Hey, fella. You look familiar. Have we served somewhere before?"

Reuben replaced his Kutto in its saya and lowered himself to get a closer look at the ragged officer.

"Carlton? Carlton Edwards? VMI class of '46, or is it '47? I was selected for early commission in '46," said Reuben with a look of remembrance.

"Reuben Duran? Is it really you? Oh for the love of heaven, it is you!" replied Reuben's old classmate from VMI in awe. "I heard you died in Mexico with Adam Stanns."

Carlton rose to his feet, as did Reuben. Carlton reached out to Reuben and embraced him.

"Damn, it's great to see you, Reuben. After all these years. What have you been doing with yourself?"

Reuben let out a low grunted laugh and said, "That... is a very long story. Probably as long as yours."

"I'm so glad all those rumors of you dying in Mexico are all wrong, Reuben. I always liked you, and to see you alive, well, I'm just glad. And you survived this tragic war, too. My heavens, you do have a long story."

Reuben indicated to Carlton to sit next to him as he was sitting himself.

"You look exhausted, Reuben. How long have you been sleeping here?" asked Carlton, motioning to the tree.

653

"Since the battle near the creek," answered Reuben, after taking a drink from his canteen and offering it to Carlton.

"Sailor's Creek?" asked Carlton before he took a drink.

"I suppose, didn't catch the name of it."

"Reuben, that was three days ago. You mean to tell me you've been asleep for three days?"

Reuben sat dumbfounded. "I couldn't have. I woke several times to eat a morsel or two and take a drink from my canteen, but I couldn't have been asleep for three days."

"Heck, Reuben, after what we've been through, we all could use a long sleep."

Changing the subject, Reuben asked, "Carlton, whatever happened to Adam's girl, Mary Alice?"

Reacting like he had seen a ghost, Carlton had a hint of shame on his face and said, "When the news of what happened to Adam arrived, I was visiting relatives in Culpepper. I thought of her right away. You remember how Adam went on and on and on about Mary Alice? Anyway, I went to offer her my condolences. She was very distraught.

"This is where you came into the picture, Reuben. What made her feel better is knowing you died with him. She felt reassured Adam wasn't alone when he died. But, of course, now you didn't die. What really happened, Reuben?"

Reuben took in a deep breath and told Carlton of the day his platoon was killed and how Adam went to help bring Reuben back to their lines only to get shot in the chest. He told of how he cradled Adam in his arms and of his last dying words.

When Reuben was finished, Carlton shook his head and placed his hand on Reuben's shoulder. "Damn, Reuben. That's amazing. Thank you for telling me. Now I can tell Mary Alice Adam died in your arms. That will give her some closure."

"You still talk with her?" asked Reuben.

Looking downward, with shame returning to his face, Carlton replied, "Eventually, Mary Alice and I got married. We have two sons, twins. One named Adam and the other... Reuben."

Thinking of his dream, Reuben shifted his body to face Carlton and took hold of his shoulders. "You married Mary Alice?"

Carlton nodded yes, his mouth quivering trying to keep from sobbing. "I... that is we eventually fell in love. We married, but the thought of taking Adam's girl bothered me. It still does even though Mary Alice seems to have let go. For some reason, I can't. That's why I entered the war. Not because of the so called glory of the Confederacy, but with hopes a bullet would have pierced me dead so I can ask for Adam's forgiveness in heaven."

Still holding onto Carlton's shoulders, Reuben stood up bringing Carlton with him. "Carlton, I had a dream while I slept! Adam came to me, along with many people in my life I have touched. He told me he's happy for Mary Alice and approves of her life. Carlton, go home and live with Mary Alice. Live with and love her and your two sons happily, for a long time!"

Reuben released Carlton's shoulders and retrieved his haversack and jo and was about to step away.

"Reuben, wait! Are you serious? You're not just saying that, are you?"

"Yes Carlton, I'm serious! You did good by taking her as your wife! Don't feel shame or guilt, Carlton! Feel love!"

Carlton nodded, deep in thought. Suddenly with a serious interest he asked, "Hey, Reuben, that girl in that picture case. The one with the long, dark hair and big, beautiful eyes, ah… Renee, what became of her?"

Reuben retrieved the image case from his haversack and opened it for Carlton to see and said, "I married her, so I must return to her and my daughter, just as you must return to your family. Go home, Carlton, and tell *YOUR* Mary Alice you love her! Bye, Carlton, I'll be in touch!"

With that, Reuben began running toward home leaving Carlton with a feeling of being… saved.

石
水
In the year of our Lord, 1865, a romantic tale continues.
The last walk home, and straight A's...

Is That Fresh Baked Bread I Smell

In the twilight hours of the day, Aarleen and Benjamin were catching and releasing fireflies while Renee and Cynthia watched beneath the oak tree as they talked about future plans for both their families. Meanwhile, Henry and Simon were fishing nearby while Evergreen and Noah were walking together hand-in-hand in circles. Inside the house, May and Doctor Chelmsford were busy making a late evening supper. It was a perfect Sunday evening. The only person missing was Reuben.

Riley let out a warning bark causing everyone to stop what they were doing and look toward the house. As if on cue, everyone at once began to make their way toward the house to see if it was Major MacKay bringing more discrete news of the war. Or perhaps he came to listen to Aarleen's Sunday, after-supper, story time. Either way, Major MacKay's visits were of hardly any concern these days. However, this visit would be much different as he made his way around the house with Riley at his side to meet everyone rather than wait in the front yard. This was very concerning, causing everyone to stop.

"Hello, everyone!" called out the major. "Please, come closer!"

Everyone did as asked.

"Is everything all right, Mr. MacKay?" asked Renee.

"It's over, Mrs. Duran. The rebellion, war, whatever you want to call it. It's over, at least here in the East. Lee surrendered to General Grant today. The news was wired in earlier this afternoon."

There was no feeling of joy. No feeling of sadness. No feeling of anger.

"What about my Da?" Aarleen asked as she took hold of one of Renee's hands. "Have you heard anything about him, Mr. MacKay?"

"You can't ask him questions like that, Aarleen," said Benjamin.

Major MacKay dropped his head and chuckled. "That's all right, young Mr. Norenham," said the major, causing surprise by calling him Norenham instead of Garrett.

"Please, everyone. As far as I'm concerned, with the end of this rebellion, I'm no longer your area inspector. Just a one armed soldier waiting for my orders to go home, so how about inviting me in for supper with the vast amount of food you have, and enjoy one of Miss Duran's stories after."

Renee had a look of dire shock and was about to speak when Major MacKay said, "Come now, Mrs. Duran, or Renee, if I may call you that now? Do you seriously think I would not have known a husband, such as your Reuben, would not have prepared you in case he had to leave?"

657

"But I don't understand," said Renee while the others looked dumbfounded.

"May I remind you, Renee, what I don't see, or don't go looking for, is up for interpretation. As long as all was seen as it should be seen, I had nothing to report. Now about that supper. I believe I smell roasted chicken."

For the first time since being assigned as the Federal area inspector, Major Jonathan MacKay entered the Duran home as an invited guest for supper. After supper, Aarleen recited one of her favorite stories. The story of a man with no name who saved the village of Itosai from rogue samurai, and becoming an adopted member of the Akagi Clan.

狼

For 35 months, Reuben marched hundreds upon hundreds of miles. Dragged away from his family, Reuben offered his service to save his brother from a position he was not cut out for. In those 35 months, Reuben protected the officers and men of Company C of the 68th Virginia Infantry Regiment from Federal troops, giving them one less thing to worry about so they could do their duty. The entire time Reuben protected these men, he believed he was substituting his service for his brother, not knowing Monroe had fallen in the farmlands of South Pennsylvania. It would be two years later when Reuben learned of Monroe's fate and travel to Gettysburg with his family to exhume his body, and bring him home to be laid to rest next to Aaron and Lucy.

Dedicated to the officers and men of Company C, and not to the Confederacy, Reuben was responsible for keeping every member of the company alive. Although Company C did its fair share of the fighting, the company never had a single fatality because of its guardian angel with the eyes of a wolf and a reverse bladed sword. Several were injured, but they would either be sent home or recover to be sent home when the nightmare was over.

In the score of 35 months, Reuben evolved from the cold-hearted killer he once was in Mexico, to a true warrior of heart maintaining the essence of the Bushido code. Although he was surrounded by the barbaric western style of warfare, he never faltered from the code except at the Chickahominy River when he took matters into his own hands causing the regrettable deaths of a Union captain and several other Union officers and men. Although Reuben rationalized their deaths were intended for his family's survival, it was too much of a cost to their families who awaited their return that would never happen.

While thousands of surrendered Confederate officers and men flocked to Appomattox Court House to be paroled, Reuben elected to turn his back to a rogue army that dragged him away from his family and forced him to fight their war. It would be a long walk home, a walk Reuben was looking forward to, a walk to provide closure and healing. It would be a walk he would take advantage of to clear his mind of the misery he endured so it would not cloud his mind when he returned to Renee and Aarleen, who no doubt had to endure misery themselves.

There was no need or want on this long walk. He encountered many gracious residences that offered Reuben food, drink, clothing, and even places to sleep. No one required him to offer payment for their hospitality, but Reuben still provided some sort of service in the means of aiding in repairs or planting, now that it was safe to begin growing crops. Many people were grateful the war was over and just wanted to get on with their lives.

Many times, Reuben would divert off the main roads and beaten paths to roam in the grassy fields, gently waving his Kutto through the tall grass, like a little boy swooshing a stick back and forth. It was a long walk, an enjoyable walk, with a true treasure at its end and as parts of the countryside became familiar, his pace quickened. He lost track of days and had no idea what day or time it was when he made it to the front doorstep of his childhood home in Norfolk to find the door padlocked. That was of no concern as he retrieved a hidden key from under a loose brick in the wall and began to pry off the latch with his tanto.

"Excuse me! What are you doing? Leave this place or I'll fetch the law on you!" shouted Mrs. O'Neal, a neighbor from down and across the street.

Reuben turned and greeted Mrs. O'Neal.

"Heaven on earth! Reuben Duran, my dear boy. Where have you been?!" she asked.

"That must be obvious," said Reuben as he let out a childlike laugh and displaying the state of his clothes.

"My, your mother, God rest her soul, would be out of her wits if she ever saw you in these grimy clothes. What are you doing here? Your family has been limited to living on the farm. The Federals sealed your house long back."

"I just walked back from… the ends of the earth it seems. Well, if you'll excuse me, Mrs. O'Neal, I have a family to return to."

Mrs. O'Neal took Reuben by the hands, and in a motherly tone, said, "Not in that condition. Your Renee won't recognize you and Aarleen will think you are a ghoul looking like that. Come over to our house. Get some rest, and a bite to eat. Trever will lend you some clothes. I would be doing your mother and father, God rest their souls, a disservice if I allowed you to return to your wife and daughter in this state of yours."

Looking up to the darkening sky, Reuben let out a huge sigh thinking of fate. "As much as I want to run home to Renee and Aarleen, you're right. After all these months, one more night shouldn't matter. I'm tired and hungry, and as you can see, filthy. You're right. My Mama would deplore it if I presented myself to my family in this state."

"Very well said, Reuben. Now come with me and Trever and I will fill you in on what has happened while you have been away. You see, it all started in the spring of '62…"

狼

The fields of the farm were bare. Nothing was allowed to be grown during the Federal occupation of the city and surrounding county, with the exception of the allotted four square yard of land per mouth of the residents on the farm. The animals were long taken away by the first Federal area inspector, Captain Oscar Grossman. However, now with the war at its end, Aarleen and Benjamin moved the hidden animals from the woods back to the farm, all under the watchful and amused eyes of Major Jonathan MacKay.

Because of an ironic act of fate, Jonathan MacKay found himself as the Federal area inspector of this region in Norfolk County including the Duran farm. The very farm owned by the man who caused Jonathan MacKay the loss of his arm at the Chickahominy River, and spared him of what could have been his death had he remained with his troops. Bitterness drove his anger toward Renee and Aarleen, and the rest of the inhabitants of the farm, once he realized it was Renee's husband who caused his injury. However, a deep rooted discussion with Doctor Chelmsford caused Jonathan MacKay to open his mind to the huge favor, and opportunity, offered to him. As he witnessed the love and devotion this family had, he felt it was his duty to watch over Reuben's family, all within the realm of his assigned duties. As his care for the Duran farm grew, his care spread to the other farms under his jurisdiction. Although he was a strict administrator, he was a good man.

The farm house had seen better days, but it wasn't from neglect. The lack of materials to make repairs were at a minimum so therefore, the house and other farm buildings looked in need of repair. May and Henry did as much as they could in their elder years, as did Noah with his war wound. What it all came down to, everyone who lived on the farm pounded in a nail, replaced a shingle, or resided a house board that became loose or fell off, including Cynthia Norenham.

Of all the people Renee had to contend with, it was Cynthia who made the greatest impact. Evergreen's attitude, in the beginning, was an issue everyone on the farm had to deal with and eventually changed for the better. However, it was Cynthia who surprised everyone with her new found sense of enlightenment.

Cynthia and Benjamin had been living in the streets for several days until Renee, Aarleen, and Henry came upon them. It was hard for Cynthia and Benjamin at first because of their pampered lifestyle, especially Cynthia. Renee had a difficult time getting Cynthia to conform to life on the farm, so Aarleen took Benjamin under her wing relieving her mother of that extra burden.

Aarleen taught Benjamin the hard work it takes to keep a farm working and also what it takes to stay alive. Much more open than his mother when they arrived on the Duran farm, he became very helpful. He was the one who made the most impact on Cynthia's attitude regarding their blessings of Renee's and Aarleen's help in their dire time of need.

Once bitter rivals in their school days, and into young adulthood, Cynthia and Renee, because of the hard times, became friends and together, kept the farm and their families alive. Cynthia showed sincere gratefulness toward Renee for showing her the rewards of being a devoted, caring, and loving wife and mother.

The only one more surprised at Cynthia's transformation was her husband Simon when he was delivered to the doorsteps of the farm by Major MacKay. Simon was sickened by those so-called friends, neighbors, and family who didn't raise a hand to help his wife and son when the Federals occupied their home over a year ago. It seemed in the city, it was everyone for themselves, especially for what was known as Norfolk's elite.

Upon Simon's return, Cynthia and Benjamin were extremely elated, as were the rest of the farm's inhabitants. Simon showed Renee great gratitude for taking in his wife and son, and also for Cynthia's transformation. He offered his services as an architect to make as many repairs to the house, cabins, and other farm structures with the limited amount of resources at his disposal.

With her husband's return, Cynthia began to have feelings of guilt because she would listen to Renee recite, in hush tones to herself, poems Cynthia could clearly interpret as Renee's feelings toward Reuben. Renee's poems were so powerfully filled with emotion, even in hush tones, Cynthia could not help but feel Renee's pain. Cynthia had come a long way.

Noah never let his disability get the better of him, especially when Benjamin designed an artificial leg for him. With the help of Aarleen, Doctor Chelmsford, and Henry, it was fitted to Noah's lower left leg, and with Evergreen's loving support, Noah was walking without the use of a crutch or cane, although he carried a jo, a habit he picked up from Reuben. Noah expressed his forever devoted service to Reuben for saving his life.

"You were not there to see him, Renee, but Reuben would have stopped at nothing to save my life, even if it meant sacrificing his own. Thank heaven it didn't come to that. For that, you and he have my everlasting gratitude and friendship," Noah told Renee one evening shortly after his return.

Doctor Chelmsford stayed on the Duran farm when he brought Noah back home from Chimborazo Hospital. He asked Renee if he could stay until Reuben's return, to which Renee gladly allowed. Having Lawrence Chelmsford stay was like having a link to Reuben. Doctor Chelmsford provided that grandfatherly feeling, especially for Aarleen who had endless questions for the doctor about her father. Her questions ranged from, *"Did my Da think of Mama often in Mexico?"* to *"When my Da used his Kutto on Federal soldiers, how exactly did he hold it?"*

Doctor Chelmsford helped out as much as everyone on the farm, but it was his profession as a physician he made use of the most. He visited the farms around the county to provide medical care to anyone in need. Although Simon was restricted to the limits of the Duran farm, Major MacKay provided Simon a pass to accompany the doctor on his rounds. Aarleen and Benjamin would also accompany the doctor on these rounds to assist. After Benjamin fashioned an artificial leg for Noah, and accompanying and assisting Doctor Chelmsford on these rounds, he acquired a great interest in the practice of medicine.

Most importantly, the reason Doctor Chelmsford wished to stay for Reuben's return was to see his friend and provide any needed assistance to cope with his experiences. The doctor was very impressed with the transformation Reuben made since his days on the battlefields of Mexico. He spent many hours with Renee as he described Reuben's sense of devotion to both the men he protected and to her and their daughter.

"I'm so worried for when Reuben comes back home. I wonder if he will be like he was when he returned from Mexico, Lawrence," Renee told Doctor Chelmsford with concern in her voice.

"Renee, when I first saw Reuben in Petersburg, I saw his outer shell. But his inside was as fresh as the morning dew. He had a spark in his eyes and he kept that spark the entire time Noah and I were with him. Do you know what that spark was, Renee?'

"Me and Aarleen?" she asked.

"That's right, Renee. No matter how horrid it was out there for everyone else, Reuben still maintained that spark of love for you both. Knowing you and Aarleen are a part of his life is what maintained his sanity. It's that spark that drove him to survive. You see, Renee, a soldier, or in your husband's case, a warrior, needs a cause to live for. While all the others around Reuben were fighting and dying for a lost cause, Reuben's cause was just and worth fighting for. Reuben's cause was you and Aarleen and he fought like a man in love."

狼

It was close to 9 o'clock in the morning. On the porch, May was tenderly snapping the ends of beans she'd gathered early in the day from a hidden plot in the woods. She was humming a tune while Renee, inside, was singing the words. It was an old Scottish lullaby Aaron would sing to Aarleen when he came to say goodnight to her as Renee tucked her into bed.

Renee was at the kitchen counter kneading dough from the last remaining sack of flour they gotten a long while ago. Her attractive frame was covered in her husband's Akagi kosode of burgundy and his deep brown hakama. Her long, dark, brown hair cascaded over her shoulders, just the way Reuben adored it. The softness of her voice stopped singing the old Scottish lullaby as thoughts of Reuben entered her mind.

Beginning to feel emotional, Renee stopped kneading the dough and closed her eyes to try to maintain her composure. From deep within her, Renee felt an urge to recite her latest passage she written the night before she and Aarleen went to sleep...

It is to you I belong
No matter how close or how far
I can still touch you with my tears and heart
You and I await your return to begin a new memoir
Show me the light
And I will show you the peace
I will cradle your fears away
With you in my arms I will never release
To hold
To cherish
To never be torn apart
You are my Stone and I am your Water
Our destiny is Love
We maintain our Faith and Love
And we are one as Love intended with Love as our anchor

Renee's eyes tightened up as she began to feel them start to water.

Cynthia sat at the table mending one of Simon's shirts, borrowed from Reuben. She looked up when she heard the words spoken by Renee. She put the shirt down, stood, and came to the counter next to her. Placing her hand gently on Renee's shoulder, she said, "I'm certain Reuben will be home soon, and without a scratch no doubt."

Renee placed a flour covered hand over Cynthia's hand and looked at her. "I know," she said and broke down and began crying.

Cynthia took her into her arms and cradled her as a sister would console a distraught sibling, much like Renee and Lucy had done many years ago. Cynthia began to laugh.

"Will you just look at us?" asked Cynthia as she cradled Renee's head on her shoulder. "There was a time when I would never think you and I would be like this."

Renee began to chuckle and lifted her head. "That's true. We were like fire and ice way back then."

"You say that as if it were many years ago, but it has only been almost close to a year since you took Benjamin and me off the streets of Norfolk."

"It seems like years. Oh, Cynthia, what if…" Renee couldn't finish her thought and again rested her head back onto Cynthia's shoulder.

Cynthia again cradled her. "There, there now. Come on, Renee. I have never known you to be weak. You never let me get you down, and trust me, I did my very best to take you down every chance I could, but you came back strong. And living with you and your daughter this past year, I'm amazed at how brave a woman you are. And the love you have for your Reuben, it's a love I never felt until I saw Simon when he arrived. Please keep your faith and love, Renee. Keep your faith and love like in your poem. Your Reuben will be home soon, I just know it," said Cynthia, with heartwarming compassion.

"I know, Cynthia, I know. But it's been over a week since the war ended," said Renee, sobbing.

It had been nine days since General Lee surrendered to General Grant. Nine long days, and still no news of Reuben. Try as hard as they could, both Major MacKay and Doctor Chelmsford could not find any type of information of Reuben's whereabouts.

During those nine days, Renee had seen former Confederate soldiers walking past, sometimes two or more at a time, stopping to cure their thirst.

"No, Miss, I don't know your husband."

"I have heard of Reuben Duran, but don't know where he is."

"No, I can't recall a Reuben Duran."

"Yes, I saw him two days ago."

"No, I heard he was kilt at Crampton's Gap a year ago."

These were the many answers Renee and the others heard from the ones passing by. No one knew for certain except that the war was over and Reuben wasn't home. All sorts of news made it to the farm. The Union President was murdered. The city of Norfolk was to be turned over to a civilian form of government. But the news Renee longed for had not reached her.

狼

Roaming his parameter, Riley trotted from one side of the field to the other. Riley, the ever vigilant German Shepard, had been on constant patrol ever since he saw his master dragged away. Riley was a blessing in disguise and took it upon himself to maintain a constant vigil until his master returned. Once again through the field, along the tree line, up to the lane, and a couple of times around the house he trotted.

He stopped momentarily to watch over Aarleen and Benjamin plowing a small plot of earth to ready for planting. With the war over, and without official notice, the two youths took it upon themselves to start planting crops.

Riley, again, was on the move and this time stopped to watch Simon patching up some falling boards on the outside of the house. Simon, keeping his eyes on the board, reached down for a hammer, but it was out of his reach. As Simon looked down, he saw Riley retrieve the hammer with his jaws and bring it to him.

"Thank you very much," he said to Riley. Riley replied with a snort from his snout, a wag of his tail, and again went on with his patrol.

His next stop was Noah and Evergreen's cabin. He pawed at the door and it was opened by Noah standing on his two legs. Earlier, Noah had been making repairs to the wagon and came into the cabin to readjust his prosthetic leg. He had been keeping a journal on his progress, as suggested by Doctor Chelmsford, and to note any time and what type of adjustments were needed. The information would be helpful for creating a more permanent form of prosthesis. Once Riley was greeted by Noah and fed a small morsel of bacon, he was again off to complete his patrol.

With his mid-morning routine completed, Riley trotted up the steps of the porch, took his usual position next to May, and sat at his sentinel post, ears and eyes always alert.

"You is the strangest dog, Riley, but I'm sure glad you is with us," said May.

Riley didn't respond, but maintained his guard.

狼

"Mama, Benji and I are finished with the plot... Mama?" Aarleen came into the kitchen along with Benjamin after preparing the small plot for planting when she suddenly saw Cynthia consoling her mother. She hastened her pace to her mother. "Mama, what's wrong? Are you okay?"

Renee looked up from Cynthia's shoulder to her daughter. Releasing her embrace, Cynthia stepped aside to let Aarleen take her place.

"Is this about Da?" asked Aarleen, "Have you heard any news?"

"No, sweetie, I just miss your father so much it hurts," said Renee, tears trailing down her face.

Aarleen wiped them away with her thumbs leaving a trail of dirt. Her eyes also formed tears. "Please, Mama. Please don't lose faith and love. You have been telling me every day since Da left to Itosai, he will return. When Da went to the city or anywhere, you told me he will return. And ever since he was stolen from us, you said every day, he will return. He will, Mama, he will." she said, full of confidence in her beliefs.

Renee cradled Aarleen's face with her flour covered hands and smiled. She kissed her forehead and pulled her into her arms. "I know, Sweetie. I just... couldn't help wondering where he could be right now. I want him home, now!" Renee cried.

Simon walked into the kitchen through the dining room and heard Renee. He said, "Listen to me, Renee. I never came across Reuben during the fighting, but I heard stories of a man with a strange sword who was too fast for any Yankee bullet to catch. And from what I know of Reuben, that man of yours is a survivor."

Benjamin stepped up to Renee and Aarleen, "Father is right. I don't know Mr. Duran as well as my father, but in the time mother and I have lived here with you and Aarleen, I feel I understand what type of man Mr. Duran is through your stories. You and Aarleen are the strongest women I have ever known, and I would think it would take a strong and cunning man to make you that way."

"You don't know Renee too well now, do you boy?" said Henry, entering the kitchen slowly. He was making his way to the table when Cynthia stepped forward to assist Henry as he slowly began to sit.

With his old shaking hand, he pointed to Renee and continued. "That woman standing there did just as much to make Reuben as strong as y'all are talking about. If it wasn't for Renee, Reuben would have kilt over many years ago, and none of us would be blessed with our present company."

Renee stepped over to Henry and leaned down and gave him a hug. "Henry, you old goat, you have no idea what you're talking about." she said as her adorable smiling face returned and gave Henry a gentle kiss on his cheek.

"Oh, yes I do, lil' missy. You and Reuben are a breed of your own, and also lil' Aarleen standing over there. What she can do with those sticks her Da showed her is amazing. She sure has knocked you around there, Benjamin," Henry said with a hardy chuckle.

Benjamin looked down embarrassed. Aarleen placed her arm around him and said "I may knock him around once or twice, but he is starting to catch on."

Laughter broke out at Benjamin's expense, and he also joined in.

"Hey, can a wounded veteran get any peace and quiet around here?" said Noah, looking in from the half-back door. "Y'all must be telling Reuben stories. Well, I have the best one of them all."

"That he has," said Evergreen, entering the kitchen as Noah opened the door.

Noah walked to the opposite end of the table from where Henry was sitting. As he took a seat, Evergreen stood behind him, placing her hands on his shoulders. "What I knew of Reuben was only of what I knew as we grew up together, but it wasn't until I took him his Kutto when I saw how powerful Reuben really is."

Noah's face was lighting up, "I'd seen him practice many times by that yonder old oak tree, but when I saw him use his skills for real, it was a sight to see. The day I lost this here leg, Reuben fought his way to me. He carved his way through Federals like a hot knife through butter. When he reached me, I told him I was gone for dead and to leave me, but he would have nothing to do with that. *'No one dies this time, especially you,'* he said. Thanks to your man, Renee, I would have lost my entire life if he had not carried me back to safety."

Everyone in the kitchen was listening to Noah wide-eyed and intently. Since Noah returned, he told Renee he had a full understanding of why Reuben was so lost when he returned from Mexico, but somehow, he felt content because he knew Reuben would return and Noah would not be alone. He told Renee the moment Reuben saw him off back to the farm, he was no longer Reuben's friend. He became Reuben's brother.

Noah continued. "When he brought me to the field hospital, the doctors were not going to treat me. They told him they only treated white soldiers and to take me elsewhere. Reuben was still carrying me in his arms and he looked around. He saw one of our officers on a table bed with his arm in a sling, smoking a cigar. Reuben asked him what was wrong and was told *'none of your business.'*"

Noah placed his hands on the table and spoke to Aarleen. "Now please, Aarleen, don't think bad of your Da for this next part, because if it wasn't for what he did next, I wouldn't be here telling you this story."

"Please tell me, Noah, please," pleaded Aarleen, although she already heard this story many times.

"Okay then," said Noah and he continued. "Your Da walked me over to that table bed and sat me down next to that officer. Reuben called him a coward and the officer drew his revolver and aimed it at Reuben's head, but Reuben twisted the officer's wrist taking him to the ground. Reuben drew his Kutto and crushed the officer's shoulder and sliced a dead soldier in half. He pointed his Kutto to the doctor who told Reuben to take me out of the tent and roared, *'You will let this doctor see to this man, or by the gods of the high mountains, I will slaughter every man in this tent starting with you!'*"

"Jesus in heaven, then what happened?" asked Cynthia.

Noah straightened his posture, looked at her and in an amused manner, he said, "Well, I'm here telling you this story now, so what do you think happened?"

"Reuben made a very smart cut on Noah's leg," added Doctor Chelmsford who was coming in through the dining room and overheard Noah's story. "I don't think any other doctor has ever done such a... precise amputation. It was Reuben's cut that allowed Noah to keep his knee."

"Yeah, if he made that cut above the knee, the only use my Noah would be is in a one legged ass kicking contest," said Evergreen.

Laughter followed and so did more stories about Reuben. Although the Norenhams didn't have any stories to share, they enjoyed listening to the others bringing Reuben to life before their eyes and ears from the memories they all shared. For the next hour they talked as Aarleen assisted Renee in kneading the bread dough.

"Dear me, Renee, is that the last of our flour?" asked Henry.

Renee looked at one of the loaves she was about to place into the oven. "Yes, it is. I know we should use it sparingly, but I had an urge to make fresh baked bread today. Reuben loves fresh baked bread."

Out on the front porch, May could hear the fellowship from the kitchen. She sat, continuing her chore of cleaning the beans and smiling as she reminisced of her own memories of Reuben.

Riley, however, caught a scent and raised his nose in the air. He began to sniff endlessly, his eyes focused toward the distant road. He didn't stop even when May slapped his snout.

"Settle down, dog. There are no more Federals out there. There's nothing here for them to take."

But Riley still sniffed the air constantly.

"Renee, this dog is sure acting strange! I fear he may have a fever! His dander is sure up!" called out May toward the inside of the house.

Suddenly Riley stood up on all four paws causing May to scream, quickly stand, and spill the beans she labored over all morning. Riley's sniffing was replaced by heavy panting and puppy-sounding yaps, his ears relaxed and his tail began to wag happily.

Renee and the others quickly made their way to the front door at the sound of May's scream and Riley's yapping. As Renee emerged from the doorway, Riley looked up at her, panting and wagging his tail. Riley nudged at Renee's leg with his snout, leaped from the porch, and ran across the yard toward the distant road as fast as his four legs could carry him. Renee and the others stood and watched.

It was May who spotted a lone man in the distance walking toward the house with the sun behind his back. "Look, Renee. There's someone coming up the lane."

Renee was puzzled because Riley usually stayed on the porch and barked out a warning and never raced to greet a visitor.

Renee watched as Riley reached the man and leaped on him, not to attack, but to welcome. Her feet turned to stone and a lump gathered in her throat. She couldn't speak as she saw the man tap the end of a long stick on the ground twice and place it in Riley's jaw, just as Reuben would give Riley his jo to carry.

It was May who broke the silence. "Dear lord, can it be? It is! It is! Renee, it's your man, I swears it is!"

Renee turned to May, and then to Aarleen, who was watching the man and Riley making their way to the house.

Renee stepped slowly down from the porch, shielded her eyes with her arm and hand from the bright mid-morning sun, and looked deeply at the man walking his way up the lane.

Startling Renee out of her haze, Aarleen yelled, "DA!!!" She looked at Aarleen who was pointing. Renee looked back at the man and noticed the distinct tsuka of Reuben's Kutto tucked into his Akagi burgundy obi.

"Reuben?" she whispered

"Reuben!!" she said.

"GEEZ OH GEEZ OH GEEZ, REUBEN!!!" she yelled.

Suddenly Renee sprinted to Reuben, as Aarleen and the others followed.

Reuben heard Renee cry his name. He quickened his pace and also started to sprint. The distance between the two quickly closed until they were within arm's reach. They stopped and stared at each other. They reached their hands toward each other, touched, and were quickly drawn together by the radiating energy coming from both of their bodies.

"My precious, Renee, I told you I would be home before noon," said Reuben, with a smile.

He quickly gathered Renee in his hands and lifted her to the sky, their eyes staring joyfully into each other. Reuben lowered Renee to the ground and she pulled him into her arms and held him as though no force could ever pull them apart.

In each other's arms, they gazed at one other. What were tears of sadness earlier in Renee's eyes this day were replaced with tears of joy. With her hands now cupped around Reuben's face, she reached up to kiss him as he pulled her tightly against his body. As their kiss ended, she rested her head against his shoulder and recited the last portion of the poem she recited earlier this day...

To hold
To cherish
To never be torn apart
You are my Stone and I am your Water
Our destiny is Love
We maintain our Faith and Love
And we are one as Love intended with Love as our anchor

Reuben gently ran his fingers through Renee's long, dark, brown hair and lifted her face to meet his. "You have no idea how much I missed you... Wickham girl."

Slapping his shoulder, Renee said with a shy giggle, "How many times have I told you never call me that, you shoddy farm boy?" and kissed him deeply again.

Reuben slowly raised his head and saw his beautiful daughter standing inches away. He reached and pulled her into their embrace, and held both his wife and daughter with adoring love.

"The test, Da... did we pass the test?" asked Aarleen.

Reuben looked up to everyone gathered around him, Renee, and Aarleen. With a very proud tone, he replied, "Yes, my little cherry blossom, all of us, we *all* passed this test with straight A's."

Reuben continued hugging both Renee and Aarleen lovingly and whispered in both their ears, "Is that fresh baked bread I smell?"

Part Four

You Are Most Welcome…

My Precious Little Angel…

石
水
Epilogue: Stones and Water, Faith and Love, Love and Devotion.
Precious legacies and gifts of tranquility…

Gifts of Tranquility

Reuben-San,

I received a letter from your wonderful wife. Renee-Dono sounds very remarkable, caring and I was very delighted to read her words about your progress. I am so very proud the lessons you have learned are still a part of your destiny.

It is with a heavy heart I must express my sadness for the loss of your mother, sister, and your brother's disappearance. Renee-Dono mentioned your involvement in your country's recent conflict. She assured me your involvement was not of vengeance, but to protect your family and those ignorant of warfare. That installed my confidence in your survival. There is no need to remind you of the code, for you have lived it here during the clan feudal conflicts with the Arata, and have learned the meaning of it well.

Every day, I am grateful of your contribution to my family. Renee-Dono mentioned your daughter Aarleen-Dono and of the training you have provided to her. From the day you protected my family, I made it clear you are to consider yourself as an adopted member of the Akagi Clan and I now extend that to the family of your blood. With that said, if ever you have the ability to return, your daughter, and her offspring, will be accepted into the halls of the dojo.

May the gods be with you and your loved ones, Akagi Genda.

狼

Atop an elegant looking thoroughbred, a very distinguished gentleman rode with his eyes focused on the distant road. He could see a curve up ahead with trees blocking the view of what lay beyond the road. He breathed heavily, not because of age, but of anxiousness. The trip from Jacksonville was quick, but this journey from the city to the Norfolk County Outreach School seemed to take forever. Since mounting his horse, he kept wondering if this trip was such a good idea. It was a needed trip for him since he was alone. His wife passed away of pneumonia back in the spring of '54. He had to correct his mistakes.

It had been eighteen years since he turned his back on his daughter for an act leading to family scandal and business failure. He literally blamed his daughter for his downfall. He wanted nothing to do with her or her child and practically erased her from the pages of the family lineage. He had to relocate further South to start his business all over again, a journey taking him to Mobile, Alabama where he had no connections. His shipping business quickly flourished, then as the blockade during the war took place, it dropped. During the crises, several of his ships

671

were converted into blockade runners, and he again began to make lucrative profits supplying the Confederacy with many materials from weapons to sewing needles.

Now with the war over, many of those who drove Franklin Wallace away began to urge him to return and help rebuild the port of Norfolk and its shipping industry. Many of his rivals heard of his contribution to the Southern cause, but most importantly, they also heard of the honorable exploits of the man Franklin Wallace's daughter chose to marry in defiance of her father's arrangements. Ironically, because of fate, it was from William Sinclair, the man Franklin Wallace chosen to be his daughter's husband, he first heard of Reuben Duran's bravery and integrity. William Sinclair told Franklin Wallace of how Reuben saved his life days prior to General Lee's surrender and he had high praise for him, and emphasized his daughter made an excellent choice.

Now, Franklin Wallace's business was once again successful, especially with the reconstruction of the country after such a brutal war. All was beginning to go his way, except he felt no happiness. With the loss of his wife many years ago, there was only one other person he had ties with, and that one person may not even acknowledge his existence. He had to try, yet hesitation still ran through his mind. The more he thought about turning around, the quicker he made his horse trot forward.

He reined his horse to slow when he noticed children walking around the curve in the middle of the road. They were taking and laughing. There were two girls skipping together arm-in-arm, which made Franklin Wallace smile bringing back memories of his daughter. He heeled his horse to speed up toward the walking children. When he got within several yards of them, he stopped his horse completely. All the children stopped, but none of them were afraid. Their fear of horsemen was long gone now with the war over, but they all looked at Franklin Wallace with questionable looks and stares.

"Excuse me, children," said Franklin Wallace in a manner of authority, out of habit. The children all stood up straight as if given an order by an army officer. Franklin Wallace suddenly felt awkward. It had been a long time since he spoken to children of this age. He cleared his throat and said, "Sorry for startling you, children. Can you tell me if the schoolhouse is near-by?"

A boy of about 10 years of age looked from side-to-side to his fellow travelers and stepped forward. "Yes sir. We were just excused from school. The schoolhouse is right around the corner yonder on the left side of the road," he said with pride in his tone as he pointed back toward the curve in the road.

Franklin Wallace stretched his neck to try and get a better look around the curve. He returned his attention to the boy, "Thank you very much, young man. You children have a nice day," he said and heeled his horse to continue.

"Goodbye, mister. You have a nice day yourself," replied the boy.

The closer Franklin Wallace got to the curve in the road, the quicker he made his horse trot until it was at a slow steady gallop. He reached the curve and as the horse rounded it, he stretched his neck to see what lay beyond. When the trees cleared, he could see a small, red church-like building with no steeple. He made the horse gallop up to the path leading to the building and brought it to a stop. He saw a young boy beneath a tree with a rake clearing the fallen leaves. Franklin Wallace dismounted and with reins in hand, he made his way toward the boy until a young girl coming out of the schoolhouse caught his attention.

It was the way she was dressed that caught his attention. It was a very unusual dress indeed, he thought. A solid royal blue skirt with a slit up the center and he realized the skirt was actually trousers. She wore a black, jacket-type of top tucked into the skirt-looking trousers. But other than the clothes, he noticed something familiar about the young girl's facial features reminding him of his wife, Margret. He changed direction from the boy to the girl.

The girl began to sweep the front porch of the schoolhouse until she noticed Franklin Wallace walking toward her. She leaned the broom against the door pane and walked toward him with a smile on her face. Franklin Wallace had a huge feeling of déjà vu as the distance between them closed.

"Hello. May I help you, mister?"

Franklin Wallace came to an abrupt halt, startling the horse. He spent several moments looking at this young girl in front of him. The girl now reminded him very much of his daughter when she was about her age, except for the peculiar form of dress. He thought she was very beautiful. Shaking his memory away from the past, he asked, "Ah, yes, young lady. May I ask who happens to be the educator of this establishment?"

Very pleasantly and politely, the young girl answered. "That would be Reuben Duran. He's inside. I can take you to him if you would like to meet him."

"Yes, indeed. I would like to meet him. By the way young lady, what is your name?"

"My name is Aarleen. Aarleen Duran and Reuben Duran is my Da." she answered with a warm, wonderful smile. "Come on in. He likes to meet new people," she said as she made her way up the steps.

Franklin Wallace stood as if he were rooted to the ground. My heavens, is this beautiful young girl my granddaughter, he wondered. He felt a sudden empty feeling deep in his gut and he fought the urge to let out tears. He turned his attention to the boy raking beneath the tree. "Excuse me, young man. Will you see to my horse?" he called out. The boy leaned the rake against the tree and quickly made his way to Franklin Wallace.

"Yes sir. I'll see to him."

"Thank you, lad," said Franklin Wallace as he handed the reins to the boy. "Ride him if you wish. He is well behaved." Franklin Wallace could not believe he said that. I am not that cordial, he thought to himself. He looked up the steps to Aarleen waiting for him. That must be why, he thought. She looks like an angel.

Aarleen escorted Franklin Wallace into the school and up the center aisle to the front of the classroom. "Excuse me, Da. This gentleman wishes to speak with you."

Reuben looked up from the letter he was reading and his eyes widened as if he was seeing a ghost. He slowly stood from the desk, gently placed the letter down, and walked around to the front of his desk where Franklin Wallace was standing.

673

Franklin Wallace was surprised at how Reuben looked. He had expected, even hoped, Reuben would be weak and broken. However, he saw a man of broad stature with the look of intelligence and strength. There was a long moment of silence between the two as they eyed one another. Aarleen stood focusing her eyes from one to the other with an odd questionable look on her face and began to feel awkward. It was she who broke the silence.

"Excuse me, Da. When Benji and I are finished with the chores, can I practice some kumitachi with him? He asked me to show him one or two techniques before we start for home."

Reuben broke his focus on Franklin Wallace to acknowledge Aarleen. "Ah, yes, of course, my little cherry blossom," he answered.

She clapped her hands twice, bowed, and skipped to the back of the room where she picked up two bokkens on the wall rack that held several jos as well. She was almost out the door when Reuben shouted to her, "Hey, be careful with Ben and don't hurt him like you did last time! I don't like explaining to Simon why my daughter can kick his son's ass!"

Reuben smiled and chuckled as he watched Aarleen run out the door and into the school yard completely ignoring the broom she placed against the doorway. "Well, I guess we'll do the sweeping and raking tomorrow," he said shaking his head as he watched her hand Benjamin one of the bokkens.

Franklin Wallace was surprised to see the boy quickly tie the horse's rein to the step post and run off with Aarleen. He turned his attention back to Reuben. Franklin Wallace had a stern look on his face. Reuben let out a breath and looked at the letter he had been reading on his desk, a letter that took several months to reach him from Japan, and returned his focus to Franklin Wallace.

"Mr. Wallace, you are looking well. Will you please have a seat?" asked Reuben.

Franklin Wallace walked around Reuben's desk and sat in his chair and placed his hands flat on top of the desk. He noticed the letter Reuben had on his desk, but he couldn't make out the writing and he looked at it questionably. "What is this? One of your students attempts at writing?"

Reuben smiled and reached for the letter and envelope. "No sir. It's a letter from my lord, master, and mentor. He sent it several months ago and I finally received it today."

"That is strange hand writing. Are you sure it's a letter?"

"Yes sir. It's from Akagi Genda-San. You met him when we picked up Renee to take him to the train station," said Reuben with no hesitation mentioning Franklin Wallace's daughter's name.

Franklin Wallace moved his head up and had a look of actual interest lasting only a moment.

"That girl, Aarleen... your daughter?" asked Franklin Wallace, gesturing toward the door Aarleen went through.

Reuben stayed standing, holding the letter. "Yes, she is. And yes, she's your granddaughter. I learned about her almost the same way you did."

"She is very beautiful. Just like..."

"Renee?"

Franklin Wallace took in a deep breath, breathed it out, and nodded. "How is she?"

"She's very well."

"Has she spoken of me? Her father?"

Reuben responded with a silent neutral look.

"I see."

Still focused on the desk in front of him, Franklin Wallace nodded. He recalled Reuben's entire family was also gone. He is all alone, just like me... with the exception of my daughter, and that beautiful daughter of theirs, he thought. Then Renee came back to his attention.

"I can't see that I blame her. You said you met Aarleen almost the same way I did. How do you mean?"

Reuben smiled. The memory of the little girl who was about to turn seven startling him out of his concentration as he was training causing him to fall on his rear end came to him so vividly. He chuckled as he rubbed his chin with his free hand. He heard Aarleen yell out a kiai and then the crack of two bokkens connecting. He turned to look out of the window behind him and saw his daughter showing Benjamin the correct way of blocking a downward cut. He walked to the open window and leaned against the pane.

"My family took Renee in and cared for her as one of their own," he said, but not in a condescending manner. "Renee gave birth while I was away. There was no way for them to contact me so I had no idea Aarleen existed. The whole time I was in Japan, I thought Renee was married to the man you arranged for her to marry. Imagine my surprise when I returned to find Renee living on our farm, and then I met Aarleen."

Franklin Wallace looked toward Reuben who was focused watching Aarleen and Benjamin. "Was my daughter angry with you?"

"No," answered Reuben, not looking away from the two youths. "Neither of us had any reason to be angry. We were just happy to be together. In a way, our separation bonded us together in ways only nature can explain."

Reuben turned his focus from Aarleen and Benjamin to the letter in his hand and out loud, mainly to himself, he spoke a small phrase in Japanese followed in English, "That is how my lord master would explain it."

Franklin Wallace frowned at the language Reuben was using, especially when he heard the term lord master used as if Reuben was a slave. "Excuse me?" he asked, quite forcefully.

Reuben turned to face Franklin Wallace, his face unaltered from the joy he gained from watching Aarleen training with Benjamin.

"I said, set things right with Divine Love. The entire time I was in Japan, I thought I was trying to forget the dark memories of my past, but my master taught me how to use my dark memories to protect my Divine Love, Renee. I don't expect you to understand. It's a very complex culture."

"What do you mean by calling this man, *'lord master'*? Were you his slave?" asked Franklin Wallace in a disgustful tone.

"No, I wasn't a slave. I was, and still am, his student and loyal retainer. Akagi Genda-San is my master, my teacher, and my friend. If it were not for him, Renee and I would never have found our Divine Love. She's my water and I'm her stone."

Franklin Wallace softened his tone and began to try to understand. "In the meantime, my daughter raised Aarleen by herself?"

Reuben turned his focus back to the two youths in the yard. "With the help of my family, yes, she did, and she did a very remarkable job." He looked at Franklin Wallace with a piercing stare, causing him to cower and in a commanding manner, Reuben said, "You should be very proud of Renee."

Awkwardly, Franklin Wallace looked away from Reuben's stare and toward the open window, "And Aarleen, is she... smart?" he asked.

"She's more than smart. She's intelligent. And strong too. Come take a look at your granddaughter. She has a lot of her mother in her."

Franklin Wallace stood up and walked to the window. He watched as Aarleen was doing bokken suburis. Her movements were so elegant and he smiled at how happy she looked as she preformed what he thought was a dance. "Did you teach her that?"

"I taught her the basics, but she has added her own personality to the suburis. Much like I did when I first began training, so, in a sense, she has evolved from my personality."

"And you believe that is a proper way for a young Virginian lady to... behave?"

Reuben snickered at the question and remembered when Noah and Doctor Chelmsford told him of the time Renee and Aarleen stopped Oscar Grossman and his troopers from confiscating his Kutto. He also was reminded of the time when Aarleen took down little Tommy Deans in the schoolyard.

"I believe Aarleen believes that's the way she should be behaving," Reuben said, nodding his head approvingly.

"So my daughter can also do... that sort of activity?" asked Franklin Wallace.

With a very proud look, Reuben said, "Renee's talent is with the jo. While I was away during the war, I didn't fear for Renee and Aarleen too much because I trained them to defend themselves. They both developed some techniques of their own in my absence. They're still teaching them to me."

With a rather impressed look, Franklin Wallace said in a concerning tone, "Impressive, but still, for a young woman to be acting in such a manner is... not proper. I would see no future for her."

Reuben let out a proud sigh, "I wouldn't worry too much for my little cherry blossom's future, Mr. Wallace. Your granddaughter is quite the storyteller."

"What do you mean?" asked Franklin Wallace, looking at Reuben inquisitively.

"A Federal area inspector was very taken by Aarleen's storytelling abilities. Before the war, Mr. MacKay was a publishing agent. With his help, your granddaughter is going to be one of the youngest female authors in American literature. Her first book will be sent to print before the end of her last year of schooling. Don't be surprised if she becomes wealthier than you, Mr. Wallace."

Turning serious, Reuben faced Franklin Wallace. "Sir, I believe, we as parents, provide our children with the tools and knowledge needed for them to chose their path. We also guide them in the right direction. We give them that nudge to start their journey. If you have done your job as the parent well, your children will make the right decisions. They will decide to take the most difficult path because it's on that path where the meaningful rewards lay. Only then can one look at their rewards. That may not make sense, but it's on the easy path where hatred, fear, and temptation lead many astray to rewards that are meaningless and empty."

With a remorseful look on his face, Franklin Wallace nodded at what Reuben said. He could not fully understand his statement, but it lingered in his mind. He began to question his motives of arranging his daughter's marriage to a man she did not love. In doing so, Renee chose to take the more difficult path leading to her happiness, with rewards she would never have received had she taken his easy path he had been forcing upon her. That path was of his own making to keep Renee in her social class and to increase his business. What he done was not for Renee, but for him. The more Franklin Wallace thought about Reuben's thought-provoking explanation, he became aware of how wrong he was and how he didn't deserve any type of forgiveness from Renee.

He was suddenly brought back from his thoughts when Reuben called out to Aarleen.

"YAME! Aarleen, we need to start for home! Did she teach you anything good, Ben?"

"Yes sir, Mr. Duran," answered Benjamin, excitedly.

"Good, you can take that bokken with you so you can practice at home if you wish, but only after your chores and schoolwork are finished."

"Thank you very much. I'll be sure to rake the yard tomorrow, I promise."

"I'll take that promise and if it's broken, I'll let Aarleen take it up a notch on you next time. Now come and walk me and Aarleen home!"

Reuben tucked the letter in his shirt pocket and closed the window while Franklin Wallace stood watching. Reuben neatly scooted his desk chair into place and slung his haversack over his shoulder. He walked to the rack holding several staffs and bokkens and took up his jo, the same one he carried throughout the war, and turned his attention to Franklin Wallace. "Well, are you coming to see Renee? I'm sure you didn't come out here just to see me."

Franklin Wallace took heavy long steps toward the door. "Wait. Do you think this is such a good idea? I mean my daughter..."

For the first time, Reuben placed his hand on Franklin Wallace's shoulder. Franklin Wallace felt positive energy radiating from Reuben's touch as Reuben said, "Listen, I lived seven years of not knowing. That's no way to live. And by the way, your daughter's name is Renee. It will go much easier if you use it. Now come. Renee will kick my ass if I don't get Aarleen home within the half hour. She usually comes with Riley to walk us home, but she has been busy this week helping Aunty May with some preserving."

677

Franklin Wallace smiled at Reuben as he led him out of the schoolhouse. He closed the door behind him as Franklin Wallace untied the reigns of his horse and was nearly pushed over as Aarleen ran into Reuben's arms.

"Oops, I'm terribly sorry, sir. That was very rude of me."

Franklin Wallace looked at the Aarleen and smiled. "That's all right."

"What's your name, sir?" asked Aarleen, curious.

Franklin Wallace looked to Reuben. Reuben shrugged his shoulders.

"My name is Frank. I am... I am, a friend of... your father," replied Franklin Wallace not wanting to reveal his true identity.

"He's also a friend of your mother, blossom. Perhaps she'll tell you how they met," Reuben said.

"Does that mean you're coming home with us for dinner, Frank?"

Franklin Wallace nodded yes, smiled, and said, "How would you like to ride on Truman, young lady?"

"May I, Da?" Aarleen asked, looking to Reuben with excitement.

"Sure, hop on up," Reuben answered, moving to help her upon the horse.

"Here, young lady. Let me help you," said Franklin Wallace as he assisted Aarleen up into the saddle before Reuben could help her. As he did so, he began to feel tears come to his eyes.

Fighting the tears back, Franklin Wallace said, "You look very impressive with that stick of yours, young lady," as they began the journey to the farm.

"Thank you. It's called a bokken and Da taught me how to use it," Aarleen replied with pride.

"Yeah," said Reuben, "but I wish you would spend as much time with your jo practice."

"But I like the bokken more than the jo. The jo is more for a woman, like Mama."

"HEY! I used my jo through the war you know," said Reuben in a mocking, angered tone.

All four of the travelers began laughing.

During the entire journey home, Aarleen sat atop Truman as Reuben, Benjamin, and Franklin Wallace flanked the horse. Franklin Wallace began to ask Reuben about the war and how he participated, but Aarleen would interrupt by talking about Reuben's years in Japan, which relieved Reuben since he didn't like to discuss the war. She would tell Franklin Wallace the stories Reuben told her, such as the blooming of the cherry blossom trees and the snowcapped mountains that never seemed to melt. She told the stories with such pride which made Franklin Wallace troubled. I never gave my daughter any reason to be proud of me, he thought as he listened to Aarleen.

"I'm hoping one of these days I'll be able to see what Da saw," Aarleen said.

"Perhaps you will," Reuben answered, thinking of the letter in his pocket.

They were coming up to the turn toward the house and Franklin Wallace stopped as that empty feeling came back to the pit of his stomach. He felt as if he was going to be sick.

"Are you okay?" asked Benjamin, concerned.

Reuben came to his side and placed his hand on Franklin Wallace's shoulder. "Let me talk to Renee first to lighten the shock. Aarleen and I will go on ahead and you make your own pace. Don't turn back now. Coming this far is the most difficult part of the journey. The rest is up to her."

Franklin Wallace placed his hand on top of Reuben's and looked to his face. It was a calm face he thought. He was truly out of his element and very confused with the new emotional feelings overcoming him, but he found them comforting.

"Thank you, Reuben. That is a fine idea." He took a large breath in and let it out, and looked up to Aarleen. "Please, will you walk Truman up to your house, young lady?"

"Of course, I'd be happy to. Are you well, Frank?" she asked with concern.

"Yes, dear, it's just I haven't seen your mother in such a long time and I'm nervous. I'm afraid she will not remember me."

"Of course she will. Who could forget a nice man such as yourself?" Aarleen asked.

Franklin Wallace turned his attention back to Reuben and snickered. "If she only knew," he said.

"We take things one step at a time around here. Everything will be fine. Come, blossom, get Noah to help you with Truman and I'll go tell your Mama she has a visitor. See you bright and early tomorrow morning, Ben?"

"Bright and early, Mr. Duran. Bye, Aarleen. I'll see you tomorrow," Benjamin said as he kept walking home swishing the bokken from side-to-side.

"Bye, Benji. Remember, we have to finish that work at school tomorrow or Da won't let us train until we do."

"Right. Give your mother a hug for me," Benjamin replied.

Franklin Wallace watched them walk on ahead. He looked toward the sky for no reason and noticed how much bluer it had become. He took in a couple of breaths and started toward the house. He got as far as the front porch when he stopped and turned around. He stared at the lane leading to the road having second thoughts, but the words Reuben said earlier, "*Look at their rewards*" kept him from walking off. Instead, as he lowered himself down and sat on the first step of the porch, he thought of the ways he could have been a better father.

Walking over the threshold, Renee silently made her way to her father who was sitting on the porch step. He looked much older than she imagined. Overwhelming emotions flowed through her such as anger, sadness, and even joy. As she watched him, she noticed he seemed to be in deep thought, like many times in her youth when she wanted to have his attention, but never got it. She always got the attention of a father's love from Aaron Duran, but never her own father. She walked closer, not knowing what to say until she was right behind him.

"Hello, father," she said, very formally in the way she was taught by her mother to speak to him.

Franklin Wallace was startled from his thoughts and stumbled up from the porch step and turned to face his daughter for the first time in eighteen years. She was dressed the same as Aarleen, but with a light brown kosode and forest green hakama, and looked just as radiant. Her face did not show emotion, but she had the beauty of his wife. He slowly stepped up on the porch staring at her face.

Renee's eyes did not avert from his stare as when they used to in her younger years. Instead they met his, her way of showing him he no longer controlled her life and not to even try. She made the first gesture and was about to speak again when Franklin Wallace cleared his throat.

"You look very well... Renee."

Renee's unemotional look turned to a pleasant smile as she heard her father use her name. She motioned to the chairs on the porch. "Would you care to have a seat, father?"

Franklin Wallace looked at the chairs, nodded, and took a seat. He was raking his mind, thinking of items to talk about when his thoughts were interrupted by Renee.

"It's beautiful how the evening sun shines through the trees. I spent many hours sitting here with Aarleen staring at the rays waiting for Reuben to come home from the war. Now that he's home, we haven't done it since. I think now is a good time to start again."

He was relieved he did not have to start speaking. Now that the silence was broken, he took the opportunity to speak.

"Yes, it is beautiful," he said, looking at the floor instead of the trees. Suddenly he looked at Renee's eyes and saw how they sparkled as the rays of the sun broke through the leaves and branches, and turned to take a look. Suddenly a joyful feeling came over him. "Yes, I see it now. It is very beautiful."

Renee's attention turned to her father and said as she smiled, "People always see more clearly when Reuben is around. He's magical."

Franklin Wallace faced his daughter and said, "Reuben... is he as good a fellow as others have told me?"

"He's the best and I'm so grateful he's part of my life. We have a wonderful home and a beautiful daughter. I believe you met her."

"Yes I have, but she does not know who I am," he replied.

"Why didn't you tell her?" she asked.

"I didn't know if you wanted her to know who I am," Franklin Wallace said as he looked away with a shameful look.

He felt a gentle touch on his arm that startled him and he looked down to see Renee's hand on his arm. He didn't know how to react and felt awkward. These emotions were all new to him. He had to be stern in his business and had no time for tenderness. He looked up to Renee's bright, brown eyes looking at him filled with joy, just as when she was a child. He remembered that look, but never had any time for it. Now that joy was right in front of him again.

Her eyes may have been bright, but Renee spoke with harshness in her voice, "You were always my father, but never my dad, or Da, as it's called here in our family. I hated you for that and what you did to keep me and Reuben apart. The worst was when you abandoned me after I convinced Reuben to seek his mentor, and I had no one. You called me horrible names and you beat me. You kicked me with Aarleen, your granddaughter, inside me and thank heaven you didn't harm her! I've never thought of that until now! You could have killed that precious gift Reuben gave me, do you realize that?" This was eighteen years' worth of abandonment talking. Her anger softened as she began to think of how much Reuben changed from when he returned from Mexico. To go through such turmoil as a jagged rock to become her smooth stone, made her think of when he told her what he said to the lieutenant she confronted defending their home, *"Don't live with grudges, they will only make you a bitter person."*

Renee looked at her hand still resting on her father's arm and her voice softened. "I had every right to curse you... but because of Reuben's family, I didn't. They took me in, even in my condition. They felt no shame toward me because they knew I loved Reuben and I had more faith and love than any of them he would return whole again."

Her gaze returned to her father's. His eyes were beginning to water. "Then Reuben returned. He went away a bitter soldier and returned as a warrior, true of heart and love, and has provided and protected Aarleen and myself with every fiber of his being. Father, of all the ones you could have chosen for me, none of them could scratch the surface of my Reuben."

Just then, Reuben, dressed in his kosode of Akagi burgundy and hakama of black, and Aarleen, still in hers, came running from the side of the house. Aarleen was armed with her bokken and Reuben with his jo. The sight caught both Franklin Wallace and Renee. Aarleen was ahead of Reuben and suddenly she stopped, and with a sharp kiai, struck at Reuben. Reuben leaped and twisted in the air to avoid the strike and landed behind Aarleen and with a fierce kiai of his own, struck at Aarleen with full force. Aarleen twisted, raised her bokken with a blocking technique, and diverted the strike with a following thrust that was blocked by Reuben. Father and daughter preformed the awase as one, meeting each strike and thrust. To Franklin Wallace, it looked as if they were connected. He looked at Renee wondering how she could allow a young lady to act in such a way, but he noticed her silently edging Aarleen on. He gazed back at his granddaughter and felt a large amount of pride, the same pride he saw Renee had. That is my granddaughter defending herself, taught to her by her father, he thought. He stood up and stepped off the porch, moving toward the two with a serious look of interest and joy. He stopped and watched as Aarleen's hair, tided in a tail, waved in the air, and her sharp shouts meeting the strikes, thrusts, and parries of Reuben's jo. He now understood what it meant to be a dad, or Da, rather than a father. Tears of affection fell from his eyes. He felt the arm of his daughter wrap around his.

"I see you understand what I needed when I was growing up," said Renee, looking to her father's face. "For that, I feel no anger or hate. I only feel your bravery for making this effort to find me, and you have... Dad."

Franklin faced Renee, eyes filled with tears and love. "Can you ever forgive a tired, foolish, grumpy old bastard of a man who does not deserve your forgiveness, Renee?"

Renee, for the first time on her own, threw her arms around her blood father and said, "I already have, long ago."

狼

In the Year of our Lord, 1866, during her last year of schooling under the instructional tutelage of her father, Aarleen Moncy Duran had her first book of short stories published. With the publishing help of Jonathan MacKay, and financial backing of her grandfather, Franklin Wallace, Aarleen's book was tremendously popular with young and old readers alike.

Upon the end of her formal schooling, Reuben surprised Renee and Aarleen with their first trip to Japan. Although he could afford the journey with the oban coins he still had in his possession, it was Franklin Wallace who provided the means for the family to make the journey.

The journey took them across the country on the transcontinental railroad. Traveling across the country by train was a first for Reuben since the last time he journeyed to Japan was by way through the Strait of Magellan. This leg of the journey was a first time experience shared by all three and significantly cut their travel time by weeks.

The first leg of the journey took Reuben, Renee, and Aarleen to Sacramento, California where Andrew and Annabelle settled with Andy. In Sacramento, Andrew and Annabelle started a new, successful mercantile and were very happy. The ship to take the Durans to Japan was not due to leave for a week, so they took advantage of the time to visit.

It was a marvelous visit. Andy was thrilled to see Aarleen and showed her as much of Sacramento as he could before the family had to leave.

Andy Klaus, for the most part, accepted the loss of his parents, but he still found it difficult to cope with the fact he was alone with no mother, father, or siblings. Seeing his cousin again did wonders for his mental stability and gave him a sense he was still a part of a family. But it was Reuben who made his future brighter when he took Andy for a walk and told him of the message Lucy asked for Reuben to tell Andy in the dream he had in the woods after the war.

Continuing on their journey, the Durans arrived in San Francisco where they met up with Renee's Godfather, James Forrest. Since the last time Reuben was in the presence of James Forrest, the Master of the *Morning Star*, he continued to sail for Franklin Wallace until the war began. He provided his service in the United States Navy and served in the Pacific chasing down Confederate runners, some of them belonging to Franklin Wallace. When the war was over, he was released from naval service and was looking for a job in Mobile when he met up with Franklin Wallace.

It was about this time Franklin Wallace was starting his period of enlightenment and pleaded for forgiveness from his old friend. It was James Forrest who encouraged Franklin Wallace to seek forgiveness from Renee.

"Your daughter may have been bitter toward you in the past, but if I know my Goddaughter, and Reuben, she will accept you back into her life. That's only if you are sincere. Renee is a very intelligent girl, and as hard as this may be for you to accept, she got that way from your abuse."

Franklin Wallace offered James Forrest partnership in his business ventures to revitalize the shipping industry in Norfolk, but James Forrest denied the offer. Instead he chose to sail for him. It was the life on the ocean James Forrest lived for and the Pacific was his playground.

So it was aboard the *Morning Star II* Reuben, Renee, and Aarleen sailed to Japan with James Forrest at the helm. However, before they left San Francisco, Renee was curious.

"You have got to show me where you met Tadashi and Captain Sean Aaron," said Renee. "I want to follow your journey step-by-step from here."

"Me too, Da!" said Aarleen, who was never without a journal and pencil.

Reuben took Renee and Aarleen, along with James Forrest, to The Olden Sword Rest House. They sat at the table where James Forrest arranged for Sean Aaron to take Reuben the rest of the way to Japan. Reuben pointed out the portion of the bar where he met Sora Tadashi.

To follow Reuben's journey step-by-step, James Forrest had to make a special stop to the village of Tatao, where Reuben and Tadashi entered the country. Reuben's original plan was to sail to Edo and from there, travel to Itosai. However, Renee's insistence to travel the same path caused Reuben to become nostalgic himself and he wanted to lead Renee, hand-in-hand, to where the water smoothed the stone.

Starting from Norfolk and throughout the entire journey, Reuben told, in great detail, of the cultural differences Renee and Aarleen were about to experience, just as Tadashi did on his initial voyage. From Reuben's stories of his previous journey, he told them of the differences, but not in such detail. Renee and Aarleen were in complete culture shock the moment they disembarked the *Morning Star II* in Tatao.

"Well, Reuben, my friend, I will return to Edo in three months. In the meantime, enjoy your visit," said James Forrest.

While in the village of Tatao, Reuben came across a magistrate and arranged transportation of a small carriage and horse to Itosai. Once the magistrate learned of Reuben's service to the Akagi, Reuben and his family were treated as honored guests. The Battle of Shun Bridge freed the Ute Province of the Arata, and because of the part the Akagi contributed, the province and its people had been grateful.

Watching her husband arrange transportation, and acquire more regional proper attire, Renee saw Reuben in a whole new light. It was as if she was falling in love with him all over again.

They traveled the same road Reuben and Tadashi took toward Itosai.

When they reached the crest of the hill where Reuben first turned back to see the *Coleen* still in the bay, he stopped and reflected on that one moment in time.

683

"This is where I first felt fear," he said as his eyes watered. "It was on this spot I felt the last chance to turn back, or I would never return."

"But you did, my love. You did as you once were and better," replied Renee wiping his tears.

They stopped at the place where the abandoned shack once stood, the first place he and Tadashi rested for the night. Reuben pointed out the area where they left the road to rest deep in the woods on the second night of their hike. Reuben took them to the battlefield where he met up with Akagi Genda-San, and had Renee and Aarleen stand in the spot where Masaru was about to kill him because he was an off-lander. They stood beneath the tree where Akagi Genda-San talked with Reuben after the battle.

As they neared Itosai, Aarleen stood in the carriage and pointed to the mountains in the distance. "HEY!!! Those are the snowcapped mountains in my dreams! And those are the hills resembling stairs! Why are those hills like that, Da?"

"That's where rice is grown and harvested, blossom. We're getting closer."

All three were tingling with anticipation, but more so for Renee and Aarleen. As they cleared a bend, a huge Shinto gate appeared across the road. Reuben stopped and softly recited a phrase in Japanese. Placing his hand on Renee's cheek and looking into her eyes with love, he translated, "My second home."

They passed under the gate and as they peaked over the hill, the road before them was lined on both sides with cherry blossom trees in full bloom. Renee's and Aarleen's faces lit up.

"Are these… cherry blossom trees, Da?" asked Aarleen in wonderment.

"Yes, they are my little cherry blossom."

"Please stop, Da! I must go touch one!"

Reuben stopped the carriage and all three climbed off. Aarleen ran to the nearest tree and wrapped her arms around its trunk. Arm-in-arm, Renee and Reuben walked up behind her.

"Oh, Da, they're wonderful," she said as she looked up as a blossom fell to her cheek.

"A kiss from the gods," said Renee.

A pleasant voice called out in Japanese causing all three to look. "Hey, what are you doing there?! Are you lost?!"

"No, my friend, I know my way, Tadashi," answered Reuben in English.

Sora Tadashi and his oldest son were walking up the path leading to the road toward Itosai when they saw the carriage and three travelers wandering among the cherry blossom trees.

"Reuben? Is that you?"

"Hai!" exclaimed Reuben, joyfully.

The two friends sprinted and embraced each other tightly and laughed out loud. Tadashi stepped back and looked at Reuben from head to toe, bringing his hand to his head in wonderment. "Look at you, my friend! You have not changed at all!"

"Come, Tadashi. I want you to meet my family," Reuben said as he motioned toward Renee and Aarleen.

"Indeed. Honored," Tadashi said, moving as Reuben motioned.

As they neared Renee and Aarleen, Tadashi's jaw dropped as he caught sight of the mother and daughter standing together arm-in-arm.

"Tadashi, this is…" Reuben began.

"Renee-Dono," interrupted Tadashi as he took Renee's offered hand. "That picture Reuben carried everywhere does you no justice, Renee-Dono. And this, your beautiful daughter?" he asked.

"Yes," answered Renee, "Aarleen."

Aarleen offered her hand and was taken by Tadashi. "Aarleen-Dono, it is a pleasure. It is because of you I have added a room to your father's cottage.

"Kazue, come quick, meet your father's friend and family. Reuben, Renee-Dono, Aarleen-Dono, let me introduce my first son, Kazue. Quickly son, go to the castle and inform Lord Genda, Reuben has returned with his family."

"Hai, father," replied Kazue, handing his father a basket so he could follow his directions.

As Kazue was about to run off, Reuben told him to take the carriage so he, Renee, and Aarleen could walk and stretch their legs. As they walked up the road lined with cherry blossom trees, Tadashi told Renee and Aarleen about how he and Reuben met. Although Reuben told them many times, to hear it from Tadashi was fresh and new.

Once they cleared the last remaining trees on the road, Renee and Aarleen caught their first glimpse of Hisano Castle and the village of Itosai behind it with the majestic waterfalls lining the gorge. They both fell to their knees to gaze at its splendor. It was like a scene out of a fairy tale.

A loud bellowing conch shell horn was heard, nearly frightening Renee and Aarleen out of their skin.

"Geez oh geez oh geez what in the world was that?" asked Renee as she rose and nearly jumped into Reuben's arms pulling Aarleen with her.

"Genda-San knows we have arrived. Now remember what I said, greet him as if this is the first time you have met him."

"This *will* be my first time, Da," Aarleen reminded him.

They continued to walk, but didn't get too far when suddenly men on horses came riding toward them, a few in full Akagi samurai armor with banners attached to their backs. The riders stopped several yards away. There were a dozen riders and to Renee and Aarleen, they looked quite menacing, yet impressive. To Reuben, they were a welcome sight. The riders opened a path and one rider trotted up next to Reuben. The rider dismounted and took Reuben into his arms and held him for several long moments.

"Reuben-San, by the grace of the gods, you are well and blessed, my loyal retainer," said Akagi Genda-San, embracing Reuben as if he were embracing a long lost, beloved son.

Watching Reuben and Akagi Genda-San greet each other caused Renee to pull Aarleen close and cry tears of happiness for them both.

Akagi Genda-San released Reuben and turned to face Renee and Aarleen.

Renee let go of Aarleen and, as instructed by Reuben, she stood straight and bowed.

"Ah, Renee-Dono. I know Reuben-San has taught you customs, but that is not necessary," he said as he took her into his arms and hugged her as a grandfather would hug his granddaughter.

"How do you like your stone?" he asked Renee.

"Oh, Mr. Akagi, he's wonderful," Renee said, smiling and looking at Reuben.

"You will honor me if you call me, Genda," Akagi Genda-San said.

Akagi Genda-San released Renee and turned his focus to Aarleen. As he was about to greet her, Aarleen wrapped her arms around Akagi Genda-San, surprising everyone.

"Thank you, Mr. Akagi. Thank you for coming to me in my dreams, and for sending my Da help and protection. Thank you for the best Da and Mama in the world," Aarleen said, sobbing in happiness.

Akagi Genda-San took Aarleen in his arms as he found it difficult to hold back his emotions and said, "You are most welcome... my precious little angel."

The three month visit was glorious. Within hours of Reuben and his family's arrival, Kaoru and Masaru arrived to the castle. Aarleen met Katsuo, the maker of her inrou and they became good friends.

"I must apologize to you, Renee," said Kaoru, once she got to know Renee.

"Why, Kaoru?" she asked.

"I'm not sure if Reuben ever told you, but I once tried to gain his affections. However, because of his deep rooted love for you, I never had a chance. His love for you was never faltering. Meeting and getting to know you, I understand why he could never love another. You are very blessed to have Reuben as yours."

Renee was speechless. Kaoru, with her long, dark hair, olive skin, and eyes of jade with a pleasant personality, was the most beautiful woman Renee had ever seen. For her to tell Renee, Reuben turned down her affections all because the love he had for Renee spoke volumes of how much Reuben loved her.

Everyone who met Renee and Aarleen adored them. Their bright smiling faces brought cheer everywhere they went and were welcome into every home and business in Itosai. Renee adored the cottage Reuben built, and told him many times if they had to live here she would be the happiest girl in the world as long as they were together. When she entered their bedroom, she thought it was rather small until Reuben slid open the wall to reveal a large covered balcony with a picturesque view of the waterfalls lining the gorge and fed into the large pond below. She stared at the view for over an hour in silent awe. Of all that Itosai had to offer, Renee enjoyed the evenings the best when she and Reuben would take long walks through the lantern lighted paths and over the bridges.

Aarleen had many opportunities to train with the Okami no Mure, the home guard first established by Reuben and Tadashi. Her skills were highly regarded, especially by Akagi Genda-San, who saw fresh new talent in her techniques.

When it was time to return to Virginia, a huge celebration was held. It was a celebration Renee and Aarleen would never forget because it was to honor them as adopted members into the Akagi Clan, a distinction Reuben earned by shedding blood for the Akagi.

"Renee-Dono and Aarleen-Dono... your Reuben-San has provided so much care, dedication, and devotion to the Akagi clan, not only with hard work but with blood as well. Renee-Dono, you have passed on Reuben-San's blood to your daughter, Aarleen-Dono, so from this day to the many to follow until the end of time, you both shall be written into the Akagi family lineage. From this day on, the family ties between Akagi and Duran will forever be as one," proclaimed Akagi Genda-San. He presented them both small medallions of the Akagi crest made from what was left over from the metal of Reuben's Kutto Isamu Gorou saved when he forged the Sword of Spiritual Power and given to Akagi Genda-San. Renee proudly wore her medallion on the same chain with the VMI button Reuben gave her during the Christmas season of '43. Aarleen wore hers on a gold chain given to her by her mother along with the gold coin Reuben gave her the evening they first met before her seventh birthday.

When Reuben, Renee, and Aarleen were returning by way of Sacramento, Andy returned to Norfolk with them. The three months while Reuben and his family were in Japan gave Andy plenty of time to think about the discussion he had with his uncle. Lucy's message for Andy from Reuben's dream caused him to believe it was time for complete closure. He decided, with his grandparent's support, it was time to return to Virginia to complete that closure, and reestablish his father's store in his parents honor.

687

石
水

Andy Klaus returned to Norfolk where he opened a new successful mercantile store. It was located close to Elmhurst Cemetery. Each day before he opened the store, Andy would visit his mother to wish her a good day, and to thank her for sending his Uncle Reuben with her message from his dream. Andy Klaus married a local girl named Patrice Hall and they had two children. Aarleen spent many days helping her cousin Andy and Patrice in the store where many of her books sold.

Henry passed on in the spring of 1868. He was well honored by the entire congregation in Norfolk County. His devotion to the Duran family was inspiring.

May passed on in the fall of 1869. Just as devoted to the Duran family, Reuben petitioned and was allowed to rename the Norfolk County Outreach School to the *May and Henry Outreach School* in their honor.

Noah and Evergreen continued to live on the Duran farm for the rest of their lives together as husband and wife. Reuben served as Noah's best man while Renee was Evergreen's matron of honor. Noah constantly experimented and invented lower leg prosthesis, some of which were patented for use with many soldiers who suffered lower-leg amputations. His favorite prosthesis was the one Benjamin originally made for him. Noah and Evergreen's two children would be the first colored children to attend and graduate from the May and Henry Outreach School.

Doctor Lawrence Chelmsford stayed on the Duran farm for a year after Reuben returned from the war. Reuben and Doctor Chelmsford spoke for hours a day about how Reuben's Budo training was the key element in Reuben's ability to cope with his darker memories of the past. Doctor Chelmsford returned to his county practice outside of Petersburg. He published several essays about his studies of the Human Psyche and the Combat Soldier. His essays earned him high regard in the developing study of psychology.

Carlton Edwards returned to Culpepper and lived a very happy, guilt free life with his wife, Mary Alice. Carlton told Mary Alice of his meeting with Reuben in the woods the day of the surrender, and of Adam's message in Reuben's dream. Although she never met Reuben, she was grateful he did not let Adam die alone. Reuben and Carlton remained in touch through the mail.

William Sinclair, Renee's once arranged fiancé, returned to Charleston, South Carolina. Like Reuben, he did not go to Appomattox for the formal surrender. William Sinclair did as Reuben suggested and released the Union prisoners and the Confederates under his momentary command. It was William Sinclair who told Franklin Wallace of Reuben's bravery and honor. He also expressed to Franklin Wallace Renee made the right choice.

Martin Doogan, Renee's only friend at the Wickham Finishing School for Girls, continued to be the groundskeeper for a couple of years after Renee graduated. With Renee gone, it was not the same, so he rendered his resignation. He and his wife relocated in West Virginia where they lived happily. Martin Doogan never forgot Renee and knew in his heart she would eventually have happiness with her Reuben.

Jacob Curtis remained a foreman on Franklin Wallace's wharf after Reuben's rescue attempt. When Franklin Wallace returned to rebuild the shipping industry in Norfolk, he promoted Jacob to manager overseeing all his wharfs for his devoted service, and also for his continued kindness he showed to his daughter.

James Forrest, Renee's Godfather, accepted Franklin Wallace's apology and became his top liaison on the West Coast. Master of the *Morning Star II*, he ferried the Duran family to and from Japan several times until he retired leaving his vessel at Reuben and Renee's disposal, as per Renee's father.

Sean Aaron continued to sail the Pacific for several years after he took Reuben on his initial voyage to Japan. He settled down peacefully in San Francisco as a lighthouse keeper. In the summer of '62, he passed on, satisfied he helped his adopted Goddaughter who he never met, but still adored as his own.

Simon and Cynthia Norenham stayed on the Duran farm for about as long as Doctor Chelmsford did. Simon purchased the old Wilcox plantation and remained close friends with Reuben. Not being a farmer, and not needing most of the land, he sold portions off at reduced prices to adjacent farms. Simon continued his work as an architect and was awarded many contracts all over the Virginia Southeast region and regained his personal wealth for his family. Cynthia and Renee became best friends and spent a lot of time helping each other in their respective homes. There were many times they reminisced and laughed about how they antagonized one another during their school years. It was a friendship Renee often compared with her friendship with Lucy. Reuben was the only person Cynthia allowed to call her *Cindy*.

Jonathan MacKay returned to his home state of Michigan where he continued with his previous position as a publishing agent. His first project was publishing a book called, *"Tales From Under the Oak Tree, a collection of short stories of love and adventure, by Aarleen Moncy Duran."* The popularity of Aarleen's book made Jonathan MacKay one of the most successful publishing agents of his agency, and Aarleen a very wealthy young lady. Reuben and Jonathan MacKay spent several days together, along with Renee and Aarleen, discussing Aarleen's written works. Reuben and Jonathan MacKay became good friends. They never spoke of the incident at the Chickahominy River or the war.

Todd Stevens and Max Warren both attended the formal surrender in Appomattox, but only from a spectator view. They never got paroled. Eventually they both made it back to Norfolk where Todd Stevens became a merchant with profitable ties to Franklin Wallace, and Max Warren became one of Franklin Wallace's foremen on his shipping wharves. They frequently visited Reuben and always brought the whiskey.

Matthew Peaks and Albert Rallins also attended the formal surrender with Todd Stevens and Max Warren. Matthew Peaks returned to Portsmouth and became a clergyman. He preached war at times is a necessary evil and should be avoided at all cost, but if it's needed, always welcome those guardian angels who carry a reverse bladed sword. Albert Rallins married his childhood sweetheart once he was made aware of the difficulties for Renee and Reuben. Albert Rallins and his sweetheart were also of two different social classes, but because of Renee and Reuben, he gave up his social standing to be with the girl he loved, and they both lived happily and had four children.

Brigadier General Sidney Doyle died from the wounds he received during the retreat from Petersburg. General Doyle held off sending the substitution orders for Monroe Duran for several months.

Colonel David McFerrin was captured by Federal militia a day prior to the Battle of Sailor's Creek. His body was amongst the pile of Confederate officers murdered by Major Oscar Grossman.

Major Jonathan Lander attended the formal surrender at Appomattox and was paroled. He returned to his home in Princess Anne County. For the rest of his life, for some reason, he avoided the city and county of Norfolk.

Company C, 68th Virginia Infantry. Every soldier assigned to Company C returned home after the war. As much fighting as they did during the course of the war, Company C suffered the least amount of casualties as any other company in the entire Army of Northern Virginia. It was the only company that did not follow normal army regulations or procedures. Rather than being split into platoons, it worked as two units each intertwined with the other allowing for quicker mobility and superior firepower for the small amount of men assigned to the company. Every soldier from Company C was forever grateful for their wolf-eyed, guardian angel who kept watch over them so they could fight without fear of death.

Tommy Deans, who at one time was Reuben's most troublesome pupil, became a university professor of history. Tommy Deans continued his education along with Aarleen during the war, and they both graduated their schooling together with Reuben as their teacher. Reuben was Tommy Deans' model and inspired him to travel across America and to Japan, where he visited

Itosai with Renee and Reuben. It was during that visit he toured the battlefield of Sekigahara with Reuben. With the assistance of Aarleen, Tommy Deans wrote several popular books about his travels that were published by Jonathan MacKay. Tommy Deans frequently invited Aarleen as a guest speaker to his university classes where she spoke of her favorite topic, her mother and father. Tommy Deans married Janet Lindsey and had three children.

Paul Cutler followed Reuben's order to the upmost of his ability and graduated school, married, and had seven children. He visited the Durans often and Renee helped him become the first Agriculture Liaison in Princess Anne County. Like with Renee, the title was all Paul Cutler needed to bring about agriculture reforms in Princess Anne County during the reconstruction period. Paul Cutler was the best man at Tommy Deans' wedding.

Tadashi and Sukuri remained in Itosai. They had three children, all of which grew and moved to Edo which became Tokyo after the Meiji Restoration. They remained good friends with Renee and Reuben and spent much time together when they would visit, and eventually live in Itosai. It was Tadashi who taught Renee the Art of Kyudo, of which she became very proficient.

Masaru, Akagi Genda-San's son, married and had four children. Masaru became the focal point in the Itosai Region after the Meiji Restoration. Because of the broad history of Hisano Castle and Itosai, the castle and village was permitted to remain in its current state under the new era for historical heritage and cultural purposes. Masaru became the regional governor, a position Masaru found dishonorable, but held for the purpose to keep the samurai heritage in remembrance. Masaru begged for both Renee's and Aarleen's forgiveness for wanting to kill Reuben when he first saw him.

Kaoru married a samurai general of the Itto region. After the Meiji Restoration, she and her husband relocated to Itosai where they lived for the rest of their lives. Kaoru and her husband, like Tadashi and Sukuri, became good friends with Renee and Reuben. Kaoru's son, Katsuo moved to Tokyo and became a teacher, with Reuben being his inspiration. Katsuo made frequent trips to Itosai.

Riley lived a long happy life as it pertains with German Shepards. After Reuben returned from the war, he was constantly at his side. Riley passed on a year after Reuben, Renee, and Aarleen returned from their second journey to Japan. Aarleen was devastated over his death. She immortalized his memory in several short stories where he was the hero. These particular stories were some of Aarleen's favorites.

Franklin Wallace embraced his enlightenment and became the father he never had been to Renee in her youth. She denied any financial support from him which he respected, but still provided to his daughter's and her husband's financial security through his granddaughter,

Aarleen. Franklin Wallace became very caring to his granddaughter and made sure she was never in need. He rebuilt the shipping industry in the region, and with his atonement to his daughter, he became popular with the community. He remained grounded and in touch, vowing never again to let social status ruin his new found relationship with Renee and her family. In the Year of our Lord 1876, Franklin Wallace passed on with Renee by his side holding his hand.

Akagi Genda-San witnessed the demise of the samurai as he predicted many years before he traveled to America where he would meet his greatest student. He prepared his region for the new era and Reuben, unknowingly, was a part of the preparation by teaching the English language to the residents of Akagi Genda-San's region. Akagi Genda-San viewed Reuben as an adopted son, especially after the Arata raid in '48. Although Akagi Genda-San loved and cherished his only son Masaru, he could not help but feel Reuben was the son he always wanted, the son whose heart and mind was open to all his teachings. In the Year of our Lord 1879, Akagi Genda-San passed on with Reuben and Renee at his side, along with Masaru and Yanna. Yanna would pass on three months later. Before Akagi Genda-San passed away, he presented Aarleen the watch her father gave him that bonded their friendship.

Aarleen and Benjamin fell in love and would marry with everyone's approval. They were married under the oak tree, and were just as happy as Renee and Reuben. They were free from any financial need, but that did not keep them from achieving their personal dreams. For Aarleen, it was becoming an accomplished author which she achieved early. Aarleen continued to be successful as an author as she wrote several volumes of short stories based on the heroics of her father, and the love and devotion he and her mother shared. She also received a teaching certificate and taught in the city school as well as the May and Henry Outreach School. For Benjamin, helping Noah with his disability and accompanying Doctor Chelmsford on his medical runs while he stayed on the Duran farm inspired him to become a doctor. Aarleen and Benjamin lived in the Duran home in the city, but spent much of their time on the farm with Renee and Reuben. Aarleen gave birth to a baby girl who was named Lucy Duran-Norenham. Reuben was to his granddaughter, Lucy, as Aaron was to Aarleen. As with Aarleen, being of Reuben's blood, Lucy was adopted into the Akagi Clan. During their third journey to Japan, Reuben and Aarleen made a father and daughter only excursion to Funashima Island where Miyamoto Musashi had his duel with the Demon of the Western Provinces, Sasaki Kojiro, the first story Aarleen's father told her.

Renee and Reuben lived happily ever after. Theirs was a classic, tragic love story with a happy ending. Spending most of their lives on the farm, and most of that time under their oak tree, they were inseparable. Reuben continued to teach at the May and Henry Outreach School and was a contributing force helping Aarleen receive a teaching certificate. They made several voyages to Japan. It was on their second voyage, Renee and Reuben took along an oak tree seedling from their oak tree and planted it in the small courtyard within their cottage in Itosai. It was a blessed life Renee and Reuben shared. With all their hardships long behind, they still embraced them. It was those hardships that made them the strong, loving, devoted couple they had become. It wasn't until Renee and Reuben were in their 60's when they decided to live out the rest of their lives in Itosai's peaceful serenity. As the years wore on, Renee began to take notice of Reuben's age and health. Fearing his time was near, Renee sent for Aarleen. Within a years' time, Aarleen, Benjamin, and Lucy, with her husband, Michael Knight and daughter, Valerie Duran-Knight, arrived to visit with Renee and Reuben. It was a joyous reunion for the entire family. Two months after Aarleen and her family arrived, Reuben passed on peacefully with Renee and Aarleen at his side in the Year of our Lord 1900. Reuben's last words to Renee were, "I'll be waiting for you under our oak tree next to the creek on the farm… my precious Wickham girl." Reuben was given an honorable samurai parting and laid to rest in the Akagi family gardens. Aarleen and Benjamin remained with Renee while she mourned Reuben's death. Each day, Renee spent it at the side of Reuben's resting place with her chest of written passages. She would read them out loud to him. One month after Reuben passed on, Aarleen saw her mother once again make her daily visit to her father's resting place. This time however, Renee took Reuben's Kutto along with her written passages. After what seemed to be an unusually long visit, Aarleen became concerned, and with Benjamin, went to check on her mother. On a warm autumn day, Aarleen found her mother lying on top of Reuben's resting place, his Kutto cradled in her arms with her last written passage in her lifeless grasp, but with a hint of a smile on her face. Renee was buried next to her husband in the Akagi family gardens. Renee's dying words were, "Here I come… my adorable shoddy farm boy."

Together for eternity
You and I
We need not search for heaven
Beneath our Oak Tree our heaven rests
With you I shall never want or need
Stones and Water
Faith and Love
We have endured and we have survived
Love and devotion we pass on to Aarleen
She takes our gifts and applies them wisely
We have raised a legacy
One who will cherish our lessons and pass them on
And she will be forever grateful
I Love You my Husband
And You Love me
Stones and Water
Love and Devotion
Those are our precious gifts of tranquility